When The Boys Are Away

AND

take a chance

Sarah Webb worked in bookselling for many years and now writes full-time. Her novels include *Always the Bridesmaid* and *Something to Talk About*, which were number-one bestsellers in Ireland. Recent novels are *Three Times a Lady, Some Kind of Wonderful, It Had to Be You, Take a Chance*, and *When the Boys are Away*. She lives in Dublin with her partner and young family.

Also by Sarah Webb

sarah webb

When The Boys Are Away

AND

take a chance

PAN BOOKS

When the Boys are Away first published 2007 by Pan Books.
Take a Chance first published in Ireland 2005 by Macmillan.
First published in Great Britain 2006 by Pan Books.

This omnibus first published 2008 by Pan Books
an imprint of Pan Macmillan Ltd
Pan Macmillan, 20 New Wharf Road, London N1 9RR
Basingstoke and Oxford
Associated companies throughout the world
www.panmacmillan.com

ISBN 978-0-330-45797-2

Copyright © Sarah Webb 2005, 2007

The right of Sarah Webb to be identified as the
author of this work has been asserted by her in accordance
with the Copyright, Designs and Patents Act 1988.

Inside illustrations by Emer Sharkey

1 3 5 7 9 8 6 4 2

A CIP catalogue record for this book is available from
the British Library.

The extracts from 'Thank You for the Music', 'Does Your Mother Know'
and 'Take a Chance on Me' by Anderson/Ulvaeus
are published courtesy of Bocu Music Ltd.

Every effort has been made to contact copyright holders
of material reproduced in this book. If any have been inadvertently
overlooked, the publishers wil be pleased to make restitution
at the earliest opportunity.

Printed and bound in Great Britain by
Mackays of Chatham plc, Chatham, Kent

When The Boys Are Away

To darling Ben, my North Star

*If one does not know to which port one is sailing,
no wind is favourable.*

SENECA

Acknowledgements

To Mum, Dad, Kate, Emma and Richard. There would have been no book without all of you. You are the wind in my sails. To Ben for all the boat-related information and for living the life of a landlubber (most of the time) for me and the kids. To Sam and Amy-Rose for all the hugs and support. To baby Jago for being easy-going. And to my 'in-laws', Bob and Janet, who are nothing like Maureen and Joe in the book, thank goodness. And not forgetting Luan, and Charlie, my lovely godson.

To my dear friends Andrew, Tanya and Nicky – for putting up with all my quirks. And to all my other kind and patient friends who always ask how the latest book is coming along. I know you don't always get a straight answer, but thanks for the interest. To Stirfry for the accidental incrimination – it's not you, honestly!

And every happiness to Andrew and Erica as they embark on their new voyage together.

To Katarina for looking after Amy, Jago and Sam so well. There would have been no book without your help.

To Ali Gunn, my agent, for all her hard work on my behalf. And to all in Macmillan for making the whole book process such plain sailing: especially my editor, the lovely, patient and wise Imogen Taylor, the two Davids – Adamson and North, Trisha Jackson, Rebecca Lewis, Liz Cowen and the eagle-eyed Liz Davis, and, of course, the ever-affable Cormac Kinsella.

To all the Irish Girls, my writers in crime. Many thanks for all the friendship, advice and encouragement. To my fellow seal-lover Martina Devlin for her wise counsel. And to the libraries who host book events and support reading and readers of all kinds, I salute you. Especially Assumpta Hickey, Jane Alger and Marian Keyes.

To all the booksellers in Ireland and the UK for supporting my books over the years. I know how important you guys are and I'll never forget or underestimate your ongoing kindness. Thanks especially to the crews in Eason, Dubray, Hughes and Hughes, and Byrne's. And not forgetting Hodges Figgis and Waterstone's, where I started as a very lowly junior bookseller. And to all the independents, including Michael in my own local, the Exchange in Dalkey. Thanks for giving me the opportunity to live a writer's life. I'm eternally grateful.

A heartfelt thanks to all my readers near and far who have taken the time to email and write to me and even send me presents. (Thanks Abby in Australia for the koala goodies and Claire in the Netherlands for the cute baby gear for Jago!) I appreciate your feedback so much, it makes it all worthwhile. Keep it up!

And finally to you, the reader. I do hope you enjoy *When the Boys Are Away*. If you'd like to contact me, my email address is sarah@sarahwebb.info. I'd love to hear from you.

PART ONE

Chapter 1

*Batten down: to secure the hatches and
loose objects on the deck and within the boat,
especially before a storm*

'Mum, they're here!' Dan yells down from his bedroom-window look-out. 'Batten down the hatches!'

'Shush! They'll hear you.' I wipe my wet hands on the front of my jeans and walk out of the kitchen into the hall. I have about three minutes before Maureen and Joe, my sort of in-laws, descend upon us an hour earlier than expected. I scamper around the hall pushing Lily's wonky-wheeled buggy against one wall, picking stray crisps off the deeply scuffed wooden floor and kicking Dan's runners towards the shoe rack under the stairs.

The doorbell shrills. I stand for a moment, take a deep breath and smooth back my hair, tucking any wispy ends behind my ears. I've been rushing around all day in preparation for the onslaught and I know my face is glowing as red as a lobster, but there isn't much I can do about that now.

As I go towards the door, Grasshopper, my brother's idiot black puppy – half greyhound, half Labrador – flies out of the kitchen and throws herself against it with a thump, her tail thrashing around like an out of control garden hose. The doorbell rings again.

'Just coming,' I say loudly.

Grasshopper jumps against the door again, spraying the floor with the special pee she reserves for visitors. She has a weak bladder and excitement sends her over the edge. Of course my brother didn't tell me this until he was out of the country and had left her with us.

I put my legs on either side of the dog, grab her by the collar and open the door a crack.

Maureen puts her twiggy fingers on the door jamb and pushes the door open wider.

'What's going on in there?' she demands. 'Are you going to let us in, Meg? Fine welcome this is.'

'Maureen.' I hear Joe's voice of reason in the background.

'I'm just trying to deal with the dog and then I'll be right with you,' I trill in my best stressed-out-but-trying-not-to-let-it-get-to-me voice. 'Don't go away now.' I close the door slowly so Maureen has a chance to extract her fingers.

'Dan!' I scream up the stairs. 'I need you. Urgently!'

He appears at the top of the stairs and looks down at me. Grasshopper yelps with delight. She loves Dan.

'Take this stupid mutt outside.'

'Did she piss on the floor again?'

'Watch the language. You know what Maureen's like.'

'Sorry. Did she urinate on the floor again?'

I stifle a smile. 'Just do it!'

He runs down the stairs, grabbing the newel post at the bottom and swinging himself halfway down the hall. The banisters shake ominously. Grasshopper barks loudly and tries to run towards Dan but I have a firm grip on her collar so, instead, her feet splay out like a cartoon dog as she skitters on the hard surface of the floor.

'Dan, would you stop doing that? How many times do I

have to tell you? You'll break the banisters and Simon won't be pleased.'

'It was Murphy who taught me how to do it,' Dan replies with a grin.

'And don't call him that. Maureen hates it. Call him Simon, OK?'

'Sure.' Dan takes Grasshopper from me and drags her towards the kitchen. 'Will I put her outside?'

'Yes.'

I follow Dan into the kitchen, grab some disinfectant spray and a large handful of kitchen roll and then deal with Grasshopper's mess in the hall.

Finally I open the door. Maureen is standing on the doorstep, her arms folded in front of her, impatiently tapping one smartly loafered foot, with a face on her that would sour lemons.

'What's going on?' she says, bustling past, enveloping me in a cloud of expensive perfume and looking around the hall. 'What's that smell?'

'Dog,' I say, leaving it at that. She'll find out about Grasshopper's bladder soon enough, I think rather wickedly. 'Watch the floor,' I add, 'it's wet.'

Joe steps forward and gives me a kiss on the cheek, his woolly salt and pepper beard tickling my face. He's a jolly man, originally from Newcastle, with rosy cheeks and a shock of white hair. the complete opposite of his tall, stick-insect, London born and bred wife, Maureen.

'Hello, my dear, lovely to see you,' Joe says, holding both my shoulders firmly and beaming at me. 'I hope we haven't inconvenienced you by arriving so early. We were going to grab a coffee first, but Maureen was dying to see Lily – you know what she's like.'

Maureen sniffs. 'The afternoon ferry gets in at four. Always has, always will. You and Simon really should communicate

5

better, Meg dear. Don't you have some sort of wall planner or master diary for the house?'

'No. Simon isn't really the wall-planner type of guy, Maureen, as well you know.'

She sniffs again. 'I suppose not. But in my day the wife—' She breaks off. 'How silly of me. The wife indeed. What *should* I call you, Meg? The girlfriend, the partner?'

Spare me, I think, not already! 'Meg is just fine,' I say through tight lips. She's only been in the house two minutes but she's already getting started. She hates the fact that Simon and I aren't married. I'd redeemed myself a little in her eyes after giving birth to Lily, her first 'proper' grandchild, but our marriage, or lack of, is a subject she never seems to tire of, unfortunately.

'Thanks for having us to stay again,' Joe said, ignoring Maureen's barb. 'We just can't keep away.' He throws a look at his wife.

'Yes, thanks for inviting us,' she adds, distracted, her eyes peering into the kitchen. She's looking for Lily.

I bite my lip. I didn't invite them. Simon didn't invite them. Maureen invited herself and Joe largely does as he's told. This is the third time they've been over since Christmas. As Joe says, Maureen just can't stay away. It has nothing to do with me, Simon or Dan, and everything to do with Lily. Maureen is completely obsessed with Lily, who, at two, is largely oblivious to the attention. But if there was an adoration of Lily competition, my own parents or Joe wouldn't get a look in: Maureen would win hands down. I've never seen anything like it.

'Simon here yet?' Joe asks as I lead them into the kitchen.

'No. His flight's delayed. He won't be here until after seven. But don't worry, he said to go ahead and eat without him. I know you like to eat before six, Maureen.'

'Are you going to the airport to collect him?' Maureen asks. 'We can look after Lily.'

'No, he's getting a taxi.'

Maureen clicks her tongue against her bottom teeth.

I give her a forced smile. 'If you'd like to drive to Dublin airport to collect him, be my guest. It's about an hour's drive there if the traffic's good, and a good hour back again.'

Joe puts his hand on his wife's arm. 'Simon spends his life in airports. He doesn't expect to be collected any more.'

'I see.' Maureen shrugs his hand away. Clearly she doesn't. Then she spots Lily out the kitchen window. 'What's Lily doing?'

I look out the window too. Lily is trying to sit on Grasshopper. She has a brown patch down one leg of her best denims. I sigh.

'Dan!'

Dan looks up from his PlayStation.

I smile at him. 'Come over and say hello to Maureen and Joe. And then I have to wash Lily. She has dog poo on her leg.'

'Yuck!' Maureen wrinkles her nose. 'How disgusting.'

'Grasshopper's always shitting,' Dan says calmly. 'Hi, Maureen.'

'Nana Maureen,' Maureen corrects him, 'and I don't think that's fitting language for an eleven-year-old.'

'Sorry. Pooing,' Dan says, correcting himself. Undeterred by the ticking off, he throws his arms around Joe's waist. 'Hello, Joe,' he says with an upward lilt in his voice.

Joe gives him a warm hug and then ruffles his hair. 'What have you been getting up to, young man?'

Dan draws back. 'Not much.'

'How's school?'

Dan scowls. 'Horrible.'

'I have something for you.' Joe reaches into his pocket and hands Dan a twenty euro note. 'Buy yourself a CD or something.'

'Thanks.' Dan gives him another hug.

'Joe! That's far too much. He's only a boy,' Maureen says.

'You've been shopping for Lily all month,' he reminds her. 'And sewing like a maniac.'

My heart sinks. Not more of Maureen's out of shape, one arm longer than the other cotton tunics. Why couldn't she be a master knitter instead? I'd love some miniature jumpers or cardigans. I only put the damn tunics on Lily when Maureen is over, otherwise they're in the back of the wardrobe with the weird Thanksgiving turkey suit my American cousins sent over last year and the tiny pink and white flowery wetsuit Simon bought for Lily in the Caribbean which I don't have the heart to get rid of, even though she has long grown out of it.

'I'll bring you to town to get a new PlayStation game tomorrow, if that's all right with your mother,' Joe adds.

I smile at him. 'Of course. What do you say, Dan?'

'Thanks! I know exactly what I want too.' While Joe and Dan discuss games, I'm left with Maureen. She's already out the back door on a rescue mission.

'Let's get Granny's little angel out of those dirty, dirty clothes,' she says to Lily. 'And away from that filthy dog.'

Lily looks up at Maureen and then back at Grasshopper. She hangs onto the dog's coat for dear life while Maureen tries to extract her.

'Come on, Lily,' Maureen coaxes her, 'come to Nana Maureen.'

'No, Ganny,' Lily says. 'Doggie! Doggie!'

I should step in to help but I'm rooted to the spot, trying not to laugh.

'Come on, now,' Maureen persists, 'there's a good little girl.'

'No!' Lily wails. 'Doggie, doggie, doggie!'

'Meg, for heaven's sake don't just stand there,' Maureen says, 'help me.'

I prise open Lily's tiny hands and Grasshopper runs away. Lily is the only one of us she's scared of, and I don't blame her.

'Don't pick Lily up . . .' I begin, but it's too late. Maureen is holding a soiled Lily to her bony chest.

'Shit,' Maureen says under her breath when she realizes what she's done.

'Shit!' Lily repeats. 'Shit, shit, shit!'

A little later, Maureen and Lily are both spotlessly clean (Maureen excels at cleaning) and dressing dolls on the rug. Lily's wearing a pair of her navy tights and a new navy tunic dress with old-fashioned smocking at the cuffs and neck, courtesy of Maureen. Joe and Dan are playing some sort of car-racing game on the PlayStation and I'm getting dinner ready. Unfortunately they've decided not to move to the living room, in spite of my gentle cajoling, so there's no getting away from them all.

I've been shopping, cleaning, making beds and cooking all day and I'm fit to drop. As I cut into a tomato, the phone rings. I wipe my hands on my by now very grubby jeans and pick it up.

Chapter 2

Swamp: to fill with water, but not sink (yet)

'Hi, doll face. Have my parentals arrived yet?' It's a cheery-sounding Simon on the other end of the phone.

'Yes.'

'Are they in the same room?'

'Yes. Let me just move into the hall.' I walk out of the room and close the door firmly behind me. 'Where are you?' I ask, trying to keep my voice calm. 'Are you nearly home?'

'Not quite. The flight's been delayed. I'll be another few hours I'm afraid.'

I hear the clink of glasses and laughter in the background. 'Where are you?' I ask again.

'In the airport bar.'

'Which airport?'

'Boston.'

'You're still in America?'

'Yes.'

Damn, damn, damn. 'You won't be home for hours.'

'I know, that's what I just said.'

I sit down on the stairs and put my head in my hands, still holding onto the phone.

'Meg? Meg?'

'I'm still here. Just get home as quickly as you can, your mother's already driving me demented.'

'I'm sorry. Hey, we won.'

'Great. Just get home, OK? Before I murder her.'

'She's not that bad.'

I hear a scream from the kitchen. It sounds like Lily. 'Listen, I have to go. I'll see you later.'

'Don't wait up. It might be tomorrow by the time I get there.'

'Have a safe flight.'

'Thanks, and Meg?'

'Yes?'

'We won the regatta.'

'Well done.' Another scream. 'I really have to go. Bye now.'

I click off the phone.

Simon really doesn't get it sometimes. While he's off fanny-ing around on some swanky yacht, I'm left holding things together at home. I should explain: Simon is a professional sailor. It sounds glamorous, but it isn't really. He spends his time flying all over the world to whichever hot and windy place the next regatta is being held, working for a bunch of rich yacht owners who wouldn't know real life if it jumped up and bit them on the bum.

Simon was born in London but studied yacht design in Southampton, before moving to Hamble, a few miles outside Southampton. Then he met me and moved to Dublin for good. Not that he spends much time in Dublin; we're lucky if we see him eight days a month. He sometimes takes a week off in the winter if he can, but he has to work while he's in demand, he says. He's self-employed and can only sail at this level for another ten or so years. After that . . . who knows?

It wasn't exactly love at first sight for either of us. Simon was in Dublin for a sailing event called the Round Ireland and the auction house I worked for at the time, Hall's, were part-sponsors of the event. A gang of us had been given tickets to the launch and the free champagne was a lure too hard to resist.

Simon was holding up the busy bar and as I waited for a fresh glass of bubbly we got into a heated argument. The conversation started off innocuously enough. I asked him where he was from and he told me he was from 'the mainland', as if Ireland was some sort of island off its coast. I wasn't going to let him get away with that. Even though I'm not usually much of a Nationalist, the remark got my blood boiling.

'You're lovely when you're angry,' Simon had said as I'd stormed off in a huff.

Later that evening we bumped into each other again and he apologized, admitting that he'd only said it to wind me up. We ended up going out for a rather drunken dinner together and quickly realized how much we liked each other.

When Simon met Dan for the first time, I knew he was some-one special. Instead of fawning all over him, as some of my ex-boyfriends had done, or ignoring him, like other, more ignorant specimens, he treated Dan as a normal, active six-year-old boy. He took us both sailing around Dalkey Island on the huge, gleaming, white race yacht that he was crewing on at the time, and when Dan asked if he could fish off the back and produced the crab line that his grampa had given him, Simon said, 'Of course, mate,' and fished with him, fashioning a 'line' from some whipping thread and a bent safety pin I provided from my broken left bra strap. When I saw the look of contentment on Dan's face as the two of them sat at the back of the super yacht, fishing, my lopsided boobs just didn't matter. Dan's real father, Sid, was a Big Mistake. In fact, before Simon, most of my boyfriends fell into the Big Mistake category.

When I got pregnant, I thought my whole world was going to fall apart. It didn't, *I* fell apart. I was twenty-two, in my first proper full-time job after college (a mediocre arts degree), and having a baby with my flaky boyfriend wasn't exactly part of the master plan. But I managed with the help of my sister Hattie, and my dad, who were amazingly supportive once they'd got over the initial shock. Mum was another matter.

Dan changed my life. I know all new mothers say this, but a twenty-two-year-old mother who goes from party girl to nappy changing in one fell swoop has even more right to the claim. Sid was pretty useless. He did offer to marry me and we were engaged for three weeks before I realized how nutty that was and broke it off. Sid was relieved. As a dad he's not all bad, and Dan worships him, but as a boyfriend or husband . . . no, no, no. Simon was different. From the very start I knew he'd make a brilliant boyfriend. Husband . . . hum. That was a different matter. It was me who had cold feet when it came to getting married.

When I got pregnant for the second time it wasn't exactly planned either. Simon and I had talked about it in the abstract and had collectively decided 'it would be lovely if it happened but let's just wait and see'. And happen it did. But this time it was a nice kind of mistake, and Simon was thrilled. He'd always wanted a baby of his own. Our baby. He loved Dan but wanted another child because he'd missed Dan's baby years. He thinks of Dan as his own, which is one of the reasons I love him so much.

But when it comes to men, there's always something. Simon has two major flaws: his job and his mother.

I walk back into the kitchen. 'Simon's flight has been delayed. You won't see him till the morning, I'm afraid.'

Maureen gives a deep sigh which I choose to ignore.

'Not to worry,' Joe says cheerfully.

Maureen is holding Lily on her knee, trying to read her *The Cat in the Hat*. Lily isn't interested. She wants to play with Dan and Joe. She hits Maureen on the hand.

'Lily, that's not very nice.' I lift her off Maureen's knee and hold her tight. 'No! No hitting.'

Lily smacks me in the face. 'No,' I say again. 'Bold Lily.'

'You bold,' Lily tells me. 'Illy good.'

'Lily bold,' Dan says, looking up from his PlayStation. 'She pulled the wires out of the back of the telly a minute ago.'

'It's time for Lily to go to bed,' I decide.

'Already?' Maureen looks at her watch. 'It's only six and we haven't given her her presents yet.'

'OK,' I concede, 'but she can only stay up for a little while longer or she'll get overtired. She missed her nap this afternoon.'

'I'll get them from the car,' Joe says, standing up.

Dan looks at me and I wink at him. 'How lovely,' I say.

Minutes later the floor is covered with bright pink wrapping paper and Lily is eating a piece of plastic packaging.

'Look, Lily,' Maureen says holding up a chubby-cheeked Baby Born. 'A new dolly.'

'She already has a Tiny Tears,' I point out. 'You gave it to her at Christmas, remember?'

'Ah, but this one poos and wees.' Maureen undoes Baby Born's vest and nappy and shows us the hole.

'We have Grasshopper to do that,' Dan says.

I laugh but Maureen doesn't seem amused. She holds up a dark green flowery dress made out of what looks like curtain material.

'I think that's a bit small for Lily,' Dan says, staring at it.

Maureen tuts. 'It's for the doll. And look, there's a matching bonnet. Let's dress the dolly, Lily.'

Jeepers, what's wrong with pink or yellow – dark green, is she mad? 'How nice,' I say. 'But she really does need to go to bed now.'

'I'll give her a bath.' Maureen stands up and eagerly holds out her hands to take Lily.

'That's OK, Maureen. She had one last night. She'll do. I don't have the energy.'

'But I've offered to do it.' Maureen's hands are still outstretched.

'Really, it's OK.' I hold Lily tightly to my side.

'But Meg, the germs from the dog. Grasshopper has been licking—'

'Maureen,' Joe says in a warning tone of voice.

'I'll be back in a few minutes and then we can all have dinner in peace, how's that?' I say brightly.

'I'd prefer to have dinner *with* my only grandchild at the table,' Maureen retorts. 'We've come the whole way from London. London, mind.'

'Maureen,' Joe says again.

'Fine.' Maureen crosses her arms over her chest huffily. 'But don't forget to do her little teeth, Meg. I know she's only two, but you have to take care of her teeth.'

It's only as I walked up the stairs I realize what Maureen has just said. 'My only grandchild.' Poor Dan.

In the early hours of the morning I wake up suddenly hearing the beep beep of the house alarm being set downstairs. I look at my bedside clock. Two thirty-four. I sigh and close my eyes again. A few minutes later Simon walks into the bedroom and sits down on my side of the bed.

'Meg? Are you awake?'

I open my eyes. The door is ajar and the light from the hall illuminates his tanned face.

'Hi,' I say groggily. 'I am now.'

'Sorry.'

'S'OK. How was the flight?'

'Not too bad.' He leans down to kiss me on the cheek.

'You stink of booze,' I complain.

'Sorry. I have a present for you.'

A present? That's more like it. I sit up and switch on the bedside light. Simon hands me a small duty-free bag.

'Here you go. I know you like it.'

I open the bag and pull out the distinctive orange rectangular box. A bottle of Happy by Clinique. The same perfume he bought me on the last trip. The same perfume he buys me every trip. By now my whole family wears it as I've given away so many bottles. I haven't the heart to tell him because it's the only perfume he can remember the name of. And don't get me wrong, I do like it, I just don't need more than one bottle at a time.

'Thanks, love.'

'I have T-shirts for Dan and Lily.'

I yawn.

Simon smiles. 'Long day?'

I nod. 'Very. And can you get Lily up in the morning? Please? I really need some sleep.'

'Sure. And remind me to tell you about Spain.'

'What about Spain?'

'I've been asked to sail with the royal family during Barcelona race week. It's a big honour.'

'That's great news, love. When is it?'

'Next week.'

Not so good news. 'You promised you'd be here to entertain your parents.'

'And I will be. I'm not flying out until Tuesday.'

'But they're here till Thursday.'

'Lower your voice, they'll hear you.'

'Sorry, but it's not fair. Why didn't you just say no?'

'To the Spanish royal family?'

'Yes, to the Spanish royal bloody family. Are they more important than your own family?'

'Of course not.' Simon pats me on the arm. 'You're just tired. Go back to sleep. We'll talk about this in the morning. I'm going to do my teeth.'

'You do that.' I switch off the light and huff back against the pillows. When Simon comes back in I pretend to be asleep. When his hand snakes across my stomach I groan.

'I'm knackered, Simon. I just want to sleep.'

He takes his hand away wordlessly. I lie there for ages, seething before finally falling into an exhausted slumber.

'Did you enjoy your lie-in, Meg?' Maureen says archly as I walk into the kitchen the following morning. It's seven-thirty and I wasn't expecting her to be up yet. I wrap my dressing gown around my body and tie it at the waist. I'm only wearing a T-shirt and knickers and I don't want to bare my white legs to the world.

'Hardly a lie-in, Maureen.' Joe lifts his head out of yesterday's newspaper. Bless him.

'Simon's been up since six with Lily,' she says. 'Haven't you, Simon?'

Simon, his mouth full of food, nods and winks at me.

'Yes, well normally I'm up with Lily *every* morning, Maureen. So I don't feel in the least bit guilty. And tomorrow morning I'm going to stay in bed until ten. Simon's off to Spain on Tuesday, you see. A bit unexpectedly.' I can't resist getting a dig in.

'Oh, Simon!' Maureen wags a finger at him. 'Naughty, naughty. You said you'd be here all week.'

'I was asked to sail with the Spanish royal family,' Simon says. 'I could hardly say no.'

Maureen beams. 'Of course not. Imagine, my son fraternizing with royalty. Wait till I tell the girls.'

Simon is sitting on the bench under the window with Dan on his far side; I squash in beside them. Simon is wearing a pair of navy sailing shorts and nothing else. He smells a little ripe.

'You need a shower,' I murmur to him.

He grunts and smiles at me. I smile back, then look at his bare, toned chest. It's nut-brown after a week in the Boston sun, lucky man. The sailors have to wear their T-shirts emblazoned with the boat's name and sail number, the size of the lettering depending on the size of the owner's ego during the race, but they strip off before and after races and on shore, hence the deep tan.

Simon's chest of drawers is chocka with once-worn sailing T-shirts, shorts, jackets, rash vests for wearing under wetsuits, caps – you name it. Each time he sails on a new boat he gets a whole new set of gear, from simple T-shirts to oilskins worth hundreds of euros. Simon doesn't need wardrobe space; all he owns in the sartorial line is one ancient 'good' navy suit which has seen better days, worn at every wedding we're invited to, one reefer – a navy sailing blazer with gold buttons – one formal white shirt, and a primrose-yellow tie which looks bloody good with his perma-tanned face. Now and then I remove some of said sailing gear from his chest of drawers and either give it to my brother Paul (sailing gear is quite in at the moment, apparently) or dump it in the nearest cloth recycling bin. Simon never even notices. If I didn't do this the house would be overflowing with the stuff, and I have enough trouble keeping it tidy as it is.

Simon stretches his arms over his head and I get a whiff of stale armpit. 'I'll have a shower after breakfast,' he says. 'Mum brought over organic sausages from her local butcher. They're delicious.'

'And a big piece of cow,' Dan adds. 'It's in the fridge.'

'Beef,' Maureen corrects him. 'Organic beef.'

'Mum calls it cow,' Dan says.

'Your mum's a vegetarian.'

'I'm not a vegetarian,' I point out, 'I just don't eat red meat.'

Simon puts his hand on my knee under the table.

'Any more sausages, Mum?' he asks.

Maureen beams at him and rolls three more out of the fat they were swimming in and onto his plate, flicking grease all over the table and onto my dressing gown in the process.

I wince but say nothing.

'Would you like a sausage, Meg?' she asks me.

Simon grips my knee tightly.

'No, thank you,' I say politely.

At that moment Grasshopper hurls herself against the window, giving us all a fright.

'Jesus, that dog,' Simon mutters. 'When's she going home, Meg?'

'Paul's collecting her this evening.'

'I hope my granddaughter is getting enough protein, Meg,' Maureen says, swinging the frying pan around rather dangerously. 'She's a growing girl you know. And only organic food of course, the rest's muck.'

I hold Simon's hand under the table and squeeze tightly.

Maureen carries on, oblivious. She turns to Lily, who is banging Dan on the head with her plastic spoon. 'Lily want another sausie wausie?' she asks.

'Sausie,' Lily says.

'She'll only throw it on the floor,' I say.

But Maureen ignores me. She runs a sausage under the kitchen tap to cool it, cuts it in half lengthways and after blowing on it ostentatiously, hands the two pieces to Lily.

Lily takes a nibble from one then throws it on the floor. Maureen avoids my smug gaze.

'So what's the plan for today?' Simon asks me.

'I'm going to have a very exciting time at the supermarket. Mum and Dad are coming over for dinner, remember?'

Simon looks at me blankly.

'Well, they are,' I continue. 'At six. So I'll be cooking this afternoon. And I'd be very grateful if you'd entertain Lily. Dan can come with me.'

Dan groans. 'Do I have to, Mum? I hate shopping.'

'I'll take you to the PlayStation shop,' Joe kindly offers. 'I promised you a new game, remember.'

'Cool!' Dan says.

'But you've just said you hate shopping, Dan,' I point out.

'Mum!'

'I'm only joking. That's very kind of you, Joe, thanks. And, Simon, are you OK to keep an eye on Lily?'

'I'll help him,' Maureen says before he has a chance to answer. 'It'll be my pleasure. My two favourite people in the whole world, isn't that right, Lily Illy?'

Lily throws her second piece of sausage at her. It lands on her cheek, leaving a greasy skid mark in her heavy pink powder.

'Nice shot, Lily,' Dan says.

I stifle a smile. The sausage lands on Maureen's lap and puts a greasy stain on her neat linen trousers. Even at this hour of the morning, she is immaculately dressed. Maureen is always immaculately dressed. She favours smart, casual, well-cut beige or navy trousers, white shirts, a single row of pearls, flat ballerina pumps, velvet Alice bands – you get the picture. Very Jackie O. I've never seen her in jeans or, God forbid, runners or a tracksuit. And I know exactly what she thinks of my dress sense as she's told me on more that one occasion.

'You'll need to smarten up a little if you want to keep a man like my Simon,' she said last time she was over. What a joke – as if he had any dress sense at all. I felt like saying Simon was only interested in what was under my clothes, but I buttoned my lip.

'Dan!' Simon chides. 'It's not funny.' He shakes his finger at Lily, who blows a raspberry at him. 'Bold Lily,' he says. She giggles.

But Simon is wrong. It *is* funny, very funny.

Dan kicks me under the table and I give him a conspiratorial wink.

Chapter 3

Fouled: something that is caught,
jammed or entangled

As I linger over the carrots in the supermarket (muddy organic versus nice clean non organic) my mobile rings. It's my one and only sister, Hattie. Half-sister really, we don't share the same mum. My real mum, Celia, died when I was little. Dad married Julie fairly swiftly after that and then they had Hattie and, a few years later, Paul. So I'm the odd one out in our family. The black sheep, at least that's what it feels like sometimes.

'Can I come over for dinner this evening?' she says, coming straight to the point.

'Maureen and Joe are over,' I say, tut tutting over the price of the organic carrots and pretending this is the reason I'm rejecting them. It's really because I can't be bothered to wash them. And yes, OK, because Maureen is an organic freak and I want to get up her nose.

'I know,' she says, 'Mum told me. I presume you're having a roast?'

'Yes. They brought a huge bleeding hunk of organic meat with them.'

'Great, what time?'

'Hattie, you're not invited. I'm already cooking for eight.'

Hattie laughs. 'Lily hardly counts. And Dan only eats meat and peas. What about if I bring dessert? Please?'

'Are you on one of your diets again?' Hattie's always on some sort of fad diet. She rotates them – Atkins, GI, cabbage, soup, Atkins, GI, and so on. Sometimes she changes the order of the diets just to give herself a bit of variety. But she's as lazy as hell in the kitchen, never goes food shopping except in the local convenience store – hence never has anything in her fridge – and always ends up in our kitchen by the weekend.

'Yes, a new kind of Atkins one. Read about it in one of the Sunday papers. So I need meat. And Mum's left nothing in the fridge.' Surprise, surprise.

'Here's a radical idea – you could always go shopping.'

'I'm *going* shopping, that's the problem. I urgently need a new pair of shoes. I haven't time for food shopping.'

'Shoes? For what? You have hundreds of pairs of shoes.' I move on to the potatoes and heft a large non-organic bag into the trolley. Joe and Simon like their spuds.

'For the date with one of Simon's eligible sailing friends.'

'What date?'

'The one you're going to set up for me.'

'In your dreams.' I push the trolley towards the deli counter. 'I'm not doing that again after the last time. Remember that poor Scottish boy? What was his name?'

'He was Welsh. And his name was Ewan, like the actor.'

'That's right, Ewan. Simon says he still talks about you.'

'He was boring. Never stopped droning on about boats and racing. Anyway, he was far too brainy for me. I'm not looking for brains at the moment, I need strong. Manly. Someone with a tan. Nothing serious. One of those grinding sailors.'

I snort. 'You're so transparent. And I think you mean grinders.' The grinders, or as Simon delightfully calls them 'grunts', are the muscle of the big boats. They work the huge winches that pull the sails in and out. And yes, they're often built like bricks. Simon started as a grinder, but now he's a sail trimmer, a couple of rungs up the ladder in the pecking order. And bloody good at his job from what I can make out.

'Yep, grinders. I want someone physical, someone who isn't afraid to get down and dirty. I need a good shag.'

'Hattie, it's ten o'clock in the morning. Please! I can't take this.'

'OK, OK. But ask Simon if he knows anyone, will you?'

'Yes, yes.'

'So I can come for dinner?'

'Six o'clock. And don't be late. You know what Maureen's like about her stomach.'

At twenty past six Simon, Maureen, Joe, my parents, Dan and Lily (in her high chair) are all sitting at the kitchen table waiting for Hattie. Lily is chomping on some cold meat left over from lunch and throwing slices of browning apple at Dan.

Maureen glances at her watch and sighs deeply. 'I'm going to have terrible indigestion this evening. I won't be able to sleep. I'll be up all night, mark my words. My stomach is on a very exact time clock . . .'

'Let's start without Hattie,' I say quickly. I know exactly how long Maureen's stomach time-clock speech is – I've heard it countless times before.

'Good idea.' Simon jumps to his feet and rubs his hands together.

I start ladling out the vegetable soup. Simon puts the first bowl in front of his mother.

'Oh, soup,' she says, 'that's more of a winter starter, isn't it, Meg? Are all the vegetables organic?'

I bite my lip.

'Meg's soup's lovely,' Simon says. 'And we're having a roast, Mum. Which is hardly summer food either, is it?'

'If it was warmer, Simon could cremate some food on the barbecue,' Dan says.

I laugh. Simon's a dreadful cook.

'I think you mean cook, Dan,' Maureen frowns at him, 'not cremate.'

'Mum always says cremate, don't you, Mum?' Dan says, looking up at me.

'Not always,' I say mildly. 'So who's for soup?'

Grasshopper barks in the garden. I tied her lead to the tree earlier and she's not amused. The back door and the glass in the patio door are splattered with dirty paw marks and I refuse to clean them yet again.

'What's Grasshopper doing here?' Mum asks.

'Paul's in Slovakia,' I say without thinking. 'He'll be back this evening.'

'Slovakia?' Dad asks, suddenly sitting up. 'What's he doing in Slovakia?'

Just then the doorbell rings. 'Must be Hattie. Simon, will you serve the rest of the soup, please?'

I walk into the hall and open the door. Hattie steps in and I lean towards her, banging my head gently against her shoulder. 'Hattie, help. It's horrible, horrible.'

She laughs. 'Enjoying the in-laws?'

I raise my head and grin at her. 'What do you think?'

'Come on.' She grabs my arm and pulls me towards the kitchen. 'I'm starving.'

'You're also late.'

'I know. Sorry.'

We walk into the kitchen.

'Hi, everyone.' Hattie totters on her heels towards Maureen and throws her arms around her, clutching her to her Wonderbra-ed chest. Not that she actually needs a Wonderbra, lucky thing. 'Maureen, how lovely to see you.'

Maureen manages to compose herself. 'Hello, Hattie.'

Hattie kisses Joe on the cheek and he blushes. He has a bit of a thing for Hattie. 'How's my favourite curry eater?' she asks him. 'Still drinking that flat brown ale?'

Joe laughs. 'Still drinking it, Hattie.'

She spots a chair beside Simon and sits down. It's actually my chair, but I don't mind. I sit beside Dan, in Hattie's place. I know exactly what Hattie's up to. Sussing out Simon's single friends.

'Let's say grace,' Dad says as soon as we're all seated. Simon and Maureen, who have already started eating, put their spoons down.

'Ah, Dad,' Hattie says, 'do we have to? It's so embarrassing. And it's not even your house. Maybe Meg doesn't want . . .'

Dad ignores her. He's very set in his ways and a dinner isn't a dinner without grace in his book. I give Hattie a grateful look. At least she tried.

'It's fine,' I say. 'Go ahead, Dad.'

Dad clears his throat. 'For what we are about to receive, may the Lord make us truly grateful. Amen.'

Maureen and Joe say 'Amen'. Mum and Dad say 'Armen', the Church of Ireland way. I smile at Hattie and she smiles back. In a country full of Catholics, Simon managed to find a Protestant girl, me, much to Maureen's disgust. She's a staunch Catholic. She doesn't actually go to Mass in London, but she always makes a point of going when she's in Ireland. Joe isn't bothered either way. He chauffeurs her there and sits in the car, listening to Radio 4 and reading the papers.

'So, why's Paul in Slovakia?' Dad asks. It's obviously still bothering him.

'He's got a new Slovakian girlfriend,' Hattie says. 'Her name's Katia.'

'And she's a stunner,' Simon says rather unhelpfully. 'Gorgeous. Lucky Paul. A real looker.' He's practically drooling.

'Thanks for that, Simon,' I say. Sometimes he's a total embarrassment.

'It must be serious if he's going over to meet her parents,' Maureen points out.

Mum and Dad gasp.

I groan inwardly. Here we go.

Mum and Dad stare at Hattie. 'Is that what's he's doing?' Dad demands. 'Meeting her parents?'

Hattie nods. 'Yes. And I think they *are* quite serious, you know. They're talking about buying a flat in town.'

'What's wrong with the flat they're in?' Dad asks.

'It's yours,' I point out, 'that's what's wrong with it. I think they want to start standing on their own two feet.'

'Have I missed something?' Mum asks. 'Isn't Paul living with a Katia? He told me she was just renting a room. Is it the same girl?'

Hattie snorts. 'Renting a room? And you believed him? Mum! Of course it's the same girl. I'd say they're at it like rabbits.'

Maureen puts her hands over Lily's ears.

'Don't fuss over that child,' Mum says to Maureen, 'you'll put her off her food.' Mum brushes her hair back off her face. Her face is red. 'And we don't all have smutty minds like yours, Hattie. You're obsessed with sex.'

'I am not!' Hattie says indignantly. 'There's nothing wrong with a healthy interest in sex.'

'Hello!' I interrupt. 'Dan's at the table.'

'I don't mind.' Dan smiles at Hattie. 'I like it when Hattie tells me about her boyfriends and stuff.'

'Hattie!' I stare at her. 'What have you been saying to him?'

'Nothing that he shouldn't already know. He's eleven. He's interested in girls. Nothing wrong with that.'

'Are you?' I ask Dan.

'What?' he asks.

'Interested in girls?'

He stares at the table. 'Maybe.' The tips of his ears turn pink.

I'm gobsmacked. I can't believe Hattie knows something about Dan that I don't. We share everything me and Dan. Partners in crime.

'Oh,' I manage to say.

'So how's everyone's soup?' Simon asks.

Later that evening, there's a splatter of flying gravel and a screech of brakes outside.

Hattie looks at me and smiles. 'Paul,' she says.

I flick my damp teatowel at her. 'Now be nice to him.'

Hattie takes her hands out of the sink and peels off the yellow Marigolds. 'Yeah, yeah. At least Mum and Dad are a few glasses of wine down. They're fairly mellow.'

I smile. 'Mum's a bit pissed. She's useless. One sherry and she's anyone's.'

Hattie laughs. 'Do you think that's why she married Dad? Access to good booze?'

'You never know.' Dad works as a rep in the wine trade and he's always bringing home nice bottles of wine.

'Do you think he'll retire soon? He's nearly sixty-six.'

I shrug my shoulders. 'Wouldn't say so. It suits him. He has cut back a good bit though. And Mum isn't exactly encouraging him to retire, is she?'

'Can't blame her. I wouldn't want him moping around the house all day either.'

'Hattie! He doesn't mope.'

'Oh yes he does. He's a right moody bastard when he wants to be, I should know.'

'Why don't you move out? Get your own place?'

'And pay out thousands of euros a year in rent when I can spend it on clothes and shoes? Get real!'

'You must be saving some money towards a flat.'

27

'On my salary? You've got to be joking. I work in a clothes shop, Meg. And the owner's a scabby bitch.'

'Hattie!'

'Well she is.'

'So why don't you find another job?'

'She may be a bitch but she's got a great eye for labels. It's a good place to work while I wait for my rich husband to come along and whisk me away from it all. Besides, I get a great discount on the clothes.'

The worrying thing about Hattie and the rich husband thing is that it isn't a joke.

'How are my favourite sisters?' Paul says sloping into the kitchen, his hands deep in his baggy jeans pockets. His hair is newly shaven and he looks much younger than his twenty-two years.

'I can see your underwear.' Hattie wrinkles her nose. 'That look went out a long time ago.'

He smiles lazily at her. 'Looking good, Hattie,' he retorts, leering at her cleavage.

She's not impressed. 'Jesus, Paul, would you stop that? I'm your sister.'

'Into a bit of the old Oedipus stuff myself.'

'Paul!' I say. 'The pair of you are as bad as each other. Oedipus is a father–daughter thing, not brother–sister.'

Grasshopper barks loudly from the garden. 'So how was my angel?' Paul asks, looking out the window. 'Why is she tied to the tree, Meg?'

'Because of Maureen and Joe,' I explain. 'And my windows,' I add honestly. 'I'm sick of cleaning them. And cleaning the pee off the floor.'

He just laughs. He opens the back door, unties Grasshopper and follows her inside. The dog goes insane, jumping up and nearly knocking Paul off his feet.

He takes her front paws in his hands and dances her around the kitchen.

'What's that on your left hand?' I ask, noticing a large silver ring.

'Me engagement ring. Katia's pregnant. We're getting hitched.'

'For feck's sake,' Hattie spits out, 'don't say anything to Mum and Dad, they're going to go ballistic. They haven't even met Katia yet. Remember what they were like with Meg when she was up the pole?'

'I'm hoping they won't go so apeshit this time,' Paul says, 'what with Meg breaking the preggers ice and everything.'

'I wouldn't be so sure,' I say darkly.

Telling Mum and Dad I was pregnant was the hardest thing I'd ever had to do in my life. Far worse than childbirth. The mental anguish was unbelievable. I still can't think about it without feeling sick to the stomach: Dad's disappointment, Mum's judgemental attitude. It was a living nightmare. I wouldn't wish it on anyone. Even Paul.

'What have I missed?' Mum asks, walking into the kitchen.

'Nothing,' Hattie and I chorus.

'*Nič*,' Paul says. 'That's Slovakian for nothing. Katia's been teaching me her language.'

'That's not all Katia's been teaching you,' Hattie says under her breath. I dig her in the ribs.

'Speak English,' Mum says. 'And stop kissing that dog on the lips. You'll catch something.'

Hattie giggles.

Mum looks over at me and Hattie. 'And what are you two whispering and giggling about? You'd think you were in your teens, not grown women in your thirties.'

'I'm only twenty-three,' Hattie says. 'Remember?'

'Hattie, you've been twenty-three for three years now,' Paul says. 'I'm catching up with you.'

'Yeah, well, I'll be twenty-three until I'm twenty-six,' she says. 'And that won't be for a few years yet. And then, I warn you, I'll be twenty-nine for a long time.'

'Jeeze,' Paul swears under his breath. 'You're as bad as Katia.'

'Ah, yes, the famous Katia. I was about to come to that. When were you thinking of telling us about her? And what age is she exactly?' Mum asks suspiciously.

Paul shrugs his shoulders. 'Dunno. About the same age as Hattie I think.'

Mum looks fit to faint. 'Hattie's real age?'

'Yeah, I guess.'

Mum frowns. 'Maybe you should find out before hitching your wagon to her.'

'Too late now,' Hattie whispers.

'What was that?' Mum demands. She's having a sense of humour failure.

'*Nic*, Mum,' Hattie says, undaunted by mum's mood. '*Nic*.'

I can't help but grin widely. God, I love Hattie.

Chapter 4

*Aground: touching or stuck on the bottom, i.e.
'Help! We've run aground!'*

On Tuesday Simon has a five a.m. flight to catch, so sex is out of the question. Well, to be honest, he's up for it but I swat him away. It's far too early in the morning for those kind of shenanigans.

We'd tried to squeeze in some sex on Monday evening but we were both too tired. Besides, having Joe and Maureen in the next room isn't exactly an aphrodisiac: Maureen's high-pitched snoring would put anyone off his or her game.

By Thursday afternoon when Maureen and Joe finally leave I'm a nervous wreck and need to get out of the house. I decide to call into my neighbour, Tina.

I first met Tina at a mothers and babies group in the local community centre. Tina was the only sane woman in the room. The others were either yawningly boring or just plain odd. Tina was neither.

I had been achingly lonely and desperate to make friends with other mothers. We'd just moved back to Dublin after traipsing around the world with Simon for four years – Europe, especially the Med, America, Hong Kong, you name it – if it had a sailing community with money, we were there. Sometimes we stayed for as long as three or four months, but mostly it was only for a few weeks.

Simon and I are the joint owners of a house in Monkstown – a rickety old Victorian two-storey terraced house in Sea View Villas that had been split into three grotty studio flats before we bought it. Dad had spotted the sign and looked at it for us, saying it was a dump, but a dump in a nice location with a lot of potential. It hadn't sold at auction and we'd managed to get it for a song when the owner had finally given up hope of shifting it. But we'd never actually lived there; Simon's career had always got in the way.

From the start, we'd fallen in love with the house's character and the sense of space and, like Dad, we could see past the dark brown walls, rickety wooden floors and filthy windows and were itching to transform it back to its former glory, to create a real family home. We had part-renovated it (we'd run out of money before finishing it) and we'd rented it out to three young nurses who didn't seem to mind the building-site state of the place because it was practically next door to the nursing home they all worked in. We'd always meant to live there permanently; Simon had promised me that as soon as I got bored following him around the sailing circuit, we'd come home. Settle.

I finally realized during race week in Antigua that it just wasn't going to happen: Simon would never settle in one place for long while he was still sailing.

Antigua is a strange place; I didn't really like it to be honest. One the one hand you have the grinding poverty of most of the local people, the shanty towns of the capital, St John's, the goats running wild all over the island, the mangy dogs yapping at your car – if you're lucky enough to own one. On the other hand you have English Harbour and all the glamour and big money of Antigua Sailing Week, a huge regatta that attracts the crème de la crème of the sailing world.

When the Boys Are Away

I was sitting in the Beach Bar in English Harbour on the last night of the race week, Dan and Lily torturing ants in the dirty sand to the left of my feet, when I had an epiphany.

Simon's boat had won its class in the regatta. I watched the men congratulate each other and fawn over the owner, Dessie, a man who'd made his money in sewerage, and I suddenly realized I'd had enough. I didn't want to do this any more. I didn't want to be the smiling wife or girlfriend sitting on shore waiting, always waiting: for Simon's boat to come in; for my half-cut man to drag himself away reluctantly from the crew in the evenings; for some time with him, some real time together without other sweaty men breathing down our necks.

I was tired of the excess, the wasted champagne, the lobster dinners, the insincere wives who were always watching their backs for the younger, skinnier girls hovering around the men like wasps around a pint of cider, snapping at the wives' heels, the bland hotel rooms, the cramped rented houses, the travel cots, the sweaty heat in some countries, the damp cold in others.

It was time to go home.

Tina lives three doors down from me on the terrace. Three doors but another world. Her house is much bigger and extended to the hilt. She and her husband Oliver paid top dollar for their house; we got ours for a song.

Oliver (never Ollie) is the head of the Allied Celtic Bank in London, a tall man with a slim yet muscular frame, a shock of red hair that he likes to keep long and foppish, just off his collar, piercing dark blue eyes and clear, slightly freckled Irish skin. He has a penchant for charcoal-black Prada suits, teamed with coloured shirts and flamboyant ties and even has a personal stylist to keep him in check. He uses a dash of false tan in his moisturizer to keep his face glowing. I know all this because Tina told me. Like having my very own walking, talking *Hello!*

magazine on tap; an in to the lives of the Monkstown rich and famous.

Occasionally Tina is flown over to London for some important bank party, leaving her brood with an agency nanny, although the parties seem to have dried up recently.

As well as their home on the terrace they also own an apartment in Chelsea, 'Oliver's bachelor pad' as Tina calls it wryly. Oliver works in London from Monday to Friday, flying home most Friday evenings, making Tina your typical Dublin 'work widow'.

I've never really taken to Oliver. I find him a bit intimidating to be honest, but Tina's a dote. I've only known her a short while but we've already become good friends.

I stand outside her door on Thursday afternoon with Lily on my hip. It's pouring and stupidly I haven't grabbed a mac or umbrella on my way out. Lily is wriggling around, trying to reach the door bell which I've already pressed.

Tina answers the door, her own one-year-old, Eric, on her hip. Her face breaks into a wide smile when she realizes it's me.

'Meg, come on in. How's my little Lily?'

Lily points to Eric and says, 'Baba.'

We both laugh.

'Where's Freddie?' I ask. It's suspiciously quiet. Freddie is a human wrecking ball of three.

'With his granny, thank goodness. And Dan?' she asks as I walk into her light and airy hall. It's painted, as the entire house is, in Farrow and Ball. Bone, I seem to remember. Odd name for a paint. A huge mirror hangs over the antique mahogany hall table and a huge crystal vase of red tulips gives a splash of colour.

'He's at home watching some noisy American teen thing,' I say. 'I like the tulips.'

'Aren't they lovely? I'll have to change them on Friday, of course.'

'Why?'

'Oliver only likes white flowers.'

'Really?'

She raises her eyebrows.

'You know what he's like.'

I smile but say nothing. To be honest, I don't really know Oliver at all. I rarely see Tina and Oliver together and I've only talked to him a handful of times.

'How were the in-laws?' She leads me into the kitchen.

I make a face and she laughs.

'Make yourself at home.' She gestures at the kitchen table.

I sit down. 'Gone,' I say.

Tina plonks Eric onto the floor and I keep Lily on my knee, jigging her to keep her happy.

'Illy play.' Lily squirms. I put her down beside Eric and watch her for a few seconds to make sure she doesn't push or hit him. When Lily's settled, I look over at Tina.

She's leaning against the black granite counter top. 'Tea? Or something stronger? I have a bottle of white wine in the fridge and I'm only looking for an excuse for a glass.'

'It's a bit early,' I say, dithering, 'but what the hell?'

She grins. 'Good.' She takes out two large wine glasses, and opens the huge stainless-steel American larder fridge and takes out the bottle.

Eric squeals and I look down. Lily is pulling a train out of his hands. He looks at her for a moment, deciding whether to cry or not. Tina hastily hands him a biscuit.

'Illy biscuit,' Lily says.

'Here you go, Lily.' Tina doles out another.

'And how are you?' I ask as Tina hands me a generous glass of wine.

'Good.' But her eyes don't say good, they say tired and down. She takes a large gulp of her wine.

I'm about to ask her what's wrong when my mobile rings.

I wiggle it out of my pocket and glance at the screen. 'Sorry. It's Dan. Better see what he wants.'

'Dan, is everything OK?' I ask.

'Mum, I heard a noise upstairs.'

'What kind of noise?'

'A gurgling noise.'

'What do you mean a gurgling noise? Have you been watching one of Simon's science-fiction movies again?'

'No! I'm serious. There's another noise now. I think there's someone upstairs!'

'I'll be right over.'

'I'm sorry, I have to go.' I jump up and grab Lily around the waist. She protests but I ignore her. 'Dan thinks there's someone in the house.'

Tina grabs Eric, who gurgles with delight. 'I'm coming with you. Will I ring the guards?'

'Not yet.'

When we approach the house, Dan's standing outside, his hair dripping from the heavy rain, his eyes wide with fear. He's nearly twelve, but an intruder in the house would scare even the bravest adult.

'Are you OK?' I ask him a little frantically.

He nods. 'There's water running down the wall.'

'Water? Where?'

'In the hall.'

I hand Lily to him. 'Hold onto your sister. Stay with Tina.'

Tina ruffles his hair. 'It'll be all right, Dan. I have my mobile and I'll ring the guards if anything happens.'

I peer in the open door. Dan's right. There's a steady stream of water running down the right-hand wall. I hear a loud crack and suddenly the stream becomes a torrent. I run upstairs and look into our bedroom. The wallpaper is bulging off the wall in large bubbles.

'It's OK,' I yell downstairs. 'There's no one up here; it's just water.' I hear the front door slam, voices in the hall and the next minute Tina is beside me.

'Bloody hell,' she says. 'I've never seen anything like that before. It's like some sort of modern-art installation.'

I groan and cover my face with my hands. I half hope when I take them away again that the whole nightmarish scene will have vanished, David Blaine style. Some hope!

The previously plain cream wall to the left of the large (draughty) sash window looks like something out of *Dr Who*. It's blistered with huge, head-sized bubbles of water trapped beneath the ancient layers of wallpaper. When Simon and I first started redecorating the house, over four years ago now, we'd discovered that if you stripped the wallpaper off, chunks of the original plaster came with it. So instead of stripping a wall we simply patched it up with new rolls of lining paper and slapped paint over the top – not exactly the most professional finish in the world, but it does the job.

Several of these blisters have already burst, depositing their tea-coloured water all over the dark blue carpet and leaving sepia-coloured stains on the cream paint. No wonder water is dripping into the hall. Several of the bubbles look ominously pregnant. I rush into the bathroom, grab an armful of towels from the hot press and the hollow plastic step that Lily uses to reach the sink to wash her teeth and dash back into the bedroom.

Tina is poking the largest of the bubbles with her finger, making it wobble ominously. 'This is fascinating,' she says with glee. 'They don't show you things like this on those house programmes, do they? *Changing Rooms* or the like.'

'Here you go, Carole Smilie.' I hand her a bunch of towels. 'Although come to think of it, I think *Changing Rooms* went out with the ark. Pity, I rather liked it. Anyway, throw these down on the carpet under that bubble.' I point at the blister she's been poking. 'And hold one under it to catch any water I miss. I'm going to burst it and try to collect the water in this.' I nod at Lily's step, now inverted.

Tina looks at my hands a little dubiously. 'OK. But maybe I should do the bursting. You don't exactly have any fingernails.'

She's right, I'm a terrible nail biter.

'I'll manage.'

'Can I do the next one?' Her eyes glint with anticipation.

'Tina! My house is flooding. This isn't some sort of school science experiment. Concentrate!' I stand with one shoulder against the wall, just beside the bubble, positioning Lily's stool.

'Sorry. But you must admit it is kind of funny.'

I try to keep a straight face but fail miserably. Tina's right, it is funny.

I relent and give her a smile. 'OK, you can do the next one.'

'Cool!'

'Right, are you ready with the towel?'

She scuttles towards the wall, lays a bundle of towels under the bubble and another bundle against the wall under the stool. 'Ready!'

'On three. One, two, three.' I press the half-nail of my bitten index finger into the blister at its lowest point and the water-soaked paper gives no resistance, it's like pressing into the film on top of custard. Water whooshes out immediately. And more water. And more water. Tina mops up furiously as the step quickly fills.

'Where's it all coming from?' she asks.

'I guess the roof's leaking.' By now the water has subsided to a spluttery trickle. 'Last time Matty had a look at it, he did warn us. Something about the flashing or was it the flushing? And the rendering. There's a gap between them apparently. It's quite serious.'

'Matty?'

'Our builder. He's a doll.'

'Cute?'

38

'Tina!'

'Only joking.'

I think for a second. Matty's tall and blond. And yes, cute enough, although a bit skinny for my taste. 'Actually he is come to think of it. But he's only twenty-six or -seven or something. Bit too young for you.'

'Says who?'

'Hey, gutter brain, back to my wall.' The step is getting heavy in my arms. 'I'll empty this out and be back in a second.'

'And I can do the next one?' she asks eagerly.

I laugh. 'Yes, yes.'

I empty the step into the bath with a satisfying slosh.

'Which one next?' she asks as I walked back in.

'You can choose.'

'That one.' She points to the biggest one of all. 'Isn't this fun?' She looks at me and I can't help but smile. 'Sorry, Meg. I know it's a pain for you, but you know what I mean. It's not something that happens every day, is it? A wall like this.'

'Don't get out much, do you?'

She laughs and slaps me with the wet towel.

'Hey!' I flick my wet fingers at her.

'Hello!' Dan shouts from downstairs. 'Can we come upstairs? Eric's getting bored.'

'No!' I yell back.

'Yes!' Tina yells simultaneously.

I look at her. 'He's going to get wet. And Lily. And Dan will want a go.'

She shrugs. 'So what? At least it will keep them entertained. It's only water.'

I jostle her with my shoulder. 'You're nuts.'

Half an hour later, we've burst all the bubbles (with Dan's help – as I'd suspected, he'd been only too delighted to join in) and I've tried to contact Simon but he's not answering his mobile.

No surprise there. He's probably sunning himself with one of the Spanish princesses, drinking royal sangria and quaffing gourmet tapas on the deck of the royal super yacht.

So I ring Matty myself. Our house was one of Matty's first jobs as a contractor, and we took a bit of a leap of faith as he was only just nineteen at the time. He's the nephew of one of Mum's friends, which is how he got the job in the first place. But he proved himself more than able, and was charming to deal with.

As we were travelling so much, Matty made a lot of the decisions himself, only ringing me or Simon when it was urgent. In the early days we'd been pretty much in weekly contact with Matty and he became a sort of surrogate landlord when we were renting our house to the nurses. They'd a never-ending list of complaints ranging from the serious (blocked drains) to the trivial (spiders in the bath) and anything in between (water shortages, ripped shower curtains, baby mouse in the kitchen).

Matty comes around at seven, after his last job. He inspects the roof and the wall inside and out and by the expression on his face, I know it's not good news. Simon eventually rings at eleven.

'Hi, love. Where have you been?' I sit down on the side of the bed. I've been kneeling on the floor, balling Dan's and Lily's socks together, a thrilling job. One of Lily's cars digs into the side of my bottom and I remove it and throw it into the washing basket with the socks. 'Why didn't you ring back earlier?'

'Sorry. We won the first race and had to stay for the prize-giving. And then everyone started to buy us drinks. You know how it is.'

'Um,' I murmur.

'Is anything wrong? You sound a little tense.'

'Tense? Aagh!' I let out a muffled scream.

'Are you all right?'

'No, this stupid house is falling down around my ears. Lily was a nightmare all evening. Dan's been giving me cheek, he's in trouble in school, and he needs a new wetsuit for his bloody swimming test tomorrow afternoon, and our bedroom is like a swimming pool.' I pause for breath. I know I'm ranting but I can't help myself. 'The carpet's ruined and the walls . . . Oh, Simon.' I can't go on, it's all too much for me. I swing my feet onto the bed and lean back against the wooden headboard.

'It sounds like you had quite a day. Did a pipe burst? Why is the bedroom wet?'

I tell him all about my afternoon's escapades with Tina and the water bubbles.

'At least Tina was there,' Simon says. I know he feels useless and I'm not exactly helping matters.

'I suppose. Matty called in this evening.'

'And?'

'He said the flashing's had it. It has to be ripped out and replaced, along with most of the rendering underneath it.'

'It's fixable though, right?'

'Yes. But it's a big job.'

'He did warn us.'

'I know, but I thought we'd get a few more years out of it. Apparently if we don't do it now the wall could be irreversibly damaged. It's going to be expensive.'

'How expensive?' Simon asked.

'Several thousand euro, minimum.'

Simon whistles.

'No kidding. But, Simon, we don't have that kind of money. We've already dipped into our savings to pay for my car. There's only a few hundred euro left. Matty says he can do it next week as one of his jobs has been cancelled. But if we don't take that slot, it'll be September before he's free again. What do you think?'

'I guess if Matty says it needs to be done—' Simon stops for a moment – 'listen, I'll give him a ring tomorrow. Maybe he'll let us pay in instalments or something.'

'Would you? Thanks. That'd be great. I have to take Dan to his swimming test after school. Tina's taking Lily for me.'

'OK. I'll ring him tomorrow. I promise. Are you all right now, Meg?'

I sigh. 'I just wish you were here to help. I hate all this building stuff.'

'I'm sorry. I don't know what to say. I'd be there if I could, but I'm working.' He pauses for a moment. 'I thought you wanted to be at home in Dublin with the kids so that Dan could go to school, make proper friends, so you could be near your family. Isn't that what you wanted?'

'Yes. But I didn't know it would be like this.'

'Like what?'

Tears spring to my eyes. 'I didn't know it would be so damned lonely.'

'You have Hattie nearby, don't you?'

He isn't helping. All I really want is a bit of sympathy. For him to tell me I'm doing OK, that I'm a good mother, not a waste of space, like I'm feeling at this precise moment. That he loves me; misses me.

'And you've got Tina now,' he adds. 'And you've only been back in Dublin a short while. Give it time.'

'Yes, yes, I know all that. But I can't help how I feel.'

'Maybe you should take a part-time job, get out of the house a bit. That might help.'

Simon always has an answer for everything.

'I'm tired enough as it is. Now you want me to go out to work too?' I worry at the skin to the side of my thumbnail.

Silence.

'Meg?'

'Yes?'

'Is it your time of the month? Is that it? Hey, you're not pregnant are you?'

'No! I've just had a very bad day. Lily's crying, I have to go.'

And by the way, you took the toothpaste again and I had to use Lily's strawberry stuff. Stop taking the toothpaste! Bye.' I practically slam down the receiver.

Pregnant indeed. Can't a girl have a bad day once in a while? I wait for him to ring back, to tell me that everything will be OK, but he doesn't. He's probably scared I'll bite his head off again. Poor man, he doesn't deserve it, but I have to take my moods out on someone. I slump back against the headboard. I hate feeling so sorry for myself.

'And I love you, dammit,' I whisper, not bothering to brush fresh tears away. 'And I really miss you.'

Chapter 5

Brightwork: highly varnished woodwork or polished metal

The next day I wake up feeling tired and groggy. I've had a restless sleep, my mind flitting from flooded houses to pretty dark-skinned Spanish girls and back again. I have no reason to question Simon's fidelity, but I've seen all kinds of things in the sailing scene and our conversation last night worries me. I don't want to drive him into someone else's arms by moaning every time he rings.

And maybe he's right, maybe I should start looking for a job. With Matty's bill on the horizon, we could do with the money. Just in the mornings, mind. I don't want to be away from Lily for the whole day, she's only two after all; and I want to be able to collect Dan from school and do his homework with him.

When Dan was a baby I'd had to go back to full-time work. It was either that or rely on social welfare.

I remember vividly handing the tiny two-month-old Dan to his minder, Diane, a very capable nurse who was taking a career break to stay at home with her own two youngsters. It nearly broke my heart. I cried all the way to Hall's Auction House and most of my first day – luckily my colleagues were reasonably understanding. Interestingly enough it was the older men, parents or not, who were the most kind.

Hall's is part of Dublin's history. It auctions everything from modern sofabeds, rickety, chipped tables and chairs, paintings and prints of all kinds right up to antique furniture, ornaments, ceramics and more esoteric items like ancient stuffed animals, human skeletons, old toys and books. It's a haven for collectors, set dressers, and people looking for a bargain, and attracts customers from all over the country. The auctions are held on a Friday morning, and house clearances are a big part of their business.

I started off in the office, a job I was lucky enough to get with only a stunningly average degree in English and History of Art behind me. I'd wanted to get into fine art auctioneering – Georgian silver teapots, Ming vases, Persian rugs – I had very highfalutin ideas. But in the early nineties there weren't any jobs going in those higher-end establishments, so Hall's it was. It wasn't exactly my dream job, but it was either that or leave the country to look for work. Practically all my friends from college had emigrated to London, New York or Europe in those job-scarce days – no Celtic Tiger for us.

So, encouraged by Dad, who saw Hall's as a way into fine art auctioneering (which it would have been if I'd worked a bit harder and taken some evening classes and exams) I took the job. And during my time there I learnt a lot and found I had a fairly good eye for things. I was no Judith Miller, but I could tell a decent bit of furniture from a fake, a decent oil painting from a cheap, mass-produced one.

I progressed from the office to helping in the auction rooms and eventually at house clearances, which I found both sad and fascinating. Some of the houses we dealt with were filthy from years of neglect and we had to wear industrial rubber gloves and overalls to protect ourselves. Once I was attacked by a huge tabby cat. It jumped down on me from the top of a cupboard, frightening the life out of me.

Other houses were full of gems that their sadly deceased owners had obviously cherished and taken exceptional care of, but now their relatives wanted to get rid of everything – the dark bulky wooden furniture and ornate picture frames deemed too large and old-fashioned for their shiny new apartments and town houses.

I'd left Hall's for good when I was six months pregnant with Lily. They held a farewell dinner in my honour and gave me a very generous gift voucher for the Brown Thomas department store which I spent rather decadently on a fantastic pair of red wedge shoes. I'd gone to buy crockery, but the shoes had called to me as only super-expensive shoes can. At the dinner my boss Desmond Hall said there'd always be a place for me at Hall's. I'd nodded and smiled at him, safe in the knowledge that I'd never have to go back. I had Simon and with a new baby on the way everything was going to change. Sometimes I miss Hall's: the camaraderie, the drinks on Friday after work, the office gossip. I wouldn't mind working there again. In fact, thinking about it, Simon's right. A job's exactly what I need. It'll get me out of the house for a few hours a day and help pay Matty.

I decide to ring Desmond and ask him for some part-time work. I'm pretty confident he'll say yes straight away. And I'm quite looking forward to getting stuck into the house clearances again. Maybe this time I'll find something really valuable which is everyone at Hall's dream: a first edition James Joyce, a piece of Clarice Cliff pottery . . .

Lily calls from her bedroom, interrupting my musings. 'Mummee, mummeeeeee!'

'Coming, Lily. Coming.'

That afternoon I collect Dan from school and drive him to Dublin Bay Marine. The owner, a lively German in his early fifties called Hans, used to be a professional sailor – that's how he knows Simon. But Hans gave it all up for love several years ago after meeting Hilda, a stunning Irish girl in her mid thirties. He settled in Dun Laoghaire and they quickly produced twin daughters, Heidi and Freya.

'Megan, my flower. How are you?' Hans booms from the back of the shop as soon as he spots me. He navigates the packed rails of sailing clothes and stands in front of me, arms outstretched.

'Give me some love.' He hugs me tight. I gasp and he draws back, unaware of his bear-like strength.

'And Dan.' Hans ruffles Dan's hair. 'Getting taller by the day. And how's Simon? Still sailing?'

'Still sailing.'

Hans shakes his head. 'Tell him when he grows out of it, there'll always be a job for him here.'

'Thanks. I will. Now I'm afraid we have to be quick. Dan has his swimming test for the sailing course right about,' I look at my watch, 'now. He urgently needs a new wetsuit and wetsuit boots.'

Hans looks Dan up and down and nods. 'No problem. Strip off in the changing room. I think I have one that will do the trick, but you'll need to try it on to make sure.'

Dan pulls a face at me. 'Do I have to, Mum? I'm sure it'll be OK.'

'Yes. I'm not shelling out a small fortune on something that doesn't fit properly.'

'Fine.' Dan folds his arms stiffly in front of his chest. I know he's nervous about the swimming test, so I decide to let his rudeness slide.

'Sorry,' I mouth at Hans.

He just smiles.

A few minutes later Dan is standing in front of us in a new blue and black wetsuit with matching black wetsuit boots. It bulges a little around his slim waist and Hans has rolled back the over-long arms.

'It's tight around the neck,' Dan complains, putting a finger between the neoprene and his skin and pulling outwards. 'And the arms and legs are too long.'

'The neck will always feel tight at first,' Hans explains. 'It'll loosen up. And you need plenty of growing room in the arms and legs. That way you should get two years out of it if you're lucky.'

'Oh, no!' Dan says. 'I'm not falling for that one. I'm not getting a wetsuit I have to grow into. Please, Hans, can't you find me a shortie?' He looks at me. 'All the kids will have shorties. Please?'

I shrug. 'This is Ireland. The sea is cold, much colder than the water you've been used to. Are you sure?'

'Yes! I can put my oilies on top if it's cold.'

I look at my watch. We're going to be seriously late if we don't get a move on, so I cave in. Lily is with Tina, and I'm hoping to get back by five.

Ten minutes later I'm standing at the side gate of the yacht club. Dan is beside me, still in his new black and red shortie wetsuit and wetsuit boots. At least this way he doesn't have to waste time changing, although we do get some funny looks while crossing the road from Hans's shop.

'Good luck.' I kiss the top of his head.

'Mum!' He squirms away from me. 'Please!'

As we walk through the gate my heart is in my mouth. Dan isn't the strongest of swimmers. It's never bothered me before because he's always worn a life jacket when out on the water, but I'm starting to get nervous on his behalf.

'You! Young man!' a plummy voice shouts.

We look over. A dark-haired man with ruddy cheeks peers over the top of his reading glasses. He's clutching a clipboard in front of his rotund stomach.

'Swimming test?' he asks sharply.

I nod.

'You're late.'

'Yes, sorry. Couldn't be helped.' Dan lurks by my side, staring at the ground.

'Name?'

'Dan Miller.'

The man runs a pen down the list on his clipboard.

He looks at me and sighs. 'No Dan Miller here I'm afraid. I have a Dan Murphy, but no Dan Miller.'

'Murphy is my partner's name,' I explain, relieved I haven't got the day wrong. 'Dan is actually Dan Miller.'

The man stares at me suspiciously and gives a tut.

'Are you a member, Mrs . . .'

'Miss Miller. And no, but Simon is. My partner.'

His clipboard drops to his side and he places one arm in front of his stomach.

'I'm terribly sorry, Miss Miller, but the sailing course is strictly for children of members. Now, if you'll excuse me.' He walks away.

I can feel my face redden. I'm mortified. I can sense Dan's discomfort.

'Let's just go,' he murmurs. I look at him, his face is beetroot coloured.

'No. I'll sort it out.' I'm damned if I'm going to let that puffed-up fart of a man treat me like that in front of Dan. Who does he think he is?

'Excuse me,' I say loudly following the man and tapping him on the shoulder. He wheels around.

'My partner, Simon, spoke to the commodore about my son. And the commodore said he'd be delighted to have him on the sailing course.'

The man narrows his eyes. He clearly doesn't believe me.

'Simon is an honorary life member,' I continue undeterred.

'And you, I presume are the head instructor, Ryan Dawson. The commodore said he'd make sure you knew Dan was coming today. Simon had dinner with him only last month.'

The man's fleshy jaw drops. He opens his mouth to say something and then closes it again. 'Let me just confer with my colleague,' he says finally.

'Giles?' A tall man in his mid twenties strides towards us. He's wearing a shortie wetsuit, a bright red life jacket and a blue sun-bleached cap and is carrying a walkie-talkie in a waterproof case. His tanned, toned calves are very cheering and I try not to stare at them. 'Any sign of the young Murphy lad yet? We're hoping to get started.'

'He's here.' I nod over at Dan who is by now cowering by the gate. 'Come on over here, Dan.'

He walks reluctantly towards us.

'I'm Meg, Dan's mum. He's very nervous and hasn't had the warmest of welcomes.'

I shoot a look at Giles.

'The lad's name wasn't on the sheet,' Giles blusters. 'Simple mistake. But he's changed and ready.'

'Good. We'll take care of him.' Ryan sticks his hand out and shakes mine firmly. 'Sorry about that. Giles is the junior organizer. He's in charge of the paperwork, isn't that right, Giles?'

'And the finances,' Giles reminds him. 'Don't forget that.'

'As if I could.' Ryan grins at me. His blue eyes wrinkle at the corners. 'I'm Ryan Dawson, head instructor. We're very honoured to have Dan on the course. I've met Simon in the bar. Great sailor.' He smiles and shakes his head. 'He's done some serious campaigns. Where is he now? Don't tell me, somewhere hot?'

'Barcelona. Sailing with the royal family,' I add, mainly for Giles's benefit and looking at him pointedly.

Ryan laughs with delight. 'Lucky guy.'

A dark-haired girl, in new-looking red and white oilskins and a matching life jacket, calls over, 'Is that all of them, Ryan?'

'Yes, just coming.' He turns back towards me. 'That's Geena, one of the other instructors. Why don't you stay and watch, Meg? There are several parents already on the slip. Is that OK, Dan?'

Dan nods. I can tell he's relieved.

'Nice to meet you, Giles,' I say. 'I'm sorry, I didn't catch your last name.'

'Cormally,' he says.

'I'll remember that,' I say pointedly. 'Cormally. Do you sail?'

'Um, not exactly,' he replies, stepping from one foot to the other. 'Used to. Bad back. Must be off. Phone calls to make, you know how it is. Be down to join you in a second.'

Ryan leads us down towards the water. He leans in towards me. 'Giles is what we call a dining member. Hasn't sailed for donkey's years but he's a big committee man now that he's retired. He's down here every day and he pays our wages.'

'Lucky you,' I say wryly.

Ryan winks at me. 'I can see why Simon's so taken with you.'

I laugh. 'Really?'

'Oh yes.' My heart gives a little hiccup. Ryan is seriously cute and a charmer too. Not that I have eyes for anyone other than Simon, of course, but I sneak a few more peeks at Ryan as I stand watching the swimming tests with the other parents. I feel a bit out of place. There are two fathers in their forties wearing suits and a handful of sleek mothers in sailing jackets and designer jeans discussing their children's swimming prowess.

'Dawn started swimming at two,' a tall bouffant blonde boasts. 'She's a natural.'

'Oh, two's far too late,' a slim black bob joins in. 'Arnold was swimming at six months.'

51

'You have to catch them before they're six months,' a tight chestnut crop says. 'My Regina was only three weeks old . . .'

Competitive parenting. I've never lowered myself and hope I never will.

One by one, the children successfully complete their test. Some easily, some with more difficulty. I'm delighted to see that Ryan has to jump in when Regina swims into the harbour instead of alongside the slip and tangles her leg in the warp of a buoy. It's all quite dramatic.

Dan opts to go last. As soon as he lowers himself into the water and swears loudly, much to my embarrassment, I know we're in for trouble.

He manages to tread water for a minute and splashes his way along the slip to complete his twenty-five metres freestyle. To finish his test he has to hold his head under the water for ten seconds. He's already tried it twice – three seconds and four seconds are all he's managed. I make my way down to the slip to see if I can help.

'I can't do this,' he says through chattering teeth after five minutes of Ryan's further cajoling. 'Too cold. Wetsuit's too tight. Can't breathe.'

Ryan and I kneel on the slip and look down at him. Some of the other parents are looking on with interest, I can feel their warm, smug eyes burrowing into my jacket.

'It's because she's not a member,' I imagine them saying. 'Isn't that right, Giles? Not a member?'

'Come on, Dan,' Ryan coaxes him. 'Just let go of the slip. You'll be fine once you're under the water. You'll get cold just hanging there like that. Simon will be disappointed if Dan can't do the course,' Ryan whispers to me.

So what about Simon? I think, Dan will be devastated. He's spent his last four summers sailing and I know he'll have severe withdrawal symptoms if he has to spend his holidays as a landlubber. Besides, from a purely selfish standpoint the thought of him moping around the house all summer at a loose end motivates me ever further. This calls for drastic action.

'Ryan, can you get in with him?' I ask.

'Sure, if you think it'll help.'

Dan looks at me. I can see the fear in his eyes. He shakes his head. His lips are turning blue. 'Can't do this, Mum. Have to get out.'

'Please just give it one more go. You can do this, you know you can. You've already done the treading water and the twenty-five metres. Now you just have to put your head under that water and hold it under. It's only for ten seconds. I'll count it out really loudly for you so you can hear.'

'Can't,' he says again, his eyes wild. 'Water's so dark. Cold.'

'But you're so close.' I put the tips of my fingers to my lips.

'What's the trouble over here?' Giles asks, striding over.

I look at his pristine sailing boots which have obviously never seen a drop of salt water and then up at his face.

'Dan's having trouble holding his head under the water,' Ryan explains, 'but he's done everything else.'

An ugly smirk comes to Giles's face.

'Not very professional swimming, eh, Ryan? We'll have to fail the lad.' Giles raises one eyebrow. 'Sorry about this. What a shame.'

Ryan takes Giles's arm and whispers something to him.

'No, sorry,' Giles says, loud enough for me to hear. 'I don't care who his father is, rules are rules.'

'No!' I exclaim. I'm not going to let this horrible man get the better of me. 'He'll do it.' I stand up, peel off my jacket and kick off my runners. 'I'm getting in with you,' I tell a startled Dan. 'We'll both do it together, OK?'

Chapter 6

Overboard: over the side of the boat, i.e.
'Woman overboard!'

Dan thinks for a moment. He stares up at me. My eyes plead with him. Don't show me up in front of this horrible man, they say. Please.

Dan nods. 'OK, but quick. I can't feel my toes.'

'You really don't have to, Meg,' Ryan begins. 'I'm sure Giles will let Dan redo the test another day.'

'Can't do that, I'm afraid.' Giles shakes his head. 'Can't make exceptions for one child.'

'Right then,' I decide. I jump into the water just in front of Giles, hoping to send at least a small splash his way.

'Feck,' I swear. 'Sorry, but it's freezing.' I haven't experienced the temperature of the Irish Sea for a long time and it's so cold it almost winds me.

'Told you.' Dan's teeth chatter beside me.

'Let's get on with this then.' I tread water furiously. 'Can you count us down, Ryan?'

'Sure.'

'Ready, Dan?'

Dan nods, his now purple lips pressed together.

'Go!' I say.

I dip forwards, plunging my head under and holding it there.

'One, two, three, four . . .' Ryan counts from the slip.

It's the longest ten seconds of my life. My ears fill with water, and I can hear horrible, hollow gurgling noises; I hold my nose tight and screw my face up to combat the cold, feeling it seep under my skin and chill my skull bones. I can hear Dan splashing beside me. I want to open my eyes and see if he's OK, but I'm too afraid. The water isn't exactly clean.

'Five, six, seven, eight. Great Dan, nine, ten.'

I explode to the surface, spluttering and then grab for the side of the slip. Water pours out of my ears. My head feels as though it's about to explode.

I look over at Dan. He's holding the edge of the slip with one hand, a grin on his face.

'Well done,' Ryan whoops. 'You both pass.'

Several of the parents begin to clap. They recognize extreme parenting when they see it.

'Brain freeze,' Dan says to me, shaking his head.

I snort with laughter, water dripping down my face. I push the hair back off my face with shivering hands.

Dan splashes me. 'You look really funny, Mum.'

I splash him back. 'Thanks. Now, get me out of here, I'm freezing.'

'You did what?' Simon asks that evening on the phone from Spain after I tell him about the swimming test. 'You're nuts.'

'That Giles man was such a pig, I couldn't let him win. I just couldn't.'

'Wait till you meet his wife,' Simon says ominously. 'Cecily. Cow of the first degree.'

'I hope never to have that pleasure. Listen, I'm sorry about last night, I was tired and a bit stressed about the house. Thanks for talking to Matty, he's starting on Monday.'

'Good. And it's OK. I'm used to it at this stage, you old bat.'

'Charming!'

He laughs. 'So what are you up to tonight?'

'Nothing. But I'm going out for pizza with Hattie tomorrow night.' Very glam, I think to myself. 'And what are you up to? Dinner with the king? Cocktails with the queen?'

Simon laughs again. 'Reception with the British ambassador actually. His wife's Irish and she loves a good party. Should be a bit of a laugh.'

'Enjoy yourself. We'll see you on Saturday night. Will you be in late?'

'Sunday night,' Simon corrects me. 'There's an extra race on Saturday as Thursday's was blown out. Gale-force winds.'

'But Dan's party is on Sunday. You promised you'd be back.'

'Ah, Meg, I'm sorry, but I have to finish the regatta. We're lying second. Sid will be there, won't he?'

'Yes, but it's not the same. He's useless at organizing things, you know that. I'll be the one running around the cinema keeping an eye on Dan's friends. You missed his party last year because of that event in Germany. In fact, have you been to *one* of Dan's birthday parties?'

'Yes. The bouncy castle one in the garden.'

'Four years ago, Simon! You'd fly back if it was Lily's party.' Oops, did I really just say that?

'What do you mean?'

'Ignore me. It was nothing. It's after twelve and my brain's going soft.'

'I'll try to ring earlier tomorrow night. And I *am* sorry.'

'About what?'

'About missing Dan's party. And what you just said about Lily. It's not true you know; I love them both. It's just unfortunate timing, that's all.'

I'm not convinced but I say nothing. Lily is only a baby and he's flown home for both her parties. 'I'll talk to you tomorrow.'

'Love you.'

'Love you too.'

I put the phone down and stare at the wardrobe. Maybe coming back to Dublin was the wrong decision. Hattie always says there's no such thing as a right or wrong decision, there's just a decision and you have to live with the consequences and make the most of things. But right now, it certainly feels like the wrong decision to me. I want the family to be together, properly together, not like this. But the only way I can do that is to convince Simon to stop sailing, and how on earth am I going to do that?

The following evening I'm standing in front of the mirror, surveying my sagging breasts. I'm still debating what to wear. I'm only going out with Hattie but I want to make a bit of an effort. Lily is clattering around the room in my high-heeled sandals, naked except for her nappy. She's just got out of the bath and her hair is frizzed around her head in a white Afro.

Lily has the finest hair I've ever seen. It's white-blonde and hasn't grown much since she was born. The most I've ever achieved by way of a 'do' is a tiny ponytail on the top of her head, like Pebbles from *The Flintstones*.

Dan is downstairs watching *Pimp My Ride* on the telly, one of his (and Simon's) favourite programmes, after stomping out of my room following yet another argument. Poor Dan, he's hopping with pre-puberty hormones, and it makes him irrational and irritable sometimes. I was very moody as a teenager, according to Mum, but I honestly don't think I was all that bad, especially when compared to Hattie, who really was a nightmare. Dan is obviously following in our footsteps.

It makes him very difficult to live with and, to be honest, I'm not sure how to deal with him. I've tried sympathy, the 'I know how you're feeling' routine complete with strong hugs; tough love 'I'm the grown-up here and you'll do what I say'; and 'let's talk about this rationally, Dan'– none of which seem to work.

Shona, the ponytailed fifteen-year-old babysitter from down the road hasn't arrived yet, which is just as well as I haven't finished running a critical eye over my near naked body.

I turn sideways and look in the mirror again. My small, B-cup breasts are suffering from the effects of gravity and breastfeeding. I cup them in my hands and push them gently upwards. That's better. Maybe all I need is a little scaffolding. Some cleverly constructed new bras, and fast, before I start to resemble one of those African tribal women you see in *National Geographic* – with digestive-biscuit-sized nipples at belly-button level. I shudder at the thought.

The doorbell rings.

'Mum!' Dan shouts up from the hall. 'Shona's here.'

'Let her in. I'm just getting dressed. Show her into the kitchen. I'll be down in a mo.'

'OK.'

Seconds later I hear footsteps on the stairs.

'Meg? Dan told me to come up and get Lily.'

Shona looks in the open bedroom doorway. I clamp my hands over my breasts.

'Sorry, Meg.' She backs away and turns her head, obviously embarrassed. 'I'm sorry . . . Dan said . . .' she faltered.

'Dan's idea of a little joke,' I say through gritted teeth. I grab my dressing gown from the back of the door and throw it on. 'Sorry, Shona. You go on down to the kitchen and send Dan up to me. I'll be down in a minute.'

'Sure, no problem.' She stares at the carpet in front of my feet. Poor girl's probably afraid to lift her eyes.

'Dan!' I hiss as soon as he walks into the room. 'What *are* you playing at? I told you I was getting dressed. Why did you send Shona up? Answer me.'

Dan looks sheepish. 'It was only a joke.'

'It wasn't funny. You really embarrassed her. Do you understand?' I sit down on the bed. 'I don't know what to do with you. Now take your sister downstairs and get her into her pyjamas. And no more messing, do you hear me?'

'Yes, Mum.'

'And apologize to Shona.'

I just have time to slip on a bra, trousers and T-shirt before Hattie arrives.

'Meg,' she calls up the stairs, 'can I come up? Dan said to check first.'

'Of course.'

She walks into my room with a grin on her face. 'Dan says Shona saw you naked. Is that true?'

'Almost.' I tell Hattie what happened.

She throws her head back and laughs.

'It's not funny,' I protest.

'It is!' .

'I suppose it is a bit,' I concede, smiling.

She sits down on the bed. 'Are you getting changed?'

'I am changed.' I look at myself in the mirror. My plain white T-shirt is clean and my black trousers won't set the world on fire but at least they still fit.

I look at Hattie. She's wearing a green and pink silk dress, pretty diamante-studded flat sandals and a fitted denim jacket. Effortlessly chic. I feel dowdy in comparison.

'Do you think I should wear something else?'

'Not at all,' Hattie back-pedals. 'You look great.'

'No, I don't. I just don't seem to have any clothes these days. None that I want to wear anyway. These black trousers are part of a suit, but I've worn them so much they're a bit shiny. And I have no tops at all. Except for T-shirts and fleeces.'

'We should go shopping together.' 'Find you some nice tops.'

'Did I mention that I'm completely broke? And with the house to fix, I'm not going to have a penny to spend on myself for a very long time.'

'I'll lend you some tops. I could do with a bit of a clear out to be honest.'

'Charming!'

She smiles. 'As could you from the looks of things.' She reaches into the depths of my wardrobe and pulls out a dark green linen suit with a long loose jacket and wide-legged trousers. 'You must get rid of some of this, Meg. It's so dated.'

I sigh. 'I know.' My wardrobe is a shambles. And my life isn't far behind.

Chapter 7

*Navigation: the art of conducting a boat safely
from one place to another*

On Wednesday I'm having another wardrobe crisis. I've been summoned for a meeting after school with Dan's teacher, Miss Myson, and I stupidly thought it would be a great idea to wear one of the new-to-me tops Hattie gave me in a pathetic attempt to impress the woman. The top is wine-red, low cut, with sequined butterflies on the front and floaty chiffon sleeves and I've teamed it with my black trousers and my only pair of decent black high-heeled boots. As I step out of the car and look at all the other sleek, confident mothers in their pristine, ultra casual, jewel-coloured tracksuits and runners or 'thrown together' Boho skirts teamed with high wedge-heeled boots I know I've made a mistake. I look overdone, like someone who's making too much effort. My outfit is more 'drinks after work' than 'meeting son's teacher'. I can't seem to get anything right these days. Some of the other mothers nod at me as I pass with Lily on my hip. I say 'hello' to several I recognize, mothers of Dan's classmates, and they look at me in surprise, as if trying to place me. It's been weeks since Dan started school and I still haven't infiltrated the school-gate mafia. But I live in hope. Dan's best friend is George, whose mum works full-time as a vet's assistant so I tend to make play arrangements with the au pair. But there are other mothers with toddlers on their hips, so maybe I'll make friends soon.

Miss Myson is one of the older teachers in the school, an experienced woman in her early fifties with a high, shiny forehead and a clipped way of speaking. Dan seems to like her well enough, he says she's fair in class and lets them read comics in silent reading instead of a book.

I'm a little nervous about what she's going to tell me. She ushers me into the classroom with a tight smile, straightening her camel-coloured finely ribbed jumper so it sits evenly over her tweedy skirt.

'Will you be OK out here with Lily?' I ask Dan. 'Keep her away from the stairs. I won't be long.'

'You could show her the fish tank in Miss Simmond's classroom,' Miss Myson suggests.

'Ish,' Lily says. 'Where 'ish?'

Dan leads Lily away by the hand.

'He's very good with his sister,' Miss Myson comments as she walks towards the large desk at the top of the room. The air smells musty: eau de pre-teens, mixed with stale sandwiches, glue and, strangely enough, pine cones.

'Please sit.' She gestures at a stiff-backed grey plastic chair.

I sit down and stare at the desk in front of me. It's very tidy. To the right are three neat stacks of exercise books, orange, blue and green; to the left is a large plastic pen holder and stationery tray, full of pens, pencils, three different kinds of sellotape, orange-handled scissors and coloured paperclips. An old-fashioned pencil sharpener with a handle is screwed to the side of the desk. As Dan isn't the most organized of children, all this neatness makes me nervous.

'I'm sure you're wondering why I called you in here today,' she says, her hands clasped together loosely on top of the desk.

I nod. 'Yes. I hope Dan's not in any sort of trouble.'

'Trouble?' She unclasps her hands and pushes her glasses up her nose. 'Not really. I wouldn't call it trouble exactly.'

My heart sinks. What has he done?

'I'll come straight to the point. I'm a bit worried about him. He seems to be spending a lot of time with the girls at break and lunchtimes. The other boys used to play football and indeed some of them still do, but Dan has introduced "kiss chase" into the playground.' She leans forwards in her seat. 'It's become rather popular. And I caught him kissing Mary Ball behind the bike shed. Were you aware of any of this, Mrs Murphy?'

'Um, no.' I'm flustered. 'No.' I'm quite sure what to say. To be honest, I'm trying desperately hard not to smile or laugh. Think of sad things, I tell myself. Sid, think of Sid.

'Are you all right, Mrs Murphy? You look rather flushed.'

'Fine thanks. It's just a little hot in here.'

'It is a little.' Miss Myson stands up and wrenches open a window.

As I watch her I think about what she's just said. Dan, a Casanova in the making. I quite like the idea as long as it doesn't go too far. I'd always been on the periphery of the 'in crowd' in school; not geeky enough to join the maths/chess/computer club gang, not cool enough for the cool kids, in social no man's land. Now and again I'd be invited to cool parties, but this tended to be a very ephemeral thing – one blink and I was relegated to social limbo.

Miss Myson sits down again, puts her hands together in prayer position and presses her fingertips against her lips. She sighs. 'It's not the kind of behaviour we expect in Monkstown National School.'

'No, quite,' I manage to say.

Miss Myson looks out the window for a second. Then she

takes off her glasses, rubs her eyes with her knuckles, and puts the glasses on again.

'I'll have a word with him,' I say, feeling sorry for her. She's obviously finding this difficult.

'Thank you, Mrs Murphy.'

'Actually it's Miss. Miss Miller.'

She looks at me for a moment and then gives a tiny nod.

'But Meg is fine,' I add. 'And while I'm here, how is Dan getting on otherwise? Is he coping with the work?'

She gives a short laugh. 'Coping? He's more than coping.' She pulls out an exercise book from the pile beside her, opens it and hands it to me. 'Here's his maths book. Take a look.'

I flick through the pages. Ten out of ten, I read. Nine out of ten, 98 per cent, 97 per cent, 90 per cent – could do better than this, Dan, 90 per cent is not up to your usual standard. I close the book and hand it back to her.

'He's close to the top of the class in all his subjects except for Irish,' she says. She pushes her glasses up her nose again. 'You've been teaching him yourself, haven't you?'

'Yes, for the last few years. He was in Dun Laoghaire National before that.'

'And how did you find him?'

'Once he concentrated, fine. But I had nothing to compare him against.'

'I suppose not. Dan is a bright boy, but as you say, he's easily distracted. He can be a little cheeky in class, but it's nothing I can't handle.'

I don't doubt it. 'So he's settling in all right?'

'Yes. A little too well it seems.'

'Ah, yes. As I said I'll have a word with him about the kissing business. Thanks for your time.'

'There is just one more thing, Meg. Several of the other mothers have pointed out to me that Dan's uniform is not quite . . . how can I put this?'

'Right?' I suggest, thinking of his non-official tracksuit.

'Exactly. He has a habit of coming to school with no socks on.'

'No socks at all?'

She nods. 'It's not that important. But I just thought I'd mention it to you.'

'Dan has lived in warm climates for the last few years. He's used to wearing sandals, I guess. But I'll make sure he's wearing socks from now on. You can be sure of it.' I'll kill him. Showing me up like that. I hadn't even noticed – how bad does that make me?

'Thanks for telling me,' I add.

Miss Myson gives me a smile. 'Dan's a bright lad and most of the time he's a pleasure to have in my class.'

'Thanks,' I say gratefully.

'You're welcome. I'll see you again.' She stands up quickly, her chair banging against the wall behind her.

'Not too soon I hope,' I say with a laugh.

'Quite.' She smiles back, this time the smile really reaches her eyes and makes her look years younger.

As soon as Miss Myson opens the classroom door to let me escape we can hear Dan and Lily in the adjacent room.

'No, Lily, fish don't like plasticine. Or scissors. Give me the scissors, Lily. No!'

'Hi, Dan.' I walk into the classroom. Lily powers towards me.

'Mummy!' She pitches her little body against my legs and throws her arms around them. For a small one, she has surprising strength.

'Easy, Lily.' I bend down to pick her up. 'How was she?' I ask Dan.

'The usual. Wild.'

'Thanks for looking after her. Grab your bag now, we're going home.'

'Am I in trouble?' he asks in a low voice, leaning towards me.

'We'll talk about it in the car.'

He bites his lip. I hear him mutter something under his breath and I throw him a look.

Miss Myson is watching us from the doorway. She steps back to let us out.

'Bye, Miss Myson,' I say. 'And thanks.'

'Goodbye, Meg. And good luck.'

As soon as I've wrestled Lily into her car seat I climb into the driver's seat, close the door and tilt my head back against the head rest. I close my eyes for a moment, take a deep breath and open them again.

Dan is watching me closely. 'Please, Mum, put me out of my misery. Am I in trouble?'

'Yes and no.' I start up the engine. 'Tell me about Mary Ball.' I look at him in the rear-view mirror.

The tips of his ears turn pink and he folds his arms in front of his body defensively. 'She's my old girlfriend. Grace Smithfield is my new one. She's in sixth class.'

'Is she now?' I'm impressed, but I try not to show it. 'And have you been kissing her too?'

'Mum!'

I turn my body around and rest my arms along the tops of the front seats.

'Stop laughing at me,' he says huffily.

'I'm not laughing, Dan. Just smiling. Wait till I tell your dad and Simon.'

Lily starts to yell. And there's nothing more stressful than being stuck in a car with a yelling toddler. 'Better get moving,' I say. 'We'll talk when we get home.'

'But am I in trouble?' Dan repeats.

'Yes, a bit. You'll have to be more polite to Miss Myson in class. And promise me you won't kiss Mary . . .'

'Grace.'

'Any girl in the playground. Or anywhere else for that matter. You're too young. There's plenty of time for that sort of thing when you're a teenager.'

'Mum!' Dan rolls his eyes. 'I'm eleven. Nearly twelve.'

'Exactly.'

I look down at his feet and wince as I see an inch of bare skin above both his shoes. 'And wear socks, for heaven's sake. You have the other mothers gossiping about neglectful parenting already, thanks very much.'

'I hate socks,' he mutters darkly. 'The make my feet sweat. And you nick all my black ones.'

'I do not!' I protest, but he's right. 'Just wear them tomorrow, OK?'

'Fine.'

'Good.'

Lily starts to kick the back of my seat and scream.

I indicate and pull out. It's going to be a noisy trip home.

I'm dying to meet this Grace and check her out for myself. Luckily I get the chance sooner than I think as Dan has invited her and her best friend Millie to his birthday party on Sunday evening. He originally wanted to have a disco and invite the whole class but I don't have the energy to be honest. Besides the rest of the boys in his class are still having far more innocent parties – barbecues, picnics and trips to the bowling alley or swimming pool. So we've compromised on a pizza restaurant, followed by the cinema. I'm dreading it.

Sid is coming to help and Hattie is minding Lily until eight, when Shona's free from another babysitting job. I'd love Hattie there with me for moral support, to protect me from Dan's friends, not to mention Sid, but Mum and Dad are at the opening of a new gardening centre, and I don't like to ask Tina to look after Lily at the weekends. She's so helpful with her during the week, it hardly seems fair.

'Hey, Megan!' Sid waves from outside Chew and Chat's bright red door. It's not the most glamorous of restaurants, the red paintwork on the door and windows has seen better days and most of the tables and chairs are a bit rickety, but it's cheap and the pizzas are excellent: thin, crispy bases, heavy on the tomato sauce and cheese – just how I like them.

I wave back and extend my arm in front of Dan. He has a habit of dashing across roads without looking and putting my arm out is a reflex action. We cross together after a motorbike and a noisy van have passed.

'You're early,' I say to Sid.

He smiles down at me, his light blue eyes twinkling in his tanned face. Sid works outside a lot and always has colour in his face, lucky man. Wasted on him of course – he has olive-coloured skin anyway. Luckily Dan has inherited his colouring and not mine. In fact, Dan is a most attractive child with Sid's skin, Sid's eyes, Sid's height, my blonde (ish) hair, Sid's aptitude for getting into trouble.

'You know what Nora's like,' he says. 'Anal about time keeping.'

'She's here?' I hiss, looking around wildly.

'Shush, she'll hear you.' He nods at the outside seating area to the right of the restaurant which is cordoned off with a low red plastic Chew and Chat awning. Nora is slouching in an aluminium chair, her high-heeled sandalled feet resting on another chair, large gold-framed designer sunglasses nestled in her dark wavy hair. She's looking annoyingly fresh in skinny-legged white jeans with an expensive-looking gold chain belt, a crisp white low-cut T-shirt exposing the top edge of a lacy pink bra. A tiny denim jacket is resting over the back of her chair. I instantly regret wearing my jeans, runners and a long-sleeved, white T-shirt. I look like a frump in comparison. Plus I have no boobs. I'm convinced Nora's are fake. No one that scrawny has such round, pert boobs. It isn't natural. And it certainly isn't fair.

'What's she doing here?' I ask Sid huffily. 'I certainly didn't invite her.' I clutch my large holdall bag to my chest.

Dan is peering in the window of the restaurant, his nose shoved right up against the glass.

'Dan asked her last week,' Sid says mildly. 'And don't go starting anything, Meg. This is Dan's night, remember? Be nice to her.'

'I'm always nice to Nora. It's her that has the problem, not me.'

'Whatever.'

'And don't you go saying "whatever" in front of Dan. It's rubbing off on him and I hate it.'

'Whatever,' Sid drawls in an exaggerated American accent.

'Stop it!' I laugh.

He gives me a wide grin, his crooked teeth showing. He nudges me in the side.

'You're so easy to wind up, Meg. Always were.'

I'm ashamed to say that my heart melts a little. Sid isn't good-looking in a conventional way, but he has buckets of charisma and an easy self-confidence that is irresistible.

I first met him at my parent's, funnily enough. Their house had been broken into while Mum was in the garden. She'd come back inside to find two teenage boys running down the stairs.

'Cooee, boys. Are you here to see Paul?' she'd asked them innocently, peeling off her gardening gloves.

They'd dropped her handbag and scarpered. When it hit her a split second later that they were burglars, she'd collapsed on the stairs. She's been horribly nervous of being in the house on her own ever since. So a state of the art alarm had been installed and Sid was employed to put security lights on the front and side walls.

'Would you look at that,' Hattie had said one Saturday morning, staring out the living-room window. I had just finished sitting my college exams and I was wiped out. I tore my eyes away from *Neighbours* (a sad addiction at the time) and looked at my sister. Her head was cocked to one side and she was gazing at a headless torso, staring into a pair of dark blue combats and beige boots resting on the rungs of a ladder.

'Jeeze, I'm going to cream my knickers.'

'Hattie! That's disgusting.' I wrinkled my nose. Hattie, at fifteen, took pride in shocking her family and friends, not to mention her teachers. On that occasion she wasn't far wrong through. I stared at the taut stomach and that delicious part of a man's side between his stomach and his hips. My eyes glanced over his crotch and down towards his boots.

'Hattie, stop gawping. He's coming down.'

When Sid's head appeared, complete with his mop of dirty blond hair, and the most piercing sky-blue eyes I'd ever seen, I knew I was in trouble. I tried not to stare but it was impossible.

'Sweet Jesus,' Hattie said. 'He's a sex god.'

'Hattie,' I warned her, 'the window's open.' But it was too late, he'd already heard her.

'Hi, girls,' he said, waving and grinning, his crooked teeth showing.

Thank you, God, I'd thought. An imperfection. Maybe I have a chance.

We were together for four years, Sid and I, right through my college days, which with hindsight was rather bad timing. I didn't see past Sid; he was my whole life at the time. He consumed me. I never went on any college trips, never travelled during the long holidays, never joined any societies or sports clubs. In fact, in many ways the whole college experience was wasted on me.

When the Boys Are Away

My pregnancy came as a complete shock to everyone I knew, myself included. I was a respectable middle-class girl with an arts degree, for heaven's sake. Things like that weren't supposed to happen. But happen it did, and I'm ashamed to admit it was largely due to my cavalier attitude towards taking the pill.

I spent the first four months in complete denial. I'd taken three home pregnancy tests – the first time my hands were shaking so much I wasn't sure if I'd sprayed the stick with enough urine. The second time, I refused to believe the cruelly etched double pink lines. Even after the third test I still wasn't convinced. At five months my previously flat stomach started to round out and I had to tell Sid.

He took it surprisingly well, but as he'd just slept with Flora, the girl from the video shop, his hasty offer of marriage was just that, hasty, and I soon came to my senses.

Sid had one fatal flaw – other women. He always came crawling back to me, his tail between his legs, and until Dan was born I'd always taken him in, fool that I was. But after Dan things were different. *I* was different.

Sid met Nora at Dan's Montessori school where she was working as a teacher's assistant while taking her PR diploma by night. And they've been together – on and off – ever since. Nora hated me from the very beginning. The feeling was and is mutual.

'Mum! Mum!' Dan runs towards me.

I stop glaring at Nora and smile at him.

'Can we go inside?' he asks.

'Of course. Sid, are you coming? And would you tell Nora not to smoke in front of Dan and his friends? She's setting a bad example and they're very easily led at this age.'

'We'll follow you in in a minute,' he says, 'when Nora's finished her ciggy.'

'Mum,' Dan cuts in, 'you smoke when you're drinking.'

'I do not.' I make a mental reminder not to do *that* again. Especially not in front of eagle-eyed Dan. 'Now come on.'

I open the door to Chew and Chat and lead him inside. The air smells of fresh garlic. As it's only six, the restaurant is quiet but I know from experience it will liven up fairly swiftly. Several family groups are seated at the smaller tables along the left-hand wall, one of them with a toddler Lily's age who is trying to climb out of his high chair.

'Hello.' A young waitress walks towards us, menus tucked under her arm and a pen behind her ear.

'Hi,' I say, 'we have a booking. Under Miller.'

She smiles. 'A birthday, isn't it?' She looks at Dan. 'The birthday boy I presume?'

He nods.

'Happy birthday. Right this way. A table for seven and a table for two.'

'Three,' I say. 'We have a gate crasher.'

'Mum.' Dan stares at me.

'Only joking,' I say lightly.

Ten minutes later, Dan's friends have started to arrive. I chat to the parents doing the drop-off while Dan ushers his friends to the larger table. He has a strict seating plan, orchestrated so that Grace is sitting beside him and her best friend, Millie, is sitting beside George. According to Dan, George fancies Millie. As long as there's no kissing involved, I've told him, and your hands are on the table at all times, you can all sit where you like.

Soon I'm sitting at the smaller table on my own while Dan and his friends read their menus and chat easily about their pizza choices. The girls seem incapable of deciding on their own and have to huddle their heads together to confer.

'My mum says pizza is terrible for the figure,' I hear Millie, a girl with wavy blonde hair and a round face, tell Grace. Grace is whippet slim, with seal-sleek long black hair that a model would be proud of.

'She's right,' Grace says. 'They're full of calories. Maybe I'll just have one slice of Dan's and a Caesar salad. And a milk shake. And ice cream.'

I put the menu in front of my face and try not to laugh out loud.

Sid walks in, spots me and makes his way over, Nora totters closely behind, her hand holding the back of his denim jacket to steady herself on her ridiculously high heels.

'This our table?' Sid asks.

I nod. 'Sorry it's so small, it's a table for two. The waitress set an extra place for Nora.' I look at her. 'Hello, Nora, nice to see you too. Not that I was expecting you. Enjoy your cigarette? It'll wreck your skin, you know.'

Nora looks at Sid. 'See! I told you I should have stayed at home.'

'Dan wants you here.' Sid pulls out the chair for her. 'Now, please just sit down.'

Nora blows the air out of her nose with a harrumph but does as she's told.

'It's Dan's evening.' Sid sits down and picks up a menu. 'Let's all try to remember that.'

When I get home at ten o'clock I'm a nervous wreck. As I walk towards the front door it opens and Simon's large frame is silhouetted against the light of the hall.

'Meg.' He grins at me and holds out his arms.

'Hi, Simon.' I give him a half-hearted hug.

'You don't seem all that pleased to see me.'

'Sorry. I've just had an exhausting evening.' I walk in the door, a sleepy Dan trailing behind me. 'Did you pay Shona?' I ask Simon.

'No, I didn't know how much to give her.'

'Don't worry, I'll do it tomorrow.'

'Where were you?' he asks. 'Dan's up late.'

I stare at him. 'We were at his party, remember? At the cinema.'

'Sorry, of course. Did you have a good time, mate?' he asks Dan.

Dan grins. 'Brilliant. I got loads of cool presents. I'll show you. Where are they, Mum?' He yawns.

'In the boot of the car. I'll bring them in. You go on up to bed. It's been a really long day and you can show Simon your presents in the morning.'

'Aw, Mum,' Dan says and then yawns again.

'Bed,' Simon says. 'I'm here all week. We have plenty of time. And there's a present from me in your room.'

Dan's eyes light up. 'Cool.' He runs up the stairs.

'Watch the banisters,' I warn him. 'And don't forget your teeth.'

Simon puts his hand on the small of my back. 'You look like you could do with a drink. Glass of wine?'

'No thanks. If you don't mind I'll go on up to bed. I'm exhausted. Lily has been getting up really early all week.'

'Oh, OK. But come into the kitchen first. I have a surprise for you.'

'A present?'

'Not exactly.'

I hear male laughter coming from the kitchen. 'Who's that?'

Before Simon has a chance to answer I push the kitchen door open and walk in.

Chapter 8

Piracy: taking a ship from its owner.
Usually done at sea

'Hi, Meg.' It's Simon's friend, Slipper. Beside him sits a tall, burly, blond man with a weather-beaten face, another sailor no doubt.

Slipper stands up and gives me a bear hug. 'How's it hanging?'

'Good, Slipper, thanks.'

'You're looking great.'

I know he's lying, but I'm pleased all the same. I'll take any flattery that's going.

'Sorry, Meg,' Simon says. 'This is Bazza.'

'Hi, Bazza,' I say with as big a smile as I can manage in my tired state. Sailors always have silly nicknames and I'm used to it by now. I presume Bazza's mum calls him plain old Barry.

'Nice to meet you, Meg.' Bazza gives me a friendly smile.

I'll have to keep them both away from Hattie I think immediately. They're just her type – tall, well built, tanned, slightly frayed around the edges – armed and dangerous.

'Are you both sailing with Simon this week?' I ask.

They nod. 'Yep,' Slipper says. 'On *Ghost*. Looking forward to it. Your man's crew boss.' He nodded towards Simon. 'She's a nice bit of kit.'

Simon laughs. 'She'd want to be. Cost an absolute fortune.'

'Who's the owner?' I ask.

'Whitey Peters.'

'The Irish betting shop guy?'

'One and the same.'

'I thought he lived in a Portuguese tax haven.'

'He does. For six months of the year. He spends the other six here. Or on his boat at various events.'

'Is he nice?' I ask. 'Single?'

Simon shrugs. 'As owners go, he's not bad. But you can tell Hattie he's married.' Simon knows the way my mind works only too well.

'Bit tight with the old spondulicks I hear,' Slipper adds.

'Maybe a little,' Simon laughs, 'but he's not the worst.'

'Does that mean you won't be bringing home a whole wardrobe's worth of sailing gear?' I ask hopefully.

'I wouldn't bet on it,' Simon says. 'Whitey likes his gear. It's the crew lodgings and nights out he tends to skimp on.'

'And where are you two staying?' I ask Slipper and Bazza.

Slipper throws a look at Simon and raises his eyebrows.

'Um, I thought they could stay here if that was OK,' Simon says a little nervously.

'We'll sleep anywhere,' Bazza adds. 'Sofa, floor. Whatever.'

'But if it doesn't suit . . .' Slipper says.

'No, it's fine.' I force myself to smile. 'Just a surprise, that's all. Simon, could you come upstairs for a minute?'

I walk out of the kitchen and up the stairs. I can hear Slipper ask Simon something.

'No, really,' Simon replies. 'Meg would love you both to stay for the whole week. Don't be silly.'

I walk into our bedroom, sit down on the side of the bed and put my head in my hands. 'Aagh,' I groan.

'Mum? Are you OK?'

Dan is standing in front of me in his boxer shorts.

'Yes, love. But would you mind sleeping on the sofa downstairs? Simon has two friends over and they'll need the bunk beds.'

'Does that mean I can watch telly as soon as I wake up?'

'As long as it's not too early. Now grab your Simpson's sleepingbag, it's in the bottom of the hot press.' I put my hands on either side of his head and kiss his forehead. 'Happy birthday, Dan,' I add gently. 'Did you have a good day?'

'The best. And Simon gave me a new PlayStation game.'

'Lucky you. Now off you go. I'll see you in the morning. Love you.'

'Where's Dan going?' Simon walks into the bedroom.

'To get his sleepingbag. He's going to sleep in the living room. I'll make the bunk beds up for Slipper and Bazza.'

'You don't have to do that, Meg. They can both sleep downstairs.'

'There's no way either of them will fit on our sofa. You can't invite people to stay and then put them on the floor, it's not right.'

'Are you annoyed with me?'

'I haven't seen you in over a week, you miss Dan's party and then you invite two strangers to stay without running it by me first. I had a hellish time at the cinema and you weren't there to help. Am I annoyed with you? What do *you* think?'

'Slipper's hardly a stranger. Wasn't Sid there to help you?'

'Sid was there all right. And Nora. She spent the whole time at dinner complaining *and* she didn't like the film . . .'

'What film was it?'

'A remake of *An American Teenage Werewolf*. Dan and the other boys loved it. But the girls spent the whole time running in and out to the loo and texting their friends. One of them,

Millie, even took a call in the middle of the film. And then the boys had a popcorn fight and nearly got us all thrown out.'

'Sounds like quite a night. I can see why you're tired. But the lads had nowhere to stay.'

'What about a B & B or a hotel? Simon we never get to spend any time alone, there's always something. If it isn't your parents, it's your sailing buddies. We never get a chance to talk.'

'We can talk now if you like.' Simon puts his arm around my shoulder.

I shrug it off. 'Thanks, but I'm too tired. And I have beds to make up.'

'Tomorrow then.'

'Will you be here in the morning?'

'Until eight, yes.'

'Eight in the evening?'

'Eight in the morning. I have to get down early to work on the mast.'

I stand up wordlessly and walk out of the room, trying to stay calm.

'Meg? Meg?'

Simon follows me into the hall. 'Where are you going?'

I wheel around. 'To the hot press to get some sheets. And then I'm going to bed.'

'Do you mind if I stay up for a while with Slipper and Bazza?'

I look at him. He's unbelievable sometimes. 'Of course not.' My voice is icy. 'It's only your first night home after all. In fact, why don't you sleep with them too? You can turn Dan's room into a bunk house.'

I pull out two single duvet covers, two sheets and two pillow cases. One of the sheets has a small rip where Dan put his foot through it and one of the pillow cases has Barbie on it, but I don't care.

I hand the armful of linen to Simon. 'And seeing as they're

your friends, you can make up their bunks. I'd advise you to lift Dan's Star Wars Lego off the floor in case someone stands on it in bare feet and hurts themselves. Goodnight.' With that, I walk into our bedroom and shut the door behind me firmly.

Just before six the following morning, Lily wakes me with her babbling and calling. I open my eyes and listen, willing her to go back to sleep. It feels like the middle of the night. She stops and I offer up a silent prayer.

I roll over, expecting to see Simon lying comatose beside me but his side of the bed is empty. I kick the space where his legs should be in case it's a trick of the duvet and the feathery bulk is hiding him, but no, nothing. He's hardly up already. Then I remember last night. Maybe he slept in Dan's room with Slipper and Bazza, like I told him to. Oops. I start to feel bad. Poor Simon. He must be on the floor. I'll go and get him, I decide.

Still a little groggy with sleep, I force myself out of the bed. The house is deathly silent expect for the occasional hum of traffic outside. Ferry traffic at this time of the morning. I pull the fleece that lives in a bundle at the foot of the bed over my head and walk into the hall.

I push open the door of Dan's bedroom. Slipper and Bazza are both present and correct, Slipper in the top bunk with his muscular arm dangling over the side, Bazza snoring gently in the bottom bunk. I close the door again and pad downstairs. Dan's asleep on the living-room sofa, but there's no sign of Simon.

As I walk out, Dan stirs.

'Mum?' he opens his eyes. 'What time is it?'

'Early, you can go back to sleep for a bit.'

Simon isn't in the kitchen or in the downstairs bathroom either. I'm starting to get worried. Thoughts start whirring through my mind like tiny butterflies. What if he's lying on the side of the road somewhere injured? Or worse (I know, I'm a terrible person), what if he's left me, sick of my nagging? What if he's found someone else? Recently I've had a recurring nightmare that I'm single again, dressed up to the nines in a dark nightclub where no one will dance with me. I always wake up, horribly relieved that I have Simon. Sad, I know, but the truth. Maybe I should have been nicer to him last night. What have I done?

As I climb the stairs I hear a noise from the bathroom. What the hell is that? I stand on the top stair, clutching the banister. There it is again.

'Ow, damn it!' A voice says. It sounds like Simon.

I push open the bathroom door and peer in. Simon is lying in the bath, fully clothed, his forehead bleeding.

'What the hell are you doing?' I demand, relief flooding through me. 'What happened to your head? And why are you in the bath?'

He rests his upper body on one elbow then reaches the other hand up to touch his head. 'Hit it on the tap. Got up too quickly.'

'But why are you in the bath?' I ask again.

'Must have fallen asleep.'

'Why didn't you get into bed? Or at least sleep on the floor.'

He shakes his head. 'No idea. Guess I didn't want to wake you up.'

I gape at him.

'Sorry,' he says sheepishly, smiling up at me.

'I'm going back to bed,' I say wearily.

'I'll come with you.' He stands up, steps carefully out of the bath and breathes on me. I'm almost asphyxiated.

'Do your teeth first. You reek of alcohol.'

'Had a few with Slipper and Bazza. Sorry.' He hiccups.

I shake my head in despair.

A few minutes later he creeps into the bedroom. I keep my eyes firmly shut.

'Meg?' he whispers after getting into bed. 'Meg?'

I play dead.

'Meg, I know you can hear me. I'm sorry.'

'Sorry for what?' I open my eyes.

'For falling asleep in the bath.'

'And?'

'For bringing the guys back without telling you and for being crap.'

I sigh. There's no point in being angry with Simon. He's only here for the week and besides, being angry is far too exhausting.

'It's fine,' I say magnanimously. 'But try to make it to bed the next time.'

'I will.'

A moment later Simon's hand snakes up my thigh. 'I did my teeth.'

'Good for you.'

'Lily's asleep.'

'Not for long.'

'We'd better be quick then.'

I'm awake now, what the hell? I shut my eyes again and lie back in expectation. Simon's hands caress my inner thighs, leisurely drifting up towards my stomach and my breasts and then back down again. He kisses me tenderly. 'I love you, Meg.' His hot breath nuzzles my ear. He kisses his way down my neck, lingering on my shoulders.

'Mummee!' Lily calls. 'Mummee, Mummee, Mummee!'

'Ignore her,' I murmur, my eyes still closed.

Simon continues to kiss me.

'Dadda, Dadda, Dadda,' Lily tries again, even louder. 'Mummee, Dadda.'

I open my eyes and sigh.

Simon rolls onto his back. 'Typical.'

'Wait there. Don't move an inch.' I'm not going to give up without a fight, not now that Simon has so kindly laid the groundwork. It's not often that I actually feel like sex these days and I'm damned if I'm going to let it go to waste.

I grab my dressing gown off the back of the door, throw it around me, push Lily's door open, lift her out of her cot and run down the stairs with her gurgling with delight in my arms.

I walk into the living room and plonk her down on the floor.

'Dan, will you look after Lily for a few minutes?' I switch on the television and the video and shove a Barney tape roughly into the slot.

'Wha?' Dan sits up and rubs his eyes.

'Look after Lily? Please?'

'Um, OK.' I lean down and kiss him on the top of his head. 'Thanks, you're a star. I owe you one.'

'It'll cost you,' he says to my disappearing back.

I don't care. Whatever the price, hopefully it'll be worth it.

I run back upstairs, close the door firmly behind me, throw my dressing gown onto the floor, peel off my T-shirt and dance out of my pants.

'Now where were we?' I ask, a little out of breath. I pull back the duvet and climb into bed.

Simon is snoring heartily. I try to wake him by prodding him in the side with my elbow but he's out cold. Then I try flicking his cheek with my finger but that doesn't work either. I lie back with my arms crossed over my chest. I can't help but smile to myself. Typical.

Chapter 9

*Cockpit: an opening in the deck from
which the boat is handled*

On Monday afternoon Hattie bullies me into accompanying her
to the yacht club as she has the day off. She arrives on my
doorstep just after three. I'm a little distracted what with Lily
being her usual boisterous self and Dan tired and crotchety.

'You're early,' I say. 'You're lucky I'm in. I've only just collected Dan from school.'

'How do I look?' Hattie follows me into the kitchen.

Dan is sitting at the kitchen table doing his homework. His
books are spread out all around him and I can see that although
he's doing his best, his handwriting assignment isn't going
terribly well. Dan, like Sid, is left handed and always smudges
his fountain-pen ink with the side of his hand as he moves it
along the page. I decide not to say anything. He finds it hard
enough without any negative feedback from me.

Lily is in the garden pulling up daisies from the lawn, chew-
ing them and spitting them out.

'Meg, how do I look?' Hattie says again.

'Sorry, did you say something?' I turn to look at her.

She laughs. 'You're away with the fairies. I asked you what you thought of my outfit.' She does a twirl.

I look her up and down. She's wearing tight white three-quarter-length trousers, silver high-heeled strappy sandals which I happen to know cost her a week's wages but are completely fab, a blue and white striped low-cut vest top which leaves little to the imagination and a white fitted blazer with gold buttons. A white sailing cap is perched jauntily on her head and she has large gold anchor earrings in her ear lobes. Her make-up is immaculate. I wonder absently where she got the cap. I certainly didn't give it to her. Maybe one of Simon's friends gave it to her as a trophy. They often give caps and jackets to girls they sleep with as a kind of reward. It didn't bear thinking about.

'Nautical enough?' she asks me. 'What do you think, Dan?'

I look at Dan who is staring up at her open-mouthed. I catch his eye and give him a wink.

'Lovely,' he says, before burying his head in his homework. I can see he's trying not to laugh.

I press my own lips together hard.

'What?' Hattie demands, putting her fists on her hips.

'Would you like a coffee?' I ask, turning my back to her and flicking the switch on the kettle. I push my hands down against the kitchen counter and will myself not to giggle.

'Sure. Dan, what's so interesting about your book? Why are you smiling like that?'

I turn around and look at Hattie again. She really does look quite comical.

Dan closes his book with a flourish. 'Finished.'

'Dan?' Hattie says again. 'Stop avoiding the question.'

'If you must know,' he says, packing his books into his grubby and ripped black and grey rucksack, 'no one wears clothes like that. Unless they don't actually sail. Isn't that right, Mum?'

Hattie stares at me.

I shrug. 'Dan's right. Sorry, Hattie, but you look like you're trying too hard. You'll stick out like a sore thumb.'

Hattie swears under her breath. 'I should never have listened to the girls in the shop.' She pulls off the hat and throws it onto the table. It skids a little on the surface of the table, like a stone skimming on water, before coming to rest against Dan's school bag. 'So what should I be wearing?' She takes the anchor earrings out and deposits them in the pocket of her jacket.

'Jeans,' Dan says.

'Flip-flops,' I suggest. 'Or deck shoes. And where *did* you get that blazer?'

'It's Mum's.' She looks glum as she takes it off and lowers it over the back of a chair. 'It's horrible, isn't it?' Then she grins. 'Got you! I'm not that stupid. I have another outfit in the car.' She runs out the door. 'Gotta hurry, or all the good men will be gone.'

'Hattie!' I say to her disappearing back, laughing.

The yacht club is heaving when we finally get there and I'm in need of a strong drink. Hattie, Dan and Lily have all changed clothes.

Hattie is now wearing spray-on jeans. Although larger than average on top, which makes her look bigger than her actual size twelve, Hattie has a slim waist partnered with annoyingly slim hips. Your average nightmare. She's kept the silver sandals on but has swapped her stripy vest top for a plain white low-cut T-shirt, her breasts straining against the cotton, and her nipples visible even through her lacy half-cup bra.

As we walk in the side gate to the club, the air is buzzing with conversation and the tinkle of glasses. The jazz band breaks into 'Summertime' as we push our way through the crowds.

'Mum, there's a bouncy castle,' Dan shouts over the noise,

his eyes widening. 'Two bouncy castles, look! A proper one and a smaller one for toddlers.' He points to the left. Sure enough, there are two red and yellow castles thronged with screaming children, arms flailing, heads bumping.

'Excellent,' Hattie says. 'That's the child-minding sorted. Dump the kids, Meg, and then we can concentrate on the men.'

'I intend to concentrate on a large glass of wine.' I eye up a woman passing in front of us with a large silver wine bucket in her hands. 'But getting rid of the kids is a great idea.'

'That's lovely, Mum,' Dan says.

'Would you prefer to stay with us then?' I smile at him. 'Help Hattie look for a boyfriend?'

Dan screws up his nose. 'Yuck! No thanks.'

'Then bouncy castle it is.'

We deposit Dan and Lily in their respective castles. Blessedly the castle for the toddlers and younger children is manned and supervised by two pretty girls in their early twenties. One of them is wearing tiny denim shorts and her legs are gazelle-like. I can't help but stare.

'I hate those young girls,' Hattie mutters as we walked away from the castle. 'All pert tits, legs up to their armpits and wide-eyed innocence. They should be banned.'

'Hattie!'

'It's not as if they're vestal virgins either. What they get up to would make your toes curl.'

I ignore her. Hattie doesn't mean to be cruel, she just hates competition. I know she feels her age sometimes, bless her. We dodge the crowds and make our way to the marquee. Every now and then Hattie grabs my arm to slow me down so she can have a better look at the talent.

The marquee is heaving – sweaty sailors, their faces still streaked with sun block, are dotted in clumps around the tent, recognizable by their matching T-shirts. Some are still wearing their oilskins, pulled down off their chests and sitting in a saggy clump on their waists.

'If someone stands on my toe again, I'll scream,' Hattie complains as she totters over the beer-sticky wooden floorboards.

'Told you to wear my flip-flops.'

'My toes would still be exposed, smart ass,' she hisses back.

'Deck shoes then,' I say, refusing to let her get the better of me.

'I don't wear other people's shoes, it's unhygienic. Don't know what you might catch – athlete's foot, verrucas, corns, bunions.'

'You can't catch corns or bunions. I'm not sure about verrucas, but I certainly don't have any.'

'If you think I'd wear any of your smelly old shoes you're sorely mistaken. I don't want to look like a complete slob.'

'Remind me why I bother talking to you again.'

'Hey, Meg! Hattie!' Simon's voice booms across the tent.

I look over to the right and scan the bodies. A splash of dark pink stands out in the sea of white and blue. *Ghost*'s raspberry-coloured T-shirts are anything but subtle.

'Simon's over there,' I say to Hattie. 'Do try and be polite, and no hitting on the married men, understand?'

'As if. I'm not that bad.'

We shoulder our way through the bodies.

'Excellent,' Hattie says, leaning in towards me. 'There are practically no women. I'm glad we got here early. I knew it was a good plan. I'll get the pick of the takings.'

'It's not a sale, Hattie.'

She laughs. 'Oh yes it is. And the first ones in the door bag the best bargains. If they know where to look. I'll start with Simon's boat and then work my way through all the big, expensive boats.'

'That's your carefully formulated plan is it?'

Hattie nods. 'Absolutely.'

'I hate to disappoint you but there *are* women here.' I nod towards some of the female sailors in the throng. 'Quite a few actually. There's obviously something wrong with your eyesight.'

Hattie wrinkles her nose. 'Not proper ones.'

'What *are* you talking about?'

'The women in here are all covered in salt and sun cream. And look at the state of their hair.'

'They've been sailing all day. What do you expect?'

'They could at least have a shower and wash their hair. I bet they smell.'

'Maybe they have better things to do. And, Hattie, I'm warning you . . .'

'Meg! Meg!' Simon waves his pint in the air at us as we approach. I smile, put my arm around him and give him a kiss. He reeks of sun cream and sweat and his hair is matted against his head – styled by his tight-fitting cap. He has two white horizontal lines on the sides of his face, where his sunglass arms rest, but otherwise his face is mahogany-coloured. I worry about his skin, it takes a right old battering from the wind and the sun. I make him promise to wear total block on his face, but I know half the time he forgets and uses whatever they have on the boat. And factor-eight sun cream just doesn't cut it.

'You look happy,' I say. 'Did you win?'

Simon beams. 'Sure did. Come here, Hattie, and give us a kiss, you beauty.'

She turns her cheek to his lips. 'Hi, Simon.'

'What brings you both down so early?' he asks. 'We've only just got in.'

'Meg needed a hand with the kids,' Hattie says brazenly. 'I was happy to help.'

I stare at her. She's unbelievable. But I keep my mouth shut because I do want her to meet someone, of course I do. Just not one of Simon's friends or anyone else I know for that matter.

'So aren't you going to introduce me to some of your friends, Simon?' Hattie purrs, getting straight to the point. She lowers her voice. 'Any of them single?'

'Hattie!' I say.

'What? I'm only asking.'

Simon laughs. 'Really single or happy to tell you they're single?'

Hattie swats his arm and giggles. 'Oh, Simon, you are awful.'

I grit my teeth. I know Hattie flirts with all men, it's just in her nature. But I hate it when the man in question happens to be Simon. She'll be batting her eyelashes at him next.

'Surely none of your lovely friends would do a thing like that?' she asks him. Bingo, there go her heavily mascara-laden eyelashes, up and down, up and down, like a butterfly's wings. Or more like a moth's, I think unkindly, heavier than a butterfly's.

He shrugs. 'Who knows?'

'Simon!' I give him a dig in the side with my elbow.

'That's the way it is. I'd be lying if I said otherwise.'

'Doesn't mean I have to like it.'

'Married men are a complete waste of time.' She arches one rather over-plucked eyebrow. 'Far too eager. Come far too quickly.'

'Hattie!' I splutter.

Simon lets out a huge belly laugh. 'That's my girl!'

She smiles. 'It's true. Anyway, it isn't right. I always think of you, Meg, sitting at home with your babies while Simon's off gallivanting. I'd hate to think of some silly slapper on heat coming on to Simon.'

The irony of what she's just said doesn't seem to register and I stifle a grin.

'Who is this vision of loveliness?' a deep male voice asks. 'I don't think we've been introduced.'

Slipper sidles into our cosy little knot. Slipper is in trouble. I can see Hattie eyeing him up appreciatively.

'This is my sister, Hattie,' I say. 'Hattie, Slipper.'

'Skipper?' Hattie's eyes glance expertly at his wedding-ring finger. I can see her mind ticking over – no ring, no tell-tale ring groove or sun-tan mark. Or sad ring-finger plaster. Bingo!

'Slipper. I'll tell you how I got the name later if you're good. Now let me buy you a drink. What would you like, Meg?'

'A glass of white wine, please.'

'Coming right up. And Hattie?'

'A vodka and slimline tonic, please.'

'You don't need slimline,' he says. 'You're perfect just the way you are.'

Hattie simpers. 'How sweet. Let me help you carry the drinks.'

'Great.' Slipper grins at her. 'Ladies first.' He gestures for Hattie to walk in front of him.

As she passes she leans in towards me and whispers 'Nice manners.'

'Just for show,' I whisper back.

She smiles at me and carries on towards the bar. As she walks in front of Slipper he blatantly stares at her curvaceous bottom. Then he turns around and winks at Simon, cupping his hands as if cupping her buttocks and licking his lips.

'Oh, *please*.' I shake my head.

'They're well matched.' Simon laughs.

I watch as they wait to be served, Slipper's elbows resting on the wooden bar counter; Hattie leaning forwards to display plenty of cleavage – 'If you've got it, flaunt it,' she always says. She's giggling like a teenager and flicking her hair back off her face with one hand, the other resting on Slipper's arm. Hattie is a consummate flirt and loves to hone her skills; she's also highly practised in the arts of flattery, simpering, pouting and ego massaging. Once she's hooked her prey, she moves on to the next poor sod, bored with the first. She doesn't see anything wrong with this at all. In fact, in Hattie's opinion men find women at their most attractive and desirable when they are being fawned over by other men. It's all about the thrill of the chase apparently. Sometimes the first man fights back and Hattie admires them all the more for it. It's fascinating to watch, if exhausting.

'So how was your day, Meg?' Simon asks. I drag my eyes off Hattie and Slipper.

'The usual. I survived.'

'It's good to see you. Thanks for coming down. I know it's not easy with the kids—' He breaks off. 'Where are the kids?'

'Bouncing their little hearts out on the bouncy castles. And tiring themselves into submission hopefully so they'll go to bed early. I'll go and check on them in a minute.'

'I'll do it,' Simon offers, 'you stay here and relax.'

'Would you mind waiting with me till Hattie comes back?'

'Of course.'

Simon understands I'm a little shy around people I don't know. Being abandoned with his new crew isn't exactly my idea of fun.

'Ryan was sailing with us today,' Simon says. 'Says he met you.'

'Ryan?'

'The instructor. Ryan Dawson. At Dan's swimming test.'

'Oh, that Ryan. Nice guy.'

As I speak Ryan's head pops out of the crowd, Simon waves at him and a moment later he's standing beside me.

'Hello again.' He towers over me. I'd forgotten how tall he is. And how cute.

'Ryan played a blinder today,' Simon says enthusiastically. 'Our bowman missed his flight from Southampton this morning and Ryan stepped in at the last minute. He was a star too. Really knows his stuff.'

'Thanks.' Ryan is clearly delighted. 'It was an honour to sail with you all. I was bricking it to be honest. I'm hardly a professional. But when we started racing I just put my head down and got on with it.'

'You've got a real talent for the bow,' Simon says. 'Ever thought of taking it further? There's a shortage of good bowmen out there.'

Ryan shrugs. 'No. Not really.'

'Maybe you should. I could put you in touch with a few heads. See what happens. Old Riggsy from Hamble, now there's a bowman . . .'

I cough lightly. If I don't stop Simon in his tracks he'll wax lyrical about sailing for hours, leaving me standing by his side like a lemon.

'Oops, sorry,' he says and smiles. 'Forgot you were there for a second. Meg has to put up with all my sailing waffle,' he explains to Ryan. 'Comes with the territory.'

'And I don't have a clue what he's talking about most of the time,' I add frankly.

Ryan smiles at me and my stomach flips a little. He really is edible.

'Here you go.' Hattie appears beside me and handing me a glass.

'Thanks.'

Hattie's eyes are glued to Slipper's. She lowers her head, bats her lashes and gives him a coy look. He's a goner, poor fellow.

'Who's that?' Ryan whispers in my ear, his eyes drinking in Hattie.

'Sorry. Hattie, this is Ryan. He's one of Dan's sailing instructors. The head instructor actually. He's in charge of the junior section down here.'

'I'd better be nice to you then.' Hattie gives him a winning smile and a wink.

'Yes, you'd better,' he says, stammering slightly. I can tell he's finding it hard to keep his eyes off her cleavage. 'Hattie. What a lovely name.'

'You're sweet.'

I watch her check out his ring finger.

Hattie's interest in Ryan hasn't gone unnoticed. 'I'm just going to show Hattie round the boat.' Slipper rests his hand on the small of her back proprietorially. 'That OK, boss?' he asks Simon.

'Fine by me,' Simon says. 'Don't be too long or we'll all come looking for you.'

Slipper grins. 'I stand warned.'

'And stay out of Whitey's bedroom.'

'Simon,' I hiss.

'Only kidding.' Simon grins. 'Even Slipper's not that bad. Are you, Slipper?'

'Course not. I'm the perfect gentleman. See you later.' He leads Hattie away.

It's Hattie I'm worried about. Hardly the perfect lady at the best of times. And I don't want to get Simon into trouble with the owner. 'Could I see the boat too?' I ask quickly, watching Hattie and Slipper disappear into the crowd.

Simon looks at me in surprise. I've seen hundreds of boats and I'm not usually all that interested. 'OK, but we'll have to be quick. The prize-giving for the first race will be on soon. Don't want to miss that, do we?'

'Of course not,' I lie. In fact, I'd love to miss the prize-giving. They're always yawn inducing.

'We can check out the kids on the way.' He takes my hand in his. His palm is hot and sweaty but I don't mind. We don't often get the chance to hold hands. Usually we have Lily hanging on us, wanting to play swings. 'Ryan, do you want to have a proper look at *Ghost*? You didn't get the full tour earlier.'

'Please,' Ryan says, 'if I'm not interrupting anything.'

'Not at all, mate,' Simon says.

'That's fine,' I say. 'Simon and I get far too much time on our own as it is.' I smile up at him. Simon presses my hand and gives me a knowing smile.

Lily and Dan are wild-eyed, red-faced, out of breath but enjoying every minute of their bouncing so we leave them to it. Lily doesn't even want to stay with her daddy, which is unusual. Normally she is ultra clingy when he's around, knowing her time with him is limited. I know there's going be hell to pay getting an overexcited and exhausted Lily to bed later, but at that precise moment I don't care.

Ghost is a stunning boat – an eighty-foot Swan, sleek and elegant, with dark wooden decks and a gleaming navy hull. I'm impressed.

'She's less than a year old,' Simon says as he clambers over the guard rail and onto the deck like a mountain goat. 'Isn't she a beauty?'

Ghost was tied alongside the floating wooden pontoon. Unlike most of the anaemic white plastic yachts Simon has sailed on, her decks are strips of mahogany, varnished and polished until they gleam.

'Beautiful,' I say in awe, thinking of the sheer amount of work it must take to keep her looking so immaculate.

'Wait till you see downstairs. Give me your hand.' Simon reaches down, grabs my hand and whooshes me up. I hold on tightly as I climb over the rail and then put two feet firmly on the deck. Ryan follows me with ease, almost as confident on the boat as Simon.

Simon nods at the wooden steps in front of us. 'You first, Meg.'

I climb into the cockpit and go gingerly down the steps, clinging to the gleaming brass rail for dear life. I step into the cabin, look around and gasp. The boys jump down the steps behind me, putting me to shame.

'Close your mouth,' Simon says with a laugh. 'Anyone would think you'd never seen a Swan before.'

'I haven't,' I say, 'not like this one anyway.'

Ryan whistles. 'So this is how the other half live. With the sewer earlier I couldn't really tell.'

'Sewer?' I look at Simon.

'That's what we call the cabin when it's awash with sails during a race.'

'Right.' Sailing is a very weird sport.

I gaze at the tidy kitchen to my right with its shiny solid-wood counter tops, double sink, state-of-the-art oven and large chrome fridge. Most of the racing yachts have tiny, perfunctory, basic kitchens. Serious racing crews eat freeze-dried and tinned food a lot of the time, like astronauts. And Mars bars. I open the fridge to check the contents. Expensive-looking wine and champagne, a huge bowl of mussels – their woolly beards still clinging to them, a cornucopia of exotic fruit and two whole glossy dark green watermelons – both with holes in the top where the vodka has been poured in no doubt – one of Simon's favourites. It's a long way from freeze-dried food and tins of beans.

'Amazing.' I close the fridge and run my fingers over the smooth, cool counter top. The air in the cabin smells of furniture polish mixed with the tangy, slightly musty smell of dried sea water. 'Is there a maid as well as a hostess?' I ask, amazed at how tidy the boat is.

Simon laughs. 'Don't let Dee hear you call her that. She's officially the boat's hostess, but she does pretty much everything from buying the food and cooking it to cleaning. Great girl. Aussie. Hard worker.'

Legs up to her armpits and perfect white teeth, I imagine. 'What age is she?' I ask, trying to sound nonchalant.

Simon considers for a moment. 'No idea. Twenty-one, twenty-two maybe. Runs the boat with her boyfriend, Raff.

Another Aussie. They live on *Ghost* and deliver her around the globe to different events. Wherever Whitey wants her, they deliver.'

'Attached. Good.' I breathe a sigh of relief.

'Good?' Simon looks at me.

Oops, did I say that out loud? 'Good for her. Attached to the boat like that.'

'Ah.'

To the left is a large seating area with a luxurious dark blue fitted corner sofa, and a wooden map table, which folds out to provide a large dining table. There are classy brass lamps with green shades attached to the wall behind the sofa. A desk, complete with computer screens above it, is scattered with charts of Dublin Bay, notebooks with strange hieroglyphic symbols scribbled on them, and a fistful of multicoloured gel pens. I wonder if anyone would notice if I swiped some for Dan. He loves gel pens, especially the ones that smell of fruit. Not that I'm allowed to tell George or any of his friends this of course, in case they think it's too 'girly'.

'That's where the navigator sits.' Simon points at the office-like black leather chair in front of the desk. 'There's a full GPS navigation system with satellite link.'

'And sonar?' Ryan asks.

Simon nods. 'Full weather system based on the American—'

I can tell he's about to launch into one of his lectures. 'Where are Hattie and Slipper, do you suppose?' I ask, cutting him off.

'Good question. I have no idea.'

A loud giggle comes from the front of the boat, or the bow as Simon is always telling me, through a closed wooden door.

'Answer your question?' Simon asks. He knocks loudly on the door. 'Coming through.'

Ryan and I follow him through the doorway and down the short corridor.

'Crew cabins to the left and right.' Simon pushes open doors as we go along.

I peer in. The cabins are small, with wooden bunk beds covered in dark blue duvets.

'Guest bathroom.' Simon pushes open the next door. The walls and floor are tiled in a creamy coloured marble and there's a decent-sized shower with one of those huge chrome showerheads that look like they've come off a giant watering can, but I'm sure are hideously expensive. They also pour a whole Niagara of water on top of you. I experienced one in a hotel in Greece that practically knocked me onto my knees, wimp that I am. I'm not all that keen on being pummelled into submission by jet-action shower nozzles either. I like my showers long and relaxing, not short and painful.

'I'd love a shower like that,' Ryan says, 'imagine what you could get up to in there.'

I look at him in surprise.

Simon notices my face and laughs. 'Ryan's not as innocent as he looks. You should hear the stories about him and—'

Ryan puts up his hands. 'Whoa there. I'm sure Meg's not interested in idle gossip.'

I most certainly am.

'What was that?' Simon asks, hearing a loud thump.

'Sounded like something heavy falling on the floor,' Ryan suggests.

Simon points at the door in front of us. 'Whitey's room.'

He puts his hand on the brass door knob and turns it. I should have warned him, but it's too late.

As the door swings open Ryan and Simon's eyes stand out on stalks.

'Close your mouth, Simon,' I say, laughing.

Chapter 10

Flood: an incoming current

Hattie is standing in front of us completely naked except for some frothy white bubbles clinging to her creamy skin. Her hair is hanging down her back soaking wet, dripping water all over the floor, and her cheeks are rosy red. Standing in front of us like that, she looks like the *Birth of Venus*, that Botticelli babe in an open shell and I'm rather proud of her, to tell the truth. Rather than shriek and run for her life as I would have done, she stands there for a moment majestically, then calmly places one hand vertically over her delightfully exuberant dark brown pubic hair (she used to shave it all off, but is now going through rather an Italian phase), and one arm horizontally over her breasts which, due to their size, is completely ineffectual.

'Slipper,' she says calmly 'we have company. Can you pass me a towel?'

Slipper comes out of the en suite, a tiny hand towel wrapped round his hips, and hands her a large white bath towel. Hattie takes it and wraps it round her body.

'That's better. Lovely ship you have here, Captain,' she says to Simon. 'Must dash.' She runs into the bathroom.

I look at Simon and he looks back at me, eyebrows raised.

'What?' I ask.

'She's your sister,' he says.

'Tell me about it.'

Slipper turns to follow Hattie.

'Not so fast, Slipper.' Simon puts one hand on his shoulder. 'What are you like?' He shakes his head. 'I can't believe you're using Whitey's jacuzzi. And look at the state of the floor.'

Slipper shrugs. 'I'll get Dee to deal with it.'

'No you won't, you'll clean it up yourself. And don't use Whitey's good towels to do it either. I'll go and get the mop. Now get dressed quickly. You'll be late for the prize-giving.'

Simon leaves the room. I can tell he's livid.

'Before you go jumping to any conclusions, Meg,' Hattie says, walking out of the bathroom, drying her hair with a hand towel, 'we weren't actually doing anything. We just fancied trying out the jacuzzi, that's all.'

I stare at my sister. 'Hattie, get dressed for heaven's sake!' She's standing in front of us in her lacy white bra and matching wispy shorts, both almost completely see-through.

Ryan has a very strange expression on his face.

'I'm sure Ryan's seen it all before.' Hattie puts her hands on her hips and looks him in the eye, a smirk playing on her lips. 'Haven't you, Ryan?'

'Hattie!' I hiss again. 'Get dressed. And stop being such a slapper.'

'OK, OK, keep your hair on.'

Slipper comes out of the bathroom in his T-shirt and jeans, wolf whistles at Hattie and smacks her playfully on the buttocks. 'Looking good, Hattie.'

'See,' Hattie says to me, and disappears inside.

Simon strides back in and hands Slipper a mop and bucket. 'You have five minutes to make this place look presentable. And the bathroom. Get on with it.'

'No problem, mate,' Slipper says easily.

'And we'll be waiting up on deck, so no funny business, understand?'

Funny business? I smile to myself, sometimes Simon can be a bit of an old fogey.

Slipper holds his back poker-straight and salutes Simon. 'Yes, sir!'

We sit on deck, waiting for Slipper and Hattie, the wood warming my bum through my jeans.

Eventually Ryan asks, 'How old is Hattie, Meg?'

I look at him. He's no more than twenty-four, so I decide to adjust the truth a little for Hattie's sake. 'She's twenty-three,' I say with confidence.

Simon snorts. I ignore him.

'Almost twenty-four,' I add to make it more authentic.

Ryan nods.

Simon lies back against the deck, closes his eyes and tilts his head towards the sun. 'Lovely day,' he murmurs. 'Been lucky with the weather.'

'Are Slipper and Hattie together?' Ryan asks over Simon's head.

I smile. He seems keen. 'They've only just met.'

'So she's single?'

'Permanently,' Simon quips.

I slap him playfully. 'Be nice.'

'Sorry,' he murmurs. 'Single, but a real catch,' he amends.

'That's better.'

'Maybe she just hasn't met the right guy,' Ryan suggests.

Simon opens his eyes, put his hands on the deck and pushes himself up. 'Ryan, please don't even think about it. Hattie would chew you up and spit you out.'

'That's not very nice,' I say.

'But it's true.' Simon smiles at me. 'Admit it.'

'She's not that bad.'

'Really? What about that time last summer when she seduced that nineteen-year-old at your cousin's wedding . . .'

'Shush, she's only downstairs, she can probably hear you. And Ryan's right, she just hasn't met the right guy yet. She needs someone strong, someone who will take her in hand.'

'They'd need large hands all right.' Simon smirks.

'That's not funny.' I give him another slap.

Ryan and Simon both laugh.

I shake my head, trying not to laugh myself. 'Boys.'

That evening, after a difficult and vocal battle to get an over-exhausted Dan to bed, I pour myself a large glass of white wine and collapse back on the sofa.

Simon joins me, after having had more success with Lily: she was so tired she fell asleep in the car. Simon simply lifted her out and plonked her straight into her bed.

'Whitey's wife arrives on Wednesday.' Simon takes my glass off me and helps himself to a good slurp before handing it back.

'Hey, get your own!'

'She hates sleeping on the boat,' Simon continues. 'She gets horribly seasick, or so she claims, so they're staying in the Royal Marine Hotel. Why don't we stay on the boat one night? We'd have it all to ourselves and Whitey wouldn't mind. He suggested it.'

I think about having a whole boat like *Ghost* to myself, with the wind in my hair and the sun on my face, being lulled to sleep by the gentle waves and, more importantly, no kids to cater for.

'It might be a bit of fun.' Simon nuzzles my neck with his nose. 'And the jacuzzi might just come in handy.'

'What about the kids?'

'I'm sure your mum would take them for the night. Or maybe Hattie would stay over.'

'Hattie? Are you mad? I think you'll find my darling sister

has other fish to fry this week. She's after a rich husband, remember?'

'But Slipper doesn't have a bean. I wonder how long he'll last.'

'As long as it takes her to find that out. He'll introduce her to some owner or other and she'll be off,' I click my fingers together, 'just like that.'

'How come you're allowed to say things like that about Hattie and I'm not?'

'Because she's *my* sister.'

Simon frowns. 'Maybe I should warn Slipper.'

'Don't you dare. He'll find out soon enough. And he's a big boy.'

'So you'll ask your mum about babysitting?'

'I'll give it a go.'

'Excellent.' Simon glances at his watch. 'Now, I have to run.' He's going back down to the yacht club to hang out with the *Ghost* crew.

He kisses me on the forehead. 'See you later, don't wait up.'

'No intention of it. Bye, love.'

I flick on the television, find some entertaining, mind-numbing reality show and sink back into the sofa to drink my wine.

On Wednesday evening I drop Dan and Lily over to Mum and Dad's at seven. Mum is out, but Dad has kindly offered to mind the kids. He's always been a bit nervous of toddlers, and babies completely baffle him, but he's always willing to give it a go, bless him. Mum says he was useless when me and Hattie were young, not that she'd really know in my case, but he more than made up for it when we were teenagers. Mum's teenage-parenting style was dictator-like, laying down the law as she saw it: 'You're not going out like that, Hattie. Put something on your legs, that's a belt, not a skirt.' 'If you bring that layabout

Sid into this house one more time, Meg, so help me I'll throttle you.'

Dad has always been fair and kind. Far too kind, Mum thinks. 'Of course you can have a tenner to buy a top, Hattie. Just don't tell your mother.' 'Keep out of your mother's way today, Meg. She's in one of her moods.'

When I got pregnant Mum didn't talk to me for weeks. If it hadn't been for Dad, I don't know what I would have done. Mum wanted me to get rid of 'it'. Dad wanted me to do what I thought best, to be happy with my decision. As if I could be 'happy' with anything at the time. I was in a right old state.

The first time Mum talked to me, after almost three weeks of silence, was to offer to accompany me to London to 'deal with my little problem once and for all'. As if my tiny, growing baby was some kind of annoying freckle that wouldn't go away. But I should be grateful for her lack of tact. It made me realize I *wanted* my baby, even if only to spite her.

Once Dan was born, she oohed and aahed over him like a proper granny, conveniently forgetting her previous behaviour. It was unbelievable. But I was in such a tired, hormonal state that I was grateful for any sort of help, even from her. When Dan was two weeks old she dragged a reluctant dad off on holiday to Spain. 'Best let Meg and Sid get on with things themselves,' she said. 'Best not to interfere.'

Sid went out and got drunk every night with his sparky mates, wetting the baby's head, leaving me literally holding the baby. It was the worst two weeks of my life. When Mum and Dad came home I was a snivelling wreck. Dad immediately called the family doctor, who made a house call and prescribed a lot of bed rest and some proper meals. I'd been too tired to shop or cook and had survived on noodles and ice cream for a fortnight.

Dad, bless him, took over, demanding that Sid took baby Dan for long walks, and coming home from the supermarket with more food than I'd seen outside Christmas. Mum kept largely out of my way. Dad had had a right go at her for making him abandon his darling daughter in her hour of need, or so Hattie, who'd been listening at their bedroom door, told me later.

Hattie was great with Dan when it suited her. But she was young and had her own life to lead. Besides, she was rarely in, unlike Dad, who was resolutely at my bedside when I needed him. I found out months later that he'd taken unpaid leave to be with me.

'Your mum's not happy that I'm babysitting this evening,' Dad says as I hand him Dan's and Lily's bags from the car. The children have already run into the house on the way to the biscuit tin, no doubt. 'I was supposed to go to the book club with her.'

'I'm sorry.'

'Don't be. They're doing Jane Austen. Not my cup of tea at all. I'm more of a Dan Brown man myself, but don't tell your mother I said that. She tells everyone my favourite author's James Joyce.'

I laugh. 'Really? Have you ever read any Joyce?'

'Of course not. But I've seen the film of *The Dead* with all that snow. Besides, your mum's worried about your relationship with Simon. She says you need to spend more time alone together. So it's good you're having a night together, just the two of you.'

'Is she now?' I slam the boot shut with more force than is strictly necessary. I hate when Mum sticks her oar in, especially when it comes to Simon. It drives me bonkers.

Dad frowns. 'Sorry, maybe I shouldn't have mentioned it.'

'You can tell her from me that there's nothing wrong with our relationship thanks very much.'

'She'd just like to see you settled, Meg. You know what she's like. First the whole Sid thing, and now Simon.'

'Two children with different fathers? Is that what you mean?'

Dad smiles sheepishly. 'Something like that. She's worried about you, that's all.'

'Worried about what her old cronies in the book club think, you mean. Imagine if I had a third child with yet another man, horror of horrors.'

'Don't be like that. There's no need to be so harsh.'

'Sorry, Dad. But I'm happy, Dan and Lily are happy, everyone's happy. And me and Simon are fine. Can't she see that?'

'Obviously not. Why don't you try talking to her?'

I sigh. 'I have tried, you know that. It's like talking to a stone. If she doesn't like what she's hearing she just clams up. She's the most difficult person in the world to get through to. I've given up. She doesn't approve of me or my lifestyle. In her day you married and had kids and that was that. Things have changed, but she can't seem to accept it.'

'I know what she's like, believe me. But you just have to be patient with her. Pick your time. Her heart's in the right place.'

'It's just buried so deep that it's hard to find sometimes.'

'Meg!'

'I'm sorry, but that's how I feel.'

'Maybe you should start standing up to her more. Tell her what's really on your mind. Your sister doesn't seem to have any problem in that regard.'

I give him a half smile. 'Hattie's Hattie. She was born stroppy.'

Dad laughs. 'That she was. But don't let it bother you. You and your mum will find your own way of communicating – give it time.'

I feel like giving him a hug but I give him a smile instead. 'Thanks, Dad. Sorry to go on . . .'

'That's OK. You go out this evening and have a lovely time.

Enjoy yourselves. What time are you collecting the children in the morning?'

'Half eight. I'll drop Dan straight to school.'

'I won't be here but I'll see you on Sunday week. You are coming for dinner aren't you?'

'Of course. I wouldn't miss your birthday, you know that.' I lean forward and kiss him on the cheek. His skin feels warm and stubbly under my lips. He smells of Old Spice. I smile. I used to buy him the tall ceramic bottles as a child, mainly because I liked using the empty bottles for making rose perfume with. My 'perfume', rose petals from the garden mixed together with water and, for some reason, sugar, always smelt of Old Spice.

After parking the car down the road from the yacht club I adjust the rear-view mirror and check my hastily applied make-up. I have some colour on my face, mainly gained from running after Lily in the garden, so I haven't bothered with foundation but now I'm regretting it. My nose and forehead are red and shiny and there's a small outbreak of new spots on my chin. Typical. Lily threw my face powder down the loo last week and I haven't had a chance to replace it, so my skin will just have to stay shiny. My mascara and lip gloss are still intact, at least that's something. I run a brush through my hair and spray on some 'Happy' perfume.

I step out of the car and pull my dress down. It has a habit of bunching up under my non-existent chest. It's silk, a plain dark green top with shoe-string straps and a summery pink and blue pattern printed on the full skirt which flirts just below the knee. I bought it in Spain last year and I've never been all that comfortable wearing it. But it was this dress or my nice but dull black trousers with a sequined vest top and I've worn that so many times before it bores me.

For some reason I have butterflies in my stomach. It's the

first night in as long as I can remember that Simon and I will have a whole night together without the kids. I hope he doesn't expect anything too spectacular to happen in the bedroom department. Don't get me wrong, sex is fine by me, and I've worn the lacy French turquoise and raspberry pink underwear he claims to like. I know he really prefers my black basque with the scratchy lace trimming and the impossibly tight lacing up the front, which trusses me up and makes me feel like Samantha Fox in her page-three glory days, but it's damned uncomfortable and far too hot to wear under clothes in the summer. Besides, underwear like that is only ten-minute underwear – it isn't supposed to be worn for long.

Once, after a particularly bad row, Simon said our sex life was in a rut and we should spice it up a bit. I'd ignored him at the time, climbing out of bed and spending the night on the sofa dreaming of French maid outfits and crotchless red leather knickers. But now and again his words come back to haunt me. I have a horrible feeling that he's right, that our sex life after Lily has become routine. But with him away so much, it's a wonder we have a sex life at all.

As I approach the side gate of the yacht club, the hum of conversation hits me; there's lively music in the background. A tall, angular man with an acne-scarred face stops me at the gate. He's wearing an official-looking navy suit and is holding a clipboard. What *is* it with this club and clipboards?

'Member?' he asks in a tight tone.

'I'm here with *Ghost*.'

He looks at me for a moment and, presumably deciding I'm fairly innocent, gives a curt nod and ushers me through.

'Meg!' Simon is standing against the side of the modern extension to the white Georgian clubhouse, one leg resting against the wall. He strides towards me. 'I've been waiting for you. What took you so long?'

'Getting Lily into her pyjamas and dropping the kids off to Mum and Dad's. The usual.'

'Well, you're here now.' He leans down and gives me a beery-tasting kiss on the lips. 'I have a surprise for you later,' he whispers in my ear, his breath tickling my neck.

'Really, what?'

He laughs. 'You'll just have to wait and see.' Paranoid images of fur-lined handcuffs and horrible leather gimp bandage masks flash in front of my eyes. I screw them shut and then open them again.

'Anything wrong?'

'No, nothing.'

He takes my hand in his and we begin to weave our way through the crowds.

'We have a table on the balcony,' he says. 'Hattie's already up there.'

'Has she dumped Slipper yet?'

'Not exactly.'

As we climb up the thronged uneven stone steps towards the balcony it's too difficult to talk, jostled by people's arms and shoulders. I narrowly miss a pint being poured down my front. It lands on my foot with a slosh and I shake it off.

'Sorry,' a man in a pink shirt says.

'It's OK,' I reply graciously. They're cheap leather and bead sandals I bought in Greece. Now if I'd been wearing my fab red fabric-covered wedges it would have been a different matter, but I know better than to wear them to a yacht club.

As we reach the top I spot Hattie on a high-backed wooden bench, a familiar red-faced man sitting beside her, having a good gawk at her cleavage. It's the vile Giles who was so mean to Dan.

'What's she doing with that horrible man?' I ask Simon.

He shrugs. 'She met him at the bar last night. Seems to be under the impression that he's some kind of millionaire.'

'What about his wife?'

Simon just smiles.

'Isn't he married?'

'Yup. She's away on some sort of golf trip apparently.'

'Why didn't you say something?'

'I thought it might be funny to see what happens.'

'Oh, right, very funny. Make a fool of Hattie day, is it?'

I storm towards Hattie and her admirer. He's not going to make a fool of my sister, I think to myself, not if I can help it.

Chapter 11

Capsize: to turn over. 'Oops, my boat capsized!'

I stand in front of Hattie and stare down at her.

'Hello, Hattie.'

'Sis.' She waves her hand at me loosely. From the amount of empty glasses on the low wooden table in front of them, they've been here a while. 'Come and meet Giles. He's adorable. He's been telling me all about his house in Portugal. Sounds divine.'

'Really?' I glare at him. 'Is there a golf course near by?'

Giles studies me. 'Have I met you before? You look familiar.'

'Yes, at the swimming test for the junior section. You wanted to fail my son, remember? I was the big eejit who jumped into the sea.'

'Ah, yes.' An angry flush scampers up his throat. He coughs. 'Delighted that the little chap will be joining us. And this beautiful specimen is your sister?' He ogles Hattie, who's falling out of her tight red wrap dress. I note she's abandoned the subtle approach.

'Yes, she is. Simon tells me your wife's away. Shame she's missing regatta week, isn't it?'

'Ah, yes.' He has the good grace to look sheepish. 'The wife.'

'Wife?' Hattie pulls her hand out of his. 'You never said anything about a wife.'

'Wife by name only, my dear,' he pats her hand in a condescending manner.

Hattie whips her hand away. 'You're not a millionaire either, are you?'

Giles, sensing trouble, stands up, wobbling a little and steadying himself on the back of the bench. 'It's been lovely meeting you all. I really must dash. Phone calls to make, you know how it is. Bye, Hattie. Pleasure.'

'Bugger that,' Hattie says with a hiccup. 'Pleasure's all yours. Thanks for wasting my time. Get some liposuction, buster. Your belly isn't natural.'

He scuttles away quickly and disappears into the bar, safely swallowed up by the throng.

Hattie picks up a glass and downs the contents in one.

'Millionaire my ass,' she says with another hiccup.

'Actually I think he is a millionaire,' Simon says mildly. 'He sold his computer firm and took early retirement.'

'A creepy *married* millionaire,' I point out. 'You're well rid of him.' I omit telling her that Simon knows Giles *and* his wife. Simon's life wouldn't be worth living if I did.

Hattie gives me a smile. 'At least I got it half right. I think I'll go and find Slipper.' She gets to her feet, staggering a little on her high-heeled red sandals, and totters down the steps and towards the marquee.

'May as well sit down.' Simon gestures at the bench Hattie has just vacated. 'Drink?'

'Love one. White wine, please.'

'Coming up.'

As he stands at the outside bar hatch waiting to be served, I watch the world go by, soaking in the heady carnival atmosphere. It's packed for a Wednesday night, but regatta week has that effect on people. Most of the sailors take the week off work to sail and party. A tall pretty blonde woman in her twenties 'accidentally' bumps into Simon, I wonder is there any truth in what Mum suspects: that our relationship is in trouble. The blonde woman starts to chat to him, wafting her long sheet of hair from one bare, bronzed shoulder to the other, smiling at him like a predatory crocodile. I try to look away, aware that I'm staring, but it's no use, I'm a sucker for punishment. To take my mind off it, I bite down on my lower lip, cross my legs, and begin to jiggle my top leg in time to the music from the marquee. I hold on to the edge of the bench, pressing my palms into the wood. I have a terrible jealous streak, and jumping up and giving the woman a good slap in the face wouldn't be beyond me. But I stay in control.

I don't know what I'd do without Simon. Yes, he drives me to distraction at times, and yes, his job isn't exactly conducive to family life, but he's a good man. I'm damned if I'm going to lose him to some tart in a low-cut dress. Just as I decide, against my better judgement, to go over there and give her a piece of my mind for flirting with my partner, Simon's drinks arrive and he walks back towards me.

I unclench my teeth and loosen my grip from the bench.

'Anything wrong?' He puts a bottle of wine and two glass tumblers on the table. 'Sorry, they've run out of wine glasses.'

I shake my head. 'It's nothing.' Just my green-eyed monster taking hold again.

'You look lovely. I like the dress.'

'Thanks.' I give him a smile and try to forget all about the blonde girl.

A little later, after finishing our bottle of wine, we decide to join the rest of Simon's crew in the marquee. As we make our way down the granite steps, worn smooth by over two centuries of feet, I feel apprehensive. Lively rock and roll music drifts up towards us from the marquee; Simon loves dancing. He's a natural – confident and self-assured whatever the music. I, on the other hand, can just about cope with straightforward pop, and flounder with any kind of dance music. I was really stuck in the 'aciiid' nineties and usually ended up drinking more than I should before flailing my arms around my head like a Duracell-bunny version of Morrissey. As for salsa and jive – forget it!

It's a balmy evening and three panels of the tent have been peeled away, revealing the innards. Couples are jiving to beat the band, flinging each other around the floor with alcohol-fuelled abandon. I pull on Simon's hand as we are about to enter the marquee.

He looks at me and smiles. 'OK?'

'Fine. Can we stay out here for a minute? Just you and me?'

'Sure. Is anything wrong?'

I pull him closer and lean my head against his upper arm. 'No. The wine's just starting to hit me, that's all.'

'You're out of practice.'

'I know.'

He drags a heavy white metal chair along the gravel, leaving a long sandy rut in the ground, and swings it around to face the marquee. He sits down and pats his knee. 'Care for a seat?'

I sit down on his lap and lean back against his firm chest. He folds his arms around me and I close my eyes. I can feel the warmth of his body through the flimsy silk of my dress, the steady rhythm of his breathing.

'I've missed you, Meg.' He gives me a squeeze.

'I've missed you.'

I can hear his breath in my ear and feel his chest moving in and out with every inhalation and exhalation. I synchronize my breathing with his, lengthening my own which is fast and shallow in comparison. I often do this when we lie in bed together. It makes me feel closer to him, more attached, part of him in some way.

After a few minutes Simon raises his head from my shoulder. 'Would you look at that?'

I open my eyes. Hattie is flinging a compliant Ryan around the dance floor to 'Rock Around the Clock'. I watch, goggle-eyed as she takes control of the floor. Unlike Simon, Hattie doesn't have natural rhythm. But what she lacks in technique, she more than makes up for in sheer exuberance. She grabs hold of the edge of her skirt with one hand, whipping it to the music, and coming very close to showing more than she bargained for. Or maybe that's her intention. You never can tell with Hattie.

Ryan's eyes are glued to her, sparking with admiration, a wide grin on his face.

'Where's Slipper do you think?' I ask Simon.

'No idea. Although he was chatting up a rather fine-looking Brazilian girl at the bar earlier.'

I shake my head. 'Such a fickle lot, you sailors.'

'Hey!' he squeezes me tightly. 'Less of that. Hattie abandoned him first for her millionaire, remember?' The band launches into a spirited version of 'Jailhouse Rock'. 'Enough about Hattie. I love this one. Let's dance.'

'Do we have to? They're such a cheesy wedding band. I'm sure they're the same one as last year. Guys and Dolls – isn't that their name? It's like bloody *Groundhog Day*. I bet you fifty euro they play "Chattanooga Choochoo" next. And the girls in the short black dresses will make engine noises – whoo, whoo – that kind of thing.'

'You're on. But they're due a slow set soon, it's nearly ten after all. So my fifty's on "The Power of Love" or "Total Eclipse of the Heart".'

'What about "Take my Breath Away"?'

'That too. Fifty euro on an eighties' power ballad.'

'My money's still on the whoo-whoo girls. I'm telling you, buster, I know this band's play list intimately.'

Simon puts out his hand. 'Fine. Let's shake on it.'

'Done.' I laugh. I reckon I'll win either way. I'll make a holy show of myself on the dance floor to 'Chattanooga Choo-choo' and be fifty euro richer. Or it'll be a slow set and I'll do the 'roundy roundy' dance, turning slow circles, with my arms around Simon, hoping I don't crush his feet too often.

The crowd claps and whoops at the end of 'Jailhouse Rock'. Hattie, modest thing that she is, takes a bow. One of the girls in the band, the one with the whitest hair and the shortest lycra dress, puts her left hand in the air, fist clenched, pumps it up and down and yells 'Whoo, whoo' into the microphone, almost deafening everyone. My heart sinks. I've won, but now I have to dance.

'You win,' Simon says. He lifts me off his knee and stands up, delving in his pocket for his black Henri Lloyd sailing wallet, which always reeks of stale sea salt. He hands me a fifty-euro note.

'You keep it. Buy me some champagne later or something.'

'OK.' He puts the note back in his wallet, stands up and holds out his hand. 'Shall we?' He nods at the dance floor. 'Just one dance, Meg. Please?'

I take his hand wordlessly, allowing myself to be dragged reluctantly towards the floor.

As we walk into the marquee the smell of stale beer mixed with sweat hits me. Bright disco lights flash into my eyes and I'm jostled by a small drunk man holding a pint. His drink slurps all down the front of my dress.

'Great,' I say sarcastically to him. 'Thanks a lot.'

'Pleasure,' he slurs, leering at me.

I realize he's all of sixteen. He staggers out of the tent. To puke on someone's docksiders no doubt. There are always loads of under-age boy drinkers at the regatta dances, all Brylcreemed hair and badly fitting reefer jackets borrowed from Dad and garish Bugs Bunny or Simpsons ties.

The girls of that age are far more sophisticated, drifting around the forecourt of the yacht club in glossy packs, exhibiting tanned midriffs, acres of leg and long, sleek hair. They must spend a fortune on hair products. I had short, untameable hair at that age, damaged by years of Sun-In hair lightener and pokerhot crimping irons. It's still recovering.

Simon takes both my hands and pulls me into the middle of the dance floor. The wooden surface feels sticky under my feet and I hope I don't land flat on my ass. He begins to dance.

'Come on, Meg.' He grins at me.

I plaster a smile on my face and move my feet. The wine helps, at least I'm not rooted to the spot, stuck like a deer in headlights, like I sometimes am. I listen to the music and try to move in time. Simon pulls me towards him assertively. I stumble a little, our chests collide and I fall. Simon catches me. He puts an arm around me and lifts me to my feet again.

'Shouldn't have worn my heels,' I joke.

'Take them off.'

'No way. The floor's filthy and I might stand on glass. I'll be fine.'

Simon holds my hands tightly. He lifts our arms up and swings them over our heads. I know I'm supposed to turn, our backs facing and then he'll flip me over his back.

When we were first dating he spent hours one evening in my small living room trying to teach me to jive. Still in the dewy-eyed stage and horribly eager to please, I'd followed his every move attentively, concentrating with all my being and revelling in his strength and ability. After several hours and with many bruises, a rather sore wrist and a tender shoulder I'd managed a reasonably competent back flip.

Our backs touch and Simon bends forward. But I misjudge the angle and one of my shoes slips, sending my leg skidding sideways. Simon pulls and instead of going over his back, I fall off it and slither sideways, my legs akimbo and my dress riding up my thighs and flashing my turquoise knickers to the world.

'Let go!' I yell.

Simon releases his hands and I flop to the floor, landing painfully on my coccyx. The music stops abruptly.

'Feck!' I swear under my breath, pulling my dress down over my exposed legs. I'd only had time to put fake tan halfway up my thighs and I pray no one has noticed. How humiliating.

'Are you all right?' Simon crouches down, the lights behind him illuminating his head like a multi-coloured disco halo.

'I think so.' I curl my feet under my body, put my hands on the floor and push myself up a little.

'Let me help you.' He puts his arms around me from the back and lifts me up. Everyone is staring at us. More humiliation.

'I'm fine, really,' I say ungraciously, pushing his hands away. 'Stop fussing. I just slipped.' My bruised bottom throbs angrily but I'm not going to admit it. I turn towards the band. 'I'm fine,' I shout. 'Thanks. Keep playing.'

I brush down the back of my dress, dislodging a beer mat that is stuck to my bottom – the final indignity – and then walk out of the tent, Simon at my heels.

'She's OK, folks,' one of the girls in the band says into her microphone. 'Cancel the ambulance. Now who's ready to salsa?' They launch into 'La Bamba'.

'Hardly salsa,' Simon murmurs. 'Probably time to retire gracefully, eh, Meg?'

'Graceful my ass!' I mutter.

Hattie and Ryan appear beside us.

'Nice one,' says Hattie. 'Just as well you're never getting married. You'd never survive the first dance.'

Simon looks at her but says nothing.

'Thanks for your concern, sis,' I say, a little annoyed. 'Why don't you dance with Simon then? Show me how it's done?'

'OK.' Hattie is oblivious to my tone. 'Come on, Simon.' She grabs his arm.

He looks at me. I can tell he's itching to dance, but doesn't want to upset me.

'Go on,' I say, rather graciously in the circumstances. 'You'll enjoy it.'

'Are you sure?'

I nod and sit down on the metal chair, wincing slightly. My bottom is still tender from the fall.

Hattie and Simon practically run onto the dance floor.

'Can I get you a drink, Meg?'

I look to my left. Ryan is perched on a table beside me.

'I'd love a glass of water. Thanks.'

'No problem.' He looks at me for a moment, as if about to say something, then stares into the tent, his eyes fixed on Hattie.

I feel sorry for him. 'She'll break your heart, you know that?'

He shrugs. 'You could be right.' He smiles at me. 'But I'm willing to take that chance. I can't help myself.'

He gazes at her again. 'God, she's amazing.'

Hattie is sitting on her legs on the dance floor, her body arched over backwards, inching her skirt up over her thighs in time to the music.

Simon bends down, puts his arm under her waist and scoops her onto her feet, not an insignificant feat. They look incredible together.

Ryan sighs. 'Better to have loved and lost that never to have loved at all.'

'Very eloquent for a sailor.'

He smiles. 'Tennyson. My mum's an English teacher, she's into her quotes. Has one for every occasion.'

'Did you do English in college?'

He grins. 'Me? No. I didn't go to college. Mum was most disappointed.'

'And your dad?'

'He died when I was seven.'

'I'm sorry.'

'It's fine. I don't really remember him. I've been teaching sailing since I left school. First job was in France, then in the States, the British Virgin Islands, the Caribbean, pretty much all over.'

'Then back to rainy old Dublin?'

'Yep. But I like being back.'

'You must miss the sun though?'

He shrugs. 'Sure. Who wouldn't? But there are other things that more than make up for that.' He stares at Hattie again.

'Why did you come back?' God, Meg, must you be so nosy? 'Sorry, you don't have to answer that.'

'No, it's fine. Various reasons really. Family commitments.' He pauses for a moment, then leaves it at that. 'But I'm happy I did. Let me get you that drink.'

'Thanks.'

As I wait for Ryan to return I pull another chair over, rest my feet on it, sit back and shut my eyes. My bottom has stopped throbbing, thank goodness, and I still feel quite mellow from the wine. I can hear the tinkle of laughter behind me, the hollow clink of halyards hitting against metal masts, the chatter of animated conversation from the balcony. As the final strains of 'La Bamba' play out, I begin to drift off.

'Meg? Meg?'

I open my eyes. Simon and Hattie are standing in front of me.

'Were you asleep?' Simon peers down at me.

'No, just resting. And thinking.' I swing my legs down off the chair. 'I do that sometimes when the kids aren't around. Think, I mean.'

Simon smiles.

'Where's Ryan?' Hattie looks around.

'Gone to get me some water. He'll be back in a minute. Don't worry.'

'Good.' She drags over a chair. The legs are a little wonky and it wobbles a bit when she sits down.

'Be nice to him, Hattie.'

She looks at me. 'What do you mean?'

'Don't act the innocent. He's Dan's instructor, try to remember that. I don't want any awkwardness, understand?'

'Awkward, smawkward.' She rubs her lips together. 'Damn, where did I put my bag? I need my lip gloss.'

'Hattie!'

'OK, I heard you. I'll be nice to Ryan. OK?' She beams at me. 'In fact I might just be very nice if he plays his cards right,' she purrs.

'Jesus! Would you stop that.'

Simon laughs. 'Ryan's not as innocent as he looks, Meg, he's been around the block.'

'What do you mean?' I ask.

'Shush!' Hattie says. 'Here he comes. Hi, Ryan.' She jumps up off her seat, presses her body against his and kisses him soundly on the lips.

'Cool down, woman. Here's your water, Meg.' He hands me a glass.

'Thanks.' I stare at him in amazement. No one speaks to Hattie like that and she seems nonplussed. She's just smiling at him.

'Speaking of cool, is that jacuzzi still available, Simon?' she asks.

Simon groans. 'You're incorrigible. No, it's taken.' He looks down at me. 'All night.'

My stomach lurches and I smile up at him.

'Meg–' Hattie stares at me – 'you saucy thing. A night of passion in the jacuzzi. And you the mother of two. Didn't think you had it in you.'

'You're not the only one in this family with a sex life.' I stand up and grab Simon's arm. 'Come on, lover. The jacuzzi awaits.'

Simon's eyes light up. He doesn't have to be asked twice. 'Excellent. See you both tomorrow. The start's at nine, Ryan, and we have to fix the spinnaker pole. So on the boat at seven thirty, don't be late.'

'I won't be, boss.' Ryan grins at him.

'Seven thirty,' I groan. 'So much for a lie-in.'

'Enjoy yourselves.' Hattie drags Ryan towards the dance floor.

'We will,' Simon shouts back. 'All night!'

'You'll be lucky.'

Ghost is still tied alongside the marina. Once on the pontoon I bend down, take off my sandals and pop them into my bag. As I've already proven, my balance isn't the best tonight and there's no sense in being stupid as the soles of my sandals are leather and quite slippery. I feel the cool smooth wood beneath my feet – delicious. I wiggle my toes.

'Lovely evening,' Simon comments as we walk towards the boat, 'can't believe it's still so warm.'

'We only get a handful of nights like this, it's nice to make the most of it.'

'We could always make love on the deck,' Simon suggests. 'Under the stars.'

'With the whole yacht club watching?' I snort. 'I don't think so. Hattie might be on for it, though. She's always been a terrible exhibitionist. She used to have a thing about having sex in public places but I hope she's grown out of it.'

'Isn't there a technical name for that?'

'Mad you mean?'

He laughs. 'That too.'

'Here we are.' Simon stands in front of *Ghost*, swings my bag onto the deck and holds out both his hands to help me clamber aboard. I take them gratefully. Years ago I'd made the mistake of putting one leg over the guard rail while the other leg was still on the pontoon. Unfortunately the boat hadn't been fully attached to the pontoon at the time and started to move sideways. I'd fallen into the sea between the boat and the pontoon, banging my hip quite badly in the process, and had a bruise for months. I'd learnt not to board a boat the hard way.

I sit on the deck and watch Simon open the hatch. I have butterflies in my stomach again. He peers into the cabin and then turns back towards me.

'Half expected to find Slipper hard at it on the map table with that Brazilian,' he says with a smile, 'but it's all clear.'

'Is the map table big enough?'

'Not really. But we could give it a go. Fancy it?'

I remember my sore bottom. 'No thanks. Is there a sail loft?'

Simon laughs. 'Not a loft, *Ghost's* not that big. But there is a fore peak, where we dumped some spare spinnakers. Would that do you?'

'Maybe.' I smile at him in what I hope is a seductive manner.

'Really?' His eyes flash brightly.

'Why not? Be like old times.'

The first time we'd made love was in the cabin of a yacht called *Catanga* on top of a huge white spinnaker. It was the early hours of the morning and we were both still drunk after a heavy night in Howth Yacht Club. Rather than get a taxi back to my place, which would have cost an arm and a leg, if we managed to get one at all, Simon had suggested sleeping on the boat. I still remember it vividly. The crisp sail was brand new and it had rustled and crackled with every move.

We'd both fallen asleep, exhausted after two bouts of rather fast and drunken sex, wrapped up in the same spinnaker, which was surprisingly warm.

During the race the next day, when the spinnaker was hoisted a pink lacy bra fell out of the sail and landed on the deck. Simon, doing bow at the time, had hastily pocketed it in case it blew away and had presented it to me that evening in front of the whole crew, including Slipper, to much hooting and jeering. I hadn't talked to him for two days.

'Are you wearing your pink bra again this evening?' Simon asks, as he leads me down a corridor to the back of the boat.

I laugh. He remembers. 'You're sweet, but I don't think it would still fit me.'

He opens a door and stands back. The smell of stale sea water and musty sails hits me but I don't care. It's the new, brazen, Hattie-like me. I walk in and he closes the door behind us. The floor is littered with huge, brightly coloured sail bags.

'But I am wearing this.' I unzip the side of my dress and lift it over my head.

Simon's eyes lap over my body. He never seems to notice my stretch marks or my jelly belly.

'God, you're stunning.' His voice is husky. 'Come here.'

He pulls me towards him and kisses me hard on the lips.

I gasp as his cool hands ran down my back and linger on my buttocks. He's always been a bottom man. He pulls my pants down my thighs and I step out of them. My breath begins to quicken. This is great. I haven't felt so turned on in a long time. He unbuttons his shirt. I unbuckle his shorts for him and start to pull them down his muscular thighs. I love Simon's legs. They're a little stocky but powerful. His erection nearly hits me in the eye.

'Simon! Why are you going commando?'

'Couldn't find any clean shorts this morning.'

He throws his shirt onto the floor and puts his arms around me. I can feel his erection pressing against my left thigh. He kisses me frantically. I stumble backwards and fall against a sail bag.

'Sorry,' he says.

'Come here.' I pull him down on top of me.

'Oh, Meg.' He kisses me again and I can feel his urgency. I kiss him back, even harder.

Then I hear a noise. 'What was that?'

'What?'

'Shush, listen.'

'I can't hear anything.' He holds my head in his hands and kisses me again.

I turn my head to the side. 'Stop, Simon. There it is again. It's coming from above us.'

We both listen attentively. Then I look up at the roof and scream. There's a face staring down at us through the porthole. I scream again and it moves away.

Chapter 12

Screw: the boat's propeller

'There's someone up there, watching us,' I say, horrified.

'They can't see anything. It's almost dark outside and even darker in here. And the glass is tinted.' Simon stands up. I grab my pants and hastily put them on and then wrap my dress around me.

'Wait, it might be a burglar.'

'Don't be daft.'

He opens the hatch and sticks his head out. 'Slipper, what the hell are you doing? You nearly gave Meg a heart attack.'

'Thought I heard something down there,' Slipper says. 'What are you doing in the fore peak?'

'Um, just checking the number two spinnaker for tomorrow. The pole damaged the leach yesterday.'

Slipper seems happy enough with the answer. 'Listen, mate, are you using the jacuzzi? Only me and Ria were thinking—'

'We're sleeping in Whitey's cabin tonight,' Simon says firmly. 'And yes, we'll be using the jacuzzi. So don't go getting any ideas.'

'We'll take the back cabin then. Catch you later.'

'Slipper! Slipper,' Simon calls.

'What?'

'Wait a minute.' Simon grabs his shorts and scrambles in the pockets for his wallet. 'Here's fifty euro. Go and buy Ria some champagne. And don't come back for at least an hour. Understand?'

'Whatever you say, boss. Have a good time, Meg. Plenty of spinnakers down there. Don't leave your bra behind this time.'

I ignore him. He can be very teenage sometimes.

Simon closes the hatch again. 'Sorry, that was your fifty.'

'It's OK. At least it got rid of him.' I'm a bit miffed. I had shoe plans for that money. But it's in a good cause.

Simon looks at me. 'Now where were we?'

I feel uncomfortable. Hattie's right, I'm a mother for goodness sake. What am I doing? 'Maybe we should go into the cabin. It might be safer.'

Simon sighs. 'OK, you're probably right.' He gathers up his clothes in a bundle. I pull my dress over my head.

'Simon, put your shorts on. What if one of the crew's out there?' I ask.

'It's fine. Nothing they haven't seen before.'

He walks out and I follow him, my eyes glued to his firm buttocks. I've forgotten he's in such good shape.

'The coast's clear,' he says.

I'm not convinced. 'Can we lock the cabin door?'

He nods.

'Good. I don't want to be interrupted by Slipper, or anyone else for that matter.'

'Neither do I.' Simon opens the door of the master cabin, switches on the lights and then dims them. He locks the door and dumps his clothes at the end of the bed. Wordlessly he walks towards me, peels off my dress and lays it over his clothes. Then he takes off my bra and pants and lifts me into his arms.

'Simon!'

He plonks me on the bed and I fall into the luxurious feather duvet. Then he jumps on top of me.

'Simon!' I say again, laughing.

He just grins and then kisses me, hard, like nothing else matters. And at the precise moment, nothing else does.

The following morning I'm woken by the noise of horribly shrill electronic bleeps.

'Bloody hell,' I mutter, opening my eyes. 'What's that?'

The air in the cabin is warm and stuffy and my mouth feels parched. I groan. 'Make it stop, Simon.' I kick him with my leg.

Simon stirs. 'Wha?'

'That noise? Is there a fire alarm on the boat? Or a burglar alarm?' I sit up and, realizing I'm naked, clutch the duvet to my chest. 'Should we abandon ship?'

He snorts. 'It's the alarm on my mobile.'

'Well, I wasn't to know. Switch it off for heaven's sake.'

A moment later he surfaces from under the duvet and crawls to the end of the bed, his white bottom exposed and his bits dangling down like, I hate to say it, a turkey's giblets wobbling around between his legs. He turns the alarm off and my ears stop ringing. It's so unfair, I only had a few glasses of wine last night. Simon's right, I'm completely out of practice. The way I feel, I may as well have made a night of it by getting completely legless. At least then I'd have some reason for my hangover. I give his naked bottom a slap.

He yelps. 'Hey! What was that for?'

'That'll teach you to wake me up so early. What time is it anyway? It feels like the middle of the night.' I moan. 'And I so need a lie-in.'

'Half six,' he admits sheepishly.

'Why did you set your alarm for half bloody six?'

'I wanted to talk to you. I have to catch an eight o'clock flight this evening, so we won't have much time later. And then I'll be away for a good bit, remember?'

I groan. 'How could I forget?'

Simon snuggles his hand under the duvet and snakes it over my naked tummy and down my thigh. I shake my leg and roll onto my front.

'Get off!'

'Ah, Meg, we won't be together again for ages.' He put his arms around me from behind and pulls me towards him, my body dragging over the expensive butter-soft sheets.

'Simon!' I flail my arms and hit him on the head, my watch impacting against his skin.

'Ow!' he says. He takes his hands away. 'No need to be so violent.'

'Sorry. I didn't mean to do that.' I wriggle my body around to face him.

He turns away.

'I'm so sorry.' I run my hands up and down his back.

He whips around and then pounces, pinning me under him with his strong arms. 'Got you.' He leans forward and kisses me. I give in. I know he'll only sulk if I don't and it's not worth it. Hell, it's only sex.

'God that was great,' he says ten minutes later, climbing off me and collapsing back against the pillows, sweat droplets popping out on his forehead. It was a bit too fast and furious for me, but I'm happy that he's happy.

'That'll see me through another few weeks,' he says. 'Damn, I'm going to miss you.'

'Few weeks?' I lift my body up on my arms and stare down at him. 'How many weeks exactly?'

'Two.'

'You said a week. You promised you'd be back for your parent's visit.'

'Did I? I'm sorry, I don't remember. Of course I'll be back to see them, but only for the last day of their visit I'm afraid. I thought I'd told you about the extra race week in Falmouth.'

'No, you didn't. I would have remembered, believe me. Where's Falmouth anyway?'

'South-west England.'

'Simon, I can't entertain them on my own for a whole week. And anyway,' I add, 'I hope to be working by then, so Lily will be with Tina. They're going to be pretty bored on their own.'

'Working? You never said anything to me about getting a job. Where?'

'You suggested it in the first place and I've been thinking about it for a while. I've decided to ring Hall's first thing tomorrow morning. I'll expect they'll find something for me pretty quickly.'

'Great. But don't be too disappointed if they don't.'

'Oh, they will, you'll see.'

Simon says nothing for a moment.

'I was good at my job I'll have you know,' I say, miffed at his attitude. 'Let me tell you, buster—'

'Whoa there, Meg.' He puts his hands in the air. 'I know you were a brilliant auctioneer-type person. Calm down.'

'Auction-room assistant,' I correct him.

Simon says nothing for a moment. Then he blows his breath out in a loud whoosh. 'I'm sorry.'

'For what?'

'For being away for so long. For my parents. For everything. I know you're not finding this easy. But it's my job.'

'I know that. But I hate the fact that we never get to talk properly, and that when something happens, like the roof leaking, you're miles away and in another time zone.'

'I'm sorry.' Simon runs his hands through his hair, leaving it sticking up in messy blond tufts. 'Why don't you and the kids join me in Falmouth? The owner has rented a big house for the crew and their families. It'll be fun and we'll get to spend some time together. It'll be like a holiday. A family holiday.'

'Oh, no. I've been on those "holidays" before, remember? Sitting on shore waiting for you. Entertaining the kids while you get drunk with your buddies. All that fake friendliness from women who you know are just dying to bitch about you behind your back. Whatever it is, it's certainly not a holiday.'

'It won't be like that this time, I promise. There will be other young families there, normal families. And the wives aren't real sailing wives, not like the ones you're used to anyway. Most of the crew are the owner's friends. Me and Slipper are the only professionals.'

'Where exactly is Falmouth? I know you said England, but what part of England?' My knowledge of English geography is shamelessly bad. But not as bad as Simon's knowledge of Irish geography, or history for that matter. At first he thought it funny to call me his 'colonial wife' until I slapped him and nearly broke one of his front teeth. I pack quite a wallop when I want to. Anyway, he deserved it, it wasn't funny.

'Cornwall. It's a beautiful part of the country and the weather's usually good. There's even a trampoline for Dan and a heated outdoor pool. Might help Dan's swimming.'

Damn, I think. He's got me there. Simon is right, it would do wonders for Dan's swimming.

'I'll think about it.'

'Great!'

'I only said I'd think about it. No promises.'

Simon grins at me.

I open my mouth to tell him not to get his hopes up when there's a loud bang on the door, someone slapping it with an open hand.

'Are you two decent?' Ryan shouts through the wood.

'No!' I squeal, pulling the sheet up to my neck. 'Don't come in.'

Ryan tries the door but luckily it's still locked.

'Ryan! You brat!' I jump up, grab my bag, run into the en suite and lock the door behind me. I can hear Simon chortling loudly.

'Hi, Meg,' Ryan says, his voice muffled by the bathroom door. Simon has obviously let him in. 'Nice bra.'

Must have left my underwear on the floor.

'Leave my undies alone, thanks. Or I'll tell Hattie on you.'

'Sure I'm wearing her knickers this morning. Bit tight on me though.'

'Ryan! I can see why you two hit it off.'

'Oh we hit it off all right. All night in fact.'

'That's my sister you're talking about.'

Ryan laughs. 'So you'll hear all about it later.'

'I most certainly won't. Hattie's the soul of discretion.'

'Ah, that's why she told me all about your own sex life.'

'Much as I'd love to leave you two to banter,' Simon cuts in. 'I'm going up on deck to fix the spinnaker pole and I need Ryan's help. Take your time, Meg. Have another jacuzzi if you like.'

'Wouldn't be the same without you. I'll be up in a few minutes.' I look at myself in the bathroom mirror, pressing a finger under each baggy eye. My skin is blotchy, streaked by remnants of last night's make-up. My mascara has left me with panda eyes and my lip gloss has slid off my mouth and onto the side of my face, giving me a lopsided clown's grin. I'm a state.

Ten minutes later, after a lukewarm shower, and a quick tidy up of my face, I get dressed and scramble up the stairs and onto the deck.

'Hi, Meg.' Slipper grins at me. 'Good night?'

'Yes, thanks.'

'Simon's at the bow.' He nods towards the front of the boat.

I step gingerly along the right-hand side of the boat towards Simon, one hand on the guard rail, nervous of slipping on the dew-covered wooden deck. The air smells fresh, with a tang of salt, and after the stuffy air of the cabin I breathe it in eagerly. 'Hey!' Simon looks at me and waves. He wipes his hands and pads towards me in his shorts, T-shirt and black reefer sandals.

'I'm off now,' I say breezily.

'Wait a few minutes, we're nearly finished.'

'I'd better get back. I have to drop Dan to school.'

Simon glances at his watch. 'He'll be very early.'

'It's fine. I'll have a coffee with Mum.'

'Are you sure?'

I nod. 'See you later.' I give him a hug. 'Enjoy the racing.'

'Thanks. And Meg?'

'Yes?'

'I had a great time last night.'

'Me too.' I smile at him, a little shyly for some reason.

He fetches my overnight bag for me from the cabin and helps me climb over the guard rail and onto the pontoon before passing it to me.

'Love you,' he calls after me. I look back.

'Love you, baby,' Slipper imitates, making kissing noises and thrusting his crotch at me suggestively.

'Simon, you big softie,' Ryan scolds him.

I'm mortified, but Simon just laughs. 'Ignore them. They're just jealous. See you later.' He blows me a kiss.

Slipper and Ryan make exaggerated kissing noises. They're such children. I decide not to blow one back and encourage them. I whip my head around and walk away as jauntily as I can. But inside I feel a little strange. Cheap almost. Like a teenager sneaking out of her boyfriend's bedroom and being caught in the act by his parents. I'm thirty-three for heaven's sake, and Simon is Lily's dad. I'm not some one-night stand. I don't need all this. Why can't sailors just be normal?

*

I sit in the car outside Mum and Dad's for a while, eyes closed, enjoying the peace. It's only a quarter to eight and school doesn't start until nine, so I have plenty of time to spare. I'm still feeling a little ropey from the wine last night.

I'm just drifting into a daydream about a sandy beach and a clear blue sky without a child in sight when there's a sharp rap on the window. I open my eyes in surprise.

'Meg, what are you doing in there?'

Mum is peering in at me. She's clutching her white cotton dressing gown around her body and looks rather dishevelled. She has bed hair, squashed down against her crown on one side, and I haven't seen her without a full face of make-up for years. I'd forgotten how prominent the freckles on the bridge of her nose are. She has tiny red broken veins on her cheeks and her eyes are bloodshot. Needless to say, Mum is not a morning person.

I roll down the window, unwilling to leave my four-wheeled sanctuary quite yet.

'You're been sitting in there for ten minutes,' she says. 'What are you doing? Have you broken up with Simon?'

'What? Of course not.' I roll the window back up, take the keys out of the ignition and step out, my flip-flopped feet scrunching on the gravel of the drive.

Mum and Dad lived in Bridge Street, a small cul-de-sac of 1970s detached houses in Killiney. Mum is always arguing with the neighbours, especially Mona Patrick, her next-door neighbour to the left. Mona's hedge is too high, blocking Mum's light; Mona's son parks his car outside Mum's kitchen, obscuring her view – of the run-down green; Mona's house is peach, unlike the other houses, Mum and Dad's included, which are all white. Mum isn't happy unless she has someone to argue with.

'Simon and I are just fine.' I lock the car. If I was Hattie I'd elaborate, telling Mum all about our night of passion on *Ghost* to shock her, but I'm not Hattie, so I don't. 'I don't know where you got that idea from. There's absolutely nothing wrong with our relationship. And I'd appreciate it if you'd keep your crackpot theories to yourself in future.'

'What do you mean?' she demands, following closely behind me as I walk towards the house.

'Thanks to you, Dad is also worried about the state of my relationship. So you can reassure him that it's just fine.'

'Good,' she says. 'I worry about you.'

'You just like a good gossip. Let's drop it, I'm tired.'

Mum snorts. 'You're tired? I'm exhausted. Lily woke at ten past six, and refused to sit in her cot and entertain herself. She wanted someone to play with her. You have that child spoiled, Meg. Mark my words.'

'I do not! Lily's always been an early riser. Count yourself lucky. I have to look after her every morning. Welcome to my life.'

We walk in the door. Dan comes running out of the kitchen, a cluster of Rice Krispies stuck to his cheek. He looks like he has some horrible skin disease.

'Hiya, Mum.' He grins, his mouth still full of snap, crackle and pop. He swallows suddenly, remembering.

'Hi.' I ruffle his hair. 'Where's your sister? I hear she's been keeping your granny busy.'

'Grampa looked after her this morning,' Dan says innocently. 'Granny's just up.'

I look at Mum. She avoids my gaze and stares at the kettle.

'Coffee, Meg?' she asks lightly.

'Please.' I ponder whether to say anything, but decide it's too early in the morning for an argument. At least it gives me the moral upper hand, not something to be sniffed at when it comes to my mother.

'Hattie didn't come home last night.' Mum fills the kettle,

clicking it on and leaning back against the kitchen counter. 'Any idea where she is?'

'No, but I'm sure she's fine. She probably went straight to work from a friend's house or something.'

'A male friend no doubt.'

'Mum!' I nod at Dan. Not that he hasn't heard it all before. He's pouring some more Rice Krispies for Lily, seemingly oblivious to our conversation. Dad always keeps his *Sunday Times* car supplement for Dan and once he's helped Lily he sticks his head in it again.

'Don't know where I went wrong with you two,' Mum mutters under her breath, just loud enough for me to hear.

I know exactly which two she's getting at – me and Hattie – but I press my lips together hard, determined not to rise to her bait. 'So how's Paul?' I ask instead. 'Haven't heard from him in a while. Lost his job yet?'

'Now, don't be so cruel, Meg. Your brother just hasn't found his vocation, that's all. I'm sure Katia will lick him into shape. Nice girl. Very solid.'

'I thought you weren't keen on Katia?'

'I've always liked Katia,' Mum says with a sniff.

I lift my eyebrows. If she's serious, she has a very short memory. 'And how is your dear friend Katia then? Any news there?' I say, fishing.

'No.' Mum narrows her eyes. 'Am I missing something?'

'Not at all, just wondering.' Ha! I have to admit, I'm quite looking forward to the fireworks. A shotgun marriage, followed by a half-Slovakian baby. That will rock Mum out of her complacency. She thinks the sun shines out of Paul's ass.

'Dan's doing the sailing course in Simon's yacht club,' I say, guiding the conversation onto a safer tack. 'Did he tell you?'

'Indeed. And are you taking a family holiday, Meg, with Simon I mean? Important to spend some time together as a family, don't you think?'

'No. He doesn't have the time. But he has suggested a week in Cornwall in a crew house. He'll be on the water most of the time, so I don't think I'll bother. It'll just mean being stuck with a whole lot of sailing wives I don't know, and I don't really fancy it.'

Mum looks at me. 'Cornwall is beautiful, Meg. And you might even get some sun. Why don't you consider it?'

'We'll see,' I say noncommittally. I turn towards Dan. 'Go upstairs and do your teeth, pet. It's nearly time for school.'

'Mum, it's only eight, I'll be way too early.'

'Please?'

He rolls his eyes. 'OK.'

Lily drops her plastic cereal bowl on the floor, sending milk-sodden Rice Krispies flying. I bend down to pick them up, the grains squishing in my fingers, and deposit them back in the bowl.

'You're not going to give that back to Lily.' Mum's eyes widen.

'No, Mum. I'm just picking them off the floor. I'm not that bad.' I empty the bowl into the bin. Unlike our permanently full bin, it has a fresh, green liner in it that smells of nappy bags and it doesn't have any sticky runs down its side either.

I clatter Lily's bowl into the sink and open the tap. The water hits the side of the bowl and splashes upwards, hitting my lower stomach. Great! I brush the water off with a deep sigh.

'Meg? What's wrong with you this morning? You seem very out of sorts.' Mum stares at me, her arms crossed in front of her chest. 'You're not pregnant again are you?'

'No! I'm just a little tired, that's all. I had a late night and an early start. Now I have to get Dan to school.'

I lift Lily out of the high chair and brush stray Rice Krispies off her dress. Mum follows me out into the hall.

'Is anything wrong?'

'No, Mum.'

She cocks her head to one side. 'Are you *sure* everything's all right with Simon?'

'Jesus H. Christ!' I snap. 'How many times do I have to tell you? Everything's fine. Just stop with the questions, please.'

As I strap a furiously kicking Lily into her car seat, I feel bad. I shouldn't have rounded on her like that.

'Mama,' Lily says, 'ice cream.'

'It's too early for ice cream, Lily. Sorry.'

'Ice! Ice!'

I ignore her, straighten up and close the car door, careful not to trap one of Lily's restless legs or feet in the process. She isn't in a pleasant mood. It's going to be a long old day. Dan climbs in beside her and gets clobbered in the head with her clenched fist for his trouble.

'Mum!' he complains. 'Lily hit me.'

'Just move away from her.'

'Easy for you to say. Why can't I sit in the front? I'm nearly old enough.'

'Dan,' I warn.

'Sorry.' He presses his body against the window, as far away from Lily as he can get.

Mum is standing in front of the car, her arms still folded across her chest, her lips pursed.

'I'm not the enemy, Meg. I'm only trying to help.'

'I know that, and thanks for having them. I really appreciate it. Sorry for swearing at you.'

'Meg?'

'Yes?'

'I think you should go on that holiday with Simon.'

'But I tried to explain to you, it's not a holiday.'

'Just go. Dan and Lily need to see their fath . . .' she hesitates, 'I mean Simon more. And you'll enjoy it once you're there.'

'I'll think about it.' I wish she'd stop trying to interfere, she always thinks she knows best. I get into the car and she steps to the side. I wind down the window.

'Thanks again,' I say.

She puts her hand on the bottom of the window frame and leans in towards me. 'I was glad to be able to help, in the circumstances.'

I bite my lip. Bloody woman.

'Bye, Dan. Bye, Lily.' Mum smiles and waves at them.

'Bye, Granny,' Dan yells.

'Bye, Gannee,' Lily copies him.

I grip the wheel and drive away.

I decide to ring Hall's as soon as I've dropped Dan to school. No time like the present and all that. I deposit Lily in her high chair in the kitchen and slot her favourite Barney tape into the battered old video. It's a miracle it still works as Lily tries to feed it with toast and toys on a daily basis.

Once she's settled I grab the phone and I sit down on the hall stairs, the phone reception in the living room is brutal, and dial Hall's number. To my surprise, I find my hands are shaking a little.

'Good morning, Hall's Auction Rooms. How can I help you?'

'Saffy, it's Meg.' Saffy is the rather ditzy but nice office manager.

'Meg?' She seems a little confused.

'Meg Miller.'

'Oh, Meg. Sorry, I didn't recognize your voice. How are you? How's that darling baby of yours? Is she one yet?'

'She's two and a half.'

'Really, how extraordinary. Doesn't time fly?'

'How are things with you, Saffy?'

'Fine. Nothing's changed really. Still engaged. We'll get hitched one of these days. What can I do for you?'

'Can I speak to Douglas?'

'Of course, I'll put you straight through.' There's a click and I hear the familiar strains of 'Greensleeves'. 'Sorry, Meg, he's on another call. I'll put you on hold, but hey, did you hear he's retiring in a few weeks? Selling the company to Bolger's. But no one's being made redundant, thank goodness. Nice talking to you, Meg.'

As I wait for Douglas I think about what Saffy's just said. Bolger's are a big Dublin auction house and Hall's main competitors; it doesn't sound like good news.

A minute later my worries are confirmed. After exchanging pleasantries I come straight to the point and ask Douglas for a job. There's a long silence on the line.

'I'm so sorry, Meg. But I've had enough problems securing jobs for everyone here as it is. Maybe some of the other auction houses are looking for staff. You could try Osborne's.'

'Thanks, Douglas, I understand. And best of luck with the retirement.'

'Can't wait, my dear. We're moving to the south of France. Lock, stock and barrel. Might open a little antique shop there, who knows? Keep the hand in. And best of luck with the job hunt.'

'Thanks.' I put down the phone, my heart heavy with disappointment. This job hunting lark isn't going to be as easy as I thought. But I'm not going to give up yet.

While Lily has her after-lunch nap I exhaust all my Dublin auction-house contacts. No one is hiring. Well, that isn't strictly true, there are some positions vacant, but without the auctioneering exams, I'm not qualified to do any of them.

The doorbell rings. Tina is standing at the doorstep, Freddie on her hip.

'Are you OK? You look a little down.'

I attempt a smile but it comes out more like a grimace. 'Not really,' I admit.

Tina comes inside, puts Freddie down and he runs past my legs and into the kitchen.

'Sorry,' she says, 'looking for food as usual.' Freddie is a round-faced toddler, with fleshy legs and arms. He has beautiful, tawny skin (inherited from Oliver) a dark mop of hair and bright blue eyes, a most unusual-looking child. And boy does he love his food.

'He's fine. I'll just go up and get Lily. She's in her cot.'

I come down a minute later, a still sleepy Lily in my arms. Tina is looking at the crumpled paper and open filofax on the kitchen table.

'I was ringing auction houses,' I explain.

'Any luck?'

I shake my head. I explain about Hall's.

'And the other places?' she asks.

'They didn't want me either.'

Tina sighs. 'I'm sorry to hear that. More fool them.'

I shift Lily onto my hip. 'Coffee?'

'Sure.'

I flick on the kettle, then deposit Lily in the sandpit in the garden. Freddie happily joins her. I'd forgotten to put the lid on yesterday evening and the sand is damp but they don't seem to mind. The sandpit is ancient, it was originally Dan's and the once blue plastic boat has faded to a strange shade of off-grey. But it keeps them happy. I pray that the neighbourhood cats haven't used it during the night as kitty litter.

Tina and I sit at the kitchen table, sipping steaming mugs of instant coffee. I'm starting to feel a little better. It's hard to be in a bad mood with Tina around, she's too darned nice.

'So what next?' she asks.

I shrug. 'No idea. Start looking for temping work I suppose. I'm not qualified to do anything else. Besides, it pays well.'

'Hang on a second,' Tina says, sitting up. 'What am I thinking? My godmother, Ivy, needs her house cleared. She moved into a smaller place two years ago and it's just been sitting there ever since, doing nothing. The auctioneers have refused to put it on the market until she tidies it up; it's too full of clutter and won't sell apparently. She is a bit of a hoarder, and she won't use one of those clearing firms – too impersonal she says. She has some nice old furniture, even if it is a little packed in. I have no idea if it's worth anything but . . .'

'I'm not really qualified to do it on my own—' I begin, but Tina cuts me off.

'In fact, it would be perfect. And I know you two will get along like a house on fire.' She pauses for a moment. 'After the initial teething stage of course.'

'Teething stage?' That sounds ominous.

'Ivy's, how can I put this? A little odd in her ways. Eccentric I suppose.'

Tina notices the sceptical expression on my face.

'But she has a heart of gold,' she continues quickly. 'She hasn't had an easy life. Her husband died a few years ago and she's living on her own now. Awful story – he was up a stepladder, putting in a new bulb in the kitchen light. Fell and hit his head on a counter top. Never recovered, poor man.'

'How sad. What age was he?'

'Eighty-six. But very healthy. Swam in the sea every day and cycled everywhere. It was a terrible shame. I'll ring her right now.' Tina pulls out her mobile.

'That's very kind of you, Tina, but—'

'I insist. Now, just to warn you she has pink hair but don't let that put you off.'

'Pink?'

Tina thinks for a moment. 'More lavender really.'

'Um, Tina, I'm not sure . . .' But she's already keyed in the number. Do I really want to work for an eccentric old lady with pink hair? If her husband died in his late eighties, she's sure to be ancient too. Heaven knows what her house will be like. Believe me, I've seen some places that would make your toes curl. I hope to goodness Ivy doesn't keep cats. But I really, really need the money.

'Hi, Ivy. It's Tina. Great, and you? Good, good. Now, I'll get straight to the point, I know you're busy. You know Hall's? The auction house. I have the ex-house clearance expert right beside me and she's looking for a new challenge. What do you think? Might be ideal for you.'

Tina beams at me and gives me a thumbs up. 'No, of course she won't rob the place, she's a professional. No, really, Ivy. Yes, of course I trust her, she's my neighbour. It's all legit, honestly.'

Charming, I think. The old bat thinks I'm going to make off with her best china.

'Really? That's brilliant!' Tina clicks off her mobile and smiles at me. 'The young Turk from the auction house has been bugging her again. He's just sold a house down the road for a record price and the under bidder is looking for something similar. What serendipity!'

My fate is sealed.

'Ivy's dying to meet you.'

'Great,' I say, trying to sound more enthusiastic than I feel. What am I letting myself in for?

Chapter 13

*Widow-maker: another term for the bowsprit,
which sticks out from the bow (the front) of the boat.
In the olden days, many sailors were killed by falling
from the bowsprit while tending to the sails*

That afternoon I'm standing on Ivy Bannister's doorstep, wondering what on earth I'm doing. Tina orchestrated everything, she arranged the meeting with Ivy and she's hanging onto Lily, collecting Dan from school and doing his homework with him. If not for Tina, I would have cancelled the meeting. But after all her kindness I don't want to disappoint her.

Tina had forgotten to tell me that Lavender Close in Blackrock, where Ivy lives, is a community of sheltered housing for older people, complete with its own velvety smooth bowling green and immaculately kept gardens. I'm debating whether to just walk away when I hear a voice to my right.

'Meg? Are you Meg?'

I wheel around. The tiniest woman I've even seen is kneeling on a ragged old pink cushion by a flowerbed. She sits back, resting her heels on her hunkers and I half expect to hear a bone crack. Huge blue flowery gardening gloves swamp her hands, almost reaching up to her bony elbows. Her arms are so thin that I'm sure if I reached out and held one in my hand I could comfortably span it between my thumb and forefinger.

'I'm Ivy,' she says, not waiting for my answer. She brushes her wiry hair back off her cheeks and I register that it is indeed pink, a delicate shade of magenta in fact. It frames her doll-like face. A pair of intelligent pale blue eyes stare up at me, blinking in the light. Her skin is caked in powdery make-up and there's a slash of bright bubblegum-pink on her lips. She's at least eighty.

'Don't just stand there,' she barks. 'Give me a hand, girl.' She peels off her gardening gloves and puts them in the trug beside her on top of her shiny silver secateurs. There's a large bucket of weeds sitting to her right.

I proffer my hand and she grips it hard. I'm taken aback by her firm hold and the strength in her arms. She's a lot sturdier than she looks, but still light as a feather.

'We'll sit outside if that's all right with you.' She gestures at the garden furniture in front of the flowerbed. My eyes linger on the solid wood seats: they look a little stiff and uncomfortable for a woman of her age, let alone mine.

'The neighbours won't hear, if that's what you're worried about. Mr and Mrs Meadows next door are as deaf as posts and old Nina Golly has a memory like a goldfish. Your secrets are safe with her.'

'It's not that.' I gulp. Ivy is very intimidating. 'Can I get you a cushion?'

She hesitates for a moment, as if deciding whether to be stoic or not.

'Please,' she says finally. 'And there's a bottle of white plonk in the fridge. And glasses in the cabinet to the left of it. I'll just fetch my paperwork. Come along. Chop, chop.'

I follow her inside. I'm instantly struck by the dramatic display of hydrangeas. There's a large blue ceramic pot of them sitting on the low ledge in front of the living-room window, in various shades of pink and purple. I'm beginning to spot a theme.

The small two-seater sofa opposite the window looks ancient, its seat sags dramatically in the middle, the dark brown tapestry upholstery rubbed smooth and shiny with age. A dark pink mohair rug is thrown over the back and you can hardly see the arms for the profusion of pink and red velvet scatter cushions. An armchair sits beside the window, a blue plastic milk crate, with a pink cushion sitting in front of it, masquerading as a footstool and there's an unruly pile of magazines and newspapers spilling over the floor to the right. The room is crammed with dark mahogany antique furniture and you can't see the surface of the walls for the original paintings and framed photographs. There are what look like regatta prizes and yachting paraphernalia in a tall cabinet against the far wall – a replica of a square rigger in a bottle with a small bronze plaque on its wooden base, a decorative brass compass, and an antique eyeglass. A handsome man in a captain's uniform features in some of the black and white photographs.

'Stop gawping, girl. The kitchen's in there.' Ivy points towards the back of the room. I walk down the short corridor and into the kitchen – its counters are heaped with all manner of small ceramic pots, glass and pottery vases, ancient-looking cookbooks and old-fashioned decorated cake and biscuit tins. A pair of Victorian china dogs sit above the fridge, their beady black eyes staring down at me. I take an open bottle of good white wine out of the practically empty fridge and find two large heavy blue wine glasses in the cupboard.

I can hear Ivy rummaging in one of the rooms off the corridor. I'm surprised she can find anything; the whole apartment is crammed full to the brim. She comes out with a large pink leather-bound folder bulging with paper in her arms.

'Do you need help?' I ask. 'I'll take the wine out and come back.'

'Tush, girl. I'm well able. Not dead yet.' She smiles at me, aware of my discomfort. 'And don't be so nervous. I don't bite. And I'm not a lush if that's what you're thinking.'

I open my mouth to protest but she cuts me off.

'I'm eighty-nine years old and if I can't enjoy myself at this stage of life I may as well curl up and die right now. Getting old is most liberating that way, Meg. Your body starts to fall apart so there has to be some compensation. Learned how to sail when I turned seventy; dyed my hair the minute I turned eighty. And for my ninetieth, well, that's where you come in. Chop, chop. Far too nice a day to linger inside.'

I follow her out, plonk down the wine and glasses on the table and go back inside for cushions.

'Take the ones off the sofa,' she says loudly through the open window. 'The ones on the armchair are just right for my back; haven't moved them in years.'

Once we're both comfortable, she opens the screw-top bottle and pours out two generous glasses.

'This is the life. Chin, chin.' She tips her glass against mine and smiles at me, her eyes crinkling dramatically at the edges. I notice a tiny smear of lipstick on her yellow teeth.

'Cheers.' I take a sip.

She takes a healthy glug and nods at the folder on the table. 'Keys, map and all the house's paperwork is in there. Insurance on two of the paintings, that kind of thing. Might help you value them, I suppose. Tina tells me you were in charge of house clearances at Hall's. That correct?'

'Yes. Not in charge exactly, but heavily involved. But I did a lot of other things too, not just the house clearances.'

Her eyes meet mine and I'm surprised by their intensity. 'Why did you leave?'

'I was pregnant with my daughter, Lily, and I wanted to

travel with Simon, Lily's dad. He's a professional sailor and his work takes him all over.'

Ivy's eyebrows rise. 'My Ron was in the Irish Navy. Officer. Different sort of life, isn't it, sailor's wife?'

'Um, we're not married.'

'Really?' Ivy considers this for a moment. 'Why ever not?'

I shrug my shoulders. 'Never felt the need for it I suppose.'

'But you'd like to? Get married I mean?'

'At some stage I suppose. But we're in no hurry.' Lord, this is getting personal.

'I see.' Ivy takes another sip of her wine. 'How interesting. But we must focus. Were you good at your job?' Her eyes bore into mine. 'Know your stuff?'

'Yes. At least I think I was.'

'Having a bit of a crisis of confidence?'

'Sorry?'

'How long have you been out of work?'

'I haven't been out of work,' I say a little indignantly. 'I've been looking after my children.'

'And following your man, don't forget that.'

I'm not at all sure I like the direction this conversation is taking. 'Yes. But I'm home for good now.'

'Living next door to Tina?'

'Yes.'

'And you liked working at Hall's?'

'Yes, very much.'

'And why haven't you asked them for work? Surely they have some work for a woman with your experience? Or what about one of the other big auction houses?'

I can feel my face colour. 'Tina told you, didn't she?'

'Told me what?'

'That they didn't want me. That nobody wants me.' I stand up to leave. 'Thanks for the wine. I'm sorry for wasting your time.'

'Sit down!' Ivy says firmly. 'Tina told me no such thing. But is that true?'

I have nothing to lose. 'Yes. None of the auction houses want to employ me. I'm not qualified you see. I have the experience all right, a lot more than most of their auctioneers, but I don't have the exams. I'm sorry; I don't know what I'm doing here. But Tina was so insistent . . .'

Ivy laughs. 'Such a sweet girl, Tina. With hidden depths. I can see why you couldn't say no. Don't be so touchy. Sit down.'

'You mean you're still interested in hiring me?'

'Of course. Sassy girl like you, friend of Tina's; why ever not? I'm willing to take a chance. As you say, you have oodles of experience and as for the self-confidence, that will come in time.'

I look at her in surprise. Whatever is she talking about?

Ivy leans forward and looks me in the eye. 'All I really need to know, Meg, is do you think you could work for me? Grumpy fool with pink hair who drinks far too much for her own good. And a nosy old bat to boot. Well?'

'I think so.'

'Then, tell me, how does this all work? What's first?' Ivy cocks an eyebrow.

I explain the process to her. I'll sort the items into different categories and then label them – furniture and bits and pieces to Hall's, paintings to an art dealer I know (if they're really worth anything), any decent furniture, rugs, silver and ceramics to Hennessy's, who specialize in antiques. As I tell her my plan, I realize I *do* know what I'm talking about and it feels good.

'Hall's and the other people take a cut I presume?' Ivy asks.

I smile. There are no flies on Ivy.

'Yes. A percentage of the sale price.'

'I see.' Ivy thinks for a moment. 'But I don't have to be involved?'

'Sorry?'

'I don't have to visit the house?'

I'm surprised. In my experience most people want to get heavily involved in the process, getting in the way, arguing that the skip items are family heirlooms and must be worth something. But Ivy must have her reasons.

'Not if you don't want to. But can I ask why? Surely you'd like—'

'Too many memories,' she cuts in. Her eyes glaze over for a moment then she snaps out of it.

I remember, too late, what Tina had said about her husband's death. No wonder she doesn't want to visit the place. I'm sorry I pressed her.

But she smiles at me, catching me off guard. 'Can't be doing with the place any more,' she says, rubbing her nose with a bony finger. 'It's only a load of old rubbish anyway – no use to me now. So what do you say, girl? Will you do it? You can work whenever suits you, as long as it gets done in the next few weeks. Damn schoolboy estate agent won't show people around until it's cleared, and I need the money, you see. I'll give you ten per cent of whatever I get for the lot. Is that fair? And once the furniture is out I'll get those Dolly Maid people to clean the place top to bottom. It'll be like I never lived there at all.'

'More than generous.' The usual rate is 5 to 7 per cent but I'm not arguing. 'But . . .' I still have my doubts.

'Yes or no?' Her eyes rest on mine and there's a twinkle in them. 'Come on now, I don't have all day. Time and tide wait for no woman.'

I consider for a moment. Ivy is certainly cantankerous; she's admitted that much herself. But in some strange way, I like her. She's a breath of fresh air. And I do need the money. It will be worth my while even if I only find a few decent pieces of furniture or even one good painting. A couple of hundred euros is nothing to be sniffed at in my position.

'Yes,' I say, 'I'll do it.'

'Excellent! When can you start?'

I think for a moment. It will take me a few days to arrange child-care for Lily and Dan. 'Monday the nineteenth? Sorry I can't start earlier, but with the kids . . .'

'Perfect. Let's drink to celebrate.' She fills her glass up again. Mine is still almost full. 'To empty houses and new beginnings.' She raises her glass and I clink mine against it.

I smile at her. 'To empty houses and new beginnings.'

PART TWO

Chapter 14

Helmsman: the sailor who steers the boat, i.e.
'That helmsman's brutal!'

Mum calls in at seven o'clock in the evening. Dan is careering around the kitchen table on his Rollerblades, leaving black marks on the tiles. I'd promised to take him skating this evening to make up for his afternoon in Tina's house but it's lashing outside. So much for June and sunny summer days. Dan adores Tina's boys, but only in short doses. A whole afternoon with the rugrats, as he calls them, isn't exactly how he wants to spend his summer afternoons. Roll on the school holidays and the sailing course.

Lily is ready for bed in pink pyjamas with an elaborate ruffle around the neck. A present from Maureen of course. She's been padding in and out of the garden in them and the ends are stained with grass and mud.

When I open the front door I plaster a smile on my face and stand back to let Mum in.

'Not calling at a bad time, am I?' she trills brightly.

'No, no, come on in.' She wafts past me in a cloud of Chanel No 5, her high heels clattering on the tiled floor. She stops in front of the hall mirror and gently pats the skin under her eyes with her fingertips.

'Ever tried Botox, Meg?'

'No. Why?' I narrow my eyes.

'The other women on the St John's committee are so much younger than me. Makes me feel ancient. I was just at a meeting at the hospital about the Christmas masked ball.' Mum heads up the fund-raising 'comedy' as I like to call it for St John's Hospital.

'Mum, you're fifty-seven.'

She clucks her tongue against her lower teeth. 'Mid fifties, please, my golden years.'

'Sorry, mid fifties. You look great for your age, and you're healthy. I don't know what you're worrying about.'

Mum sighs. 'That's all very well. At least you have an excuse for looking so washed out all the time, but I have no young children waking me up at all hours of the morning.'

'Thanks a lot.' I thought I was looking reasonably chipper these days, but obviously not.

Lily screams. I walk into the kitchen, Mum following at my heels – my flat, ballet-pumped heels. I'd break my neck running around after Lily in real heels, but I do miss wearing court shoes, wearing suits, dressing up for work. Hated it at the time – trying to find a clean top first thing in the morning (I always left it till the last minute), tights that weren't laddered; but I miss it now. Pity I won't need to wear a suit in Ivy's house; I can always dress up to meet the auctioneers though. Shit, I wonder, do I actually have a suit that fits?

Lily has managed to pull all the kitchen roll out of its wooden holder and wrap the white paper around her upper body, head and neck. She looks like a tiny Egyptian mummy. Dan is laughing at her attempts to free herself from her paper prison.

'Dan,' I say, 'don't just stand there, help your sister, please.'

He skates towards Lily a little too quickly, his left roller-bladed foot catching on the kitchen roll and bringing him down.

'Ow, shit!' he says, landing on his bum.

'Daniel!' Mum says in her best 'I'm shocked' voice.

'Sorry,' he says from his prone position.

I pull the paper off Lily's head then hoist Dan up by the arm. He's rubbing his bum and wincing. After my own escapades on the dance floor at the regatta, I know how he feels.

'Are you OK?' I ask kindly.

'I think so.'

'Take off the Rollerblades and go up and put your pyjamas on, there's a good lad.'

'It's too early.'

'Please.'

'OK, OK.'

I pat him on the back as he skates into the hall. 'Take off your skates. Have you done your homework?'

'Nearly.'

'You can finish it when you have your pyjamas on. And do your teeth while you're at it.'

I can hear him muttering to himself as he throws his skates onto the hall tiles and stomps up the stairs.

'Sorry about that,' I turn towards Mum, 'he's a bit hormonal today.'

She waves her hand in the air, her silver charm bracelet tinkling on her slim wrist. 'It's fine, really. But Dan's language . . .'

'I know, I know.' I bend down to finish helping Lily, who is being very good considering she's still mummified.

I peel the layers of paper off her body, balling it up and stuffing it into the already overflowing bin. Eggshells fall on the floor. I kick them towards the base of the bin with the side of my foot. Mum tuts, picks them up and puts them on the draining board. I feel like such a slob. The sink is full of lukewarm suds, I'm soaking the cereal-encrusted breakfast bowls from this morning as the dishwasher is acting up again. The table is littered with the dirty plates from dinner, a Heinz bottle with sticky red ketchup oozing down its side and an empty milk carton which Lily knocked over earlier and is still lying prostrate.

Mum takes it all in, her carefully plucked eyebrows lifting higher and higher. A plastic bucket of wet laundry squats in front of the open washing machine and Lily has left dirty footprints on the tiles. It can't get any worse, unless Grasshopper happens to be staying over, of course. Which reminds me, Paul rang earlier. He and Katia are taking a two-day break on Monday and Tuesday so we will have the 'pleasure' of Grasshopper's company. Aagh! Strange days to take a break, but maybe it's the only time Katia can take off work. Grasshopper will be handed over on Sunday at Dad's birthday lunch.

Mum takes off her expensive black tailored jacket (which I happen to know she picked up for a steal at a designer sample sale), pulls my yellow Marigolds over her manicured hands, wincing as her fingers hit the damp pools lodging in the fingertips. She peels them off, shakes the drips out over the sink and puts them on again.

'You don't have to do that.' I lift Lily onto my hip and rest her weight against the side of the kitchen counter. 'Please, I'll do it later.'

'It's no trouble.' She lifts out the crockery, changes the water in the sink, and puts the breakfast bowls back in with a clatter. Then she squirts them with thick worms of green Fairy Liquid and gets scrubbing, the bowl white with suds. Mum always uses far too much washing-up liquid – you can taste it on the glasses in her house.

I stand watching, waiting for her to come to the point. She rarely calls in for a casual visit. There's something preying on her mind.

'Hattie tells me you went for a job interview today,' she says, scrubbing the frying pan a little too vigorously.

Aha. I'm right: there is something on her mind. I'd talked to Hattie on the way back from Ivy's house, buoyed up by the prospect of a new challenge, and gagging to tell someone all about her pink hair. I'd tried Simon first but his mobile wasn't on so I couldn't even leave a message. He hadn't rung last night either. Hattie had been delighted for me but a little apprehensive when I told her about Ivy.

'What if she dies, Meg? Not great job security working for a wrinkly that old.'

'She's not going to die, Hattie.'

'She will at some stage, stands to reason. Or worse, what if she breaks a hip and you have to mind her? Sponge baths and commodes, wouldn't fancy that myself.'

'Hattie! She's really strong and healthy for her age and she's not going to break a hip. And if something does happen to her there's a full medical team on hand in the sheltered housing. Hell, she gets all her meals delivered to her door and a doctor visits her every week. There's a social club and a bowling green and everything. In fact, I might go and live there myself, get a bit of peace.'

'Mum's not going to be pleased,' Hattie said ominously. 'You know what she's like about working mothers.'

'She can go to hell. It's my life. And besides, I'll only be working a few hours a day. Mum will be fine about it.' But it looks like Hattie was right.

Mum sniffs. Here we go. 'Hattie says the woman you'll be working for is nearly a hundred, is that true?'

I snort with laughter, giving Lily quite a start. She begins to cry but I give her a tight hug, which seems to reassure her. She hiccups loudly and then settles down again.

'Shouldn't Lily be in bed?' Mum asks, her voice critical.

'No, she's fine. Eight o'clock is her bedtime. And Ivy's

eighty-nine; a very healthy and active eighty-nine. Don't be so ageist. It's only a bit of part-time work, clearing her house in Blackrock. Nothing major. I can fit it in around the kids.'

'But what about Dan? He's at a difficult age. He needs you around.'

'I know,' I say through tight lips. I'm quite au fait with Dan's hopping hormones. 'And I will be, most of the time.'

She empties the sink, peels off the rubber gloves, puts them together and places them carefully over the tap. 'Finished.' She looks around. 'Will I hang out that washing for you?' She walks towards the basket and swings it onto her hip.

'It's too late to put it out now. I'll do it in the morning. Just sit down and relax. Please!'

'There's no need to snap.'

'Sorry.'

She puts the basket back on the floor and sits down at the table, her arms resting on the wood. Her wrists look thinner than I remember and I'm reminded of Ivy's tiny childlike wrists. 'I'm only trying to help.'

I sit down beside her and swung Lily onto my knee. 'I know, Mum. But It's exhausting just watching you.'

'You'll be even more exhausted going back to work, Meg. Do you think it's the right thing to do? It's not even a proper job. What's the point?'

'It's all I could find. And it's a start.'

'You didn't try very hard, did you? This is the first I've heard of you looking for work.'

'Ivy's a nice woman and I want to help her. Can't you just be pleased for me?'

'Sounds more like community work than a proper job. Can't it wait? Lily's so small. She needs you.'

I think I know what's coming. I press my lips together, trying not to rise to the bait.

'Remember how tired you used to get working for Hall's

and looking after Dan?' she continues, oblivious. 'I'd hate you to have another nervous breakdown.' She pats my hand.

I pull it away. 'I didn't have a nervous breakdown,' I say through gritted teeth. 'I was run down and needed a break, that's all. A week in Spain did the trick, remember? You were very good to take Dan for me.'

'All that crying all night,' Mum goes on, ignoring what I've just said, 'the panic attacks.'

'One! One panic attack. And the doctor said it wasn't even a proper one. Don't exaggerate.'

'I was so scared when you rang and said you couldn't breathe. And when we got to your house, Dan screaming the place down and you collapsed on the floor and gasping for breath . . .'

'Mum, please! Stop! It was a long time ago. I'm fine now; more than fine.'

'I just don't want to see you getting into that kind of state again.'

'It's different now. I have Simon for support. I was on my own then with a small child and working all hours. It won't happen again. Ever. I won't let it.'

'But what about the stress, Meg? The doctor said it was stress that tipped you over the edge last time.'

'There won't be any stress. I can work whenever it suits me and Tina's offered to mind Lily and Dan until I can get something else sorted.'

'Tina? Tina next door?'

'Yes.'

'She hardly needs the money.'

'Maybe not, but she offered to help.' In fact, after some persuasion Tina had agreed to accept the going rate for her work. 'Might come in useful at some stage,' she said. 'My own little nest egg.' I was glad, I didn't want her to think I was taking advantage of her.

Mum frowns. 'You could have asked me.'

'Could I?'

'I'm always happy to babysit when I can, you know that.'

'I know, but you couldn't do it all the time. Not with all your committees and everything.'

'I suppose not. But do you really have to go back to work? Can't you wait until Lily is in school?'

'No, I can't. I presume you noticed the scaffolding as you came in – the house is falling down around our ears and we're having enough trouble just trying to make the mortgage repayments.'

'I hadn't realized you were desperate. You could always ask your father . . .'

'I'm not asking Dad for a handout. And, anyway, it's not just the money. I need to do something else. I'm not good at being in the house all day, I get cabin fever. I need to do something that doesn't involve the kids. Something for myself.'

'And being a mother isn't enough for you?'

'Not all the time. I know it's a selfish thing to say, but it's true.'

'It was enough for me.' She steeples her fingers and puts them to her mouth.

I keep my mouth firmly shut. Whatever I say now I can't win, knowing her parenting history. She worked as a psychiatric nurse, and was a pretty good one according to Dad. She left nursing to look after me. I know I should be grateful, but I didn't force her to do it and it's hardly my fault she still has a chip on her shoulder. Not that we've ever talked about it. Yes, she was a full-time housewife, but a reluctant one.

I get up. 'Can you hold Lily for me for a second?' I ask her.

'Of course. Come to Granny.' Mum puts her arms out and Lily clings to me like a little monkey, her nails digging into my skin.

'Lily, go to your granny.' I prise her hands off me and hand her over. Lily protests for a moment and Mum distracts her by jingling her charm bracelet.

I busy myself making Lily's bottle. As I open the fridge and pull out the last of the milk, my mind goes into overdrive. I marvel at Mum's ability to rewrite the past.

Once when Dad and I were discussing Hattie's career or lack of one (we used to do this a lot before we both gave up on her) he'd suggested nursing. I'd laughed so hard that I'd given myself a stitch.

'It's not that ridiculous, Meg,' he'd said. 'Your mum was an excellent nurse, one of the best. She even looked into going back to it.'

'Really? When?'

'When you were small. Before Hattie came along. We'd been trying for a baby for a few years. She was a bit . . .' he paused, 'a bit disappointed, I suppose.'

'I had no idea.'

He shrugged. 'It's irrelevant now. Then Hattie came along and your mum gave up on the whole idea. It's a shame really, she would have made a great matron.'

I smiled. 'I can just see her in a navy uniform with a starched white apron and a doily thing on her head. Bossing all the younger nurses around. Like that woman in the *Carry On* films, only slimmer.'

Dad laughed. 'Hattie Jacques? Don't let your mother hear you say that. Not exactly glamorous, Hattie Jacques.' He stopped smiling. 'I shouldn't have told you any of this; your mother would kill me. You know what she's like.'

I made a zipping motion with my hand on my mouth. 'My lips are sealed.' What Dad didn't know was that I'd seen Mum in her nurse's uniform, a vivid memory I could never seem to wipe from my mind. She was the prettiest nurse I'd ever seen. And the most scary.

Ironically Mum now helped hospitals in another way, by raising funds for them.

'Stop fussing. I'll be fine,' I say firmly.

'And what about Simon?' she asks, staring at the dirty ends of Lily's pyjamas.

'What about him?'

'What does he have to say about all this?'

'Mother, it isn't the Dark Ages. He's happy for me to work if I want to.'

'There's no need to be so short with me.' She stands up. 'This is exactly what I'm talking about. When you get overtired, Meg, you get—'

'I'm not overtired,' I cut in, 'I'm fine.'

Lily, no doubt sensing the tension in the room, begins to cry. I pull her away from Mum. 'You're all right, Lily.'

'You really are impossible sometimes. I'm only trying to help.'

'No, you're not! If you were really trying to help you'd be supportive of my decision to work and you'd be happy for me. But you're not, are you? Because I'm not doing things your way, the Julie Bloody Miller way. Because I'm not a perfect mother like you were, sacrificing everything for her children. I hate to say it, but you weren't all that perfect.' Yikes, now I've done it. Me and my big mouth.

Mum opens her mouth to say something and then closes it again.

'I think I'll go now.' She slips her hands into the arms of her jacket and shrugs it over her shoulders. 'I'm happy to mind Lily and Dan when you're stuck, but I do have my own life. Not that you or you sister have any interest in it. And if you're coping so well why does your house looks like this?' She waves her hands around the room.

I glare at her. Tension shoots up my back and into my neck and I can feel my pulse quicken with anger. 'I have two young children. Mess is normal.' Lily fusses on my hip and I jiggle her. 'I'm sorry but I have to get Lily to bed.'

We both walk into the hall wordlessly. I want to tell her I'm sorry, that I know she is – in her own weird twisted way – only trying to help. Sorry that I'm not the perfect stay-at-home wife, the kind of daughter she can be proud of. But I don't want to let her win.

'Goodbye, Meg,' she says stiffly, turning the latch of the front door. She tries to open it but it sticks.

'Put the chain in and pull it towards you,' I say. 'It's the damp.'

She gives it a strong yank and it opens. She stands in the open doorway and looks at me for a moment. 'Your father's birthday is next weekend. I hope we'll see you for lunch.'

'I'll be there.'

She kisses the top of Lily's head. 'Bye, Lily. And I hope you'll be in better humour then, Meg. Get some rest.'

'Goodbye, Mother.' She has to get the last bloody word in. I close the door behind her and rest my back against it. I feel completely drained. Lily grizzles again. 'Let's get you to bed, little one.'

Simon rings later that evening and before he's a chance to say a word I give him a blow-by-blow account of my conversation with Mum. I also fill him in on Ivy and her house.

'Maybe your mum's right for once,' he says. 'Maybe you are taking on too much. And Ivy does sound a bit eccentric.'

'Not you too. It'll be fine, I know exactly what I'm doing. What *would* make life easier is if you were home more to help out.' Oops, my mouth runs away with me again, why can't I keep my thoughts to myself today?

Silence.

'Are you still there? I'm sorry, I didn't mean that.'

'I know things aren't easy for you, and I'm sorry you're so tired.'

'I'm not tired! I'm just overworked.'

'And about to put even more pressure on yourself,' Simon points out.

'Oh, this is hopeless. First my mother and now you. Not forgetting Hattie of course. Great to see you all have such confidence in my abilities. I used to be quite good at my job you know. In my youth. Before I became a mum and obviously lost all my marbles.'

'Don't be like that.'

'Like what?'

'You know.'

'No, I don't.'

He sighs audibly. 'You're impossible to talk to sometimes.'

'Well, I'm sure there's a blonde at the bar who will hang on your every word.'

'Now you're just being silly.'

'Make your mind up, Simon. Which is it to be: incompetent, impossible or just plain silly?'

'Meg!'

'And your children are fine by the way, not that you bothered asking.'

'You didn't give me a chance. I can't—' The phone cuts out. I wait for him to ring back but he doesn't. It's not like him. I dial his mobile number but there's no answer. I feel an icy wave rush through my veins. What if I've pushed him too far this time? What if I've pushed him right into some racer chaser's arms? Aagh! I'm so stupid. I try his mobile again.

He answers immediately. 'Meg? What happened? Is anything wrong? I don't know what happened to my phone. I tried to ring you back but it was engaged.'

Relief floods over me. 'Must be your reception. The line

went dead this end too. I'm sorry for being ratty. I've just had a long day.'

'I'm sorry too. I understand, really I do. I miss you, and I'm sorry I can't be there more. But I'll see you in Cornwall.'

Yikes, I'd forgotten all about that. Did I say I'd go or did I say I'd think about it? I really can't remember. 'About Cornwall.' I twist the phone's coiled wire around my little finger. 'I'm starting this new job, and Matty will still be working on the house. It's not great timing.'

'Please, Meg. I really want you to come. Please? For me? I really want you and the kids to be there.'

'And you promise you won't dump us with a gang of hideously awful sailing wives all week? That you'll spend some time with us? As a family?'

'I promise. I'll even book the flights. You won't have to do a thing.'

'I'll see.'

'Thanks. I know you'll love it.'

I yawn out loud. 'Oops, sorry.'

Simon laughs. 'You sound wrecked. I'll let you go to bed. I'll ring tomorrow. Love you.'

'Love you too.'

I put the phone down and lie back against my pillow. What am I doing? Maybe they're all right, Simon, Mum *and* Hattie. Maybe I am taking on too much with Ivy's house. I yawn again. I'm too wiped to think about it any longer. I click off the light and get into bed in my clothes.

Chapter 15

Hull: the main body of a yacht or boat

By Friday morning Matty is in full swing, adding to the green, blue and yellow mix and match scaffolding which looks like he's salvaged it from the local dump. Knowing Matty, he probably has.

'Are you sure that scaffolding's safe?' I shout up to him, shielding the dappled sunlight from my eyes with my hand. 'It looks a bit rickety.'

'Course it is, Meg.' He pauses for a second. 'Not for children though. Keep Lily and Dan away from it.'

'Will do.'

Now I really am nervous. Lily is a mountaineer in training, has been since she was first able to pull herself up and coast around the furniture. Last summer I was sitting in France outside the yacht club in La Rochelle under a dazzling white awning, shading myself from the blazing sun. Lily was playing with a small colony of ants at my feet, heaping sand on them with a spoon, and Dan was sitting beside me re-reading one of his Anthony Horowitz spy books. We were waiting for Simon to come in from sailing (what's new?). I took my eyes off Lily for a moment to gaze in envy at a woman in the most beautiful aquamarine-coloured chiffon dress, and when I looked back, Lily had vanished.

'Dan, where's Lily?'

He lifted his head from his book. 'Lily. She's—' He looked down at the ground. 'She was there a second ago.'

'Shit!' I said, standing up and looking around frantically.

Dan put his book down on the table. 'She can't have gone far,' he reasoned, taking in my stricken face. 'She's probably hiding behind a boat. Don't worry.'

'She could be in the water,' I said, running towards the sea, my flip-flops slapping against the soles of my feet, my heart pounding in my chest. Lily couldn't swim.

Dan followed me.

There was a group of tanned children in shorts and sailing-event T-shirts playing on the concrete slip at the edge of the water.

'Excuse me,' I shouted down, have you seen a little girl?'

'No, sorry.' They shook their heads.

'Thanks.' There were only changing rooms to the right, and all the doors were closed. Still no sign of Lily. I ran left, towards the boat park, Dan at my heels.

What if she'd been abducted by some weird Frenchman? You heard about things like that in the papers. I felt sick just thinking about it. Or she could have bumped her head and be lying unconscious in a pool of blood, her little body—

'There she is!' Dan pointed upwards.

I looked up. She was standing on the deck of a small white J24 yacht, holding onto the guard rail. The boat was on its trailer and Lily was at least fourteen feet off the ground.

'Ma, Ma,' she said in delight, her face lighting up. 'An, An,' she called to Dan. She looked proud as punch. She gave us a wave.

'How the hell did she get up there?' I said.

'The ladder I guess.' Dan stepped onto the first rung of the aluminium ladder which was resting against the hull of the boat. 'I'll get her down.' And he did. He handed her to me and I hugged her tight, my heart still hammering in my chest.

So you can see why I'm worried. I'll have to warn Matty about leaving tall ladders around for Lily to climb. And warn Matty's men too – if you can call them that.

The wiry dirty-blond fellow in his early twenties, Matty's labourer, doesn't have a word of English. He's Polish and none of the others can pronounce his name, Piotreck, so they called him Trekie instead. Stoney, Matty's right-hand man, is all of nineteen. He's a dark-skinned lad with a bumpy, shaved head and an unfeasibly long face. If it wasn't for his kind puppy-dog brown eyes, he'd look like a convict. He rarely wears a shirt and his smooth, tanned torso is rather a bonus. It certainly cheers up my day. And then there's sixty-something-year-old Kev, originally from England, with his shock of white hair and saucer-like green eyes and his enormous, spade-like hands. Kev is a plasterer and builds the best stone walls in Ireland, according to Matty, and was a ballet dancer in his youth, Matty told me one day in confidence. And this is the motley crew I've entrusted my precious house to. The mind boggles.

I go back inside, wondering if you can buy safety gates for ladders. Hopefully, Matty can rig something up, otherwise Lily will be under house arrest for the next few weeks and I don't know if I can cope with that. She's developed an ear-piercing scream of late and a few minutes of it can transform me into a quivering wreck. My nerves can't take a whole day of her vocal cords indoors. Cornwall is becoming a distinct possibility.

Its five o'clock and I've decided to cook something decent for Dan and Lily, but my heart isn't in it. I open the fridge door, survey the contents, close it again, lean back against it and groan loudly. God, cooking for kids can be boring at times. Give me a day to rustle something up for a dinner party and I'm fine, but the daily scramble and squabble of the kid's tea really gets me down.

'OK, Mum?' Dan asks, tearing his eyes away from his beloved *Simpsons*.

Lily is watching it too, sitting with her back against his stomach, her thumb in her mouth. I have no idea what she's making of Homer's marital inadequacies but it keeps her quiet and in one place, so I'm not complaining. She spent all morning running around the park like a lunatic and then refusing to take her nap, even though she was exhausted, so I don't feel too guilty about her evening telly fix.

An idea pops into my head. 'Keep an eye on Lily, Dan. I'm just calling into Tina's for a second.'

'Sure. No problem.'

'Thanks.'

I knock on Tina's door. Seconds later she opens it, Freddie on her hip and Eric clinging to her trouser leg.

'Meg.' She smiles. 'Welcome to the mad house.'

'You too?' I grin at her. 'Hi, Freddie.' I reach over and pat his head. He curls his face into Tina's chest and starts to roar. 'Oops, sorry.'

Tina sighs. 'He's been like this all day. Teething, I think. I haven't got a thing done.' She nods down at the floor. There are toy cars and coloured plastic balls all over the floor of the usually immaculate hall.

'Connie's been sick all week and the place is a tip.' Consuela is her South American cleaner who comes three times a week, lucky Tina. Tina kicks a yellow and black Caterpillar truck with the side of her foot, sending it scuttling towards the skirting board.

I bend down and start to pick up some of the toys.

'Ah, leave it, Meg. You have enough to do in your own house. Oliver's not back this weekend so it hardly matters.'

I straighten up again. 'Why don't you all come over for tea? Have the boys eaten yet?'

Tina sighs. 'Is it that time already? They've barely had lunch.'

I grin. 'Some days just get away from you, don't they? Do the boys eat spaghetti and meatballs?'

'Yep.' Tina jiggles Freddie on her hip. 'But are you sure? This one's pretty grizzly.'

'We can walk him around the garden. Show him the builders and their cement mixer.'

'If you're sure.'

'Positive. I'd enjoy the company.'

Ten minutes later Tina is helping me cook and Dan has taken the little ones off our hands in return for an hour of uninterrupted PlayStation after tea.

'Dan's doing a great job in the garden,' Tina says peeling the brown outer skin off an onion and chopping it in half. 'Who's the man playing with Lily?'

'Man?' I lift my head and stare out the open French doors. Matty is swinging Lily around in circles by her arms. She's squealing with delight.

'Ah, that's the famous Matty. Our builder. We're actually paying him to fix the side of the house. But he seems to have morphed into Mary Poppins.'

'He's great with Lily,' Tina says. 'Does he have any of his own?'

'No, he's single. At least he was last time I asked.'

Tina's eyes are now glued to Matty and Lily.

'Do you miss Oliver?' I ask.

'Oliver?' She peels her eyes away. 'Oh, I suppose. Sometimes.'

'How do you cope? You must get lonely.'

Tina looks at me. 'Same way you do. I just get on with it. And the kids keep me more than busy.'

'But at least when Simon's home it isn't just for the week-end.'

Tina says nothing for a moment. Then she lowers her head again. 'No one's life is perfect,' she murmurs, holding an onion firmly with one hand and slicing it quickly with the other; her eyes start to water. She seems a little down. I hope I haven't upset her.

'I'm sorry, I shouldn't have pried. I know how much you must miss him.'

Tina's eyes are streaming. I'm not sure if it's from the onions or whether she's really crying. I am a ninny.

She wipes the tears away with the back of her hand and looks at me as if she's about to say something.

At that moment Matty bounds in the door, dangling Lily over his shoulder by her feet. 'Hello, ladies. Does this little scallywag belong to anyone in here by any chance? Only her bottom seems to be leaking.'

I laugh. 'Matty, this is Tina, my neighbour. Tina, Matty.'

'Nice to meet you, Matty. Sorry about the eyes,' Tina says. 'Onions.' She holds out her hand politely.

He grins at her and shakes her hand firmly. 'I can smell them.'

Tina lifts her hand to her nose and smells it. 'Oh, I'm so sorry . . .'

'I didn't mean your hand,' Matty says. 'I meant in general.' Matty's eyes linger on the onions and the meat.

I suddenly feel sorry for him, driving home all alone in his ancient red truck to a builder's banquet of curry Pot Noodles and tea, no doubt.

'Would you like to stay for some food?' I find myself asking him. 'It's only spaghetti and meatballs but there's plenty to go round. You probably have something else planned though,' I add, giving him an out.

Matty's eyes light up. 'Thanks, Meg. I'd love to. If you're sure.'

I look at Tina for affirmation and she smiles and nods.

'Positive,' I say. 'We'd love to have you. But I should warn you, it might be a bit noisy with the kids.'

'I don't mind that.'

Tina is watching us with interest, while mixing the onions with the meat and shaping it into balls with her slim fingers and rolling them lightly in flour.

'I'll finish up outside,' Matty says.

'No rush,' I say. 'It won't be ready for a while.'

Matty lingers for a moment, shifting his weight from one foot to the other, looking a little uncomfortable. 'Right. Back to work so.' He lopes off and, once outside, tickles Lily, who is lying on the grass. I watch them for a moment, smiling to myself and suddenly missing Simon horribly. I notice Lily's sagging bottom. Right, nappy changing.

An hour later we're all sitting around my kitchen table. It's like one of those Italian meals you see on the television advertising pasta sauces. Except at our table there's not much family bonding going on: the children are crying, arguing or shouting; Lily is leading the fray, wailing to beat the band; Freddie is also crying, only not as noisily; Dan is holding his knife and fork vertically in his hands and complaining that he's starving; and Eric is moaning that he doesn't like meatballs.

'Just eat the spaghetti,' Tina says firmly, putting a plate of plain pasta down in front of him. Then she serves Dan, Lily and Freddie. Instant silence.

Lily decides to shovel the food into her mouth with her hands, but at least it stops her crying. I put a plate piled high down in front of Matty and hand Tina a smaller helping.

'Looks great,' Tina says encouragingly. She flashes me a smile. 'Thanks, Meg.'

'Yeah, thanks.' Matty swallows his first mouthful. 'Great chow.'

I'm just about to sit down and tuck in myself when the doorbell shrills. 'What now?'

'I'll get it,' Dan jumps up.

'Thanks. And if they try to sell you anything just say no. Or tell them you don't speak English.' I sit down and raise my wine glass in the air. Tina has been rather generous with the wine, but that's fine by me. It's the end of the week after all, and a busy week at that. 'Cheers everyone. *Bon appetit.*'

Matty and Tina clink glasses.

'Ahem,' I cough, nodding at my glass which I'm still holding out.

Tina clinks her glass against mine. 'Cheers, Meg.'

'Can Dad have some meatballs?' Dan walks back into the kitchen with Sid just behind him.

'Smells good.' Sid rubs his hands together. He's wearing his work clothes, navy combats, a grubby white T-shirt covered in paint and filler stains and a pair of ancient boots, once camel but now grey. His hair is streaked white with plaster dust and there's a dirty black smudge on his left cheek.

I catch Dan's eye. He has a hopeful expression on his face and I hate to disappoint him. He sees little enough of Sid as it is.

'I suppose so,' I say grudgingly, rubbing Dan's hair backwards, the long dirty-blond strands falling back against his scalp. 'You need a haircut young man,' I add. 'Maybe your dad will take you next week.'

Dan ignores me. He hates getting his hair cut. Like father, like son, I think looking at Sid's unruly mop.

'Sit beside me, Dad.' Dan scoots down the wooden bench against the wall to make space for him. Sid sidles in, swinging his long legs under the table.

'You know Matty and Tina,' I say.

Sid nods and smiles. 'Sure. Hiya. Where are you working at the moment, Matty?'

Matty laughs. 'Here! The side of the house has had it. We're replacing the plaster.'

'I wondered what the scaffolding was in aid of.' Sid whistles. 'Expensive business.'

'Yes, thank you, Sid,' I say. 'Luckily Matty's offered to work for free.'

Matty chokes on his wine, splattering some down his T-shirt. Luckily the wine and the T-shirt are both white.

'Only joking.' I grin at him.

'Glad to hear it,' he says. 'So where are you working, Sid?'

'Blackrock. Old place overlooking the sea. Nothing major. Be finished tomorrow. Thought I'd call in and see Dan while I was in the area.'

I dish out some more food and hand the plate to Sid. He tucks in immediately.

Lily starts to cry again and Dan kindly takes her outside, Eric and Freddie toddling behind him.

'Ten minutes,' Dan calls in the open door from the garden. 'Then I'm playing SimCity, OK?'

'No problem,' I say, closing the door behind him.

'Peace,' Tina says, 'we'd better make the most of it. More wine anyone?' She lifts up the bottle.

'Why not?' I say.

Sid thrusts his glass towards Tina but Matty puts his hand over his own.

'Not for me,' Matty says, 'I'm driving.'

'Live a little,' Sid cajoles. 'We could make a night of it. The four of us. I'm sure Meg would let you kip on her sofa.'

Tina looks at me, a smile playing on her lips. I shrug. Sounds a little crazy to me, but with the week I've just had, crazy is good.

'What about Nora?' I ask Sid. 'Won't she be wondering where you are?'

'Na, she's at a hen night in Galway.' Sid puts his finger in his wine and flicks some at my face, hitting my cheek. I wince.

'Hey!'

'So I'm all yours,' Sid says.

'Hardly,' I say drily.

Sid laughs. 'Metaphorically speaking, of course.'

'Woo, big word for a sparkie.' I pat my face dry with my sleeve.

'That's not nice,' Sid says. 'Behave.'

'Coming from you, that's ripe.'

'Oh really? And why's that then?'

'Because you're the epitome of the word misbehave.'

'Woo, big word for a mother of two.'

I flash him a look.

'Hey, stop it you two!' Tina grins. 'Anyone would think you're still together the way you carry on.'

Sid snorts. 'Thankfully not.'

I slap him on the arm, a little harder than I intended. His skin flares bright red where my open hand struck.

'Hey! I'm only joking, Meg. Letting you go was the worst mistake I ever made.'

I look at him in surprise.

'Weren't expecting that, were you?' he asks me, his eyes soft.

'No,' I say. I take a sip of my wine. I hadn't been expecting that at all.

An hour and a half later Tina and I have miraculously managed to settle Freddie, Eric and Lily in Tina's house. They're all wiped out from dashing around the garden with Dan. This way we can enjoy the rest of the evening together without having to worry about babysitting.

Freddie and Eric are in their own beds – a red moulded

plastic Ferrari in Freddie's case and a solid wood pirate ship, complete with its own slide, mast and sails for Eric. Lily is in her well-used travel cot in the stark white spare room. I hope to goodness she doesn't leak over the plush white carpet.

Dan is lying in his sleepingbag on the sofa in Tina's family room, a large area off the kitchen with huge floor-to-ceiling glass windows and an ultra-modern set-into-the-wall fireplace. I promised him he could watch a film before he went to sleep as he'd been so good with the toddlers, and I've left him with his favourite, *The Empire Strikes Back*, magnificent on Tina's huge wide-screen TV with surround sound. He's in his element. It *is* rather spectacular and I'm half tempted to snuggle down beside him.

'Now where's that wine?' I ask Tina, walking back into the kitchen.

'Isn't this great?' she asks, passing me a glass. 'Is it just me, or do you feel deliciously decadent drinking wine with your ex and your builder no less while the kids are asleep?' Tina hugs her arms around her body. 'I haven't had so much fun in ages.'

'You need to get out more.' I nudge her gently with my shoulder.

She laughs. 'You're right. And I've made a decision. Things are going to change around here. I'm going to have a lot more fun from now on, starting tonight.'

'I'm glad to hear it.'

Tina pours sticky, molten cheese into a tall, white porcelain fondue dish. A delicious smell wafts up, sweet, nutty and alcoholic.

'We got this for our wedding,' she says, noticing me staring at the alien-looking dish. 'I've only used it once or twice. Got addicted to fondue skiing. They always served delicious après ski fondue at the hotel in Val d'Isère. Haven't been skiing since the kids were born though.'

She puts the bowl down on a large plate, lights the tea light under the dish and sets four tiny two-pronged forks along the side. She hands me a basket of French bread chunks and four matching white side plates.

'I'm impressed,' Sid says as we walk into the living room brandishing our wares in front of us like two of the three wise men. He's lounging on the immaculate white Italian linen sofa, his large frame dwarfing the seat, his legs splayed out in front of him – dirty boots off, thank goodness. His socks aren't as clean as Matty's. Sitting like that, he reminds me of Paul as a teenager, all legs and testosterone. Thinking about it, Paul's testosterone has calmed down a bit, but Sid's certainly hasn't, even at thirty-four.

Matty jumps up, takes the bowl off Tina and puts it on the smoked-glass coffee table in front of the sofa.

'Thanks.' She gives Matty a winning smile. 'You two OK for drinks?'

Sid lifts his can of Budweiser in the air with a flourish. 'Sorted.' He has two more cans by his feet, still paired by their plastic handcuffs.

Matty lifts his wine glass off the oak floor and takes a sip. 'The wine's lovely.' His large, manly hands look incongruous set against the delicate Waterford crystal glass.

'Should be,' Tina says mildly, 'it's one of Oliver's best.'

I stare at her. Oliver's best wine is no laughing matter.

'Don't look so shocked, Meg. He's miles away. What he doesn't know won't hurt him.'

This new bravado is refreshing but a little scary. Must be the hundred-euro-a-bottle wine, I surmise. She's had rather a lot already.

'Good attitude.' Sid lifts his can and salutes her. 'I'll drink to that.' His eyes linger a little too long on Tina's pert breasts. He catches me staring at him and looks away.

'Thanks, Sid.' Tina plonks herself down on the white sheepskin rug to the far side of the coffee table.

'No problem, Teeney.'

Tina giggles. 'No one's called me that since school.'

'I'd say you were a divil in school.' He gives her a knowing wink. 'Convent girls are the worst.'

Tina snorts. 'Is it that obvious?'

'It is. All Bambi eyes and dark souls. Isn't that right, Matty?'

Matty shifts uncomfortable on the sofa. 'I wouldn't really know.'

'Come off it,' Sid continues, 'a good-looking guy like yourself. You must have had hundreds of girls in your day.'

'Um, no,' Matty stammers. 'Not at all.'

'Sid!' I break in. 'Would you give Matty a break. He's a decent law-abiding citizen who likes to date his women one at a time. Unlike some men I know.'

Sid sits up and pretends to look offended. 'I sincerely hope you're not referring to my good self, Meg Miller. I'll have you know that I've changed a lot since—'

'Your alley-cat days?' I suggest.

Sid has the good grace to grin. 'Yes, I suppose. I'm a one-woman guy these days.' He pauses for a moment. 'One woman at a time that is.'

'Sid!' I throw one of Tina's glossy magazines at him and it lands on his head and slithers down his chest.

He picks it up and looks at the cover. An olive-skinned beauty with pneumatic lips stares out at him, in a tiny green and blue tropical-print bikini. 'That's lovely, Meg. Death by *Vogue*. Thanks a lot.' He slaps it down onto the table and touches his forehead, red where the hard edge of the magazine caught it.

'No less than you deserve,' I snip.

'Children, stop that squabbling.' Tina stands up. 'And no one's touched my fondue.' She puts her hands on her hips and throws her honey-coloured hair back. 'I'm most offended.'

Matty instantly leans forward, forks up a piece of bread and carefully dips it into the cheese mix. 'Delicious, Tina. It's got a real kick. What's the secret ingredient?'

'Vodka,' Tina says. 'Oodles of it.'

'Vodka?' Sid grabs a piece of bread and dips it straight into the bowl with his fingers, swirls it around, loading it with cheese and pops it into his wide-open mouth. 'Umm, s'good,' he says, his mouth still half full.

'You're supposed to use a dipping fork,' I say drily. 'That's why they're there, numbskull.'

Sid looks at the forks. 'That looks like far too much work. Tina doesn't mind if I use my fingers. Do you, Tina?'

'You don't know where those hands have been,' I warn her.

Sid holds his fingers up to his nose and sniffs them. 'No fishy smells, Meg, you're all right. I've washed them since this morning.'

I wrinkle my nose. 'Sid, you're gross. Grow up, will you? Your son's in the next room, remember?'

Tina laughs. 'Meg's right, that was pretty bad.'

'Bad?' Sid looks from Tina to me and back again. 'Jeepers, girls, I'm only getting started. The night is young.'

'God spare us all.' I stand up. 'Now, who wants more wine? I think I need a top-up before the night completely disintegrates.'

'And what sort of disintegration are you expecting?' Sid asks me, his eyes lighting up. 'A bit of an orgy maybe? Or some one on one action?' He puts down his can and lifts his hips off the sofa with his hands, pumping away enthusiastically, his eyes closed and his mouth open. By rights he should look ridiculous but, Sid being Sid, he looks horribly, pornographically erotic. For a moment, I feel a wave of adrenaline rush up the back of my legs and my knees go weak. Sid has always had a terrible effect on me. I pull myself together, willing my body to stay immune to his rather obvious charms. He stops his simulation and gives me a leery wink. 'I'm all yours, Meg. I think you should know that.'

I give him a withering look. 'Please. I'm not that desperate. And sit down would you, you big eejit. You're making a show of yourself.'

'Really?' Sid looks at me far too knowingly for my liking. I frown at him. It's all getting far too close to the bone and I know exactly what type of bone is on Sid's mind; my blood rises to my cheeks just thinking about it. The drink has me all befuddled. 'So who's for wine?' I whip my head around too quickly, and put a hand on the back of the sofa to steady myself.

Tina holds out her glass eagerly and I top it up generously.

'I'm OK for the moment.' Matty says.

'Go on,' Tina says, 'live a little. Tomorrow's Saturday. No school.'

'There is if you're working for a certain slave driver,' Matty points out.

'Meg!' Tina slaps me on the leg. 'You're not making poor Matty work weekends, are you?'

'No, I mean yes. He's working tomorrow but only because he offered. You're getting me in trouble with Tina. You tell her.'

'Meg's right,' Matty sits up a little on the sofa. 'I did offer. I often work weekends if I have a lot on. Working for myself I don't have much choice, I have to take the work when it's there until I build up more contacts.'

'Are you very busy at the moment?' Tina asks.

Matty nods. 'It's pretty mental all right. After Meg's job I'm down to Bray. Kitchen extension. Then up to Shankhill to do a bathroom. Sorry, I won't bore you with the details, but I'm mad busy. I'm not complaining. I like it that way.'

'It's not boring at all. I was just wondering if you'd have time to squeeze in a small job at some stage. Before the summer's out.'

'How small?'

My ears prick up. What is Tina up to?

'The guest bathroom upstairs is in an awful state. Horrible white tiles that need to be replaced urgently, I don't know what possessed me; they're terribly industrial-looking. Makes the place look like an abattoir. And maybe a new bathroom suite. I'm sure it wouldn't take you long. Not if you're as good as Meg's says you are.'

Have I said he's good? I can't remember, but I'm a bit miffed that she's trying to steal my builder, right under my nose. And she renovated that particular bathroom a mere six months ago. If her six-month-old tiles are dated, our green ones are positively prehistoric.

Tina senses my gaze. 'I've never liked those white tiles,' she says firmly. 'They were a mistake. Looked much better in the magazine.'

Matty rubs his chin. 'Might be able to fit it in. Can't work on Meg's place if it's raining . . .'

Now I'm getting irritated. 'Yes, you bloody well can.' I'm not going to get bumped for my richer and thinner neighbour, even if I do love her to bits. 'That render stuff's wet anyway, isn't it?'

'But if it gets too wet it won't hold to the wall.' Matty explains the physics of it all to me patiently. I'm not really interested but I listen out of politeness.

'I stand corrected,' I say a little stiffly when he's finished.

'I'll have a look at your bathroom on Monday,' Matty says to Tina. 'Give you a quote.'

'Oh, don't worry about the money,' Tina says lightly. She waves her hand in the air. 'Whatever. I just want to get it done.'

'Do you need new lights?' Sid asks hopefully, euro signs pinging in his eyes.

'I don't think so.' Tina looks doubtful.

Matty looks at Sid and then back at Tina. 'Why don't I go up now and have a look? I'll check the lighting for you while I'm at it.' He's probably trying to protect Tina from Sid's predatory electrics. I know Sid puts in extra lights where they aren't strictly necessary as he's admitted as much to me on several occasions. I wonder if Matty is aware of this too.

'Would you?' Tina beams at him. 'You're an angel.'

Matty stands up and puts his empty wine glass on the coffee table with a little chink. 'No trouble.'

Tina scrambles to her feet. 'I'll show you where it is. Back in a sec, guys,' she trills at Sid and me.

As soon as they have left the room Sid grins at me and pats the sofa seat beside him. 'May as well make yourself comfortable.'

I'm currently perching on the edge of Tina's imitation Le Corbusier chaise longue, all black leather and chrome. It looks great but it's bloody uncomfortable. I push myself up and sit down beside Sid. He puts his arm around my shoulders and I shrug it away.

'Loosen up, Meg,' he drawls. 'We may as well get cosy, they won't be back for a while.'

'What do you mean by that?' I sit up poker straight.

'Did you catch the way they were looking at each other?'

'Sid! Tina's married. And her kids are upstairs. You have a one-track mind.'

'Don't tell me you haven't noticed that she's spent the whole evening flirting with him. And that bathroom ruse!' He snorts.

'No, she hasn't,' I insist. 'Tina just wants people to like her, that's all.'

'Wants Matty to like her – a lot,' he adds suggestively.

'Let's stop this conversation right now. I'm sure it's all completely innocent. And the new bathroom isn't a ruse, Tina's always changing things in this place. This floor's only a few months old. She's obsessed.'

'Not surprised. Nice gaff, must have cost them a pretty penny to get it looking like this. Those lights alone are worth a couple of grand.' He points up at the elaborate track lighting over our heads.

'You should see the lighting in the master bedroom. State of the art.'

'I think you'll find it's Matty who'll be seeing that.' He lifts his eyebrows.

I sigh. 'You're as bad as Hattie. In fact I don't know why the two of you didn't get it together years ago. You're like two peas in a pod.'

'Wasn't for lack of trying.' Sid drains his can, puts it down on the table and opens another one with a crack.

'What? Hattie tried it on with you?' I'm flabbergasted.

Sid looks at me, an amused expression on his face. 'No, I made a pass at her. Several in fact. She turned me down every time.'

I'm lost for words.

'She didn't tell you?' he asks. 'I thought you guys were close.'

'We *are* close. I can't believe you made a pass at my sister. You really are scum, Sid.' I start to stand up but he puts his hand across my body.

'Wait one minute,' he says, pushing me down again. 'Don't come over all virtuous. It's me, Meg, remember? And you're not exactly all that innocent yourself, are you?'

I can feel my face colour. My head is reeling, like a baby's spinning top.

'What have you two been talking about?' Tina steps back into the room with Matty close behind her.

I study her face carefully. There are no obvious signs of any romantic dalliance. Her cheeks are a little flushed and her eyes shining but that's probably just the wine. Her white cashmere cardigan is buttoned almost up to the neck. Matty on the other hand looks dishevelled, the back of his blue shirt is hanging out of his jeans and he's fastened it up too quickly, missing a buttonhole out, but that's nothing out of the ordinary, Matty always looks dishevelled.

'Track lighting,' I say. 'And how was the bathroom?' I ask, eager to deflect the conversation.

'No problem,' Matty says. 'A couple of days' work. Week tops.' He turns to Sid. 'And the lights are grand. Sorry, mate.'

'No worries,' Sid says easily. 'I've enough on my hands as it is.'

'Enough talk about work.' Tina claps her hands together. She slots a Van Morrison disc into the streamlined Bang & Olufsen stereo. The opening bars of 'Brown Eyed Girl' ring out.

'Matty, can you dance?' Tina holds out both her hands to him. Matty takes them eagerly and gets to his feet. They start dancing, a kind of fast waltz, Matty throwing Tina away from him and pulling her back against his chest. She snuggles into him and they move slower, swaying to the music.

Sid nudges me in the side, a smile playing on his lips.

I bite the inside of my mouth. My God, I think, staring at Tina, maybe Sid's right.

'Dance with me, Meg,' Sid says.

'No.'

'Why?' He slides his lean body down the sofa so that his mouth is beside my ear. 'Afraid you might like it?'

I give a dramatic sigh. 'You're really sad. You know that, don't you?'

'One of these days you'll change your mind. I'm just going to bide my time.'

I shake my head. 'Sid, it'll never happen.'

He puts his hand on my leg. I push it away. 'Stop it. I'm not going to tell you again.'

'Let's go upstairs. I'm sure Tina won't mind. Be like old times.'

'That's it!' I stand up. 'I'm leaving.' I glare at him. 'And the next time I see you, I hope you'll be a lot more sober and a lot less delusional.'

'I'm only joking, I can't believe you're taking me seriously.'

Am I completely over-reacting? Maybe he is just playing with me. And maybe I'm making a complete fool of myself. But I know from experience that calling his bluff is dangerous. I'm not going to take any chances.

I ignore him. 'Tina, I'm sorry, but I have to go. I'm exhausted.'

Tina breaks away from Matty and studies her watch. 'But it's only early.'

'I know, and I'm sorry.' I kiss her on the cheek.

'I had a lovely evening. See you, Matty.'

'Why don't you leave Dan and Lily here?' Tina suggests. 'There's no point waking them up now.'

'Are you sure?'

'Positive.'

'I'll be in for them first thing in the morning,' I promise her. 'Thanks. And thanks for the fondue and the wine.'

'My pleasure. I'll see you out.'

'You stay there, Tina.' Sid jumps to his feet. 'I'll do it.'

As we walk silently towards the door I have a strange feeling in the pit of my stomach.

Sid opens the door a crack, then changes his mind, turns and rests his back against it, closing it behind him with a clunk.

'Are you going to let me out or not?' I glare at him.

'Don't be like that, Meg. I'm sorry, I didn't mean to offend you.'

I say nothing.

He cocks his head to one side. 'Are you annoyed with me?'

'No. I'm just tired.'

'Give me a kiss and then I'll open the door.'

I screw my eyes tightly closed and then open them again. My hands are balled on either side of my body and my shoulders are rigid with tension. God, he's so annoying; worse than a child. 'Just get away from the door,' I clip.

'You didn't say that last Christmas.'

'That was a mistake.'

'Didn't seem that way at the time. In fact, you were pretty keen if I remember rightly.'

My stomach lurches. 'You promised never to mention that again. Ever!'

He shrugs. 'When have I been known to keep my promise?'

'You bastard! It'll never happen again, understand? Now, let me out or I'll scream.'

He gives a snort of derision and then opens the door for me. As I pass through he puts both his arms around me from behind.

'Let go of me.'

'I could have you if I wanted to,' he whispers into my hair. 'We belong together. I love you, you know that. Always will.'

I push my body against his arms and he loosens his grip. I storm away and my heart doesn't stop thumping until I'm safely at home with the door bolted and the chain on. I hate him. Hate how he makes me feel. Hate the power he has over me.

As I lie in bed my mind races. I shouldn't have left Tina and Matty like that but I had to get out of there. Last Christmas I'd made a mistake, a stupid, stupid mistake, but I'm not going to let it ruin my life.

'How long are you here for, Meg?' Sid had asked on the night before Christmas Eve. He was slouching on my parent's couch in front of the television in the family room cum conservatory at the back of the house. We were back for Christmas, Simon was out with Hans from Dublin Bay Marine, Hattie was out with a gang from work, and Mum and Dad were at a drinks party. I was babysitting. We were supposed to have a romantic night in, just me and Simon, but it hadn't turned out that way. In fact, we'd just had an almighty row after he told me he was flying out to Greece on New Year's Eve to sail in a New Year's Day race on one of his regular boats. I nearly throttled him. We'd planned to spend New Year's Eve together for once. I'd even managed to book a lovely fish restaurant in Monkstown – no mean feat I can tell you. I was still seething, sitting in front of the television watching a re-run of *When Harry Met Sally*, settling into my fourth or fifth glass of wine of the evening.

I tore my eyes away from the screen where Sally was faking an orgasm in a cafe. 'Another ten days. Then we're joining Simon in Spain for a few weeks.'

'Still thinking of coming back for good in the spring?'

'That's the plan.'

'Thanks, Meg.'

'For what?'

'For bringing Dan back to Dublin. I've missed him.'

'I'm not doing it for you.' I wasn't in the mood for Sid. I wasn't in the mood for anyone. I just wanted to sit on my own and watch television, glass in hand, open bottle at my feet. I had no idea why Sid was still here when I was making it fairly obvious that I didn't want his company. He'd called in to see Dan, had put him to bed and was now lingering like a bad smell.

He shrugged. 'Thanks anyway.'

'Where's Nora this evening? Shouldn't you be getting back?'

'She's gone home to her parents.'

'For Christmas?'

'For good, I think.'

I looked at him. His eyes were fixed on the television screen. He was more subdued than normal and he'd been drinking. 'I hadn't realized. I'm sorry.'

'S'OK. Probably for the best.'

I said nothing for a moment, but then curiosity got the better of me. 'What happened?'

His eyes met mine. They were strangely soft and unfocused. 'She said there were three people in the relationship.'

I sighed. 'So who is it this time? Someone you've been working for?'

He shook his head and held my gaze. 'You know very well, Meg. You've always known.'

'What are you talking about?'

He gave a short laugh. 'Doesn't matter.'

'Yes, it does. Go on.'

'It's you. You're the other woman. Always have been.'

I was speechless for a second. 'Me? What? I don't understand.'

He sat up a little. 'Don't play games with me. I'm not in the humour. Maybe I'd better go.' He moved towards me, his eyes flashing. 'Should have married you when I had the chance.'

'Married? Us?' I gave a gentle laugh. 'That would have been a disaster.'

'Would it? Do you really think so? We were mad about each other.'

'You seem to have conveniently forgotten why we broke up in the first place.'

Sid ran his hands through his hair, making it stick up in tufts. Irrationally, I wanted to reach out and smooth it down.

'I know, and I'm sorry about all that, really I am. But I've changed.'

'Yeah, right.'

'Come outside with me. I need some air.'

'Are you still smoking?'

'Cigarettes you mean?' he asked.

'Those too.'

Sid gave a laugh. 'A little. But don't give out to me, Meg, not tonight.'

'Actually, I was going to ask you to roll up.'

Sid grinned at me in his lopsided way. 'You see. That's why I love you. You're so bloody unpredictable.'

I suppose I could blame the wine, the joint, the cold air hitting me and making me even woozier, but when Sid leaned down to kiss me I didn't move away. When he nipped at my neck, teasing my skin gently, I didn't move away. When his hands roamed over my body, tucking under my jumper, I didn't move away. When he carried me inside and deposited me on the rug in front of the television, ripped my jumper and shirt off me, kissing every part of my bare flesh, I didn't move away. When he balanced above me on his strong arms, looking down at me with those blue, blue eyes, I grabbed his neck and pulled him towards me, hungry for his mouth, for his body, for absolution. From what, I didn't really know. But we had unfinished business, me and Sid, and we both knew it.

'No,' I said as his hands moved down towards my jeans. 'I can't. Sid!' I pushed him away.

'Please,' he pleaded.

'No, it's not right. No.' I sat up and gathered my clothes together. 'I'm sorry.'

He shook his head but said nothing.

Afterwards, I felt strangely calm and utterly relieved that nothing more serious had happened. We shared a cigarette, sitting outside shivering, staring up at the stars in the clear winter sky.

'This doesn't change anything you know,' I told him, dragging deeply and allowing the smoke to fill my lungs with its creeping nicotine fingers. 'Simon and the kids – that's my life now. That's what I've chosen. Kissing you was a mistake. Promise me you'll never mention it.'

'I won't,' he said simply, staring into the distance. 'I promise.'

*

It was the first and last time I've ever let myself slip. And now I'm paying for it. If Simon finds out . . . it makes me sick just considering it. And as for Dan. I shudder to think.

At six in the morning I wake up, my mouth is so dry my lips are practically stuck to my dehydrated gums and I'm gasping for a drink of water. I stagger into the bathroom and stick my head under the tap. Straightening up again I yawn deeply, almost pulling a muscle in my chest in the process. I know I should really get Lily, the little scamp is bound to be up soon if she isn't already up and I have a key to Tina's house after all; but I just can't face it. Another hour in bed, that'll do the trick. Another blissful hour.

The next thing I know I'm being prodded in the side.

'Wha?' I mutter.

'Mum, Lily wants you,' I can hear Dan's voice above me but I screw my eyes closed even tighter, willing him to go away. 'She's in the kitchen. I've been giving her biscuits to keep her happy, but that's not working any more.'

I drag my eyes open, the dim light of my bedroom piercing my eyeballs. My head is throbbing ominously and my mouth is desert-dry again. I've obviously been dribbling in my sleep as I can feel crusted saliva at the edge of my mouth. I rub it away with the back of my hand and sit up gingerly.

'What time is it?' I ask Dan.

'Nine.'

'Nine? Has Lily been up long?'

'Since half six.'

I wince. 'Yikes! Poor Tina.'

'It's OK, I looked after her. Tina was still asleep. Lily knocked over a glass of water in the living room but I cleared it up.'

'What was she doing in the living room?'

'Wandering around; you know what she's like.'

I nod grimly.

'It was funny, Dad was asleep on the sofa, snoring. Lily put her finger up his nose and he didn't even wake up.'

'Yuk. And have you had any breakfast?'

'Tina made us all sausages and rashers.'

'All?'

'Dad and Matty. And me and Lily and the boys.'

'Matty?'

'He stayed over too. But I didn't see him until he came down the stairs later. He seemed a bit surprised to see me.'

'Maybe he'd forgotten you were staying over.' My mind mulls over this nugget of information and jumps to the obvious conclusion. I should never have introduced Tina to Matty, I'm a marriage wrecker. I hold my head in my hands. First Sid and now this. What class of idiot am I?

Chapter 16

*Fender: a cushion placed between two boats or
a boat and a pier to stop them banging together.
Can also be used as a verb . . . 'Fend off, quickly,
we're about to crash!'*

'Meg, where the hell are you? I'm here on my own and Mum's in one of her ve-have-vays-of-making-you-talk moods. Help!'

I laugh. 'We're on our way with reinforcements, Hattie. Hold the fort till we get there. And don't let her wear you down. The future of the Miller family depends on it. Be there in ten minutes.'

'Hurry!'

I click off my mobile and throw it onto the passenger seat. I'm not exactly looking forward to Dad's birthday lunch as it is; now I'm an even more reluctant celebrant. I'm still a little hazy from Friday night, which is most unfair as I'd spent all day yesterday paying for my excesses: lolling around on the sofa in front of the television, trying to ignore the throbbing between my eyes and the somersaults my stomach was turning, while entertaining Lily to the best of my grumpy ability. This largely meant blowing bubbles for her (and making myself dizzy in the process), handing her Pringles and allowing her watch Disney's *Cinderella* over and over again. Dan spent the day at George's house which was good; he deserved time out from Lily. And from me!

Matty rang at eleven, apologizing for his no show. 'Wouldn't be safe to work today. The way I'm feeling right now, I'd fall off the scaffolding.' I felt like asking wouldn't love lift him up where he belonged, but I thought better of it. Whatever my suspicions, I had no proof and besides, it wasn't really my business: not that that usually stopped me.

I'd seen Tina briefly in the afternoon when I raised myself off the couch and called in with Lily to check how she was feeling. She didn't seem to be suffering at all which irked me. In fact, she was very chipper, with the kind of grin that sneaks onto your face at the start of a new romance and stays there whatever the circumstances. It was the kind of grin that made me very suspicious.

When I quizzed her about the adult sleepover she'd dismissed it all breezily.

'Matty was far too drunk to drive home,' she said, 'so I offered him the spare room. Sid slept on the sofa. He was so out of it, he would have slept anywhere. After you left he practically threw a bottle of vodka down his throat.'

As I pull into Mum and Dad's drive Katia and Paul are climbing out of Paul's boy-racer car. The left wing mirror is hanging off the side, attached by a thin black wire, like a tooth attached to the gum by a slither of skin. The glass is shattered and there is a deep white gash along the corresponding door panel. Grasshopper is skipping around the boot, his slimy pink tongue licking the rear window excitedly as if it tasted of dog food, smearing the glass. Stupid mutt.

'Wa-Wa,' Lily says, staring doe-eyed at Grasshopper.

I wind my window down. 'Been rally driving again?' I ask Paul caustically.

'Hi, sis.' Paul beams at me. His hair is even shorter than normal if that's possible and his white Calvin Klein boxer shorts are yet again strikingly visible above his low-slung jeans. Katia is her usual well-groomed self in a tight black top, black Lycra trousers, black high-heeled strappy sandals with a crocheted cream bolero over her shoulders. Her white-blonde hair is tied back tightly, gathered in a pink hair clip and lacquered to within an inch of its life. I feel decidedly underdressed in my own combats and white T-shirt with a decent-enough cardigan thrown over the top. But Lily makes up for my sartorial inelegance.

Lily has far more clothes than I do. Today she's resplendent in a yellow linen dress with tiny ties on the shoulders and butterfly embroidery along the hem and the edges of the sleeves, with a matching yellow top and her favourite pink sandals with a daisy on each ankle strap. The sandals barely fit her any more, her little toes peek rather dangerously out the end – just asking to be stubbed – but it was sandals or her wellies. I couldn't find any other toddler shoes this morning. Mum and Dad gave her the dress for her birthday, hence its outing. Lily, with Simon's dark skin, is one of the few Irish children who can carry off yellow without looking ill.

'Are you here for the fireworks?' Paul winds down each of his car windows a little.

'What do you mean?' I ask.

'We're announcing our engagement today to Mum and Dad.'

'Really?' I look at Katia for confirmation.

She nods, her hair not moving an inch. 'I keep telling him to wait, but he insists. No patience, your brother. Rasher.'

I stop for a moment. Rasher? Is that Paul's new nickname?

'She means rash,' Paul says.

I stifle a laugh. Katia's English is excellent, who am I to judge with my three words of Spanish and my scant Leaving Cert

French? She also speaks Russian and German. 'Ah, yes. Very rash.' I turn to Paul. 'But can't you wait until after lunch at least? I'm starving.'

He gives a bark of laughter. 'OK. Just for you and your stomach we will. If that's OK with you, Katia.'

Katia shrugs. 'They're your parents, Paul.'

'Good, then that's decided,' Paul says. 'We'll break the news after lunch. And I'll leave Grasshopper in the car for the moment. He's not exactly Mum's favourite beast after all.'

As Katia walks on with Dan and Paul helps me lift Lily out of her car seat, I wonder if I should warn him not to be too optimistic. There's no telling how Mum will react to the prospect of a Slovakian daughter-in-law. But I decide to keep schtum. No point in worrying him. And perhaps she will be fine about it – and pigs might fly.

Lily clings to Paul like a little bushbaby, her strong hands anchoring onto his T-shirt, her legs gripping his slim waist. She adores Paul, blindly in my opinion. He never pays her all that much attention, which is probably why she worships him. I hope to goodness she grows out of that particular pattern of female behaviour, attaching herself to unworthy men, it will only end in tears.

'Hey, Lily.' Paul tickles her waist. 'Have you been a good girl for your mummy?'

'Lily best girl,' she says proudly.

Paul laughs and tickles her again. She giggles with delight and hits his hand away ineffectively.

'Paul, do you have to tell the parentals *today*?' I swing Lily's grubby nappy bag and a canvas 'I Love Boston' shopping bag, one of Simon's hastily grabbed airport presents for Lily, holding Dad's presents onto my shoulder. I slam the car doors, including the one Dan has forgotten to close, lock up, then walk towards the house, Paul by my side.

'Why do you think we're going on holiday first thing

tomorrow morning?' he says with a wink. Katia walks on ahead and rings the doorbell.

'You have it all planned you evil bastard.' I shake my head in admiration. 'You're *unbelievable*.'

'It was Hattie's idea.'

'Why am I not surprised?'

Paul frowns a little. 'Hattie says Mum might need a little time to adjust to the news.'

I look at him. 'She might be right,' I say gently. 'But Mum might surprise us all, you never know. And the holiday's a great idea because you need a rest with all that work you're doing.'

He pulls a face. 'Don't be like that.'

'Sorry, just jealous. You know that.'

He nudges me with his shoulder. 'Course.'

'Darlings!' Mum opens the door wide. She holds her arms open to embrace Paul and Lily. 'How's my favourite little girl?'

'Fine, Mum,' I say.

'Isn't your mum a silly?' she says to Lily.

Paul twists his body around to hand Lily over to her.

'No, no.' Mum backs away from him. 'You keep her. I'm too busy in the kitchen to mind Lily as well.' She looks at me pointedly.

She always manages to make me feel guilty. It's not as if I foisted Lily on Paul; he'd taken her quite happily.

'No, it's grand,' Paul says with a smile. 'It's good practice.'

I shoot him a look. Luckily it seems to have gone over Mum's head.

'Come in.' She steps back. 'Don't linger on the doorstep like that. Your dad's in the sitting room.' She waves her hand at the open doorway to the left. 'Go on in.'

Only Katia follows her instructions, polite as always.

'Where's Hattie?' I ask.

'Wafting around the place,' Mum says with a sigh. 'Won't sit still for a second. Don't know what's got into her.'

'She's afraid you'll pin her down and interrogate her about her love life,' Paul says.

I give a snort.

Mum tut tuts. 'As if I'd do such a thing.'

Paul looks at me, his eyebrows raised. 'As *if*.'

'There you are.' Hattie lopes down the stairs, two at a time. She gives me a firm hug. 'Wondered where you'd got to. I was just tidying my room.'

Mum makes a horse-like harrumphing noise.

Hattie's room is a notorious tip. Most days there are so many clothes on the floor it's impossible to push the door open, let alone see the well-worn cream carpet. She has more clothes than anyone I know, including Tina, who has a vast walk-in wardrobe. Unlike Tina, whose shelves look like a stray Benetton employee has been let loose on them, Hattie seems to keep most of her clothes draped over the end of her pine queen-sized bed, thrown over the chair, or on the floor.

Hattie ignores Mum and swings Lily's changing bag off my shoulder and onto her own. 'Paul, give me Lily and go and help Mum in the kitchen.' Hattie puts her hands out to take Lily, but Lily clings firmly, burying her head in Paul's chest. 'We'll go in to Dad.'

'No, 'attie,' she says.

'I do need some help in the kitchen, girls,' Mum trills. 'And leave your poor brother alone, Hattie. Cooking is not his *forte*.' She sniffs the air. 'Think something's burning.' She runs into the kitchen.

Paul pats Lily's bare lower leg. 'Lily's fine here with me. Katia can help Mum.'

'Don't be so sexist,' Hattie snaps.

'And don't *you* be so sensitive. I didn't mean it that way. It'll give them a chance to get to know each other a little better, that's all.'

'Oh, that's a great idea.' Hattie sniggers. 'Go for it. They'll get on famously I'm sure.'

'Stop being sarky,' Paul says.

I shake my head. It's going to be a long afternoon. I open the sitting-room door and walk in. Dad stands up and smiles. His face looks pale and a little gaunt and the checked brown-and-white brushed-cotton shirt I gave him last Christmas is hanging off him. He's lost weight again and it doesn't suit him. Hattie and Paul don't seem to notice, but I'm worried.

'Hi, Dad.' I lean over and give him a gentle kiss. 'Happy birthday.' His freshly shaven face feels cool and smooth under my lips and I smile at the familiar waft of Old Spice. Some things never change.

'Thanks for coming, Meg. And Paul, of course.' He nods at Paul. The Miller men aren't ones for public displays of affection. 'Katia's just been telling me about her brothers. Delighted to hear they'll be coming to Ireland.'

'What's that?' Mum asks, sidling in the door, not wanting to miss anything.

'Katia's brothers. They're coming to Dublin. To stay with Katia and Paul.'

'Only until they find work,' Paul adds. He sits down on the floor, Lily still on his hip. She puts her feet on the floor and toddles off to find the toy box behind the sofa.

'Do you have room?' Mum asks Paul.

He shrugs. 'We have a sofabed. It's only short term.'

'As long as the entire village doesn't decide join them,' Mum sniffs. 'Seems like the whole of Slovakia wants to move to Ireland. Lots of my friends' cleaners are Slovakian.'

'Mum, we should be embracing our new European neighbours, remember?' Hattie says. 'Don't be so disparaging.'

Mum throws Hattie a look. 'I have no problem with foreigners *per se*. I'm no racist, if that's what you're implying, Hattie.'

'Wasn't implying anything of the sort,' Hattie says drily. 'You're always telling us how you gave your pocket money to the black babies, isn't that right, Mum?'

Mum looks at Hattie again, unsure if she's being made fun of or not. 'That's right. And it is easier to find a cleaner now, I suppose,' she concedes.

'Oh, well, that's OK then,' Hattie says. 'As long as the houses of the great and good of south county Dublin are spick and span.'

'Hattie!' Dad says, before I have a chance.

'Sorry,' she mumbles.

'Must get back to the roast.' Mum flutters her hands to her face and pushes back some stray wisps of hair. For a woman in her fifties Mum has fantastic hair, a thick, brown, shoulder-length mane. I've always been jealous of it. Hattie has inherited her hair, although it's been dyed for so long everyone thinks she's a natural blonde.

'Why don't I help you in the kitchen, Mrs Miller?' Katia asks.

'There's no need. I'm sure Hattie or Meg . . .'

Katia puts both her hands up and blows the air out of her mouth with a rather French 'pah'. Her pillar-box red nails emphasize her elegantly long, young-looking hands. I glance down at my own stubby nails and dry hands and try not to compare them.

'I insist.' Katia strides into the kitchen.

'Isn't that nice of Katia?' Dad says. 'Such a sweet girl.'

I look over at Hattie and she gives me a wink.

'Can I give Grampa his presents now?' Dan dives into the Boston bag and pulls out the longest of them, hastily wrapped in silver paper in the car on the way over. I suddenly realize that the paper's embossed with Happy 21st. I hadn't spotted that in the rather dingy shop. If Dad notices he's far too kind to mention it.

'You shouldn't have,' Dad says as Dan hands him the package.

'That's from me,' Dan says proudly.

'And Lily,' I add.

Dad opens it and hands Lily the paper to play with. 'A remote-controlled plane.' He grins at Dan. 'Just what I've always wanted. How did you guess?'

'We can fly it together in the garden,' Dan says. 'It was Mum's idea.'

'That sounds like a good plan,' Dad says. 'We can give it a test run after lunch.'

I hand him two more parcels and an envelope. He takes them eagerly. 'I think I know what this is.' He opens the plain white envelope and reads the card inside. 'A subscription to *Irish Gardener*. Thanks, girls.'

'You're welcome,' Hattie says. We give him the same present every year so it's not exactly much of a surprise.

'Can I open the others?' Dan's eyes are gleaming. He's hopping from one foot to the other.

'Course you can.' Dad hands him the parcels.

Dan tears the paper off in record time. 'A book and a pen and a weird jar of something.' He hands them to Dad. 'Not as good as the plane.'

'No.' Dad smiles. 'But still nice.' He turns his presents over in his hands. 'Roy Keane's new biog. The very one I was after. And a new fountain pen, you shouldn't have. *And* Gentleman's Relish, my favourite. You remembered. Thanks, both of you.' He beams at me and Hattie. I feel it would be churlish to add that those presents are from me, and me alone. But I say nothing. It irks me a little that Hattie is getting the credit for my initiative.

While Hattie studies the plane's instructions with Dan, Dad winks at me. 'Thanks, Meg,' he mouths.

I smile at him. He holds my gaze, his eyes soft, thoughtful. His eyes look different, watery almost. Is he crying? I wonder with a start. Dad rarely cries; in fact the last time I'd seen him teary eyed was at my bedside after Dan was born. I want to ask him if everything's all right, if there's something on his mind, something he wants to tell me, but then Paul interrupts my musings.

'Here you go, Da,' he hands him a second envelope. 'This is from me and Katia.'

Dad's eyes widen as he reads the letter within. 'A weekend in Dromoland Castle. Paul, I can't accept this. It's too much.' Dromoland is one of Ireland's most exclusive and expensive hotels.

'Katia's friend is a manager there. She got us a good deal. Anyway you deserve it. You and Mum.'

Dad is visibly moved. He sits back in his favourite seat, the blue tweed reclining armchair, with the footrest that lifts up. Hattie and I look on as Paul and Dad joke about dirty weekends.

'Buttering up the old man before he drops the bombshell,' Hattie whispers in my ear. 'Smart move, baby bro.'

I smile. 'He's not a Miller for nothing.'

Suddenly we hear a loud bang and raised voices in the kitchen. Hattie puts her hand on my arm. 'What was that?'

There's another shout. 'No idea, but I think we're about to find out.'

'I'd better go and see if Katia's all right,' Paul says a little nervously.

'Maybe Mum's stabbed her,' Hattie suggests.

Paul's face pales.

'I'm only joking, Mum may have a temper but she's not that bad.'

Paul practically runs out of the room. Hattie and I jostle with our elbows to be the first after him. Hattie wins.

Paul has disappeared into the kitchen and Hattie and I linger in the hall, as close to the ajar kitchen door as we can get, nudging each other and trying not to laugh.

'Is everything all right?' we hear Paul ask.

'Great,' Hattie whispers, 'we can hear everything.'

'Shush,' I hiss, not wanting to miss a thing. This is better than *Coronation Street*.

'No!' Katia and Mum say in unison.

'She's not the girl for you—' Mum begins.

'She wants me to be your maid—' Katia says simultaneously.

'One at a time,' Paul says. 'Katia, what's wrong?'

'But, Paul,' Mum interjects. 'She—'

'Mum,' Paul warns, 'let Katia speak.'

Mum mumbles something I don't catch. I look at Hattie but she shakes her head and shrugs.

'Your mother expects me to cook and clean for you, Paul,' Katia's voice rings out clear and strong. 'She thinks I'm taking advantage of your good nature, making you do things you don't want to do when you're tired after work. Like cleaning the toilet. What have you been telling her, Paul? She says *I* should be cleaning the toilet, and doing all the housework. I'm not a toilet cleaner, do you understand? I have a masters in biochemistry.'

Katia says something in what I presume is Slovakian. From the way she spits it out, I'd say it's a fairly strong swear word. Then she continues, 'As for you being tired, is she mad? I pay the rent, *all* the rent. Don't forget that. The least you can do is help around the house. It's not as if you have anything else to do.'

'Hey,' Hattie whispers, 'sounds like Paul's lost his job again.'

'Shush,' I say. 'This is good.'

'I think there's been a bit of a misunderstanding,' Paul interrupts Katia's flow.

'Are you going to let that little madam speak to me like that?' Mum asks. 'Or to you for that matter?'

'Mum, I think we should all calm down here,' Paul says, rather bravely.

'Calm down? Calm bloody down?' Mum hisses.

'He's in *real* trouble now,' Hattie says. 'Mum's swearing.' Mum only swears when she's hideously angry.

'I'm perfectly calm, Paul,' Katia says. 'And Mrs Miller, I have no intention of waiting on Paul hand and foot. I'm not a cleaning lady. He is a grown man and either he pulls his weight or I walk. I don't care if he's the king of Prussia, he helps with the housework, it's as simple as that. Everyone's equal in our house, and that's how we intend to bring up our children.'

'Children?' Mum's voice quivers.

'Wait for it,' Hattie says.

'If we have any,' Paul says quickly.

'Damn,' Hattie says, 'foiled again.'

'What was that?' Mum asks. 'I heard something in the hall.'

Chapter 17

Wake: the waves a boat leaves behind it when moving through the water

The next thing we know Mum is standing in front of us, her shoulders so tense they're almost up to her ears. There are two flaming red spots on her cheeks.

'Move, the pair of you,' she snaps. 'I didn't bring my children up to eavesdrop. Go into your father at once.'

'We weren't eavesdropping,' Hattie says, jutting her chin out. I wouldn't have dared. 'It's not our fault if you were shouting at each other in there.'

Mum opens her mouth to say something. A tiny bead of spittle is sitting on the corner of her upper lip and her eyes are dark with anger. I haven't seen her look this furious for a long time and I've forgotten how scary it is.

'Go on.' Mum tosses her head at the sitting-room door. 'Get!' She turns on her heels and hustles back into the kitchen, closing the door firmly behind her.

'Get?' Hattie says, miffed. 'Who does she think she is? We're not bloody sheepdogs.'

'Better do as she says.' I move towards the living room.

'Shame. It was just starting to get interesting.'

'What's going on in the kitchen?' Dad asks, raising his head from the Dr Seuss book he's been reading to Lily.

'Mum dropped a pan,' Hattie lies smoothly. 'Nothing to worry about.'

'Good.' Dad sticks his head back in the book. I know he realizes there's more to it than that, but he wisely decides not to get involved.

As Lily is being so ably entertained, and Dan is lying on the carpet on his stomach reading about cars, I sit down beside Hattie on the sofa and begin to flick through the Sunday supplements.

'Style magazine, please.' Hattie holds out her hand.

'I've just started reading it.'

'But it's the only bit of the paper I like.' She bats her eyelids at me. 'Pretty please.'

I thrust it into her waiting hands. 'Here. But don't go ripping out any pages until I get a chance to read it.'

'Of course I won't.'

I don't believe her, but I hand it over regardless. My stomach rumbles and I clench my muscles, willing it to stop.

'Lunch is served,' Mum calls from the hall, a little too brightly.

'Thanks heavens for that.' Hattie slaps the magazine closed. 'I'm starving. And Meg's stomach is about to take off from the sound of things.'

Mum places us around the dining-room table. The huge chocolate-coloured mahogany slab has been in Mum's family for donkey's years. It's far too big for the average-sized dining room: you have to wiggle and slide into your seats and once there, getting out again is nigh impossible, but it *is* a grand piece of furniture. It's also more than a little wonky as it sits on a central plinth instead of the more usual four legs, and one of Hattie's ex-boyfriends surfed down the smooth, shiny surface at a party, almost snapping the joint. Dad tried fixing it, but to this day you can't rest your elbows on it without a wobble and you have to put the heaviest object – the turkey or the roast usually – bang in the centre, over the plinth, just in case.

Which is why Dad's upper body is perched over the table, long slim arms hovering over the roast chicken like a praying mantis, preparing to carve.

My mouth waters at the wafts of lemon and garlic coming from the steaming bird. Mum isn't much of a cook, but she has lemon roast chicken down to a T.

Katia is sitting opposite me, beside Paul. Their hands are out of view and when I duck down, ostensibly to pick up my napkin but really to have a look, yes, they are laced together. As I bob up again I smile at Katia in what I hope is a supportive manner – with the prospective mother-in-law from hell she needs all the support she can get.

Mum and Katia seem to have settled their differences for the moment, although Mum is still on edge and the angry spots remain tattooed on her cheeks. She's bustling urgently in and out of the room, bringing dishes of vegetables from the kitchen to the table, fussing with mats and serving spoons.

'Sit down, Hattie,' Mum says. Hattie is on her tippy toes, pressing her palms against the windowsill to push herself up and straining her neck, swan like. 'What on earth are you doing?' Mum demands.

'Does Con next door have a new car? A red one?'

Mum sniffs. 'Yes, silly fool. Ancient Porsche he bought on ebay. It keeps breaking down and yesterday the exhaust fell off. Mona's in despair. She thinks Con's having some sort of mid-life crisis.'

'Hardly a mid-life crisis.' Hattie moves away from the window. 'Unless he expects to live to a hundred and twenty. More like an old-age crisis.'

Mum narrows her eyes. 'Are you calling me old?'

'You're in your prime,' Paul says smoothly. 'Give me that dish and sit down. It all looks delicious.'

'Big lick,' Hattie says under her breath.

'What was that?' Mum asks. She doesn't miss a trick.

'I called Paul a big lick,' Hattie says easily, 'because he is.' She sticks her tongue out at him.

Mum isn't amused. She presses her lips together into a rigid line.

'Let's eat,' Dad says firmly. 'Sit down, Julie. I'll start carving and I need you to pass me the plates.'

Mum doesn't respond.

Dad tries again. 'Julie? Sit down.'

Mum is still glaring at Hattie. 'Yes, yes.' She smooths her pleated cotton skirt down at the back with her hands before sitting. 'I heard you the first time.' She seems a little defeated. Normally she'd give Hattie a right earful for displaying her pointed pink tongue.

Dad and Paul gamely try to keep the conversation on an even keel while we eat, a gargantuan task which Hattie tries to sabotage on more than one occasion by throwing out barbed comments and making controversial statements about everything from politics (Mum hates political talk at the dinner table), to one of her old bugbears, the price of a decent apartment in Dublin. Paul was offered the tenancy of Dad's investment property, a small apartment in Dublin city, before she was, and it still aggravates her to this day. She was sharing a house with a girl from work at the time and Paul was still living at home, so you can see why Dad offered it to him: he was dying to get him out of the house.

Lily is sitting in the ancient metal and plastic high chair, held together by industrial-strength black duct tape. Mum isn't one for throwing anything out, even if it's falling apart. Lily's food antics are gross: flicking peas at Dan, masticating and regurgitating her chicken, like a seagull feeding her chick, and feeding it to Hattie's one-eyed, no-haired Tiny Tears, but at least they keep us all distracted.

Dan does his bit by entertaining us with tales from school – stink bombs, pencils being poked up noses, giggling girls and kiss chase.

'Oh, I used to love kiss chase,' Hattie says dreamily.

'In college?' Paul asks archly.

'Ha bloody ha.' Hattie turns on him. 'So, smart ass, when are you going to tell the parentals your news?'

'After dessert,' I say quickly, remembering the apple pie from the local deli I'd spied earlier on the kitchen table, with its gently browned egg-glazed pastry, skin bumpy with generous lumps of fruit. My mouth waters just thinking about it. 'Isn't that right?' my eyes plead with her.

'Good idea.' Katia lays her hand over Paul's and smiles at him, her eyes softening. 'Let's tell them now.'

Drat. I'll kill Hattie later if I miss out on dessert.

Mum and Dad look at Paul and Katia expectantly.

'You're moving to a new job, is that it?' Dad asks hopefully.

'Moving?' Hattie mutters. 'Off the sofa you mean?'

'Hattie,' Dad warns her.

'Just saying.'

'Don't.'

'Sorry.' She clatters her knife and fork together on her plate and sits back, arms folded over her chest. When she does that she looks just like mum, I realized with a start, who is sitting in exactly the same self-protecting manner.

'Go on, Paul,' she says unperturbed, 'why don't you put Mum and Dad out of their misery?'

He looks around the table a little nervously. 'Um. Yeah, OK.' He presses his palms against the table top, causing a dangerous wobble, water glasses ringing against wine glasses, plates and dishes sliding towards him. After he's steadied the table, he looks up again. By now he has a captive audience. Even Lily and Dad are watching him.

'I've asked Katia to marry me.' He beams at his bride-to-be. 'And she's said yes. We're going to get married as soon as we can.'

Mum gasps. The colour drains from her face. She stares at Dad wordlessly.

'Congratulations,' Dad manages to say. 'Wonderful news.' He's blinking a lot and appears rather shellshocked.

'Cool!' Dan jumps up and down in his chair. 'Can I be best man?'

'We'll see.' Paul smiles at him. 'Maybe not best man, but you'll be something important, I promise.'

'Pageboy might be better, Dan,' Hattie says. 'Or usher. I'm sure Paul will want one of his crew to be best man, like Dopey or Sneezy.'

'What are you talking about, Hattie?' Dad shakes his head.

'Paul's gang are all named after the seven dwarfs.' Hattie picks up her dessert spoon and turns it over in her hands. 'Didn't you know? Let's hope he doesn't pick Grumpy for all our sakes.'

'Not the seven dwarfs,' Paul says with an exaggerated sigh, 'the seven samurai.'

'Oh, that's OK then.' Hattie gives a snort of laughter. 'So you'll have a guy in a saffron robe brandishing a sword as your best man. I can just see it. The rev in Monkstown church will just love that.'

'Hattie!' Mum stands up.

'What?'

Mum seems lost for words. Her lips are pressed together again and her eyes are flashing. She gathers the plates on the table in front of her, scraping them off into an empty serving dish and clattering them furiously into a pile. I sense she's about to blow. Luckily she just picks the plates up and storms out the door.

'Now look what you've done.' Dad frowns at Hattie.

She turns both palms up. 'What? It's Paul you should be giving out to, not me. He's the one who—'

'Go after her,' he says sharply. 'She's obviously upset.'

'Me?' Hattie blinks at him. 'I don't think that's such a brilliant idea, do you? Meg, you go.'

'I'll go,' Katia offers.

'No,' Hattie and I say simultaneously. Katia has rather missed the point.

I leap to my feet. 'I'll go.'

I find Mum sitting down in one of the kitchen chairs, her head bent over the table, resting in her hands.

'Mum,' I say gently, putting my hand on her shoulder.

She lifts her head. There are tears in her eyes.

'Where have I gone wrong?' her voice hiccups a little. 'If it was Hattie marrying a refugee or you, I could just about cope. But *Paul*.' She gives a throaty sob.

I decide it's not the time to take offence. 'Katia's not a refugee. She's a very bright woman with a master's degree. And she's *good* for Paul.'

'But they're so young.'

'And so in love. He'll be fine. It'll be the making of him, you'll see. If anyone can lick him into shape, Katia can.'

'What if she's only marrying him for a visa or a work permit?'

'Mum, Katia doesn't need a visa or a work permit, Slovakia's in Europe now, remember?'

She shakes her head and wrings her hands together, their heels resting on the table. I notice with a start that there are age spots on the back of them, faint brown splodges on her otherwise pearly skin.

'And as for Hattie,' Mum groans, 'still living at home at her age and not a decent man in sight.'

'Hattie's fine, Mum. When the time's right she'll meet someone. She has no shortage of admirers. She's just not ready for commitment yet. Stop worrying.'

She looks at me, the hazel specks in her irises standing against their darker grey backgrounds, eyeballs still swimmy with tears. 'And *you*, Meg.'

Oh, here we go.

'Having babies left, right and centre. And not a wedding ring in sight.'

'Two babies.' I know she's only lashing out because she's upset but it still hurts.

'Why can't my children just be normal?' She moans.

'We are normal,' I protest.

She rounds on me. 'What's normal about living like you do? Miles away from Simon, leaving the children with no proper father figure.'

'But Sid—'

Her eyes darken. 'Don't get me started on Sid. Why can't you just make some sort of commitment to Simon, a proper commitment? And as for refusing to go on holiday with the poor man—'

I grip the side of the table. 'I *am* going to Cornwall.' I decide for sure right at that moment.

'Really?'

'Yes, yes. Next week.' God help me, if it proves a point to my mother then I'll be the first onto the bloody Air Southwest aeroplane.

Mum seems to pick up a bit. 'That's great.' She stops for a moment. 'And you and Simon could always have a double wedding with Paul and Katia, couldn't you?'

I stifle a snort. 'That's not going to happen. Simon and I are not getting married in a rush.'

'But you will one day? Soon?'

I ignore her question. 'Paul and Katia *are* getting married however. Soon,' I say. 'And I'm afraid you're going to have to accept that.'

'But it doesn't mean I have to like it.'

I say nothing for a moment. Mum is stubborn and I don't want to say the wrong thing. I know I have to tread very carefully.

'Paul deserves to be happy. And Katia makes him happy. We all have to respect that. Can't you just be pleased for him?'

'No, I don't think I can.'

'You're going to have to try.'

There's a rap at the door.

'Yes?' Mum says.

Paul sticks his head into the room. 'Everyone OK in there?'

'Fine.' Mum wipes away her tears with the back of her hand.

'I didn't mean to upset you,' Paul says moving towards her and putting his arm around her shoulder. 'I'm sorry.'

'I'm not upset.' She sits up straighter and tucks her hair behind her ears. 'Just a little surprised that's all. It's all so sudden.'

'I guess. But when you know, you know. And me and Katia are right together.'

'Are you sure? There's no need to rush into anything.' Mum cocks her head to one side. 'Goodness, Paul, she's not pregnant is she?'

I frown at Paul and give a tiny shake of my head. I have a feeling that that particular piece of news might push her over the edge.

'No, no,' he assures her. 'And yes, I'm sure. Dead sure.'

'I'll just go back inside,' I murmur. I figure I'll leave them to it.

As I enter the dining room, Dad, Katia and Hattie all look up expectantly. Dan is nowhere to be seen. He's probably escaped to fry his brains in front of the television again, sensible chap. Lily is gurgling milk in her mouth and spitting it out onto the tray of her high chair. Tiny Tears is on the floor at her feet, covered in stray food.

'Mum's fine,' I say breezily. 'Paul's announcement came as a bit of a shock to her, I think. But she's looking forward to the wedding,' I add. 'A lot.'

'Good.' Katia smiles. 'And you and Hattie will be my bridesmaids. I have no sisters, only brothers. What do you say?'

'Yes!' Hattie shrieks immediately. 'Bridesmaids get the pick of the best-looking men, it's an unwritten rule. Tell me about your brothers, Katia. Any of them single? Do you have any photos?'

Bridesmaid? I'm far too old to be a bridesmaid. I exchange a look with Dad. He gives me an encouraging smile.

'You'll make lovely bridesmaids,' he said. 'Both of you.'

Katia looks at me.

'I'd be honoured,' I manage. The die is cast. Yikes, I'll need to lose my spare stone before the wedding. And as for squeezing myself into a bikini before Cornwall, my stomach lurches just thinking about it.

Chapter 18

Adrift: loose, not attached

I've never seen Dublin Airport so busy. It's teeming with hopeful pasty-faced holiday out-bounders, and tanned, weary-
looking in-bounders wearing sombreros, carrying giant furry
donkeys under their beefy arms. The taxi ride was uneventful –
Lily fell asleep in her car seat which we're schlepping all the
way to Falmouth for the team van on Simon's instructions. I'd
suggested holding Lily on my knee, but Simon was shocked
at my *laissez-faire* attitude to his angel's safety. He's right of
course, but he's not the one travelling with the children and all
their associated paraphernalia. Namely :

1. *One heavy, navy metal-framed car seat. Chosen by Simon naturally.*
   I liked the light plastic sky blue (and cheaper) one myself but I was
   overruled by Simon and the shop assistant.
2. *One heavy navy and grey (spot a theme yet?) full-on pneumatic*
   wheeled pram whose folding mechanism needs a degree in engineering to
   work it. Personally I'd set my sights on a nice neat little buggy with
   small, swivel wheels, ideal for zipping around the shops or the
   supermarket. In red*. But once again, I was overruled.*
3. *One large beige sailing bag with a slight taped-over rip in one corner*

214

containing Lily's bedding and favourite toy dog, Wa-Wa. She refuses to sleep without him.

4 *Lily's pink and green travel cot. I chose this particular piece of equipment so it's blissfully light, reasonably compact and doesn't need brute force to erect it.*

5 *One large black sailing bag containing Dan's and Lily's toys and books.*

6 *Lily's changing bag crammed full with nappies and wipes. I know they probably have nappies in the wilds of Cornwall, but I don't want to take any chances.*

7 *The Miller in-flight entertainment kit: assorted food, toys, books, sweets, etc. Basically anything to keep the kids quiet on the plane.*

8. *And, finally, a large dark blue sailing bag crammed with clothes.*

I've had to limit myself to a very scant, pared-back wardrobe, which was not difficult, to be honest, and Dan would happily wear the same T-shirt and shorts all week given the choice. Lily is a different matter. She's getting desperately fussy about her clothes and will only wear dresses, not trousers or jeans. So I've packed a selection of her favourite outfits, shoes and her beloved wellies of course. There's no telling when she'll refuse to wear her shoes and insist on her wellies, even on the hottest day.

After checking-in, we queue up for the X-ray machines. Lily, freshly awake and refusing to sit in her buggy, is perched on my hip and Dan is carrying the Miller in-flight entertainment kit. The way my life with Simon has panned out, I'm no stranger to flying with Dan and Lily and I've learned to cover every eventuality.

The tan-coloured bag, made by one of Simon's friends from an old sail, is packed full of Lily's travelling essentials, nappies, baby wipes, nappy bags, little plastic bags of food, chopped cucumber rounds, carrot and cheese sticks, browning-at-the-edges apple boats. She never eats any of these of course, but they make me feel virtuous when she tucks into a whole tube of Pringles. At least I'm trying to keep her on the nutritional straight and narrow. But an enclosed metal bird isn't the place to enforce a healthy eating regime with the resulting toddler tantrum, not if I want to stay on speaking terms with the cabin crew or my fellow passengers.

The bag also contains Lily's favourite books: a battered and bitten board book called *Yummy, Yucky*, an ancient copy of Richard Scarry's *Busy, Busy World* which used to be Hattie's, and *Where's Spot?*, a lift-the-flap book which has long ago lost all its flaps. Plus assorted cuddly toys, stacking cups, a ratty old A4 pad and a new box of Crayola chubby crayons.

Dan is content with a Lemony Snicket book and his Game Boy. Easy peasy. I haven't bothered with a book or a magazine for myself, no point with Lily around. But I have rather optimistically packed two new paperbacks with my clothes. No doubt they'll come back unopened, but a girl can dream.

The security officers wave us through the X-ray area, after stopping briefly to pat down Lily's pram and to discuss the Game Boy version of *Destroy All Humans* with Dan. I'm tempted to linger in the brightly lit, hospital-clean cosmetics shopping area but Lily starts niggling. I swap her onto my other hip and we trundle towards gate B. The terminal is heaving and it smells of stale fast food and sweating bodies. I look around for a seat but a buzz of people swarms in front of me, all on the same futile quest.

I spot some space to the right of the departure lounge. 'This way,' I tell Dan, who is pushing the buggy, the in-flight bag sitting in it like a squat, ugly baby. Dan's erratic driving clips several holidaymakers on the heels but I'm past caring. My hips and arms are aching from Lily's dead weight, my mouth is parched dry and I just want to sit down. As I park myself and Lily on the wide ledge in front of a huge plate-glass window, I let out a huge sigh of relief. Finally!

Two hours later I'm *still* sitting down. This time on the aeroplane. Due to some sort of technical glitch which hasn't been properly explained, something to do with the doors apparently, we haven't been able to take off yet. Lily is past merely restless. She's already depleted the emergency Pringle stash and even making Wa-Wa dance and sing wouldn't pacify her. She's more interested in trying to clamber over the seat and hit the tall, poker-necked woman with the bouffant hair sitting in front of us. Unfortunately the woman doesn't have much of a sense of humour and loudly asks one of the air hostesses in a pinched voice if she can change seats.

'I'm being interfered with,' she says to the bemused young woman. I cringe and tell Lily off roundly. The air hostess clips off in her heels and moments later kindly hands me two packets of crisps. I wriggle to get my wallet out of my jeans pocket.

'Don't worry,' she smiles, showing a mouth glittering with metallic braces. 'On the house.'

As you can imagine, I'm heartily relieved when we finally take off.

Simon meets us at Newquay Airport. He waves as we walk through the doors in the small arrivals area. He looks even more tanned than usual, his blue eyes twinkling out at me from his berry-brown face. His hair is bleached light brown and the fine hairs on his arms are white blond.

'Meg. Over here.' He waves again.

I'm so relieved to see him. 'Coming.' As I approach him, pushing the loaded trolley in front of me, I lean over and give him a peck on the cheek. 'Sorry to keep you waiting so long. There was some sort of technical problem and we were grounded in Dublin for hours.'

'I was actually running late myself,' Simon admits. 'I rang the airport to see if your flight had landed and they told me about the delay. I've only been here ten minutes or so.'

'Oh good,' I say a touch drily.

Lily holds her arms out and starts to yell. 'Dada. Dada.' Dan pushes her forwards and backwards in her buggy, but she won't stop.

I bend down and click her out of her buggy. 'Here.' I hand her to Simon. 'You take her. Let's keep moving. If I stop I'll keel over.'

'Difficult flight?'

'You could say that.' I'm still seething from the bouffant woman's put down. After Lily had finished her crisps, she'd started crying, her ears were popping, poor child; it was hardly her fault. But the woman didn't see it that way. She repeated her request to be moved, but the hostess told her there was nothing she could do – as the plane was full. Then Lily started to kick, banging her feet into the woman's seat. When Lily started to throw crushed Pringles from the bottom of the tube into Dan's hair, and he growled at her, making her collapse into giggles and squeal, the woman tutted so loudly I'd finally had enough. When she reached her hand up to call the air hostess again I snapped.

'I'm sorry if my daughter is annoying you,' I said to the woman's back. 'But she's only two. Complain to me, if you must, leave the poor hostess alone.'

The woman turned around and gave me a withering look. Her pale skin was taut on her face and she looked much younger than her crêpey neck implied. She opened her mouth to say something but just then the seatbelt signs pinged on and she closed it again. She turned back wordlessly. I was almost weak with relief when the captain announced he was beginning the descent.

As I left the plane the air hostess gave me a reassuring smile.

'I have a toddler at home,' she told me in a low voice. 'Right little minx he is too. Nightmare to travel with. Far worse than your little poppet.'

'Thanks,' I said gratefully.

The bouffant woman sniffed loudly in front of me. I felt like ramming her in the skinny ass with Lily's restless feet but I refrained.

After I tell him about my ordeal, Simon puts his arm around my shoulders and gives me a firm squeeze. 'Hopefully you'll never see her again. Silly old bat. Now, the van's just outside. Hope it hasn't been clamped. I parked it in the drop-off zone.'

I slap a holiday smile on my face. 'Where's this swimming pool? I'm so sticky I could melt.'

As we bump along the Newquay roads on the way to Falmouth I stare out the window. Cornwall reminds me of West Cork, but with bigger villages and grey stone houses, instead of the smaller candy-coloured painted houses of the Irish villages. Maybe this holiday is just what we need, I think as we wind through a particularly pretty mining village; a chance to be together as a family, a chance to relax and just do nothing.

'The crew are going to dinner in Rick Stein's restaurant tonight,' Simon says as we arch over a humpback bridge, my stomach lurching.

'The fish guy from the telly?'

'Yes. It's in a place called Padstow. Bit of a drive but worth it, I'm told. It's impossible to get a reservation, but Donna pulled some strings.'

'Donna?'

'The boat owner's wife.'

'I thought you said she was called Debra?'

'That was his last wife. Traded her in for Donna. Younger model and all that, but still a "D". Beautiful girl. Probably has the right idea.'

I slap Simon's thigh.

The van slurps sideways as it winds around a tight bend. 'Better slow down a little,' I say, holding onto the armrest as we swerve around another corner. 'No hurry. Unless you want to see the contents of my stomach all over the windscreen.'

'There is, I'm afraid,' Simon says, leaning forward like a rally driver, his hands gripping the wheel determinedly, his eyes glued to the road. 'I have to take a look at one of the halyards before tomorrow morning. It's catching on something in the mast.'

I stare out the side window again. So much for the family holiday – I should have known. There's nothing but short green hedges and unexciting fields, so I flick through the CD case that's resting on the dashboard instead. Pink Floyd, Pink Floyd, Eric Clapton and more Pink Floyd, yuck. Boys' CDs. I drop it in disgust.

'Meg? Are you all right?'

'Sure. Are we bringing Lily and Dan to the restaurant?'

I glance in the rear-view mirror, afraid if I turn my head that Lily will want to get out of her seat. I needn't have worried: she's fast asleep, her sweaty hair matted against the back of the seat. Dan is also snoozing, his head lolling against the headrest, mouth open and dribbling a little. I open my window to give them some air.

'Simon?' I say again. 'The restaurant?'

'I'm afraid it's fully booked. It was such late notice you see. You guys coming, I mean. They don't have space for both of us. I'll stay in the house with you, it'll be a good chance to catch up. Anyway, I'm not sure if taking Lily out to dinner in a nice restaurant is such a good idea.'

'That's OK. You go if you like. I'll babysit.'

'No, I'd prefer to spend the evening in with you.'

I smile at him. 'Thanks.'

A little later we trundle along a short rutted drive, turn a corner and Harbour House appears in front of us.

I gasp. 'Talk about wow factor.'

Simon laughs. 'I knew you'd like it.'

'What's not to like?'

I gaze at the huge, rambling house, painted a stark, eye-searing white. It has a large central block, framed by two double-storey castellated turrets with picture windows on the upper floors opening out onto steel and glass balconies that glint in the sun. To the left, a curved wall snakes away from the main body of the house and an arched door in eggshell blue complete with a halo of light pink rambling rose is cut into its chunky surface.

'What's behind the wall?' I ask.

'The pool, the herb garden, and the servants' quarters.'

'Servants?' I squeak. This gets better and better. Visions of tanned young men in scanty white shorts feeding me peeled grapes by the pool flash through my mind.

'Earth calling Meg.'

I snap out of my reverie. 'Sorry, did you say something?'

'I said I was only joking about the servants. Staff I should have said. A maid and a housekeeper. She's off until tomorrow. Some sort of family bereavement or something. And a couple of nannies.'

I'm taken aback. 'The house comes with its own childminding facilities?' I ask hopefully.

Simon laughs. 'No, no. Some of the women have nannies with them.'

I slide down in my seat and fold my arms across my chest, thinking about what he's just said.

We park and he switches off the van's engine.

'Are you getting out?' he asks. 'What's wrong?'

Lily's eyes flash open and she begins to cry.

'I'll deal with her.' Simon clicks off his seatbelt and climbs out of the van.

I push my head back into the headrest and squeeze my eyes shut. What am I doing? I should never have agreed to come here. Nannies! I'm way out of my league. Why did I let Simon talk me into this? But it wasn't Simon's fault, not really. If I hadn't been so eager to prove Mum wrong. I'm my own worst enemy.

'Where are we?' Dan interrupts my musings.

I open my eyes, turn and smile at him through the gap in the front seats. 'I have no idea,' I murmur.

He squints at me. 'Huh?'

'Harbour House.' I recover myself. 'In Cornwall. Remember? Let's go and find that swimming pool.'

The house is just as amazing inside. All the interior walls are white, posh Farrow and Ball white, no doubt. There's an enormous dining room to the left of the hall containing the biggest table I've ever seen outside a stately home or a hotel. It's gargantuan, a huge rectangular slab of dark conker-coloured wood so shiny you can see your face in it. It seats sixteen; Dan counts the red leather high-backed chairs just to make sure.

There's a large L-shaped kitchen off the dining room, complete with a racing-green double Aga, more Nigella Lawson eggshell-blue crockery than I've ever seen in one place before, dinky little oval mixing bowls that fit into each other like Russian dolls, neat lemon squeezers, tubby storage jars with their old-fashioned metal and rubber clasps that always remind me of the Dutch beer we used to drink in college. I'm gobsmacked. Even the kitchen is like something out of *Elle Decoration*.

I breathe it all in, eyes out on stalks like a child in a sweetshop. I've always dreamed of having a house like this.

'Hi there,' an American voice trills from behind the enormous brushed-steel larder fridge. A tiny woman in her mid twenties pops her head around the door. She's wearing cut-off denim shorts, a white T-shirt with some sort of green stain on her left breast, and blue beaded flip-flops.

'Hey, you must be Meg.' She wipes her hands on the bum of her shorts and gives me a surprisingly firm hug.

'Lovely to meet you,' I say, a little taken aback by the warm greeting.

She draws away. 'I'm Pat, short for Patricia. The boys call me Pixie, but I prefer Pat. I'm the general dogsbody. This house is something else, isn't it?' She beams at me, her nose scrunching up a little. 'Best-equipped kitchen I've ever worked in. Plenty of space too. I'm used to galleys on boats and believe me, it's hard to knock up a three-course meal for twelve hungry sailors in a space no bigger than your average armpit.'

I laugh. I like Pat already. She has an easy manner you can't help but warm to. It doesn't occur to me to be shy with her. Her sandy-blonde hair is tied back with a piece of grimy ribbon and the bridge of her snub nose is peppered with pinhead-sized freckles.

'And where's the lovely Simon?' she asks, looking around.

'Showing Dan his room. Dan's my son.'

'I've heard all about the kids. Simon never stops talking about them.' Pat winks at me. 'That man's a keeper. You're lucky. Some of the rest of the other guys on the boat are arrogant shits, if you'll pardon my French. And as for some of their wives, not mentioning any names, *ooh la la*.' Both her eyebrows rise dramatically.

'Really?' This doesn't sound good.

'Sorry, I shouldn't have opened my big, fat mouth. Forget it. Hey, I'm Irish too, my mom moved over to Boston in her twenties. She's a Sullivan from Kilkenny. How about that?'

I nod, not knowing quite what to say.

'I see you've met Pat.' Simon walks in with Lily on his hip and Dan following behind him with a long face.

'What's up, Dan?' I ask.

'There are two women sunbathing beside the swimming pool. One of them said I can't swim until after five. And I'm boiling.'

I look at Simon. 'Why?'

'Kids' pool time is between eleven and twelve, and five and six apparently.'

'What? Says who?' I'm getting a little irate now. I'm relying on the swimming pool to keep Dan away from his Game Boy.

Pat snorts. 'That would be either Donna or Mary.' Pat looks at Dan. 'Tall, skinny woman with dark hair and a gold bikini?'

Dan nods. 'That's the one.'

'Donna then. She rules the roost.'

'But what about the other children?' I ask. 'Surely they want to swim?'

'Donna doesn't have kids and Mary has a full-time nanny, Caga. Lovely girl, Aussie. All the kids are at the beach with Caga and the other mums. You should hang out with them. Far more fun than sunbathing with the rich bitches.' She puts her hand to her mouth. 'Oops, sorry, Dan.'

'That's OK. They are bit—'

'Dan,' I warn him. 'Why don't you go upstairs and have a rest?' I look at my watch. 'Another hour and it'll be pool time.'

'All right,' he says grudgingly.

'Let's go outside and I'll introduce you to Donna,' Simon says after Dan has left the kitchen. He moves Lily onto his other hip and she giggles as Pat tickles her bare toes.

'Do I *have* to?' I ask a little trenchantly.

He nods. 'Rude not to.'

'See you later then, Pat,' I say, reluctant to leave the safety of the kitchen. 'And if you need any help, I'm not too bad at cutting things up. Or stirring.'

Pat laughs. 'Hey, thanks. I might just take you up on that. I get kinda bored in here on my own. One of the men likes to keep me company while I'm cooking dinner in the evenings but I don't think his motives are all that honourable to be honest.' She lowers her voice. 'He pinched my bum last night.'

'No!'

'Hey, I just waved a carving knife at him and he got the message.'

'I'm sure he did. It wasn't Slipper by any chance?'

'Slipper, na. It was the owner, Nick.'

'No!'

Pat looks at Simon. 'Not a word to the others, you hear?'

'My lips are sealed,' he promises.

'There's lots of fancy wine in the fridge.' Pat grins at me. 'I'll pour you a large glass and you can have it after meeting the princesses. You'll need it.'

'Cheers, Pat.'

'She's great,' I whisper to Simon as we walk through the long living room on the way to the swimming pool. There are immaculate chocolate-brown leather module sofas running down two of the walls, enough seating for a small army. The room is dominated by a cinema-sized flat-screened television.

'*Shrek* will look great on that,' I say.

Simon gives a laugh. 'You're right.'

I can see the pool through the enormous plate-glass windows at the far end of the room. Lying by it are two women. Although women isn't really the appropriate term for them. One is a gazelle-limbed bean pole, the other a more voluptuous, golden-haired woman with sleek, groomed, movie-star looks.

'Simon,' I hiss, 'you didn't tell me they're models.'

'They're not. Donna was but she retired when she married Nick. I doubt Mary works, her husband's loaded. He owns a huge contract-cleaning company. She's from Belfast originally – you'll like her.'

I stare at the women. If Donna is the one in gold, then Mary is the voluptuous one in a black cut-away swimsuit.

As we walk closer my eyes linger on Mary. Her stunning strawberry-blonde hair fans out behind her on the white lounger cushion like a golden arc. Her skin is lightly tanned and she has a slightly crooked aristocratic nose. She's reading a

highbrow novel but as soon as we walk onto the creamy marble tiles of the courtyard she puts her book down and sits up,
pushing her sunglasses onto the top of her head.

'Hey, Simon, is this Meg? And Lily?'

'Hi, Mary.' Simon pulls me by the hand towards her. 'Yes,
these are my girls.'

'Hey, Donna, wake up,' Mary says to her dozing friend.

Donna, who looks like a young Catherine Zeta Jones, sits up.
I'm dismayed to see that her stomach stays taut even when she
bends forwards. Mine doesn't even look toned when I'm lying
down. Damn. I'll look like a heffalump in my new blue flowery
tankini. I'll just have to stay entombed in my sarong, or avoid
the pool completely. Maybe I can invent a chlorine allergy?

'Hello,' Donna says, getting to her feet. She towers over me,
all six-foot something of her.

'Nice to meet you, darling,' she says, holding out her hand.
It's hot, sticky and limp. I try not to wince.

'Welcome to my little summer house.' She waves her hand in
the air regally. 'Do you like it?'

'You own this place?' I said before I could stop myself. 'I
thought it was rented.'

She blinks and gives me a look. Oops, maybe rented is the
wrong word.

'Nick takes it every year,' she tells me. 'Timeshare. We live in
Chelsea.'

'It's stunning,' I gush, trying to make up for my faux pas.
'Amazing. You're so lucky. And I met Pat too.'

'Pat?' Donna lifts her mane of hair off the back of her neck
and then lets it drop again in a waft of expensive shampoo. My
own minty Head and Shoulders doesn't have quite the same
effect, I suspect.

'Your cook?' I clarify.

Donna laughs, the skin on her face barely moving. Surely
she's a little young for Botox? 'Oh, you mean Pixie. Pixie's the

maid. She's just helping out while Mrs Pilks is away. She's not a bad cook, but she does chatter on a bit.'

'I like her.' I jut my chin out. 'I'm looking forward to a swim in the pool.' I almost add, with my children, but I stop myself. No point in making an enemy so early in the holiday. I should give her a chance.

'Haven't been in myself.' Donna preens her hair. 'Not much of a swimmer.' She turns towards Mary, who's watching with interest from the safety of her sunlounger.

'Hey, Mary's Irish too, so I'm sure you'll get along.' Donna gives a strangled squeak. 'But she's from Northern Ireland, that's different isn't it? I hope you girls won't fight. Politics and all that. You're not in the IRA, Meg, are you?'

Mary gives a healthy snort. 'Of course she's not. They're a terrorist organization, Donna, not a political party.'

Simon puts a calming hand on my shoulder.

'We'll try to be civil to each other, Donna,' I say through gritted teeth.

Donna waves her hands in the air again and gives a tinkle of laughter. 'All that political nonsense goes way over my head. I've no interest in any of it. Nick doesn't even like me watching the news. I find it all terribly upsetting – all those famines and floods and everything. Nick says I'm just a very sensitive person.'

I stare at Donna, longing for Hattie. She'd know exactly how to deal with this supercilious airhead. I'm lost for words. Simon's hand massages my left shoulder and the base of my neck.

Donna continues oblivious. 'So, Meg, have you brought anything fabulous to wear for our little party? Mary made her own dress, imagine that? What a little Martha Stewart, eh?'

'Oh, stop going on about it, Donna.' Mary smiles at me. 'And I didn't make it, I altered it. It's hardly brain surgery.'

'But, darling, it's just so unusual. On your own, without a dressmaker.'

'To you, maybe,' Mary says. 'Not to normal mortals like myself. Hey, Donna, I even clean my own house sometimes. And I do my own nails.'

Donna gasps, her hands rising automatically to her mouth.

Yes, I think. An ally. Things are looking up.

Chapter 19

Fathom: six feet

'I can't believe you didn't tell me about the party,' I say, rounding on Simon as soon as our bedroom door is closed.

'I'm sorry. I didn't think it was important.'

'No, I'm sorry. I'm being petty.' I flop down on the king-size bed, the plump feather-filled duvet deflating under my bum with a whispery sigh. 'It's just Donna,' I admit, 'she makes me feel inadequate.'

'She's quite something all right.' He sits down beside me. Lily is checking out her travel cot from the inside, happily placing Wa-Wa on her pillow and arranging her other cuddly toys against the mesh sides. She's sharing our large airy room on the first floor of Harbour House's left turret, opposite Donna and Nick's room. Dan's room is just beside us, smaller than ours with a French-style white queen-size bed, eggshell-blue curtains and matching upholstered chair.

Lily and Dan are the only children sleeping in the left turret, Simon told me on the way up the stairs. All the others are in the main block or the right turret. Which means I have to keep Lily quiet in the wee small hours and stop Dan bouncing on his bed at six in the morning. From the look of her, I'd say Donna really, really likes her beauty sleep.

I rub my temples. I'm in way over my head and I know it. I'll never survive a week with Donna unless I come up with a strategy. Women like her are just plain mean to women like me. Normal women. Mere mortals as Mary would say. I've come across more than my fair share of trophy wives in my day and they're a breed apart. They're the school bullies who've married rich, who have clawed their way to the top of the food chain and are determined to stay there, whatever the cost. I think they're terrified of losing their newly found place in society, poor deluded creatures. It *is* built on fairly shaky foundations after all – a nice pair of boobs, a pretty face, a slim, toned body. All these things fade and they've witnessed their predecessor, no slouch in her own day, being booted out the door and know damn well they'll be next in line unless they dig their claws in.

Even producing sprogs is no guarantee of keeping their man. I know one owner Simon has sailed for who has eleven children by three different wives and an ex girlfriend.

Trophy sailing wives see me as a threat, Lord knows why. My highlights are halfway down my scalp, I haven't shaved my legs in a week, my fake tan is blotchy around my ankles and my wardrobe is Primark rather than Prada, but I don't buy into the sailing-world pecking order, never have. I'll happily chat away to the waitress in the yacht club and invite her children to come and play with Dan and Lily in the hotel pool. The other women don't like this one little bit. Upsets the natural order of things, they think.

And as for some of their husbands! I remember one English guy in his forties, Lewis, a millionaire who'd made his money in hire cars, telling me proudly during Antigua Week that he'd never changed a nappy in his life and never intended to. When he saw my shocked face he said, 'My wife rarely changes nappies either. She's afraid of getting baby poo under her nails. Not surprised. They cost enough. Top of the range gel ones. Gets them done by a Filipino girl every week.'

I need a plan. And quick. For the second time that afternoon I wish Hattie was with me.

At five o'clock on the dot Dan jumps into the pool, sending a huge splash of water slurping onto the marble tiles. I cheer. 'Nice belly flop, Dan,' I say as he surfaces.

He shakes his head and wipes the water out of his eyes with his arm. 'That was a dive, Mum, not a belly flop.'

Caga, Mary's nanny, an athletic Australian girl in her early twenties with a strangely flat face and a button nose, cute rather than pretty, gives a yell, holds her nose and jumps in beside Dan. She's the only nanny here. One of the other mothers, Susan, has one but has given her the week off, so I feel a lot less out of place than I thought I would.

'Caga!' Dan complains. 'You nearly hit me.'

'Tough.' Caga splashes him with her hands. 'Deal with it. Are you getting in, Meg?'

'No. I think I'll just watch. The pool's busy enough without me.' I'm on a sunlounger enjoying the rest. Lily is upstairs taking a nap, still wiped out from the journey and the heat. It's surprisingly warm, much warmer than in Dublin which is a huge bonus.

Four excited and shrieking children are already splashing in the water with their mums or nanny. I can't remember all the children's names, even though they've all been pointed out to me.

Roberta, another of the sailing wives (married to Alistair, a bit public school for my taste but a nice enough man), is sitting on a sunlounger beside me. She's refreshingly normal-looking after Donna and Mary, with a friendly face, a sunburnt and peeling nose and long light brown hair tied back in a ponytail.

She's wearing a red vest top and a pair of combat shorts and her flip-flops look almost as old as mine. Her son, Jason, who's almost one, is nuzzled on her shoulder, napping.

I ask Roberta to tell me the children's names again and she kindly obliges.

'Mary's little girl is the one with the mop of curly black hair – Matilda or Tilly for short – she's five,' she lowers her voice. 'Bit of a madam. And her brother, Shane, the red-haired lad,' she points at a boy who is spitting water out his mouth, 'is seven and a handful. Caga's their nanny. Fab girl. The perfect-looking blond boy with the tan is Susan's son, Zac. He's eight and very much an only child.'

Susan is tall, with wide, muscular shoulders. Her hair is pushed under her cap and she's wearing a sporty navy Speedo swimsuit. She's swimming alongside Zac, coaching his splashy breaststroke.

'Breathe,' she tells Zac. 'Pull harder with your arms. Breathe!'

'Susan takes her swimming quite seriously,' Roberta comments. 'She was a pretty hot dinghy sailor in her time, did two Olympic trials but she gave it up when she had Zac.' She lowers her voice again. 'IVF,' she whispers.

I find out Susan is married to Dean Kelly, an ex-Olympic sailor turned motivational speaker. I remember Dean because he's a hulk of a man, six feet eight no less, with a huge mouth that could hold a dinner plate. He makes Simon look Lilliputian. Won a gold medal for Great Britain in the Sydney Olympics in the Star boat, no less. Obviously Susan is as competitive as her husband.

We watch the swimmers for a few minutes, and bask in the late-afternoon sun. The air is heady with delicious minty scents, wafting over from the herbs at the far end of the large walled garden.

'What are you wearing this evening?' Roberta asks after a

while. 'Is it dressy? Will I get away with black trousers do you think?'

'I don't know,' I say honestly. 'We're not going. There's no room, the restaurant's fully booked.'

Roberta says nothing for a moment. 'You know, they managed to squeeze in one of Donna's friends and her actor husband only this afternoon. Donna made Caga pretend to be her PA and ring the restaurant. I'm only telling you so you understand what Donna's like.'

'I see.' I feel about an inch high. 'I'm clearly not glitzy enough to be in her gang.'

'Forget about Donna,' she says. 'You're worth ten of her.'

'Thanks,' I say, touched. 'And what about Mary? She seems nice.'

'Humm.' Roberta seems unconvinced. She shifts Jason, who's now awake, onto her knee. 'It's always the quiet ones,' she says a little cryptically. 'Duty calls.' Jason bangs his head against her breast. She lifts her top, sits back and starts to feed him.

'Who's organic, but doesn't eat red meat?' Pat asks brandishing a plate. We're all sitting at the large oak table in the kitchen surrounded by assorted children. Except Donna and Mary, of course.

'Me,' Susan says.

'Hawiian chicken with sweetcorn.' Pat puts a plate down in front of Zac with a flourish. Susan hovers behind him, cutting up his chicken and pouring him more orange juice from the jug on the table.

A moment later Pat comes back from the Aga with a copper saucepan. 'Vegetarian, organic, pureed?'

'Me,' Roberta says.

'Vegetarian goulash.' Pat ladles a dollop of brown goo onto Jason's plastic Thomas the Tank plate.

'Atkins diet?' Pat asks.

'No!' I say in shock. 'You're not serious?'

Pat gives a hoot of laughter. 'Not quite.' She winks at me. 'Low-carb, high-protein, organic?' she calls out.

'Me,' Caga says, raising her hand and waving it in the air. She leans over towards me, lowering her voice. 'Unfortunately. Poor children. Mary thinks they're a little chubby. I keep telling her it's only puppy fat, they'll grow out of it, but she doesn't listen.'

I'm genuinely shocked. At both Mary's attitude and at the amount of work it causes Pat. It's just as well their parents are going out to dinner. I'd hate to think how many she has to cook for normally.

'We usually cook for the children ourselves,' Roberta says, reading my mind. 'But Pat offered tonight as all the adults are out for dinner. Oh, sorry, Meg, I forgot you're not going.'

'That's OK,' I say easily.

'I'm not sure if I'm going either,' Susan says, a deep frown creasing her forehead. 'Zac's not used to strangers babysitting.'

Caga smiles at him. 'I'm not all that strange, am I, Zac?' She makes her eyes squint and he laughs. 'Go on,' she says to Susan. 'He'll be fine.'

'But Zac's—'

'Eight,' Caga finishes for her. 'And we have the movie all planned, don't we Zac?'

Zac stares down at his plate.

Caga ruffles his immaculate blond hair which Susan must have blow dried. All the other children still have damp heads.

'What movie?' Susan asks.

'The first Harry Potter. Zac says he's dying to see it.'

Susan purses her lips. 'Zac doesn't like scary films like that, do you, poppet? He likes Disney films.'

Caga raises her eyebrows but says nothing.

'What about *Shrek*?' I suggest. 'Dan likes that. It's good fun.'

'I'd prefer it if Zac read,' Susan says. 'He's working his way through the Narnia series,' she adds proudly.

'Mum,' Zac pipes up, 'please?'

'We'll talk about it after your tea.'

When Susan isn't looking, Caga winks at him and he gives her a shy smile. Caga then picks a piece of chicken breast off Shane's plate and pops it into her mouth.

'Hey!' he protests.

'Mum thinks you're fat,' Tilly says to her brother, a sneer on her face. 'Maybe you shouldn't eat so much.'

'Tilly,' Pat said, 'that's not very nice. He's not fat at all.'

'Yeah, right.' Tilly pushes her plate away from her. 'And that chicken is barf. I want something else.'

Pat puts her hands on her hips. 'Oh, really?'

Caga jumps to her feet, sensing trouble. 'I'll do it,' she tells Pat.

'It better be organic,' Tilly says, tossing her blonde hair back, looking remarkable grown-up for a five-year-old. 'You know what Mum's like.'

'Yes, yes,' Caga mutters barely audibly. 'Organic, I'll give you organic. You're lucky to have food.'

'And what will your two eat?' Pat asks me. 'I'm sorry, I haven't made them anything yet.'

'Oh, whatever you have,' I say. 'They're not fussy.'

'Have you any chips?' Dan asks. 'Or sausages?'

Pat grins. 'I might have some special supplies hidden away. You never know. I might just have some chips in the oven.'

'Chips?' Tilly sits up in her chair. 'Can I have some?' She seems highly excited, her eyes are shining and she's licking her lips.

'No, Tilly,' Pat says. 'I'm so sorry. You know what your mother's like.' She gives Tilly a smug grin.

'I want chips,' Tilly shrieks. 'I'll scream if you don't give me chips.'

'Like the girl from *Just William*,' Dan says. 'Violent Elizabeth.' We sometimes listen to *Just William* stories in the car. They're Simon's favourite.

'Violet Elizabeth,' I correct him with a smile.

Tilly, livid at being ignored, starts to scream. Dan puts his mouth to her ear and screams even louder. She stops immediately, shocked into submission. She looks at him with a mixture of scorn and admiration.

'Can you come back to London with us?' Caga calls over from the open fridge. 'I could use a boy with your talents.'

Dan smiles. 'Can I have some chips first?'

'Course you can.' Pat laughs. 'You must be starving after all that swimming. And Lily's being very quiet.'

'That's because she's helping Zac with his chicken,' I point out. Lily reaches across and takes yet another piece of Zac's dinner.

Caga plonks two plates in front of Tilly and Shane.

'What's this?' Shane asks, prodding some pink meat with his finger.

'Organic ham,' Caga says. 'Potato salad and grated cheese. Just eat it,' she adds sternly.

Shane jumps to his feet, his face red. 'I'm not eating *that*. It's cold. There's some steak in the fridge. Call me when it's ready. And don't burn it again.' He stalks off and a moment later we can all hear the drone of the television from the sitting room.

'And I want chips,' Tilly says, glaring at Caga.

Caga sighs. 'Anyone want a job?'

Later that evening, I'm sitting in the living room with Simon when Donna clicks down the bare wooden stairs like an exotic stick insect dressed in all her finery. Simon is freshly showered and the ends of his hair are still damp and curling into the nape of his neck. My legs are thrown over his solid thighs and we're sipping wine companionably.

When the Boys Are Away

Donna is wearing a silver dress made of a heavy material that slides over her body when she moves. It's low cut, with tiny spaghetti straps, her pert breasts poking out of the viscous material likes two small, firm melons. I didn't notice earlier, but her cleavage looks a little strange, her breasts seem to have a definite edge to them and I wonder if they're implants. It wouldn't surprise me.

I remove my gaze from her chest, aware that I'm staring, and look at her shoes instead. Silver peep-toes with skyscraper heels and red Laboutin soles. I know my shoes from Tina's extensive collection. When I'm feeling down, she kindly lets me slip them on and parade around on her bedroom carpet. Sadly Tina's a size four, I'm a five, so wearing them outside her bedroom is out of the question unless I cut some of my toes off. And, believe me, I've been tempted.

I swivel around and tuck my own rather grubby plastic flip-flops (free with *Elle* magazine) under my thighs.

'Simon,' Donna trills as she threads a rock of Gibraltar sized diamond stud earring into her right earlobe. 'My dear friends Blossom and Jude have cancelled. Meeting with a Hollywood agent or something. *Very* tedious.' She waves her hand in front of her face. 'Nick's invited Paul Knox-Davis, but we have room for one more if you want to come.'

'And Meg?' Simon asks.

'Oh, we could probably squeeze her in at a pinch.'

Donna gives my thighs the once over. Silly cow. OK, so they're not exactly svelte, but they're not that bad. And do tell us about the cancellation now, just as you're about to leave.

Simon sits up a little. He's gawking at Donna. '*The* Paul Knox-Davis. The America's Cup skipper?' There's no hiding the interest in his voice. Even *I* know who Paul Knox-Davis is: only the most successful and the most famous skipper in the business and Simon's hero.

237

'We should definitely go.' Simon looks at me beseechingly. 'I'm sure Caga will keep an eye on the kids.'

'I don't know,' I say. 'I'm kind of tired—'

'That's settled then.' Donna says with a tight smile. 'You stay here and rest, Meg. Simon can come with us. There are two taxis already outside waiting.'

I'm not all that impressed with her tone, or her suggestion, but I don't want to cause a scene. Besides, I know Simon will talk sailing all night with Paul and the rest of the crew and I don't relish being stuck beside Donna for the duration.

'Are you sure?' he asks me.

I can see the anticipation on his face. 'Go on,' I say with a smile.

'Thanks, Meg. I'd better go upstairs and change.' Simon jumps to his feet and looks down at his shorts and sailing runners.

Donna waves her hand in the air, her chunky silver Tiffany's bracelet clunking on her slim wrist. 'You're fine. With the amount of money Nick will be shelling out tonight, you could arrive in a chicken suit and they wouldn't care.'

I wince. Nice attitude, Donna, I think. Can you *be* more crass? Bet you click your skinny fingers at the waiting staff too.

'Are you coming, Meg?' Mary wiggles down the stairs in a tight black satin dress, emphasizing her hourglass figure. Beside Donna, she looks all woman. 'It won't be the same without you.'

'I'm going to stay here, but thanks for asking. It's nice to feel wanted.' I look at Donna, labouring the point a little, but I don't care.

So an hour later, I'm watching television alone in my room, lying on my stomach on the bed. As *ER*'s credits roll, I push myself up and look around. Personally, I think whoever's put together the room has gone a little overboard with the finishing touches. The bed's headboard is upholstered in dark green silk, studded with tiny pearl buttons; there are matching upholstered chairs opposite it, a mouldy-green coloured distressed chest of drawers, complete with fake woodworm holes, clear Perspex bedside tables with horribly pointy edges, and the *pièce de résistance*, an enormous ceramic chandelier-style light over the bed, complete with 'leaves' that unfurl when you switch the bulb on and close up tightly like a bud when you switch it off. Dan has already played with it for ages, entertaining Lily while I unpacked.

The en suite is fit for Julius Caesar himself, wall-to-wall soapy-to-the-touch Travertine marble with a huge oval tub under the window, a walk-in shower with dark pebbles set into the floor to massage your feet and the largest showerhead I've ever seen.

I'm not quite tired enough to go to sleep and I don't feel like reading either, my mind is too restless. Suddenly I have a delicious thought. Donna's out, Caga and Pat are busy downstairs, Dan is in his room, exhausted from travelling and from his splashy lengths of the pool. If he's only allowed in the water for a limited time each day, he reasons, he's going to make the most of it. So avoiding the babies and toddlers, he wove up and down the pool for almost an entire hour with his emerging front crawl.

So I could . . . No, Meg, I tell myself. It's not right. Then Donna's whippet-thin face floats in front of my eyes, her fake boobs, cutting comments, tight smile and condescending manner. Why the hell not? I decide boldly. I glance at Lily who's snoring quietly, more of a rattle than a real snore, an arm tossed around Wa-Wa, a bare leg thrown out from under the towel. It's too warm for her duvet, so I've improvised with a bath sheet.

I walk out of the room and close the door gently behind me. My heart is hammering in my chest and I feel deliciously wicked.

Chapter 20

Avast: a command which means
'Stop what you're doing'

I step slowly towards the door of Donna and Nick's bedroom, wooden floor cool and slightly tacky under my bare feet. I reach out my hand, touch the chrome door handle and then draw back as if I've been electrocuted. What if I'm being watched? What if this house has some sort of state of the art alarm system and my every move is being recorded?

I look around, studying the white walls, picture rails and ceiling. Nothing. I'm being paranoid. But better safe than sorry. I'll cover my tracks – starting with my fingerprints. I wiggle my hand under my saggy pyjama top and stretch it out towards the knob. I press down tentatively, half expecting to set off an alarm, but nothing happens. The door swings open. Immediately there's a heady sweet smell of expensive perfume. Bingo! Donna's boudoir.

I step in and close the door, unable to take my eyes away from the enormous bed in the centre of the floor. It's surrounded by an elaborate iron frame, draped with yards and yards of off-white muslin. Over the foot of the bed is what looks like a real fur throw. Ocelot no less. Tina has an ocelot coat that her granny left her – not that she ever wears it. It sits in her walk-in wardrobe in its posh leather suit bag. She hasn't the heart to get rid of it.

Dan did a project on endangered animals, big cats in particular, for school last year and informed us that it took up to twenty ocelots to make one fur coat. Donna's throw is far bigger than a coat. I hope to goodness it isn't real fur, but I'm too scared to reach out and stroke it just in case.

The bedroom is immaculate. There isn't a pillow out of place, let alone a messy pile of shoes, a dirty towel bundled in the corner or a heap of discarded clothes draped over the chair. Hell, there isn't even a hairdryer or a shopping bag on view. It's not natural. The opulent black silk curtains are still wide open and at the far end of the room there's a door, to the en suite no doubt. I feel a wave of excitement. Sad I know, but I can't help myself. I just have to know what a woman like Donna uses on her skin.

Walking into the bathroom I gasp. It's amazing, a riot of creamy marble, with a glass-enclosed walk-in shower with space-age nozzles angled in every direction, an enormous double curvy-ended bath with striking geometric chrome fittings, and a marble counter with two sinks cut into the surface. I want it; it's my dream bathroom. And spilling all over the marble counter is a sea of beauty products, acres of pots and jars and at least seven different perfume bottles.

I lap up all the labels – la Prairie, Prada, Eve Lom – and I haven't even moved on to the make-up yet. My own tatty washbag contains one almost empty bottle of Johnson's Holiday Skin, a Clinique moisturizer that Hattie gave me for my birthday, Boot's cleanser, and cottonwool robbed from Lily's changing bag. A far cry from Donna's hoard. Imagine having the money to buy any beauty product your heart desired. What must that be like? I'm unlikely to ever find out.

Does it bother me? I'm ashamed to say that, yes, at this precise moment it bothers me a lot.

Donna's large bright pink make-up bag is open and I poke my fingers into it, flicking through the lipsticks, eyeshadows and blushers. A make-up brush tickles my fingers and I jump. Calm down, I tell myself. Stop right there, my prissier inner conscience says, rummaging through other people's things is despicable. I begin to feel slightly dirty. I take one last look at the beauty treasures, and then my eye catches on something. A large lurid pink thing, hanging in the shower. I walk towards the glass and peer in. It's a bubblegum-coloured Hello Kitty showercap. Then I look back at the pink make-up bag. Same pink Hello Kitty design. Donna also has a matching Hello Kitty electric toothbrush and hair dryer. How sad is that? I walk out of the bathroom smiling to myself.

But I am a little disappointed to tell the truth. What did I expect to find? Jars of lizard tongues? Pots of anti-ageing cream made from stem cells? Syringes labelled Botox? I'd found nothing incriminating at all. Just a mild kitten fetish. I leave the bedroom feeling strangely flat. I step out of the room, turning to close the door behind me.

'What are you doing?'

My hand jumps off the door handle as if scalded and I whip around. Luckily it's only Dan.

'What are you doing?' he repeats.

'I thought I heard something.' I check I've closed the door properly and push him down the corridor by the shoulders.

'What was it?'

'Nothing. I must have been imagining things.'

Dan cocks his head to one side and smiles at me. 'You were snooping, weren't you, Mum?'

'Of course not!' I try to sound suitably indignant.

But Dan's not going to give up that easily. 'Remember the time Simon caught you going through his wallet?'

'I was looking for a receipt.' At times I wish Dan didn't notice so much.

'And the time Granny Maureen found you wearing her pearl necklace and—'

'Yes, yes.' I cut him off. I can feel my face redden. I'd rather not re-live that particular incident. I'd sworn after that never again to nose around other people's belongings. Ever. Best-laid plans and all that.

'And why are *you* roaming the halls?' I ask, eager to deflect his attention.

'I woke up.' He brushes his sticky hair back off his face. 'I'm hot. I was going to get a glass of water in your bathroom but you weren't there, so I went to look for you.'

'Well, the noise seems to have gone now,' I say, briskly, moving towards the stairs. 'I'll get you a glass of water from the kitchen. Go back to bed.'

As I tramp down the stairs I feel ashamed. I'm such a bad role model.

I'm woken in the early hours of the morning by a sudden dead weight across my chest. I open my eyes. Simon is spreadeagled on top of the covers, fully clothed, breathing heavily.

'Simon,' I mutter, lifting his arm off me and giving his body a shove with my shoulder. He murmurs something under his breath.

'What?' I say a little irritably, cross at being woken up.

'Sailing for my country. Huge honour.' He begins to hum what sounds like 'Rule Britannia'.

'What are you on about?'

He snaps open his eyes and gives me a bleary grin. 'Oh, hi, Meg? What are you doing here?'

I sigh. There's no talking to him when he's like this. 'Move over, you big eejit. And roll onto your side or you'll snore all night.'

'OK.' He rolls over to face me and immediately falls asleep.

I lie there listening to Lily's breath whistling in and out and Simon's heavier, more laboured breathing. I suddenly miss home, grotty bathroom, overgrown garden, leaky roof and all. At least at home I can go and sleep on the sofa.

When I finally get back to sleep I dream I'm back in first year in school, being taunted by the school bullies for wearing a vest instead of a bra.

Chapter 21

Bitter end: the last part of a rope or chain

The following morning, the sun is beaming through the cracks between the Roman blinds and the window frames. I'm relieved. It's far easier to entertain Dan and Lily when the sun is out. I look at my watch. Almost nine. Jeepers, a lie-in. How exciting! Simon left over an hour ago to go sailing, but Lily isn't in her cot: I'd better go and look for her. I drag myself up, pull my saggy-bottomed pyjamas back onto my waist from around my hips, rub my eyes and comb my hair back from my face with my fingers.

As I walk out of the room I hear voices from outside. The double doors onto the balcony are open so I step out onto the large wooden and glass platform. I stick my head over the side and peer down. The voices stop instantly and two pairs of eyes stare up at me, taking in my bedraggled state. Donna and Mary, both looking as fresh as designer-bouquet daisies. Mary is immaculately dressed in a crisp sky-blue cotton sundress, and Donna's wearing a white crochet bikini top and tiny white shorts. I cringe inwardly, cursing my old pink cotton pyjamas.

'Why don't you get dressed and join us?' Donna shades her

eyes with her hand. 'Or is that a tracksuit you're wearing? Pixie made some delicious smoothies earlier. You have to try one.'

'Have you seen Lily?' I ask Donna.

She looks a little puzzled.

'My daughter?' I prompt.

'The kids have all gone to the beach with Caga and the others. Did Lily go with them, Mary?'

'Yes, I think so. And Dan too.'

At least Mary remembers his name. My hands grip the wooden rail of the balcony tightly. 'But what about their swimsuits and towels? And Lily needs her sunhat.'

'I'm sure they organized all that,' Donna says. She doesn't seem all that interested.

'Are you joining them after breakfast?' I ask hopefully, directing my question at Mary. The beach sounds like a great plan on such a lovely day.

Mary laughs. 'We're going to the spa. Donna's booked us both in for the whole day. Her treat. Isn't she a darling? Want to join us?'

What a waste of such a glorious day. The beach sounds like far more fun. Besides, I can't leave the others with Lily and Dan, it wouldn't be right.

'I think I'll join the gang on the beach,' I say brightly. 'I'm sure they're expecting me. Better go and get ready. Have a great time at the spa.' I have no idea how I'm going to get to the beach but I'm damned if I'm going to ask Donna for help. I'll get a taxi if I have to.

I linger in the shower, letting the warm jets pummel my body. At home, three minutes in the shower without either Lily or Dan banging on the door is a luxury, so this is sheer bliss. I get dressed in my only decent sundress, a jaunty red and white patterned one Hattie lent me from her extensive collection and pack a bag for the beach, humming away to myself, enjoying being alone.

Pat very kindly offers to give me a lift in the team van; it's a rather bumpy ride down tiny back roads.

'You're so lucky,' she says. 'I'd love to spend the day on the beach. Might take a quick dip myself before I turn around; set me up for all the onion chopping and potato peeling later. Mrs Pilks is back at work this afternoon and she always makes me do all the crappy jobs. Have you seen her yet? She's been knocking around since yesterday. Arrived just before you guys.'

'No, what's she like?'

'Let's not talk about her it's too depressing. Here we are. Sandy Beach.'

The sea shimmers in front of us. Framed by rolling green hills, the silvery strand stretches out, the sand carved up by tongues of glistening water, small streams being dammed by enthusiastic young engineers and their even more enthusiastic fathers. It's not a huge beach, but it's beautiful.

I smile at Pat. 'It's perfect.'

She smiles back at me. 'I know. *And* you get to eat the fab picnic I prepared for you with my own fair hands. Salmon sandwiches and the works.'

I can feel bubbles of anticipation well up from the pit of my stomach. I love lazy days at the beach, always have.

'I can't wait,' I say, 'or, as you Yanks say, *bring it on!*'

Pat laughs and puts her foot down on the accelerator.

At five o'clock Pat rolls up again to collect the troops. I'm exhausted, but in a nice sandy, sun-satisfied way. The day's flown by. Roberta tends to be a bit of a fusspot when it comes to Jason's diet, but otherwise she's good company. Susan's just plain neurotic. She spends most of her time tending to Zac – plastering him with organic sun lotion, watching him as he splashes with the other children in the water, accompanying him to the ice-cream van and to the toilets in case any strange men try to peek at his privates.

Caga is a great laugh, she reminds me of Hattie and we're getting on famously. Her charges, Tilly and Shane, are remarkably annoying but she tends just to ignore them. She's really taken to Lily, who loves being thrown about in the water. Caga and I even have a go on the kids' boogie boards, much to Dan's amusement.

We load some of the damp, sun-sozzled children into the van with Pat. Caga is driving Mary's monster eight-seater jeep with the rest of the mob.

'Looking forward to the party?' Pat asks as I climb into the van beside her, Dan between us.

'Party?'

'Donna and Nick's big party. It's tonight. That's why Donna and Mary have spent the day at the spa. Pampering themselves and getting their hair and make-up done.'

'Jeepers, I hadn't realized it was tonight. I've nothing to wear; I thought this was just a family beach holiday and they're all going to look so glam.'

'Best not try to compete,' Pat says sagely. 'They're not normal, Meg, really they aren't. Maybe one of the other mums will have something you can borrow.'

'Ah, no, Pat, it's OK. That's very kind of you, but—' It's no use, Pat is off.

'Hey, Susan. Got anything Meg could wear at the ladida party?'

'I have a red dress that might fit her.'

'I have a fake Prada,' Roberta offers. 'It's black and really easy to wear. You're welcome to it if you like.'

'Prada,' Pat says with a grin. 'Now you're talking. Perfect. And what size are your feet, Meg?'

'Five.'

'Me too. I have a pair of knockout silver sandals that'll be perfect.'

'I couldn't,' I say. 'You're all so kind, but—'

Pat is having none of it. 'And Caga will do your hair and face. Her mum's a beautician and she's inherited the touch. You'll knock Simon's socks off. Wait till you see yourself.'

'I don't know what to say.' I'm touched. 'Thanks.'

'Our pleasure,' Roberta says. 'You have to promise to up-stage Mary and Donna for us, though.'

'Hear, hear,' Susan adds heartily.

'Meg, you look amazing.' Simon walks into the bedroom and dumps his sailing bag at the foot of the bed. He looks me up and down. Roberta's dress is rather daring, but with the other women's encouragement I've decided to brazen it out. It's slashed to the top of my waist, hanging in black, silky, Grecian folds. I've insisted on wearing a bra underneath, showing off my saggy breasts being one step too far. Luckily, my best black Wonderbra with the diamanté trim looks part of the outfit and I just about get away with it. The heavy dress material skims my hips in a flattering manner and Pat's sandals are perfect, if a little uncomfortable. Caga curled my hair with her ceramic tongs, teasing it into large fluffy seventies hoops and I love it. She also spent almost an hour doing my make-up and I have to admit I don't look half bad – all smoky eyes and dramatically slicked red lips.

'Thanks.' I give him a twirl. 'The girls leant me a dress and shoes, and looked after the kids while Caga did my hair and make-up.'

'I'm so glad you're all getting on now. Is it Donna's dress?'

'Donna's?' I laugh. As if I'd fit one of *her* dresses. 'No, it's Roberta's. And you'd better have a shower. You have salt crystals all over your face. And a red streak. What's that?' I put my finger up and smear the oily red mark. It feels tacky to the touch.

'Lipstick,' Simon admits. 'Mary kissed me on the cheek. She was just being friendly. I'll jump in the shower and see you in a few minutes. You go on down if you like.'

'It's OK, I'll wait.' I'm nervous about going downstairs, nervous of what Donna and Mary will say about my outfit, my make-up, my hair. Pat has made me promise that I'll lie and say I got the dress in a little boutique in Dublin, but I'm not sure I can carry it off.

As I walk down the stairs on Simon's arm I feel flutters of nerves in my stomach.

'Here's Simon,' Donna says from the bottom of the stairs. 'And is that Meg?'

For the second time that day I feel her eyes locking onto me, boring under my skin. It's horrible. I stumble a little and Simon supports my weight and pulls me erect.

'Not used to heels?' Donna says as we reached the bottom, giving a girlish laugh.

I refuse to be goaded. 'Not much use for running around after the kids. Not that you'd know anything about that, of course, lucky you.' I give her a wide smile.

'Meg's more of a flip-flop girl,' Simon adds, giving my arm a squeeze. I know he's only standing up for me, but right at the moment I wish he'd proclaim me the high-heel queen of Dublin. Instead, I feel like a country bumpkin. I'm not going to let Donna get to me, I tell myself, still high on the pep talk from Pat and the girls. Not tonight.

'Is that Prada?' Mary asks, giving me the quick once over.

I nod and bite my tongue.

'Last year's Prada,' Donna says, cutting me down to size. 'I used to have it in white. Now let's move outside. Mrs Pilks can greet the guests.' She gestures at a figure standing with her back to us in the outer hallway.

Hearing her name, the woman spins around on her neat navy heels. Our eyes lock. It's the bouffant woman from the plane. Just my luck.

She walks towards me. 'Hello again,' she says coolly.

'How do you two know each other?' Donna demands. 'From Ireland?' Is it my imagination or does she sound a little edgy?

'No, no,' Mrs Pilks says in a clipped tone, her eyes still on mine. 'We met on the plane.' She stands rigidly and puts out her hand. 'Mrs Pilks. Mrs Brody's housekeeper.'

'Mrs Brody?' I ask.

'Donna.'

'Oh, of course. Nice to meet you properly, Mrs Pilks.' I take her hand and wince at her pincer grip. Don't mess with me, it says.

This is just getting better and better.

There's a buzz of conversation from the terrace, peppered with laughter. Looking through the window, I can make out Pat in a white shirt and black skirt nipping among the guests with a tray loaded with full champagne glasses.

'There's Skipper,' I say to Simon, pointing towards the far side of the terrace. I'm eager to get way from Mrs Pilks and glad to see a familiar, friendly face. 'Excuse us.' I pull Simon's arm and we walk outside. 'That's the woman from the plane, the one I was telling you about,' I tell him as soon as we're engulfed by the crowd and out of earshot.

He gives a snort. 'Really? From the look of her I'm not surprised. I'd keep out of her way if I was you, she looks like a harridan.'

'No kidding. I have no intention of going near her, she might bite me or something.'

Simon laughs.

We make our way through the throng, my heels clipping on the marble tiles. I hold onto Simon's arm for dear life, nervous of landing flat on my face. I'll have to ditch the shoes soon for my black flip-flops, I'm just not able for the full two inches, sadly.

'Meg! Simon!' Slipper slaps Simon on the back and leans down to give me a rather slobbery kiss on the cheek. 'Great to see you both.' He beams at us. 'Some of the people here are as dry as old maids' p—' he pauses for a moment, noticing my nose wrinkling. 'Sorry, Meg. As dry as old sticks. Is that better?'

'Yes. And what on earth are you drinking, Slipper?'

He holds up his champagne glass, which looks like a miniature doll's house glass in his large hand, and stares at the viscous pink liquid. 'No idea. Some sort of strawberry cocktail Pat concocted for me. It's potent. She must be trying to get me drunk.' He gives me a leery wink.

'That must be it,' I say with a smile.

'And may I just say how stunning you're looking this evening, Meg.' Slipper's eyes linger on my cleavage. 'Very classy.'

'Scrubs up well, doesn't she?' Simon squeezes my hand and smiles at me.

'Thanks, Slipper,' I say, delighted by their attention, even if it is only Simon and Slipper, but it doesn't last for long.

'Simon, Slipper, darlings.' Mary trips towards us. Her painted-on green satin dress leaves nothing to the imagination and her pert breasts shoot out in front of her like two cruise missiles, nipples alert. Her eyes dart around in their sockets, making her look slightly wired.

'Mary, you're a sight for sore eyes.' Slipper licks his lips. 'And where's that lucky husband of yours?'

'Banging the nanny,' Mary says lightly, with a dangerous glint in her eye.

I'm horrified for Caga's sake. How dare she say that? Caga wouldn't go near the man.

'Really?' Slipper nearly drops his glass.

'No,' Mary purrs, 'but that got your attention, didn't it? He's having a nap. Sex always exhausts him, poor pet. Doesn't have much stamina these days. Not built for marathon sessions like some.' She bats her eyelashes at Simon. Simon! The cheek of her.

I pull him closer to me. 'Simon doesn't have that problem,' I hear myself say. Damn, trust me to get drawn into this.

'Really?' Mary asks with interest. 'Would you lend me him later? Or maybe we could have a threesome?'

I stare at her. Is she serious? Yuk, yuk on both counts. The very thought of a threesome makes me feel queasy.

'Look at your face, Meg,' Slipper says. 'Anyone would think you'd just been invited to a threesome with your own husband.'

'Oh heavens, Meg.' Mary puts her hands on her hips. 'I'm only joking. Don't look so shocked. Besides, we're all adults here. Consenting adults.' She turns her attention to Slipper. 'So why's a nice guy like you still single, Slipper?'

'Predatory females,' Slipper says.

Mary laughs. 'I'd say you're not averse to a bit of predatory behaviour yourself, am I right? A bit of rough. I've heard the stories.'

'All highly exaggerated, obviously,' Slipper says, the smile dropping off his face.

I'm intrigued. I thought Slipper would be all over Mary like a rash, but apparently not.

Mary is unabashed. 'Will you join me upstairs for a line of charlie, Slipper?' She rubs the side of her nose with her forefinger. 'It's good stuff. Really pure. I've heard if you put a dollop of it on your—' she stops and smiles, 'you know where, it's pretty exciting for both parties. Fancy trying it?'

I'm rooted to the spot, my mouth caught in an 'O' of surprise. Mary has two kids, not to mention a husband. I hate to admit it but I'm fascinated.

'Is that safe?' I find myself asking.

'Oh, yes,' Mary says breezily. 'Maybe you and Simon should try it.'

'Our sex life is quite exciting enough as it is, thanks. Sizzling, in fact.'

'Really? Can I watch?' Mary asks, moistening her lips with the tip of her tongue.

'No, you can't!' I splutter indignantly.

'Shame.' Mary puts her hands on her hips. 'You don't know what you're missing. So how about it, Slipper?'

'No, I don't think so. Coke has never been my thing really. Up the nose or up anywhere else. But I'm sure Donna will happily join you. For the nose part anyway. I've heard she's quite the fan. And you never know, Mary, she might swing both ways. Like yourself. A match made in heaven I'd say. You should give her a go.'

'Oh you!' Mary swats his arm playfully. 'I'll catch you later. And if you change your mind . . .'

'I won't,' Slipper says firmly, 'but thanks for the offer.'

She gives him a saucy wink and sashays away.

'Sorry about all that, Meg,' Simon says. 'I had no idea she was, well, into that kind of thing.' He seems genuinely perplexed.

'I know,' I say. 'She seems so . . . well, nice.'

'Mary is nice,' Slipper says. '"Nice 'n' easy". That's her nickname. She's a bit of a legend on the south-coast sailing circuit.'

I laugh. 'I know it's very provincial of me, but I am a bit taken aback to be honest. You don't encounter much swinging in south county Dublin, and our friends aren't really into coke either. The odd spliff maybe, but nothing stronger.'

'The odd spliff?' Simon laughs. 'Would you listen to you, you big druggie. Anyone would think you roll carrot-sized joints every evening while listening to Bob Marley.'

I dig Simon in the ribs. 'Yeah, right. Chance would be a fine thing. But I'll have you know I was a bit of a wild thing in my college days. Very cool. I used to have a biker jacket and every-thing.'

Slipper begins to sing the old Troggs' song 'Wild Thing'.

'Go on, laugh,' I say, a little miffed that they don't believe me, 'but it's true.'

Simon hugs me to his side and kisses the top of my head. 'I can well believe it. That's why I love you.'

Two hours later I'm sitting on my own by the swimming pool. Most of the guests have meandered inside, as there's no cloud cover and it's a cool evening, but I don't mind. It's a clear, starry night and I'm enjoying the peace and the star-gazing. I'm tak-ing a break from holding onto Simon's arm, trying to feign interest in his sailing conversations. Most of the other women inside are clumped together in groups, chatting and laughing among themselves. It's like a teenage disco, with the boys on one side of the room and the girls on the other. I find it difficult to break into a group of women I don't know and start up a conversation. Susan's upstairs with Zac, surprise, surprise, and Roberta is sitting on her husband's knee, leaning back into his expansive belly; I don't like to interrupt.

Pat comes outside and picks up an empty glass from the ground.

'Hey, Pat,' I call.

She comes over, dumps her tray of dirties on the ground and sits down beside me, flips off a shoe and begins to massage her foot, sighing with relief.

'Tough night?' I ask.

'You could say that.' She grins at me. 'Where's Simon?'

'Last seen inside. Talking about guess what?' I put my hand over my mouth and feign a large yawn.

'Sailing?'

'What else.' I shift my bottom on the surface of the low stone wall we're perched on. 'Or he and Slipper could be having a threesome with Mary I suppose,' I say wryly.

Pat raises her eyebrows. 'Ah, so the leopard's revealed her spots. Good.' She gives me a small nod. 'Watch her around Simon, Meg. She's dangerous. She's already managed to break up two marriages, and I'd hate to see anything happen to you too. You seem good together. Happy.' She stops for a moment. 'I'm not suggesting that anything like that would happen of course. I'm sure Simon's—'

'A man just like the rest of them,' I cut in. 'And thanks, I appreciate the warning. I'll certainly keep an eye on her.'

'Pat? Pat?' Mrs Pilks' shrill voice from inside interrupts our conversation.

Pat jumps to her feet. 'Sorry. Duty calls. We'll talk later.'

'See you.' I sit for a while, collecting my thoughts. I know I should go back in and make a bit of an effort but my heart isn't in it. No one will notice if I sneak off to bed. Simon is enjoying himself, maybe I'll just leave him to it. I'm about to stand up when I suddenly hear Donna's voice to my far right. She's just stepped outside with Mrs Pilks.

'Mum, it's not good enough,' Donna snaps at Mrs Pilks. 'Some of the guests have empty glasses. Where's that stupid Pixie girl? I thought she was in charge of the bar? And where's the caviar? It was supposed to be served hours ago. The guests are all half cut now, they could be eating fried cockroaches for all they'll know.'

Mum? I sit up poker straight. The horrible Mrs Pilks is Donna's mum? As I stare at the older woman's face, it begins to make sense; there's a distinct family resemblance around the sharp blue eyes and the thin-lipped mouth. Donna's lips are fuller of course, but she's probably had them done.

I move my foot and it catches a glass which falls over with a hollow ring.

Donna swings around and glares at me. 'What the hell are you doing hiding in the shadows, Meg?'

I say nothing, knowing that for once I have the upper hand.

'And what are you staring at?' she demands.

'A rather touching family scene,' I say. 'Although I don't think you should speak to your mum like that, Donna.' I've had enough of Donna and I'm not in the mood for mincing my words.

Donna gasps, her perfectly manicured hand rising to her mouth. 'Don't tell anyone, will you, Meg? It's so embarrassing. Mum needed a job you see and our old housekeeper left. She begged me for the position. What could I say? She wouldn't accept money from me, though I did offer.'

'I like to pay my own way. And I hardly begged you, Donna.' Mrs Pilks isn't impressed. 'As I remember, it rather suited you at the time. Not exactly interested in ruining your nails in a bowl of washing-up water, were you?'

'Yes, well, I still gave you a job when you needed one, didn't I, *Mother*?' Donna puts her hands on her hips and cocks her head.

I feel a little sorry for Mrs Pilks. Even if she is a female version of the child catcher on *Chitty Chitty Bang Bang*, she doesn't deserve Donna as a daughter.

'That was very big of you, Donna,' I say drily.

'You won't tell anyone, will you, Meg?' Donna says again, giving me a smile which has no warmth in it.

I shake my head, not trusting myself to say anything. I'd love to land Donna in it, but that would just be petty. I don't want to be mean for the sake of it. Surely I'm a better person than that? Anyway, who would be interested? Come to think of it, Mary would probably be very interested; not to mention Caga, Pat and the other mothers. 'Please excuse me, Mrs Pilks,' I say, standing up and nodding at her. 'And I'm sorry about all that business on the plane,' I add, mainly because I feel sorry for her.

Is it my imagination or do her eyes go a little swimmy?

'It's forgotten,' she says. 'I was on the way back from my sister's funeral and I was very out of sorts. She was on holiday in Wicklow and died in a car crash with her only grandson. Your little girl is about the same age as—'

'Meg doesn't want to hear your sob stories, Mum,' Donna cuts in.

I stare at her. She's gone too far. 'Yes, I do! Of course I do. I'm so sorry, Mrs Pilks, how tragic. Donna, you're a horrible person. Horrible. I wouldn't want anyone to know that Mrs Pilks has such a vile daughter so I'll keep your tawdry little secret, for her sake, but you'd better start treating her with some respect or I might change my mind.'

'Well!' Donna huffs as I walk through the double doors, back into the main house. 'Meg,' she shouts after me, 'ask Simon about New Zealand. He has great plans, you know, and I don't think they include you or your bastard children. By the way, he's upstairs in my bedroom with Mary.'

I stand rooted to the spot. What a complete bitch! How dare she call my children such a thing. And have I heard right? Simon and Mary. I feel sick to the stomach.

'That's *enough*, Donna!' I hear Mrs Pilks snap. 'Meg's right. I don't know why I put up with you. I won't be talked to like that by my own flesh and blood. I quit!'

'You can't quit, Mother,' Donna shrieks. 'I won't allow it.'

'Watch me. And, Donna Pilks, it was far from housekeepers and fancy houses you were raised. I worked my fingers to the bone to send you to a good school when your father walked out on us. And what have you done with your education? Nothing! Parading around in your undies for photographers and then marrying Nick. What happens when he trades you in for a younger model? You won't be so cocky then.'

I collect myself and manage to walk away, towards the stairs. As I climb upwards, I can still hear their voices, Donna's shrill and frantic, Mrs Pilks' low and calmer.

I have no idea what's going on in Donna's bedroom, but I'm about to find out.

As I reach the top of the stairs I hear shrieks and two leggy blondes in their early twenties gallop down the hall and rather rudely brush past me, giggling frantically. Donna's bedroom door is closed but I can hear laughter and a male voice coming from inside.

'Mary,' the voice chants. 'Mary, Mary! Simon, Simon!' It sounds like Slipper.

I put my hand on the familiar doorknob and press down.

PART THREE

Chapter 22

Dock: a protected area where boats are moored.
A safe place for a boat to stay.

'Meg!' Simon stands behind me as I swing the last bag into the back of the van. Dan and Lily are already strapped into their seats, waiting patiently.

'Please,' he continues, 'listen to me. We need to talk. I'll cancel sailing today and stay with you guys, have a family day. That's what you want, isn't it?'

I whip around and glare at him. 'After last night? I don't think so. It's too late, Simon, you've burned all your bridges this time.'

'At least let me drive you to the airport,' he begs. 'We can talk on the way.'

'No. Pat's already offered, and I have nothing more to say to you.' I slam the boot. 'You go sailing with your new friends, on the glitzy America's Cup boat. *Revenge.* Isn't that what it's called?' I snort. 'Ha! *Revenge.* What a stupid name. They shouldn't let men name boats, their testosterone always gets in the way.'

'That's what this is really about, isn't it? New Zealand.'

'Simon, it's about *everything*,' I say. 'New Zealand, last night, the lot. I want to go home. I'm sorry. It's over, I've had enough.'

'What are you talking about? What's over?'

'*We* are. Look, we can't talk about it now, Dan and Lily are watching us.'

Simon runs his hands through his hair. 'You can't be serious. Tell me you're not serious.'

I shake my head, blinking back the tears. 'I don't know. I need to be on my own for a while. I'm sorry.' I gulp.

Pat appears beside us. 'Ready?' she asks me.

I nod and give her a half-hearted smile.

'I'll leave you two to say your goodbyes.' She hops into the driver's seat and closes the door. She must know something's up. After all, we were supposed to stay until Saturday, but she doesn't pry, for which I'm grateful.

Simon stares at me. 'Meg,' he puts his hand on my arm, 'don't leave like this.'

'I'm sorry, I have to.' I open the van door.

'I'll ring you later,' he says. 'We can talk.'

'Please don't. I need some time. Bye, Simon.' I feel numb. What is this? Am I really leaving him?

'What happened last night?' Dan asks me as we trundle away from Harbour House.

'Nothing, pet.' I brush tears away with the back of my hand. I wonder what else he overheard. I should have said goodbye to Simon inside, privately. 'Nothing for you to worry about.'

As soon as we get home to Monkstown, I plonk Dan and Lily in front of the television, go upstairs and sit on the edge of my bed to ring Hattie. It was a rather uneventful trip home with no Mrs Pilks to add colour, thank goodness. Dan was brilliant with Lily, sensing there was more to our hurried departure than met the eye (I'd told him I had to get back as Matty needed me urgently to advise him on finishing the wall – feeble I know, but it was the best I could do in the circumstances), he entertained her on the plane while I stared into space, going over and over the previous night's events.

'Hattie?'

'Meg! Are you having a great holiday? How's Cornwall? What are the other women like? Are they total bitches? I bet they are. Go on spill.'

As soon as I hear Hattie's friendly voice I begin to cry.

'Is everything all right? Is it Simon? Has something happened?'

I let out a wail, unable to speak.

'Where are you?'

'Home,' I manage to say through the tears.

'In Dublin?'

'Yessss.'

'Stay right there. I'll come straight over.'

'But you're in work.'

'Sod that. They can do without me, it's an emergency. I'll pull a sickie. I'll be with you in half an hour. Hang in there.'

I put the phone down and collapse on the bed, sobbing. What have I done? I'm thirty-three, with two children, a house that's falling down around my ears and no job, not a proper one anyway; Ivy's house clearance may only be a one-off. Without Simon's income, I'm in trouble. I'll have to move back in with the parentals. I shiver at the thought, hot tears rolling down my cheeks. I've made such a mess of my life, yet again.

True to her word, Hattie bursts into my room what seems like only minutes later.

'Dan let me in.' She sits down on the side of the bed and looks at me with concern.

I wipe my damp cheeks with the edge of my duvet. I crawled under the bedclothes after speaking to Hattie, craving comfort.

'Meg, what's wrong? Tell me.'

I open my mouth but there's a lump as big as a bowling ball in my throat and all I can manage is a groan and a hiccup. The tears have stopped but the after-effects remain – raspy, uneven breath, swollen eyes, lead-heavy heart.

Hattie leans forward and put her arms around me. 'There's no rush, take your time.' As she holds me tight, my breath begins to even out and the lump dissolves a little.

'I've left Simon,' I say eventually into Hattie's hair, needing to talk about it so badly that it hurts.

Hattie draws back, startled. 'Why?'

I give her a mournful look. 'I'm not really sure. I've just had enough. Worrying what he's up to when he's away, the arguments when he gets back, coping with the kids on my own. And then there was the party.'

'What party? In Cornwall you mean?'

I nod. 'He was kissing this woman and we had a huge row—'

'You caught him at it with another woman?'

'Not exactly.' Images of the previous night's shenanigans come flooding back to me in Technicolor detail.

'Why don't you start at the beginning?' Hattie is practically rubbing her hands together with glee. She loves scandal.

I tell her all about Harbour House, about Donna, about Pat and Caga and the other mums, about Mary and, finally, about the fateful party.

'Let me get this straight,' she says, enthralled. 'You found out about Donna's mother and Donna told you Simon was in her bedroom with this Mary woman, then what?'

'I went upstairs to look for him. I heard voices so I opened Donna's bedroom door and there he was, kneeling on the floor in his boxers, British flag around his shoulders, kissing Mary.'

Hattie's eyes are out on stalks. 'Was he, you know, *with* Mary?'

I snort. 'No, thank goodness. There was a whole gang of

them, and before you ask, it wasn't an orgy. At least I don't think it was. They were sprawled on this fur-rug thing on the floor.'

'Is Mary the floozy who came on to Simon and Slipper earlier that night?'

'Yes. She was holding her arm over her naked breasts and I can tell you, it didn't cover much.'

Hattie's trying not to laugh. 'Go on.'

'I was so embarrassed. I just stood in the doorway with my mouth hanging open, like a bloody goldfish, staring at Simon. It wasn't just a peck, Hattie, it was a full-blown snog. Eventually, one of the girls noticed me and the room went quiet. Simon must have sensed the change in the atmosphere. He opened his eyes and looked over.'

Hattie shakes her head. 'I don't get it. What were they all doing exactly?'

'Playing Truth or Dare. Apparently it got a bit out of hand and turned into strip Truth or Dare. Kissing Mary was Simon's forfeit. It was either that or take off his boxers. But originally they'd gone upstairs to drink champagne and celebrate. Simon and Slipper had been asked to join the British team for the America's Cup.'

'Wow! That's brilliant. When's it on?'

'Next year. Two of the team had dropped out injured, hence the vacant slots. The team's currently living in Auckland.'

'Auckland?' She stares at me. 'Are you moving to New Zealand?'

'Simon might be. I most certainly am not.'

Hattie's eyes begin to mist over. 'I've always had a thing for Kiwi men. All that sun and surf, it would be amazing. Think of the tans, the barbies on the beach . . .'

'You're thinking of Australia, and you're not listening to me. I'm not going.'

'Not going? But what about Simon? Haven't you discussed it?'

'No. The first I heard about it was when Donna walked into the room behind me and said,' I put on Donna's simpering voice, layered with sarcasm, '"Simon and Slipper are going to New Zealand with *Revenge*, isn't that exciting, Meg? Don't tell me he hasn't told you yet? Naughty Simon."'

I stop, remembering how stupid and angry I'd felt.

'What happened then?' Hattie asks, dying to hear the rest.

'I ran out of the room and Simon followed me. We had a huge row on the balcony and I told him he was a complete shit for not telling me and for showing me up in front of Donna.'

'What did he say?'

'That he wanted to go, but he knew how much being at home in Dublin meant to me.' I look at Hattie, tears in my eyes again. 'But that sailing in the America's Cup had been his dream for as long as he could remember. "What about the kids?" I said. "What about me?" And he said we could come with him, live in Auckland. Hattie, I can't do that to Dan and Lily, not now they're settled in Dublin. I don't want to live like that again. I'd go mad.'

'Live where exactly?'

'In a hotel.'

'A hotel? Really?' Hattie's eyes light up.

'It's not as much fun as it sounds, believe me. I've done it and it's a pain in the ass. The same food day after day, nowhere for the kids to play . . .'

'No housework, a pool on your doorstep,' Hattie points out. 'There *is* a pool, isn't there?'

'I don't know, but that's not the point. He never said a word about New Zealand. He let me find out from bitch-face Donna.'

'What happened after your argument?'

'Simon went back into Donna's bedroom to get his clothes. Then I made a complete fool of myself.' I cringe at the memory.

'Really?' Hattie is on tenterooks.

'You seem to be taking a perverse joy in my misery.'

'Ah, no. It's not like that. But you have to admit, it's a great story.'

'It gets better. I stormed back into Donna's room to give Mary and Donna a piece of my mind. I wanted to tell Donna to sort out her life, that money didn't buy happiness. To tell Mary to play with her own husband instead of hanging out with Simon and Slipper. How Mary's children deserved to see more of her, how she was missing out on one of the best experiences – being a mother . . .'

Hattie's eyebrows rise dramatically.

I wince. 'Maybe it's just as well I didn't say all that. I would have sounded like a sanctimonious prat.'

'So what did you say?'

'I told everyone that Mrs Pilks was Donna's mum. Oh, and that she had a Hello Kitty fixation. And I told Mary to keep her hands off my husband, and then I told her she had droopy boobs.'

Hattie laughs.

'And I think I spat in her face a little.' I groan at the memory. 'I was so mad, Hattie, I just wanted to hit her.'

'I guess you did, with your spittle.'

I put my hands over my tingling cheeks. 'God, how embarrassing.'

'You should have gobbed in her eye, the stupid cow.'

'They were all staring at me. It was awful. Then Donna .asked how I knew about the Hello Kitty thing. I'd been snooping in her bathroom, you see, but I wasn't going to tell her that, obviously.'

'Obviously. So?'

'I ran out of the room and back into our bedroom, and Simon ran after me. I asked him what he'd been thinking of, kissing

Mary like that. He said it was only a bit of a laugh and that she'd launched herself at him.'

'It was part of a game, I suppose,' Hattie says. 'I'm sure it didn't mean anything.'

'It did to *me*. Then I told him I'd had enough, I couldn't take it any more, that it was me or the sailing.'

Hattie sucks in her breath. 'What did he say to that?'

'Nothing. He tried to give me a hug, but I pushed him away. Then Lily woke up and started crying. I told Simon to get out and he did. I didn't see him until the following morning; he must have slept on a sofa or something.'

Hattie says nothing. I know she thinks I overreacted about the kiss, but hell, it wasn't her partner showing her up like that. And with Mary!

'So then this morning I packed our bags and we left before any of the other women were up. I couldn't face seeing Donna or Mary again. I wanted to be home; I'd had enough of the place.'

'And Simon?'

'Before we left for the airport I told him it was over.'

Hattie strokes my hand. 'Do you really mean that, Meg? Maybe you're just tired and upset. It's a big decision.'

I shake my head. 'I don't know, but I can't go on like this, I just can't. I thought if I were in Dublin, everything would be fine. I'd have friends nearby, and you and Dad and—' I break off. 'But I miss Simon; it's just not working.'

'You need to talk to him, to sort things out.'

I blow out my breath loudly. 'You're right, I suppose. But after this regatta he's flying straight to San Francisco. He won't be home for nearly three weeks.'

'You have to talk to him otherwise you'll be a nervous wreck. You have a lot to lose.'

'You think I don't know that?' I say a little snappily. 'But living like this is hopeless. I may as well be a single mother for all the help I get from Simon. At least on my own I'll know where I stand.'

'You don't mean that.'

'I'm not so sure. Maybe I do. Oh, I don't know. Hattie, don't tell anyone about this, please. Especially not Mum. In fact, don't even tell her I'm home. Promise?'

'Promise.'

'I'm sorry, I've been rabbiting on about me and my pathetic life. How's Ryan? Have you been out much?'

Hattie seems to slump a little. Her eyes dart around the room before settling on mine. 'I don't really know what's going on with him,' she admits. 'One minute he's all over me, the next I don't hear from him for days. I've only seen him once since you went away. We went out for a drink after work, but he left at nine, saying he had to be somewhere urgently. It's all a bit strange.'

'I'm sorry. I know you like him.'

Hattie shrugs. 'There's something on his mind, but he doesn't want to share it with me.'

'Why don't you ask him what's wrong? Maybe you could help.'

'Ask him?' Hattie laughs hollowly. 'Meg, you can tell you haven't been single for years. You can't just ask a guy you haven't known all that long things like that. Personal things.'

'Why not?'

'It's a sure fire way to get rid of him.' Hattie stops for a moment. 'Sometimes you have these long, intense conversations quite early. Sometimes even on the first date. You swap stories, personal stories. But with Ryan, it hasn't happened. I know very little about him.'

'I had a night like that with Simon. The second time we went out, in fact. We went for a walk after dinner and sat on a bench on Dun Laoghaire pier. I told him all about Dan and Sid and getting pregnant and—'

'You told Simon all your sad stories,' Hattie's eyes widen, 'and it didn't put him off?'

'No! Of course not. He told me about getting hurt by ex girl-friends – that kind of thing.'

Hattie stares at me for a moment. 'I wish I could find some-one like that.'

'You used to tell me a man like Simon would bore you rigid, that you needed excitement in your life, not certainty.'

'Maybe I've changed.'

'Overnight? I don't think so. You're not ready for a Simon. You're miles away from a Simon.'

'Maybe I am ready.' She folds her arms over her chest defiantly.

'I'll believe it when I see it. Until then, talk to Ryan, ask him what's wrong. And if he doesn't like it, tough. If he doesn't want to communicate there's not much point being together, is there?'

'Um.' Hattie murmurs non-committally. Then the corners of her mouth turn up and she begins to smile. 'Suppose not. Although he is rather good in bed. And very, very cute.'

'Hattie!'

'I'm only twenty-six. Plenty of time for talking in my thirties.'

I shake my head. 'You're *so* not ready for a Simon.'

She nudges me on the shoulder with her head and leaves it resting there. 'I know, it was just a momentary lapse. I'm glad you're feeling a little better.' She sits up straight. 'Now have you any food? I'm starving.' She stops for a moment. 'And speaking of food, I have an idea. I think you might be able to help with Ryan.'

'Yes?' I ask warily.

'Come out to dinner with us. I'll leave the table, go outside to make a phone call or something, and you can suss him out.

Ask him questions, see if he's hiding anything. Give him a Meg interrogation special.'

'Thanks a lot! I'm not that bad.'

She smiles. 'It's a very useful trait. Don't knock it. What do you say?'

'I don't know—'

'It'll take your mind off Simon. I'm asking for your help. Pretty please?'

Hattie is always listening to my woes and doesn't ask for my help all that often. 'OK,' I say. 'Can I bring Tina for company? I'd feel like a bit of a gooseberry on my own.'

'Will you still be able to interrogate Ryan?'

'Of course. Tina can be my wing woman. We can play good cop, bad cop. I'll train her up; she'll be brilliant.'

'Sounds like a plan.' She nudges me with her shoulder again. 'Now, about that food . . .'

Chapter 23

Planing: a boat is said to be planing when it's moving over the top of the water rather than through it — it tends to be going rather fast at the time

First thing the following morning, after a restless night's sleep, I'm woken by a series of sharp raps on the front door.

'Cooee, it's Mum,' her sharp voice cuts through the letter box and up the stairs. 'Open the door, Meg.'

I debate putting my pillow over my head and ignoring her. Maybe she'll go away. How the hell does she know I'm home? I'll kill Hattie!

'Mum.' Dan flies into my room in his pyjama bottoms, his hair stuck in clumps against his head and sleep in the corners of his eyes. 'It's Granny. Will I let her in?'

'No!' I push myself up with my hands, clutching my throbbing head. I feel slightly nauseous for a moment. I smooth down my hair, rub the corners of my mouth, grab my dressing gown off the back of the door and tie it firmly around my waist.

'Where's Lily?' I ask him.

'She's been up for ages. I took her downstairs and put on her *Dora* video in the living room. And I gave her some Rice Krispies.'

I smile at him gratefully, hoping that said Rice Krispies aren't all over the sofa by this stage. 'What would I do without you?'

'Does that mean I don't have to go into school?' Dan asks hopefully. I look at my watch. It's already half eight. I'll have to really get my act in gear to get him to school by nine. I just don't have the energy. Besides, they're not expecting him – officially he's still in Cornwall. And they never do any proper work in the last week of term.

'Yes. But come Friday you'll be the best student in the class, agreed?'

He beams at me. 'OK.'

Mum bangs on the door again.

'I'd better talk to her.' I walk into Dan's bedroom, stepping over small hillocks of dirty socks and underpants, and slide open the large sash window. Then I kneel on the carpet and stick my head out.

'Up here, Mum,' I yell down at her.

She puts her hand over her eyes and peers up. 'What are you doing up there? Come down and open the door.'

'I can't. Lily's sick.'

'Sick?' she asks a little suspiciously. 'What's wrong with her?'

'She has some sort of rash. It might be chickenpox. Or measles. She could be contagious. We had to come home early because of it.'

'But I thought you said—' Dan pipes up from behind me.

I spin around and shush him.

'Go down and check on Lily, please,' I tell him, 'and pull up your pyjama bottoms – you have builder's crack.'

He scuttles away.

'Who were you talking to?' Mum asks.

'Dan.'

'Why isn't he in school?'

'I don't want him to infect his class.'

'Is he sick too?'

'No, but you can't be too careful. He might be a carrier.'

'What does the rash look like? Have you called the doctor?'

'Not yet, the surgery doesn't open until nine. It's very early,' I add pointedly.

'Oh, this is ridiculous.' Mum puts her hands on her hips, her smart brown handbag swinging on her lower arm. 'Open the door and let me in. I've had everything under the sun at this stage of my life, Meg, believe me. I'll just come in for a quick cup of coffee. I need to talk to you.'

I stare down at her for a moment, cursing her stubborn nature. Then I stand up and close the window with a bang that makes the glass rattle in the frame.

'Are you all right?' Dan is standing behind me. He's hitched his pyjama bottoms up and the elasticized waist is now sitting inches over his belly button like an old man's trousers.

'I thought you were going downstairs.'

'I was waiting for *you*. You seem a bit funny this morning.'

'I'm just tired. I didn't sleep all that well last night.'

'Does Lily really have chickenpox? I thought you said her spots were just an allergy to something in the garden at Harbour House.'

'It probably is just a touch of heat rash, she often gets it. But don't tell your granny that.'

He digests this. Then asks, 'Are you and Simon fighting?'

'Why do you ask?'

'When you and Dad were fighting you were always tired.'

A lump comes to my throat. I feel like crying, but I know once I start I won't stop. I grip the tie of the dressing gown and press my thumbnail into it, hard.

'I'm sorry,' I say, a little lost for words.

'It's not your fault. All men are trouble.'

'Who told you that?'

'Hattie.'

I should have known. 'Most men are decent nice people, Dan, just like most women. But sometimes people are a little unkind to each other, I think that's what Hattie was trying to say.'

'No, she was complaining about a boy who never rang her back.' He doesn't miss a trick.

I sigh. 'Hattie's just Hattie. Pay no attention to her. And don't be worrying about me and Simon; it'll all be fine. Trust me.'

'OK. But I'm here if you need to talk.'

Tears come to my eyes. 'Thanks, Dan, but I'm fine, really. Everything's fine.' I smile at him, pressing my fingertips under my eyes to stem the wet flow. 'Now go and get dressed.' I pat him on the bum.

'Hey!' He jumps away from me.

I pad downstairs and unbolt the front door. Mum is standing there, her arms still folded in front of her chest, her foot tapping against edge of the granite doorstep.

'About time.' She brushes past me as I stand back to let her in. 'I'm dying for a coffee.'

'Nice to see you too,' I say under my breath. I shut the door and follow her into the kitchen. I stand watching as she flicks on the kettle and takes a jar of instant coffee down from the cupboard. She peers through the glass and shakes the jar.

'Is this fresh?' she asks.

'It's freeze-dried.'

'You know what I mean. It looks a bit clumped together. How long has it been in the cupboard?' She takes the lid off and sniffs the grains.

'It's not going to kill you.' More's the pity, I think acerbically.

She looks at me, clicking the jar down on the kitchen counter. 'I suppose you're wondering why I'm here.' She rests her back against the counter, closes her eyes for a moment and then opens them again.

Now for the lecture on Simon and family values. I brace myself. I'll triply kill Hattie if she's told Mum everything. Looking at her properly I notice her face is pale and she has dark shadows round her eyes. Her usually perfect hair is hanging limply around her face and she's missed a button while closing up her cotton jacket, making the material bunch. There's an expression in her eyes I can't quite fathom.

'Your dad's in St John's,' she says without preamble, 'having tests. He's been feeling sick for months now.'

I feel as though the floor's moving under my feet and I put a hand on the kitchen counter to steady myself. 'In hospital? What's wrong with him?' I feel about an inch high. Here I am worrying about my own pathetic life while Dad is sitting on a hospital gurney, wearing one of those draughty cotton robes that don't close properly at the back.

'It hasn't been confirmed,' Mum says after a pause, 'but from the tests they've done so far it looks like bowel cancer.'

The muscles in my stomach tense at the news. Tears prick my eyes and I press my lips together to stop them. I gulp down a breath. 'Grampa died of bowel cancer,' I manage to say after a moment. 'In his sixties.'

'I know.' She puts out her hand to comfort me but I step away.

'He died just after Mum— Before you and Dad—' I break off, tears streaming down my face. I take the few steps towards the kitchen table, pull out a chair and sit down, putting my elbows on the table and resting my head in my hands, fingers pressing into my eye sockets again.

'I know this is all a bit of a shock for you, Meg.'

'Dad can't have cancer. He doesn't even drink tea or coffee. I don't believe it. Maybe it's just stomach ulcers or something. Or gallstones.' My eyes are swimming with tears, my efforts to stop them coming to nothing. 'He's the healthiest person I know.'

'I'm sorry, but they have to operate as soon as possible.'

'Operate?' I sit up straight. My God, what if he never wakes up again after surgery? It happens. My mind is racing. 'Where is he? I have to see him.'

'He's in St John's, remember. But I think you should wait. You've had quite a shock. And Hattie told me about Simon. I—'

'Don't say it!' I jump off my seat and stand in front of her, my voice edgy. 'I've fecked everything up this time, haven't I? Stupid Meg. Useless with relationships. "I told you so." That's what you're thinking, isn't it? I'm sorry, Mum. Sorry for disappointing you. Sorry for constantly disappointing you.'

'Oh, Meg, I was going to say I was sorry to hear things were—' she pauses for a moment – 'difficult. And I hope you can patch things up. But you do need to consider the children in all this.'

'The children? I do nothing but consider Dan and Lily. Why do you think I spent all that time traipsing around the world after Simon? For the good of my health? I moved back here to give Dan and Lily a more normal life. I'm doing my best, Mum, I really am. But none of it's working. I'm exhausted.'

She looks at me for a moment. 'You're not pregnant again are you?'

'Pregnant?' I start to laugh a little hysterically. 'Why do you always ask me that? You're obsessed. It would be the icing on the cake for you, wouldn't it? Another illegitimate baby—'

'Stop it, Meg!' Mum's eyes are flashing. 'That's enough. That's not what I meant. I'm just concerned for you, that's all.'

My heart is racing and I pull breath into my lungs in jagged spurts.

'I don't know what's got into you,' she adds. 'You're impossible to talk to sometimes.'

'Maybe I have my real mother's temperament,' I say, jutting my chin out defiantly.

She looks at me with hurt in her eyes. 'Maybe you do,' she murmurs. 'It's probably best if I go now.'

'What about your coffee?'

'It doesn't matter. I'll tell your dad you'll be in after lunch. Is that OK? He's in St Patrick's ward, in a private room.' Her eyes are wet. 'Meg,' she begins, then breaks off. 'I'll see myself out.'

I stand in the kitchen, watching her walk away, listening for the front door to close. I feel wretched. I sit down at the table again and run my fingers over the slightly sticky wooden surface. I press my finger down on a pool of dried yoghurt, breaking its skin. Dad. His smiling face floats before my eyes. What would I do without him?

I remember thinking he'd been looking thinner recently. Poor Dad, sick for months, and never once complaining about it. Not to me anyway. He's always been there for me and I haven't made things easy for him. I remember all the time we spent together when I was a child, just me and him. Sitting on his knee while he read me stories from fairy tales (*Beauty and the Beast* was always my favourite) and *My Naughty Little Sister* to the *Famous Five* and the *Secret Seven* long after I could read for myself. Pottering in a motorboat hired from one of the fishermen in Bullock Harbour, 'fishing' off the back of it with orange string wrapped around a piece of stick, a rusty old fish hook attached to the end. I never caught anything, but it was fun trying. Picnics on Dalkey Island in the rain, Dad's big raincoat over our heads like a tent; walks on Dun Laoghaire pier, making him stop every few feet to pat any friendly dogs being walked by their owners. Me and Dad, always just me and Dad.

Hattie was born when I was seven. My baby half-sister. For several weeks I took to pinching her and making her cry, according to Dad. I don't remember that. I *do* remember running away – packing a bag with all my favourite books and toys, and walking out of the house and down the road towards the train station. He found me sitting on the pavement outside the station. I didn't have any money and I knew the station man wouldn't let me on the train without a ticket. One of our neighbours had driven past, noticed me and rung Dad. Dad gave me a huge hug and started crying. He said he loved me and that I wasn't to scare him like that ever again. We sat for ages. I asked him if we could give the baby back. He said no, but that me and the baby would be friends in no time. He was right. But 'no time' turned out to be several years. Now we're as close as real sisters. Closer maybe.

The phone interrupts my thoughts. I pick it up and answer it, wiping my tears away with my free hand.

'Meg? Is Mum still there?' It's Hattie.

'No, she's just left.'

'I'm so sorry for breaking my promise, but I knew you'd want to see Dad before his operation and Mum wanted to tell you herself.'

'That's OK. I understand.'

'And you had enough on your plate yesterday without me adding to it.'

I give a sigh. 'I guess it does put things into perspective.'

'I guess it does.'

'How is he?'

'OK. Hanging in there. I think he's nervous about the operation, but he's putting on a brave face.'

'And how are *you* coping with it all?'

'I'm not too bad. It came as a bit of a shock, I suppose. How was Mum this morning?'

'I wasn't very nice to her, Hattie. I thought she was going to lecture me about Simon.'

'And did she?'

'A bit. But I kind of snapped at her.'

'You were upset. She won't take it personally.'

'I hope not. Listen I'd better go and get Lily and Dan dressed. I'll talk to you later. I'm going in to see Dad this afternoon.' I feel tired just thinking about everything, Dad, Mum, Simon, the works.

'Tell him I'll see him this evening, after work. And Meg?'

'Yes?'

'Did Simon ring last night?'

'I don't know, I took the phone off the hook.'

'Ring him, please. For me? For yourselves?'

'I know we need to talk, it's just—'

'Just get on with it.'

'OK, OK. I will.'

'Good! Take care of yourself. I love you. Even though you're a stubborn pain in the ass sometimes.'

At twelve I call into Tina's.

'What are you doing back?' she asks, worry flitting across her face.

'I had a bit of a row with Simon. And now Dad's sick.'

'You poor old thing. Come in.' Tina stands back from the door to let me past.

'I've left Lily with Dan so I'd better not. Dad's in St John's and I'd really like to see him. I was wondering—'

'Of course,' she interrupts, reading my mind. 'Lily and Dan are always welcome, you don't even have to ask. Drop them in now if you like. Freddie's asleep but Eric's in the garden. He'd love the company.'

'Thanks.' I give her a grateful smile.

'Your dad?' she prompts.

I come straight to the point. 'They think it's bowel cancer.'

I can tell Tina is trying not to look shocked. 'Poor man. But there's a lot they can do these days. Is he having surgery?'

I nod, not trusting myself to speak.

She leans forward and gives me a hug. 'I'm so sorry, Meg. But he's a strong, healthy man. He'll pull through.'

'Thanks.' I swallow the lump in my throat and draw away. 'Better get the kids ready. I don't know how long I'll be.'

Tina waves her hand in the air. 'I'm here all day. Take as long as you need, really.'

'Thanks,' I say again.

As I drive towards Ballsbridge I realize I hadn't even asked Tina how she is. I'm so wrapped up in my own little world I've forgotten my manners. At a red light I pull my mobile out of my bag and ring her. To hell with the penalty points.

'Tina.'

'Meg? Is everything OK?'

'Yes. I just wanted to ask how you were. I'm so sorry, I was a bit distracted earlier and I never asked.'

'Don't be silly. You have a lot on your mind. And I'm fine. No, I'm good actually. Matty's here finishing off the bathroom. He's great company, isn't he?'

I hear a muffled voice in the background.

'It's Meg,' Tina says to the voice. And after a moment. 'Matty says to say hi.'

I feel like telling him to get back to work on my wall immediately, but I hold my tongue. 'Say "hi" back to him,' I say. 'Light's green. Have to go.' I click off my phone, throw it onto the passenger seat and accelerate away. It slides off the upholstery and onto the floor. Typical.

There's something going on between Tina and Matty, I just know it. Tina is scarily transparent, but I have enough to worry about without adding my friend's infidelity to my list.

As I pull into the hospital car park I feel shaky. I forgot to eat this morning and I curse my stupidity. I always feel rotten when I skip breakfast. I'll have to grab a chocolate bar in the hospital shop and something for Dad. But what do you give someone with cancer? Chocolates seem strangely flippant and flowers, I shiver, inappropriate. Will he be strong enough to read a book or a magazine? I lock the car door and walk towards the hospital, my teeth nibbling on my inside lower lip.

I linger in the shop for a few minutes, looking at the covers of the glossy magazines, but nothing looks right. He's not exactly the sex and shopping or celebrity-scandal type and *Business and Finance* looks a little heavy going for someone who isn't well. I curse myself for not stopping in Blackrock on the way to nip into the bookshop.

I hand over the money for a KitKat and a bottle of water and walk towards Dad's ward, cramming the chocolate into my mouth, piece by piece. My mouth is dry and the chocolate and biscuit feel like sawdust and stick in my throat, but I take a swig of water and force myself to swallow.

Dad is in a private room on the third floor: the oncology wing. As I walk along the swirly green and white lino my runners catch and squeak on the tacky surface, making me wince. I've always hated that noise. I can hear my heart pounding in my chest. I walk faster, looking from left to right and reading off the numbers in a mumble. There it is – Dad's room – 29b. I lick the corners of my mouth in case of chocolate residue and take a deep breath before rapping lightly on the beige door.

'Come in.'

It's Dad's voice all right, but a softer version. His 'indoors' voice, as Lily's friend Barney might say. I snort a little, thinking about the purple dinosaur – this isn't the kind of indoor-voice situation Barney had in mind on his show – before collecting myself and opening the door.

Dad is sitting in the hospital bed, propped up by a wealth of plump pillows behind his back and around his shoulders. His left arm is attached to a drip and he's wearing maroon and navy striped pyjamas that, from the razor-sharp creases and flat matt appearance, are brand new out of the box. No doubt Mum bought them for him. Appearances mean a lot to Mum, even in hospital.

I close the door behind me with a gentle click.

'Hi.' I walk towards him and lean over to give him a kiss on the cheek. His skin feels cool and papery beneath my lips and he smells clean, like a baby, unlike his usual more musky, Old Spice self. I'm unnerved by his appearance and busy myself looking around for a chair. There's an armchair by the window but it looks too heavy to move easily.

'Thanks for coming in,' he says. 'You didn't have to.'

'Course I did. I wanted to see you.'

I smile at him, then get an orange plastic chair and plonk it next to the bed. I look down at his left hand, the needle of the drip poking through his pale skin, held in place by an old-fashioned material plaster. There's a small ring of dried blood on it and I pull my eyes away, my heart sinking.

Dad looks small and fragile in the large bed, like an old man. I realize with a start that he's sixty-four, not 'old' by any stretch of the imagination, but not in the first flush of his youth either. Dad has always been my champion, my protector. I know I can always rely on him to fight my corner, take my side. But maybe not for much longer. I shiver at the thought.

'Are you cold?' Dad asks. 'You can close the window if you like.'

'No, no I'm fine. In fact, it's quite muggy in here. Will I open it wider for you?'

'That's as far as it goes. It's to stop the inmates jumping out when they hear the food trolley.'

I know he's trying to lighten the mood so I play along. 'Is it that bad?' I ask.

'Worse. I asked your mother to sneak me in pizza last night. Their fish pie was slopping all over the plate. Couldn't touch it. I was starving.'

'And did she?' I doubt if Mum has ever ordered pizza in her

life. She certainly never gave us pizza as children – it was all meat and two veg and don't forget your piece of fruit in our house.

'No. I got some of her home-made shepherd's pie instead.' I give a laugh.

He smiles. 'But it was worth a try.'

'I'll bring you in pizza if you like. After your . . . you know.'

'Operation?' he says gently.

I nod.

'I probably won't be able to eat for a while, Meg. But it's a nice thought. When I'm home, eh? Or maybe you can cook me a good hot curry.'

'Yes. When you're home.'

His eyes settle on mine and I look away, unable to hold his gaze for fear of dissolving into tears. I stare out the window instead. The leaves on a tall willowy tree flutter in the breeze. 'It's a nice room,' I say when I trust myself to speak.

'Are you all right?'

'Sure.' I blink back some rogue tears. 'I just – you – being in here. The operation. I'm sorry.' Tears start to stream down my cheeks.

'It'll be OK. The doctors are all very hopeful that they've caught it . . .' he pauses for a moment, 'the cancer, in good time. I have your mother to thank for that. She frogmarched me to the doctor even though I kept telling her there was nothing wrong with me, that I was just tired. You know what she's like.'

I press my lips together and try for a smile but the edges of my mouth won't cooperate. I clench my hands together in my lap and play with a ring. I open my mouth to ask something but then forget what I was going to say.

'I'm lucky,' Dad continues. 'The doctors don't think it's spread into my lymph nodes yet, or anywhere else for that matter. They should be able to treat it with a simple operation.'

I wince. Simple? Cutting bits out of your body? The more I

look at Dad, his pale face, his familiar strong features somehow
diminishing before my very eyes, I can't help thinking that I'm
going to lose him. I know I'm being selfish, that he needs me to
be strong but I can't. In my heart I believe he's going to die. Just
like my mum.

'You're thinking of Celia, aren't you?' he asks quietly. 'I'm so
sorry, Meg. If I could have protected you from all of that – from
all of this.' He waves his right arm around the room.

Tears stream down my face. 'It's hardly your fault.'

'You've been through so much, if only I had been there more
for her, maybe she'd have coped better. And after she lost the
baby – and then—'

'It wasn't your fault. Mum wasn't well. There was nothing
you could have done.' I wipe away my tears with my shirt
sleeves. He hasn't mentioned my real mum for as long as I can
remember, not since Dan was born. As he held Dan for the very
first time he told me how proud Celia would have been at that
moment. Her first grandchild. 'You certainly didn't ask to get
sick,' I add.

'I'm not going anywhere,' he says strongly, sounding more
like the dad I know. He takes my hand in his. 'Do you understand?'

I try to believe him, but it's hard. I nod.

'Good. There's a box of tissues in there.' He points at the
bedside locker.

'Thanks.' I help myself to several large man-sized Kleenex,
blow my nose and dab my face dry. 'Sorry,' I murmur.

'Don't be daft.'

We sit in silence for a few minutes, faint hospital sounds
drifting in – the clink of a trolley, shoes squeaking on the floor,
someone in another room with a hacking cough, nurses chatting as they walk past.

'How long will you be in here?' I say, finally remembering
what I had wanted to ask him earlier.

'It depends on how the operation goes. A few weeks tops.'

'And then?'

'Back home. Your mum says she's happy to look after me herself, but we'll see. I'll just have to rest and take it easy. Allow my poor old body to get back to normal.'

'She *was* a nurse, I suppose,' I say a little grudgingly.

'Yes, but we might drive each other crazy. I'll be on my feet in no time. Back to work before I know it. Back to normal.'

'And they'll keep an eye on you afterwards? Just in case.'

'Of course. Just in case.'

I start to feel a little more reassured. The picture Dad is painting doesn't seem all that bad. But I know it won't all be plain sailing. I suspect the dark shadow of cancer will hover over all our heads like Banquo's ghost, no matter what he says.

'I'll just have to get on with my life,' he says, reading my mind again. 'We all die at some stage; it's a fact of life. We all have to live each day as if it's our last. Each day, Meg, starting now.'

My eyes threaten to fill up again but I manage to control my overenthusiastic tear ducts.

'What happened in Cornwall?' Dad asks gently. 'Why did you come back early? Your mum and Hattie said something about an argument with Simon.'

I sigh. It all seems rather petty in the circumstances. 'I may have overreacted a bit. But he wants to move to New Zealand. To sail.'

Dad's eyes widen. 'For good?'

'For six months. But it's not just that. He was acting the eejit in Cornwall. I just lost all patience with him.' I tell him everything, even about the kiss with Mary. I don't mean to, but once I start I just can't stop.

Dad smiles gently. 'I can see why you were annoyed. There's nothing worse than drunk people whooping it up, especially when you're sober. Can't have been much fun seeing Simon with another woman like that either. Still, I suppose he just got a bit carried away.'

I stare at him. I feel as though he's giving me a dig for not entering into the party spirit, but I decide to let it be. Maybe I did overreact a little.

'When's Simon home?' he asks.

'That's just it. He won't be home for weeks. He's flying straight to San Francisco tomorrow morning. More sailing. Farr 40 World Championship this time.'

'Farr 40?'

'It's a kind of yacht.'

'Ah, I see.' Dad thinks for a moment. 'Why don't you go with him? Leave Dan and Lily with your mum.'

'I can't do that. She has enough on her plate.'

'Might be good for her. Take her mind off things.'

'It's too much. She's under enough stress already.'

'She could share them with Hattie. Might do your sister some good. Stop her gadding about so much. She can take some holidays. She was complaining only last week that she had more than two weeks left and no one to go away with.'

I feel bad. Poor Hattie. It isn't easy being single when it comes to planning holidays. I remember it only too well. And single with a young child and very, very broke is even worse. I spent most of the holidays in my pre-Simon days in a rented holiday cottage in Galway with Dad and Mum. Hattie sometimes came down for a weekend, but otherwise there were just the four of us.

But she certainly wouldn't want to waste her holidays looking after my two. There's also the cost to think about.

'It's a nice thought,' I say, 'but I couldn't afford it. I'm completely broke as it is.'

'Bung it on your credit card.'

I stare at him. Dad is a stickler for keeping finances in order and he's always giving out to Hattie and me for paying for things on the never never, as he calls it.

'I'll think about it.' I don't like to tell him that my credit card was frozen weeks ago.

'Do that,' Dad says, 'and talk to Simon. Ring him when you get home and sort things out. Please? For me?'

I nod. How can I refuse? Besides, I need to tell him about Dad. 'I will. I promise.'

'Good.' He lies back against the pillows and smiles at me. 'Good.'

I stay with him for a little longer, revealing Lily's latest escapades and Dan's rather colourful school stories. After a while he begins to look tired.

'I'd better go now. I've left the kids at Tina's. I'll be back in the morning.'

'The operation's scheduled for nine. They don't usually operate on a Saturday, so I was lucky to get a slot. Hopefully it will all be over quickly. And I'm not sure if I'm allowed any visitors until Monday. Except for your mum, of course.'

I'm a little miffed that *she* is sanctioned and I'm not, but I try to hide it. 'Of course.'

Dad smiles at me. 'Nearly out of the woods now. Hang in there, Meg.'

I feel ashamed. He is so sweet, so unselfish. I don't deserve him. 'I'll say a prayer for you,' I say, surprising myself. But it seems the right thing to say and it can't hurt. I stand up. 'Good luck tomorrow. I'm sure it'll all go swimmingly.'

He smiles at me again. 'I'm sure it will. And best of luck with Simon.'

'Thanks. I'll go easy on him.'

Dad laughs. 'You do that. Poor man.'

'Hey, less of that.' I give him a kiss. 'Bye, Dad. I love you.'

'Love you too.'

As I walk down the corridor, tears spill over again. I wipe

them away and, to take my mind off Dad's operation, think about what I'm going to say to Simon.

That evening, just after eight, Mum calls in again. She thrusts a large white A4 envelope into my hands. 'From your dad. And please get the doorbell fixed. All this knocking is ruining my nail-varnish. Now I have to get back to St John's. They kick everyone out at nine. *Ciao.*'

I turn the envelope over in my hands. A horrible thought creeps into my mind. It's not a copy of his will is it? I couldn't deal with that. Not now. 'What is it?' I ask her.

'Open it and see.' With that she jumps into her car and drives off at quite a pelt, scattering gravel in her wake.

I rip open the envelope and gasp as I read the printed pages inside. Of course it isn't a will. What was I thinking? To speak in Monopoly terms, Dad has just given me a Get Out of Jail Free card. What the hell am I going to do now?

Chapter 24

Underway: a boat that is moving is 'underway'

On Sunday evening Hattie drags me to Bella Mama, a new Italian restaurant in Dalkey. Dad's operation went smoothly enough, but he's still in recovery. I'm not in the mood for socializing, but Hattie insists.

'You have to eat,' Hattie said logically when she rang earlier to make the arrangement. Shona had agreed to babysit, so I didn't really have an excuse. 'So it may as well be somewhere nice. It'll keep your mind off Dad. And before you say it, no, we shouldn't be at home thinking about him. He wouldn't want that. He'll be fine, you'll see. Lighten up. See you at eight. And don't forget Tina.'

When I call in for Tina, Oliver answers the door.

'Hello, Meg,' he says rather formally. 'Long time no see.'

'Oliver,' I say, feeling as if I should proffer my hand.

He steps back to let me in. 'Tina's just changing her shoes – again. The woman has far too many to chose from.'

'Too many Choos,' I quip.

He stares at me blankly, making me feel a little pathetic.

'Sorry,' I murmur. 'Bad joke. Jimmy Choos?'

'Right.' He leans back on his heels and then sways forwards, his arms crossed in front of his chest. He's wearing a crisp white shirt, black denims and shiny black boots and with his immaculate grooming, he looks like he's just stepped off the pages of *Vogue*.

I wish to goodness Tina would hurry up, the silence is making me feel very uncomfortable. I scramble for something intelligent to say. My eyes linger on the large crystal vase with its heady and rather messy profusion of red and dark pink buds. 'Lovely flowers.' Brilliant, Meg.

He looks at the vase and then back at me, his eyebrows raised and a smirk on his lips. 'Do you think so?'

I remember Tina saying he only likes white flowers and I wonder if he's annoyed at the racy splash of colour.

'How's work?' I ask, still struggling with the silence.

'Busy.'

'Good,' I say. 'Good.' Where the hell is Tina?

I try again. 'How was your flight?'

He narrows his eyes a little. 'Fine.'

'And, um, are you flying back tomorrow?'

'Yes. Five in the morning.'

'Gosh, that's early. How do you cope?'

'I'm used to it.' He unfolds his arms and walks towards the stairs. 'Tina,' he shouts, 'get a move on.'

'Coming,' Tina says, appearing at the top of the stairs, a pair of silver shoes dangling by their straps from her hands. She's wearing a floaty red chiffon dress with a matching cardigan. I feel rather underdressed in my jeans and one of Hattie's cast-off tops. But I have worn my wedge sandals and thrown on some make-up, so at least I've made a bit of an effort.

'Jeeze, you're only going for pizza,' Oliver says. 'Hurry up. Meg's waiting.'

'Lower your voice,' Tina warns him, 'you'll wake the boys.'

'Have you checked on them?' Oliver asks. 'I'm not changing any nappies or anything, I have work to do.'

'They're both fine,' she says, walking down the stairs. 'Stop worrying.' She leans a hand against the wall and pops on her shoes.

'And if you're back after eleven I'll leave them on their own,' Oliver says, his chill tone shocking me a little. 'I have to be in town by half past.'

'Yes, yes,' Tina says wearily. 'I won't be late.'

'Better not be,' Oliver mutters.

Tina ignores him and links my arm. I'm aware that I'm staring at the man, but I just can't help it. He's being really unpleasant. Tina doesn't seem to notice.

Tina picks up her bag from the hall table, fingers one of the red roses and then turns to me. 'Ready, Meg?'

I nod and she ushers me out the door. Oliver has already disappeared.

As I unlock the car, I ask, 'Is something wrong with Oliver?'

'No, why?' She hikes up her dress and sits in the passenger seat.

'He seemed a bit—'

'Gruff?' she suggests.

'Yes.'

'He's just tired. Pay no attention.' She closes the door, ending that conversation.

I sit behind the wheel for a second before starting the car. 'Are you sure nothing's wrong, Tina?' I get the feeling there's something she's not telling me.

She gives me a toothy smile. 'Positive. He's just in one of his moods. You know what men are like. Now hurry up, I'm dying for a glass of wine. I've been looking forward to it all evening.'

When we walk in the door of Bella Mama, Hattie and Ryan are sitting at a table in the corner in front of the window, bodies almost touching. The two tables beside them are vacant. There are starched white tablecloths on all the tables, almost touching the wooden floor. The walls are dark red and the chairs are upholstered in dark red velvet. Elaborate gold-coloured candle holders snake out of the walls, their flickering light reflected in oval mirrors behind them. It's all very baroque, but it works.

One of Ryan's hands is on Hattie's bare shoulder and he's tracing the other hand over her collarbone and playing with her hair.

'I won't be able to eat if they paw at each other all night,' I say to Tina.

She laughs. 'Leave them alone. I think it's rather sweet.'

'Sweet?'

'Don't be such an old killjoy.' Tina waves at the engrossed couple. 'Hi, Hattie,' she says, walking towards the table.

They part quickly. Ryan looks up at Tina quizzically. Hattie whispers something in his ear and he smiles and stands up. 'Tina, I've heard a lot about you. Nice to meet you.' He gives her a kiss on the cheek.

She touches her cheek gently and smiles. 'What a charmer. You must be Ryan.'

'Sit down,' Hattie says. 'Meg, you sit beside Ryan. Tina, beside me.' She pats the chair to her left.

'Three beauties no less,' Ryan says when we've settled ourselves. 'Lucky old me.'

'Lucky old you indeed,' Hattie says, giving me a kick under the table.

The evening flies by. Hattie is in sparkling form, regaling us with stories about the clothes shop and its well-heeled customers. I watch Ryan as he listens, seemingly enrapt. Now and again his gaze drifts from Hattie's face to her cleavage, but as she has sprinkled her décolletage with golden glitter, he can hardly be blamed for that. Tina tells us about her new bathroom and how wonderful Matty is, her eyes lighting up when she mentions his name, and I describe Donna's house, avoiding all mention of the party or my current stand-off with Simon. Everyone's far too polite to mention it, except Hattie of course.

'And have you talked to Simon yet?' she launches straight in.

'Yes,' I say, mentally crossing my fingers. 'And I've decided to go to San Francisco on Tuesday, if I can arrange everything in time. Mum's offered to take the kids. I just have to confirm the flights.'

'Cool!' Hattie says. 'A good bonking session with no interruptions from the minors will put you back on track.'

'It's not as simple as that,' I protest.

'Yeah, right.' Hattie picks up her glass of wine and takes a good glug.

'Sorry, Ryan,' I say, embarrassed.

'I'm well used to it.' He smiles at me. 'Anyone for dessert?'

'I couldn't, I'm stuffed,' Tina says. 'But I do fancy a cigarette. Will you keep me company, Hattie?'

'Take Meg with you,' Ryan says. 'I need Hattie for a second.'

'No problem.' Tina gets to her feet and drags me out by the arm.

'You don't smoke,' I hiss in her ear.

She leans in towards me. 'Ryan doesn't know that.'

As soon as we're outside she says, 'Damn, foiled. I was trying to get you and Ryan alone together like you said in the car. What on earth are they up to now?'

It's dark outside and we stare into the romantically lit restaurant. She points through the window at our table.

'Where's Hattie going?' I ask, watching my sister slither down in her seat.

Tina begins to giggle. 'Under the table I think. Maybe she's dropped her napkin. But she doesn't seem to be coming up.' She looks at me, shocked amazement on her face. 'She's not giving him – you know, is she? I thought things like that only went on in movies or novels.'

'Judging by Ryan's face, I think she is,' I say. I don't know whether to laugh or cry. Ryan's mouth is half open, both his hands are pressed against the seat of his chair and his eyes look glazed. I stare at his face for another moment before tearing my eyes away. I feel sordid watching. It's *my* sister under the table after all.

'I can't believe no one's noticed,' Tina says, her eyes still glued to the scene. 'I think she's coming back up. Gosh, that was quick.'

I look back again. Hattie is sitting beside Ryan, dabbing the edges of her mouth in a ladylike fashion with the linen napkin. What *is* she like?

Ryan leans over and kisses her fully on the lips.

'Interesting taste I'm sure,' Tina comments.

I laugh. 'Tina!'

She grins at me. 'Now I've seen it all. I can't go back in and look Ryan in the eye now.'

'You stay out here and I'll send Hattie out to you. I'll talk to him. Maybe his little escapade will have softened him up. Maybe he'll be ready to talk.'

'Softened him up?' Tina laughs and gives me a wink.

'Would you just stop?' I say. 'You shouldn't drink. It has a bad effect on you.'

'A good effect I'd say,' Tina says. 'Look, Hattie's coming out.'

'Hey, Meg. I'll keep Tina company.' Hattie stares at us. 'Where are the cigarettes? Jeepers, you two are useless. You're supposed to be out here smoking. Ryan's going to get suspicious.' She sashays across the road to a pub and scabs two cigarettes from a man smoking outside, lights them both, then jay walks back again, narrowly missing being clipped by a beeping car. She gives the car a wave. 'Keep your knickers on,' she yells at it. She hands Tina a cigarette and pats me on the bum. 'Go on, hurry up. We can't stay out here all night.'

'But I don't smoke,' Tina tells her.

'Just make your breath a bit smelly,' Hattie says. 'Were you two looking in the window a few minutes ago?'

'No!' Tina and I say overenthusiastically.

'You were, weren't you? What did Ryan look like? Were his eyes open?'

'Hattie!' I shake my head.

'Don't be such a prude,' she says. 'Tina doesn't mind, do you, Tina?'

'No. You go inside, Meg. I'll fill Hattie in on the details.' She gives a cackle.

'Don't corrupt my friend,' I say, poking my finger in Hattie's shoulder.

'Hey, that hurt,' she says, rubbing her bare skin.

'Serves you right.'

'Stop procrastinating, Miss Marple, and get inside.'

'OK, OK.' I leave them to it.

Ryan looks up. 'Enjoy your cigarette?'

'I only had a quick puff,' I say, playing along with Tina's story. I sit back down at the table.

Ryan smiles at me. 'It's nice to see you, Meg. Give my regards to Simon. Lucky devil. I'd love to be in San Francisco right now.'

'Really?'

He nods.

'Wouldn't you miss Hattie?' I ask, fishing for information.

He looks at me for a moment, no discernible emotion on his face. 'Course I would.' He picks up a dessert spoon and turns it over in his hands before putting it back on the table. 'Is there something on your mind, Meg? Something you want to ask me?'

Shit, am I that obvious? My days as a private investigator are obviously numbered. 'Nothing really.'

He raises his eyebrows. 'Want to know if I've fallen for Hattie, is that it? I know you and Simon warned me about her.'

I laugh a little hollowly. Help, get me out of here.

'You have nothing to worry about. Hattie and I understand each other perfectly. It's nothing serious, we're both just having a bit of fun. I know she's not ready for real commitment. So what we have suits us both.'

I open my mouth to protest, but then close it again. Ryan has no idea how Hattie really feels about him, and I'm not about to rock the boat or embarrass her. Besides, how's he supposed to know if she hasn't told him? No wonder he's not exactly Mr Reliable if he thinks it's all just a bit of a laugh. Yikes. I wish I'd never been bullied into talking to him. Now I have to tell Hattie. Maybe I can drop Tina home and then – I glance at my watch. Ten past eleven. Shoot, have to get Cinderella home, Oliver's going to kill her.

Five minutes later Tina and I are driving back like the clappers.

'So what did Ryan have to say for himself?'

'That it's just a bit of fun, nothing serious.'

'Ah.' Tina leans her head against the head rest and closes her eyes. 'Not what Hattie wants to hear.' She opens her eyes again. 'Or have I read it all wrong?'

'No. I wish I'd never agreed to talk to him in the first place. She's going to kill me.'

'It's strange, he was all over her in the restaurant.' Tina's right, they'd launched at each other, full throttle as soon as we left. 'I just don't understand men sometimes.'

I dump the car outside my house and walk Tina next door. As we crunch over the gravel on the drive, the light clicks on in the porch and the front door swings open.

Oliver's tall frame is silhouetted against the glow.

'You go on home,' Tina says.

Oliver lurches a little sideways and I wonder if he's drunk. I feel uneasy. I don't want to leave her with him. I feel protective towards her. If he's still in a mood, maybe he'll be kinder to Tina in front of me.

'Are you not going to offer me a coffee? Shona's not expecting me back for a while—'

'Tina,' Oliver's voice cuts through the dark, 'what time do you call this? Hurry up!'

'Just coming,' Tina says evenly. 'Probably best if you go,' she says to me in a low voice.

Oliver strides towards us and grabs her by the arm.

'Hey!' she protests. 'No need for that.'

I'm shocked. Simon wouldn't dream of grabbing me like that. I stare at Oliver.

'What are you looking at?' he demands.

Tina manages to shake off his arm.

'Not much,' I say before I can stop myself. It's one of Dan's choice retorts.

Oliver looks at me and I can see he's trying to intimidate me. He moves closer and I can smell whiskey on his breath. I square my shoulders and stare back at him.

'Meg's coming in for coffee,' Tina tells him. 'Don't you have to be in town? You'd better get moving.'

He looks at Tina and then back at me. He mutters something under his breath, turns on his heels and walks inside the house.

'Are you OK?' I ask Tina.

She shrugs. 'Sure. I'm sorry about all that.'

A moment later he comes out again, black leather jacket thrown around his shoulders, and opens his car.

'Should he be driving?' I ask Tina.

'Try stopping him.'

He revs his engine noisily and we both step back as he powers away from the drive, scattering gravel in his wake.

'I'm so sorry,' Tina says as he races down the road.

'It's hardly your fault.'

'I was late.'

'That's no excuse. I don't know what to say.'

'Neither do I. Listen, do you mind if we leave coffee. I'm exhausted.'

'No problem.'

'He's not always like that. Sometimes he can be quite charming.'

'Did he hurt your arm?'

Tina shakes her head. 'No, I'm fine. He just gets frustrated and takes it out on me. He'll be a pussy cat in the morning, honestly.'

I decide to button my lip. I'm not convinced. No wonder Tina likes Matty. If I had to put up with Oliver's behaviour I'd covet someone gentle and kind like Matty too.

'Night, Meg. And thanks for driving. I had a really nice evening. Well, apart from Oliver acting the prat.' She leans over and kisses my cheek. 'Sleep well.'

'And you.' As I walk home, I jiggle my keys in my hands. All in all it's been an eye-opener of a night.

Hattie rings at ten the following morning. 'Well?' she demands. 'What did he say?'

I sigh inwardly. 'Where are you?' I ask. Her voice is echoing.

'In Ryan's bathroom,' she admits. 'It's tiny. So, what did he say? Spill. And hurry up, I'm late for work.'

'I didn't really get a chance to talk to him for long,' I begin. 'And he didn't really say anything specific.'

'Meg! Just tell me. I'm a big girl, I can take it. What *did* he say?'

Hattie always knows when I'm lying, it's most annoying. I decide to come clean. It's probably for the best in the long run. As long as she doesn't shoot the messenger, so to speak.

'He said it was just a bit of fun, nothing serious. That you both knew that.'

'Yeah, right. What did he really say?'

Oops, I'm stuck now. How do I dig myself out of this one? I open my mouth to say something. 'Um, well, um,' is all I manage.

'Meg! *What did he say?*' I hold the receiver away from my ear as she's nearly deafening me. I hear a knock and a muffled voice in the background.

'I have to go,' Hattie says. 'Ryan needs me.'

'What about work?' I ask.

'It can wait.' She gives a sniff. 'I have no idea why you're lying to me. Maybe you're jealous of our amazing sex life or something. But it's not funny. I'm going to have sex now. Fast, furious, mind-blowing sex with Ryan. And I don't want to talk about this again, get it?' She cuts me off.

'Fine,' I say to myself. 'Next time get someone else to do your dirty work.' I feel sorry for her. She's obviously in complete denial. But I sense that it's only a matter of time before Ryan shows his true colours.

On Tuesday morning at five a.m. I'm standing under the shower, trying to wake up. The warm water caresses my body and I shut my eyes and think about the last two days. I've tried ringing Simon, not to tell him I was on my way to San Francisco, I wanted to keep that a surprise, but to tell him about Dad, and to say I was sorry. I'd left a few garbled messages on his voicemail. He'd rung me once, but it was a terrible line and it had gone dead after a few seconds. He only had time to say 'hi', but at least I know he's still speaking to me.

And I'm nearly there, in San Francisco, in his arms again (I hope). It's been quite a struggle, but I've managed to get everything organized in time. Miraculously Hattie said she'd take a few days off and help Mum with the kids. I think she's still a bit annoyed with me over the whole Ryan thing, but she managed to be civil to me yesterday and I didn't bring him up. I'm not totally stupid.

I spoke to Dad briefly on the phone yesterday, he sounded tired but in good form, all things considered. 'I'll be in to see you as soon as I'm back,' I promised him.

'I look forward to it,' he said. 'Enjoy yourself, Meg. You deserve a break.'

'Thanks, Dad. And thanks again for the ticket.'

'My pleasure.'

I also rang Ivy. I was supposed to start working on her house yesterday morning, but when I told her about Simon and about Dad and his present, she'd been very understanding. 'Life comes first, Meg,' she'd said. 'My place can wait. You go and make up with your young man.'

So everything is set – the kids stayed at Mum and Dad's last night with all their week's bags and baggage and so far all is going to plan.

As I rub the water out of my eyes and bend down to pick up the shower gel, I hear a noise downstairs. Then a bang. I freeze. There's someone in the house. A burglar. I turn off the shower and stay rooted to the spot. Have I locked the bathroom door? I look at the lock. I haven't put the bolt across. But as it's practically falling off the door it wouldn't hold Lily's weight, let alone a grown man's. I step out of the bath and grab a towel as quietly as I can. I wrap it tightly around my body and look around for something to defend myself with. My eyes rest on something. It's not exactly the most threatening of implements, but in my distracted state I pick it up and open the door, brandishing it in front of me.

'Meg! What the hell are you doing? What's the loo brush for?'

It's Simon! I've never been so relieved to see him in my entire life.

'What are you doing here? You're supposed to be in San Francisco.'

He takes the loo brush out of my hand, walks into the

bathroom and puts it back in its holder. Coming back out he gives me a hug. 'God, I've missed you,' he says into my dripping hair. 'I'm so sorry.'

'I'm sorry too,' I say. 'I acted like an idiot.'

He draws away and wipes some water off the side of his face. 'No, I meant about your dad.'

'You got the message?'

He nods. 'I'd just arrived in San Francisco. It was a nightmare flight; I won't go into it. I checked my messages as soon as we landed. Then I went to the ticket desk and changed my return flight and got straight back on the same aeroplane. The girl at the desk thought I was mad at first, but when I told her about your dad she was very understanding. She bumped me up to first class and I slept the whole way back.'

'And the sailing?' I ask.

'Slipper's covering for me.'

I start to cry. 'I'm so happy to see you. I was on my way to San Francisco. That's why I'm up so early.'

'With the kids?'

'No, I left them with Mum and Hattie.'

'Hattie?'

I smile. 'I know. Wonders will never cease.'

'So I ruined your holiday?'

'I don't mind. This is even better.' I hug him again, tightly, and kiss him on his raspy cheek. I draw back and grin at him like a loon.

'I'm not going anywhere. Not now, not ever again. I don't want to lose you, Meg. So I'm giving up the sailing. For good.'

I stare at him incredulously. Am I hearing things?

He smiles at me. 'Don't look so shocked. I *can* do other things, you know.'

I shiver in my towel, drips from my sopping hair running down my bare skin.

'Go inside and get dressed.' He pushes me gently towards

the bedroom. He steps into the bathroom and out again, holding a hand towel. 'Here.' He hands it to me. 'For your head.'

I flick my head down, sending a shower of water onto the carpet and wrap the slightly musty smelling towel over my wet hair. Lord knows how long it has been in the bathroom, but I don't really care.

I follow Simon into the bedroom and pull on old tracksuit bottoms and a T-shirt. I look at the unmade bed longingly.

'Get in.' Simon nods at the bed. He knows how much I like my sleep. 'We can talk in bed.' He pulls off his clothes and spoons in beside me. Irrationally, I wish he'd move away a bit, give me more space, but I humour him.

'I'm so sorry for giving you such a fright,' he begins, his left hand running up and down my arm.

'It's just so unexpected. It's a big step, quitting sailing.'

He gives a laugh. 'No, I meant scaring you in the bathroom like that.'

'Oh, right. That's OK. I was getting ready to fight off an intruder.'

'With the loo brush?' he teases me, nuzzling his chin into the back of my neck.

I draw away and turn around, getting slightly caught up in the duvet but kicking myself free. I can just about make his face out in the early-morning light filtering through the white curtains.

'What's wrong?' he asks.

'Are you really giving up sailing or are you joking?'

'Joking? I wouldn't joke about something like that.'

'So what are you going to do?'

'I thought I might give Hans's place a go. He's always said there's a job there for me whenever I want it.'

'How much will it pay? Will we manage?'

Simon shrugs. 'It won't be as lucrative as the sailing but I know Hans will make it worth my while. And if I do some corporate sailing in the evenings we should be OK.'

'It sounds like you and Hans have talked about this before. Am I right?'

'Yes. Professional sailing is like any sport, you only have a certain shelf life. And if you get injured—' He stops for a moment. 'Best to have some continuity plans.'

I realize with a start that in my innocence, I've never considered that. But one of Simon's friends recently lost two fingers in a winch accident, so I know it can happen. I guess I didn't want to give myself yet another thing to worry about. 'I see. But why? I thought you loved the sailing.'

'I do. But it's starting to come between us, Meg.'

'No, it isn't,' I protest feebly. 'It's not really the sailing. It's more the whole lifestyle.'

'Which comes *with* the sailing. It's a fact of life. And to be honest, I miss you and the kids. I don't want to miss them growing up. Plus I'm putting you under a huge amount of stress, coping with everything on your own for most of the time. And now with your dad being sick, you'll need some extra help. It's time for me to pull my weight.'

Simon's right, I *am* under a lot of stress, and I do want to be there for Dad. I should be over the moon. Simon is giving up his dream job for me and the kids. Why do I feel so uneasy?

'Are you sure about all this?' I ask. 'What about New Zealand?'

His eyes flicker away from mine for a moment and I know I've touched a nerve.

'Simon, I don't want you to wake up years from now regretting that you never did the America's Cup. I know it's like the Holy Grail for sailors.'

He meets my eyes again. 'You and the kids are more important to me than sailing, even in the America's Cup. You're the most important thing in the world to me, Meg, and I don't want to lose you – not over a sailing event. Or over something stupid I did when I was drunk. I'm so sorry about Mary—'

I cut him off. 'I overreacted. Forget about it. I have.'

'Are you sure?'

I nod at him, tears forming in my eyes. Oh, not again. I'm like a faulty Tiny Tears. One emotional squeeze and I'm away. And I know the America's Cup isn't just another sailing event, but I don't want to rub salt into his wound by pointing this out.

'I'm only going to say this once. You can change your mind. If you want to go to New Zealand, I'll cope. We'll all cope.'

'You'll come with me?' he asks. There's a flash of hope in his eyes and I feel terrible, but I have to be honest with him.

'No. It wouldn't be fair on the kids, especially Dan. I'm sorry, I meant if *you* wanted to go. On your own,' I add, just to be crystal clear.

He shakes his head. 'I don't want to be away from you all for that long. No, it wouldn't work. As I said, I'm going to work with Hans. I've made up my mind.'

'A hundred per cent?'

'Yes. A hundred per cent.' He gives me a hug.

'Welcome home,' I whisper into his neck.

Later that morning we drive over to Mum and Dad's to collect the kids. Mum answers the door, her gardening gloves tucked under one arm and a pair of secateurs sticking out of her trouser pocket. Unusually, her face is bare and her hair is scraped back into a ponytail. She looks a lot younger that way. Less matronly.

'Meg!' she cries as soon as she realizes who it is. 'Simon! What are *you* doing here?'

'I never made it to San Francisco,' I explain. 'Simon beat me to it.'

Simon tells her the full story, including details of his new career change.

307

Mum smiles. 'How extraordinary. I hope Meg appreciates the sacrifice you're making.'

I look at her. Sacrifice? Simon puts his hand on my arm. 'It's no sacrifice, Julie. I want to be with my family. No sacrifice at all.'

Mum pushes back a strand of hair. She looks at me, her lips pressed tightly together.

'Can we come in?' I ask.

'What am I thinking of? Of course. Come in, come in,' she ushers us inside. 'Dan and Lily are in the garden with Hattie.'

Just then we hear a shriek.

'They're playing on the swing. Leave them be for a minute. Sit down and have a cup of coffee with me.' She waves at the kitchen chairs.

'Are they new?' I ask, pointing at the red and white checked seat cushions.

'Yes, I made them last night. Do you like them? They match the new blind. Thought I'd brighten the place up before your dad gets back.'

Personally I think it's all a little Italian bistro for Dad but I keep my mouth shut.

'Sit down.' She clicks on the kettle.

'How is he?' Simon asks as Mum busies herself with coffee mugs and the cafetière. 'Meg said the operation went well.'

Mum stops dead for a moment and then turns around to face us. 'You might as well know—' Her face darkens. 'The cancer has spread into other areas. They thought it was just in the bowel, but, um . . . well . . . it isn't.' She's stumbling over her words and although I can see the anguish in her face, I'm too caught up in my own pain to register her feelings.

'What does that mean?' I ask. Simon reaches over, takes my hand and holds it firmly.

'He has to have chemotherapy.'

'Can't they just cut the affected bits out? I thought that was what the surgery was all about.'

'It's not as simple as that, apparently.' Mum picks up a coffee cup and holds it tightly in her two hands, staring at it. 'It's in a lot of different areas. I'll know more after I've been in today and talked to the consultant. I was in shock yesterday and I didn't ask enough questions.'

'Of course,' Simon murmurs.

'Why didn't you tell me?' I demand. 'You were going to let me go to San Francisco not knowing? How could you do that?'

'It wouldn't have made any difference, Meg,' she says gently. 'Your dad's stable and doing well. They're not starting the chemo until he recovers from the operation. There was no point worrying you.'

'You should have told me!' I pull my hand out of Simon's and stand up. 'He's my dad. I have a right to know.'

'I agree.' Mum looks me in the eye. 'And it was your dad who made me and Hattie promise not to say anything.'

'I don't believe you. He wouldn't keep something like that from me.'

Mum sighs. 'He wanted you to go to San Francisco to see Simon. He did it because he *loves* you.'

I know she's telling the truth. Dad was only trying to help me, to love me in the best way he knew how. I run out of the room, up the stairs and lock myself in the bathroom. I sit down on the lid of the toilet and begin to cry hot, angry tears. It's not fair. Why Dad? He doesn't deserve this.

A few minutes later I hear footsteps on the stairs and then a knock on the door.

'Meg? It's me. Are you OK?' It's Simon.

'Yes.' I dab at my eyes with some loo paper. 'I'm fine. I just need to be on my own for a few minutes.'

'I understand. I'll be in the garden when you're ready.'

I listen to his steps as he walks away and take a few deep

breaths. I have to pull myself together. Dad needs a strong, capable daughter, not a snivelling wreck. I splash some cold water on my face, look at myself in the mirror and wince. My eyes are red and the skin around them is puffy and blotchy. My cheeks are pale and because I fell asleep with a towel on my head, my hair is sticking out from my scalp at strange angles, even though I've tamed the worst of it with hair clips. I look a fright.

There's another knock on the door.

'Meg? It's Hattie.'

I let her in.

'It's terrible, isn't it?' She gives me a sad smile. 'I'm so sorry I didn't tell you, but Dad made me swear I wouldn't. I couldn't break my promise.'

'I know.' I blow out my breath in a rush. 'I just feel so bloody helpless. What if he doesn't make it?'

'He will, he's as tough as old boots.' She stares at my head. 'What the hell have you done to your hair? It looks mad.'

I laugh despite everything. 'Hattie!'

'Sorry, but Dad would want us to laugh about things.' She gives me a gentle shove with her shoulder. 'He'll fight it, you'll see.'

'Do you think I'd be allowed in to see him today?'

'I don't see why not. I'll look after the kids if you like.'

'That's OK, Simon's home now.'

'For good he tells me.' She looks at me. 'Is that for real?'

'I think so. He seems fairly certain. We'll give it a go anyway.'

'Will you cope having him around all the time?'

'It'll be great. What do you mean?'

'You're used to being on your own, that's all. Having things your own way.'

'It'll be great,' I repeat. 'We'll just have to be flexible, give each other some space.'

'Um,' Hattie murmurs, a smile on her lips.

'What?' I demand.

'Nothing. I'm sure you're right. Why don't you give him the afternoon off to unpack and relax? Leave the kids with me. I have the day off anyway, so I might as well use it. You could go shopping or for lunch or something after seeing Dad, take your mind off things. Or make a start on that old one's house, what's her name?'

'Ivy. That's not a bad idea. Thanks.'

Hattie smiles at me. 'Hey, I might go and visit Tina this afternoon with Lily and Dan. Do you think she'd mind?'

'I'm sure she'd love it.' And it would give Simon a chance to visit Hans. Until he has a definite offer of work, I know I'll be a bit twitchy. I got the phone bill this morning, and it wasn't pretty. 'I'll give her a ring and see what she's up to.'

'Great. See you in a minute.' Hattie walks out of the bathroom.

I sit back down on the loo and punch Tina's number into my mobile. Hattie has lifted my spirits and I'm feeling better, a little more positive. I'm glad she's back to normal with me, I hate it when we argue.

I haven't seen Tina since the other night, and I'm a little nervous about ringing her for some strange reason. I'm afraid she'll mention Oliver, but I'm also afraid she won't. How can we be proper friends if we don't talk about the things we find difficult to discuss, if we have secrets from each other?

'Meg! Are you there yet? Is it sunny?'

'I'm still in Dublin.' I tell Tina all about Simon's surprise trip and his plan to stay at home.

'Ah, Meg, that's great. I'm delighted for you. Gosh, it'll be strange having him around all the time, won't it?'

'That's what Hattie said, but it'll be fantastic.'

'Oh, I'm sure it will be. It'll just take a while to get used to, that's all. Don't expect it to fall into place instantly. There will be teething problems, but nothing serious, I'm sure.'

Not Tina as well. I'm beginning to get a little nervous – what if they're right?

'Listen, are you around this afternoon? I'm going to see Dad and Hattie was thinking of calling around to your place with the kids.'

Tina pauses for a moment.

'Only if it suits,' I add.

'That sounds great. Around three? I have someone over for lunch.'

'Anyone interesting?' I ask, ever curious.

'I'll tell you all about it later. I promise.' There's a crash and a wail in the background. 'Ooops, have to run. Eric's just fallen off a car. Don't ask. Bye, see your gang at three.'

'Meg, are you still in there?' Simon asks, walking in the door which Hattie left ajar.

Lily's sitting on his hip, snuggling into his side.

'Go 'ome?' Lily says hopefully.

I stand up and gave her a kiss on her peachy cheek. 'Let's all go home.'

Chapter 25

Below: beneath the deck

Simon insists on driving me to the hospital. He's arranged to meet Hans later that morning, so I can hardly complain. Besides, I appreciate the offer.

As we're stopped at the traffic lights in Blackrock a tall, elegantly dressed woman walks past the car. She reminds me of Simon's mum.

'Have you told your parents about your plans to stay in Dublin?' I ask him.

'No, not yet. I want to get everything sorted first.'

'What do you think they'll say?'

'Mum will be delighted. She's always complaining about not seeing enough of me. They can come over a lot more now.'

Jeepers, I hadn't thought of that. I pick at the skin on the side of my thumbnail.

'Only if it suits *you* of course. They wouldn't want to impose.'

I say nothing.

'I know you find Mum difficult—'

'No, I don't.'

Simon makes a tiny coughing noise at the back of his throat.

'Maybe a little,' I concede. 'It's just an awful lot of work. Having them to stay, I mean.'

'I know. But I'll be around to help now. Changing the beds and all that lark.' Simon pulls into the hospital car park. 'Here we are. I'll sit in the car and wait for you.'

'Don't be daft. Dad would love to see you.'

'I know you'll want to talk to him on your own, so I'll just stick my head in and say hello.'

Simon puts his arm around my shoulders as we walk towards the entrance. Several patients and visitors are huddled in clumps, sucking deeply on cigarettes, the smoke lingering in grey plumes in the still air.

We stand outside Dad's room for a moment. Simon gives me a hug and kisses the top of my head.

'It'll be OK,' he says in a low voice.

I bite my lower lip, almost drawing blood, promising myself I'm not going to cry this time.

I knock on the door, hear Dad's familiar voice, open it and walk in.

'Meg,' Dad says with a smile. His upper body is resting against a barrage of pillows, more of them than the last time I visited. He looks even smaller now, his shoulders slumped, his face pale and slack.

'Hi.' I step towards him and kiss him gently on the cheek, holding my breath. I need to remember my Old Spice dad, not this freshly washed baby-smelling dad. 'How are you?'

'I've been better,' he admits. 'Your mum rang and said you'd be in this morning.' He smiles at Simon. 'And *you* must have given Meg quite a surprise.'

Simon laughs. 'She thought I was a burglar. She tried to attack me with the loo brush.'

Dad laughs, then stops and gives a hollow cough. 'Lucky you weren't. You might have been brushed to death.' His eyes twinkle.

314

'It's not funny,' I say. 'He gave me a real fright. I could have had a heart attack.'

'I'm glad you didn't,' Dad says. 'Wouldn't wish this place on anyone.' He looks around his room a little despondently.

I wonder how long he'll be in for, with the new diagnosis, but I'm too afraid to ask.

'Mum told you about the complications?' Dad says, sensing my unease and coming straight to the point.

I nod wordlessly.

'I'll be getting the best treatment available, and the doctors say with the chemo I have an excellent chance of beating this completely.'

I nod again, this time unable to meet his eyes.

'I should go,' Simon murmurs.

I shake my head. With Simon by my side I feel stronger. I know as soon as he leaves the room I'll dissolve into tears and that isn't what Dad needs right now.

'No, stay.' I slip my hand into his and hold it tight. I look at Dad. 'If you don't mind.'

He smiles at Simon. 'Course not. I'm so glad to see you back, son. I believe this time it's for good.'

'That's right,' Simon says confidently.

Warmth surges through my veins. Simon is by my side. Simon will be there every day, helping me through this.

'I hope it works out for you,' Dad says. 'For all of you.'

'Thanks.'

'Why don't you both sit down? You're making me nervous hovering like that.'

Simon pulls over the armchair and a plastic chair. I sink down into the armchair, instantly regretting it, as I'm now much lower than Dad. Simon notices and stands up. 'Take this one.'

I pull the plastic chair towards Dad until the metal legs hit the bed frame with a hollow ring.

'I'm sure you have a lot of questions, Meg,' he says. 'And I'll do my best to answer them. But remember this is all new to me too. And everything's a bit of a blur.'

'I'm sure you're in shock. It's a lot to take in.'

'Once I'm back home, it'll be easier. I always think being in hospital makes you feel sicker than you really are. I'm looking forward to sleeping in my own bed. This one's darned uncomfortable and I hate blankets.'

I smile at him. He likes his creature comforts.

'When will that be?' Simon asks.

'In about ten days. Then I'll have to come back in for chemo every few days until the cancer's gone. Hopefully not for longer than three months, but they can't be sure of that.'

'Are you scared?' I ask before I can stop myself. Great, Meg, that's very positive. Your brilliance knows no bounds.

Dad holds my gaze. 'Yes. I won't lie to you. I am scared. Scared, but determined to fight this. I have a lot to live for, after all. And I have no intention of leaving any of you. Especially *you*, Meg. I know how hard all this is on you.'

I feel terrible. 'It's not *me* this is happening to, it's you,' I blurt out. 'And you should have told me as soon as you knew. If I'd gone to San Francisco and something had happened to you—'

'Nothing's going to happen to me. Everything's under control. The doctors and nurses are keeping a careful eye on me. Too careful if you ask me. I'll be back to normal in no time, you'll see. I wanted you to go to San Francisco. But I'm equally as glad to see Simon back in Dublin.'

'I'm sorry about the wasted ticket,' I say. 'It was so sweet of you.'

'It's not important. I just wanted you and Simon to talk. And now you're here, together. That means a lot to me.'

I nod at him tight-lipped, afraid of saying the wrong thing.

'So tell me about your plans, Simon.' Dad asks after a moment.

I realize I've been sitting rigid and I try to relax as Simon tells Dad about Hans's shop. I listen to them chat, and yet again I'm grateful for Simon's presence.

Coming out of Dad's room a little later, closing the door gently behind us, Simon squeezes my hand to get my attention. 'Isn't that Ryan?'

I follow his gaze down the corridor. Ryan is walking out of the nurse's station.

'Should we say hello?'

Just then Ryan turns on his heels and begins to walk away from us quickly. His head is bowed a little. Has he seen us?

'Wonder what he's doing here?' I ask.

'Same as us probably,' Simon squeezes my hand. 'Visiting someone. Now, let's get you home.'

'Hattie didn't say anything.'

'Maybe he didn't tell her. Best not to mention it. I'm sure if it's someone close to him he'll tell her in his own good time.'

'You're probably right.'

The traffic is light and ten minutes later we're back home.

'Do you mind if I scoot straight down to Hans's place?' Simon asks, opening the hall door, pushing it open and stepping back to let me in first. The house is eerily quiet without the kids. 'Meg, did you hear what I just said?'

'Sorry?' I look at him blankly.

'I'm going to walk down to the chandlery now, to meet Hans, is that OK?'

'Yes, fine.' I look at my watch. It's only half eleven. The day is dragging – it seems like at least one. 'In fact, I might just do a couple of hours work in Ivy's house. I might as well get on with it. Might help take my mind off things.'

'Good idea.' Simon leans over and kisses me, a peck on the cheek first, followed by a deeper kiss on the mouth. He puts his arms around me and holds me tight. 'But seeing as the kids are out, and we have the house to ourselves—' He dances me around a little in his arms.

'I'm not really in the mood,' I say firmly. What is he thinking? Sometimes Simon's testosterone levels drive me mental.

'Sorry.' He lets go of me, his arms dropping to his sides. 'Not appropriate. It's just so great to see you, and to have some time to spend together, proper time.'

'I know. But at the moment I'm a bit preoccupied and we have oceans of time ahead of us.'

'I understand.' He grabs a light grey sailing jacket from the new stash of them on the coat hooks.

'Where did that come from?' My eyes linger on the unfamiliar jacket.

'Cornwall. New team gear.' And before I get the chance to moan about our house being taken over by sailing clothes yet again, he kisses me firmly on the cheek. 'Better run. See you later.'

'What time?' I call after his disappearing back.

'No idea. Sixish?'

'I'll make dinner for us then.'

'Great,' he calls over his shoulder. 'Look forward to it.'

I look around the hall. Simon has dumped all his bags along one wall. I unzip one and am almost asphyxiated by the smell of damp, festering sailing clothes. I close the bag quickly. He can deal with that himself. I'm not going to slave over his laundry any more, not now he's home for good. I give one of the bags a good kick to move it closer to the wall and then walk into the kitchen.

I flick on the kettle, get Ivy's folder from the top of the fridge and settle down at the table. There's also a Jiffy bag. I empty the contents onto the wood with a clatter: a set of keys and a sealed envelope. There's no name on it, but I presume it's for me so I rip it open. Inside is a single piece of writing paper, folded over twice. I open it out and smooth it down on the table. There's one sentence in Ivy's spidery handwriting. I have to squint a little to read it, her writing is minuscule. 'Tread softly because you tread on my dreams,' it reads. It's a line from Yeats. I remember it from school. I pick up the keys and turn them over and over in my hands. 'Tread softly because you tread on my dreams,' I repeat out loud. I know exactly what she means. I've helped at dozens of house clearances and I'm aware how invasive and upsetting the whole process can be – favourite sofas proclaimed worthless and dumped in the skip; years and years of family photographs ending up in the same metal grave; old ball gowns, softly coloured jumpers and even wedding dresses put aside for the charity shop. House clearances are a real leveller. I'll do my very best to respect Ivy's wishes.

Driving the short distance to Blackrock, I wonder what, if anything, would be deemed of any real value in our house. One painting that had been my mother's, a snowy Parisian scene of two young children throwing snowballs into the Seine, their red woolly hats the only splash of colour on the otherwise white canvas. The small Victorian dressing table in our bedroom perhaps, also my mother's. It's a shiny conker-coloured walnut with its original mirror, a bit cloudy around the edges, and small curved drawers flanking the mirror. Her antique, square-set silver, diamond and sapphire engagement ring. She was buried wearing her wedding ring, I remember with a start. Dad had insisted on it. I don't know how I know this, I was so young at the time and it's not exactly the kind of thing you tell a child.

It isn't much – one painting, one ring and a battered dressing table. I hope Ivy's house holds a lot more treasures. I'm a little worried about overlooking something valuable but Ivy assured me that if that happened, and she was sure it wouldn't, that it didn't really matter. 'Just do your best,' she said on the phone when I voiced my concerns. 'I'd much prefer someone I know rifling through my things. And a woman too. You'll recognize what's important and what's not, Meg, I know you will.'

It's a big responsibility – I hope I don't blow it. But if I get it right – with the promised 10 per cent commission – it will go a long way towards solving the problem of paying Matty. He's already been very patient, but I know he runs his business on a shoestring, and at the very least he has to pay his men.

I pull up outside 11 Church Close and sit in the car for a moment, collecting my thoughts. The cul-de-sac is quiet and still, no one walking dogs or pushing buggies, no one pottering in their front garden. Not so much as a car pulling in or out of a drive. Ivy told me that most of her neighbours are retired and keep themselves to themselves and I can see why the retirement village suits her down to the ground. It's far livelier than Church Close.

I open the car door, grab my carrier bag off the passenger seat and lock up. Ivy's front garden is looking a little bedraggled. The late summer perennials have started to bloom, red and dark purple flowers thrusting their heads rather bravely through the overgrown foliage of the main beds. Clumps of browning bedding plants and crumbling-leaved geraniums give the narrower beds beside the drive a dejected look. She'll have to get a gardener in before viewings start. And a cleaner, I think, looking at the murky windows and the dull door brasses, which need a good rub.

I put the key in the door and open it. I quickly punch in the alarm code and wait until the shrill beeping stops. The air in the hall is stale and I wrinkle my nose. I close the door behind me, walk into the small sitting room to the right, and swing both the windows wide open. Then I stand back and survey the room.

I have my work cut out for me. It's crammed with a mishmash of furniture: a battered teak veneer seventies sideboard, probably made of chipboard from the look of it, runs along the right-hand wall. It's lurching dangerously to the left and on closer inspection I notice one of its stubby wooden legs is broken and another is skew-whiff. To the left is the fireplace, flanked by two tall mahogany glass-fronted cabinets, one jammed full of dozens of dolls in intricate traditional costume, the other displaying crystal glasses and elegant curved decanters, which I know just from looking at them weigh a ton, assorted china and what looks like an old doll's tea set.

There's a stiff-backed, uncomfortable-looking modern two-seater sofa to one side of the fireplace and two ornate, slightly battered wooden-framed armchairs, whose gold-coloured upholstery has seen better days. French doors lead into the overrun garden. The walls are littered with pictures and prints of all shapes and sizes, some in the most beautiful, highly decorated frames, some in simple clip frames.

The two highly detailed berry-red and faded-blue rugs on the floor look promising, as does the wonderful set of Georgian fire irons with a matching coal bucket sitting in the hearth.

As is so often the way with houses belonging to older clients, some of the pieces are exciting, others are skip fodder. I have no idea where to start. I look around the crowded room once more and then sit down on the small sofa (I was right, it's most uncomfortable), get my large spiral-bound notebook and a pen out of my carrier bag and open it.

Ivy's House, I write and underline it twice. *11 Church Close*, I add, just to be clear.

Room 1: Sitting Room.

Ivy said most of the decent things are in here. She said there's the odd interesting picture or ornament in the rest of the house but nothing of much value.

Room 2: Hall. I write next.

I go into it. There are four doors. I open the one opposite the front door which leads into the kitchen, and have a look around, pulling open cupboards and rooting in drawers. I find some nice silver cutlery, a heavy Victorian silver openwork fish slice, its handle an ornate fish head, a rather fine Waterford crystal water jug and a matching pair of Victorian silver candlesticks, melted wax still encrusted on their feet. I put them all on the kitchen table and record them in my notebook, before moving them back into a cupboard for safe-keeping. The rest of the kitchen crockery and bits and pieces will need to be boxed up for a charity shop.

Ivy's right, there are slim pickings in the other three rooms – the bathroom, master bedroom with tiny en suite and the guest room. They have been stripped of all personal belongings and look rather sad: naked mattresses on the beds, a lone empty toothbrush mug with a snake of hardened toothpaste running down its side. I note the beds, bedside lockers and two prints in nice ornate wooden frames for Hall's and move back to the main event, the sitting room.

I sit back down on the sofa, prop the notebook on my knee, take a good look around and start writing. *Paintings*, I jot down. *Prints, tapestries, needlepoint and other 'crafty' framed artworks. Framed photographs (on wall).* I let out my breath in a whoosh. I start to get into my stride and begin to writer faster.

Rugs, I write next. *Antique furniture, 'Hall's furniture', 'other' furniture (no commercial value).* I usually write skip furniture, but I can't bring myself to call it that yet. Hopefully the skip heading won't feature too highly on my lists. But I know in the business side of my head, I've already earmarked the sideboard and the clip frames for dumping.

I work my way down the page, making lots more headings. *China, Glass, Misc (Dolls!).* Once I'm satisfied I've covered everything, I reach into my bag and take out my stickers. I've come up with a colour-coded system for marking every item. Red for the antique dealers, yellow for Hall's. Pink for the art dealers. Blue for the book specialists. Green for the skip. Black for the set dressers and prop buyers. One prop buyer in reality – Gwen Barker, a lovely woman, if a little eccentric, in her mid fifties, who sources props for both television and films. She was always looking for bits and bobs when I worked in Hall's, the odder the better – things like human skeletons (Victorian medical thriller), stuffed monkey hands which had been made into gruesome candlesticks (horror film). The dolls and the doll's tea set are a distinct Gwen possibility.

Once satisfied I've covered everything, I begin by stickering the paintings. When I open the clip frames to remove the prints I'm surprised to find old photographs hidden behind the generic Impressionist scenes. The photos all seem to be of one particular woman – tall, in her twenties with carefully set platinum-blonde hair, Marilyn Monroe style, and a slash of dark red lipstick. I presume it's dark red, it's hard to tell in the black and white photos. In one of them the woman is lounging on a beach towel, large Jackie O sunglasses perched on the end of her nose, engrossed in a paperback. Her legs are crossed daintily at the ankle, and I notice with a start that along with her rather modest stripy swimsuit that comes way down over her generous hips, she's also wearing high-heeled sandals. My curiosity is piqued and I resolve to ask Ivy about her. I put the photographs in the padded envelope that held the keys and carry on.

As I put red stickers on the antique rugs, my stomach begins to rumble and I push up my sleeve and look at my watch. After two. Not wonder I'm hungry. I sit up on my hunkers and roll my shoulders a little. I've been so absorbed in cataloguing and labelling that I've lost all track of time. And it feels good.

Driving home, I feel like ringing Ivy and thanking her over and over for giving me this opportunity, but I rein myself in. It's only the first day after all. There's plenty of time for that later. Instead I switch on the radio and sing along to 'Hey Jude'. Badly.

Stopping at traffic lights, my eyes are draw to a chemist's window to the left. They're advertising a new vitamin C wonder pill. Suddenly my heart sinks. Dad. How dare I feel so chirpy when Dad is so sick? I grip the steering wheel tightly in my hands. He wouldn't want me to feel so guilty – he said as much in the hospital.

So I decide to stop being so hard on myself. Working has taken my mind off it, that's all. Just as I hoped it might. Nothing wrong with that.

'Mum!' Lily wraps her arms around my legs and almost grounds me as soon as Tina opens the door.

I smile down at her. 'Are you glad to see me by any chance?'

She beams up at me. 'Play, Mama. Play.' She loosens her grip on my legs and starts to pull my arm instead.

'OK, Lily,' I say, gently taking my arm away.

She hears a shriek and runs towards the noise.

Tina laughs. 'The boys are out in the garden, soaking each other with the hose. Hattie's sunbathing and trying to keep dry.'

I follow her down the steps, into the kitchen and out through the French doors into the immaculately landscaped garden. The garden is in full bloom, a spectacular explosion of colour, all Tina's gardener's work is finally coming to fruition. The large curving beds were redesigned and replanted last year with a themed colour scheme – hot pink and stark white flowers, lush green foliage – and it all looks fantastic. Like one of those show gardens you see at Chelsea.

'Would you like something to drink?' Tina asks as we walk towards Hattie and the children, whose shrieks are ear piercing. 'Or some lunch? There's loads of salmon and brown bread left over, and some potato salad and other bits and pieces. Have you eaten yet?'

'No.' My stomach gives a lurch followed by a loud gurgle.

I've been trying to ignore its protestations but the words salmon and potato salad have sent it into overdrive. 'That would be great if you wouldn't mind. I'm starving. I'll just say hi to Hattie first.'

'Sure. I'll be in the kitchen.' Tina stops for a moment and then says, 'And your dad? How is he?'

'OK. Tired. But bearing up.'

Tina nods. 'I'm here if you want to talk about it.'

'Thanks,' I say gratefully. 'I'll probably take you up on that at some stage.' I give a short laugh. 'Bore you with all my woes.'

Tina's eyes rest on mine. I can see the sympathy and the understanding behind them and I feel a lump in my throat.

'Bore away,' she says softly. 'Any time. I mean that.'

I nod, unable to say anything.

Tina puts her hand on my shoulder for a moment and then takes it away. 'See you in a minute.'

'Hey, Hattie,' I say loudly, walking towards her. She's slouched in a pink and lime-green striped deckchair, her head resting against the canvas, eyes shut, legs splayed in front of her, looking the picture of relaxation. She opens her eyes slowly, squinting in the sun. She pats her hair for her sunglasses and then slides them down over her eyes.

'Jeepers, it's bright,' she says, hoiking herself up a little. She looks towards the far end of the garden, where the children are dashing around on the grass, Eric and Freddie stark naked, Lily in her nappy and a soaking wet T-shirt, Dan in a pair of light blue cotton boxer shorts.

Dan is wielding a hose and threatening the young children with a drenching. They don't seem to mind, running purposefully under the wide arcs of water and yelling and laughing.

'Keeping dry?' I ask Hattie, crouching down on my hunkers beside her.

'Just about. Although there has been the odd splash.' She

points at the sleeve of her white T-shirt, which is darker than the rest of the material. 'Moved just in time, or else it would have been a bit of a wet-T-shirt competition moment.'

I laugh.

'Sorry the kids are so wet,' she continues. 'Their clothes are a bit damp too. Tina took them inside to stop them getting even worse. But it's such a nice day. They were dying to get out of their clothes.'

I smile at her. 'It's fine. They may as well make the most of it. How were Lily and Dan for you this morning?'

'Great. Not a bother. And Dad?'

'He's OK. It was good to see him.' I don't elaborate. I look over at Lily, whose nappy looks distinctly sodden. It's only a matter of time before it sniggles down her chubby thighs.

Hattie puts her hand on my arm and squeezes it. Maybe, like Tina, she senses that I don't want to talk about it right now. But I'm wrong. This is Hattie after all. 'Ah, Jesus,' she says after a moment. 'It's shitty, isn't it? Poor Dad. All those bloody chemo drugs and everything. And the side effects. His hair will fall out, not that he has much left anyway. And I hate to think what that poison does to your—'

'Hattie!' I cut in. 'Not now, please.'

'Oh, right, sorry.' She pushes her sunglasses up her nose a little and rearranges her bottom in the deckchair. 'It's hard to sit up straight in these things,' she comments. 'Listen, I wasn't thinking. I didn't mean to mention the chemo, it just came out.'

'It's all right, Hattie. Just forget about it.'

'I know you're very sensitive when it comes to things like needles—'

'Hattie!' I stand up quickly. My right leg has gone all pins and needles and I shake it out.

'Are you all right?' she asks, staring at me.

'Cramp in my leg,' I explain.

'Ah, I see. And I promise I won't mention any more medical procedures, OK?'

'Good.' I know being annoyed with her is pointless. She doesn't mean to be so tactless. And I know I'm a bit sensitive at times.

We watch the children for a while. Dan is showing Eric how to slide along the wet grass and I only hope he doesn't get a prickle or a splinter in his bottom. Lily and Freddie are examining a snail on the granite paving stones, poking its shell gently with pieces of stick.

'Who was that woman with Oliver?' Hattie asks, breaking the silence.

'With Oliver? Was *he* here?'

'Yes. For lunch. You just missed him. He was with a small dark-haired woman. They were leaving as I arrived. Tina introduced me to Oliver but not the woman. He's a bit of all right, isn't he? Those piercing blue eyes.'

I'm far more interested in Oliver's companion. 'And the woman?' I prompt.

'I asked Tina about her when they left. She just said "All will be revealed" rather cryptically. What's all that about?'

'I have no idea,' I say. I'm intrigued. 'Maybe it's his sister or something.'

Hattie thinks for a moment. 'She didn't look anything like him. Plus she was huge.'

'Fat you mean?'

Hattie grins. 'No, preggers. At least six or seven months, although I'm no expert.'

'Pregnant?' I exclaim. The plot thickens. 'I'll go and ask Tina who she is.'

Hattie gives a snort.

'What?' I demand.

'You're practically chomping at the bit. You're such a nosey old bat.'

I poke the tip of my tongue out at her. She's right but I can't help myself. I walk quickly towards the kitchen.

Tina is pottering at the kitchen table, pulling cling film off a plate of fresh light pink salmon wedges and humming to herself under her breath.

'You're in a good mood,' I remark, watching her.

She smiles at me, balling the cling film between her palms. 'I guess I am. Must be the sunny weather.'

She turns her back to me, pulls a large white dinner plate out of a cupboard and places it on the table. Taking a fork in either hand she looks down at the fish. 'One piece or two?' she asks me. 'It's a bit flaky, mind. I'm not sure piece is the right word. Scattered lump might be more accurate.'

'It looks delicious. I'll start with one. And I'll help myself to salad.' There are several ceramic bowls on the table of varying sizes filled with salads and I can't wait to get stuck in – chunky tomato pieces with shiny black olives and lashings of French dressing, potatoes covered with creamy mayonnaise and punctuated with spikes of green chives, and pasta with rich-looking pesto sauce. Tina has played a blinder.

'You've been busy,' I remark, gesturing at the table.

'The deli in Dalkey has you mean. Fire ahead.'

I know Tina is itching to sunbathe, she loves the sun and she's wasting valuable baking time but curiosity gets the better of me. 'I hear Oliver was over for lunch. Who was he with by the way? It's quite a spread.' I try to be as nonchalant as possible, but I'm not fooling Tina.

She laughs. 'I wondered how long it would take Hattie to tell you. Eat first and then I'll tell you all about Rozalia.'

'Rozalia?' I jump from one foot to the other. 'Is that the pregnant woman's name?'

'It is. She's Hungarian.'

'Ah, Tina, tell me now. Put me out of my misery.'

She laughs again. 'I'm only joking.' She pulls out two

kitchen chairs, their wooden legs complaining against the tiled floor. 'Sit down and tuck in. You eat, I'll talk.' I do as she requests, crossing my knees under the table and hitting my kneecap on the wooden lip in the process. I stifle a yelp.

Tina smiles at me and shakes her head a little. I'm always catching my knees on her table. Then she pours two large glasses of orange juice and slides one along the table towards me.

'Thanks.' I pick it up, take a long gulp, and look at her expectantly. 'Well?'

She rests her elbows on the table and steeples her fingers. She stares at them for a moment and then looks up.

'It's a long story, so I'll start at the beginning. When Oliver moved to London it was a relief to be honest. Things hadn't been great for a long time.'

What? I feel like interrupting already, but I hold my tongue.

'At the beginning I thought it was just teething problems. Two individuals trying to adapt to living together, to being married. But the constant bickering wore me down. Oliver wanted everything done his way, from how the house was decorated, to what we ate for dinner, to where we went on holiday. At first I used to disagree with him, to fight my corner; but after a while I realized it wasn't worth the hassle and only caused bitter arguments; Oliver was a nightmare to live with when he was in a bad mood. It was easier just to humour him, to let him think he was in control of everything, me included.'

She pauses for a moment and looks at me. 'Go on,' I encourage her, hanging on every word.

'When I got pregnant with Eric, Oliver was delighted. He'd just been promoted to Irish MD of the bank and he was dying to play the role of big family man. We bought this house, which was far larger then we needed, but to Oliver it was the perfect status symbol. He made me give up my job in the bank which I wasn't exactly thrilled about at the time, but there was no talking to him. He was earning good money and we didn't exactly need my pittance of a salary. I was tired and riddled with pregnancy hormones, so I did as I was told. And to be honest, it was far easier not having to scramble out of bed in the mornings to go to work. And Oliver liked me to look nice, so he never minded me spending a fortune on clothes. I practically became a professional shopper until Eric was born.'

You still have a rather severe shopping habit, I think to myself, but she reads my mind.

'I know I'm still a bit of a divil with the credit cards, but I'm not half as bad as I used to be, Meg. Honestly. You should have seen me a few years ago. I was just spending money for the sake of it. I guess it was like a hobby.'

'Nice hobby if you can afford it.'

Tina's face colours a little.

'Sorry, that wasn't kind,' I say, annoyed with myself.

'It's OK. I deserve it. But money isn't everything. And I've never rubbed your face in it, have I? I'm sorry if I have.'

'No, no.' I feel terrible. Tina is trying to tell me about her shitty marriage and I'm selfishly bringing the conversation back to me and my problems. What am I like? 'Of course you haven't. I'm just in a funny mood. Ignore me. What happened after Eric was born?'

'Are you sure you want to know all this? I'm not boring you rigid?'

'Don't be silly. Please, go on.'

'Where was I? Oh, yes. Eric. Oliver was never much of a hands-on dad with Eric. He was always far too busy working. I knew when I got pregnant with Freddie that I was on my own. To this day, Oliver has barely changed a nappy.'

I raise my eyebrows. 'So much for being the big family man.'

'Quite. When the London job came up, MD of the whole UK operation, I knew he'd take it. I was relieved to tell the truth.

Things had deteriorated between us and I'd started to resent him. I know it's terrible.'

I snort. 'Tina! Are you mad? You had every reason to resent him. He sounds like a nightmare to live with.'

Tina shrugs. 'There were two of us in the marriage,' she says, rather overgraciously I think. 'Oliver wasn't happy either. I think I deeply disappointed him; marriage disappointed him. He never said anything, but I could sense it. His mum was devoted to him and his dad, you see. She's a decent woman, don't get me wrong, but she wears flowery aprons and starches shirts. She even looked a little like Doris Day when she was young. I'm just not that type of woman.'

I'm shocked. 'Course you're not. Who is? This isn't the nineteen fifties.'

'I see that now. But I didn't at the time. He just chipped away at any self-esteem I had. I thought I was doing everything wrong. He criticized everything I did: how I dressed the boys, any changes I made to the house, the way I dressed, my hair, everything. It was horrible. So when the job came up in London we both agreed he should take it and commute home every weekend. Some weekends we got on OK. I made a huge effort not to rile him; but other weekends . . .' She whistles and shakes her head.

I remember his horrible behaviour the other night after dinner and I shudder.

'Has he ever hit you?'

'No, no, nothing like that. It was the coldness and the arguments. Although I guess they weren't exactly arguments, more like Oliver ranting at me for hours. He realized that by being away during the week, he'd lost control of the day-to-day things – the shopping, the house, what the boys were doing. I changed the curtains in our bedroom without asking him – to annoy him more than anything else, I think. To prove to him that I was capable of making decisions without him. And then gradually I began to change more and more things in the house, scoring points against him, I suppose. It made me feel a little more in control of my life. It became yet another addiction.' She gives a bitter laugh. 'It's sad, isn't it? Petty.'

She stops and flexes her hands on the table. I notice she's no longer wearing her wedding ring and there's a pale mark on the skin of her ring finger.

'When Eric was six months old it all came to a head. Oliver came home one weekend and said he wanted us to live separate lives, that he wasn't happy.'

I blow out my breath. I'm upset that Tina hasn't told me all this before, confided in me. 'You never said a thing.'

'I know. But that was part of the deal.'

'Deal? What deal?'

'Oliver wanted to maintain the illusion that he was a happily married man. Better for business he said – banks being very traditional institutions and all that. So he'd see the children as usual most weekends. The only difference being we'd have separate bedrooms, not that sex had exactly been top of his agenda since Freddie was born. He hated my post-pregnancy figure. He said my tummy was like a marshmallow. He used to poke it in disgust and tell me to get rid of it. As if there was just some sort of magic drug I could take to tighten it up. I wish.'

I'm horrified. What a pig. 'He was lucky you let him near you so soon after having Freddie. It was months before I let Simon touch me, poor sod.'

'He was always a bully, I see that now. But he said he'd only keep paying the bills as long as I didn't tell anyone.'

'Talk about control freak. And you went along with it?'

'What choice did I have?'

'You could have separated,' I suggest gently.

'And lose all this.' Tina waves her hands around the kitchen. 'I wasn't ready to lose my home, Meg, not then. Not after I'd put so much work into it.'

'And now?'

'Things have changed.' She cups her hands around her glass and stares into it as if it was a mini aquarium filled with exotic fish. 'Oliver wants a divorce. He told me the other night, before you and I went out for dinner. Rozalia's having his baby at Christmas. She wants to get married as soon as possible. I think he expected me to be upset, to beg him to come back, but I didn't. I wouldn't give him the satisfaction, even if I did want him back, which I most certainly don't. I told him it was an excellent idea, a long time in coming. He wasn't at all pleased. That's why he was in such a foul mood that evening.'

I nod at Tina. It's all starting to slot into place, like a jigsaw puzzle.

'And how do you feel about her, Tina? Are you all right?'

'I don't know. I had a feeling he was seeing someone, not that he admitted it. He's mellowed a little in the last while and he hasn't been over to see the boys as much. But now that I've been proved right—' She breaks off. 'I just don't know. It all seems so final. Divorce.'

'And Matty?' I ask softly. I want to know how he fits in. I don't want to see him get hurt and I know where divorce is concerned, things can get messy.

'He's a lovely guy,' she says. 'I'm very fond of him. But nothing's happened. Not really. I kissed him that night you and Sid were over and we've been spending some time together, but that's all.'

'Does he know about Oliver?'

'Yes, I told him everything. It was only fair. He needed to know what he was getting himself involved in.'

I'm relieved but hurt. Tina confided in Matty, but hadn't felt she could tell me.

'Matty's lovely,' she continues, 'but it's all such a mess.'

'It doesn't have to be,' I say. 'Maybe it's what you need. A new start. Maybe the divorce will be a positive thing for you.

For Oliver too. Not that I have much sympathy for him. Horrible man. I still can't believe the way he grabbed your arm the other night.'

'We all do things we regret from time to time. And he did apologize the next morning. But I feel a bit of a failure. Maybe I should have worked harder at our marriage. If I'd been less bolshy—'

'Bolshy? Tina you have to be kidding. You're one of the kindest, most forgiving people I know. Oliver's a fool. Let him go off and play happy families with Rozalia. What's she like anyway?'

'Pretty,' Tina admits. 'Young. Twenty-three I think. She adores Oliver. Her eyes follow him around the room.'

'Sounds a bit creepy if you ask me. It was a bit insensitive of him to bring her to see you.'

Tina shrugs. 'It had to happen at some stage, I suppose. She wanted to meet the boys.'

'I still think it was a shitty thing to do. I presume he told you she was coming?'

'Yes.'

'At least that's something. But you're too nice. I would have told him where to take his little Geisha girl. And it's just as well you didn't tell Hattie any of this before she met Rozalia. She would have given the pair of them a right dressing down.'

'Why do you think I left her in the dark?'

I laugh. 'Just tell me one more thing. She isn't his secretary is she? Rozalia, I mean.'

'No, she helps his PA. Updates the computer files or something.'

'So she *is* practically his secretary. What a cliché. Sad bastard.'

'He is, isn't he?'

'That's the spirit. So what happens next?'

'We hand over lots of cash to lawyers,' she says wryly. 'Oliver wants to sell the house and split the proceeds.'

My eyes widen. 'You're not going to let him, are you? It's your home.'

'Might be for the best. As you say, a new start for us all. I don't really need five bedrooms and four bathrooms.'

'But your beautiful house!'

'It's only bricks and mortar. Matty says I could buy a lovely old two-bedroomed cottage with half the proceeds and he'd help me fix it up. It would be fun, working on a project like that.'

'But you can't move away, what would I do without you?'

'I won't move far,' Tina promises. 'I like this area and it's convenient for Matty's work.'

'Matty? He'd be living with you?'

'No! At least not for a long time. But he might stay over. If he wanted to that is.' Tina goes all shy and stares at the table.

'But you've discussed moving? With Matty?'

'Yes.'

I feel monumentally left out. I pick up my glass and turn it in my hands.

Tina senses my unease. 'I'm sorry, Meg. I should have told you about Oliver a long time ago.'

'Why didn't you? I don't understand.'

Tina sighs. 'I was scared, I suppose. Scared of what you'd think of me. Your friendship means a lot to me and I didn't want to lose you.'

'Lose me? What are you talking about?'

'I didn't want you to think badly of me, living on Oliver's money, living a lie. I thought you'd—' she breaks off.

'What? Judge you?' The penny drops.

'I guess so,' she says.

'Oh, Tina. Why did you think that? Please, I need to know.'

She sighs again. 'I just get the feeling that you don't approve of the way I live, not working and spending all that money—'

I cut her off. 'Most of the time I'm just plain jealous. It's not a nice thing to admit to, but it's true. I'm the one who should be sorry.' I stand up, move towards her and give her a rather awkward hug. We're not really huggy sort of friends, but that's another thing I intend to change. 'I just want you to be happy,' I say, giving her one last squeeze and then drawing away. 'I'm the one who should be sorry. Sorry for being such a green-eyed monster who didn't see that underneath all the new bathrooms and shoes you weren't happy. I don't deserve you as a friend.'

'What's going on in here?' Hattie says, striding in the French doors. 'What have I missed?' She looks at me and then at Tina. 'So who's the pregnant one? Come on, I'm dying to know.'

Tina looks at me and we both begin to laugh.

'What's so funny?' she demands. 'She's his mistress, isn't she? Come to blackmail you, Tina. Although I still can't figure out why Oliver was tagging along. You'll need to explain that bit to me.'

'Hattie!' I say.

Tina just laughs. 'Let's open a bottle of wine to celebrate. And you still haven't touched your lunch, Meg.'

I look down at my plate. I've been so distracted I've forgotten to eat. My stomach is now crying out for sustenance. I dig my fork under a piece of salmon and begin to wolf it down.

'What are we celebrating?' Hattie asks suspiciously.

'A new start?' Tina suggests.

I nod, my mouth full of food.

'Someone had better explain what's going on around here,' Hattie says huffily, 'or there'll be no more free child-minding for either of you.'

Chapter 26

*Ballast weight: a weight placed low
in a boat to provide stability*

The next few weeks gallop by in a blur of Dan's sailing and
sleepovers, and lazy sand-pit and paddling-pool days in the
garden with Tina's crew, with the odd trip to the seaside
thrown in, weather permitting. Simon's time is taken up with
sailing, more sailing, and work in the chandlery. I'm spending
most of my time ferrying Dan around, looking after Lily, and
surprise, surprise, waiting for Simon.

I've almost finished working on Ivy's house. It turns out that
the jewel-coloured rugs in the sitting room are nineteenth-
century Persian, picked up by Ivy's husband on his world
travels. They fetched a hefty sum from a specialist rug dealer in
Temple Bar, a lovely Iranian man called Imad, recommended
by Douglas, my ex boss from Hall's.

In fact, Douglas has been a sweetie. I think he felt bad about
not being able to offer me a job and all, so he went out of his
way to help me, opening his contact book wide and even ringing two of them, a slightly dotty ceramics expert from Howth,
and Imad, on my behalf. As I suspected, Gwen loved the dolls
and the miniature tea set and snapped them up. One of the

watercolours, a gentle pastoral scene by a collectable Irish artist, fetched just over ten thousand euro at an art auction and one of Ivy's vases, another of her husband's finds, turned out to be an original Chinese Fu Dog vase made at the end of the Qing dynasty. Not as valuable as Ming, but worth a pretty penny all the same.

I just have to return the black and white photos to Ivy, hand over the cheques from the various auctions (minus the vendor's commission of course, but still very impressive) and get the skip collected. All the rooms are cleared now, ready for the cleaners, followed by the estate agent, and I must say I'm rather proud of myself. Job well done. And I enjoyed it. I'd love to do it all over again. Douglas suggested setting up my own house-clearing company, but that sounds a bit grand to me. Still, it's worth thinking about in the future. Especially as Dan will be back at school soon and Lily will be starting playschool, so the mornings will be my own. But right now I have plenty of other things on my mind to keep me busy.

Like Simon. There's no easy way to say this but Simon is slowly driving me demented. From the very first day of his new life I realized that things were going to be very different between us. I just hadn't understood how different.

The first week wasn't so bad. Simon slotted into his job at Dublin Bay Marine without a hitch. Once word got out in the small Irish sailing community that he was available to give advice on their boats and equipment, the most competitive of the owners immediately sat up and took notice and Simon's mobile went into overdrive. He was inundated with calls from all over the country. At first he said no to any request that involved sailing or crew training. His job, after all, was to sell the equipment in Hans's shop, not to become a professional sailor again. And sell he did. People were so eager to talk to him and to cajole any nuggets of advice they could out of him, they bought far more than they needed for their boats, including expensive instruments like satellite radar and hand-held navigation systems. Hans's figures had never looked better.

The first weekend at home as a family was strange. There were no piles of ropes, sailing gear and equipment on the hall floor waiting to be boxed up for a trip; no last-minute dash to the airport when the taxi failed to show up. No groggy good-byes in the early hours of the morning; no tears from Lily when she realized her dad had left without giving her a kiss. Just a normal family weekend.

On the first Saturday morning of his new life Simon painted our bedroom wall – it was still streaked with light brown tea-like water stains from the roof problem. Then he tackled the jungle grass in the garden, the weedy beds and even cleared the smelly, leaf-clogged outside drain. All the small jobs that I'd been at him to do for months. It warmed my heart to see him pottering around the garden with the kids trailing behind him, 'helping'.

Two of Simon's sailing bags were still sitting on the floor of our tiny utility room, moved from their resting place in the hall only the previous day. I'd left them in the hall on purpose. I wanted to see how long they'd sit there before Simon dealt with them. Our hall is short and narrow: in order to get to the front door you had to climb over the bags, so there was no missing them. In fact, I'd been lifting Lily's buggy over them all week, purposefully wheeling the dirty wheels over the stiff beige sailcloth, leaving tracks of mud and soggy leaves in my wake.

Every morning I'd ask Simon to shift the bags into the utility room. Every morning he'd forget. Eventually I gave up, exasperated, and did it myself. He hadn't even noticed.

My next 'experiment' involved the dirty socks and underwear on the bedroom floor. Dan had caught me kicking a pair of grubby-looking white sports socks under the bed one morning.

'What are you doing?' he'd asked with interest, creeping in the door.

'Dan!' I jumped back in fright.

'Are you not going to pick those up?'

'No, they're Simon's.'

'You pick mine up.'

'I know.' I sighed. 'But you're eleven.'

Dan looked at me sideways. 'Can I kick my socks under my bed?'

'No, you can't. Don't even try it. If I see one smelly sock under there, you're in trouble, understand?'

Dan put his finger to his forehead and twisted it, mouthing 'loco', under his breath.

There was method in my madness, I should point out. I wasn't losing it. I was determined not to become Simon's skivvy. It was different when we were living out of sailing bags in a hotel, that was acceptable, but this was our home. There were no chambermaids here. I wasn't going to spend my life picking up after him.

I stared at the wet blue towel on the floor under the bedroom window. That was going to stay there too. It was all going to stay exactly where it was until Simon finally did something about it. I'd made up my mind. Rational? Probably not. Strangely satisfying? Yes.

'Do you mind if I go sailing this afternoon?' Simon asked breezily that first Saturday as we munched on bacon sandwiches at noon. After the painting, the gardening and the tickling, I could hardly say no.

And so it all began. Now, three weeks later, Simon is spending every Saturday afternoon, Sunday afternoon, Tuesday and Thursday night sailing. Do I mind? Of course I do. But it's only until the end of the summer, he's promised me. Once the sailing season finishes in September things will change.

On the first Sunday in September, me and the kids troop over to Mum and Dad's house for a family lunch. Simon is sailing, an autumn season in Howth yacht club, every Sunday in September and October. As he's getting paid good money to do so, I can hardly object. He took the kids to the park on their bikes (tricycle in Lily's case) yesterday morning giving me a much needed lie-in, so he's in my good books, regardless of the sailing.

'Where's Simon?' Hattie asks opening the door and leaning forward to give me a kiss on the cheek.

'Guess.'

'Not again.'

I say nothing, giving her a wry smile.

'You're a saint. I'd murder him. Come on in. Paul and Katia arrived just before you. They're in the living room with Dad. Mum's in the kitchen slaving away. Or so she'd like us to think. She's actually sitting at the kitchen table reading the paper.'

'Anything wrong, Hattie?' I ask her as I usher Lily off the doorstep and into the hall with my hands.

'No. Why?'

'No reason. You just seem a little, oh, I don't know.' I want to say snappy as I know she won't appreciate it. She can't still be annoyed with me over that Ryan business, can she? I thought she'd got over that.

She glares at me, her eyes flinty. 'I'm fine. And you?'

'Fine.'

She gives me a curt nod. 'Good.'

I follow her into the living room. Paul and Katia are on the sofa, Dad is sitting by the window in his reclining armchair. He rises to his feet.

'Meg, Dan. And Lily,' he says. 'How lovely to see you all.' He looks pale but his smile lights up his face.

Lily runs towards him, her arms stretched out. 'Gampa. Sit knee, Gampa.' She loves Dad's reclining chair.

'No, Lily.'

'It's fine, Meg.' Dad scoops her up in his arms, and sits back down, Lily on his knee.

'Are you sure?' I ask anxiously.

'Yes. She's only light.'

'Ride, Gampa. Ride.' Dad leans back and the chair reclines. Lily giggles delightedly. 'More, Gampa, more.'

I leave them to it, sitting down on the sofa beside Katia. She's wearing a baggy grey jumper and looking closely I can see her bump is starting to show.

'How are you, Katia?' I ask with a smile.

'Not bad.' She leans towards me. 'A little sick still,' she says in a low voice, 'but getting better.'

'That'll pass soon enough.'

'I don't know,' Hattie joins in. 'One of the girls at work had morning sickness the whole way through.'

I give Hattie a look. 'Shush.'

She nods her head towards Dad. 'He's not listening.'

'Still,' I warn. 'Go easy.'

Hattie wriggles her bum in her armchair huffily. 'Fine.' I sense trouble.

'And how's the new job, Paul?' I ask. He started working in a clothing warehouse two weeks ago.

He gives me a grin. 'The hours didn't really suit. So I'm looking for something else at the moment.'

Hattie gives a click of disgust but we all ignore her.

'What kind of work are you looking for?' I ask, eager to keep the conversation on an even keel.

'Something with regular hours so I can see Katia more. Something in town.'

'Ever thought of using your degree?' Hattie asks snidely.

'Dan got his first stage,' I cut in. 'At sailing. He really enjoyed the course, didn't you, Dan?'

'What?' Dan's head is stuck in a book.

'The sailing course,' I prompt.

'Oh, yeah. I got my first-stage badge,' he says proudly. 'And I won two races in the last week.'

'Well done,' Paul says. 'That's great, isn't it, Katia?'

Katia smiles at Dan. 'Well done, Dan.' She glances over at Dad, then, satisfied that he's occupied with Lily rubs the side of her stomach. 'I've been getting these pains in my side, Meg. Is that normal?'

'Sharp pains or muscular pains?'

'Muscular pains.'

'That's normal all right. Try to get as much rest as you can. It's just your body settling in really. Are you managing to keep food down?'

'Most of the time. Paul's been great. He runs down to the chipper when I get a chip craving.' She smiles warmly at him.

'Oh, I'd say he's been really helpful,' Hattie remarks.

'Lunch is ready.' Mum swings open the door, wiping her hands on her red and white flowery apron. Her cheeks are flushed and wisps of loose hair hung around her face. The rest is tied back in a neat chignon.

'Great.' Paul jumps to his feet. 'I'm starving. Can I help with anything, Mum?'

'You could bring the soup bowls through.'

'Is it tomato?' Dan asks. 'I only like tomato.'

'It's always tomato,' Hattie says drily.

'Good. I like tomato,' Dan says.

I ruffle his hair.

'Mum,' he complains, moving away from me.

'Help Paul with the soup, there's a good lad.'

'OK.'

We sit down at the table – Dad and Mum at either end, Paul, Katia and Hattie on one side, me, Lily and Dan on the other. Lily insists on moving her high chair nearer to Dad and he's chuffed.

'I'm her favourite.' He puffs out his chest.

'It's only because you give her all your ice cream,' Mum says with a smile, 'and you let her put her vegetables on your plate. She's no fool.'

'She's smart,' he says, 'nothing wrong with that.'

'The soup looks lovely,' Katia says. 'Thanks for having us, Mrs Miller.' They've obviously got over their differences, thank goodness.

'Julie. Please, Katia. Mrs Miller sounds so . . .'

'Old?' Hattie suggests.

'Formal I was going to say, Hattie.' She smooths down her skirt and sits. 'Now let's eat.'

'So how did your treatment go this week, Dad?' Hattie asks, spooning up some soup.

'Hattie,' I say, 'Dad may not want to talk about it.'

'No, it's fine.' His kind eyes rest on mine. 'I don't mind at all. In fact it's healthy to talk about it.'

The irony of the word 'healthy' isn't lost on any of us. There's silence for a moment.

'And to answer your question, Hattie, it went well. I've offered to do a clinical trial for the hospital. I have to put E45 cream on my skin before the radiotherapy, to see if it helps with the burning.'

'And does it?' I ask.

'No. At least it hasn't so far. But hopefully the results will be useful for the doctors.'

'What's radio thingy?' Dan asks with interest.

'It's a treatment to zap the badness out of my body. To make me better.'

'Oh.' Dan accepts this and goes back to his soup.

'There was a lovely Northern nurse doing the chemo, Marian was her name. We got talking and she said her fiancé is a sailing instructor in Simon's yacht club. Maybe Simon knows him. His name's Ryan. Ryan Dalton or Dawson maybe. Something like that.'

Hattie's face blanches and her spoon stops halfway up to her mouth.

'Yes, I think Simon knows him,' I say quickly. So that's what Ryan was doing in the hospital. It all makes sense now. The little snake. Shoot, I wish I'd told Hattie I'd seen him after all. Poor Hattie.

'Ryan was my head instructor,' Dan pipes up. 'He's cool.'

'Fiancé?' Hattie asks, clattering her spoon back in her bowl. 'Are you sure?'

'Oh, yes,' Dad says. 'She's over the moon. Apparently they'd been engaged before but he got cold feet and moved away for a while.'

'Really?' Hattie says, her eyes flashing. 'Isn't that lovely for them?'

'Do you know him, Hattie?' Dad asks, sensing there's something wrong. 'Is he a friend of yours?'

'No,' she says, getting to her feet abruptly. 'Ryan's no friend of mine. Excuse me for a moment.' She walks out of the room.

'Was it something I said?' Dad looks around the room in confusion.

'She's just in one of her moods,' I say. 'Too many late nights. Nothing to worry about.'

'I thought Ryan was Hattie's boyfriend,' Dan adds, thinking he's being helpful. 'That's what she told me.'

I stand up. 'I'd better go after her.' I look around the room. 'Probably best not to mention Ryan again, just in case.'

'I'm sorry, I had no idea,' Dad says.

'It's not your fault,' I assure him. 'Honestly.'

'Some men,' Katia says as I'm walking out the door.

'Quite, Katia,' Mum agrees. 'Present company excepted, of course.'

'Hattie?' I knock on her bathroom door. 'Hattie, are you in there?'

'I'm on the phone,' she shouts through the door. 'Be with you in a second.'

I put my ear to the door but can hear only a murmur, then she raises her voice 'When were you thinking of telling me exactly?' A long pause and then, 'You're unbelievable!' followed by, 'I most certainly will not. And it'll be a lot worse than bananas the next time, believe me, buster!' then silence.

There's a click as she draws back the lock.

I open the door gingerly. Hattie is sitting on the closed toilet seat, her eyes flashing. She looks up at me. 'Bloody men. I thought Ryan was different. Everything you said was right. I just didn't want to hear it. How could I have been so blind? He's been engaged for months now. He said he couldn't help himself with me, but that Marian is the one for him in the long term and he realizes that now. She's his rock apparently. Then he blathered on about her and what a good little nursey she is. Bollocks to that! As if I wanted to hear anything about the stupid cow!'

'I'm so sorry. I don't know what to say.'

She bites her lip. 'I really liked him, Meg.'

'I know. But I have to ask, what was that banana bit all about?'

She gives a snort. 'Serves him right. After what you said to me, after the pizza, I mean, I started watching him. I saw him leave his house one morning with this blonde girl in the passenger seat; it must have been her. Marian.'

'You were stalking him?'

'No. Watching him.'

'And the banana?'

'When he parked outside the hospital I put a banana in his exhaust. Jammed it right in, good and tight. When he came out later it blew the exhaust off the car.'

'Hattie! Did he know it was you?'

'No. But then I set up a small ad account in his name with

his mobile number. Male model wants to meet older woman for afternoon delight. Must love a sailor. That kind of thing.'

I laugh, horrified yet impressed. 'You didn't.'

She shrugs. 'No one messes with me and gets away with it. You were so right. I was just a distraction for him. A bit of fun, nothing serious.' She stares down at her hands. 'That's the worst thing. He never really loved me at all.'

I don't know what to say. 'I'm sorry.'

She sighs. 'Hey, these things happen.' She gives a short laugh. 'Is Slipper still available?'

You have to admire her resilience, even though I know this time it's mainly an act. I can see the hurt in her eyes. Ryan's behaviour has obviously cut her deep. 'No. He's still seeing Pat. The nice American girl from Cornwall. They're coming over on Friday in fact.'

'Oh, well. Plenty more fish in the sea.' She stands up. 'Coming downstairs? I've done enough wallowing for one day.'

'Did he get many calls?' I ask. 'Ryan, I mean. From bored housewives?'

'Loads.' Hattie grins. 'It drove him mad.'

I squeeze her arm. 'You're priceless.'

'I'm sorry for being short with you,' she says. 'I guess in my heart I knew you were telling the truth, even if I didn't want to hear it. I shouldn't have said those things.'

'That's what sisters are for.' I smile at her. 'And Ryan's an idiot for letting you go. Forget about him.'

'He's ancient history.' She waves her hands in the air. She'll bounce back. Hattie's nothing if not resilient.

'Everything OK?' Mum asks as we sit down again at the dining-room table.

'Fine,' I assure her. 'Everything's fine.'

Dad's eyes meet mine and I give him a nod and a smile. He looks relieved.

347

'I was just telling Granny about Katia's morning sickness, Mum,' Dan says.

My heart sinks. Today's just getting better and better. Dad wasn't listening earlier, but Dan obviously was.

I give a hollow, 'Oh,' and look at Dad.

'Isn't it wonderful news, Meg?' Dad says jovially. 'Another baby Miller for the clan. We're delighted, aren't we, Julie?'

Mum smiles gently at him, her eyes a little misty. 'Yes. New life is always a wonderful thing.' A tear rolls down her cheek and she wipes it away with her hand. 'Something to be cherished.' She gives a sob. 'I'm sorry.' She bows her head.

'Mum, Granny's crying,' Dan whispers to me. 'Will I go and give her a hug?'

'Yes, you do that.'

But Dad beats him to it. 'Hey, Julie,' he says stroking her hair. 'Hush now.'

She wipes her face with her napkin. 'I'm sorry everyone.' She blows out her breath and gives a brave smile. 'It all just gets to me sometimes.' Dad's standing behind her now, his hands on her shoulders. She looks up at him and pats both his hands tenderly.

'It's only when something like this happens, you really realize how much someone means to you.'

'Jeepers, don't go all Oprah on us, Mother,' Hattie says. 'What's for dessert?'

After a large helping of apple pie and cream, I'm stuffed. The rest of the lunch goes without a hitch, which makes a change. Katia and Paul discuss their wedding plans, postponed until after the baby has arrived. Dan tells us all about his sailing course, Lily entertains us with her dog impressions, licking Dad's face with her sticky tongue. Hattie is rather subdued, but seems all right, all things considered. In fact, everything is on a surprisingly even keel.

'We'll do the washing-up,' I say after coffee, standing up and hitting the front of my thighs against the lip of the table, making it wobble precariously. 'Me and Hattie.'

'And I'm sure Paul would love to help us,' Hattie adds. 'Wouldn't you, Paul?'

'Yeah, whatever,' he says a little doubtfully.

'No, no, it's fine,' I say firmly. 'You clear the plates and dishes into the kitchen, Paul. We'll manage the washing-up.'

'We'll look after Lily and Dan while you are in the kitchen,' Katia offers. 'Won't we, Paul?'

'Yeah, love to. It'll be good practice.'

'Wonders will never cease,' Hattie mutters under her breath.

'Any time you need more practice, Paul,' I say, 'you know where we live. We're always looking for babysitters. Any time,' I add pointedly.

Hattie follows me into the kitchen. 'This is going to take ages.' She glares with loathing at the baking tray that's sitting in the sink, complete with chicken grease and nippets of skin.

I pass her a clean teatowel from the cupboard. 'I'll wash.' I pull Mum's yellow rubber gloves over my hands. Unlike my pair at home, they're dry inside and the slightly furry lining is still intact. I take the baking tray out of the sink and clatter it on the counter to my left with the dirty saucepans and dishes. Then I fill the sink with fresh, clean hot water and squirt in lemon-smelling washing-up liquid until it froths.

'You're as bad as Mum with that stuff.' Hattie points at the furiously bubbling sink.

Paul walks in and clunks several dirty plates down on the kitchen table.

'Scrape them into the bin,' Hattie says. 'Go on, you muppet. Don't leave them like that.'

'Sometimes, Hattie, you're a pain in the—' Paul begins, stopping in his tracks as Katia walks in the open doorway.

'He must be such a help to you in the flat, Katia,' Hattie says, giving Katia a sickly sweet smile.

Katia looks at Hattie. The sarcasm isn't lost on her. 'You know, Hattie, he's getting better,' she says after a moment. 'Paul's kind to me and he doesn't hit me, unlike my last boyfriend. There's a lot to be said for kindness in a man. And faithfulness.'

Hattie is rendered speechless, but it doesn't last long. 'I'm sorry, I had no idea.'

'Paul is a good man,' Katia says to Hattie. 'He's not perfect, but then what man is? Now, I'm going to play with Lily.' She strides out the door, closing it behind her.

'Jeepers, I didn't mean to upset her.' Hattie flaps her teatowel around in her hands. 'She's a bit touchy.'

Paul shakes his head. There's a smile on his lips. 'She's well able for you, sis. And did you hear what she said? I'm a good man. And kind too.'

'Poor girl, she needs her eyes tested,' Hattie says. 'Go on, get. I'll do the plates. Help Katia with Lily.'

'One of these days you'll realize I'm not a teenager any more,' Paul tells her, his hand on the door knob. 'I'm an adult, with my own life. And maybe one day you'll start treating me like one, Hattie. Stop speaking to me like I'm some sort of special-needs kid.'

'He's right, Hattie,' I say, trying not to laugh. It's not like Paul to be so serious.

'I wouldn't be so smug, Meg,' he says. 'You're not much better.'

'But, Paul—' I splutter.

But it's no good, he's left the room.

'What was all that about?' I ask, flabbergasted.

'Little brother's asserting his manhood,' Hattie says. 'Don't worry, it won't last long. He'll be back to his usual eejity self soon enough.'

'Maybe not,' I muse. 'Maybe like he says, he's grown up. Become an adult.'

Hattie laughs. 'Yeah, right. I'll believe it when I see it. Ten quid he's upstairs right now on the PlayStation with Dan.'

I think for a moment. 'No way. Five quid. I only have a tenner on me and I need money for some milk on the way home.'

'Deal.' We shake on it, Hattie wincing as her bare palm meets my wet rubbery one.

'Now what did you want to talk to me about?' she asks. 'I'm useless at drying up, as well you know. There must be some reason for you dragging me in here.'

Hattie's right. She *is* useless. She never dries the plates properly and always leaves suds on the glasses. I usually do the washing and the drying with Dad. The parentals have a dishwasher, but it's a family tradition to do the Sunday dishes by hand mainly because we use the best non-chipped glasses, ancient hand-painted blue plates that have been in the family for ever, and wooden-handled cutlery, things you can't put in the dishwasher. All wedding presents coincidentally. What is it with wedding presents? Is there some unwritten rule that they all have to be hand washed?

'Dad needs a rest,' I say. 'And yes, I suppose I did want to ask you something.'

'What?'

'We'd better get going on the glasses. Will you pass me some from the table?'

'Stop stalling.' She hands me two glasses and I plunge them into the hot water and hand them back to her, one at a time.

'It's Simon I guess. Me and Simon.'

'Go on.'

'He's been back nearly a month now and things aren't going all that well, to be honest.'

'What kind of things?' Hattie asks.

'It's all got a bit routine, I suppose. Every day is the same.

351

We get up, give the kids their breakfast, Simon goes to work, he comes home late and we exchange a few words before going to bed.'

'Sounds exciting all right,' Hattie says drily. 'And what about the sex? You haven't mentioned that.'

I shrug. Unlike Hattie, I'm not all that comfortable talking about that side of things.

'Don't be so coy.' She swats me with the teatowel. 'The sex is boring too, I take it.'

'Not exactly boring,' I begin. 'Maybe a little,' I admit. 'It was different when he was away. We'd, you know—'

'Bonk each others brains out,' Hattie suggests.

'Make love—'

Hattie gives a snort.

'OK then, have sex when he came home. And then before he left. And maybe while he was here at the weekends. But now he wants it all the time and I'm just too tired most nights.'

'And I guess it's lost a bit of its excitement?'

'Yes.'

'And he's not as tanned now, is he? And he's putting on a bit of weight too.'

'That's got nothing to do with it.'

'Really?' She looks at me knowingly.

'Maybe a little. He keeps complaining about my pyjamas and my underwear too.'

I can see Hattie is trying not to laugh. 'Meg, your pyjamas are mostly leggings and old T-shirts. I don't blame the poor man. And the last time I checked out the contents of your underwear drawer I was shocked. I swear you've had some of those grey cotton knickers since you were a teenager.'

'What were you doing snooping in my bras and knickers?'

'I was waiting for you to get out of the shower. I was bored. If you must wear saggy cotton knickers at least wear black ones.'

'I'm not like you, I can't wear thongs every day. They go up my bum and I never feel properly dressed in them.'

Hattie laughs. 'There goes your future career as a lap dancer.'

I smile. 'Am I really that pathetic?'

'Lost cause I'd say. But I think you should talk to Simon. Tell him that you love sex with him, but not every day. And then maybe you need to spice things up a little.'

'I was afraid you were going to say that.'

The glasses, soup bowls and side plates are finished. I refresh the water and move on to the dinner plates.

'We're flying,' Hattie says, looking at the growing stack of gleaming, clean crockery on the table. 'All this sex talk must be good for us.'

'Hum,' I murmur. Hattie isn't taking this very seriously.

'Anyway,' she continues. 'Back to spicing it up. Have you tried—'

'Before you suggest it, I'm not interested in threesomes.'

'Shame, I rather fancied a go at Simon myself.'

I wrinkle my nose. 'Hattie!'

She laughs. 'Look at your face. I'm only joking. He's not really my type. And I've already seen you naked.'

I laugh. 'Lucky you. Have you ever, you know?'

'Had a threesome?'

I nod.

'Not exactly.'

'What do you mean, not exactly?'

'It almost happened once, with two guys now, not a girl and a guy.'

'And?'

'We all fell asleep. Too much tequila. But one of them woke up halfway through the night and we had sex with the other guy lying beside us. That was quite exciting. We were trying to be really quiet and not move around too much so we didn't wake him.'

'And did you? Wake him I mean.'

'Yes. But he pretended to be fast asleep. He only told us the truth the following morning. But I wouldn't do it again. I've grown out of all that kind of stuff. One guy is enough for me now.'

She lowers more dirty plates into the water with a slosh. It wets the top of my thighs, leaving a damp line on my jeans. 'Thanks a lot,' I say.

'It'll dry. Back to sex. The pair of you should go away for the weekend, somewhere romantic.'

'Can't really afford it at the moment,' I say glumly. 'And Simon's busy most weekends.'

'You need to spend some time together alone. Forget about the money; your relationship is more important than money. Anyway didn't you make some good moolah selling that old dear's stuff?'

'She's called Ivy,' I remind her.

'Yeah, Ivy. You'll get your commission soon, won't you? So treat yourselves, go somewhere nice. Without the kids. Hey, why don't I mind them for you here next Saturday night? Give the pair of you a night off. It'll be a start.'

'Slipper and Pat are coming to stay on Friday night. And then on Saturday they're moving to a B & B, bless them because Maureen and Joe are arriving.'

'Again?'

'Tell me about it. They're dying to see Lily. It's my own fault, Joe rang the week before last and I told him all about her new trick.'

'Which is?'

'You know. Pretending to be a dog. Sticking her tongue out and panting.'

Hattie raises her eyebrows. 'And they're coming over to see Lily be a dog?'

'Sad, isn't it?'

'You'll have to start keeping Lily's circus tricks to yourself.'

'I know.'

'So how about Thursday night?'

'Thursday night would be great. The evening sailing races have stopped now thank goodness. Are you sure you don't mind?'

'Course not. Mum will help. And Dad. It'll be brilliant.'

'Thanks. I really appreciate it.' My eyes light up. 'I'll cook Simon a nice dinner and dress up.'

Hattie raises her eyebrows.

I laugh. 'Nothing like that. My nice black dress.' I can feel my eyes shine just thinking about it. 'It'll be great.'

'Speaking of dressing up, I have something upstairs that might come in useful,' Hattie says with a sly grin. 'Let's finish these dishes, leave the pans to soak and then I'll show you.'

'What is it?'

'You're so impatient.' She passes me a dish. 'Just something to get you in the mood. Here, wash!'

Ten minutes later I follow Hattie up the stairs. As we walk past the television room we can hear the droning noise of a car-racing game. The door is ajar and we stick our heads around.

Dan and Paul are both sitting on the floor, inches away from the television screen, PlayStation joysticks in their hands. They're oblivious to our collective gaze.

'You owe me a fiver, sis,' Hattie whispers.

'I guess I do.'

Hattie's bedroom is its usually tippy self, clothes strewn over every available surface. It smells stale; she doesn't believe in fresh air and never opens her curtains properly, let alone her windows. She closes the door firmly behind us and opens her wardrobe door.

'It's in here somewhere.' She burrows under the shoeboxes and posh-looking empty carrier bags. 'Aha.' She pulls out a plain brown cardboard box.

'Shoes?' I ask hopefully. Visions of delicious, seductive high heels flit through my mind.

'Far more interesting.' She hands me the box. 'I ordered one for myself last year and it didn't arrive for weeks. So I rang them and gave out. The next day my first order arrived and two weeks later another order arrived, free. So now I have two.'

I open the box and gasp.

'Hattie!'

Chapter 27

Bowline: a knot used to make
a temporary loop in a line

Hattie grins at me. 'Don't look so shocked, Meg. It's only a vibrator. Surely you've seen one before?'

'No. Not exactly. In magazines and on the telly. Not in real life.'

'I don't know. The older generation.' Hattie shakes her head and tut tuts.

I take the pink and white instrument out of its box and turn it over in my hands. It's surprisingly heavy. 'What are the marbles for?' Halfway down the shaft is a bulging see-through panel full of Smartie-sized multi-coloured balls.

'They jiggle around and massage you,' she explains.

I can feel my face redden. 'Oh.'

'The little rabbit ears are for your clitoris,' she continues, oblivious to my embarrassment. 'Or depending on your anatomy, the rabbit's nose might work, I suppose. Look at its little face. Isn't it cute?'

'Cute?' I stare at the pink plastic features.

'The head has a face too,' she says. 'Look.'

So it does, a chubby face with a wide, satisfied grin. The

whole contraption looks like some sort of obscene child's toy. 'Does it really work?' I ask.

Hattie stares at me and then laughs heartily. 'What do you think? Course it does. I use mine all the time whenever I'm feeling in the need of a little pick-me-up or a treat. It's a bit noisy, though, so I have to be careful when Mum's around.'

'I can imagine. I don't think she'd be all that impressed.'

'I don't know. They have a fairly healthy sex life. At least they did until Dad got sick. These days they're—'

'Hattie!' I put my hands up. 'I *really* don't want to know, thanks all the same.'

She shrugs. 'I live here. And sex is part of life, Meg. You've always been a bit hung up about it.'

'I have not!'

'You have a bit, admit it. Sid was a revelation to you. In fact, he's the only one of your boyfriends who'd do anything for me. I'd say he's good in bed. Is he?'

I redden even more. 'Find out for yourself if you're so interested.'

'Would you mind?'

'Of course I'd mind. He's Dan's dad, for heaven's sake. Anyway, I hear he tried it on a few times already.' I wasn't going to bring it up, ever, but it just slipped out.

'He told you?'

'Yes, but it's fine. He's a sleazebag.'

'But cute.'

I glare at her. 'And out of bounds.'

'Point taken.' She takes the rabbit out of my hands and puts it back into its box. 'Anyway, have fun with this, Meg. Get Simon to use it on you, it'll be a real turn-on for both of you.'

'I couldn't,' I splutter, cringing at the thought.

'Why not? He's seen you give birth to Lily for goodness sake. It can't get more intimate than that. All that blood and gunk.' She shudders. 'Yuck.'

'You're absolutely charming.'

'Hey, I'm only telling it like it is. Promise me you'll give it a go?'

'OK,' I say reluctantly, 'but only on my own.'

'For feck's sake, you'd think I asked you to amputate your own foot. Lighten up, Meg. You'll love it, wait and see. The orgasms are only amazing. There was this one time—'

'Hattie! Enough! Please.' I put my hands over my ears theatrically.

By Thursday night I'm dying for my romantic night in with Simon. I have to admit that Hattie is right, the vibrator's amazing. I've become quite attached to my pet rabbit, a little too attached maybe. I worry that even Simon's best efforts at foreplay won't quite match my long-eared friend, but I'm so satisfied after an early-evening bath and a sneaky orgasm, courtesy of my new buddy, that I don't think I'll be all that bothered one way or the other.

Hattie, true to her word, collected Dan and Lily at five. She was delighted at her success and made me promise to indoctrinate Simon into the rabbit's charms some time in the near future. 'I'll show you where to put it on his balls to give him a real thrill,' she said with a wink. I told her she should have her own sex show on the telly and she just laughed. 'There's an idea,' she said. I hope she was joking.

I sit on the side of the bed waiting for Simon to come home. I'm wearing his favourite underwear, a lacy black bra, matching thong, suspenders and stockings. Amazingly as I'm not exactly all that well endowed, the bra is too small for me; Simon bought it in Boston where all the women must have even smaller boobs than me. But if I loosen the back strap fully it almost fits. There's also a small ladder in the left stocking running from the heel to the back of my knee, but I don't think he will even notice. I dot some nail polish on the run to stop it getting any worse.

I think about the rabbit again but stop myself succumbing to the temptation. Simon will be here at any minute; I'll save myself for the real thing. As I lie back on the bed and close my eyes, I realize that I haven't felt like this in a long time: actually looking forward to sex. I must have dozed off, because the next thing I know Simon is standing over me with a peculiar expression on his face.

I smile up at him lazily. 'Hi, you,' I say in what I hope is a sexy manner.

'Meg.' He leans down and kisses me on the lips. I put my arms around his neck and pull him towards me.

'Oh, Meg,' he says, drawing back. He frowns and gives a guttural moan.

'What is it?'

'Mum and Dad are downstairs.'

'What?' I sit up, one of my breasts flopping out of the bra. I cup it back in quickly. 'They're not supposed to be here till Saturday.'

'They got the day wrong.'

'How did they manage to do that? What about Slipper and Pat?'

'Mum and Dad have already offered to stay in a B & B until Saturday night.'

'Good.'

Simon looks at me. 'We can't let them do that.'

'Why not? It's their mistake.'

'I've already told them not to be so silly, that they're staying here with us.'

'Oh you did, did you?' I scowl at him. 'I haven't anything ready. I was going to go shopping tomorrow morning.'

'That's OK. We'll go out to dinner tonight.'

'But it was supposed to be our night in together. Why do you think I went to all this trouble?' I wave down at my trussed-up body. 'It wasn't for the good of my health, I can tell you.'

'What do you mean by that? I thought you liked that under-wear.'

'I do. But it's a bit snug,' I admit, dying to pull the thong from where it's painfully lodged between my buttocks. I look at my watch. 'It's only half six. Go down and tell them you need to have a shower.'

'I'm sorry. Dinner's booked for half six. We have to go.'

'Come here then,' I throw my arms around him. 'If we're quick—'

Simon grins down at me. 'Feck it.' He jumps up and pulls down his shorts. He has no boxers on and I can see he's ready for action.

'Mr Murphy,' I gasp as he lunges towards me.

I've just about managed to wiggle my thong down my thighs when there's a rap on the door.

'Simon,' Maureen shrills, 'it's six thirty-five. We'll be late for dinner. And you know what my stomach is like. Can I come in?'

'No!' Simon and I yell simultaneously.

'I'm just getting changed, Mum,' Simon says. 'I'll be down in a minute.'

'Nothing I haven't seen before,' she says. The handle begins to turn.

'Wait!' Simon shouts. 'Please.'

I pull the bed covers up to my chin and Simon pulls his shorts back up his legs.

'Shit, shit,' he curses, his erection still clearly visible under the cotton.

'Sit down,' I hiss.

Maureen stalks in. She's wearing a sky-blue twin set, beige trousers and her signature navy velvet Alice band. Immaculate as usual. She looks down at me. 'In bed at this hour, Meg? You're not pregnant are you? You look rather flushed.'

'Wouldn't get the chance in this house,' I say under my breath.

'Sorry, dear,' Maureen says, 'what was that?'

'No, Maureen. I'm not pregnant.' I'd love to tell her what we're really up to, but Simon would kill me so I hold my tongue.

'You'll have to start eating some red meat. Iron levels are most important in the early stages of pregnancy.'

'I'm not pregnant,' I repeat.

'But if you are—'

'We'll be down in a minute, Mum,' Simon says, cutting her off. 'I promise.'

'Your father's starving,' she says. 'Poor man. All that driving. He's wasting away.'

I smile to myself. Whatever you say about whippet-thin Maureen, Joe is certainly not wasting away.

'OK,' Simon says, 'we get the message. We'll be down in a minute.'

She fingers her pearls, gives us one last beady look, and then walks out, leaving the door wide open behind her. I can hear her clicking her tongue against her teeth as she walks down the stairs. She's got the loudest tongue click in the world.

'Do you think she sussed us?' I ask, feeling bold and not really caring one way or the other.

'Na, I doubt it. Wouldn't occur to her. Although she'd love another grandchild all right.' He runs his hands through his hair. 'Sorry, Meg. We'll make up for it later.'

'OK,' I say, horribly disappointed. I'm already starting to feel tired. All this excitement is too much for me. I built myself up for this evening and I know dinner with Maureen and Joe will be a complete libido blocker. 'You go on down. I'll join you in a minute.'

He nods. 'Do you know where my clean boxers are? I couldn't find any this morning.'

'You could try under the bed,' I say nonchalantly. 'Or there might be some dry ones in the utility room.'

Simon looks under the bed. 'Holy moley. How did all that get there?' He pulls out a pair of boxers and gives them a sniff. 'These will do.'

'No they won't!' I say sharply. 'That's disgusting. Go and find some clean ones in the utility room. And take all the dirty ones downstairs while you're at it.'

Simon looks at me for a moment as if deciding something. 'We're running late. I'll do it tomorrow.'

'If you leave them for much longer they'll start to grow fungus. We'll have a whole mushroom crop under there. The room is already starting to smell musty.'

'I won't forget,' he says. 'Tomorrow. I promise.' Famous last words.

Dinner is a nightmare. We'd only been in the place (Hogan's pub up the road, great pub food) for ten minutes and Maureen had already lectured our unfortunate waitress about organic chicken as opposed to free-range chicken, and out of season (according to her) vegetables. Eventually she agrees to eat an omelette, after being reassured by the chef himself that the eggs are local. The poor man came out of the kitchen to talk to her. Luckily he seemed a decent type, at least I thought so until I spotted him giving Maureen the two fingers as he walked away. He probably spat in her eggs, but she deserved it. Calling him 'my good man,' in her clippy London accent is bound to get a reaction.

After dinner, Maureen starts to tell us how disappointed she is that 'her Lily' wasn't there to greet her at the door.

'I miss her so much when I'm away,' she says with a dramatic sigh. 'The poor child is growing up without her grandparents.'

'She still has my parents,' I point out, 'she sees them all the time.' But as soon as I say it I know it's the wrong answer.

'Don't make us feel any more guilty than we already do, Meg. In fact, we have news, don't we Joe?'

'We haven't really discussed it properly, Maureen,' Joe says, looking startled. He's sitting back in his seat, letting his dinner settle. Unlike Maureen, he'd found several things he rather fancied on the menu and really went for it – deep-fried Brie, Cumberland sausage and mash, and banoffi pie heaped high with extra cream. 'It's only an idea. No need to tell them yet.'

But Maureen will not be deterred. 'We're thinking of moving to Ireland. To be closer to Lily. And all of you, of course. What do you think of that?' She looks from Simon to me and back again, a wide smile plastered on her thin lips.

Simon puts his foot on mine and presses down hard. I gulp back a moan.

'That sounds interesting, Mum,' Simon says diplomatically. 'But what about all your friends in London? Wouldn't you miss them?'

Maureen waves her hand in the air and a discreet gold bracelet slides down her wrist. 'Family is the most important thing, isn't it? And we're not getting any younger, Simon. One day you might even have the pleasure of one of us under your roof.'

I gasp audibly. Simon presses down harder and grabs my hand. 'You're both in your prime,' he says. 'In your prime.' I can tell he doesn't know what else to say.

Joe waves his pint of lager at his wife. 'Simon's right. We have years ahead of us. Stop being so morbid.'

She glares at him. 'I'm not being morbid, just practical. We could sell our house and Meg and Simon could build a granny flat in their back garden.'

I hardly think—' Joe begins but she cuts him off.

'Wouldn't that be lovely, Simon? We could see Lily every day. Imagine that.' Her eyes glaze over and I know she's imagining dressing Lily in the horrible stiff cotton dresses and fancy cardigans she favours.

I feel like putting my head in my hands and screaming.

'Excuse me,' I say, standing up. 'I have to use the bathroom.'

'Now look what you've done,' I hear Joe say to her as I walk away. 'I told you not to come on so strong, but oh, no, you had to—'

I walk around the corner and out the back door. Then I allow myself a small scream. A passing waitress almost drops her tray.

'Sorry,' I mouth at her.

I stay outside until my heart has stopped beating a tattoo against my chest. My fists are balled and I can feel the tension rising up the back of my neck. What have I done to deserve a mother in-law like Maureen?

My mobile rings. It's Simon.

'Where are you? Are you OK?'

'I'm out the back. Just getting some air. Where are you?'

'Out the front. Wait there.'

Seconds later he appears beside me. 'I'm so sorry about Mum. She can't help herself sometimes.'

'If she comes to live with us I'll kill myself,' I say dramatically.

Simon stifles a smile. 'It's not going to happen. She'll change her mind. You'll see.'

'She's as stubborn as Hattie,' I point out. 'We should just send Lily over to live with them in London and be done with it.'

'You know, that's not such a bad idea,' Simon says after a moment.

'I was joking,' I splutter. 'You don't think I meant it, did you?'

'Course not. But maybe a few days alone with Lily is just

what she needs,' Simon muses. 'Fancy a weekend away, Meg? Just the two of us?'

'Are you serious?'

Simon nods.

'Your mum would never agree to that. She's over to see you too, Simon. We can't just bugger off for the whole weekend. And what about Slipper and Pat?'

'They can come with us. And I don't flatter myself – it's Lily she's after. She'll jump at the chance to spend a whole weekend feeding and dressing her darling granddaughter.'

'And Dan?'

'He'll need to stay with Lily, to make sure she's all right. But he might be allowed to have a friend or two over.'

I raise my eyebrows, getting his drift. 'A sleepover you mean? With George and some of their other buddies?'

Simon nods.

I begin to grin. 'Simon Murphy, you're one evil man. And you know, it might just work.'

He kisses me hard. 'And we'll have the whole weekend together,' he says, pressing me up against the wall and kissing me again. 'With no children in our bed at six in the morning.'

'Let's do it,' I say, kissing him back.

Chapter 28

Squall: a sudden, violent gust of wind

By eleven the following morning, the plan is all in place. Simon and I will collect Slipper and Pat at the airport at midday and drive straight down to the Dolphin House Hotel in Wicklow. Hans happily gave Simon the day off. Being autumn, things have quietened down in the shop and Hans is delighted with Simon's work so far. He's is no fool, he knows he has me to thank for Simon's career change, and he practically gushes every time we speak.

Just before we leave, I call in to Tina's.

'Meg, come on in.' Tina holds the door wide open, smiling at me. I always feel so deliciously welcome in her house. I'll miss her like crazy if she moves away. I follow her down the steps and into the kitchen. There's loud banging outside. We both look out the window. Matty is hammering away at something in the back garden; Tina's two boys are looking on with rapt attention.

'Matty's building them a house on stilts,' she explains. 'They've always wanted a tree house, but we don't have any trees, so Matty suggested stilts.' She looks at me, worry in her eyes. 'He's brilliant with them, Meg. Sometimes I feel it's all too good to be true and that one morning I'll wake up and everything will be back to the bad old days. I'm so lucky, so grateful to get a second chance, but I don't feel I deserve it.'

'You've been through the mental wringer recently, of course you deserve it.' I pause for a moment. 'But I do know what you mean. Sometimes I wake up in the early hours of the morning, convinced that Simon doesn't really exist, that I'm on my own with Dan again. It's silly, I know, but we all do it. Remember the bad times I mean. But I guess you just have to enjoy being happy while it lasts and take things day by day.' I smile at her. 'There's no point in either of us worrying about things that may never happen.'

'I suppose you're right. Hey, are you going all Zen on me?'

I laugh. 'Zen? I don't think so. But speaking of going, I'd better get a move on. We're due at the airport in less than an hour.' I explain about Pat and Slipper and our weekend away.

'Have a great time and don't worry,' Tina says 'I'll keep an eye on the in-laws for you.'

'Thanks. And say hi to Matty for me.'

'I will. And Meg? I never thanked you.'

'For what?'

'For introducing us in the first place.' She smiles at me a little shyly. 'Thanks.'

'You're more than welcome. He deserves someone like you, Tina. Be good to each other.'

'We will.'

As I walk the few steps home, I ring Hattie on my mobile. She's not answering so I try her at work, but her boss says she phoned in sick. The woman sounds a little ticked off. I'm not all that surprised. I'd hate to be Hattie's boss, she's not the most reliable of employees. I wonder if she really is sick. Maybe she's upset about Ryan and can't face work. I ring Mum and Dad's to check up on her. Mum answers the phone. She says Hattie never came home last night and she presumes she went straight to work.

'I'm sure you're right,' I say. 'I'll try her there. Sorry to bother you.' I click off the phone before Mum has a chance to say anything else. Hattie's probably taken a day off to go shopping or something. Or maybe she's met someone else already, I wouldn't put it past her.

Ten minutes later we're driving through Blackrock on the way to the airport. Simon's at the wheel so I rest my head against the headrest and close my eyes. Before I know it, I've dozed off.

'Hey, sleepyhead,' Simon says as I open my eyes. We're sitting at traffic lights at Santry. 'We're nearly there.'

'Sorry.' I squeeze my eyes tightly closed and then open them again. 'Hope I wasn't snoring.'

'No, just dribbling a bit.'

I rub the sides of my mouth, then check out my face in the passenger mirror and, satisfied, click it shut again.

'I'm dying to see Pat,' I say, opening my window a little. The air is thick with dust from road works and fumes from passing trucks so I quickly close it again.

'I know, she's a great girl. Slipper's mad about her. I've never seen him so besotted.'

'He's not acting the maggot with her?' I ask cautiously, not sure if I really want to know the answer.

'No, he's a changed man. Completely faithful to Pat. Or so he says. Besides, I can't see her standing for any nonsense, can you?'

'No, I suppose not. But love can do funny things to people,' I muse, thinking about Ryan and Hattie.

Simon looks over at me but says nothing.

When Pat and Slipper walk through the arrivals door I hardly recognize either of them. Slipper is wearing snug-fitting denims, a plain white T-shirt, and Reefs. His hair is close shaven, and it suits him. He looks amazing. Pat is wearing a red cotton on-the-knee skirt, a plain white vest top with spaghetti straps and Roman slave-style sandals, leather laces snaking up her slim, tanned calves. Her hair is in braids, topped by a jaunty straw cowboy hat.

Simon gives a breathy whistle. 'Jeepers, they look like movie stars.'

I look down at my own seen-better-days jeans and plastic flip-flops and wince. No film-star looks for me. Simon, in his shorts and sailing T-shirt, smeared with hardened boat filler and varnish, fares little better.

'Meg!' Pat grins and runs towards me, her arms outstretched. She gives me an almighty hug. 'It's good to see you again.'

'And you,' I says, hugging her back. I'd forgotten how spontaneous she is.

She draws away. 'You look great. Thanks so much for inviting us over.'

I give Simon a sideways look. Guess who proffered the invitation – without asking me I might add. He winks at me. 'No problem,' I say graciously.

Slipper slaps Simon on the back. 'Hiya, mate. So what's this posh hotel like? Big bar?' Simon had filled them in by phone and they'd been only too delighted to join us in Wicklow.

'Huge,' Simon says, 'and a swimming pool and jacuzzi for the girls. And I've booked them both into the beautician's tomorrow morning.'

'How sweet of you,' Pat says.

'There's a soccer match on,' I say wryly.

Pat laughs. 'It's still a nice thought.'

As we drive towards Wicklow on the motorway, I listen as Pat and Slipper tell us their news. They're finishing each other's sentences and laughing loudly at each other's jokes, like two teenagers. Simon and I used to be like that, I think a little wistfully. But I guess we've just got used to each other over the years and some of that early spark has gone. But that's life. I stare out the window and wonder why I'm in such a contemplative mood. Maybe I'm just tired. I don't feel like getting involved in the conversation so I lean my head against the closed window and pretend to be asleep.

'Is Meg all right?' I hear Pat ask Simon quietly a little later.

'She's just wiped out,' Simon replies. 'My parents are over and she doesn't find my mum easy. And her dad's sick; she's got a lot on her plate at the moment.'

'Slipper was telling me about her dad. I hope it goes OK. All the treatment and everything. My aunt had breast cancer but she was given the all clear recently. If he's as strong as Meg is, I'm sure he'll fly through it.'

Thank you, Pat, I say to myself. Thank you.

The Dolphin is an old cut-stone castellated house that has been extended and converted into a luxury hotel and as soon as I flop back on the huge double bed I know Simon has made the right choice. It's part owned by a man he sailed with over the summer, and Simon managed to wangle an amazing deal; there's no way we could have afforded it otherwise.

We've bagged the presidential suite and Slipper and Pat are in the Oscar Wilde suite, much to Pat's delight. Pat is a big Oscar Wilde fan apparently, after seeing a Hollywood version of *The Importance of Being Earnest*. I'm not sure Slipper knows who Oscar Wilde is, but he likes the green wallpaper and huge bed. We agree to meet in an hour for lunch, after we've unpacked and checked out our rooms, which both include generously sized en suites, and small sitting rooms with sofas and TVs.

Simon lies down beside me, his bulk making the mattress wobble.

'Hi there.' He brushes some of my hair back with his hand.

'Hi yourself.'

He rolls over onto his stomach and looks down at me. 'No kids, no in-laws, big bed all to ourselves. Are you thinking what I'm thinking?'

I smile at him. 'I'm thinking I'd kill for a nice big bubble bath.'

He groans. 'Typical.'

I laugh. 'There's plenty of time later for that kind of thing.'

'That kind of thing.' Simon smiles wryly. 'I guess that puts me in my place.'

'I'm sorry. I didn't mean it that way.'

'It's OK, I understand. You must be tired, you've had a long week. You stay here, I'll run a bath for you.'

'Thanks. You're an angel.' I listen as he turns on the taps, the water thundering against the bottom of the huge roll-top bath.

Lunch is delicious, fresh salmon served with lots of home-made brown soda bread and lashings of butter, followed by rhubarb fool – and several bottles of chilled white wine. Then a lazy afternoon's walk by the sea and a potter in some of the shops and galleries in nearby Wicklow town.

The evening is punctuated by more good food and more good wine. We all get on famously and I find myself being drawn out of my mood by Pat's lively personality.

After dinner we adjourn to the huge squashy sofas in the hall and sit in front of the biggest open fire I've ever seen. It's as tall as Simon and at least ten foot wide, with stone seats on either side for very cold people to sit and warm their bones. The walls of the hall are hung from floor to ceiling with tapestries of hunting scenes in faded reds and browns, originally designed to keep the draughts out.

By the end of the evening, Pat is leading a sing-song, with Simon accompanying her on the piano in the corner. One of the waiters, a local lad, has a great voice and is belting out old Beatles tunes, although his grasp of the words is a little suspicious.

By midnight, I'm fading. Simon, Slipper and Pat are still in full swing, so I excuse myself and go outside for some air. The night is clear, if a little nippy. I wrap my arms around my body in an attempt to keep warm and stare up at the stars. I wish I'd paid more attention to Dad when he'd tried to teach me the constellations when I was little. On clear nights, we used to lie out in the back garden in the winter, a rug under us and our coats firmly buttoned up to our throats. Dad had an old pair of binoculars and we took turns staring through them. I'd seen several shooting stars on our star-watch nights and the binoculars really brought the Milky Way alive. I smile to myself, remembering the silence, the vast sky laid out in front of us, the easy companionship of those nights. Tonight, if I concentrate, I can just make out Orion's belt. Or is it the Big Dipper? Or the Plough? I'll have to invest in a star book.

'Meg, what are you doing out here?' Pat appears beside me. 'Are you feeling OK?'

'I just needed some air. It's a beautifully clear evening.' I nod up at the dark sky.

She smiles. 'I used to love looking at the stars when I was little. Still do. Ever seen a shooting one?'

'Yes, lots.'

'Really?'

'Sure. They're not all that unusual.'

'I've never seen one. Must be something to do with my short attention span.'

'If you look for long enough at certain times of the year, you will.'

'When?'

I shrug. 'I can't remember. But I'll find out for you. My dad will know. He's into that kind of thing.'

Pat gives a laugh. 'Dads always know everything, don't they? It's part of their job.' She pauses for a moment. 'Slipper told me about your dad. I was sorry to hear about the cancer. How's he doing?'

'OK, I think. He seems to be responding well to the treatment. But we just have to wait and see.'

'It's the waiting that gets to you, isn't it? The not knowing?'

'Yes.' I want to say more, but there's a lump in my throat.

Pat seems to understand. We stand in silence for a few more minutes, looking up at the stars.

'No shooting stars for me tonight,' she says after a while.

'Another night.'

'Now, are you coming back inside? It's getting kinda chilly out here.'

'I'm going to go on up to our room I think. I'm wrecked and that bed is just calling to me. Will you tell Simon for me? I don't want to disturb him.'

'No problem. I'll see you in the morning. How about a swim before the beautician's? Say ten o'clock. Breakfast at half nine?'

'Sounds a bit early to me.' It will be our first lie-in together for as long as I can remember and I don't want to squander it.

'Breakfast at ten?'

'Perfect. See you then.'

I sleep like a log and the following morning I'm woken by a strange noise coming from the sitting room.

'Simon,' I hiss, rolling over. But the other side of the bed hasn't been slept in. I look at my watch. Nine o'clock. Where the hell is he?

I get up and stand at the open doorway. There's the noise again. It sounds like a low rumbling. I grab my phone from the bedside table and key in Simon's number.

I hear it ringing and from the sitting room comes the sleepy reply. 'Hello?'

I click off my phone and walk in. The room is a state. And in the middle of the mess, sprawled over the two sofas are

Simon and Slipper. Slipper is still holding an empty wine glass, cradled in his two hands. The coffee table is littered with three more empty glasses, one on its side spilling its dregs onto the smoky glass top. The room has that horrible pub-the-morning-after smell – stale and reeking of alcohol. The rumbling noise is Slipper snoring.

I give Simon a gentle kick with the side of my bare foot. He groans and then rolls over, falling off the sofa. He groans again and opens his eyes.

'Hiya, Meg.' He smiles blearily up at me. He's still drunk.

'Get off the floor, you big eejit. You're lucky you didn't hit the side of your head on the table. Be careful.'

'Have to sleep,' he moans. 'Tired. Where's the bed?'

I bend down, holding his arm a little harder than is strictly necessary, and drag him up. 'This way.' I deposit him at the side of the bed and he falls onto it, face first, and begins to snore. I put the covers over him and find a blanket in the wardrobe to throw over Slipper, who's still snoring. Then I run myself a bath. So much for my romantic weekend!

A little later I hear a tentative knock on the door. 'Meg? Are you awake?' It's Pat. I sigh and put my hands on either side of the bath, levering myself up. The water sloshes over the side but I don't care. For once I don't have to mop it up.

I open the door in a towel, leaving a trail of bubbly steps in my wake.

'Oh, I didn't mean to disturb you. Were you and Simon having a bath?' She gives me a knowing wink.

I laugh. 'Yeah, right. Chance would be a fine thing. He's comatose and Slipper's as bad. He's still on the sofa. Have a look.' I gesture into the sitting room.

She peers in. 'Just where I left him at four this morning.' She smiles at me. 'What are they like?'

'Teenagers?'

She laughs. 'Without the stamina. Hey, speaking of stamina, I'm starving. Ready for breakfast?'

'Can we swim after eating?'

'Swim? Honey, I'm going to lie in the jacuzzi. Swimming sounds far too energetic for me.'

'Breakfast it is then. Just give me a second to get dressed.'

Pat sits down on the side of the bed, which is a little disconcerting. I'm quite shy about changing in front of other women. I always use those private booths in the swimming pools, pretending it's to make life easier with Lily as it contains her in one place and stops her running around the changing room starkers, but it's really for me. I figure Pat will see my wobbly bits in my swimming togs, so there's no point in being coy.

I slip on my underwear and then a top and jeans, and slide my feet into flip-flops. Then I tie my damp hair back and grab my swimming bag. 'Ready,' I say.

'That was quick.' Pat has been flicking through a glossy *Discover Ireland* magazine. 'Hey, that Giant's Causeway sounds cool. Is it near here?'

I smile. It's in Northern Ireland, miles away. 'Not exactly. Now let's eat.'

After a hearty Irish breakfast of bacon, sausages, mushrooms, beans and potato cakes we stagger out of the dining room, towards the pool.

'Just as well we're not swimming now,' I say. 'I'd sink from all that food.'

Pat laughs.

Minutes later, we're lowering ourselves into the jacuzzi, the frothy bubbles tickle our toes.

'Jeepers, it's hot!' I exclaim.

'You'll get used to it.'

I sit down and lift my chin to stop the bubbles going up my nose. This is the life. I give a satisfied sigh.

'So Simon's working for Hans?' Pat asks after she's got herself settled.

'Yes. Do you know him?'

'Sure. Met him a couple of times at events. Nice guy. Irish wife, is that right?'

'Yes. And when's Slipper off to New Zealand?'

'Tuesday. This is our last weekend together. I'm thinking of joining him over there.'

'Really? How exciting.'

'I know. Don't say anything to Simon yet. Or to Slipper for that matter. I'm trying to get a work visa. I'd be bored stupid otherwise. But I'll know in a week or two.'

'That's great. I hope it works out for you.'

'Hey, if it doesn't I'll go over for a long holiday, maybe two. It's only six months after all. It'll fly by.'

I feel a little uncomfortable. Pat's right, it isn't long at all. Maybe Simon is missing out on a chance of a lifetime. Maybe I've been short-sighted.

'What's on your mind?' she asks.

I shake my head. 'Oh, nothing.'

She gives me a sceptical look.

'New Zealand,' I admit.

'Having second thoughts?'

'I guess so. But it's too late now. And Simon seems happy to be in Dublin.'

'Does he ever talk about New Zealand?'

'No. Never. He avoids any America's Cup talk in general.'

'Before the America's Cup offer came up I mean.'

'No, why?'

Pat's face is flushed. She puts a hand in the water and brushes some hair back off her face. There's a look in her eyes that makes me nervous. I pull my body up with my arms until my shoulders and arms are out of the water.

'Pat, what is it?'

'I've been thinking about this a lot over the last few days. Ever since Slipper told me in fact.'

'About what?' Now I *am* getting worried. What is Pat talking about?

'There's no easy way to say this. I was hoping you already knew. But if you don't, I want you to promise me you won't do anything rash.'

My heart sinks and I begin to feel knots in my stomach. Simon's having an affair. He's going to leave me for some young racer chaser and there isn't a thing I can do about it. How can I compete with a skinny—

'Meg, are you listening?'

'Sorry. Yes. Please, whatever it is just tell me, Pat.'

'I'd want to know. That's why I'm telling you. And I don't know if I'll get another chance this weekend—'

'Just get on with it. Simon's having an affair, isn't he?'

'An affair?' She snorts. 'Simon? God, no.'

'What then? You're doing my head in.'

'He has a child. A daughter. In New Zealand.'

'What?' I haven't heard right. What Pat just said doesn't make any sense.

'Simon has a daughter.'

I feel the blood drain from my face. 'It's not true,' I say in a tiny voice.

'It is, I'm afraid. The baby's mum, Kira, used to work with Simon on the boats. As a hostess.'

'But I don't understand. He never said a word. Are you sure?'

Pat nods. 'Yes.'

'But he would have told me. Slipper's got it wrong.' I jump up and step out of the jacuzzi. 'You're wrong.' I grab a towel and wrap it around me.

Pat looks up at me, her face even more flushed. 'Go and talk to Simon. I'm so sorry.'

I glare at her. 'You shouldn't spread nasty gossip, Pat.'

She looks hurt. 'I'm sorry. I just thought you should know.'

I turn my back on her and storm off, skidding and nearly coming a cropper on the wet tiles. I steady myself before marching into the changing room. Then I throw my clothes on and run up to our room. I swing the door open, dump my swimming bag on the ground and stand at the foot of the bed.

'Simon! Simon! Wake up.'

He moans, then opens his eyes.

'What's wrong?' he asks, catching my no-nonsense tone.

My hands are straight down at my sides, my hands balled, my body one big volcanic mass of tension. 'Do you have a daughter? In New Zealand?'

He sits up, a horrified expression flitting across his face. I know the answer immediately. My hands fly to my mouth and I gasp for breath. 'Jesus.' I stare at him, anger rising through my veins. 'Why didn't you tell me?'

'I didn't want to lose you. Meg, I'm so sorry—'

'What kind of idiot are you?'

'Meg—'

'I don't want to hear it. Get out.' I begin to thump his chest with my fists. 'Just get out.' I slap him across the face and he grabs my hands.

'Meg—'

I pull my hands away from him and glare at him in disgust. 'I have nothing to say to you. Get out!' I grab a lamp from the side table and try to hurl it at him but the flex stops me. I pick up Simon's shoe instead.

'Meg, stop. I'm going.' He stands up, his hands over his face. 'I'll wait outside.'

As soon as he leaves I throw all my clothes into my bag, and clear the bathroom in record time. My blood is pulsing through my veins and I'm too angry to think straight. I swing my bag over my shoulder and push the door open.

Simon is standing outside, one leg against the wall.

'Meg,' he says, straightening up and holding out his palms, 'we need to talk.'

'I have nothing to say to you. Don't ring me, don't follow me. Understand?'

He reaches out a hand to touch me, but when I back away he drops it.

'Get away from me,' I spit. 'Leave me alone.' I turn my back on him and walk down the stairs. I expect him to follow me, but he doesn't. I'm relieved, yet disappointed. He's not even going to fight for me. My stomach lurches and tears prick my eyes. What have I done to deserve this? Why is this happening? Am I such a terrible person?

Pat is sitting in the hall and jumps to her feet as soon as she sees me. I feel terrible. None of this is Pat's fault, she was only trying to help.

'Meg, are you OK?'

'No, not really. But I'm sorry, I shouldn't have taken it out on you.'

'So it's true?' she asks gently.

I give a small nod.

There are tears in her eyes. 'I should never have said anything. I'm so sorry. I just thought you had a right to know.'

'You did the right thing. I'm sorry, I have to go home now.'

'I understand. Will you be all right to drive?'

'I'll manage.'

She gives me a hug but I'm too wound up to respond. 'Take care. It'll work out in the end. Go home and give those lovely children of yours a kiss from me.'

I give her a half smile and then shrug. 'Sorry to wreck your holiday.'

'Hey, I wrecked yours.'

'Don't worry about it.'

*

I drive back from Wicklow like a maniac, my eyes hot and prickly with angry tears, my breath ragged. My mind is racing, but I can't think straight. What happens now? We can't go on as normal, that's for sure. Simon abandoned his baby. A baby I had no idea existed. What am I supposed to do? In a way it would be easier if Simon was still sailing for a living. That way I could avoid him for a few days and then he'd leave for some exotic clime, and I'd have time and space to think. With Simon at home, I don't have that luxury.

I switch on the radio to drown out the thoughts in my head, but the dulcet tones of Dido don't exactly help my mood; I need something with a bit more bite. I scramble in the glove compartment and find an old Tom Petty CD of Simon's. That will do. Soon 'Free Falling' is blaring out of the speakers, suiting my mood better. I turn it up and sing along, banging the steering wheel in time to the music like Tom Cruise in *Jerry Maguire*. Luckily the road is quiet and I manage to get home safely in record time, before Tom Petty has a chance to sing his last tune. I hate to think what my speedometer was reading.

I sit outside the house for a moment attempting to collect my thoughts. Maureen and Joe are inside and I don't want them to see how upset I am. Besides, I don't want to be near Simon or anyone close to him. I'll go home, I decide suddenly. I'll pack some bags, and me and the kids will go and stay with Dad and Mum until I can bear to speak to Simon again. I know it isn't the ideal solution, especially with Dad so sick and everything, but it's all I can think of in my distracted state.

I check my face in the rear-view mirror, smooth my hair back and rub away the mascara marks from around my eye sockets. I look terrible, but I'm past caring.

I let myself into the house as quietly as I can and creep up the stairs. I go into our bedroom, open the wardrobe and pull out two sailing bags from the top shelf. I also manage to pull several old fleeces of Simon's down on top of my head. I stare at them before giving them a swift kick.

'Bastard,' I mutter, kicking them again. I leave them and walk into Lily's room.

I've never seen it so tidy. The floor is clear of all toys and clothes, you can actually see the pink carpet; the cot has been freshly made up with crisply ironed Barbie bed linen; the carpet has Hoover scratches on its surface.

The clothes in Lily's wardrobe have all been refolded and colour ranged. I know I should be grateful, but it just makes me feel inadequate and horribly sad. Lily's clothes are usually shoved randomly onto the shelves. I do try to keep her tops and trousers on separate shelves, but it doesn't always turn out that way. At the heart of it, I resent Maureen's interference. I didn't ask her to sort out Lily's room. Still, at least she's made packing easier.

I begin to throw Lily's little tops, jumpers, skirts and trousers into the first bag. I add an assortment of socks and tights, a blue and green fleecy jacket from the back of her door, a half-full packet of nappies and a suspiciously light box of wipes. Then I close the door behind me and open Dan's door.

'Mum.' Dan looks up from his *Simpsons* comic book. He's sitting on his top bunk. I'm strangely relieved to see his room is still as messy as ever. 'Is today Sunday?' he asks.

'No, Saturday. I came back early.'

'Can I watch telly? Granny said I'd watched enough last night to last me all year, so she said I had to come up here and read.'

'You can, of course.'

Dan's face lights up. He drops his book and jumps off the bunk, making the floor shake ominously under my feet.

'Dan!'

'Sorry I forgot.'

'You can watch telly as soon as we get to Granny and Grampa's. Now, I'd be grateful if you'd help me pack.'

'Cool! Can we leave Lily here? She's being a pain. Even Granny Maureen says so.'

I smile despite myself. So Simon was right, a good dose of Lily at her worst was just what Maureen needed. 'No, we have to take her too.'

'Where's Simon?'

'He's in Wicklow still, when he gets back he'll stay here with Maureen and Joe.'

Dan looks at me. 'Why?'

I sigh. It's probably best to tell him the truth. It'll be easier in the long run. 'We've had an argument. I'll tell you about it later, I promise. Right now we have to pack.'

As he throws what clean clothes and underwear he can find into the second bag, I go into my room and pile some of my own in on top of Lily's. There isn't much space left, but I don't need much. I already have my weekend bag in the car, and what I've forgotten I can always borrow off Hattie.

As I debate whether to take something decent, after all we could be staying there for a while and I might feel like going out with Hattie, I hear footsteps on the stairs. I brace myself.

'Mummeee.' Lily launches herself at my legs, her face the picture of happiness. Maureen has cut her fringe and it's a little crooked, making her face look lopsided. She's dressed in a navy velvet dress I haven't seen before. It has uncomfortable-looking tight gathers around the collar and the wrists and I'm sure it's cutting into the poor child's skin.

I pick her up and hold her to me, breathing in the clean scent of baby shampoo from her hair. 'How's mummy's little angel?'

'What are you doing here, Meg?' Maureen strides into the bedroom. She puts her hands on her hips and stares at me. 'I thought I heard someone up here. Joe said it was just Dan jumping off his bed, but I knew I heard voices.'

'I'm packing,' I say, trying to stay calm. My heart is racing and my palms are getting a bit sweaty.

'Packing? Did you forget something? I don't understand.'

'We're going to stay at my parents' house. Me and the kids.'

'What are you talking about?' Maureen demands. 'Why aren't you in Wicklow? Where's Simon?'

I ignore her questions. 'Dan,' I shout, 'can you take Lily downstairs for me?'

Dan appears at the door. 'Come on, Lily,' he says, peeling her off me.

'No! Want Mummee,' Lily protests, kicking her little legs.

Dan is well able for her. 'I'll get you a bicky,' he says. 'And we'll watch *Thomas the Tank*. You like Thomas, don't you, Lily?'

'Thomas,' Lily repeats. 'Bicky.'

'Thanks, Dan.'

When they've left the room, Maureen turns on me. 'Those children watch far too much television. No wonder Lily doesn't sleep properly. She was up until ten last night, Meg. Ten! And Dan and his friends giggled like girls all night. I didn't get a wink of sleep. Lily kicked me all night; she has frightfully sharp little heels, that girl.'

I smile to myself. Good girl, Lily, I think rather ungraciously.

'And as for Dan's friends, I'm sure they all need retinol. I've never seen such behaviour. Jumping around like monkeys, playing basketball in the kitchen, the pillow fights with your good cushions. Oh, they had my heart scaled. Eventually I let them watch a film, but it wasn't at all suitable. I suggested one of Lily's Disney films, that nice *Robin Hood* or *Sword in the Stone*, but oh, no, they wanted James Bond. James Bond! What kind of a role model is James Bond for young boys—'

James Bond? She was lucky they hadn't insisted on one of Simon's science-fiction gore fests.

'I'm sorry you had a hard night, but I have to get going.'

'What's all this about?'

I look at her. She's fingering the pearls around her neck and she looks a little nervous.

'I'm leaving Simon,' I say without preamble.

She gasps. 'What? You can't! Why? Did something happen in Wicklow?'

'Yes. I found out about his other daughter.'

She sways a little on her feet. 'Tia?' She stops for a moment and shakes her head. 'I have to sit down.' She backs towards the bed and sits on its edge. Her face is grey and she clasps her hands tightly in her lap.

She looks up at me, a strange expression in her eyes that I can't read. 'I see. What did he tell you exactly?'

'*He* didn't tell me a thing. That's just the point. I had to hear about her through one of his friends.' Not wanting to get Pat in trouble, I don't go into details.

'It was a long time ago,' Maureen says. 'It wasn't Simon's fault. You see Kira, Tia's mother—'

I can't bear this. I don't want to hear the details from Maureen of all people. I cut her off. 'Maureen, I just want to go home. I'm sure you understand. I need to think.'

'But can't you and Simon work this out? I know he should have told you . . .'

There's a cough from behind me. I swing around. Joe is standing there, his bulk taking up most of the doorway.

'Is everything all right?' he asks gently.

'She knows about Tia,' Maureen says.

Joe nods. 'About time too. I'm so sorry, Meg. Simon should have told you a long time ago. I tried to talk him around, but Maureen had the poor boy convinced that he'd lose you if he came clean. Silly woman.'

'Joe!' Maureen looks shocked.

'You've always been so obsessed about losing Lily that it clouds your judgement. We've never met Tia you see,' he continues, 'never even talked to her. The whole business broke Maureen's heart. That's why Lily's so precious to her.'

Maureen stares down at her clasped hands. Then she looks up, her eyes damp. 'That's enough.'

'Meg's family,' Joe says, putting a hand on her shoulder. 'She needs to know the facts. It's important, Maureen.' He turns back to me. 'After she found out she was pregnant, Kira wouldn't have anything to do with Simon, you see. Flew back to New Zealand before they had a chance to talk about things properly. Simon really loved the girl. Would have married her; but she didn't want anything more to do with him. Didn't love him enough, you see. And, well, I don't rightly know what happened next.' He shrugs. 'Poor lad was devastated. It was nearly the end of him. If it hadn't been for the sailing and his friends I don't know what he'd have done. We were so pleased when he met you, Meg. You were stable, you see. And a good mother. And we knew you loved Simon.'

Tears stream down my face. 'I presumed . . . the worst, I suppose. But he still should have told me. It's such a huge thing to keep secret.'

'We've all made mistakes,' Joe says gently. I can tell he's directing this at Maureen, but she isn't biting.

'So you'll stay, Meg?' she asks hopefully.

I falter. Maybe.

'Put all this silliness behind you,' she adds.

Joe shushes her, but it's too late.

I stare at her. 'Silliness? Simon's silliness you mean? *I* haven't done anything wrong, Maureen. It's your son who's in the wrong here.'

'But you haven't always been the most supportive partner, have you, Meg? It takes two to —'

'Maureen!' Joe says sharply. 'What's got into you? The girl's been through enough today. Maybe it's best if you do go and stay with your parents for the moment, Meg. You can leave Lily and Dan here with us if you like. We're here until Tuesday after all.'

'I'll take them with me, but I am grateful for the offer. Please tell Simon not to ring me or call in. It'll only make things worse. I'll be in touch with him as soon as I'm ready.'

'When will that be?' Maureen asks.

I ignore her.

'Take as much time as you need, lass,' Joe says. 'And I really am sorry.'

'I know you are.' I give him a hug. I glance down at Maureen, who is still perched on the bed. She looks defeated and I feel a little sorry for her. 'Bye, Maureen.'

'Bye, dear. And by the way, Dan eats far too much junk. His teeth will suffer you know.'

'Yes, thank you,' I say through gritted teeth. 'I am aware of dental hygiene.' As I walk down the stairs I can hear her saying, 'What? Can I not give her some parenting advice?' and I have to smile. Maureen just can't help herself, she's a lost cause.

I swing Lily onto my hip and ring the doorbell at Dad and Mum's. Dan follows and stands just behind me, eager to get to the promised goggle box no doubt. Hattie answers in her dressing gown. 'What time is it?' she says sleepily, rubbing her eyes.

'Three.'

'Oh, right. What are you doing here? I thought you were in Wicklow.'

'I was. I came home early. If you let me in, I'll tell you all about it.'

'What did Simon do this time?' she asks. 'Men! Big feckers the lot of them.'

'Ha, I knew it!' Dan says. 'I called George a fecker last night when he hit me over the head with a cushion and Maureen freaked out. But Hattie just said it. It's not a bad word at all.'

'It *is* a bad word,' I say. 'And for heaven's sake don't use it in front of Maureen. Hattie just had a momentary lapse of sense, didn't you, Hattie?'

'What? Oh, yes. I did.' She hits her forehead with her hand. 'Don't know what got into me. Bad Hattie.'

Lily copies Hattie but manages to hit herself in the eye. She begins to wail.

'Dan will you take Lily into the garden?' I thrust her at him. 'I have to talk to Hattie. Urgently.'

'Again? Do I have to? I minded her all morning.'

'Please, Dan? It's important.'

'Oh, all right. But you promised me I could watch telly.'

'After I've talked to Hattie, you can watch telly until it comes out your ears. I promise. Right now I need you to entertain Lily for a few minutes.'

'Fine,' he says huffily.

'Not exactly thrilled at the prospect, is he?' Hattie asks wryly as we watch him storm past us with a crying Lily on his hip.

'Don't blame him, he's been really good.' I watch through the window as he puts Lily in the swing and pushes her. 'What am I doing? I'm a terrible mother. I should be the one out there, soothing Lily. I'm so selfish.'

'Sit down and tell me what's happened. They're fine. And you *are* a great mother most of the time. But you're allowed to have bad days every now and then. That's life, Meg. Stop fretting over Dan, he's grand.'

I smile at her gratefully. 'Where are Dad and Mum?'

'They went out for a walk. They won't be back for a while.'

I'm relieved.

I collapse into a chair and rest my elbows on the kitchen table. 'Wait till I tell you.' I unfold the whole sorry story of Simon's secret, from start to finish, including Maureen's hurtful 'unsupportive partner' barb.

'That women should be shot,' Hattie says, her eyes flashing. 'Her sense of timing is extraordinary.'

Despite everything, I smile. 'Isn't it? She should be on one of those reality telly shows – Mothers-in-Law from Hell.'

Hattie laughs. 'Too right. I'm so sorry. You've had a lot to deal with lately and now this. I don't know what to say. Simon's a dark horse, isn't he? You have to admit, it does make him a bit more interesting.'

'Be serious. What am I suppose to do now? I can't stay with him after he's lied to me for so many years.'

'He hasn't exactly lied to you, has he?'

'As good as. What if we'd gone over to New Zealand and bumped into Tia or her mother? What then?'

Hattie snorts. 'Hardly likely. It's a big place.'

'So's Ireland, but it happens all the time over here.'

'Ireland's not as big as New Zealand.'

'It's got the same population.'

'No, it hasn't.'

'Yes, it has. Four million or so. I know it's bigger physically, but most people live in the main cities. I know what I'm talking about, Hattie. I did some research on the internet.'

Hattie sniffs. 'OK, don't get your knickers in a twist. You're such an oldest child.' She rubs her finger backwards and forwards over the kitchen counter and then looks up at me. 'And you haven't always been strictly honest with Simon, have you?'

'What do you mean?' I demand.

'There are things you haven't told him.'

'Like what?'

'Like the time you kissed Sid last Christmas.'

'How do you know about that?' I stare at her. I've never told a soul.

'Dan told me. He saw the pair of you at it, poor pet. He asked me did it mean you and Sid were getting back together.'

I groan and put my hands over my face. 'I don't deserve to have children.' I'm so ashamed.

'It's not that bad, Meg. Dan understands more than you give him credit for.'

I peel my hands away. 'Don't you see? That's just the point. He's eleven. He's far too young to have to worry about things like that.'

Hattie shrugs. 'Some kids have to worry about a lot worse, like where their next meal's coming from, or whether their dad's going to belt them again. Dan's fine. Granted he's a bit put upon at times, when you can't be bothered with Lily yourself. But he's a good kid.'

I stare at her, wincing. 'You can be very hard sometimes, do you know that? I'm in the middle of a major trauma here and you're giving out about my mothering skills.'

'*You* just said you were a bad mother, not me.' She snorts. 'Major trauma? You can be a right drama queen when you want to be. So, Simon made a mistake.'

'A *mistake*? But—' I try to interrupt her but she's having none of it.

'Hear me out. At heart Simon's a good guy. Give him a chance. Talk to him. From what Maureen and Joe said, he only kept it from you because he thought it was for the best.'

'I can't talk to him.'

'Why?'

I shrug. 'I don't know what to say.'

'Let him do the talking then.'

I know in my heart Hattie's right but I hate to admit it out loud. 'I'll think about it.'

'Promise?'

I nod. So much for getting a sympathetic hearing from my sister. I should have known better.

'Good. Now let's go and rescue Dan from Lily.'

A little later, my mobile rings. 'Meg, please don't put down the phone.' It's Simon. Heeding Hattie's advice, I let him speak.

'Yes?' I snap, not trusting myself to say anything else.

'Come home. I'm going to stay in Hans's place for a few days and Mum and Dad have moved into a hotel until tomorrow.'

'Tomorrow?'

'They're going home early. Dad thinks you need some space.'

I say nothing.

'Are you still there? Listen, I'm so sorry about everything. I know how you must be feeling.'

'You have no idea how I feel. You've been lying to me for years. I had a right to know about Tia.'

'I know, and I'm sorry. And if there was any way I could go back and change things, believe me, I would. But can't we just talk? Please? I need to explain what happened with Kira.' He sounds genuinely contrite and upset but I just can't say yes. It's easier to be angry and I embrace the waves of prickly crossness I feel.

'Goodbye, Simon. I'll move back home, it's better for the kids that way. I don't want to drag them into all of this. Not because of you, do you understand?'

'Of course. But can't we just talk?'

'No! I'll ring you. Please, don't try to contact me. You'll only make things worse.'

'OK,' he says meekly. 'I love you. And the kids.'

'All three of them?' I ask.

He says nothing and the phone clicks dead. I feel bad for getting that final dig in, but not as bad as he's made me feel.

I manage to get out of the house before Dad and Mum get back, for which I'm grateful.

As I drive home, Hattie's parting words ring in my ears. 'No one's perfect, Meg. Remember that.'

Chapter 29

Luff: when a boat is sailing too close to the wind the sail begins to shake or luff

'Dan rang me last night,' Sid says the following morning. 'Asked me to call over.' He puts one arm on the door jamb and rests his body weight against it. 'Can I come in?'

'It's early for you,' I comment. 'We don't usually see you before midday on a Sunday.' He strolls past me as if he owns the place. 'Dan sounded a bit upset. Something about Simon moving out.'

'He's exaggerating.'

Sid raises his eyebrows. 'Really? Sounded serious to me. Dan said there'd been an argument.'

I'm starting to get annoyed. Trust Sid to stick his oar in. And what was Dan doing, gossiping to him like that?

I fold my arms over my chest. 'It's really none of your business. All couples have their ups and downs, you know that better than anyone. Now, are you taking Dan out or what?'

'I thought we'd stay here for a change.'

'It's not really convenient. I have things to do.'

'Work away. I won't stop you.'

I glare at him. 'You'll be in the way. Why don't you take him out for lunch or something? Or to the cinema? He'd like that.'

'You could come with us.'

'What about Lily?'

'Lily too. Like a family outing.'

'Family?' I snort. 'What are you playing at? Did Dan put you up to this?'

'What do you mean?'

'You hate toddlers. Always have. And Lily is no exception. I practically had to bribe you to take Dan when he was little. You seem to have a rather selective memory.'

'I've changed,' Sid says with a grin. 'I've grown up. I just wasn't ready back then.'

'And you're ready now? Is that it?'

He nods. 'One hundred per cent.'

'Is Nora pregnant?'

'What?' he splutters. 'No, of course not.'

I look at him suspiciously. 'Something's brought this on. Have you broken up with her? Have you got a new girlfriend, with children?'

'What are you talking about? You're not making any sense. Listen to yourself. Can't I spend some time with Dan without being accused of God knows what?'

'No. Something's up. I've known you for long enough.'

'I keep telling you, I've changed. Come out for lunch. To that nice bagel place on the seafront. With Lily. Then we'll go to the park. Humour me.'

I'm hungry and I don't exactly have anything else to do other than mope around the house.

'Lily could do with some fresh air,' I admit. 'OK. But I'm keeping my eye on you.'

I demolish my bagel in record time, Sid passes me a napkin and points at the side of my mouth where the mayonnaise has gathered. After eating I feel much better, almost human. I collect a take-out coffee and we wander up the pedestrian path towards Dun Laoghaire park. Dan is walking behind us, messing with Sid's mobile. Sid is holding the pole at the back of Lily's tricycle, pushing her along. We walk in companionable silence and for a split second I wonder if this is what life with Sid would really be like – before banishing the thought to the back of my mind.

When we reach the park, Sid plonks Lily in a toddler swing and begins to push her as I watch. Dan is climbing on the monkey bars, his long legs almost touching the ground. The park is busy, the open-air market in full swing, and there's a lively buzz from the food and gift stalls. I watch the other parents as they navigate the packed playground and I wonder if they're happy or just acting out parts – doting father, dutiful mother.

'Mummee. Wheee,' Lily shrieks at me, enjoying being pushed higher and higher by Sid's strong hands.

'Meg,' says a voice behind me and I whip round. It's Simon. I instantly feel horribly guilty.

I gawk at him. 'What are you doing here?'

'Collecting some hot dogs for me and Hans.' He gestures at the grease-stained paper bag in his hand. 'I'm working today.'

'Oh.' I can't think of anything else to say.

'I'd better go,' he mumbles. He gazes at Lily and then realizes who's pushing her. He looks back at me, confusion in his eyes.

'Sid was taking Dan to the park anyway,' I say, feeling the need to justify myself. 'Lily needed some air so we tagged along. He's great with her, isn't he?' I add, kicking myself for being so unnecessarily cruel.

Simon mutters something under his breath which I don't catch. I know I've hurt him. I feel rotten.

'I'd better go,' he says. 'See you, Meg.' He strides away.

'Simon, wait,' I say to his disappearing back. He doesn't respond and I don't run after him.

As we walk back to the house, Sid bumps my shoulder with his. 'That wasn't too bad, was it?'

'No, it was nice. Thanks for lunch.'

'No problem.' He checks that Dan is well behind us before asking 'What did Simon have to say for himself?'

'Nothing really.'

'Why didn't he say hi to the kids?'

'He just didn't.'

'Why?'

'I don't want to talk about it.'

'Things are obviously bad if you can't even communicate with each other.'

I spin around on my heels, my eyes flashing. 'And you're the expert on relationships, are you? Don't make me laugh. You broke my heart, remember? Then spat on it and stamped on it, time and time again. I can't believe *you're* giving me a lecture on relationships.'

'Meg!' Sid holds my arm tightly. 'Calm down. Dan's right behind us. No wonder he rang me. You're in quite a state, aren't you?'

'I'm *not* in a state,' I hiss at him. 'How dare you, you sanctimonious pig. Just feck off and leave me alone.'

'I thought you said feck was a bad word,' Dan pipes up from behind us.

'It is. Sorry, I shouldn't have said it. But sometimes it just slips out when I'm annoyed.'

'Are you annoyed with Dad *and* Simon?' Dan asks me, his eyes wide.

'Yes. Yes, I am.'

Dan holds my gaze. His eyes start to blur with tears. Then he blinks and stares down at the ground. I step towards him and put my hand on his arm but he shrugs it away. 'Get off.' He runs away from me, up the road.

'Dan,' I call after him.

'Leave him,' Sid says, but I ignore him and sprint after Dan, my legs and lungs complaining. Eventually I catch him up as he waits to cross the road.

'Dan,' I say, bending over double with the exertion and gasping for breath, 'please wait.'

'Why should I?'

'Ah, Dan, give me a second to catch my breath.' I straighten up, my breath still ragged. 'What's wrong?' I ask.

'Why do you always have to argue with people?'

'I don't always argue with people.'

'Yes, you do. Granny and Sid and Nora and Simon and Granny Maureen. You never stop.'

'That's not true.'

'It is. You were just fighting with Dad back there.'

'We weren't fighting—'

'Yes, you were. I'm not stupid. Why can't you just be happy?'

'I *am* happy, Dan, most of the time, anyway. But sometimes things happen, adult things. Life isn't always easy for me, you know.'

'I do my best,' he says. 'I help as much as I can. I play with Lily.'

A lump forms in my throat. 'I know. But this has nothing to do with you.'

'What is it then? Why do you keep fighting with Simon?'

I shake my head. 'It's complicated.'

He looks at me in disgust. 'You only tell me things when it suits you.'

'No, I don't.'

'Yes, you do. When I was little you used to tell me about all the horrible things Sid had said to you. Remember?'

'Did I?' My pulse races. My God. Did I really? Maybe I did. I honestly couldn't remember. Maybe I'd shut it out of my mind, relegated it to the closed and padlocked box marked 'Sid'.

Dan nods. 'I didn't mind. You said I was your only real friend. The only person you could trust.'

I feel about an inch high. How could I have used Dan as my emotional sounding board? It's not right.

'I shouldn't have worried you like that,' I say, putting my hand in the small of his back. 'Let's go home. Please, Dan.'

'Only if you tell me what's wrong. With you and Simon I mean.'

I chew the inside of my lip for a moment. I have no idea how he'll react if I tell him the truth. But if I don't tell him and he finds out anyway . . .

'Simon has a daughter in New Zealand,' I say finally, after weighing up the odds.

Dan's eyes light up. 'Really? What age is she? Can I meet her? Is she related to me and Lily as well?'

Whatever reaction I was expecting, it wasn't this. I'm so relieved I feel weak at the knees. 'I suppose she's Lily's half-sister. And she's a few years older than you. Thirteen.'

'Cool!' He looks at me. 'What's so bad about that?'

I smile down at him. My baby, my wonderful grown-up baby. 'Nothing,' I say. 'Nothing at all.' And then I'm off, crying my eyes out. I just want to hug him, to hold him tight and never let him go.

'Mum?' Dan says. 'Are you OK?'

I nod and wipe the tears away with the back of my hand. 'Yes. Sorry.' I laugh through the tears. 'Just being silly. And I'm sorry for fighting with everyone. I'll try not to from now on. Things are going change, Dan, you'll see—' I break off, making wild promises to myself in my head. No more arguing with people, even Mum, no more relying on Dan as a cheap babysitter. I come to a halt when I start thinking about Simon though.

Dan shrugs, oblivious to the machinations of my mind. 'OK. Hey, can we have chips for tea?'

'Sure. If it makes you happy.'

'Deadly!' He grins. 'Thanks.'

There's a solution for everything when you're eleven. Chips, I think. If only life were that simple.

'Is Dan all right?' Sid asks as we join him again just outside the house. He's carrying Lily under one arm now, dragging her tricycle behind him.

'He's fine.' We walk towards the house and I turn the key in the lock. 'Inside, you two,' I say to Dan and Lily. 'And dump your muddy shoes at the bottom of the stairs.'

'Can we watch telly in the sitting room?' Dan asks me.

'Sure.'

He yelps with joy and runs in, Lily toddling behind him.

'Thanks for lunch,' I say again to Sid, once they've disappeared. 'And sorry for snapping at you.'

'That's OK,' he says easily. 'Can I call round this evening?'

I look at him suspiciously. 'Why?'

'To see Dan of course.'

'He has school tomorrow. It's not a great idea.'

He rests his hand on my shoulder. 'Fine. But if you need to talk—'

I move away from him. 'Listen, I don't know what you're playing at, but I'm not buying this sympathy act. What are you after?'

'Nothing. I just thought if this break with you and Simon is final—'

'Go on,' I say, my eyes narrowing.

'We might give it a second chance.'

I give a rather harsh laugh. 'Second chance? Seventh chance more like. Are you joking?'

'No.' He looks a bit affronted. 'I know Dan would like it.'

'Leave Dan out of this.'

'Why? He's our son.'

I shake my head. 'It's not going to happen. Not now, not ever. And what about Nora?'

'I like her, but she's not you.'

'Sid, I'm tired of all of this. Whatever happens with Simon, that's certainly not what I want. Let's get this absolutely straight. I don't love you.'

'Yes, you do.'

'No, I don't,' I say firmly.

He smiles and shakes his head a little. 'Yeah, right.'

'Why don't you believe me?'

'I see the way you look at me. I know you want me.'

I start to laugh a little hysterically. I can't help myself. 'This kind of look?' I ask, putting on my best bemused and exasperated look. The kind of look I usually give him when he's annoying me.

'Exactly.'

'That's not lust, that's exasperation. Believe me, I'm not in love with you. I haven't been for a long, long time. I'm sorry.'

'But what about Christmas?'

'That was a mistake. Things just got out of hand.'

'But you must have fancied me a bit to snog me like that.'

I smile. I may as well give him that much. 'I suppose I must have. But it won't happen again. *Ever.*'

Sid bites his lip and then makes a noise at the back of this throat. 'Pity,' he says after a long pause. 'But I guess there's always Nora.'

'Lucky Nora,' I say drily looking at the door. I'm tired and I just want to sit down and veg for a while.

He gets the message. 'I guess I'll go then.'

'You do that.'

'I'll see Dan the weekend after next.'

'What's wrong with next weekend?'

'Stag do. In Kilkenny.'

Ah, back to the Sid I know and understand. 'Enjoy yourself.'

I see him out, then walk into the living room and put my arms around Dan from behind.

'Everything OK, Mum?' he asks, his eyes still glued to the screen.

'I think so.' I kiss the top of his head.

'Get off,' he complains, swatting me away. I sit down on the sofa with Dan on one side of me and Lily on the other. Like a proper family.

Mum rings in the early evening. I'm in no mood to talk to her but I don't want to be rude and I have decided to be a better person after all which includes being a better daughter. Stepdaughter. After a perfunctory chat about the weather, Dan's school and my stay in Wicklow (I'm vague on that subject) I can hear Lily calling from her bed.

'Mum, I'm sorry. Lily's crying. Is there anything in particular on your mind? I'm sorry to rush you.'

'Yes, I suppose there is. Hattie told me about you and Simon. About the baby, well, child I suppose.'

Hattie! I'll bloody kill her; she's landed me in it, yet again.

'Meg, are you there?'

'Yes, yes,' I reply irritably. 'And she's thirteen.'

'Gosh, really, a teenager?'

'Yes.' I wait for Mum to come to the point.

'How are you taking it all, Meg? It must have come as quite a shock.'

'You could say that,' I say, a sarcastic edge to my voice.

'I just wanted to let you know that I'm here if you want to talk.'

'Thanks.' I'm pleasantly surprised – no judgemental comments, no backhanded remarks?

'But don't do anything rash, Meg. Do you hear me?'

I knew it was too good to be true.

'Rash? Like what? Like telling Simon to take a hike? Is that what you mean? Because it's too late, Mum. I asked him to leave.'

'Was that wise?'

'Wise? He's been lying to me for years. Is *that* wise?'

'There's no point in talking to you if you're in one of your moods.'

My 'always arguing' conversation with Dan comes back to haunt me. I rein myself in. 'I'm not trying to pick a fight. I'm just extremely upset and very confused. What am I supposed to do? Welcome him back with open arms? Act like nothing's happened? He has a daughter. A daughter he's never met. Think about it. She's Lily's half-sister.'

'I suppose she is,' Mum says grudgingly, 'but sometimes things are best left lie. Don't go looking for trouble, Meg. From what Hattie said, the girl's mother doesn't want anything to do with Simon. Don't ruin your life over something that happened a long time ago.'

'A long time ago? He's never even seen her. Shouldn't he at least have made some effort—'

'Don't go poking your nose into other people's business.'

Now my blood is beginning to boil. I've had enough of this. 'Simon's daughter *is* my business. And if you can't see that—'

'Of course I can. I just don't want you making things worse. All I'm saying—'

'I know what you're saying. Stupid Meg's making a hames of things again.'

'That's not fair!'

'Really? I've had it up to here with you and your judgemental attitude. You've never approved of the way I live my life. Admit it. You want to see me all nice and settled. I hate to point it out to you but your real children aren't such hot shots either.

One's a nymphomaniac and the other's about to give you yet another illegitimate grandchild.'

Mum gasps. 'Stop this at once. Why are you being so cruel? And what do you mean "real children"?'

'Oh, work it out yourself, and leave me alone!' With that I slam down the phone, feeling angry beyond words. I put my head in my hands and close my eyes tightly. Dan's right, I do pick arguments with everyone. Silly, pointless arguments, and I hurt everyone around me. But she was asking for it. All that guff about making things worse. Who does she think she is? As if she really cares about me.

Ten minutes later the phone rings again. I pick it up and hold it wordlessly to my ear.

'Meg, are you there? It's me. Hattie. Say something.'

'Hi,' I say, relieved it's not Mum.

'Are you OK? Mum says you're pretty upset.'

'Oh, does she now?'

'Don't be like that. She's worried about you.'

'Yeah, right.'

'She's in the kitchen crying.'

'Oh.' I feel deflated. It's much easier to be angry with Mum when she's being her usual bossy self.

'She's only trying to help.'

'I can't believe you told her about Simon,' I say, shifting the focus. 'You little toerag.'

'Charming,' she says easily.

'What were you thinking?'

'It'll come out eventually. She may as well know now.'

'Hattie!'

'Oh, quit the moaning. It's starting to annoy me. And I can't believe you called me a nympho, you wench. Jealousy will get you nowhere.'

I give a short laugh. Then something dawns on me: Mum

hardly told Hattie that. 'You were listening on the other phone, weren't you? You nosy cow.'

'Don't sound so shocked. You used to do it all the time.'

'*Did*, Hattie. Past tense. I haven't lived at home for years, remember? Not like you, you sad thing.'

She gives a sniff. 'Anyway, you shouldn't have said that to Mum about not being her "real child". She's very sensitive about that. She loves you just the same as me and Paul. More probably. And believe me, you're not all that easy to love.'

'You really know how to make a girl feel better,' I say sarcastically.

'I aim to please.'

'And that's bollocks. Mum's never liked me, I came to terms with it years ago.'

'Like you? Of course she doesn't bloody like you. She loves you, you stubborn cow.'

'She's not my mother.'

'Oh, not again. No, she's not your biological mother. But she's as much your mum as she is mine. Just stop all the semantics. It's boring.'

'Fine, but you know I'm right. Let's change the subject. Where were you last night? I rang you loads of times.'

'Out,' she says a little too breezily.

'Out where?'

'Jeeze, Meg, you're not my minder. Out, OK?'

'Who is it this time? What poor soul have you seduced now?'

'Drop it. I'm not in the humour.'

'Hum, you sound rather guilty. Not married, is he? Like that awful Giles man.'

'No! Not married – not yet anyway.'

The penny drops. 'Were you with Ryan?'

'So what if I was?'

'After everything that's happened? Tell me you're joking.'

'We spent the night together, end of story. Satisfied?'

'Is he breaking up with his nurse?'

'What do you think?' she snaps. 'No! According to Ryan, he had a temporary lapse. I led him astray. He turned up at the shop yesterday and waited in his car like some sort of stalker. Fecking eejit.'

I don't like to point out that up until last week she'd been stalking him. 'I'm sorry. But next time, it's probably best to tell him where to go if he comes looking for you.'

'Looking for sex you mean.' She sighs. 'But I still like him, Meg. When I saw him waiting for me, I just thought . . . it was stupid, I know. But I hoped he felt the same way. Lying bastard.'

'So you won't sleep with him again?'

'I'll try not to.'

'Hattie!'

'Like I said, I'll do my best.'

Last night wasn't the first time in the last week I'd been unable to reach Hattie, I wonder if this 'thing' with Ryan has been going on for a while. It wouldn't surprise me. Poor Hattie. I've never seen her like this over a man and it's most disconcerting. She's usually the one in control.

'If you feel tempted and you need me to sit on you or handcuff you let me know,' I say.

Hattie gives a throaty laugh. 'Sounds kinky. I have lovely pink handcuffs with fluffy linings too.' She pauses for a moment. 'Although, oops, I think I may have . . . sorry, Meg, have to go.' She puts down the phone abruptly.

Hattie rings back ten minutes later. 'Wait till I tell you. I rang Ryan.'

'Hattie!'

'No, nothing like that. Let me finish. I realized I'd left the handcuffs at Ryan's and apparently Marian found them earlier this evening. She stormed out of the house calling him a pervert. She thought he'd bought them for her. Apparently she's a bit of a missionary girl and anything else freaks her out.'

'And she's a nurse?' I ask.

'I know. Gas, isn't it? Anyway, Ryan's taking me out to dinner, tonight! He realizes Marian's not the girl for him. Oh, Meg, isn't life wonderful?'

'Hattie, just wait a minute. A minute ago you were calling him a bastard. And if he'll cheat on this Marian girl —'

But Hattie isn't listening. 'Sorry, Meg, I have to run. Ryan will be here any minute and I have to wash my pits. I stink.'

'Hattie—'

But the phone goes dead.

Jeepers, what am I going to do with her? Ryan's a train crash waiting to happen, but she seems oblivious to the truth when it comes to this sailor boy. Bloody sailors! They have a lot to answer for.

Later that evening, Dad calls in unexpectedly. He wipes his feet carefully on the mat, avoiding the mossy part to the left.

'I want to talk to you,' he says. 'Alone.'

I pull my dressing gown around my body and tie it firmly. It's only eight and I'm already in my pyjamas, which is a bit embarrassing.

'I had a bath with Lily,' I explain, gesturing at my attire. 'Didn't bother getting dressed again.'

Dad nods. He seems a little distracted.

'Would you like a cup of tea?' I ask him. 'Or something to eat?'

'No, no, I've had dinner thanks. But tea would be nice.'

He follows me into the kitchen and I begin to worry. Maybe his treatment isn't working; maybe he's coming to tell me the worst – that he hasn't much time left. I have to know immediately.

'Dad, is it bad news? About the cancer? Tell me, I can take it.'

He smiles at me gently. 'It's not about me, Meg. It's about you.'

'Me?' I have an inkling of what's coming. I decide to cut him off at the pass. 'Dad, I know you think I should take Simon back, but I just don't know if I can trust him any more.' I flick on the kettle, my finger catching on the switch. I put it in my mouth and suck it.

'Simon?' Dad pauses for a moment. He pulls out a chair and sits down at the kitchen table. 'I think you and Simon need to spend some time apart to think about everything and about your life together. No, I'm here about your Mum.'

I sigh, fold my arms in front of my body and rest my back against the kitchen counter. She's obviously been telling tales. Typical! That's just like her. 'What's she been saying this time?'

Dad looks at me. 'She hasn't said anything to me. Why? Did you two have another argument?'

'It was Hattie then. She never knows when to keep her mouth shut. Some sister she is.'

'Hattie may have mentioned something, yes, but that's not why I'm here. Look, I'll come straight to the point. I have to face facts – this illness may get the better of me. And I want to say something to you while I still have the chance. Something important. Now sit down and stop hovering around like that.'

I pour him a mug of tea, added sugar and milk and plonk it on the table in front of him. A little slosh goes over the top and lands on the table. I swipe at it with a piece of kitchen roll.

'Please sit down,' Dad says firmly.

This time I do as I'm told.

'Well?' I say.

Dad holds my gaze. His eyes are soft and he leans forward a little, his palms resting on the table, index fingers touching.

'Stop pushing your mum away. You've been jealous of her your whole life. Just let it go. She's a good person and she loves you.'

'Loves me? That's a joke. If she really cared about me she would never have married you. She knew I hated the very idea of it.'

'You were six years old when we married. Julie saved me. I was barely coping before she came along. It wasn't easy bringing you up on my own and trying to hold down a full-time job.'

'What do you mean? Everything was great. I used to go to Granny Mona's house all the time. And Rita next door's after school.'

'I know, and they were both a godsend. But my mum was in her seventies and she found it all a bit much at times, especially when you were a toddler. And Rita was a nice woman, but it wasn't ideal. She smoked like a chimney and gave you the same dinner every night – sausages and chips. I'm surprised you didn't get scurvy. I wanted something better for you, something permanent. A proper family.'

'But we *were* a proper family. Just me and you. We had a brilliant time together. Remember our sandwich nights and pyjama Sundays?'

Dad sits up a little and gives a short laugh. 'Sandwich night. I invented that because some nights I couldn't deal with the thought of cooking. And on Sundays I just wanted to sleep on the sofa all day, I was so wiped out. Looking back, I suppose I was a bit depressed. It's not normal for a man in his thirties to be so tired all the time.'

'But it was still fun, spending all that time together, just the two of us.'

'Yes it was,' he says carefully. 'But remember when there was just you and Dan? The lonely weekends and Bank Holidays when everyone else was busy doing other things? The endless nights longing for someone to talk to? The sinking feeling when another bill came in? Putting your pillow over your head at night so that your child couldn't hear you cry? The worry, the constant, daily worry.'

'How do you know all that?' I ask, a little upset. 'About the crying at night?' A lump begins to form in my throat as some of the bad times come flooding back. I'd blocked them out, forgotten them. It seems such a long time ago now.

'I'm talking about me, Meg. Not you.'

Tears come to my eyes and I blink them back. When it comes to my childhood I suddenly realize I've been wearing rose-tinted glasses for a long time. 'You used to shout at me,' I say in a small voice, 'and then hug me and cry.'

'I know. And I'm so sorry. I was under a lot of pressure.'

Suddenly something comes to me. I'd been jumping on Dad's bed. He'd walked in, slapped me really hard on the thigh and started calling me names. 'You called me a little bitch,' I say, my voice cracking. Tears begin to run down my face.

'Jesus, Meg. I'm so sorry. You were only four. You remember that?' He put his head in his hands. 'I'm so, so sorry. I was in a bad place. I shouldn't have taken it out on you. You didn't deserve it.'

'I shouldn't have been bouncing on your bed. It was my fault.'

'Ah, no, it wasn't your fault. You were only little. I was at the end of my tether and I snapped. It was my fault.'

'I understand. Really I do. I slapped Dan once when he broke a glass. Hard too. I made him cry. I felt terrible afterwards but he was so good about it.'

'Kids are very forgiving.' Dad looks at me. 'Do you forgive me? For everything?'

'Course I do. You were a great dad. *Are* a great dad.' I wipe away my tears with the back of my hand. 'Most of the time anyway.' I try a laugh but it comes out as a hiccup.

We sit in silence for a moment. My eyes feel hot and my head throbs a little but I've stopped crying. Dad's cheeks are flushed. I know this isn't easy for him, revisiting the past.

While sitting there I have an epiphany. Dear God, I've been

enormously, catastrophically selfish. Julie didn't take Dad away from me; she gave me the real Dad back. The kind, patient loving Dad of old. She gave us both a life. I give a tiny moan.

'Are you all right, Meg?'

I nod, scared to open my mouth. 'Julie,' I manage to say, willing him to continue talking.

Dad nods at me. 'When I met Julie things became easier almost overnight. I had someone to talk to, to share my worries with.'

'But you already knew her.'

'What do you mean?'

'She was Mum's nurse. In that hospital.'

Dad stares at me. 'You remember the hospital? You never said anything. You were very young, Meg. Are you sure?'

'I *do* remember. You took me there once because Rita was out shopping and Granny was sick. It was near the place we used to go and see Santa.'

'I should never have taken you there. It wasn't the place for a child.'

Memories come flooding back to me. 'I thought Julie had planned it you see, that she'd planned it all along, to take Mum away from you, to have you all for herself.'

'That doesn't make any sense. I met Julie again two years after your mum died. At the Forty Foot. We were both swimming. You know that.'

'I can't help what I thought, Dad. As you say, I was little. For a long time I believed that Julie was responsible for Mum's death, in that hospital.'

He stares at me, a haunted look in his eyes. 'Jesus. No wonder you didn't take to her. But Meg, your mum, didn't die in hospital.'

'What?' I stare at him.

'She died at home. While you were at school.'

'You told me she died in the hospital. That she took too many pills by mistake.'

'She was taken to the hospital. Afterwards. To try to resuscitate—' His voices catches. 'It was too late. She didn't die in hospital, she died in her bed. Our bed.'

I put my hand over my mouth and groan. 'Why didn't you tell me the truth?'

He shakes his head. 'I don't know. It was all so awful. I didn't know what to do. Taking her own life like that. I didn't know what to say. It seemed better —' He breaks off.

'She was sick for a long time,' I say, realizing that he's distressed. 'There wasn't anything you could do. You told me she'd suffered from manic depression since she was a teenager. And losing the baby pushed her over the edge. There was nothing anyone could do.'

'It should never have happened. I should have been there. I should have realized something was seriously wrong that day. But she actually seemed quite calm, happy even. It was only when she didn't collect you from school. Your teacher rang me. Thank God you were downstairs in the kitchen when I found her. And then Rita collected you—' He presses his hands against the wood of the kitchen table. His face is ashen.

I put my hand on his. 'There's no point in going over it. What happened, happened. There was nothing that you or anyone else could have done for her. Her mind was obviously made up. She's in a happier place now.' I wince, remembering something else a few years later. Lotta Carmichael. Religious education class. Six years old. She told the whole class that my real mum was in hell, because everyone who killed themselves went to hell. That it said so in the Bible. The teacher, a gentle country woman in her early twenties, tried to rectify the situation, but it had cut deep and I've never forgotten it to this day.

'That girl in school,' Dad says, reading my mind, 'should never have said that to you, Meg. It upset you for weeks.'

I nod. I wonder where Lotta is now. Silly cow. I also remember what Julie said at the time. 'Your Mum's with the angels, Meg. Looking down on you, keeping you safe. When you need her, she'll be there. Just like I'll be there. Always.' I'd just pushed her away, run to my room, slammed the door and wept my tiny eyes out.

'Did you really believe that Julie had something to do with your mum's death?' Dad asks.

'Yes. Until I was about eleven. Then I realized it didn't make any sense, that Julie wasn't the killing kind.' I smile wryly.

'I'm so sorry. What a terrible misunderstanding. Julie was the one helping to keep your mum alive. She nursed Celia back to health after two previous suicide attempts. Often she just sat with her in the hospital, holding her hand.'

'I never knew that.'

'God, we're a right pair,' Dad gives a short laugh. 'You and me.'

'I'm sorry I've been so hard on Julie.'

Dad gets up wordlessly, walks towards me and puts his arms around me from behind. He holds me for a while, saying nothing, then removes his arms and rests his hands lightly and reassuringly on my shoulders.

'Hey, Mum, Lily's writing on my walls again,' Dan skids into the room in his pyjama bottoms. The atmosphere is broken. Dad smiles at me as if to say everything will be all right.

Dan stares at me. 'Have you been crying? Your eyes are all red.'

'Just a little,' I admit, in the spirit of honesty. He must be used to my tears at this stage, poor pet.

'Oh. Will you come and take Lily out of my room? She keeps throwing toy cars at me. Look, I'm injured.' He points at a red mark on his forehead. 'I've put her in prison, but she's not happy.'

411

'Prison?' I get to my feet. 'She's supposed to be in bed. Little terror.'

'I have to see this,' Dad says, following right behind me.

The following day I try to stick to my normal routine. I've been up most of the night, thinking about Dad, Mum, Simon, Hattie and Ryan, and I feel completely drained. I drop Lily into Tina's, Dan to school and then call into Ivy's to go through the final auction details and deliver the photographs I'd found.

'Meg.' Ivy greets me at the door. Her eyes twinkle in her bird-like face. 'You look terrible. Come in and sit down.' She gestures towards the comfy armchair and I sink into it grate-fully. She perches on the sofa opposite me.

'Thanks.' Lord, do I really look that bad? I press my fingers under my eyes. The skin feels loose and baggy to the touch.

'Not sleeping?' Ivy says without preamble.

I shake my head. 'No.'

'What's on your mind? Not work, I hope,' she says with a smile and I know she's joking.

I give a short laugh. 'No. Things at home are just a little difficult at the moment. Simon—' I stop for a moment. Ivy doesn't need to hear my tales of woe. 'It's complicated.'

She looks at me carefully but says nothing. She doesn't press me for information, for which I'm grateful.

'I brought you these,' I say, thrusting a large brown A4 enve-lope into her hands. 'I found them behind some of the prints in the clip frames.'

She opens it and takes out the largest black and white photo-graph. The blonde woman in the striped bathing suit with the film-star looks smiles up at her. She studies the image for a while, running her finger over the woman's full lips.

'She was twenty-two when this was taken,' she says, her voice flat. 'My beautiful daughter. Loved to swim. Spent all her spare time on Killiney Beach.'

'Daughter? I didn't know you had a daughter. Tina never said.'

'It's not something we talk about. She died, you see. Years ago. She'd just turned twenty-three. She didn't want to live any more.'

'What was her name?' I ask gently.

'Rowena. Rowie.'

When Ivy looks over at me, her eyes have lost their sparkle. 'She took her own life. Went swimming on Killiney Beach in the dead of night, fully clothed, middle of winter.' She pauses. 'It was a terrible, terrible thing. Nowadays maybe it would have been different. There might be drugs that could have helped her, but back then—' She sighs.

I don't know what to say. My stomach is churning and my eyes prickle with tears. It's too close to home for comfort.

'Rowie was schizophrenic, not that it was diagnosed properly until it was too late. She had treatment—' Ivy broke off and looked down at the photo again. 'Awful, brutal treatment. It seemed the right thing to do at the time, but it didn't help. Scared her half to death in fact. She was a gentle soul. It was all just too much for her in the end. Living a half life.'

'I'm so sorry,' I say, clutching my hands in my lap tightly. 'I didn't mean to bring it all back.'

'That's all right. I like to think of her sometimes. Ronnie, my husband, couldn't deal with her death. Men aren't as strong as us that way. He preferred just to block it out, pretend she'd never existed. But she did. I thought he'd destroyed all the photographs, but he can't have had the heart to in the end. I'm glad. Rowie was a wonderful girl. She should be remembered.'

I want to tell Ivy I understand, to tell her about my own mum, but I can't find the words.

'I'm sorry,' she says, reading my unease as discomfort. 'Depressing stuff. Ignore me.'

'No. Thank you for telling me,' I manage to say. 'Really.'

She holds my gaze and then looks down at the photograph again. 'Life's so short, Meg. Embrace it while you can. Time and tide wait for no woman. Rowie used to say that before she went swimming. "Mum, have to dash. Time and tide wait for no woman."' Ivy gives a laugh. There are tears in her eyes. 'God I loved her. Still miss her every day.' She puts the photograph back in the envelope. 'Be happy. Things happen we have absolutely no control over. Patch things up with that young man of yours. He sounds like a keeper. Family is the most important thing in the world. I wish I'd had more children, but it wasn't to be. You're a lucky woman.'

After a moment she stands up.

'I'm very happy with what you've done with the house, child,' she says, getting back to business. 'You've been so help-ful. The estate agent is most impressed. Delighted I've got rid of all the old junk as he calls it.'

'Did you tell him what we got for the rugs? Or the painting?'

'Not at all. Stupid man. Wouldn't know a Persian rug if he was rolled up in one. Still, he's hoping to get a good price for the house. Set me up nicely for my world cruise.'

'Really? A cruise?'

Ivy smiles. 'Cruise ships are riddled with old people so they have great doctors on board. If I have to die, Meg, I intend to go in style. In Egypt, or Greece, perhaps. Lots of history in Greece. No point freezing my rear end off in Dublin when I could be sunning myself somewhere exotic, now is there? And keep an eye on Tina for me. She was always a bit of a soft spot. I don't trust that Oliver of hers one little bit.'

I'm sorely tempted to tell her about Oliver's shenanigans, but I know it's not my place. I'm sure Tina'll tell Ivy and the rest of her family in her own good time.

'Speaking of Tina, I'd better get going,' I say, standing up. 'She's minding Lily for me this morning.'

'Pleasure doing business with you, Meg.' Ivy holds out her

hand and I take it, almost wincing at the paper-thin skin and the bones pressing through it.

'Can I call in again?' I ask suddenly, realizing that I'll miss her. 'Just to see you, I mean?' Some day, I'd like to tell her about my real mum, Celia. But I'm not quite ready yet.

'Of course, my dear. Any time you like. I won't be going on my cruise for a few months yet. You're always welcome. And you can bring those children of yours, you know. They might like the bowling green. This place could do with some livening up. I do love children.'

'I'll do that. See you soon then.'

'I look forward to it.'

Chapter 30

Following sea: an overtaking sea
that comes from behind

On the way home from Ivy's house I make a decision. As soon as I get home I take action.

'Joe, it's Meg. I need your help. I want to find Kira and Tia.'

'What? Are you sure?'

'Yes, positive. I need to talk to Kira. I can't see any way forward without talking to her.'

'She moved just after having the baby. Simon has no idea where she is.'

'I know, but is there anything you remember, anything at all that might help me?'

'She was studying history of art in Auckland. And her mother was a teacher. That's all I know.'

'What's her second name?'

'Te Kooti.'

'Te Kooti? Is that how you pronounce it?'

'Yes, it's Maori.'

'Maori?'

'Yes, Kira and her family are Maori.'

I'm flabbergasted.

Joe laughs. 'Weren't expecting that, were you, lass?'

'No,' I reply honestly. 'No, I wasn't. Maori. Wow.'

'Are you sure you want to find them? Absolutely sure?'

'Yes. Thanks for your help. I'll try googling their names and see what I come up with.'

'Good luck.'

For three days I try to find a record of a Kira or Tia Te Kooti on the internet, with no luck. I find plenty of Te Kootis all right, including a famous Maori soldier. It's easy to get distracted on the internet, and I spend far too long looking up all sorts of Maori family sites, all of which are fascinating but lead me no closer to Tia and Kira.

At the end of the week I've almost given up hope when a letter arrives that changes everything.

Dear Meg

Please don't tell Maureen or Simon about this letter. It's a delicate matter and I don't want to see either of them hurt unnecessarily

I think you're right, I think talking to Kira might help. But there are a few things you should know first. Kira never told Simon she was pregnant, you see. Simon first heard about Tia through a Kiwi sailing friend; he tried to contact her but she wouldn't talk to him. He arranged to fly over to New Zealand to see her but decided against it in the end. He was in bits and didn't want to be rejected again.

When he told us about the baby, I managed to get Kira's mother, Hana, to talk to me. Kira was a stubborn girl and wanted to do everything on her own, without any help from Simon, but she also wanted to finish college. She'd taken a year out to work on the yachts before doing her finals. Then she was going to go to

*Wellington to do an arts administration diploma. Hana
agreed to look after Tia until Kira finished her studies,
but it meant she had to give up her own part-time job as
a teacher. Her husband had died several years before.*

*To cut a long story short, I offered to send Hana
money for Tia on the understanding that she sent regular
photographs and news about the baby, which she did. She
in turn made me promise not to tell Simon or Maureen
about our arrangement. Once Kira got her diploma and
started working in a museum in Wellington, Hana
refused to take any more money, but she still keeps in
touch, and I send Tia presents at Christmas and on her
birthday. Hana's a lovely woman. She's had a hard life
and she adores Tia.*

*I rang Hana yesterday. She's spoken to Kira and Kira
wants to talk to you. Her number is at the end of this
letter.*

*Meg, please do not tell Simon or Maureen any of this.
I'm not sure how you'll explain finding Kira and Tia, but
I know you'll think of something. I have enclosed a
recent photo of Tia.*

*With much love,
Joe XXX*

I stare at the photograph. A pretty girl with glossy black hair in
tidy plaits smiles out at me. She's wearing what looks like her
school uniform, a neatly ironed white short-sleeved shirt and a
grey skirt. Her skin is a delicious honey colour but tears come
to my eyes when I notice her ears – the left one sticks out at the
top, just like Simon's. I peer closer. She has Simon's nose too,
and his strong cheekbones. It's only then it really begins to sink
in, Tia is Simon's flesh and blood. I turn the photo over and
over in my hands. I know what I have to do.

My heart is hammering in my chest and my palms are sweaty but if I don't do it now, I never will.

'Hello, is that Kira?'

'No, Hana speaking. Who is this?'

'Oh, hello, Hana, this is Meg. Joe . . . Yes, that's right, Simon's partner. Is Kira there? Can I speak to her? I'm sorry, it's not the middle of the night is it?'

'No, no, the morning. No worries.'

In the background I hear a young girl ask, 'Who is it, Nana? Is it for me?'

'No, for your mum. Can you get her, there's a girl?'

'Mum, phone for you,' she shouts.

Hana laughs. 'I'm sorry, there's not much privacy in this house. But Kira will take it upstairs.'

'Thanks.' I gulp.

'And don't be nervous, child. She's a good girl, my Kira. A good mother.'

'Thanks,' I say again, touched.

'Kia ora?' a strong, clear voice comes on the line.

'Kira, this is Meg.'

'Hiya, Meg. I was wondering when you'd ring. Joe's been on to Mum several times.' She pauses for a moment. 'Bloody hell. This is a bit weird, isn't it?'

'Yes, it certainly is. I'm sorry, I've forgotten what I was going to say. My mind's gone blank.'

Kira gives a laugh. 'Happens to me all the time. Comes from having ankle biters.'

'You're probably right. Has Joe told you about what's been happening over here?' I ask.

'Sure, and I'm sorry. It must have been difficult for you, finding out like that. But I was a different girl then. I gave Simon a hard time. But I have two more kids now, twin boys. I got hitched last year.'

'How nice. Joe didn't say.'

'Mum lives with us. She loves the babies. Minds them for me when I'm working. We live in Wellington.'

'And you work in a museum there, Joe told me.'

'Yes, the infamous Te Papa. Huge old barn of a place. I love it, even if it is a bit touristy. So, what can I do for you?'

'You know, I'm not sure. I just wanted to talk to you. Things over here are a bit of a mess and I thought it might help.'

'Does Simon want to see Tia?'

'What?' I wasn't expecting that.

'Sorry, I thought that's why you were ringing. On Simon's behalf. He was always a bit scared of me.'

'Was he? How funny. I think he's a bit nervous of me too.'

'Oh aye? Good. He needs someone to keep him on his toes. He can be a lazy bum when he wants to be.'

I laugh. I like Kira, she reminds me of Hattie.

'So, when are you coming over?'

'Coming over?'

'To see Tia. She's started asking about Simon recently. I think it's a teen thing myself, but she has a right to meet him. And her half-sister. Lily, isn't it?'

'That's right, Lily.'

'Listen, I was a stubborn cow when I was younger. Didn't want Simon anywhere near me or Tia. Wanted to do it all myself. But hey, things are different now. I'm a settled married woman and all that. And the other half, Ralph, is cool with it. Simon will like him, he sails too. Not professionally, thank God. He's a carpenter. Come over, all of you. You're welcome any time.'

'Are you sure?'

'Yeah! Tia would love it. And Mum. And it would be wicked to see Simon again. And Joe will have to come too. But leave that Maureen at home. She sounds like a right snarky cow.'

I snort with laughter. 'Kira, you'll be well able for her.' I feel a surge of joy. 'Thank you,' I say simply. 'I was terrified of ringing you.'

'And I was convinced you'd have my guts for garters. For dumping Simon.'

'Not at all. I'll be in touch.' We swap email details and I give her my phone number.

'Nice talking to you, Meg,' she says.

'You too.'

'Tell Simon I said hi. And, tell him – tell him I'm sorry. For everything.'

'I will.'

As I put down the phone, I feel happier than I have in a long time. Maybe things will slot into place for me after all. There's always a first. I'm almost ready to talk to Simon – almost.

The following day I go for a walk with Dad. He pushes Lily in her pram, splashing through last night's puddles. We potter along the seafront, stopping every now and then so Lily can admire a passing dog. I want to tell him about Tia and Kira but I don't know where to start, so we chat amicably about how Dan's doing in school. He's been back a few days now and I haven't heard from Miss Myson recently, thank goodness. I've also checked Dan's feet every morning for socks, so far he's been wearing them.

'And Simon?' Dad asks when there's a lull in the conversation.

I stare out to sea. There's a lone swimmer braving the water and I shiver.

'Still swimming?' I ask Dad, eager to change the subject.

'Haven't been in yet, but I plan to any day now. So, Simon. Have you two talked yet? Properly I mean?'

'Not exactly, but we will. I just have a few things to sort out first.'

'Like what?'

I sigh. 'Dad! Just things, OK?'

'I was only asking.'

'Sorry, I didn't mean to snap at you. It's a little complicated at the moment.'

He follows my gaze out to sea. 'Don't leave it too long. You've always been so stubborn. Sometimes you have to accept people's mistakes and just get on with things.'

'I'm beginning to see that,' I say in a quiet voice. 'Really I am.' I stop for a moment. 'I talked to Kira you know.'

'Kira? Tia's mum?'

'Yes. Last night. She's really nice. Reminds me of Hattie.'

'What did she say?'

'That Tia would like to meet Simon.'

'And how do you feel about that?'

I shrug. 'OK I guess. But they live in Wellington.'

'And Simon's been offered sailing work in New Zealand, hasn't he?'

'Yes.'

'Well?'

'Well what?'

'Meg, don't be so obtuse.'

'We can't up sticks just like that.'

'Why not?'

'We've only just moved back for one, and I'd have to pull Dan out of school.'

'I'm sure they have perfectly good schools in New Zealand. He's only in fifth class. Anyway, he's used to travelling.'

'There are other things too.'

'Like what?'

'Just things. OK?' I look at him, at his thin, pale face. I can't move halfway around the world, even if it is only for six months. What if anything happened to him while I was away? I'd never forgive myself.

'Don't stay on my account,' he says gently. 'Please. I want

you to be happy; for you all to be happy. And if that means doing without you for a while, then so be it. I'm not going anywhere for a long time yet. And we can come over to visit. I've always rather fancied a trip to New Zealand. Travelling around in one of those camper vans. It would be a good excuse. '

I shake my head. 'I'm not going.'

He takes my hand in his, his warm palm pressing against my cold skin. 'Stop being so stubborn.'

'OK, I'll think about it,' I say eventually. I rest my head against his shoulder.

'Good, you do that. Fancy some lunch?'

I nod. Lily has dozed off in her buggy so we might even get some peace.

We walk up to Dun Laoghaire and sit outside a coffee shop. It's just about warm enough to eat outdoors and I park Lily's buggy beside a table and sit down.

'What can I get you?' Dad asks.

'A chicken salad sandwich and a coffee, please, with milk and one and a half sugars.'

'And Lily?'

'Cheese, thanks. And orange juice if they have it. Milk if not.'

'See you in a few minutes.' He goes inside to order.

I slip my sunglasses over my eyes and enjoy the peace. The fresh air has perked me up a bit, I felt very groggy this morning after a restless night of strange, nonsensical dreams.

'Meg?'

I turn my head. Mum sits down at the table, her hands encased in smart dark brown leather gloves. It's not *that* cold, I think to myself.

'What are you doing here?' I ask.

'Meeting your dad.'

I snort. 'So this is a set up.'

'Not exactly, but I did want to talk to you. Your dad just helped me a little, that's all. But he wanted to see you too.'

'Well?' I demand, cutting to the chase.

'Why are you being so confrontational?'

Because I owe you an apology, I think, but I'm damned if I'm going to tell her that.

'I have a lot on my mind,' I say instead.

'I know.' She picks up a plastic take-away spoon that someone has left behind and begins to tap it on the table top. 'So, where do we go from here?'

'What do you mean?'

'We can't go on like this, Meg.'

'Like what?'

'You snapping at me every time we meet. Your dad told me what you thought when you were little, about me killing Celia.'

'Oh that.' I feel deeply embarrassed and ashamed. 'I'm sorry,' I mumble.

'No, I'm sorry. I remember the day you came to the hospital. Your mum really bucked up for a while after that. You gave her a reason to go on. You were wearing a little red dress that was a bit short for you. And a matching red coat with a black ribbon around the waist.'

'My Christmas outfit,' I say. 'I made Dad put it on me. I wanted Mum to love me, you see. I thought if I was very good she might come home. I thought I'd done something wrong, that it was my fault she was sick.'

'There was nothing you could have done. You know that, don't you?'

'I do now. But I didn't at the time.' I pick at a bit of loose skin at the side of my thumb. 'Dad shouldn't have told you about that other thing. I know you had nothing to do with her death. I was young; I didn't understand. I was just looking for someone to blame.'

'And there I was.' She pauses for a moment. 'Am I really that judgemental? The other day you said I was judgemental. Did you mean it?'

'Yes, I suppose I did. But I shouldn't have lashed out at you like that. I just feel you're always on my case. I can't do a thing right in your eyes.'

'I've made mistakes, I know that. But I do love you, and Dan and Lily, with all my heart. I'd do anything for you. I want to tell you something, but you have to promise never to tell your dad.'

'Um, all right,' I say, a little uncertainly. I want to cross my fingers under the table but I know that would be infantile.

'You were the main reason I agreed to marry him. I wasn't at all sure about it, to be honest. He was a bit of a mess. A depressed widower with a young child to look after – not exactly love's young dream for a girl in her early twenties, you have to admit. But I could see how much he loved you, what a good father he was. And I adored *you*. So I overcame my misgivings and I said yes. And I hoped he'd love any children God blessed us with as much as he loved you.'

I don't know what to say, so I keep quiet.

'I know I'm not your real mother, as you keep pointing out to me.'

I open my mouth to say 'I'm sorry,' but she puts one gloved hand up to stop me.

'And that's fine. I do understand. And I know you're not going to like what I say next, Meg, but hear me out. I think there are issues surrounding your mother's death you haven't come to terms with yet. I think a good grief counsellor would really help you.'

'Counselling! I'm not a bloody basket case!'

'I'm not saying you are. I just think you need to talk to someone about your feelings, that's all. Someone who's qualified to help.'

I stand up. 'Oh that's lovely. You're telling me I'm mad like Mum, is that it? That I'm going to crack up.'

'No. Meg, please sit down. You're not listening to me.'

'Oh, I'm listening all right.' I click the brake off Lily's pram.

'Meg, sit down,' Dad's voice booms out. He puts a large wooden tray of food on the table and then faces me. 'What's going on here? Why can't you just be civil to your mum for once?'

'She's just called me a basket case!'

'Julie, what's going on?'

'I just suggested she might need some counselling, that's all.'

'What did I say to you earlier?' Dad's eyes are sparking with anger and I'm delighted he's taking my side. 'Meg has other things on her plate right now. Didn't I tell you to wait, that she isn't ready?'

'I'm sorry,' Mum whispers. 'I was only trying to help.'

'What do you mean wait?' I ask Dad, picking up on what he said.

Dad puts a hand on Lily's buggy. 'I think Julie's right, talking to someone might help you in the long term. But not right now.'

'You think I'm mad too?' I demand.

'Of course I don't. Stop overreacting. Can't you two just stop bickering, please? It's exhausting.' Dad looks drained and I feel instantly guilty.

'Sorry,' I mumble.

'Let's sit down and have lunch together.' Dad gestures at the table. 'I know you will always have a bit of a fiery relationship, you're far too alike for it to be any different.'

'Alike?' I splutter.

Dad smiles. 'As stubborn as each other. A right pair of drama queens too.'

'Dad!'

'Hey!' Mum says.

Dad just laughs. 'Here you go, ladies,' he hands out the food. 'Chicken salad and a coffee for both of you. Milk and one and a half sugars.'

I smile at him. Maybe he has a point.

'Truce?' Mum says to me.

I nod. 'Truce.'

The thing is I know we're always going to fight, that's partly how Mum and I communicate, but if we can manage to see the funny side of things, we have a chance of not killing each other. And I hate to admit it, maybe she's right, maybe talking to someone about my mum's death might be helpful. Now and again I have dark and unsettling dreams about that hospital and at the very least it might stop those. But I'm not going to admit that she's right, not yet anyway. A girl has her pride.

'Hey, Mum said you freaked out earlier, in a coffee shop or something. What's that all about?'

'Hello, Hattie.' I move the phone to the crook of my shoulder and finish fastening Lily's nappy. She's just out of the bath and is a divil for peeing on my bed while I'm drying and dressing her. 'I did not. She was having another go at me and I wasn't taking it, that's all. No big drama.' I sit down on the bed and Lily flies out the door, her bum waddling in its fresh nappy. 'But don't worry, we're talking, if that's what you're worried about.'

Hattie snorts. 'No big drama? With you pair? Yeah, right. Anyway, glad it's sorted out. Any news?'

'Not really. Sid's calling over later. I want to talk to him about Dan. I'm thinking of going to New Zealand, after I've talked to Simon of course.'

'What? No news my ass. When did you decide this?'

I tell her all about my conversation with Kira.

'I can't believe you didn't ring me last night, you cow,' she says.

'Stop calling me names or I'll put the phone down.'

'So when are you thinking of going?' Hattie asks.

'If everything works out, as soon as possible. But I haven't talked to Simon yet. He may not want to go any more.'

'Yeah, right. And pigs might fly. Of course he wants to go. It's the bloody America's Cup, you ditz. Even I know how mega that is, you big eejit. So you've forgiven him?'

'You're going to run out of derogatory terms for me if you're not careful. And yes, I guess I have forgiven him. He made a mistake, but as you said, no one's perfect. Do you think he'll forgive me for being so—' I sigh. 'Stubborn I suppose. Maybe he won't want to come back at all. Maybe I've blown it.'

'Simon?' Hattie gives a short laugh. 'I don't know why, but he adores you. Of course he'll want to come back. Are you crazy? He's a man in love, bless him. Not that you deserve him, you moany old thing.'

'Thanks,' I say. For once I'm grateful for Hattie's honesty. 'Would you please stop calling me names? Listen, there's the door. It's probably Sid, I'd better go.'

'Should be interesting,' Hattie comments.

'What do you mean?'

'He's hardly going to be thrilled about New Zealand, is he? Taking Dan away from him for six months.'

'Do you think?'

'Doh?'

My heart sinks. I've had enough confrontation for one day. Hattie may be right.

'You're in a very snappy mood,' I say. 'Is there anything wrong?'

'Apart from the usual?'

'Ryan you mean?'

'Got it in one.'

'What's up now?'

'It's complicated.'

'Isn't it always?' I hear a noise from downstairs.

'Sorry. Have to go, Someone's at the door, I think. Talk to you tomorrow.'

As I walk down the stairs Sid is in the hall talking to Dan. Lily is on his hip, naked apart from her nappy.

'Hi,' he says, smiling up to me, 'I have a rather cold little lady here.'

I smile back at him. 'Thanks. I'll just take her back upstairs and get her dressed. I'll be down in a minute. Make yourself a coffee if you like.'

'Thanks, but I'm OK.'

Ten minutes later I leave Lily playing with her train set and Dan car-racing on his PlayStation and I join Sid in the kitchen. He's standing with his back against the counter, his legs and arms crossed lazily. 'How's tricks?' he asks.

'Fine.' I sit on the side of the table and put my slippered feet on the seat of a chair. If I sit down properly I'll feel too small and I'm nervous enough as it is. I decide to come straight to the point. I'm tired and my bed is calling to me. The sooner I talk to Sid the sooner I can succumb to its warm comfort. I clear my throat. 'Sid, I have something to tell you.'

'You're getting married?' He cocks his head to one side.

'No!' I laugh.

'You want me back then?' He grins.

'No!' I shake my head. 'Nothing like that.'

'What then?'

'Simon's been offered a job,' I say a little awkwardly. 'A really good sailing job. Away. And I'm thinking of going with him. With the kids. I wanted to talk to you before any final decision was made.' You see, I wanted everything to be sorted before I talked to Simon. I couldn't raise his hopes about the America's Cup only to dash them again. I feel bad talking to Sid before Simon, but that's how it has to be.

'For how long?'

'Six months.'

Sid looks at me for a moment. 'Where exactly?'

'Auckland.'

'New Zealand?' he demands.

I nod.

'Jesus, Meg, you can't do that. You can't take Dan away just like that. It's not right. What are you thinking?'

'I know it's a lot to take in, but it will go really quickly and you can talk to each other on the phone.'

'But, Meg, half a *year*!' His eyes are bulging and his lips are twisted in anger.

I say nothing. There's no talking to Sid when he's like this. It's best to let him calm down a little.

'Can I make you a coffee?'

'No! And stop offering me coffee. I said no a minute ago, remember?'

'Yes, sorry.' I stare down at my hands.

'I won't let you,' he says finally. 'I'll get a lawyer.'

'Don't overreact.'

'Overreact? He's my son. I have a right to see him when I want to. I'll bring you to court if I have to.'

I'm starting to get tired of this. How dare he come over all high and mighty? Where had he been when Dan was a baby and then a toddler, when he needed night feeds and nappy changes? Oh, it was easy now that he was a walking, talking boy, but in the early days I hadn't seen Sid for dust. And the months without any maintenance payments. Don't get me started.

'Actually you don't really have any rights,' I say firmly. 'We're not married. You have very few rights in the eyes of the law. And you stopped paying maintenance over four years ago, remember?'

'I can't believe you're throwing the law back in my face.'

'You started it by saying you'd take me to court.'

'Anyway, I don't believe you. Of course I have rights, I'm his dad.'

'I'm not saying it's right, Sid. But I looked into it a long time ago. Check for yourself if you like.'

Sid glares at me, his arms hugging his chest tightly now. 'Don't do it. What about Dan? He's just getting settled in school. It's hardly fair to pull him out now. Have you thought about *him*?'

'Of course I have. I haven't stopped thinking about him, but I'm not going without him.'

'Then don't go!'

'I have to go.' Suddenly it dawns on me: if I want to make things work with Simon I have to go, it's as simple as that and I have to make Sid understand.

'Why?' he demands. 'What's so bloody important about New Zealand?'

I decide to take a chance. 'Simon has a daughter over there. A daughter he's never seen. They need to spend some time together.'

Sid gives me an ugly leer. 'Not so perfect now is he, your lover boy? An affair was it? Some young blonde?'

'It happened before I met him, if you must know. His daughter's thirteen for heaven's sake. And I thought you of all people would understand. About people making mistakes,' I add pointedly.

'Understand? All I understand is that you're taking Dan away from me. I can tell you now, I'm not going to let it happen.' He points at me, jabbing his finger in the air several times. 'Understand?'

'I think you'd better leave.' I jump off the table. He's showing a nasty side I haven't seen in a long time and I don't want to hear any more.

'Fine. But this isn't the end. Dan's *not* going to New

Zealand.' He storms out of the kitchen, into the hall and slams the front door behind him.

As soon as he's gone I realize my heart is racing and I've been practically holding my breath. I take a few quick gulps of air. What the hell am I going to do now? I can't leave it like this. Dan loves Sid; he's his dad and I've spent years building up that relationship. I can't let it fall to pieces now. I lean against the wall and put my hands to my face, pressing my fingers into my eye sockets. Just when things were looking as if they might just work out. Tears well up in my eyes. I thought going to New Zealand with Simon was the answer, meeting Kira and Tia, living in Auckland as a family. But I can't go to New Zealand now, I just can't. For Dan's sake. But what about me?

The following morning there's a knock at the door just after ten. Dan's in school, I dropped him off hideously late – I was still in my pyjamas with a jacket thrown over them. I'd had another restless night, worrying about Dan and Sid, and I felt like death warmed up. Lily's playing on the floor with her trains and I'm pottering around in my dressing gown, picking up pieces of toast from the floor and wiping the milk sploshes and crusty breakfast cereal off the table. I should have dressed ages ago, but I just don't have the energy. In fact, I wonder if I'm coming down with something; my head is throbbing and my throat is a little sore.

'Coming,' I yell towards the front door, presuming it's the postman. We have an annoyingly narrow letter box that the previous owners screwed a piece of wood across to stop it opening wide, making it even smaller. The postman is always having problems with it. I look at Lily, she's still engrossed with her toys, so I answer it.

I pull it open and nearly faint. Nora! In full work mode – natty, expensive-looking black suit with tight pencil skirt, flat pointy black to-the-knee boots, red designer bag. I wince and wrap my dressing gown firmly around my body.

'Where's Sid?' I ask, looking behind her nervously. Hiding in the bushes with a shotgun no doubt. But there's no sign of him.

'Can I come in?' she asks.

'Why?' I look at her suspiciously.

'Just let me in, Meg. I've come to talk about Dan.'

Grudgingly I let go of the door and stride into the kitchen as well as I can in my slippers, letting her close the door and follow me if she wants to. Rude, I know, but I'm not in the mood for her ladyship and I know exactly what she's going to say to me.

'Dan's at school,' I say, leaning against the kitchen counter.

Nora nods. 'Good.'

Lily looks up for a moment, vaguely interested by the new voice in the kitchen.

'Hi, Lily,' Nora says, holding her bag against her chest. 'How are you?'

Lily ignores her and goes back to the television. Usually I'd reprimand her for being rude, but this morning I don't care. Anyway, it's Nora, for goodness sake. She deserves it.

'Listen, I have things to do,' I begin, my arms crossed protectively over my chest. 'I presume Sid has told you about New Zealand and you've come to threaten me as well. As I told Sid, it's no use—'

'No.' She cuts in. 'I'm not here to threaten you.'

'You're not?' I look at her with interest.

'No. I think Dan should go to New Zealand with you and Simon. And Lily.'

'Oh.' I'm flummoxed. There must be some sort of catch.

'Meg, I'm going to be brutally honest here.' She takes a deep breath. 'I've always been envious of you.'

'Envious?' I give a laugh.

'Let me finish. You'd just have to click your fingers and Sid

433

would come running back to you. Don't deny it, I'm not stupid.
I've seen the two of you together. And I know what he's like –
always wanting what he can't have. I've overlooked his other
indiscretions over the years, but when it was you . . . that time
last Christmas.' She shakes her head.

'You know?' I stare at the kitchen table, embarrassed beyond
belief. My cheeks are burning and I feel pretty shoddy.

'Not until this moment.' I can feel her gaze on me and I lift
my eyes.

I'm so stupid. She tricked me. Why didn't I just deny it? 'I'm
sorry, Nora. It shouldn't have happened. It was a mistake. He
told me you were having problems, that you'd left him.'

'And you believed him?'

'Yes, fool that I am, I did. But nothing really happened—'

'Nothing?' Nora snorts. 'He didn't come home for two days.'

I look at her in confusion. 'That had nothing to do with me.
We kissed, I freaked out and he left. End of story. He certainly
wasn't with me for two days, if that's what you're implying.'

Her eyes open wide.

'Really?'

'Yes.'

'Can I sit down?' she asks in a low voice.

'Of course.'

She puts her handbag on the table top and sits down in front
of it, reaching over to play with the large brass buckle. 'Let me
get this straight, you're saying nothing happened? That Sid
wasn't with you for two days?'

'Yes.'

'And why should I believe you?'

'Ask Dan. He'd know if his dad was staying with us.
Anyway, why would I lie to you?'

'I'm sorry. It's just, I thought—' she shakes her head. 'I'm
sorry,' she says again.

I feel bad for being so sharp with her. 'Listen, I was vulnerable and I made a mistake. But I'd never do anything like that. And Sid was just being Sid. You know what he's like.'

'Yes. I also know he still loves you.'

'But he's with *you*. Doesn't that tell you something?' I thought it prudent not to tell her about the other night's shenanigans.

'You could have him if you wanted him,' she says matter of factly.

'You keep saying that, but it's not true. He'd run a mile if I started showing any real interest. With Sid, it's all in the chase. He loves you, Nora, but I don't think he's going to change. You just have to accept him as he is, warts and all.'

'I don't think he does love me.'

'He's crazy about you. Are you blind? He never stops talking about you. He's like a man obsessed. He was never like that with me.'

'Really?'

'Really.'

Nora begins to rub at a scratch on her bag. Then she looks up at me. Her eyes are still wide and I realize with a start how young she is, younger than Hattie.

'I'm scared of losing him,' she says. 'Scared that one day you'll take him away from me.'

'Why would I do that? I'm with Simon now.' It's a white lie, but easier than going into details. And I will be, I hope, at least if he'll have me, once I've sorted everything out.

'You were with Simon when you kissed Sid,' she points out.

It's like a slap in the face but I know I deserve it. 'I'm sorry; I don't know what to say. I was confused about Simon, and Sid was just there.' I shrug. 'It all got a little out of hand.'

'A little out of hand?' She snorts. 'He broke up with me. I was in bits. And I guess when he realized you didn't want him he came crawling back to me. And I took him back, big eejit that

I am. But I couldn't take all that again.' She locks her eyes on mine. 'I've always hated the power you have over him.'

'It'll never happen again,' I say. 'I promise you. Never.' I stop for a moment, something niggling at the back of my mind. 'That's why you want us on the other side of the world, isn't it? To keep me away from Sid.'

'That's part of it,' she says honestly. 'But it's really for Dan.'

'Dan?'

'Meg, I love Dan. Like it or not, he's part of my life as well as Sid's. And he deserves a proper dad, someone who's there all the time for him. At the moment he has two part-time dads and it's not good enough, he deserves more.'

I feel my blood turn cold. 'Have you talked to Sid about all this?'

She shakes her head. 'I wanted to talk to you first.'

'I see.' I stare down at her hands. I know beyond a doubt that Nora is right. Why haven't I seen it before? Dan deserves better. By trying to keep everyone happy, I've failed him. Tears come to my eyes.

'Maybe he should live with you and Sid,' I say. A tear runs down my cheek.

Nora stares at me. 'You'd do that? Let him live with us?'

I nod, a huge lump forming in my throat. 'If it's best for Dan. If it's what he wants.' I brush my tears away with the back of my sleeve.

'Jesus, Meg, there's nothing I'd like more,' Nora says.

I give a sob. My throat constricts and I screw my eyes shut. What am I doing? This can't be happening. Nora says something.

'What?' I ask, looking at her through bleary eyes. 'I missed that.'

'I said it wouldn't be right for Dan. Sid's not ready for that kind of commitment and I've just been promoted. There'd be no one at home for Dan after school or anything. It's a nice idea but it's just not practical. He's better off with you.' She gives me a gentle smile. 'You're a good mum, Meg. Even I can see that. And Dan adores you. Go to New Zealand. Take him with you. All of you, as a family. Let me deal with Sid.'

I try to smile through my tears but it comes out as a grimace.

'You look terrible. Your eyes are all swollen. Go and wash your face.'

'Thanks a bunch.' But I know she doesn't mean to be cruel, it's just her way. Appearances mean a lot to her, too much probably. Look at her fatal attraction to Sid.

She stands up. 'I'm going now. And Meg?'

'What?'

She opens her mouth to say something and then shuts it again. 'Nothing. Bye.'

'Bye.' I see her to the door, wondering what's on her mind. As she lingers on the doorstep for a moment, I say, 'Thanks,' and give her a smile. I have no real reason to hate her any more. When it comes to Sid, I've won, and I think we both know that. He still loves me in his own deluded way and I suppose I still love him too and probably always will. He *is* Dan's dad, warts and all. But Nora and I are grown up enough to leave the past be and to get on with our lives. I think she's satisfied that the Pandora's box labelled Meg and Sid is firmly closed. For good.

I feel sorry for her. I certainly couldn't spend my life wondering who else Sid was shagging, it would do my head in. I don't know how she copes. But she seems to accept it as part of the deal.

'Meg, let Simon be Dan's dad,' she says finally. 'Stop taking Dan's side all the time. He's not your friend, he's your son. Let Simon be a real parent. And leave Sid to me, he'll calm down, you'll see. I'll talk to him this evening and I'll ring you afterwards, let you know how I get on. You must want to make plans.'

Astute of her. Maybe she's smarter than I've realized.

'Thanks. What do you mean about Dan?' I ask a little defensively.

'Think about it. Bye.'

I watch her walk down the street towards her car. It's the first time I've ever seen her in flat heels and I realize with a start that she's even smaller than me. I close the door and rest my back against it. My eyes still sting from crying. But I feel lighter. I know I'll spend all day worrying and waiting for her phone call, but at least there's hope. But there's another vital phone call I've been putting off – to Simon.

Chapter 31

Cast off: to let go

The following morning, hands shaking, I ring Simon on his mobile. 'It's Meg, can you talk?'

'Of course, give me one minute.'

I can hear the murmur of voices in the background. He comes back. 'I'm going into the office. Meg? Are you still there?'

'Yes.'

'Good. I'll be just a second.'

He sounds nervous. I don't blame him. For all he knows I'm about to give him a right earful.

The phone clicks. 'Meg'

'Still here.'

'That's better. I was in the shop.'

'How's work?' I ask, more out of politeness rather than any real desire to know. We have other things to talk about, but right at this moment I don't know where to start.

'Fine. Getting busier. People ordering things for Christmas.'

'What sort of things?' I say, stalling with small talk.

'Model boats, special high-tech gadgets—' he tails off. 'And how are you, Meg? How are the kids?'

'Fine.'

'Good.'

The phone goes silent for a moment as both of us scramble for the right words.

'I need to talk to you,' I say eventually. 'Can you come up to the house this evening?'

'Of course.' He stops for a moment. 'Can't I come now? I'll go mad wondering what you're going to say otherwise. I don't know if I can bear it. Let's just get it over with.'

'It's nothing bad,' I say, hearing the misery in his voice and feeling guilty for putting him through hell over the last few days.

'Really? You mean I can come home?'

'We have a lot of talking to do. Let's not rush into anything.'

'But you've forgiven me? Please, Meg, I need to know.'

'Yes,' I say in a low voice. 'Yes, I have. We've both made mistakes, I know that now. But come up to the house. We need to talk in person.'

'I'm on my way.' The phone goes dead.

I smile to myself. I look over at Lily, who's playing with an old wooden jigsaw puzzle of Dan's, slotting two-dimensional jungle animals in and out of their cut-out spaces. I kneel down on the rug beside her and give the top of her head a kiss. She's still in her night things and smells a little fusty. 'Dada's coming to see you,' I say. 'Let's get you dressed.'

'Dada.' Her eyes light up. She scrambles to her feet and runs towards the door. 'Dada, Dada.'

I follow her. 'He won't be here for a while, pet,' I tell her. But miraculously Simon is standing in the hall.

'Hans's jeep was just outside the shop,' he pants. 'I borrowed it.'

'Dada!' Lily throws herself at his legs. He scoops her up and kisses her on both cheeks. 'Still in your pyjamas, Lily?'

She grins at him. 'Dada,' she says again. She's gazing at him at if he's Santa, Baby Jesus and the Tooth Fairy all rolled into one.

'She seems pleased to see me,' Simon says.

I nod, feeling strangely awkward. 'Coffee?' I ask.

'Sure.'

He settles himself at the table, dandling Lily on his knee. 'Can I do anything?'

'No, I'm fine.' I'm happy to keep busy, finding clean mugs and smelling the milk to check it's still fresh.

Simon plays with Lily while I wait for the kettle to boil. Now and again he looks up and gives me a half smile. I know he's giving me time to collect my thoughts and I'm grateful for that.

Finally, when we're both sitting down with steaming mugs in front of us, I can delay it no longer.

'Things have to change around here.'

'I know. And if it means giving up all the sailing, I'll do it. I'll sell curtains, mend washing machines, anything. I just want you back.'

'You'd do that?'

'Yes, of course. Whatever it takes.'

I sigh. 'I don't want you to give up sailing. In fact, quite the opposite. I've been selfish, I see that now. I should never have stopped you sailing. It's in your blood. It wasn't fair of me. And in a strange way I miss the sailing life. I miss being with you all the time, even if it is only at night and on the odd day off. I miss talking to you every day. Properly talking, not just the perfunctory talking we do late at night when we're both wrecked.' I take a deep breath. 'And if New Zealand is still on offer, I'm happy to live there for a while. It's only six months after all. And it might be fun.'

'Are you serious?' Simon gives a whoop of delight, springs up, Lily clinging to his hip, and kisses me on the cheek. 'I was talking to Slipper yesterday. They still haven't found anyone for the slot.'

'Yes. On one condition.'

'Name it.'

'That we all meet Kira and Tia. Dan, Lily, Maureen, Joe, everyone. I've spoken to Kira, it's what she wants too.'

'How did you find her? I don't understand.'

'Your dad told me her second name and I managed to find her on the internet. Kira Te Kooti is quite an unusual name. Took me a while, but I tracked her down eventually.' I hoped Joe would tell Simon the truth one day, about the letters and the support he'd given Kira and her family over the years, but it wasn't my secret to tell. Instead I tell him all about my conversation with Kira.

Simon says nothing for a while. He sits back down and stares into space. Then his eyes meet mine and they're wet with tears. For a horrible moment I think I've made a mistake.

'Thank you, Meg. I'd like that. Are you sure?'

I nod.

'But what about Dan's schooling?'

'He'll manage. He's only in fifth class. He can go to school in Auckland and I'll do some extra with him if I have to. It's not for long. It's more important that we're together as a family.'

'And what about Sid?'

'I was just getting to that. I spoke to Nora.'

'Nora?'

I smile. 'I know, I know. She thinks we should go to New Zealand too. Sid wasn't all that thrilled with the idea at first but she's managed to talk him around. In fact, they're getting married.'

'What? Sid's getting married? You must be joking.'

'I'm serious. And they want Dan to be their best man.'

Simon laughs. 'He'll love that. When's the wedding?'

'That's the catch. Nora's hoping to have it in December, New Year's Eve in fact, new beginnings and all that. So Dan will have to fly back from Auckland on his own. And the plan is they're going to honeymoon in Australia, and Dan will fly back with them and join them for two of the three weeks. What do you think?'

'Sounds perfect. How on earth did Nora manage to talk Sid into all that?'

'She's one smart woman,' I say, keeping it vague. 'Gave him an ultimatum. Marry me or I'm leaving you basically.'

Simon nods. 'I see.'

'Don't say anything to Dan yet, they want to tell him themselves.'

'No problem. He'll be thrilled.'

There's a bit more to it than that, but Nora swore me to secrecy. Turns out she's quite a wily customer, all in all. She's been keeping track of Sid's indiscretions for the last year, and relayed them back to him, names, dates, telephone numbers, including photographs taken from her car. She's wasted in PR, she'd make one hell of a private investigator. She said she'd overlook his past behaviour and marry him on one condition – that he'll attend hypnotherapy and counselling every week to cure him of his sex addiction. When Sid started spluttering about marriage and 'too soon', she played her trump card, threatening to publish his story in the *Sunday World*, her brother being a sub editor there, which would ruin Sid's life for ever more.

Why she still wants to marry him knowing exactly what he's capable of, I don't understand. Just goes to show that love really is blind. Maybe she's also an addict, her poison of choice being feckless men, or one feckless man in particular. But who am I to judge? She'll certainly keep him on his toes.

'And Dan'll love flying on his own,' I say. 'It'll make him feel very grown up.' I could offer to go with him, but financially it wouldn't make sense, and besides, I'd have to take Lily on the twenty-something-hour flight. My skin crawls just thinking about it. In fact, it was Nora who suggested that Dan might like to fly on his own. She even rang the airline and checked he'd be looked after properly.

'And Lily?' Simon asks. 'Will she like Auckland do you think?'

I smile. 'Are you kidding? She'll love it. Think of all that sun and sea. And I presume there'll be a swimming pool at the team hotel?'

'Yep, a big one apparently. With a baby pool and a hot tub.'

'What's not to like? She'll be in water-baby heaven.'

He chatters on about the hotel, the city itself and the other team members as I listen, asking the occasional question from time to time. I haven't seen him so excited for a long time. Not since Lily was born in fact. But my mind is elsewhere. All the time I'm wondering how to break it to Dan.

After two hours a chipper Simon goes back to work, promising to take us all to Chew and Chat for pizza later to celebrate. I collect Dan from school and he's full of a soccer game he played at break.

'I scored two goals, Mum. Two! George scored one and—'

I zone out, my thoughts racing in my head. Am I really going to do this? Pluck Dan out of school, just when he seems so happy and so settled?

'Have you been listening?' Dan asks as we pull up outside the house.

'Not really,' I admit. 'Sorry. What were you saying?'

'It doesn't matter.'

I look back at Lily but she's fast asleep. I decide to leave her be. She could do with a nap. 'What is it?' Dan asks astutely.

'Nothing.'

'Yeah, right. You look like you're sleep walking. Is it about New Zealand?'

'New Zealand?' I repeat.

'Hattie rang last night when you were putting Lily to bed.

She told me all about New Zealand and Simon doing the America's Cup and all. It sounds pretty exciting. Can we go? Please? Hattie says they have good schools there if that's what you're worried about. She looked it up on the internet. And we don't need any shots 'cause there are no snakes or anything like in Australia.'

'Did she now?' Bloody Hattie. 'But do you really want to go away again?'

'Sure. New Zealand sounds cool. All that bungee jumping and white-water rafting. Much better than rainy old Ireland. It'll be fun. And hey, will I get to meet my sort of sister? Tia? Doesn't she live there?'

'Yes, that's right.'

'Cool,' he says easily.

I'm completely taken aback. I thought he'd rail against moving yet again.

'I thought you were tired of travelling?' I ask, confused.

'No, that was *you*. What are you talking about? I miss all the sailing and the hotel food and the swimming pools.'

'Won't you miss George?'

He shrugs. 'Sure, but we can email. It's no biggie. It's not like you and Hattie. We don't have to talk to each other all the time. We're not girls, you know.'

'Hey!' I give a laugh.

'Only joking. So can we go?'

'I'll think about it.'

'Cool, does that mean I don't have to do my homework?'

'No, of course you do!'

'It was worth a try.' He gives me a lop-sided grin. 'Stop worrying so much. Things will work out fine.'

I smile back at him. 'I'll try. Now you run on in, I'll deal with Lily.'

'Are you sure? I can lift her in if you like.'

'No, I'll do it. Go on in and get yourself something to eat.

Your dad and Nora are calling over this evening. They have news. And Simon will be home soon.'

'He's coming back? So you guys are talking again?'

'Yes. Everything's back to normal.'

He smiles at me. 'Really? No more arguments?'

'No more arguments. I promise. With anyone. Life's too short. You see, everyone makes mistakes, Dan, and we're all just trying to find our own place in the world. A place where—'

'Mum, I'm eleven, stop with the philosophy.'

'Sorry. Now go and eat.'

'Cool!' He jumps out of the car, opens the door with his own (new) front-door key, his school bag dancing on his back. I close my eyes and sit in the car for a few minutes, listening to Lily breathing. A smile lingers on my lips. My little boy has grown up.

'Meg, it's Maureen, and before you say anything I want to apologize for calling you a useless partner.'

'Maureen!' I can hear Joe's voice in the background.

'I know I was a little out of order but I was upset. But I believe, from what Simon's told me, that you've decided to see sense.'

'Maureen!' This time Joe's voice is even louder. 'Give me the damn phone. Meg, are you still there? It's Joe.'

'Hi, Joe.'

'Who is it?' Simon calls down the stairs. He's been upstairs having a shower and he stands on the top step with a towel wrapped around his waist, his torso dripping. He's put a little weight on around his middle but he still looks good to me.

'Your parents,' I say.

'I'll take it upstairs.'

'Joe, Simon will take it upstairs.'

'But it's you we wanted to talk to,' Joe says.

'Charming,' I hear Simon's voice join in on the other phone.

'Both of you,' Joe corrects himself.

'Maureen wanted to apologize to Meg, Simon,' he continues.

'Apology accepted,' I say, rather magnanimously, I feel. It wasn't much of an apology. But this is the new improved Meg. The Meg who doesn't argue with anyone, even if provoked.

'I'm here too!' Maureen's voice rings down the line. 'I'm on the phone in the kitchen.'

'Isn't this jolly? A foursome?' I say. 'So did you hear that, Maureen? I accept your apology.'

She sniffs. 'Yes, well there was one more thing.'

'Maureen,' Joe warns.

'I was just going to tell them about our holiday plans,' Maureen says. 'We've never been to New Zealand, so we were thinking we might come over for a few weeks, spend some time with you and Simon, Meg, and then do some travelling. Joe has this idea about a camper van, but I'm not so sure.'

'Mum and Dad are thinking along the very same lines,' I say, before I can stop myself.

'Isn't that wonderful?' Maureen says. 'I have a brilliant idea. Seeing as we'll all be in New Zealand, why don't you and Simon—'

'Maureen,' Joe warns.

But it's too late. 'Have a lovely Kiwi wedding? With the whole family. Wouldn't that be nice?'

Simon cuts in. 'Mum, please. It's not the time—'

'Maureen, can't you just leave it be—' Joe says.

'What a lovely idea, Maureen,' I say. 'We'll think about it.'

'What?'

'What?'

'What?' Simon, Joe and Maureen all ask, like a shocked Greek chorus.

'Meg?' Simon asks. 'Are you serious?'

'I just said we'll think about it, Simon. I mean, we do intend to get married at some stage, don't we?'

'Of course. But I thought you were dead set against the idea. Remember?'

'I was. But maybe I've changed my mind. Anyway, lovely to talk to you, Maureen, Joe. We have to go now, I'm afraid.'

'Yes, yes of course,' Maureen says. 'And I'll start looking at venues right away.'

'Venues?' I ask.

'Wedding venues. In New Zealand.'

'Maureen,' Joe says.

'I've started doing computer classes in the local library,' Maureen continues, ignoring Joe. 'I adore the internet, wonderful contraption. And I believe that's how you found Kira and Tia, Meg.'

'That's right.'

'Maybe they could come to the wedding too,' Maureen says.

'Mum, Meg has said she'll think about it,' Simon says. 'If you want to ruin everything, just keep banging on like you are now. If you actually want it to happen you'd better give us some space and time to ourselves. Starting right now.'

'Oh.' Maureen squeaks.

'Well said, son,' Joe says.

'I think this is goodbye for the moment, Maureen,' I say. 'Thanks for ringing.'

But Maureen is undeterred. 'I think you'd look lovely in ivory, Meg, and I do like those old-fashioned pink tea roses—'

'Bye, Mum. We're putting down the phone now,' Simon says.

'Bye, Maureen.'

Simon appears a minute later, still in his towel. I whip it off him.

'Hey!' he protests.

'Let's do it on the kitchen table,' I suggest, pushing him playfully with the palms of my hands. 'The kids are in bed.'

He lies back on the wood before giving a squawk, jumping up and trying to look at his back.

It's peppered with dark red indentations. Scatterings of pink, blue and green beads are stuck to his skin.

'Lily's beads,' I explain. 'She was making a necklace earlier. Sorry.'

He smiles. 'Let's go up to bed.'

'I'd thought you'd never ask.'

'And Meg, were you serious, about, you know?'

'Getting married?'

'Yes.'

'Ask me in Auckland. If you win the America's Cup, then we'll see.'

He laughs. 'You're a terrible woman. Do you know that?'

The next day Hattie demands to meet me in a coffee shop in Blackrock during her lunch break. She says it's urgent. I drop Lily in to Tina, along with a large bouquet of flowers – freesias in all sorts of bright colours. There are clothes on the banisters, and toys on the hall floor, but Tina doesn't seem worried. She's wearing an old pair of jeans that I haven't seen before, Matty's perhaps, a pretty white cashmere jumper with what looks like a grass stain on its sleeve and flip-flops. Her hair is tied back in a messy ponytail and her bare skin is glowing. I've never seen her looking so relaxed.

'Thanks, Meg,' she says as I hand the flowers to her. Lily runs past me into the open door of the sitting room where the boys are building a fort with some of Tina's Egyptian cotton sheets and cushions from the sofas. 'Beautiful smell. You shouldn't have.'

I smile at her. 'You're always so helpful with Lily, I wanted to give you something.'

'Your friendship's enough,' Tina says. Her eyes are dancing.

'Something up?' I ask her. 'You seem in a good mood.'

'Nothing special.'

'How are things with Matty?'

'Great. I never knew a relationship could be like this.'

'Like what?'

'Equal. No trouble. No ups and downs, just nice.'

'Nice?' I wrinkle my nose.

'Better than nice. Brilliant!'

'I'm so pleased for you. You're right, he's a lovely guy, one in a million. There are good guys out there. I just hope Hattie finds her own one day.'

'How's she getting on? Still with Ryan?'

'Lord knows. I'll hear all about it at lunch no doubt.'

'Give her my love.'

'Will do.'

'In case I forget to say it later, I'll miss you when you're in New Zealand.'

'Thanks, I'll miss you too. You've been the perfect neighbour. And friend of course.'

She gives me a hug and then draws back. 'Perfect is boring. I've decided not to be so perfect any more.'

I laugh. 'Good plan.'

The coffee shop is jammed but Hattie has managed to bag a small table by the window. She waves at me as I walk in.

'Hi,' she says as soon as I sit down. She gives a dramatic sigh. 'I'm so glad to see you. I ordered you a coffee and a sandwich.' She nods at the mug and plate on the table in front of me.

'Thanks. What's wrong?' I ask. 'Are you sick?' I study her face. Her cheeks are slightly flushed, but other than that she looks normal.

'Sick to the teeth, yes. Sick sick, no. Oh, Meg.' She gives a rather strange-sounding sob and puts her head in her hands.

'What is it?' I ask, worried. Goodness, she's not pregnant, is she? I take a surreptitious look at her stomach. She's wearing a stretchy wrap-over dress on top of skinny-fit jeans. If anything, she looks slimmer than usual.

Hattie raises her head. 'It's Ryan. He's going to marry Marian after all. Never broke it off in the first place, lying bastard. Said he just had cold feet and I made him realize what he really wants – and that's her.' She gives a high-pitched wail, nearly bursting my eardrums. Everyone in the cafe stares at us. I'm mortified, but Hattie, caught up in her own drama, seems totally oblivious. 'I feel so stupid.'

I lean over and put my hand on her arm. 'I'm so sorry, I don't know what to say.'

She sighs deeply. 'They've set a wedding date. In four months time. I'm so sick of men.'

'I'm not surprised. Poor you. Ryan doesn't deserve you. You're well rid of him. When did you find this out?'

'Yesterday afternoon. The prick texted me. Can you believe it?' She gives a dramatic sniff. 'I have to get away, Meg, I'm in bits. I've handed in my notice. I've made a decision: I'm going to New Zealand with you.'

'You're what?'

'I'll protect you from all those mad sailing wives. It'll be fun.'

'But—'

'I *have* to go, don't you see? I have to get out of the country to let my poor old heart recover. I think New Zealand would really help. Otherwise I might bump into Ryan and Marian and that would be the end. I'd die, I really would!' She rolls her eyes dramatically, squeezing her eyelids together tightly. 'And Dan would really like me to come. He says I can help you with Lily, get him off the hook.'

I have the feeling I've been set up by Dan *and* Hattie. 'New Zealand *men* might help, you mean?'

'Who needs men?' She snorts through what I now suspect

451

are crocodile tears. 'But you never know.' She clutches at my hands, her silver rings cold against my skin. 'So what do you say? Please? I'm begging you. Mend my broken heart, sis. I can't stay here in Dublin all on my own. I'll be lonely. Dad's already planned a big road trip of South Island. Can you imagine Mum in a camper van? Ha! So we don't have to worry about him. Come on, live a little. Say yes.'

I think for a moment. I *would* miss Hattie, and she may have a point about helping with Lily. I decide to take a leap of faith.

'OK then, yes. You can come,' I say bravely.

She whoops, jumps up from the table and gives me a kiss, spilling hot coffee down my jeans in the process. I wipe it away. Hattie's right, New Zealand will be a lot more fun together. A lot more dangerous, but a lot more fun.

'Excellent!' Hattie says. 'A family affair. The Millers on tour.' She pauses for a moment. 'Listen, Meg, I'm a bit broke. Any chance you could bung my plane ticket on your credit card? Mine's maxed out.'

'Hattie!' I smile at her. Some things never change.

*To Ali Gunn and Imogen Taylor
for pointing me in the right general direction.
One day I might just get there.*

'If you cannot get rid of the family skeleton,
you may as well make it dance'

GEORGE BERNARD SHAW, 1856–1950

This book is about being a sister, and I'm blessed to have two fantastic sisters of my own, Kate and Emma. Thank you both for being not only my sisters, but also my best friends. And to Mum, Dad and Richard for putting up with me.

To my own family, Ben, Sam and Amy Rose for all the love and support. And to the Cookes.

To my dear friends Andrew, Nicky and Tanya – for being there no matter what.

To Denise, best wishes on your new 'voyage'; and to Carolyn, a strong woman and much loved friend.

To Anne Christine Ronvel and Katarina Zemkova for looking after Amy so well. There would have been no book without your help.

To Ali Gunn, my agent, for all her hard work on my behalf. And also to Stephanie.

To all in Macmillan for making the whole book process such a pleasure, especially my editor, Imogen Taylor, a real lady and a pleasure to work with; the two Davids – North and Adamson; Trisha Jackson, Rebecca Lewis and Cormac Kinsella.

To all the Irish Girls, my partners in (writing) crime,

Acknowledgements

especially Martina Devlin, for all the hand-holding and physical sustenance.

To all the booksellers who have taken a chance on me – a million thanks! I won't name you all, as I know I'll leave someone out. Thank you for making me so welcome in your shops. A special mention to my local bookshops – the Exchange in Dalkey, and Eason and Dubray Books in Dun Laoghaire. And to the gang in Eason, shops and wholesale, for your ongoing support and kindness. And all my new friends in Dubray.

And a special mention for Maria Dickenson, a woman with impeccable taste in books, among other things.

To all my supporters in Dalkey village – Country Bake, Senso Studio and Dalkey Arts in particular.

To all in Abbasolutely, the best Abba tribute band ever, especially Eoin and the Moussoulides family – the book wouldn't have been half as authentic without your help and inspiration. All mistakes are entirely my own!

And to Abba, thank you for the music. It never fails to make me smile.

To all the readers I've met on my bookshop tours and through my website – thanks for all the encouragement, emails and kind letters. And a special thanks to Oonagh for her dedicated reading.

And to Pauline and all the girls of 6th class in St Kevin's in Kilnamanagh. Keep reading, girls!

And finally to you, the reader. I hope you enjoy *Take a Chance* as much as I enjoyed writing it. If you'd like to contact me, my email address is sarah@sarahwebb.info.

1 'Waterloo'

'Gemma!' Wendy Redden watched in horror as her sister lurched forward at the end of their feisty rendition of 'Waterloo', ripping the seat of her snug-fitting blue satin jumpsuit in the process. Gemma landed awkwardly on her ankle, her long blonde Agnetha wig slipping down and obscuring her eyes.

'Are you all right?' Wendy asked her over the wolf whistles and applause. 'What happened?'

'I'm not sure,' Gemma said from her prone position, straightening her wig so she could see. 'I think someone must have spilt a drink on the stage, it's wet.'

'Probably champagne,' Wendy muttered. 'Bloody rich hooligans.'

AbbaFab were singing at Saffron Wolfe-Remington's twenty-first. Saffron was a spoilt, if rather beautiful girl whose parents had more money than sense and whose 'closest friends' (all three hundred of them) left a lot to be desired. The Wolfe-Remingtons' stately pile, Wolfe Castle, was in the wilds of County Wicklow.

1

'I'll help you.' Wendy held out her hand, but when Gemma tried to move her right leg she felt a searing pain.

'I've think I've done something to my ankle,' Gemma said. 'Can you get Ronan to lift me up?'

'I'll manage.' Wendy put her hands under Gemma's armpits, took the weight in her strong arms and hoiked Gemma's body up off the wooden stage floor. Gemma put her uninjured foot down, Wendy supporting her, and straightened her knee. Then she stood upright on her left leg with Wendy's help. Her right leg was bent at the knee, her foot inches off the floor.

'Try putting some weight on it.' Wendy nodded down at Gemma's rogue ankle.

Gemma put down her right foot, but winced the moment she tried to shift her balance. 'Not good,' she managed, her face turning pale even under the heavy stage make-up. She felt nauseous with pain. 'I think it may be sprained or broken. I'd better get my boot off before it swells up.'

'We'll sit you down first. Don't want you losing your balance again.'

'What's happening?' Ronan asked, coming out from behind his keyboard. He was dripping with sweat and his blond Benny beard glistened under the strong stage lights.

'Gemma's in trouble,' Wendy said. 'It's her ankle. Can you keep the audience distracted? I'll help her off the stage.'

Luke, the other member of AbbaFab, came over to

2

see what was going on. 'Everything all right?' he asked.

'Keep playing,' Ronan told him. 'Gemma's hurt. Wendy's sorting her out.'

Luke nodded and went back to strumming his electric guitar. Ronan jumped behind the keyboard and launched into playing the opening bars of 'Does Your Mother Know?' with his feet and his bum, always a crowd-pleaser with that kind of audience.

'Wendy, it's fine!' Gemma protested. 'I'll stay up here and sing. We only have a few more numbers to go. Put me on a chair behind the keyboard, beside Ronan, pull my boot off and hand me a microphone. I think the seam's gone in the bum of my costume again, so it's probably just as well to have me seated. Although this lot wouldn't even notice,' she said, gesturing with her free hand at the audience, 'they're all half cut.'

'Are you serious?' Wendy said. 'You want to stay on stage?'

Gemma nodded. 'I'll be OK. Really. You sang through labour contractions, remember? In Bray?'

Wendy winced. 'Don't remind me. We nearly didn't make it to the hospital in time. But are you sure?'

The young crowd started clapping at the end of Ronan and Luke's song, stamping their feet and shouting.

Gemma attempted a reassuring smile. 'Yes. The show must go on and all that. Better hurry, the natives are getting restless.' Luke and Ronan were now playing an ad-libbed instrumental which wasn't going down too well.

3

'We want more!' someone in the audience yelled out. 'We want more,' several voices joined in. Followed by a loud 'Spit on me, Frida!'

Wendy sighed. 'OK, if you're positive, Gemma. But we're never playing at a twenty-first like this again, trust me.'

'Too right,' Gemma said. 'They're animals!'

As Wendy pulled a chair for Gemma on to the stage her mind raced. They'd played some rough gigs in their time, but this party was something else. They'd already had cold sausages thrown at them, and a leering boy with a face full of spots had grabbed her leg a few minutes earlier. She'd given him a swift kick with her white platform boot for his trouble, but he'd just laughed. She should never have agreed to let the band play. Baroness Wolfe-Remington, the matriarch who had booked AbbaFab, was just plain rude and for all the family's old money, Wolfe Castle was a run-down shambles. The young guests had been fed sandwiches and sausages instead of a proper meal, and now they were all careering around the large ballroom as the result of an excess of cheap champagne and a lack of soakage.

But there's no time for regrets, Wendy told herself, there's work to be done. She settled Gemma on to the chair, pulled her boot off carefully (Gemma had to bite on her thumb with the pain), and then took centre stage again as Ronan and Luke played the opening bars of 'Super Trouper'.

As Wendy waited to sing, swaying to the intro music, she suddenly realized that if Gemma really had broken her ankle – and it looked pretty likely from the swelling – AbbaFab was in serious trouble.

But what Wendy didn't realize was that her life was about to change forever.

After the gig, Baroness Wolfe-Remington tried to get Ronan and Luke to help the bouncers dismantle the stage, but Wendy was having none of it.

'Are you mad?' she exploded. 'We have to get my sister to hospital. She fell on your stupid stage and I think her ankle's broken. We should sue you for personal injury.'

'Sue?' The Baroness recoiled and wrinkled her nose as if 'sue' was a dirty word. 'It was hardly my fault.'

'No? The stage was wet, Baroness.'

Ronan put his hand on Wendy's arm. 'We're ready. You go with Luke and Gemma. I'll travel in the van with Pat. He loaded up the lights and sound equipment with Luke and the bouncers while we were packing the costumes.'

'Bless him,' Wendy said. Pat was their loyal and hardworking roadie, a good man to have around in a fix. She turned back to the Baroness. 'Baroness Wolfe-Remington,' she said, giving the woman her ridiculous full title, 'I don't have time for this. We're leaving now. Please excuse me.'

'You won't really sue, will you, dear?' the Baroness called after her.

Wendy ignored her. Stupid cow hadn't even asked about Gemma.

'How's Gemma?' Wendy asked Ronan as they walked out of the castle.

'She's coping. We've put her across the back seat of Luke's car. But the sooner we get her to hospital the better. I'll follow you in the van with Pat.'

Wendy got into the front of Luke's car and turned her body right around to face Gemma, her knees on the seat. Gemma was still in her blue satin jumpsuit, sitting sideways across the rear passenger seat. Luke and Ronan had placed coats behind her back and had propped her right leg up with bags and rolled-up costumes. Her face looked white and drawn.

'Ready to go?' Luke asked.

'Yes,' said Wendy. 'How are you doing?' she asked Gemma as he started up the car.

'OK,' Gemma replied.

'I still think we should have taken an ambulance.' Wendy had rung St John's Hospital and they'd offered to send an ambulance, but Gemma had refused it. At least the hospital was expecting her now, though. Plus St John's had the best orthopaedic department in the country, with surgeons who worked at the weekends, which was why Wendy had chosen it and not the small, local hospital.

'It would have taken them ages to get down here,' Gemma said. 'It's quicker this way. And I'm OK, really I am. Stop worrying.'

'I can't help it, you know what I'm like.'

Gemma smiled at her sister. Wendy was a born worrier.

They went over a bump and Gemma gasped.

'Sorry, Gemma,' Luke said. 'I'll go a little slower. The surface of this drive is in bits.'

'Thanks,' Gemma said. 'And Wendy, put your seat belt on, please. You're making me nervous.'

'OK, OK.' Wendy clicked herself in and then extended the belt so that she could still turn round. She looked at Gemma again.

'Stop staring at me!' Gemma said. The pain was starting to make her a little edgy.

'Sorry,' said Wendy.

'No, I'm sorry, I didn't mean to snap.'

'That's all right. I understand.'

After a few minutes Gemma asked, 'Do you think we should ring Mia?'

Wendy looked at her watch. 'It's after one. Maybe we should leave it till the morning. Or till later in the morning – you know what I mean. There's no point waking her up. I'll ring her first thing.'

'OK,' Gemma said. Personally she thought Wendy was wrong – their younger sister Mia hated being left out of the loop and would be livid that they hadn't rung her. But Gemma didn't have the energy to argue. Her ankle was swelling up like a balloon and had started to throb ominously. She wished it wasn't such a long drive to the hospital.

'I'm heading on to the main Wicklow road now,' Luke said, turning left. 'It should be a lot smoother. We'll have you there in no time.'

'Thanks,' Gemma said. She lay back against the

7

coats, staring out of the passenger window at the darkness, trying not to think about the pain.

Wendy, Luke and Ronan sat in the Accident and Emergency waiting room. They hadn't had time to change, and their Abba costumes, even with their jackets thrown over the top, had raised a few eyebrows, but they were all too tired to care. Gemma was on a trolley in one of the cubicles, waiting for a bed. A doctor had already seen her and, as she'd suspected, her ankle was badly broken. The surgeon would see her in the morning to decide what was to be done. The nurses had been amused by Gemma's blue jumpsuit, and when she'd explained had asked for a song.

'Go on, love,' one of them cajoled. 'Give us a few bars of "Dancing Queen". It's my favourite.'

'Later,' Gemma joked, feeling a little better due to the strong painkillers she'd been given. 'Fix my ankle and then I'll give you a song.'

Wendy's head was resting on Ronan's shoulder, her eyes closed. She'd gone past exhaustion at this stage.

'Are you OK, Wendy?' Ronan asked, taking one of her hands in his.

'Humm,' she murmured.

Luke yawned and stretched his long white satin-covered legs out in front of him. Pat had left after dropping Ronan off, but Luke had insisted on staying to drive Ronan and Wendy home. One of the nurses had already warned them that due to the serious nature of Gemma's break, she'd have to stay in hospital for at least a couple of nights.

A nurse approached them. Ronan nudged Wendy gently and she opened her eyes and sat up. 'We've found her a bed,' the nurse said. 'In St Patrick's Ward. We'll bring her up now. The other patients are asleep so . . .'

'We'll come back later on,' Ronan said. 'We don't want to disturb anyone.'

'Can I just say goodbye to my sister?' Wendy asked.

'Of course,' the nurse said.

'I'll go and get the car,' Luke said. 'I'll pick you both up outside the door.'

As Wendy and Ronan walked down the brightly lit corridor after saying goodbye to Gemma, Wendy said, 'Frida's mother died in a hospital, you know,' referring to the dark-haired Frida Lyngstad from Abba.

'Um,' Ronan grunted non-committally. He was well used to his wife's Abba obsession. And he knew better than to show any interest in what she'd just said or he'd get a ten-minute diatribe on everything from the nature of the woman's death to the colour Frida wore at the funeral. Wendy had an encyclopaedic knowledge of everything Abba had ever done, especially her idol, Frida. She'd been consumed by the band for as long as he'd known her. It was sad really but, Ronan reasoned, everyone had their strange obsessions and an Abba fixation probably wasn't as bad as most.

'She was only twenty-one when she died, poor woman,' Wendy continued, undaunted.

'Really?' Ronan asked, forgetting himself.

'Yes. Have I ever told you about Anni-Frid's mother and the German soldier? Tragic story. It was during the Second World War when Norway was invaded by Germany. Her mother . . .'

'There's Luke,' Ronan said as they walked out the door, glad of the distraction. He'd heard the German soldier story many, many times. 'Let's go home and get some sleep.'

At eight o'clock that morning, after a few hours' sleep, Wendy dialled Mia's home number. As she waited for a reply, she tapped her nails on the desk in front of her. Even though it was Saturday, she'd been up since just after seven doing accounts and dealing with the email bookings, and she was already exhausted. Most of their bookings came through their impressive website www.abbafab.ie (which Wendy had designed herself) and she fielded several hundred AbbaFab emails a week.

Wendy had been managing AbbaFab and singing as Frida from the band's inception almost seven years ago. It had been Ronan who'd had the idea initially, after spotting Wendy and Gemma singing 'Dancing Queen' at a karaoke pub in Blackrock called the Singing Tree. They had real stage presence and their voices meshed together perfectly. He'd been toying with the idea of putting a tribute band together and as soon as he heard the girls he knew exactly which band to replicate.

Mia wasn't answering, which wasn't unusual – it was the weekend, after all, and she wasn't exactly a morning person. She didn't own a mobile either and often let her house phone ring out, much to her sisters' annoyance. Deciding she'd try again later, Wendy clicked off the phone, rose from her chair and walked into the kitchen. Her two young sons were sitting at the table. The boys were worlds apart in both temperament and looks – Steve was a blond and stocky six-year-old with a strong personality and a fiery temper, and everyone said he was the spitting image of Wendy. Greg, a year older, had a slimmer build and dark hair and was placid by nature, more like his father.

'Hiya, Mum!' Steve said enthusiastically, his mouth crammed with cornflakes.

'Steve,' she said. 'What have I told you about speaking with your mouth full?'

He closed his mouth and grinned. 'Oops,' he said, opening it again. A stray cornflake fell on to the table.

Wendy stifled a smile. She clicked her tongue against the back of her teeth.

Steve swallowed and said, 'Sorry, Mum.'

She ruffled his blond head. 'Try to remember.' Steve nodded and resumed eating.

'And how are my two fine boys this morning? Don't answer that, Steve.'

Greg looked up at her and swallowed down his own mouthful. 'Mum, will you be at home this afternoon?'

11

he asked. 'Can we go to the park? I want to ride my bike.'

'No, sorry. But I'll get Nadia to take you instead. I have to visit Gemma. She'll be in St John's Hospital for a few days and I promised.'

'Hospital, cool!' Steve said. 'Can we come too?'

'No.'

'What's wrong with her?' Greg asked.

'She broke her ankle last night. Someone spilled a drink on the stage and she slipped. Like that time you spilled milk all over the floor and I slipped and hurt my elbow, remember, Steve?'

'Was Gemma's leg covered in blood?' Steve asked, his eyes widening, relishing the thought. He ignored his mother's cautionary tale.

'No!' Wendy said forcefully, eager to nip Steve's morbid visualizations in the bud. He had such a well-developed blood fixation that she wondered if her firstborn had been a vampire in a former life.

Wendy looked around the kitchen. She liked to keep the house looking nice and this required constant vigilance. There was orange juice spilled on one of the kitchen counters and the fridge hadn't been closed properly. She nudged it shut with her elbow, tore a piece of kitchen paper off the roll and mopped up the juice. 'Where's Nadia?' she asked.

The au pair agency still hadn't found Wendy a new girl and she was losing patience with their current 'help', Nadia – a flaky nineteen-year-old from Paris who was in the habit of pursing her lips and 'pahing' at the slightest provocation. Nadia hadn't quite decided whether she was staying in Ireland for two more weeks or two more years, which was most annoying and made it difficult for Wendy to plan ahead. The boys loved Nadia, of course, as she was quite happy to roll around on the floor wrestling with them, getting them all excited and out of breath.

'Dunno,' Steve said with a shrug.

'She's tidying our room,' Greg said.

Wendy shook her head. 'She shouldn't have to do that, boys. What have I told you time and time again?'

'But she doesn't mind,' Steve insisted. 'She likes it.'

'Unlikely,' Wendy murmured, an image of their hastily discarded dirty Simpsons' socks and Man United underpants flashing through her mind. But she had too much to do this morning to worry about it.

Less than an hour later Wendy was racing around south County Dublin, trying to get all her errands run before visiting Gemma in hospital. There were two house viewings pencilled into her diary for that afternoon – a special treat: a Victorian villa in Dalkey that used to belong to a well-known Irish artist, and a three-storey red brick in Sandycove. But there was no way she'd get to them now. And it was the very last viewing of the Dalkey villa before it went to auction – damn! She did so want to see it. She had no intention of buying the properties she visited, even if she could afford any of their hefty price tags – she and Ronan were quite happy with their modern semi in Monkstown. But she was strangely addicted to viewing

13

houses, especially period properties, picking up tips for the interior of her own home and seeing how the other half lived.

She also had to phone all her music contacts to find a short-term replacement for Gemma. Ronan was ringing round the agencies while she was out. Luckily most of them worked on Saturdays. She had already collected her new Frida wig from the costume store in Blackrock, and bought a new school jumper for Steve in Dun Laoghaire. Steve was always leaving his jumpers and coats behind him and she spent her life chasing his clothes and sewing name tags on to new ones. Now she was in the Credit Union waiting to deposit last week's payments.

As she waited in line, the tanned, blond male teller behind the counter caught her eye. He looked strangely familiar. Bert, she thought with a start. That's who he looks like, Bert from the cruise ship. Wendy put her hand on the counter beside her to steady herself. Lord, she was tired. She closed her eyes.

In a matter of seconds she was back on the *Emerald Star*, dressed in all her finery – dark pink feathered and sequinned headdress, gold-sequinned leotard that plunged rather indecently at both the back and the front, tan tights and gold high-heeled sandals – and high-kicking her way across the stage while belting out 'Shall We Dance?', accompanied by four other backing dancers dressed in similar costumes but without the headdress. The feathers marked Wendy out as the principal, and on the *Emerald Star* she was *the* star of the highly regarded cabaret show, *Broadway on*

14

Board, with its repertoire of popular songs from musicals such as *South Pacific*, *The King and I* and *My Fair Lady* to the more modern *Grease* and *West Side Story*. The average age of the holidaymakers was sixty-seven, and their tastes tended towards the conservative. To them, *Grease* was very risqué.

Wendy had been living in London for several years, singing and dancing in various musicals, always in the chorus. When she was offered the chance to star in a show, even if it was only on a cruise ship, she jumped at the chance. At twenty-three, she already had six solid years of experience behind her and she was eager to use it.

Wendy was treated like a princess on board, eating at the captain's table and socializing with the crème de la crème, and she lapped up the attention. She worked hard – there were three shows a day for starters, not to mention the dance and singing classes she organized and taught for the on-board Active Retirement Fitness Programme. And as the star of *Broadway on Board*, she also had her pick of the co-stars, a motley crew of ex-ballet dancers, wannabe entertainers and even the odd Eurovision singer. Like Bert from Norway who had represented his country twice. At least, Bert was what everyone called him, his real name being something traditionally Nordic and completely unpronounceable. He first attracted Wendy's attention when he'd told her that his father (who worked on the oil rigs) had known Anni-Frid from Abba when they were both children. This impressed Wendy, a huge Abba fan even in her twenties, no end. Bert was an attractive

man in his early thirties, a little cleaner-cut than the
Irishmen she was used to, with his full head of wavy
blond hair and perfect rows of pearly-white teeth,
honed from gnawing on raw fish in his native Norway,
no doubt. He was a generous and adventurous lover,
gently encouraging Wendy's burgeoning sexual confidence and delighting in her increasingly excitable
libido. He'd always heard that Irish girls were shy and
nervous when it came to sex, but not his Wendy. After
six weeks together, they'd made love all over the boat:
in her tiny cabin; in his even tinier cabin; in the
cramped dressing rooms in the middle of a show; on
stage, behind the curtain in the small hours of the
morning – the more risky the location the better, as far
was Wendy was concerned. In fact, they'd once made
love on deck, Wendy conveniently 'forgetting' to put
any underwear on under her chiffon skirt. Late one
evening they'd climbed to the deserted top deck, and
while Wendy held the ship's rail and gazed out to sea,
Bert had lifted her skirt above her waist, unbuttoned
his jeans and entered her, making her gasp. It was all
the more exciting knowing that at any second someone
could happen upon them. They were almost caught –
only once – when they'd shut themselves into the small
cinema mid-afternoon and were interrupted by a cleaner.
Luckily it was gloomy in there as the cleaner hadn't
flicked all the lights on and they'd had time to scramble
into their discarded clothes before she happened upon
them.

Of course, the ship's entire staff and crew were well
aware of Wendy and Bert's antics, but as they hadn't

been caught by any of the holidaymakers they'd all turned a blind eye to their behaviour. Many of them were impressed and more than a little envious, to tell the truth, especially the men. Wendy was one popular lady. And no one was surprised when she broke up with the rather boring Bert and set her sights on the far more glamorous Captain, a fit and attractive divorced man in his early forties. Except for Bert, that was. He left the cast of the show in disgust several weeks after Wendy and the Captain had been caught in flagrante in the ship's kitchen late one night by a retired couple from the Home Counties who were looking for some milk for their cocoa. The Captain promised the couple seats at his table if they over-looked his little, ahem, indiscretion, so no harm was done.

As for the Captain, Noel Stone, there was a man . . .

Wendy heard a loud cough. 'Excuse me, I think you're next,' the woman behind her in the queue said kindly.

'Um, thanks.' Still a little caught up in her day-dream, Wendy moved forward and smiled at the young blond bank teller. 'Hi,' she said with a flirtatious smile.

'Good morning,' he replied rather formally.

The smile dropped off Wendy's face and she came back down to earth with a bump. She passed the cheques under the glass partition. 'I'd like to lodge these. Thanks.'

*

On Wendy's way home, Gemma rang.

'Wendy, I saw the surgeon this morning and I have news.'

'One second, I'm driving.' Wendy pulled the car in. 'OK, fire ahead.'

'I'm going to be out of action for ages, my ankle's pretty badly broken according to the surgeon. They're operating on it late this afternoon or this evening.'

'But it's June!' Wendy said in a panic. 'We're wall-to-wall with weddings and summer festivals. I haven't found a replacement yet.'

'I know, and I'm so sorry. I'll be in plaster up to my knee. There'll be no "Waterlooing" for me for quite some time.'

'How long exactly?'

'A couple of months at least.'

'A couple of months! Poor you.' Wendy's heart sank. Finding someone to replace Gemma for a week or two was one thing, but for several months . . .

'Have you tried any of the agencies yet?' Gemma asked, aware of the pressure she'd put Wendy under.

'Ronan's at home doing just that. And I haven't tried all my contacts yet. But don't you worry, we'll find someone.'

'I was thinking about it this morning and I had an idea,' Gemma said.

'Yes?'

'What about Mia?' There was silence on the other end of the phone. 'Wendy, are you there?'

'Sorry, yes. But – Mia? Are you serious?'

'Why not? She's got a great voice. And from the sound of things, the music school's about to be sold to a developer.' Mia taught the piano at the Dublin Academy of Music.

'I don't think she's ready for that kind of pressure,' Wendy said. 'She's so young.'

'She's twenty-four,' Gemma pointed out.

'But a very young twenty-four, you have to admit. She's not emotionally ready.'

'I'm not so sure,' Gemma said. 'Besides, it might be good for her. It would give her confidence, stretch her a bit.'

'Hum,' Wendy murmured. She wasn't convinced. 'I'll try the rest of my contacts and then we'll see.'

'It was just a suggestion.'

'I know, thanks. But you just concentrate on getting better, do you hear me?'

'I will.'

Gemma said goodbye to Wendy and clicked her mobile off. Her ankle was hurting badly and she felt tired and irritable. It was broken in several places and the surgeon who'd been in to see her earlier said he was so busy he couldn't operate until after five. He warned her the moderately lengthy surgery would involve inserting a metal plate and two pins under her skin and muscle to hold the ankle joint together as the bones were badly fractured, and to tell the truth she was very nervous.

She'd had a horrid morning all in all and she felt lonely and weepy, which wasn't surprising seeing as she'd had enough painkillers pumped into her to tranquillize a baby elephant. But at least Wendy would be in later, and Mia too. And if anyone could cheer her up, her baby sister could.

2 'I Have a Dream'

Mia Redden had the strangest feeling that something momentous was about to happen. She was lying on the sofa in the living room of her Monkstown flat in her pyjamas, her legs thrown over one of the sofa arms, when her body suddenly chilled and she gave an involuntary shudder. It was the very same feeling she'd had just before her mum had died. When Mia was only five, her dad, Seamus, a sales rep for a printing company, had been killed in a horrific car crash. She had only vague memories of him, mostly gleaned from old family photographs and the stories Wendy, Gemma and her mum, Miriam, had told her over the years. But she'd been a feisty fifteen when her mum had died after a second, fatal heart attack, only two days after the first. Soon after Miriam's death, Wendy, at the tender age of twenty-nine, became Mia's legal guardian.

Miriam had never quite got around to telling her eldest daughter about her will, although she had of

21

course meant to, and the new role had come as quite a shock to Wendy, not to mention Mia. Wendy moved back to Dublin, leaving her life on the cruise ship reluctantly behind her, and took to her new 'job' with the impeccable organizational skills that she brought to everything. She threw herself into looking after Mia's practical needs from day one. It helped deaden the pain of losing Miriam. And after Wendy and Ronan's marriage, Mia had lived with them for several years until she moved into the Monkstown flat two years ago.

The phone began to ring shrilly in the hall. I was right! Mia thought. She swung her legs down and sat up poker-straight. Something *is* about to happen. She listened and waited, willing the phone to ring out. She chewed on the inside of her lip and fixed her eyes on the fireplace in front of her. Who would be ringing on a Saturday morning? It must be one of her sisters, she surmised. Something was wrong, she just knew it. The phone rang out.

What seemed like seconds later, it started to ring again. This time Mia walked into the hall, took a deep breath and picked it up.

'Yes?' she answered nervously.

'Mia, thank goodness,' said Gemma. 'I rang a few minutes ago, why didn't you answer?'

'Where are you?' Mia asked, ignoring her sister's question. She could hear voices and something rattling in the background.

'In St John's Hospital.'

Mia sat down on the chair beside the hall table, her

heart pounding. 'I knew there was something wrong. What are you doing there? Are you OK? Has something happened to Wendy?'

'I'm fine and Wendy's fine. There's nothing to worry about, honestly,' Gemma soothed, hearing the anxiety in her sister's voice. 'I've broken my ankle and I'm going to be in here for a few days. They have to put a pin in it later.'

Mia winced. She hated anything to do with hospitals or surgery. 'That's terrible. How did it happen?'

Gemma told her the story.

'I'll come in straight away,' said Mia. 'You should have rung me last night.'

'It was late, Mia, and we didn't want to disturb you. I'm sorry, you're right, we should have. I wasn't really thinking straight. And Wendy said it was better not to worry you.'

Mia said nothing.

'Wendy tried to get you several times already this morning,' Gemma continued, 'but you weren't answering.'

'It's Saturday morning,' Mia said. 'I've just got out of bed.'

'Sorry. Of course. I hope I didn't wake you up.'

'No, it's fine. I was up.'

'Listen, Wendy's coming in early this afternoon, how about visiting later on instead, say at four? It'll be a bit less manic then and we can have a proper chat. I'd love the company to tell the truth. I'm really nervous about the operation – it's supposed to be at five but I'm sure it will be delayed. You could help take my mind off it. Any news about the music school?'

'No. Not yet. I'm expecting a phone call from the director today or tomorrow.' Mia picked up a pencil from the hall table and started to doodle on the notepad beside the phone. 'I was in yesterday but lots of my classes had been cancelled. I think it's a lost cause at this stage. The owners of the building are determined to develop the site. And we can't afford to relocate.'

'Surely the building is listed?' Gemma exclaimed. 'It's Georgian, isn't it?'

'Yes, but there are so many alterations and extensions tacked on to it that it has no architectural value any more apparently.'

'So it really is closing for good?'

'It certainly looks like it.'

'Oh, Mia, I'm sorry to hear that. But you'll find something else, won't you?'

'Yes, I suppose so. But I've been working there since college.' Mia sighed. 'It's just a bit of a shock to the system, I guess.'

'I understand. Will you be OK? If you need money . . .'

'Thanks, but I'll manage. I'll find some other job to tide me over. Maybe in a café or something, I wouldn't mind that. Anyway, enough about me. Is there anything *you* need?'

'No, I'm fine. But thanks for asking.'

'Are you in pain?'

'No, they're giving me something for it. I'm a little

spaced out but I can't feel a thing. Listen, I'd better go, the battery on my phone's running low.'

'Ring Wendy,' Mia suggested. 'She could bring in a re-charger for you. I'm sure she has one or two lying around the house in case of emergencies. In fact, she probably has a whole rake of them carefully filed away in a box under the stairs.'

Gemma laughed. 'You're probably right.' Her phone beeped ominously. 'I really must go now. We'll talk this evening. See you later, alligator.'

'In a while, crocodile.'

Mia sat in the hall for several minutes, allowing her heart rate to return to normal. Gemma had given her quite a fright when she'd mentioned St John's. Mia didn't know what she'd do without Gemma and Wendy, and even the mere thought of losing either of them made her decidedly anxious. At a pinch, there was always Alva, although you never quite knew where you were with her. Alva was Mia's oldest friend; they'd been inseparable since childhood and were as close as sisters, but Alva could be a little self-absorbed at times, to put it kindly.

Eventually Mia got to her feet and walked up the three steps into her kitchen, situated at the rear of the old house, overlooking the back yard. Mia loved its lofty fourth-floor perch, from which she could see into a whole area of neighbours' back gardens. The house, divided up into four smallish flats in the seventies, was in a slightly rundown Victorian square, and many of the other old houses, despite the paint cracking off the window frames and flaking off the exteriors, still had large, meticulously kept gardens. She flicked the red switch on the kettle and gazed out of the window at the gardens directly beneath her.

As Mia watched, a white-haired woman pulled off her gardening gloves, ran her fingers through a small green shrub and placed her hands over her face, taking in the scent. Mia smiled. Her mum used to do that. She looked away. That was twice she'd been reminded of her mum today. She concentrated on spooning instant coffee into her favourite chipped Beatrix Potter mug, poured boiling water over the granules and sat down at the table to read yesterday's copy of the *Irish Times*.

Later that day, Mia made her way along the seafront towards Monkstown train station. It was a fine evening and as she walked at a brisk pace her red leather satchel swayed jauntily from side to side on her back. Mia loved walking, which was just as well as she didn't own a car and relied on the haphazard Irish public transport system to get her around the city.

She'd found some 'homemade real lemonade' in the local deli, which she happened to know was Gemma's favourite, and although the large glass bottle was rather heavy, she was lugging it, together with a new hardback crime novel, into the hospital for her sister. Gemma was an avid reader and was always complaining that her busy life didn't leave her nearly enough time to devour all the books she'd like. Gemma will have plenty of time to read now, Mia mused. Gemma liked to be busy, however much she bemoaned her time-poor lifestyle, in fact, she positively thrived on work and activity-packed days. Unlike Wendy, who was a born worrywart, she took problems and setbacks in her stride. Perhaps not ones that literally stopped her in her tracks, however. Mia wondered how her sister would cope with her ankle-imposed rest. She had a feeling that ankles took a considerable time to heal.

Mia reached the station and bought a ticket from the young (and dishevelled-looking) stationmaster, whose eyes didn't leave the soccer game playing on the portable television screen once while he served her, a feat in itself. As she clicked down the metal steps to the platform she thought about Italian policemen, dressed in their crisp white uniforms, their snug-fitting trousers ironed to perfection, a sharp, precise crease cutting down the centre of each leg, and sighed. She'd visited Rome on a school trip in fifth year and had fallen in love with the bustling, bubbling romantic city, not to mention the dark-skinned and tantalizingly (to a teenager escorted around by her teachers) out-of-reach men. There wasn't much fear of coveting the young Irish stationmaster, that was for sure, or the local Gardai, the Irish police force. Most of them seemed to be female these days, for a start.

After a few minutes a green DART train pulled into the station and Mia hopped on. The carriage was deliciously empty and she swung her rucksack off her back and sat down on a vacant seat beside the window, the bag resting on her knee. As she stared out of the window, she noticed a family on Sandymount strand. A young mother with long dark hair streaming behind her in the wind was holding a toddler by the hand, both splashing in their wellies in a puddle of seawater. A tall blond man, the dad Mia presumed, was standing beside a little boy, watching him draw on the sand with a stick. Mia looked away and stuck her head into her dog-eared paperback copy of *The Secret Garden*. She'd read it countless times, but it was one of her favourites. The words swam a little in front of her eyes at first, but she persevered and soon she was engrossed in the story.

'Gemma.' Mia leaned over and gave her a kiss on the cheek. 'How are you feeling? How's the ankle?'

Gemma pulled herself up in the bed and smiled warmly at her little sister. 'Not too bad, thanks. I'm dreading the operation though. The surgeon has put it off until tomorrow morning as he's swamped with operations. Which gives me lots of time with you.'

'Lucky me.' Mia winked and smiled.

Gemma smiled back. 'Less of that, Madam.'

Mia sat down on the chair beside Gemma's bed. The ward was quiet, with only the gentle hum of conversation and the odd clink of water glass against vase on a bedside table breaking the silence.

'I feel like I should be whispering in here,' Mia said looking around. 'It's as quiet as a church.' Most of the other beds were occupied by older women, many of whom were asleep.

28

'I know what you mean,' Gemma agreed. 'It's mostly hips. I feel like the baby of the ward.'

'Hips?'

'The other women – hip operations.'

Mia nodded. 'Ah, I see. So Wendy and her gang were in earlier?'

'Just Wendy. She said the boys would be too much for the ward so she left them at home with Rónan.'

Mia smiled. 'She was probably right. They're not exactly shy and retiring, are they?' She pulled the book and the bottle of lemonade out of her bag. 'I brought you a book, it's a new one, I hope you haven't read it. And I found this lemonade in a local shop, I know you love it.'

'You are an angel.' Gemma grinned at her. 'Wendy brought me in some interiors magazines but they're frightfully boring.' She picked up the book and studied the cover. 'No, haven't read it. Excellent! Thanks.'

'Let me pour you some lemonade.'

'You're a star. I've run out of 7-Up – the water in here is lukewarm and tastes of plastic.'

Mia handed the full glass to Gemma, who downed the tart liquid in one. 'You're thirsty.' Mia laughed and poured her another.

'It's always so bloody hot in hospitals. Makes you dehydrated.'

'So how was Wendy?' Mia asked, putting the bottle down on the bedside table with a sharp clink and settling herself on the edge of Gemma's bed.

'Fine. As hectic as ever. She brought me a huge box of chocolates. She's trying to find a replacement for me at the moment. We have another big gig at the weekend.'

Mia whistled softly. 'That's not going to be easy. Has she had any luck yet?'

'No. It's a really busy time of the year for everyone.' Gemma decided to bite on the bullet. 'Mia, I've been thinking,' she said as casually as she could manage. '*You* could take my place in the band while I'm in plaster. Actually it's quite good timing, what with the music school closing and everything. What do you think?'

Mia stared at her incredulously. 'You're joking, right?'

'You'd be well able for it, Mia. You have a fantastic voice, you know you do.'

Mia blew out her breath in a noisy rush. 'Yeah, right.'

'You do. You sang the lead in all the school musicals, remember? *Calamity Jane* and *Grease*.'

'That's different. It was a long time ago. I haven't sung in years.'

'Will you just think about it?'

'Gemma, there's no way I'm singing with Abba-Fab.' Mia narrowed her eyes. 'Anyway, what about Wendy?'

'What about her?'

'What does she think? I presume you both talked about it earlier. Does *she* want me in the band?'

Gemma hesitated for a second. A second too long.

'Wendy doesn't think I'm good enough, does she?' Mia asked astutely.

30

'No, it's not that,' Gemma began. 'She's just worried . . .'

'You're far too nice for your own good.' Mia combed her long blonde hair off her face with her fingers and lifted it away from the nape of her neck. 'Wendy's right, I'd be terrible. And anyway, she'll find someone to replace you eventually. She has loads of contacts in the business and she won't give up until she's found someone good.'

'Mia, let me finish. Wendy's just worried that singing with AbbaFab might be too much pressure for you. Being on stage and everything. But she'll come round. I think you'd be great. Really I do. I wouldn't have suggested it otherwise. Why don't you think about it, please? Maybe the music school is closing for a reason, have you considered that? Maybe AbbaFab is your destiny.'

Mia laughed. 'And maybe you're out of your tiny little mind, Gemma! I think those drugs are getting to you. Now, you mentioned chocolates. Hand them over.'

Gemma looked at Mia. Mia met her gaze for a moment and then looked away. Gemma sensed confusion and understood that the subject of AbbaFab was firmly closed, for the moment at least. 'They're in the locker,' she said instead. 'Help yourself. But lay off the toffees, they're mine.'

Later that evening Mia pottered around her flat, making sure everything was in its place. She moved the square red rug so that it lay against the hearthstone of the original black marble fireplace. She lifted the silver-framed photograph of AbbaFab off the mantelpiece and ran a yellow duster over the glossy stone surface. She looked at the picture as she dusted it. The group were dressed in their 'Arrival' outfits – snug-fitting white flight jumpsuits – and Ronan was holding a tiny toy helicopter in the palm of his hand. She put the frame back in its place and, still staring at the photo, sat down on the sofa opposite the fireplace.

AbbaFab. The band had played such a huge part in her life for years now. When AbbaFab first formed Mia was only sixteen and still in school, her whole life stretched out before her, a blank page. At that age, joining the band was the last thing on her mind. A long time ago, before her mum died, she had dreamt of being a professional singer like Wendy. But things had changed. Now she was a music teacher and she enjoyed it most of the time. She had an ordinary life, a quiet life, unlike Gemma and Wendy. And mostly she was satisfied with her lot. So why, at this precise moment, did she feel like life was passing her by? Mia sighed. Wendy had Ronan and the boys, Gemma always had plenty of admirers and it was only a matter of time before she settled down with one of them. Where would that leave her? The spinster of the family. She winced at the word. Spinster. It sounded hopelessly old-fashioned and out of date. But that's what she would be – a spinster living all alone in a flat with her cats. She'd die alone and her cats would eat her. She shuddered. Stop being so morbid, Mia, she told herself.

She looked at the photograph again. What if she did take Gemma's place? What would happen then? For a fleeting moment she saw herself up on a stage in a white karate suit, white PVC boots up to her knees, dancing and singing 'Take a Chance', her favourite Abba song, with Wendy by her side. Then she came back down to earth. She wasn't good enough, Wendy had as good as said so. There was no point even thinking about it. AbbaFab wasn't for her. Not now, not ever.

A little later that evening, Mia's phone rang.

'Mia, I've had a fight with Sean,' Alva said in a rush. 'Can I sleep on your sofa, just for a night or two? Please? It's an emergency.'

Mia groaned inwardly. 'Alva, not again. Can't you just talk to him? I'm sure it's not all that bad.' Alva had a terrible temper that often whipped up out of nowhere like a desert sandstorm, and she and her long-term boyfriend, Sean, had regular fights triggered by anything from Sean's devotion to his job as an electrician, to his obsession with restoring his Victorian cottage, which had been sadly neglected by its previous owners. Alva hated spending their weekends sanding floors, filling holes and grouting tiles, but Sean loved fixing the place up, tinkering with his toolbox and making weekly visits to the local DIY store.

It was all a bit awkward for Mia, as she and Sean were also old friends; they'd been in school together and it was Mia who'd introduced Alva to Sean all those years ago. But at the end of the day, Mia's loyalty lay with Alva, although she wasn't naive enough to think that she was easy to live with, far from it. Mia didn't know how Sean put up with her at times.

Mia was quite used to her friend's frantic phone calls after an argument with Sean, so she took Alva's request with a large pinch of salt.

'It's serious this time!' Alva protested.

'I'm sure it is,' Mia said calmly. It always was.

'Sean walked out yesterday morning and he hasn't come home yet.'

'What?' Mia was taken aback. Sean had never stayed out all night before. 'Have you tried ringing him?'

'Yes, he's not answering his mobile. I think he's switched it off.'

'I see.' Now Mia *was* shocked. That wasn't like Sean at all. He rarely turned his mobile phone off – to him, it was like another limb. Alva and Mia often teased him about his devotion to it. 'What happened?'

'Oh, I don't know. I lost my temper with him, I guess. He's always leaving his dirty work boots in the hall, so I left them outside the back door overnight to teach him a lesson. It rained and they got wet.' Alva sniffed. 'It was his own fault for leaving them in the hall in the first place. And then he said he couldn't live with me any more, that I was selfish and impossible. I threw his keys at him and told him to get out if he felt like that, and so he did. But he didn't come back. What am I going to do?'

Mia could hear the anguish in her friend's voice. And then Alva began to sob. 'Oh, Mia. He's gone. He's really gone. When I got home from work last night, he'd left me a note. It said to leave the house and take all my belongings with me. That it was over. Mia, how could he be so cruel?'

Mia took a deep breath. 'Alva, he's just annoyed, he doesn't mean it. Pack some things and come over here. Of course you can stay.'

She sighed inwardly. All in all, it was shaping up to be quite a week.

3 'Super Trouper'

'Hi, Mia.' Wendy was standing on Mia's doorstep at nine on the button on Monday morning. 'Lovely day, isn't it?' She lifted her oversized sunglasses from her eyes and settled them on the top of her head. Even at this hour, she was perfectly made-up, her lips red and glossy, the gently blushered pink apples of her cheeks sparkling in the light.

'Wendy.' Mia faltered as she opened the front door and blinked in the bright morning sunlight. 'Is anything wrong? It's pretty early.'

Wendy seemed a little nervous, hopping from one foot to the other as if she needed to go to the bathroom. 'No, no, not at all. Can I come in?'

'Of course.' Mia was still in her pyjamas. The directors of the music school had finally admitted defeat and vacated the premises after weeks of speculation: she'd received the official phone call yesterday evening. There was no question of any redundancy payments; the school had always run on a shoestring budget, leaving its entire staff, Mia included, high and dry. Regardless of this, Mia had decided to postpone worrying about her jobless state and to make the most of her newly acquired free time by having a lazy morning, reading all the parts of the Sunday newspapers that she normally didn't have time to get round to, even the travel and sports sections.

She had promised herself that she'd start looking for a new job first thing the following morning. There were several Dublin secondary schools with well-developed music departments, she'd ring around and see if any of them needed a new music teacher. It was a long shot but it was better than doing nothing. At least it would stop her thinking about her jobless state and worrying about Alva and Sean. And it would show Wendy and Gemma that she was actively looking for work. At the end of the day, Mia knew that both her sisters were good for a loan (Gemma had already offered, after all) and this made her rather more relaxed about her precarious financial state. Alva had offered to pay rent, but Mia had refused this. After all, Alva's tenancy was only temporary, she hoped.

Mia hadn't realized quite how difficult living with someone could be, especially when that someone was Alva. She had taken over the living room with her clothes and toiletries, not to mention her shoes. It was only a fraction of her wardrobe, for which Mia was grateful, but it still took up a lot of space. Alva was incredibly messy, and quite frankly Mia had no idea how Sean had put up with it for so long. Alva never thought of tidying up after herself and was genuinely surprised when Mia pointed out that she'd dirtied every coffee mug Mia owned and hadn't once rinsed one out in the sink, let alone washed one properly. It hadn't occurred to Alva to bother – Sean always did that kind of thing in their house.

'I'm not interrupting anything, am I? Were you asleep?' Wendy said, taking in Mia's pyjamas.

Mia blushed and crossed her arms self-consciously over her chest. Her blue cotton Snoopy pyjamas had seen better days. In fact she'd owned them since she was in her early teens and it was a wonder that the threads still held together.

'Of course not, I've been up for ages. I was just about to get dressed. Come on in.' She stood back from the door and led the way up the stairs and into her flat, holding her pyjama bottoms up with one hand as the elastic was shot and they had a habit of sniggling down her waist. She really would have to invest in new ones and throw these away, even if they were her favourites. As they walked into the living room she winced. 'Sorry about the mess,' she said. 'Alva's staying with me at the moment. Sit down. Would you like some coffee?'

'No thanks, I'm fine.' Wendy lifted a pair of black lacy pants off the sofa, held them up gingerly between two fingers and smiled. 'Alva's, I presume.'

'Just throw them on top of that pile.' Mia pointed at the mound of clothes to one side of the sofa.

Wendy did as suggested, then moved the over-flowing and rancid-smelling ashtray, which had been balanced dangerously on the sofa cushions, on to the floor, swatted the velvet covering with her hand to remove the stray ash and finally sat down. Mia sat opposite her on the small armchair.

'Why is she staying here?' Wendy asked. 'Is Sean pulling down walls in the cottage again?'

'Something like that.' Mia didn't really want to get into it at this hour of the morning. Wendy would probably try to help the rowing couple, and Mia didn't think either Alva or Sean needed any outside interference, however well intended. Besides, hopefully they'd be back together again by this evening, if they weren't already. 'Can I get you anything, some coffee, a glass of water?' she asked.

'No, really. I've just had breakfast. I'm fine.' Wendy smiled at her sister again, a little too brightly, Mia thought, immediately becoming suspicious. It was quite obvious that Wendy wanted something. The last time she'd arrived on the doorstep at such an early hour (with Steve and Greg in tow) she'd asked Mia to babysit the boys while she had her roots touched up in the salon in Sandycove. She was talking about AbbaFab on a daytime chat show and was convinced that the strong studio lights would illuminate the slightly darker blonde slash of her parting. The irony was that Wendy, like Mia, was a natural blonde. A slightly darker blonde than Mia, whose hair was an almost Nordic white, yet a blonde none the less. But Wendy had been highlighting it for so many years that she now felt powerless to stop the chemical enhancement.

'I was sorry to hear about the music school finally

closing,' she said. 'There was something about it in the arts section of Saturday's *Irish Times*. I did try to ring you as soon as I read it but you weren't home.' Wendy knew better than to implore Mia yet again to get a mobile phone. Mia was adamant that she didn't need one.

Mia nodded. 'I was out with Alva. But thanks for trying. As you know, it's been on the cards for a while. One of the directors rang last night. They're moving out this morning. So I'm now officially out of a job.'

'Will you be all right?' Wendy asked gently. 'I know you'd been half expecting it, but it still must have come as a bit of a shock.'

'I'll be fine. Hopefully I'll find another teaching job at a school or something. I'm going to start looking tomorrow. Otherwise . . . well, I'll just have to wait and see what comes up.' She shrugged.

'If you need any money to tide you over, you only have to ask,' Wendy said.

'Thanks. I appreciate that. But I'm all right for the moment.' Mia paused for a moment. 'But I might have to take you up on that next week if I still haven't found anything.'

'Sure.' Wendy seemed distracted. 'Let me know how much you need.'

Mia stared at her. 'You're being a little odd, Wendy. What's up?'

'I guess you're wondering why I'm here so early in the morning?'

Mia nodded.

'There is something.'

40

'You mean you didn't call in to check if I was OK about the music school business?' Mia raised her eyebrows and stifled a grin.

'Of course I did,' Wendy assured her. 'But there's something else.'

'Yes?' Mia stared at Wendy. Surely her über-confident sister wasn't finding it difficult to ask a simple question? Mia noticed that she was clutching her hands together in her lap.

Wendy looked around the room and her eyes settled on the AbbaFab photograph on the mantelpiece. 'I want to ask you a favour.' She took off her wedding ring and jiggled it around in the palm of her right hand.

'Go on.' Mia was more than a little curious now. It really wasn't like Wendy to be so on edge.

'I've been mulling it over and I think Gemma's right, you'd make a great Agnetha.' Wendy put up her hand as Mia opened her mouth to protest. 'I know Gemma already said something to you about it in the hospital, but she suggested I should talk to you about it myself.'

'But . . .' Mia protested.

'Please, hear me out before you say anything. When Gemma first suggested you, I have to admit I wasn't convinced. You haven't been on stage for so long, I was worried it would all be too stressful for you. It's pretty exhausting work, to be honest, and I know you love the teaching. But I thought it over and Gemma's right, you'd be brilliant. You have an amazing voice, you know you do, and we could work on your confidence

41

and your stage presence. With a bit of practice you'd be perfect. And it's only for a few months. You might even enjoy it, Mia. What do you say?'

'*No!* No way.' Mia stared at her wide-eyed.

'Mia, please?'

'Wendy, I can't. I'm sorry. I know you're pretty desperate and you've tried all the agencies but . . .'

'Is it because I didn't ask you first,' Wendy cut in, 'before I tried the agencies?'

'No,' Mia said. 'Well, maybe a little. And maybe you're just desperate, maybe you don't *really* think I'm good enough.'

'That's ridiculous, Mia. You're the best singer of the three of us, you know you are. You've got an amazing voice. I've been thinking about it a lot, Mia, and I think you're ready to perform again. And more importantly, I think you need AbbaFab as much as we need you.'

'What are you talking about? I don't need AbbaFab, I'm perfectly happy without all of that glitzy stage stuff. Just because you and Gemma feel the need to be the centre of attention all the time doesn't mean that I do too. It's not genetic, you know, that need to be important, to be . . .' Mia looked at her sister's stricken face. 'Ah, Wendy, I didn't mean to upset you.'

'Is that what you think, that me and Gemma sing to make ourselves feel important?' Wendy asked. 'Do you really believe that?'

'No, of course I don't. I don't know why I said it. I'm sorry.'

'Mia, we sing because that's our job. And it pays well, far better than working in an office or singing in

42

a chorus line, which is probably what I'd be doing otherwise. Gemma's OK, she has her Leaving Cert, but I don't even have that. I left school at seventeen to sing in that show in London, remember, *Cats*? It's not as if I'm exactly qualified to do anything else. And it means I can be around my family and not stuck on some god-forsaken cruise ship half-way around the world.'

Mia was taken aback. Wendy rarely lost her temper. 'Wendy? Are you all right?'

'Yes, sorry, I didn't mean to raise my voice.'

'And I'm sorry I said ... you know ... about you and Gemma. I just wasn't thinking.'

'That's OK.' Wendy stood up, walked towards the window and stared out at the park across the road. The wind was whipping the trees around and stray litter was swirling in the gusts. 'And I'm sorry for bothering you so early in the morning.' She turned back and faced Mia. 'But I'm going to ask you one last time. Please, fill in for Gemma, be Agnetha. It'll only be for a few weeks and I wouldn't ask unless I really thought you could do it, Mia. And however much you protest, I think it would be the making of you. And we need you. *I* need you. Please, do it for *me*. I'm begging you.'

'Wendy, you don't understand, even if I want to, I can't. I just can't physically do it. I'd freeze on stage or something and let you all down. I'm terrified of singing in public now, you know I am. I haven't stepped foot on a stage since ... you know.'

'You weren't always terrified. Your confidence just took a bit of a knock when Mum died, that's all,'

Wendy said gently. 'But you're a different person now. I'd be there to help you. And Gemma has promised to train you in herself. Plus Ronan would prompt you if you forgot any of the words. And Luke's such a gentleman, he'd take care of you too. It would be so much fun, you and me together. Please?'

'I can't. Leave it, won't you?' Mia was almost in tears. 'You'll find someone else. Someone better than me.'

Wendy decided to give it one last shot. 'We really do need you, Mia, I'm not exaggerating. The band's in trouble otherwise. I've tried all the agencies and all my contacts, believe me. Unless we find someone by this weekend, I'll have to start cancelling gigs, word will get out and no one will book us ever again, especially not for weddings. I've already had to cancel a slot in the Olympia Theatre this week. Please? For the sake of the band. For your sisters' future?'

Mia sighed. She'd never forgive herself if AbbaFab had to break up when there was some way she could help save it. It was Wendy and Gemma's life, not to mention their livelihood, and she owed it to them. Maybe she could give it a try. She *was* out of work now, after all.

'I'll think about it,' she said tentatively. 'But only until Gemma gets better,' she added.

Wendy jumped up and gave her a huge hug. 'Oh, thank you, Mia. You've saved my life. What a relief!'

'I only said I'd think about it,' Mia insisted as Wendy pulled back and kissed her on both cheeks. There were tears in her eyes.

Wendy smiled. 'There's no time for thinking, Mia. First practice is tomorrow morning. Ten o'clock at my house. I'll tell Gemma – she'll be over the moon. We'll lick you into shape in no time.'

'I'm not sure . . .' Mia began.

Wendy ploughed on. 'And Ronan. He can accompany us and teach you some of the lyrics and routines. And I wonder if Luke's free? Actually, maybe we'll go hen at the first rehearsal, it might be less intimidating for you, Mia.'

'But Wendy . . .'

'Mia,' Wendy beamed, 'welcome to AbbaFab. You've made me one happy sister.'

That evening when Mia got back from a walk along the west pier in Dun Laoghaire, she found Alva slumped on the sofa digging a large spoon into a carton of chocolate ice cream.

'Dinner?'. Mia asked, raising an eyebrow. Alva was a junk-food addict – it was amazing she maintained such a slim figure with the amount of ice cream, biscuits, cakes, hamburgers, chips and chocolate she threw into her system. Alva had some metabolism, lucky thing. She didn't believe in the gym and drove everywhere, even to the local shops. She reminded Mia of a sloth with her long, spindly limbs and her general distaste for anything that involved moving off the sofa, especially anything that smacked of healthy living or fitness. Ironically, she worked as an account manager for an Australian sportswear company called Bluewater.

But for all her faults, Mia adored Alva. She had been there for her when Mia's mum died, distracting her and making her leave her room when all she wanted to do was to curl up in a ball and weep her little heart out.

Alva looked up at her. 'Just a snack.' She licked the spoon and put it and the empty carton down on the sofa beside her.

Mia leaned over and picked them both up wordlessly. 'Do you want anything in the kitchen?' she asked.

'Just a glass of orange juice. With ice if you have it. Thanks.'

'OK.' Mia walked into the kitchen, rinsed the spoon in the sink, tossed it on to the draining board and put the empty ice-cream carton in the bin. She was getting a little fed up with Alva treating her like a servant. She opened the fridge. She could have sworn she'd left some lasagne on the top shelf.

'Have you seen the lasagne?' she shouted into the living room. 'It was in a dish in the fridge.'

'Sorry, I think I may have eaten it earlier,' Alva shouted back over the excited hype of a supermarket ad on the television. 'Hope you don't mind,' she added.

'No, it's fine,' Mia replied before sighing deeply and noisily, not that Alva could hear her over the blare of the television. She was dog-tired and Alva's company was beginning to grate on her nerves. Alva had brought her own portable television with her, knowing that Mia's house was goggle box-free, which in Alva's humble opinion was simply unnatural. She was a big television fan and claimed she'd suffer terrible withdrawal symptoms without her daily fix of the soaps, especially *Coronation Street* and its Irish counterpart, *Fair City*. Mia also missed silence. Alva rarely turned the television off, even when having a conversation. And if she played music or the radio, it was always at top volume. At least the small kitchen was quiet, expect for the gentle hum of the elderly fridge and the soft constant drip, drip of the cold tap, which no one except Ronan could ever fully turn off. Indeed the last time he'd turned it off for her he'd closed it so tightly Mia had had to borrow a wrench from one of her neighbours to turn it back on again.

'Either you ate it or you didn't,' she muttered, peering into the murky depths of the fridge. If they weren't such good friends Mia would have said something, but instead she bit her tongue. She'd just have some cheese on toast instead. She searched for the lump of red Cheddar that she knew had been there last night as she'd hacked off a slice to eat with an apple, but it had disappeared, along with the entire sliced loaf. All that was left in the slightly frosty interior was a bag of decidedly brown-around-the-edges iceberg lettuce, some squashy tomatoes and a chunk of cucumber that had also seen better days. 'Salad and crackers again,' she murmured. 'And the fridge needs to be defrosted,' she added with irritation. She hated defrosting the fridge – it was such a thankless task and she always managed to get water all over the kitchen floor, no matter how carefully she covered the tiles with newspaper and kitchen roll. She looked over at the fruit bowl on the table. It hadn't been touched. 'And fruit.' Not that she needed to diet. Mia was blessed with great skin and a good figure – she had never dieted in her life, much to her sisters' chagrin. She seemed to be able to eat what she wanted without putting on weight, assisted by the fact that she didn't have much of a sweet tooth, unlike Gemma, or a body that constantly craved carbohydrates, like Wendy's did. Mia's favourite treat was a bowl of cashew nuts or sea-salted peanuts, a large bag of cheese and onion crisps, or if she was feeling really decadent, a tube of Pringles. None of which, however calorific, seemed to put an ounce on her.

Alva's eating habits were just plain weird. She grazed in the evenings but never seemed to eat a proper meal during the day. She also smoked like a chimney, much to Mia's annoyance. She tried to make her go outside to smoke, but Alva paid no attention to her. 'You don't mind really, Mia, do you?' She'd smile and light up yet another. 'Sure, didn't you used to smoke yourself?'

'Alva, I smoked for two days when I was fourteen. That hardly counts, does it?'

'Reformed smokers are always the worst,' Alva replied with a smile.

Mia said nothing. Sometimes there was no talking to Alva.

Mia poured the last of the orange juice into a glass and added some ice. She'd have to go shopping again

48

tomorrow – thanks to Alva she was out of practically everything.

She walked back into the living room and handed the glass over. Alva was watching an awful Irish teenage soap, set in a strict Catholic boys' school, called *Paddy's Place* – a peculiar hybrid of *Dawson's Creek* and *Father Ted* – and had lit up again, the blue-grey smoke wafting up towards Mia's face.

'I'm going to the supermarket tomorrow,' Mia said, stepping back to avoid the fumes. 'Is there anything you'd like in particular?'

Alva peeled her eyes off the screen and looked up at her. 'I'll give you a list,' she said. 'That's what I do with Sean. I think I'm out of cleanser. Do they have Nivea in your supermarket? And I need some razors. Oh, and some shampoo.'

'I meant food, Alva,' Mia said, trying to remain calm.

'Sorry,' Alva murmured. She fished out the remote control from the side of the sofa where it had become lodged, flicked the television off and turned her full attention to Mia. 'I'm not the easiest house guest, am I?'

'You're not that bad,' Mia said. Yes, you're terrible and you're driving me mad, she felt like saying but bit her lip.

'I really appreciate you letting me stay,' Alva said. 'I don't know what I'd do without you, Mia. I'm lucky to have you. I know that. You're so patient with me. I know I'm not the best at housework or shopping and that kind of thing. But I'll try and be more helpful. I've just been a little . . .' She shrugged and gave Mia a half-smile.

'Down?' Mia suggested kindly.

Alva nodded. After a moment she said, 'I'll take you out for lunch next weekend to make up for it. What about Guilbauds?' Guilbauds was one of the most exclusive (and expensive) restaurants in Dublin and one of the few establishments in Ireland with two Michelin stars.

'It's fine, you don't need to do that,' Mia protested.

'I'd like to,' Alva insisted. 'We could get all dolled up and drink champagne. Sean took me there for lunch on Valentine's Day last year – the food's delicious.'

'It would be fun,' Mia said hesitantly. 'Are you sure?'

'Yes. It's a date.' Alva gave what sounded like a cross between a hiccup and a sob. Tears began to well up in her eyes.

'Oh, Alva, what's wrong?'

Alva looked at Mia, large drops spilling from her eyes. 'Mia, what have I done? I miss Sean so much and he hates me.'

Mia sat down on the sofa beside her friend and put her arms around her. There was nothing to be said. There was no point in giving Alva false hope, after all. That would only make things worse in the long run. She knew that she had been ringing Sean several times a day, to no avail – he steadfastly refused to answer her calls. When Alva had tried ringing from different numbers he'd hung up as soon as he realized who it was. She had even called by the cottage, but Sean had left her standing on the doorstep like an idiot, ignoring her increasingly frantic raps of the doorknocker. She'd been so embarrassed when one of the neighbours had come out to see what the commotion was. Alva had murmured something about a misunderstanding and had run back to her car in mortification, tears streaming down her face.

Mia stroked Alva's hair. 'You'll be OK,' she soothed. 'And you can stay here as long as you need to.'

'Thanks, Mia,' Alva sniffed. 'You're so good to me. I do appreciate it. You're the best.'

Mia's heart softened. What were a few dirty coffee cups between friends, after all?

Just after ten the following morning Mia found herself opening Wendy's gate and crunching up the short gravel drive. Unusually, she'd woken before six and had been unable to get back to sleep as her mind started to race with conflicting thoughts about the band. AbbaFab had played such a huge part in her life for so many years now and her secret childhood daydream of joining Wendy on stage was about to come true. But now the dream had become reality, she was terrified. Singing on a stage again – the very thought made her nauseous. Could she really do it?

Mia took in the new duo of bay trees on either side of the front door, standing straight and proud in their square terracotta pots, slightly incongruous against the white pebble-dash of the modest semi. Delusions of grandeur, Mia smiled to herself as she stroked one of the leaves between her fingers, holding her hand up to her nose and inhaling the strong, distinctive smell.

She lingered on the doorstep, dithering. Should she ring the doorbell, thus sealing her fate, or should she walk away? It was her last chance; once she'd stepped inside Wendy's house she knew there'd be no going back. She heard the crunch of gravel behind her and whipped her head around, catching a nerve in her neck in the process. 'Ouch,' she exclaimed, raising her hand and massaging the tender area she'd tweaked.

'Are you all right?' asked Wendy. She was standing in front of Mia, a two-litre container of milk cradled against her body like a plastic baby. She was wearing a snow-white velour tracksuit, matching white runners and her obligatory sunglasses, and she was panting a little.

'It's just my neck,' Mia said. 'I caught a nerve, I think. I'll be fine in a minute.' She looked at Wendy. 'Where were you?'

Wendy gestured at the carton. 'I ran down to the shop. The boys used up all the milk making hot chocolate last night with Ronan. Made one hell of a mess too. I've told them a thousand times not to put empty cartons back in the fridge, but do they ever listen? Honestly, I'll swing for those three one of these days. Now, are you coming in?'

'Um, of course,' Mia murmured. 'I was just . . .'

'Good,' Wendy said firmly. She pulled her keys out

of a pocket and opened the door. 'We have one hell of a lot of work to do if you're to be ready for the Blackrock Music Festival tomorrow evening.'

'Tomorrow!' Mia's stomach lurched. 'You never said anything about that yesterday. I thought the next gig was at the weekend.'

'Must have forgotten,' Wendy said mildly. 'Sorry, I have a lot on my mind. But it's only a short set – six songs at the most. It'll be a doddle.'

'Wendy!' Mia said, following her sister into the kitchen. Gemma was sitting at the kitchen table, a mug of coffee in front of her.

Gemma looked up at Mia. 'Hi, Mia. How are you this morning?'

'OK,' Mia said and then added, 'but a little nervous.'

'You'll be fine,' Gemma said with a warm smile.

Mia opened her mouth to continue but Wendy leaned over her, put the carton down on the table, opened it and handed it to Gemma. Wendy was in one of her slightly manic, let's-get-everything-done-nice-and-quickly moods.

'Now you can drink your coffee,' Wendy said. 'If it hasn't gone cold, that is.'

'You really didn't have to go out for milk, I could have had it black. It's a little lukewarm all right, but if you throw my mug into the microwave for a second it'll be fine,' Gemma said.

'I most certainly will not!' Wendy protested. 'It'll taste awful.' She took the mug from Gemma's hand and sloshed the coffee down the sink.

'Wendy!' Gemma said, a little shocked at the waste.

'There was no need for that. I wouldn't have minded, honestly.'

Wendy made her fresh coffee in the cafetière and handed a mug to her. 'I know you don't like it black. And I needed milk anyway so it was no trouble. This should be perfect.'

'Thanks.' Gemma sloshed milk into her mug. 'What were you saying, Mia?'

'Nothing,' Mia mumbled.

'Go on, tell me. What's up?' Gemma cajoled.

'Wendy's just told me about the Blackrock gig and I'm not sure about any of this, Gemma. I'll never be ready by tomorrow and I'll be useless.' Mia bit her lower lip. 'Can't you find someone else? Please?' She looked at Gemma beseechingly.

'You *can* do it, Mia,' Gemma reassured her. 'You have a great voice and once you're in costume you'll be the mighty Agnetha, not Mia at all. And Wendy will be there with you, and Ronan and Luke.'

'But,' Mia began. 'I don't think . . .'

'Let's get started then,' Wendy said firmly. She winked at Gemma who smiled back at her. They both knew that sometimes it was best to jolly Mia along. 'We're wasting time, girls. You can drink your coffee in the garage, Gemma. I'll carry it in for you. Come on, Mia. We have work to do.'

Wendy opened the door at one side of the kitchen and led Mia and Gemma into the garage, which was fitted out as a practice room for the band. Gemma sat down on the old, well-worn sofa, demoted years ago from Wendy's sitting room, which slouched in all its flowery finery against one of the walls. She put her crutches on the floor in front of her.

'Come on, let's get started,' Wendy said, picking up two microphones and switching on the large black amplifier. She clicked the small switches on the base of each microphone and tested them both with a flick of her nail. They gave a metallic 'thunk'. Satisfied they were working, she lifted one to her mouth and began to sing the opening bars of 'Thank You for the Music'. *"I'm nothing special, in fact I'm a bit of a bore."'*

Gemma joined in, singing loudly to compensate for the lack of amplification. '*"If I tell a joke, you've probably heard it before."'*

'Come on Mia, next line,' Wendy encouraged, handing her the other mic. '*"But I've got a talent . . ."* – go on!'

Mia took a deep breath, put her mouth up to the mic and began to sing. '*"But I've got a talent, a wonderful thing, everyone listens when I start to sing, I'm so grateful and proud. And I want to sing it out loud."'*

Wendy and Mia sang the chorus together, Gemma dropping out this time to listen. It didn't sound half bad. As soon as they'd finished, Wendy put her arm around Mia's shoulders. 'That's it, you see, you *can* do this,' she whispered into Mia's hair. 'You're my Little Star, don't forget that. You're going to be great.' Wendy kissed the top of Mia's head tenderly. Mia felt tears prick her eyes. Her mum used to call her that – 'Little Star'. Wendy gave her a tight squeeze and then let go. 'We're going to start with "Waterloo", Mia, are you OK with that? Do you know the words?'

'I'd want to,' Mia said, 'I grew up with you and your Abba obsession, Wendy. It's part of our family's history. You told me how you used to make Abba costumes for your Sindy dolls and dress them all up as band members. You made Gemma be Bjorn and Benny, and you were Agnetha *and* Frida. And you made Mum choreograph a special dance for "Nina, Pretty Ballerina". And when I was three, just before you left for London you dressed me up in your old tutu and taught me the dance, remember?'

'Ah, yes.' Wendy grinned. 'That was a great dance. Hey, that's an idea. We could resurrect that dance. It was a mini-ballet, wasn't it?' She looked at Mia. 'What do you think?'

'No.' Mia frowned. 'Definitely not. I refuse to wear a tutu, Wendy. It would look ridiculous.'

'Quite right too,' Gemma said, dragging the conversation back to safer territory. 'No tutus. Speaking of costumes, what are you thinking of wearing tomorrow night?'

'The cats. The karate suits are in the dry-cleaner's until Thursday. And your blue jumpsuit will need to be, um, altered a little to fit Mia. No offence.'

Gemma smiled. 'None taken. I can't help it if I'm more voluptuous than my little sis, can I?' Gemma was a curvy size fourteen and proud of it.

'Cats?' Mia asked. 'You mean the white dresses with the matching skirts that come off? Aren't they a bit Bucks Fizz?'

Wendy snorted. 'Not at all! Abba had the idea back

56

in 1975. They had these amazing Swedish costume designers called Owe Sandstrom and Lars . . .'

Gemma nipped Wendy in the bud. They didn't have time for her Abba stories today. 'I'll pop on the Blackrock backing track,' she said, crutching herself over to the stereo in the corner. 'Ronan prepared it for you last night, Mia. It has the music for all six songs on it. He also printed out all the corresponding lyrics, just in case. Here.' She handed Mia a sheaf of paper.

'Thanks.' Mia took the pages and began flicking through them. She felt slightly better when she realized that most of the words were more than familiar to her. She just hoped she'd remember them all on stage.

Gemma pressed play on the stereo and the room was flooded with the opening bars of 'Waterloo'. 'Wendy, you go through the movements with Mia. I'd suggest you keep them simple. Cut out the twirling bit at the middle, just do the swaying and the singing to each other. I'll watch and advise.'

'OK,' Wendy said, slightly miffed. She was used to giving directions, but she knew it made more sense for Gemma to watch them both and to give Mia feedback.

Mia stifled a smile and winked at Gemma. 'Ready when you are, Gemma,' she said. Wendy coughed. 'And Wendy, of course.'

By lunchtime Mia and Wendy had practised four out of the six songs, with Gemma looking on and making suggestions, and all three were ready for a break. Mia and Gemma flopped down on chairs in Wendy's kitchen and leaned over the table.

'I'm exhausted,' Mia moaned. 'I haven't done so much exercise in years. My legs are killing me.'

'It's the dancing,' Gemma commiserated. 'It'll take a while to get used to it.'

'I'm just popping out,' Wendy said, still on her feet and glancing at her watch. 'I won't be long. Make yourself something to eat, you know where everything is. We'll get going again at two if that's all right.'

'Where are you off to?' Gemma asked, sitting up. 'Are you collecting the boys from school?'

'No, Nadia's collecting them and taking them to the park to give us some peace,' Wendy replied. 'I've just got an errand to run.'

'What kind of errand?' Gemma asked, her curiosity tweaked.

'I have to buy some stamps,' Wendy said. 'And, um, send a parcel.'

'But Wendy,' Mia began. 'I think we need to talk about the costumes, I don't think . . .'

'Sorry, have to dash.' Wendy had grabbed her bag and flown out of the house before Mia had had a chance to finish her sentence. Seconds later, they heard the sound of Wendy's car screeching away. She'd left the handbrake on again.

'Is the post office in Monkstown even open now?' Mia asked. 'I thought it closed for lunch.'

Gemma shrugged. 'I have no idea. Who knows where she's really going?'

'What do you mean?' Mia asked.

'Nothing.'

'Tell me.'

Gemma lowered her voice and leaned towards Mia. 'Maybe she's having an affair.'

Mia's eyes widened and she gave a surprised little squeak. 'You don't really think . . .'

Gemma hooted with laughter. 'Of course not. I'm only joking, Mia. This *is* Wendy we're talking about. I bet she's off to some interior design shop, to order some hideously expensive curtains or cushions or something. You know Wendy. Now, let's get some lunch. I'm starving.' Gemma stood up. 'Wendy's fridge is usually groaning with nice things from that deli in Dalkey.' She opened the tall, baby-pink Smeg fridge, which didn't exactly match the stainless-steel kitchen cupboards but was very 'cutting edge' according to Wendy. Besides, it made her smile every time she looked at it, and that was enough to earn its place in her kitchen. Keeping the cupboard doors clean and smear-free, not to mention little boys' greasy fingerprints-free was a chore, but Wendy loved the lustre and gleam of the metal. Personally, Gemma thought it looked cold and uninviting. Give me good old natural wood any day, she thought to herself. But she did like the fridge.

Gemma was right, the fridge was crammed full of food. She took out some delicious-looking pâté, a generously full cheese box and some ready-made cartons of potato and pasta salad. Then she took a loaf out of the bread bin and placed it all on the table.

'Here we go,' she said, placing everything on the kitchen table. 'Why don't you set the table?'

'Sure,' Mia said. 'Will Wendy be joining us, do you think?'

'I shouldn't think so. But put a place out for her anyway, just in case.'

Funny, Mia thought as she clinked the heavy, gleaming knives and forks out of the perfectly ordered cutlery drawer, I'm actually quite enjoying myself.

'What are you smiling at?' Gemma asked her.

'Nothing really,' Mia said. 'I'm starving too, let's eat.'

'You're a funny one,' Gemma said affectionately and smiled back. 'Always were.'

The estate agent was standing at the door of number 7 Eagle Terrace as Wendy dashed up the path. 'Sorry I'm late,' she said to the dark-suited woman. 'The traffic was brutal.'

'Not to worry,' the woman said pleasantly, handing her a brochure. 'It's guiding at seven hundred thousand; I'll let you have a look around at your leisure and if you have any questions just ask. The auction's on Thursday week. There's another couple here as well and two more are expected.'

'Thanks.' Wendy took the brochure and flicked through it. Nice big colour pictures of the newly renovated living room – excellent. She walked into the white, wooden-floored hallway. It smelt of fresh paint and there were framed prints of shells on the walls.

Nice, Wendy thought, but a little bland. As she walked into the kitchen she winced as a whole rail of chrome halogen spotlights struck her in the face. She located the light switch and flicked them off. The room was immediately thrown into shadow, daylight struggling to illuminate the large open plan space. 'Very little natural light, shame really,' she murmured, looking around and admiring the cream cabinets and Belfast sink. There was a huge vase of lilies on the round kitchen table and a door led to a wooden-decked patio area to the left. She flicked the light switch back on and continued her rounds.

After a perfunctory look at the tasteful but safe cream bedrooms and white, fully tiled bathroom Wendy found what she'd been looking for – the living room. The room that had been featured in last week's property supplement of the *Irish Times*. It was a generously proportioned rectangular room painted an unusual shade of green; the walls had been profession-ally dappled with a highly specialized paint-on-damp-plaster technique that Wendy recognized from one of her interiors magazines. Must have cost them a pretty penny, she thought as she ran her finger down one of the tactile surfaces. The room was full of dark wood furniture and the two small sofas were upholstered in purple velvet and artfully finished with lime-green and raspberry-pink scatter cushions in various shapes and sizes. Those are nice, Wendy noted, picking up one of the smaller cushions and turning it over in her hands, looking for a label. There wasn't one – how disappointing. She replaced it and turned her attention to the green velvet drapes, complete with elaborate swathed pelmet. Personally I would have kept the window dressing much simpler, Wendy thought as she peered at their immaculately piped tiebacks. The curtains are just a little too much. The room had clearly been put together by an over-enthusiastic interior designer. Still, the sofas with their contrasting cushions certainly worked.

'What do you think?' the estate agent asked eagerly, as she walked through the doorway. 'Need any help?'

'No,' said Wendy politely. 'I've seen everything I need to see. It's not quite what I'm looking for. But thank you anyway.'

4 'Summer Night City'

Mia was woken on Wednesday morning by the sound of the phone ringing. 'No, no, no!' she muttered, opening her eyes and sitting up quickly. She looked at the clock on her bedside table: it was just after eight and her alarm was set for a quarter past. But she resented being woken up early all the same. 'Who's ringing at this hour?' She staggered to her feet, walked into the hall and whipped the phone off its cradle.

'Yes?' she answered irritably.

'Mia?'

'Hi, Sean,' she said, recognizing his voice instantly. 'What's up?' She didn't have time to mess around; Wendy and Gemma were expecting her at nine for a costume fitting and final rehearsal before the music festival that evening.

'You sound a bit groggy,' Sean commented.

Not surprising as I've just been woken up by the bloody phone, Mia felt like snapping, but it wasn't Sean's fault that she'd had such a bad night's sleep, and it wasn't all *that* early after all. 'To be honest, I didn't sleep very well,' she admitted. 'I have to sing with AbbaFab later and I'm a little nervous. Actually I'm terrified. I had this really bad nightmare last night – a taxi driver had locked me into his cab and he wouldn't let me out until I'd recited all the lyrics to "Knowing Me, Knowing You" backwards. It was very scary.'

'Sounds it. But what's all this about AbbaFab? It's news to me. When did you join?'

'Only yesterday. Did Alva not tell you about Gemma's accident?' Mia asked without thinking.

There was a deathly silence on the other end of the line.

'Sorry,' Mia said, berating herself. 'I forgot. But while I have you on the phone, what *are* you thinking of? Alva's in bits, Sean. Why won't you talk to her? It's not like you.'

'Ah, Mia, I don't know what's going on in my head to tell the truth. I'm not proud of my behaviour, but I don't know what else to do. Listen, I really need to talk to you. Are you free for lunch?'

'Oh, Sean, I'm hideously busy today. I'm sorry, but lunch is out. How about sometime tomorrow? I'm supposed to be at Wendy's in half an hour so I can't really talk now. But I do think you should ring Alva.'

'Tomorrow is fine,' he said, ignoring her comment about Alva. 'I'll survive until then. I'll give you a ring in the morning to arrange a time.'

'And how are *you*?' Mia asked, feeling a little guilty for being so abrupt with him.

'Not too bad in the circumstances,' he said.

This annoyed Mia. He *had* walked out on Alva after all. 'Sean, I don't want to take sides or anything and I know you're probably upset too, but Alva is *very* upset. Please, return her calls; at least let her know you're all right. She cried herself to sleep last night.' Mia bit her lip. Damn, she thought, I shouldn't have said that. Alva will kill me.

Another deathly silence.

'Sean?' Mia asked. 'Are you still there?'

'Yes,' Sean answered tightly. 'And you're right – I should talk to Alva, I know. I just don't know what to say to her. It's all such a mess.'

'Are you sure you're all right?' Mia asked gently. He sounded very despondent.

'I miss her so much,' he said in a rush. 'I love her, Mia, really I do – I just can't live with her. She's impossible at times.'

'I know what you mean,' Mia said before she could help herself.

Sean snorted. 'Helping around the house, is she?'

'She's not the worst,' Mia insisted, back-pedalling furiously. 'She's taking me out at the weekend. To Guilbauds no less. *And* she went to the supermarket with me yesterday.'

'Really? Food shopping?'

'Yes.'

'Well, there's a first.'

'Alva has a good heart,' Mia said. 'Can't you just talk to each other? Work things out?'

'But, Mia, I've met someone else,' Sean blurted out.

'*What?*' Mia demanded incredulously. 'Already? You're joking?'

'No. She's called Sadie. I rewired her house a few months back and we kept in touch. Nothing's happened yet, but we have a date on Saturday night.'

'A date? Sean, are you mad? What about Alva?'

'I don't know, Mia. I'm just trying to get on with my life. Sadie thinks . . .'

'Please don't tell me you've been talking to *her* about all of this?'

'But she's been very helpful.'

'I'm sure she has,' Mia muttered darkly. Any woman who muscled in on another woman's territory was bad news in her book, very bad news. Mia glanced at her watch. She wanted to hear more about this Sadie woman, but she really had to go or she'd be very late and Wendy was a stickler for punctuality. 'Sean, I'll talk to you about this tomorrow. I'm sorry, I must dash or I'll be late for band practice.'

'Just one last thing,' Sean added. 'Please don't tell Alva about Sadie.'

'What do you take me for? Of course I won't! I'll leave that to you. I'll see you tomorrow, we can talk more then.'

'Thanks, Mia. See you tomorrow.'

'Damn, damn, damn,' Mia swore as she ran into the bathroom and turned on the shower. She didn't have time for one, but she needed to freshen up as she'd be trying on costumes this morning. She stepped into the shower cubicle and winced as she felt something cold and slimy under her left foot. She looked down. A soapy, matted loop of dark hair peeped out from under her toes. 'Yuck!' She reached down, picked it up between her fingers, opened the shower door and threw it into the sink. 'Oh, Alva!' she sighed.

Wendy and Gemma stood back and looked Mia up and down.

'The skirt needs to come in a good bit,' Gemma commented. 'It's practically a hipster at the moment.'

'And I might put a couple of tucks into the top,' Wendy mused. She walked towards Mia and took a clump of white satin in her hands, pulling in the back of the top.

'That's better,' Gemma said. 'Shows off her figure.'

'Hello,' Mia said, waving both her hands in the air. 'I am here, you know.'

'Sorry, Mia.' Wendy took her hands away and lifted a white-blonde wig off the sofa. 'It seems a shame to cover up your own hair, it's the perfect colour for Agnetha. But if you don't wear this, the rest of us will look wrong. It'll look like our heads are much bigger than yours.' She handed Mia the wig. 'Try it on for size.'

Mia put the wig down for a moment, twisted her own hair into a roll and then slipped the wig over her head. Wendy tucked some stray strands of Mia's real hair under the wig and then smiled. 'It suits you. What do you think, Gemma?'

Before she had a chance to answer, Ronan and Luke crashed through the door carrying a large silver flight box, which held the heavy stage spotlights.

'Sorry, ladies,' Luke said with a grin. 'Hope we're not interrupting anything?'

'Mia's just trying on her costume for tonight,' Wendy said. 'What do you think?'

Luke wolf-whistled. 'Looking good, Mia. The skirt's a bit long though, you can't see the boots properly. We need to see more leg.'

Mia blushed, then pulled the wig off her head and handed it to Wendy. 'I'll just go and change,' she mumbled, brushing past Luke and Ronan.

'Was it something I said?' Luke asked Wendy.

'She's just nervous,' Wendy said, putting the wig down on the sofa. 'I'll go after her. You guys stay here.'

'I'm sorry,' Luke said, 'I didn't mean anything by it, really I didn't.'

'Don't worry, Luke,' Gemma said. 'Mia's just a little sensitive sometimes.'

'Luke, stop standing around gabbing and put the box down,' Ronan said, puffing under the weight.

'Sorry, boss,' Luke said. He turned towards Gemma again. 'Was it the leg thing – saying we needed to see more leg? Did she think I was, you know, flirting with her?'

Gemma gave a laugh. 'Luke, stop worrying. Mia's fine. Wendy's right, she's nervous.'

'So what's the plan for the afternoon?' Ronan asked. 'Wendy asked us to meet her here.'

'Confidence building,' Gemma said glancing at the doorway to make sure Mia wasn't on her way back in.

'Got it,' Ronan said. 'We're all yours.'

'Mia has no reason to worry. She looks a million dollars in that costume,' Luke said. 'As far as the audience is concerned she doesn't even have to sing a note. She could mime all night and they'd be perfectly happy. Actually that's not a bad idea. Why don't we get Mia to mime the songs?'

'The men might be happy with that,' Gemma said dryly. 'But the women might not be so amused. Abba songs are sacrosanct to women, you must know that by now. And delivery is everything. Miming just won't cut it.'

'But can Mia actually sing?' he asked.

Gemma winced and shook her head. Luke followed her gaze to the doorway. Mia was standing there, fixed to the spot. She felt their eyes resting on her and she turned on her heels and ran straight into Wendy.

'Mia!' Wendy said. 'You nearly winded me. What's wrong?'

'I can't do this!' Mia cried. She ran past Wendy up the stairs and locked herself in the bathroom.

'What happened?' Wendy asked, looking at Ronan. 'Did you go and say something?'

'Don't look at me like that,' Ronan said. 'I didn't say a word.'

'It was me,' Luke said sheepishly. 'I was just asking Gemma if Mia could actually sing, and Mia overheard me. I'm sorry. I should have kept my big mouth shut.'

Wendy strode towards the tape recorder in the

corner and pressed rewind and then play. She turned the volume up. 'Listen!' she commanded. 'I was taping her earlier.'

Mia's voice rang out clear and sweet.

'I asked her to sing "Dancing Queen" on her own so that I could listen. She had no idea I was taping her.'

'Wow, that's some voice,' Luke said. 'I feel like such an idiot.'

Wendy said nothing. She was annoyed with him for upsetting Mia, but there was no point in making him feel any worse than he already did.

'Can I borrow the tape recorder?' Luke said. 'I have an idea.' He turned it off and unplugged it before Wendy had a chance to protest. 'Back in a second,' he said. He strode out of the practice room through the kitchen into the hall, then popped his head around the living-room door.

Greg and Steve looked up from the table against the window where they had been doing their homework under Nadia's supervision.

'Have you seen Mia, lads?' Luke asked.

'No,' Steve said. 'But I heard someone go upstairs. Will I help you look for her?' he asked eagerly.

'Not at all, you stay there and do your homework like a good chap,' Luke said.

Steve groaned. 'Great.'

Nadia shushed him.

Luke walked out of the door and bounded up the stairs. Seeing the bathroom door closed in front of him,

70

he rapped on it with his knuckle. 'Mia, are you in there?'

No answer.

He rapped again and tried the door. It was locked.

'Mia, listen, I'm sorry about all that business downstairs. I'm always putting my foot in it. I know you're probably feeling a little nervous right now and I'm sure I didn't help matters. But you have an amazing voice. Really. And I'm not just saying that. Every bit as good as your sisters'.' He thought it better not to say 'Even better than your sisters' just in case he was overheard again.

'How can you say that?' Mia said through the door, incised by his audacity. 'You've never even heard me sing.'

'Oh yes I have.' Luke found a socket and plugged in the tape recorder. He pressed play and sat down on the carpet outside the door. Mia's voice rang out, pitch perfect.

After a few minutes Mia unbolted the door, opened it and stepped out. Her eyes were a little red but there was a shy smile lingering on her lips. 'Is that me?' she asked.

Luke nodded. 'Agnetha Faltskog, eat your heart out. Are you coming back downstairs?'

Mia looked down at him. 'Yes,' she said in a small voice.

He jumped to his feet and grinned at her. 'Great.'

Mia noticed the tiny wrinkles fanning the outer edges of his eyes when he smiled. She looked away quickly, embarrassed to be caught staring at him. But he didn't seem to notice.

The rest of the afternoon passed in a whirlwind of 'Mamma Mias', 'Super Troupers' and 'Fernandos', and Mia was quite worn out by the end of it; worn out but excited. It was as if someone had discovered the loose end of the little ball of hope she'd kept buried in her heart for all this time, had given it a gentle tug and was slowly unravelling it. A scary feeling, Mia thought, scary yet exhilarating, and she felt more alive than she'd felt in a long, long time.

After a swift bite to eat in Wendy's kitchen, Ronan and Luke left in Luke's car. The three sisters piled into Wendy's car and, after screeching off the driveway ('Handbrake, Wendy!'), arrived in Blackrock just after five.

'What time are we on stage again?' Mia asked nervously.

'Seven,' Wendy said. It was the third time Mia had asked her in the last hour. 'I know we're a bit early, but we're on first and I want to make sure that everything's in order. The stage, lights, sound, that kind of thing,' she added for Mia's benefit.

'And it usually takes at least an hour to wangle a cheque out of the organizers,' Gemma said with a grin. 'Money up front is the only way to go, isn't it, Wendy? Wendy's great at getting them to pay up.'

'Years of practice.' Wendy laughed. 'Debt collection isn't exactly one of my favourite jobs. But as Gemma so rightly pointed out, it's always best to get paid up front. Here we are.'

Wendy pulled into the Frascati Centre car park and drove the car head first into a parking space (she found manoeuvring into the tight spaces in the Blackrock Shopping Centre car park difficult and had scraped her car on the huge concrete pillars more than once). The music festival was being held in a large marquee in Blackrock Park, and Mia's hands had been shaking through the entire car journey at the mere thought of it.

Mia stepped out of the car and held her hand out to Gemma. 'Here you go, Gemma,' she said, pulling her sister out of the car. Gemma rested her body against it while Mia retrieved her crutches. 'Here,' Mia said, handing them over. 'I'll hold them while you put your arms in.'

'Thanks.' Gemma smiled gratefully. 'I feel like such an invalid these days.' When she was sorted, she leaned over towards Mia. 'Do you think we'd have time to have a quick look around the shops?'

Mia looked at Wendy who was pulling bags out of the boot and muttering to herself. Wendy seemed a little frazzled.

'I wouldn't say so,' Mia said.

'What was that?' Wendy asked, looking over at Mia. 'Did you say something to me?'

'Nothing,' Mia said. 'Can I give you a hand, Wendy?'

'Please.' Wendy lifted the plastic-covered costumes out and placed them on the top of the car. The edges of the thin, clear plastic fluttered in the breeze and Mia shivered as she surveyed the cat outfits underneath their flimsy see-through coverings. Suddenly she felt her face blanch and she felt terribly queasy, as if her stomach was turning elaborate somersaults.

'Are you all right, Mia?' Gemma asked with concern. 'You've gone very pale.'

Mia gulped. 'Um, I'm fine. I just feel a little . . .'

At that moment she felt her blood rushing to her head with all the force of a tidal wave and her legs went from under her. 'Mia!' she heard Gemma cry out. 'Wendy, Wendy, help!' and then – nothing.

Moments later Mia opened her eyes. She was lying on the tarmac beside Wendy's car and her left arm hurt dreadfully. Wendy and Gemma were crouched over her, Wendy holding Mia's head gently in her cupped hands.

'Mia?' Wendy asked with concern. 'Can you talk?'

'Where am I?' Mia said. 'What happened?' She felt extremely cold and her whole body was shaking.

'You fainted, Mia,' Gemma explained. 'Wendy managed to catch you, but you landed a little awkwardly on your arm.'

'I'm sorry, I should have moved quicker,' Wendy said.

'Wendy, Flo Jo herself couldn't have moved any faster,' Gemma insisted. 'You did brilliantly. I was no help. Bloody cast.'

'I need to . . .' Mia pushed her upper body up with her hands.

'You should stay lying down,' Wendy said firmly. 'You need to get the blood back to your head, that's what you need.' Mia put her head down again and allowed it to rest in Wendy's warm, firm hands.

'You used to faint a lot when you were younger.' Gemma smiled down at her. 'Remember that time in school? You passed out in Assembly and they let Alva bring you home in a taxi as Mum was in Wexford at a funeral.'

'And we spent the whole day watching really bad daytime television,' Mia said. 'And Alva made me drink a whole bottle of Lucozade. She said it would be good for my blood-sugar levels.' She laughed. 'That was a really good day. And no, we didn't feel a bit guilty about missing school, before you ask, Wendy.'

'I wasn't going to,' Wendy said, although the thought had crossed her mind. 'Gemma, do you think you could pass me something soft for Mia's head? I'd better ring Ronan and let him know what's happened. He'll be wondering where we've got to.'

'And you should ring the organizer of the festival, Wendy,' Gemma suggested.

Wendy looked at her. 'Why?'

'To cancel.'

Wendy said nothing for a moment. 'Cancel? Do you think?'

Gemma stared at her. 'Of course. Mia was unconscious a few minutes ago. What are you thinking of, Wendy?'

'I'm starting to feel a lot better,' Mia protested from

75

her supine position. 'I can do it. There's really no need to cancel on my account.'

'We're cancelling and that's that,' Gemma said firmly.

'Now wait a second,' Wendy snapped. 'I make the decisions around here when it comes to the band, Gemma. Or have you forgotten that?'

Gemma glared at Wendy. 'But Mia's still my sister. You can't be serious about making her sing.'

Mia sat up and leaned back against the car.

'Mia!' Wendy said, but her sister ignored her.

'No one's making me do anything,' Mia said. 'I'm singing and that's final. I'm all psyched up, so I may as well get it over with. Now, I'd like some water, please. Is there any in the car, Wendy?'

'No. Sorry, I'll go and buy some,' Wendy said. 'Wait here.' She flashed Gemma a look and then strode off in search of a shop.

'You shouldn't let Wendy bully you like that,' Gemma said as soon as Wendy was out of earshot.

'She wasn't bullying me.'

'Yes she was and you know it.'

'I don't want to argue with you, Gemma. I *have* to sing this evening, don't you see? If I don't, I'll be even more nervous by Saturday for the wedding. And besides, I can't let everyone down.'

'Let Wendy down, you mean?' Gemma said gently.

'I suppose so.'

Gemma sighed. 'Mia, are you sure you're up to it?'

'Positive. I fainted, that's all. And my arm seems

76

OK.' She moved it gingerly. 'It's just bruised, I think. Please, no more arguing with Wendy, OK?'

'OK. And Mia?'

'Yes?'

'You really have nothing to worry about, you'll be great.'

'Thanks.'

'And I'll be right there in the wings, watching your every move. If you feel in the least bit faint or queasy just wave at me and I'll make sure Wendy stops the show. Understand?'

Mia nodded. 'Thanks, Gemma,' she said. 'But I hope I won't need to.'

'But I'll be there for you, just in case.'

Mia smiled. 'Thanks. Now, here's Wendy, and it looks like, yes, an entire fridgeload of water.'

Gemma looked over at Wendy who was fast approaching, cradling five bottles of water in her arms, and began to laugh. 'Hey, Wendy,' she said loudly. 'Expecting a drought?'

'Ha, bloody ha,' Wendy replied. She dumped her load into the boot of the car. The bottles rolled towards the back of the almost empty boot, following the natural slope. 'I'm sorry for snapping at you, Gemma, I'm just tired. I don't know what came over me. And you're right, what was I thinking? Mia's not well. I'll cancel the gig immediately.'

'You'll do no such thing,' Mia said. 'Now, stop it, the pair of you, I'm fine. I'd just like some water. What have you got there, Wendy?'

'Sparkling, still, oxygen-enhanced, lemon-flavoured and orange-flavoured. What would you like?'

'Just plain still,' Mia said. 'Sparkling gives me hiccups.'

Wendy fished out a bottle, opened the cap and handed it to her sister. 'Take your time, Mia. Don't bolt it down.'

Mia took a long swig of the deliciously cool liquid, droplets escaping from her mouth and running down the sides of her face like two tiny streams.

'Mia!' Wendy exclaimed. 'Take it easy.'

'What?' Mia said. 'I'm thirsty.'

'She's grand, Wendy,' Gemma said. 'I think we should both stop fussing over her. Is that Ronan?' She pointed to the far side of the road.

'Yes.' Wendy began to wave at him frantically to catch his attention. 'Cooee!' she called. 'Over here!'

Ronan looked over, waved back, and crossed the road, jaywalking rather dangerously between the cars. Luke followed closely behind.

'Are you all right, Mia?' Ronan asked as soon as he reached them. Mia was still sitting on the ground, her back against Wendy's car.

'Fine,' Mia insisted. 'It's nothing to worry about, really. I just fainted.'

'Wendy rang me a minute ago. She was really worried about you,' Ronan said, looking at Wendy. 'She blames herself for pushing you so hard at practice this afternoon. She's feeling very guilty.'

Gemma and Mia looked at each other and then at Wendy. 'Really?' Gemma asked. Wendy was always a

78

worrier, but today she seemed to be even more stressed out than usual. 'It's not your fault, Wendy,' Mia said. 'Honestly. There's no need to feel bad. Like Gemma said, I'm prone to fainting. I just haven't done it for a while.'

'I suppose you're right,' Wendy said. 'But I still shouldn't have pushed you so hard.'

'As I keep telling you,' Mia said, 'I'm fine.'

'If you're sure,' Wendy said, 'I guess we'd better start getting organized. Ronan, can you help Mia up and keep an eye on her? And, Luke, would you mind carrying our costumes and bags over to the changing area? I believe there's a caravan in the park for us to use as a changing room.'

'A caravan?' Luke whistled. 'A whole caravan for the four of us? How posh can you get!'

'Don't be so sarcastic!' Wendy said, trying not to laugh. 'It's better than a tent.'

'Or the back of the van,' Ronan pointed out.

'True.' Luke smiled. 'Such a glamorous life we all lead, eh?'

'Too right, mate!' Ronan snorted.

At half past six, Mia was still sitting in the caravan staring at her rather paler than usual face in Wendy's large portable mirror. Wendy and Ronan had finished their own stage make-up and were helping Pat with the sound check. It would only take them a few minutes to pull on their costumes, they told Mia, so she should stay in the caravan and have a rest. Gemma was reading the crime novel that Mia had given her in the hospital and Luke was keying a long text message into his mobile phone.

'Writing an essay?' Gemma said archly, looking up from her book. The electronic pips were starting to irritate her, making it difficult to concentrate on the plot. She was finding her leg plaster more and more irritating, curtailing all her usual activities and making her unusually crotchety. How she longed to be able to drive once more, walk to the shops, or even walk down the stairs unhampered. Gemma promised herself that she'd never take the simple everyday things for granted again once she was mobile.

'No,' Luke said mildly and resumed his texting.

'Who are you texting?' Gemma asked, ever curious.

Mia looked over and smiled at Luke. 'Pay no attention to my nosy sister,' she said.

'I'm quite used to her,' Luke said. 'It's hard to keep any secrets when she's around. Besides, AbbaFab are like one big, happy family. Isn't that right, Gemma?'

'Absolutely! Or should I say Abbasolutely.'

Mia and Luke laughed.

'So, go on,' Gemma continued, 'who's the lucky girl?'

'I'm sending my mother a birthday message if you must know,' he answered patiently.

Gemma snorted. 'You expect me to believe that? Who's the latest? Go on, spill the beans.'

'Gemma, I don't have a girlfriend at present, as well you know. But as soon as the future Mrs Jackman comes along you'll be the first to meet her, I promise.'

He looked over at Mia and smiled. 'See what I have to put up with, Mia? I have absolutely no private life. And as for my text, I'll prove it to you, Gemma.' He handed Mia his mobile phone. 'Would you mind reading the message out loud for your sister, Mia?' he said rather smugly.

'Hi Mum,' Mia read from the screen of his mobile. 'Will ring later. Hope U R having a lovely birthday. Will call in at weekend with present. Have a great dinner this eve – know Mona is taking you out. Best and much love, Lukey.'

'Lukey!' Gemma laughed. 'I've heard it all now. But I stand corrected. My apologies, Luke. Your reputation is safe for the moment. But Lukey, really!'

'Thank you, Gemma,' Luke said. 'And what does your mum call you then? I'm sure you have a nickname.' Luke's smile dropped off his mouth quickly when he realized what he'd just said. 'Sorry,' he murmured.

'It's fine,' Gemma said evenly. 'And Mum used to call me Charlie if you must know,' she remembered. 'Charlie the Clown, as I always made her laugh. Wendy was Super Star, she was terribly bossy as a child and always wanted to be on the stage.'

Luke laughed. 'No, I can't see that at all.'

'And Mia . . .' Gemma looked over at Mia who was listening with interest.

'I was Little Star,' Mia said softly.

'Yes, you were.' Gemma smiled at her. 'Mum's Little Star. Mum used to say that Mia had the voice of an angel.'

Mia stared at her hands. They didn't talk about Miriam very often, especially in front of others, and she wasn't all that comfortable with the conversation.

'Your mum obviously spotted your potential from an early age, Mia,' Luke said kindly. 'I like that – Little Star. And speaking of stars, you'd better get changed, Mia, or there'll be no Agnetha on the stage this evening.' He studied her face. 'Um, have you started your make-up?'

She laughed. 'No. Don't worry, I'll get cracking.'

'Phew,' he breathed a sigh of relief. 'I didn't want to put my foot in it again, but you don't exactly look ready. Trowel on some sparkly blue eye shadow and some false eyelashes, there's a girl, and you'll be laughing.'

'I'll have a go.'

'Why don't I do it for you?' Gemma suggested. She sat up straighter. 'It'll make me feel useful.'

'Will you do mine too?' Luke asked, lifting one eyebrow suggestively.

'I will not, you big fool.' She swatted him on the leg. 'Go and do your own.'

'Charming,' Luke complained, a smile on his face. 'See what I have to put up with, Mia?'

'Terrible, isn't she?' Mia agreed.

'You'd better be nice to me or I'll give you an Ugly Sister of a make-up job, Mia,' Gemma warned.

'But wonderful at the same time,' Mia corrected herself with a grin.

Luke winked at her and Mia felt the strangest

sensation in the pit of her stomach. She smiled to herself.

'You're always smiling at some private joke or other, Mia Redden,' Gemma said as she dabbed some creamy foundation on to a make-up sponge. Luke had gone into the small caravan bedroom to change. 'I often wonder what's going on in that strange little head of yours.'

'Not much really,' Mia lied. 'Nothing very interesting anyway.'

'Humm,' Gemma murmured. She wasn't so sure. But Mia had always kept herself to herself and she knew she'd get nothing more out of her, especially with Luke practically in the same room.

'He's nice, isn't he?' Mia whispered as Gemma carefully applied Mia's black spider-like false eyelashes.

'Yes, very,' Gemma whispered back, 'but don't go getting any ideas. He's much older than you are.'

'He doesn't look all that old. What age is he?'

'Twenty-eight, I think, or maybe twenty-nine, I can't quite remember.'

'Only four years older than me,' Mia pointed out.

Gemma said nothing.

'But he'd have no interest in someone like me,' Mia continued, fishing. 'I'm sure his girlfriends are all very glamorous.'

'Humm,' Gemma murmured non-committally.

'What was his last girlfriend like?' Mia asked.

'Mia! He's in the next room and the walls are paper-thin. He'll hear us talking about him.'

'Not if we keep whispering,' Mia said, lowering her voice. 'Go on, what was she like?'

'She was a nurse, if you must know.'

'A nurse? Really?'

'Now, you're going to have to keep your lips still while I do your lip-liner. So no more talking, understand? And don't distract me while I finish your false eyelashes either unless you want glue in your eye.'

'OK,' Mia said, 'my lips are sealed. But just one more question. When did they break up?'

'Mia!' Gemma hissed.

Mia cocked her head to one side and gave Gemma one of her Bambi looks.

Gemma gave a tut. 'OK, but this is the last question I'm answering, I mean it.'

'Well? Go on then, when?' Mia asked again.

'Ages ago, before Christmas. Satisfied?'

'Very.' Mia sat back in her chair and closed her mouth. But there was no disguising the smile playing on her lips.

Gemma sighed inwardly. Mia was very naive when it came to men and she didn't want to see her get hurt. Mia had had a serious boyfriend in college, a kind, rather gentle French boy called Yves, but it had all ended in tears when he'd gone back to Paris after graduation. As Gemma pressed the false lashes gently against her sister's eyelids, waiting for the glue to take effect, she told herself there was no point worrying about something that hadn't happened yet. Mia was right – she was hardly Luke's type after all. She'd talk to Wendy about Mia and her crush later, Gemma decided. Maybe Wendy could have a word with Luke. Warn him off. It couldn't hurt.

Mia stood at the back of the large marquee and studied the stage in front of her. It had been constructed from matt grey scaffolding and worn-looking wooden planks and boards, and Mia wondered if it would take their combined weights. They'd given it a brief trial run earlier, but that was without the strains of an hour's worth of moving and dancing to contend with. Mia also hoped her costume didn't rip at the seams. Wendy had made it a little too snug for Mia's liking. And what if she forgot the words of the songs? Or the dance moves? And what if she fainted again? Mia bit her lower lip anxiously. She could both smell and taste the sickly-sweet strawberry lip-gloss that Gemma had doctored her pout with. Mia ran her finger over her top teeth, removing a bright pink gloop of gloss. Great, now I'm going to get gloss all over my white costume, she thought. She wiped the pink residue on to the back of her hand and rubbed it into her skin. It made her hand glisten and she held it up to the light and stared at it.

Luke looked over at her and smiled warmly. His dark blue eyes twinkled in the dim light. Even dressed as Bjorn, in his stage make-up, wig and white jumpsuit, he was a sight for sore eyes. Mia could feel herself blush and thanked Gemma for the heavy stage foundation, concealing her discomfort.

'OK?' Luke whispered.

She nodded. 'Think so,' she whispered back.

'You'll be great,' he said. 'Chin up.'

'Thanks.' He really was nice, Mia thought, smiling to herself again.

The band was waiting backstage listening to the Mayor of Dublin's preamble to an opening speech. The marquee was heaving with bodies – the band had all had a peek several minutes earlier – and the excitement in the air was palpable. AbbaFab were the first band on that evening, and the whole Blackrock Music Festival seemed to have caught the attention of the punters and the local and national media alike. The Mayor was currently talking about Blackrock and its place on the music map, citing south County Dublin luminaries from Bob Geldof and Bono to Sinead O'Connor.

'Get on with the music,' a member of the audience shouted up at him rather rudely. The crowd clapped and cheered in agreement.

'Right, I will,' the Mayor retorted, nonplussed. 'And now, to get the evening off to a stellar start, I have the great honour of introducing one of the most popular tribute bands in Ireland, the great, the amazing Abba-Fab!' The atmospheric 'Arrival' music began to drift from the huge speakers on either side of the stage.

Wendy put her hand on Mia's shoulder and squeezed it. 'Here we go. Break a leg,' she said softly.

Mia nodded wordlessly, gulping back her fear.

Wendy led the band on to the stage. 'Hello, Blackrock,' she said in her mock-Swedish accent. 'I'm Frida, this is Agnetha, Benny and Bjorn, and together we're

AbbaFab.' Ronan and Luke went straight into the opening bars of 'Waterloo', Luke as Bjorn on lead guitar, and Ronan as Benny on keyboards. The crowd cheered. Mia opened her mouth to sing the first line but no sound came out. Wendy, sensing that something like this might happen, was well ahead of her and also kept silent. Ronan and Luke played on as if nothing had happened, embellishing and extending the opening riffs.

Mia looked out into the sea of faces and then back at Wendy. Wendy smiled at her, her eyes twinkling. 'You can do this,' she mouthed. 'Sing.' In the left wing, Mia could see Gemma, whose eyes were glued on her supportively as she gave her a thumbs-up sign. Mia took a deep breath. She had two choices here – she could either sink or swim. And she was damned if she was going to let Wendy and the others down. You can do this, she told herself in Wendy's words, gripping the microphone tightly in her right hand and concentrating on the music. *I* can do this. There was the cue – she opened her mouth and no one was more surprised than Mia at the strength and bell-like clarity of her voice as she sang the first line. Wendy joined in for the second line and the crowd whooped and clapped. By the first chorus, Mia realized that she was operating on autopilot and she wondered why she'd been so nervous. Singing the wonderfully upbeat Abba pop songs, songs she remembered so fondly from her youth, wasn't a chore, it was fun. She turned to the crowd and wiggled her bottom.

Wendy gasped. Gemma cheered Mia on in the wings. Was that really her little sister playing to the audience?

Ronan raised both his eyebrows at Luke. Luke leaned in towards Mia as the last strains of the song filtered out and the crowd began to clap and cheer wildly. 'Well done, Little Star,' he said warmly. No one except Wendy, Gemma and her mum had ever called her that, but after a moment Mia decided that she quite liked it. In fact, she liked it a lot.

'Thanks, Bjorn,' she replied, and gave him a huge smile.

After their set, including a storming encore during which the whole tent joined in, dancing and singing along to a second rendition of 'Waterloo', the band collapsed on to the caravan cushions in one sweaty and excited heap.

'You were fantastic, Mia!' Gemma enthused. 'You're so much better than me.'

'No I'm not!' Mia said, delighted with herself. 'You're just being kind. But I did enjoy it. And the crowd were great, weren't they?'

'Yes, they were,' Ronan agreed, swigging back some water from Wendy's reservoir of bottles.

'I can't believe it was your first gig,' Luke said to Mia. 'You looked so professional out there. You've got some career ahead of you if you want it, Mia.'

'Thanks,' she said a little shyly, smiling at Luke.

He smiled back at her. She blushed and tore her eyes away from his.

Gemma glanced at Wendy. Wendy looked back at her and raised her eyebrows as if to say, 'Did you see that?' Gemma nodded almost imperceptibly.

'Anyone free for a drink after we get changed?' Luke asked, oblivious to Wendy and Gemma's disapproving looks. 'McCarthy's pub on the main street serves a decent pint.'

Ronan looked over at Wendy. 'Wendy?' he asked. 'Fancy a drink?'

'Not really. But you go ahead if you want to,' she said. She was exhausted and a noisy pub was the last place she wanted to spend the remainder of her evening. 'I'd better get back to Nadia and the boys. Don't be too late, mind.'

'I won't be,' Ronan promised. 'Anyone else?'

'Count me in,' Gemma said. 'And I'm sure Pat will join us.' Pat was loading the van with their instruments.

'Actually he's going straight home,' Ronan said. 'He'll see us on Friday at the wedding in Killiney.'

Mia pricked up her ears. 'I though the wedding was on Saturday.' She turned towards Wendy. 'You said the weekend, Wendy.'

'Did I?' Wendy said a little vaguely. 'Sorry, I probably did. I guess the weekend always starts early for us, I'm afraid. You can still do it, can't you?'

'Yes,' Mia said. 'And at least we're not working tomorrow.'

Wendy sighed. 'I wish that was the case, Mia. But we need to spend a couple of hours practising to get you up to speed for the wedding. And I still have to alter Gemma's blue jumpsuit for you, you'll be wearing it on Friday. The alterations shop is too busy so I'll have to do it myself. I'll need you to try it on for me. I'm sorry.'

'That's OK,' Mia said evenly. 'There goes my life!' She smiled.

'So how about that drink, Mia?' Luke asked. 'Wendy won't need you all day, will you, Wendy?'

'I suppose not,' Wendy said. 'I have bookings to confirm, I can do that in the morning and give you a bit of a lie-in, Mia.' Wendy had no idea why she was encouraging Mia to go out drinking with Luke, but she didn't have the energy to protest. It would sound petty. And besides, Ronan would be there to chaperone.

Luke grinned at Mia. 'See! All the more reason to come out for a little while this evening.'

'Thanks,' Mia said, 'but I have to go home. My friend Alva is staying with me and I don't like to leave her on her own for too long.'

'Still? How long is she staying for?' Wendy asked.

Mia sighed. 'I'm not exactly sure, to be honest.' She figured she might as well tell Wendy the truth – there didn't seem to be any point in keeping it a secret any longer, not now that Sean seemed to have another girlfriend. 'Alva and Sean have broken up. I was hoping they'd work things out but it doesn't look like that's going to happen, unfortunately. So she'll be staying with me until she finds her own place.'

Ronan whistled. 'Poor Alva.'

'That's awful,' Gemma agreed. 'They seemed so happy.'

'Appearances can be deceptive,' Wendy said. There was silence for a moment.

'Well, why don't you ring your friend and tell her to meet us there?' Luke suggested. 'If she's feeling a little down right now a night out might be just what she needs.'

Gemma snorted. 'Yeah, right! So you can hit on her, Luke?'

'Gemma! That's a terrible thing to say,' Luke said.

Mia felt uneasy. Maybe Luke wasn't the gentleman she thought he was. Otherwise why would Gemma have said such a thing? 'I don't think she'd be ready for . . .' she began.

'Mia,' Luke said gently. 'Do you really think I'd take advantage of someone when they're that vulnerable? Going through a break-up is hard on everyone. Were they together long?'

'Years,' Mia said quietly. 'Since school.'

Luke winced. 'Poor girl. I know how tough that can be.'

Wendy laughed. 'Luke Jackman, you're not telling us that you've been unlucky in love, are you?'

Luke smiled enigmatically at her. 'Wendy, there's a lot you don't know about me.'

Mia looked at him. He caught her eye and smiled

back. 'Do ask your friend to join us, Mia. Trust me, I'll be the perfect gentleman.'

'OK,' she said, for some reason believing him, 'I will.'

'That's sorted then,' Luke said. 'Now, let's get out of these bloody costumes, troops. McCarthy's awaits.'

'Can I have a word with you before you go to the pub?' Wendy asked Ronan as he stepped carefully over Gemma's plaster-flexed leg on his way to the far side of the caravan. 'After you've changed.'

'Sure,' Ronan said a little uneasily. There was a slight edge to Wendy's voice and he feared he was in for a private roasting. When Wendy was tired she had a tongue like a whip when she chose to unleash it.

Wendy leaned against the car and waited for Ronan who was bantering with Mia. 'No more of that bum-wiggling now, you hear, young lady?' he joked as he finished packing Wendy's car full of the AbbaFab costumes. 'We don't encourage that sort of behaviour.'

'Yeah, yeah. Course you don't,' Mia thumped Ronan's arm playfully, then turned towards Wendy. 'Anything else to do, Wendy?' she asked as Ronan slammed the boot closed.

'No, that's it,' Wendy said shortly.

'Right,' Mia said. She knew Wendy wanted to talk to Ronan alone and she pitied her poor brother-in-law: Wendy was definitely in a bad mood. 'See you tomorrow. What time?'

'Is two OK?' Wendy asked.

'Two's fine. See you then.' Mia skipped off in the direction of McCarthy's pub. Luke and Gemma were already waiting for her there. She'd phoned Alva a little earlier and Alva'd said she'd be more than pleased to meet them after she'd changed. It would help take her mind off Sean, she'd said.

'Ronan, please try not to wake up the boys when you come in,' Wendy began. 'Or me for that matter. I'm wrecked and I could do with a good night's sleep.'

Ronan gave her a hug, but she didn't respond with all that much enthusiasm so he drew back quickly. 'I'll try not to. I'll have a few pints and then come straight home. I want to do some writing in the morning. The closing date for the Irish song contest for the Eurovision is only a few weeks away and I think I'm on to something.'

Wendy smiled. Ronan had been writing songs for as long as she'd known him, but he had yet to have one recorded or win any of the competitions he'd entered. But she admired his eternal optimism.

'And don't forget about fixing the spare mic,' she reminded him. 'And we have to do some more work with Mia in the afternoon, remember? For the wedding.'

'Gemma has already said she'll help. And Luke can fix . . .'

Wendy cut him off with a deep sigh. 'I'm a bit worried about Luke and Mia, to tell the truth,' she said in a low voice. 'Did you see the way she was looking at him earlier, all puppy-dog eyes? He'd chew her up and spit her out! I really don't want to see her get hurt.'

'Wendy!' Ronan said. 'That's unfair. Luke's a good guy and he'd never do anything to hurt Mia.'

'Ronan,' she continued, 'he might not mean to, but Mia . . . well, Mia's Mia.' She shrugged. 'I worry about her. I can't help it.'

'There's no need to, Wendy. She's not a child any more. Stop fussing.'

Wendy's face dropped and he instantly regretted his last comment. 'Sorry,' he said, 'I shouldn't have said that. You have every right to worry about her, but really, Wendy, there's no need, she's fine. But I'll keep an eye on her tonight if it will make you happy. Listen, why don't I come home now and we can have an early night together? I can ring Luke. He won't mind.'

'No, it's OK,' Wendy said. 'You need a night out. I'll go home and take a long bath and watch some bad television. I need to do the supermarket shopping on the Internet anyway if we're to have any food for the weekend. I don't have time to shop tomorrow. Honestly, Ronan, it's fine. Go on, I'll see you later.'

'Are you sure?'

'Yes! Sorry for being snappy. I'm just tired.'

Ronan smiled at her. 'You go home and put your feet up, you deserve it. Watch a movie or something. I'm sure Nadia will have the boys in bed by now.'

'Good idea,' she said. 'And I'm sorry for having a go at you about the mic, it'll wait. Or as you say, Luke can do it. Have a nice evening. And try not to wake me up when you come in.'

'I won't,' he promised again. 'And I'm sorry for saying that about Mia. I know you and Gemma worry about her. But she's fine, really she is.' He leaned over and gave her a kiss. 'See you later.'

Wendy stood and watched as Ronan walked away from the car. She opened the car door and stepped in. And there she sat, arms slumped over the steering wheel, analysing what had just happened. She and Ronan seemed to spend their lives apologizing to each other at the moment. And she was getting tired of it. It hadn't always been like that. What had happened to their relationship, their marriage? They hadn't spent an evening alone together for weeks. She couldn't remember the last time they'd gone out for a meal or to the cinema together, and their sex life had become more of a chore than anything else. Frankly, she was so tired most evenings that she just couldn't be bothered. If it weren't for Ronan's persistence, they wouldn't have a sex life at all.

Wendy looked up. The sky was darkening and a light spitty drizzle was falling on the windscreen. She'd better get home. She turned the key in the ignition and before reversing out, switched on the radio and tuned it to Lyric FM. She needed to listen to something calm and soothing as she could feel her nerves jingling and jangling under her skin. She thought about Ronan. Maybe they could take a holiday, just the two of them – a two- or three-day break to somewhere like Rome or Paris, somewhere romantic. They certainly needed a romantic injection of some sort to get their relationship back on track. Wendy sighed. She was worried – worried about Mia, about her marriage, about her workload. And she hated worrying, it was so tiring and not in the least bit productive. Yet she couldn't help it. She wished she had something to take her mind off things.

'Stop it!' she admonished herself. 'Get home and have a bath. You'll feel better then. Stop feeling so sorry for yourself – and thank God that there's nothing really wrong with you or your life.' But she knew there was something wrong – she just couldn't quite put her finger on it.

Later that evening, on their way home from the pub, Mia and Alva decided to satisfy their drink-induced carbohydrate craving in the local chipper. It was heaving: most of Blackrock's pub dwellers had obviously had the same idea. Ronan and Luke were bringing Gemma home in a taxi as she was legless, in more ways than one. When Luke had ordered champagne to celebrate Mia's first gig, the barman had looked at him sideways.

'Champagne?' he'd asked. 'Don't know if we have any, mate. Not much call for it in here to tell the truth.' But he managed to find some dusty bottles of Moët in the cellar, which had turned out to be very nice indeed and he'd insisted on giving them to Luke, makeshift ice bucket and all (a small plastic basin), for next to nothing. They'd had to drink it out of wine glasses, champagne flutes being one request too many, but no one had minded.

'Special night for the blonde lady, is it?' the barman had said kindly. 'Thought I recognized her all right from AbbaFab – hard to be sure with those wigs on though – caught the first few songs before I had to come in here. Good band. The Missus loves Abba.' One bottle had turned into three by the end of the night, and, with a couple of pints each, except for Mia, who was restricting herself to champagne, the evening had ended on a decidedly high note.

And Luke had, as he'd promised, been the perfect gentleman. He'd even spent a good hour listening to Alva talk about Sean and how much she missed him. Mia had felt more than a little jealous until just after eleven, when Alva had slipped to the toilet. Gemma and Ronan were deep in conversation at the far side of the table.

'Alva's lovely,' Luke said to Mia, shifting along the pub seat towards her. 'It's such a pity that things with Sean didn't work out. But I'm sorry.'

'For what?' Mia asked.

'For not spending more time with you this evening.'

'Oh?' Mia's heart lifted.

'I wanted to get to know you better. We will be working together after all.'

'Oh,' Mia said, disappointed. She'd been hoping that their connection went deeper than mere work. But maybe it had all been in her mind.

Luke looked into her eyes. 'Are you all right?'

'Sure.' She took a sip of her now flat champagne. Apt, she thought to herself. To be honest, she'd had quite enough to drink and was only sipping to find something to do with her hands.

'Do you need some air?' Luke suggested. 'I could go outside with you if you like.'

Just then, Mia spotted Alva walking back towards them. 'Thanks, but I'm OK, really,' she said, disappointed again. She would have loved to go outside with Luke – to have him all to herself – but she couldn't leave Alva. Besides, the cool night air always had a bad effect on her at first when she'd been drinking and she'd be mortified if she did or said anything inappropriate. Plus, Alva was a little drunk and it was about time they started to make tracks. Mia wanted to get her friend home in one piece. 'We'd better get going. Alva has to work tomorrow and I have to practise with Wendy, remember?'

'Lucky old you.' Luke smiled. 'Maybe we could go out for dinner one night? What do you think?'

'Um,' she murmured. 'I'm not sure. With the band, you mean?'

'No, just the two of us.' He smiled at her. 'A proper date,' he added just to make himself crystal-clear.

'I'd like that,' she murmured as Alva sat back down beside them. Her heart leaped. Yes! she thought to herself. It wasn't my imagination. He does like me.

'What are you pair talking about?' Alva asked with a grin. 'You look as thick as thieves.'

'You, Alva,' Luke said smoothly. 'And how lovely

you look tonight. Green really suits you. It highlights the hazel flecks in your eyes.'

Alva laughed. 'You old charmer,' she said, chuffed that he'd noticed.

As Alva and Mia waited in the queue at the chip shop, Alva checked her face on the surface of the diamond-shiny stainless-steel counter.

'I'm getting fat,' she moaned. She pointed at her flushed face and poked her cheek with a finger. 'Look!'

'No you're not,' Mia insisted. 'You look great.'

Alva lifted her head. 'Speaking of great, that Luke's a bit of all right,' she said. 'What do you think?'

Mia shrugged her shoulders. 'He's not bad if you like that kind of thing.'

'What's not to like?' Alva demanded. 'He's not exactly hard on the eye. And he's a really good listener. A real sweetie.'

'I wouldn't have thought of him as sweet, to tell the truth,' Mia said.

'Two singles,' the woman behind the counter said loudly.

'That's us!' Alva said wryly.

The woman smiled at her. 'Join the club, love. Wrapped separately?'

Mia nodded. 'Please.'

'Salt and vinegar?'

'Lots!' Alva said.

As they walked out of the chipper, steaming, greasy brown paper bags in their hands, Alva said, 'I'm starting to feel a little better about the whole Sean thing.'

'Really?' Mia asked.

'Yes. Thanks to you.' Alva gave her a hug, stumbling slightly on the pavement and sending Mia lurching sideways.

'It's nothing,' Mia said, supporting Alva's weight. 'You're squashing my chips, woman!'

'Sorry,' Alva said, letting go and straightening up. 'I love you, Mia.'

'I love you too.' Mia grinned. 'Now, let's get you home.'

Early the following evening, Mia was sitting in a café in Monkstown waiting for Sean. She was a little paranoid that Alva would somehow find out about their rendezvous, so she'd chosen a discreet table towards the back of the café, tucked behind a rather large and leafy potted plant. He'd rung to say he was on his way, but he was already ten minutes late. Still, Mia didn't mind. She'd just spent three hours with Wendy and Gemma practising songs over and over again, as well as being prodded, poked and needlepricked by Wendy, so she figured she deserved a large coffee and something sweet and full of calories. After the bustle of the afternoon, she was rather enjoying sitting quietly on her own, flicking through the newspaper that someone had fortuitously left behind them.

'Hi, Mia.' Sean bent down and kissed her on the

cheek. 'Sorry I'm late.' He pulled out the chair beside her and sat down.

Once they'd placed their order Mia said, 'So, tell me all about Sadie.'

'Jeepers, woman,' Sean complained. 'You don't waste much time, do you?'

Mia cocked one eyebrow.

'OK, OK.' He smiled. 'On the understanding that you hear me out without interruption, Mia.'

Mia put one hand in the air. 'Scout's honour.'

'You weren't in the Scouts,' he said. 'You were in the Guides, remember.'

'Sounds better than Guide's honour,' Mia reasoned.

'I suppose it does.'

'So?' Mia asked. 'Go on, tell me all about Sadie.'

Sean satisfied Mia's curiosity. And she didn't like what she heard. Not one little bit. She decided she'd have to do something about this Sadie lady. But what?

5 'Voulez-Vous?'

In the early hours of Thursday morning, after the session in McCarthy's pub with Luke, Mia, Alva and Gemma, Ronan jabbed his door key in the general direction of the lock of his front door. 'Clink.' He'd hit metal all right – but the doorknocker, not the lock.

'Damn,' he muttered. 'Must try harder.' He squinted up his eyes and tried to focus on the lock. It was no use, Wendy hadn't left the outside light on and the navy-blue door was only dimly illuminated by the grubby street light on the opposite side of the road to their semi.

'I know,' he murmured. He put both hands on the door and felt his way along the paintwork, Braille-like. 'Aha,' he said as he came across the lock. He tried the key again, this time it went in a little way but then stopped. He thought he'd better not try and force it – even in his less than lucid state, he knew that Wendy would kill him if he broke the key in the lock again.

He pulled out the key and then had a brainwave.

Maybe it was upside down. He tried again, this time with more success.

'Bingo,' he said as the door swung open. He staggered in and slammed it behind him with his shoulder.

'Oops.' He snorted with laughter. 'Quiet!' Wendy was going to be mad with him for waking her up – she was a light sleeper and usually woke at the slightest disturbance.

He cocked his ears. Nothing. Good, she must still be asleep. And the boys and Nadia were all heavy sleepers so he didn't have to worry about them.

Ronan looked at the stairs ahead of him – Will I manage all of those without waking Wendy up?' he wondered. Doubtful, he decided after a few moments swaying on his feet. Maybe I should drink some water. And take some of those fizzy vitamin C tablets. And some painkillers. Might have a bit of a headache in the morning otherwise. Shouldn't have drunk all that champagne. Or gone to that nightclub with Luke after dropping Gemma home. And that red wine in the nightclub wasn't the best.

Ronan walked slowly into the kitchen. 'Shush,' he told himself as he closed the kitchen door carefully behind him, remembering Wendy this time. He flicked on the lights and winced slightly as the brightness hit his pupils, causing them to widen.

As soon as he saw the fridge he remembered that he hadn't had dinner, and sure, wouldn't a nice feed be just what the doctor ordered? He wrenched open the fridge door with a loud clink of the sauce and jam jars. Excellent! Ronan smiled to himself – eggs, sausages *and* bacon – his mouth watered in anticipation. He could have a lovely big fry-up!

He pulled a frying pan out of the pan drawer with a clatter and clunked it on to the ceramic surface of the hob. Then he gnawed open the thick plastic packaging on the bacon, wrestled out three rashers and threw them into the pan. He listened for the satisfying sizzle. Nothing. Then he remembered – he hadn't turned on the hob. So he turned the dial and waited. Within a few seconds the ring began to glow red and the bacon started to sizzle. He then dropped four sausages into the pan, jumping back as hot fat splattered on to his hand.

'Damn,' he muttered, licking the fat. He turned down the heat. Then he pulled an egg out of its cardboard egg-carton bed and cracked it on the side of the pan. Unfortunately he applied a little too much force and the sticky innards fell straight on to the kitchen counter and then slithered their way on to the floor tiles.

'Feck!' he swore, bending down to pick it up. He tried to scoop the egg yolk up with his hand but lost his balance and banged his forehead on the kitchen cabinet instead. He stood up gingerly, rubbing his temple. He looked at the egg carton. Maybe eggs weren't such a good idea after all.

He abandoned the eggs and prodded a sausage with his finger. It was warm but still a sickly pink colour. He decided to sit down at the kitchen table and take the weight off his feet. The tiles were slippery under the soles of his shoes, still covered in an egg slick, and he almost lost his balance again. 'Slowly,' he murmured, 'slowly.' Once sitting safely on a kitchen chair, he slumped over the table and rested his head on his hands. He was feeling rather sleepy so he thought he'd have a rest, a little one mind you, just until his fry was ready.

Wendy sat up in bed, startled. She looked to her left; no Ronan – he couldn't have come home yet. What the hell was that shrill noise? It sounded like the smoke alarm. She listened for a moment. It *was* the smoke alarm, she decided. She immediately pushed herself up, swung her legs out of the bed, ran to the door, threw it open and stepped into the hall. There was a terrible smell of burning – she sniffed the air and put her head over the banisters – and it seemed to be coming from downstairs. Her heart began to race and her head was thrown into a blind panic. The house was on fire! The boys! She rushed into their room.

'Get up, quickly. There's a fire.' She put both her hands on Greg's shoulders – he was the heavier sleeper of the two – and shook him firmly.

He opened his eyes and looked up at her. 'A fire?' he mumbled sleepily. 'Where?'

'Downstairs,' Wendy said, trying to keep calm. Please God, she thought, give me enough time to get my boys out.

'What's happening?' Steve asked, his head hanging over the top bunk, blond hair spilling over his rapidly blinking eyes.

'There's a fire in the house. You both have to go outside, quickly. I'll wake Nadia. Wait for me in the front garden, OK?'

'What about Dad?' Greg asked, climbing out of bed.

'He's still out,' Wendy replied. 'Hurry up.'

Nadia met them all on the landing. 'What's that noise?' she said sleepily.

'Outside boys, now!' Wendy said loudly.

For once they did as they were told, racing down the stairs, opening the front door and walking outside. They're going to freeze, Wendy thought as it registered that Steve had no pyjama top on.

'Where are the boys going?' Nadia asked in confusion.

Wendy put her arm around the girl's shoulders and ushered her towards the top of the stairs. 'There's a fire, Nadia. Come on, we have to get outside.' She grabbed some coats from the hooks by the door on her way out.

Once in front of the house, Wendy turned towards Nadia. 'Keep an eye on the boys, I'm going back in.' She handed Nadia the coats. 'Here. Keep warm.'

'Is it safe to go back?' Nadia asked, taking the coats off Wendy. 'There's many smoke in the hall.'

'I'll be careful,' Wendy promised. 'And I have to get to the phone to ring the fire brigade.'

'You go, I look after the boys.' Nadia shivered. It was a cool evening and she was only wearing a skimpy vest top and some thin cotton pyjama bottoms. She threw one of the coats, a large black fleece of Ronan's, over her shoulders, swamping her slight frame. 'Come here you two,' she said kindly. 'I get you warm.' She shrugged coats over their slight bodies. Greg and Steve watched their mother walk back into the house with wide eyes.

'Mum!' Greg said, running towards Wendy, the coat falling off his shoulders and landing on the grass in his wake.

Wendy turned back and put her hand up. 'Stay with Nadia!' she said firmly. 'I'll be fine. And don't get cold.'

She walked back inside. The hall smelt of smoke. She looked at the kitchen door. There were curls of noxious-smelling smoke wafting under it. She put her hands on the surface of the wood – it felt cool to the touch. She put her ear to the door; she could hear something all right, but couldn't quite make out what it was. What was going on in there? She knew she probably shouldn't open the door but she wanted to know the extent of the damage before she rang the fire brigade. After all, she didn't want to call them out unnecessarily. But if it was bad ... she suddenly remembered the fire extinguisher and fire blanket under the stairs. She pulled open the cupboard and reefed them both off their fixtures on the wall. At least this way she'd go in prepared.

Suddenly she felt a tap on her shoulder. Her heart leaped into her throat and she screamed in fright. She swung around violently.

'Wendy?' Ronan was standing in front of her. 'Easy! It's only me. Do we have a fire blanket?'

The door to the kitchen was open now and smoke was billowing out in a foggy, swirling mass.

'What the hell are you doing?' she shouted at him. 'Close that door. There's a fire. Where were you?'

'In the kitchen,' he said loudly over the still-ringing smoke alarm. 'The pan's on fire.'

'What pan?' Wendy demanded in confusion. What the hell was he talking about?

'I was frying some rashers and I fell asleep,' Ronan explained.

Wendy stared at him: his eyes were droopy and his facial features slack – it was a look she was all too accustomed to. 'Are you mad?' she screamed, pushing past him. 'You drunken idiot.'

She dropped the fire extinguisher at his feet and pushed roughly past him, opening the fire blanket as she entered the kitchen. Ronan was right – flames and smoke were engulfing the frying pan. Wendy screwed her eyes up, the smoke was starting to make them water. She walked towards the hob and placed the fire blanket over the burning pan. Within seconds the smoke diminished. She ran over to the back door, turned the key with her shaking hands and swung it open. Then she grabbed the oven gloves, pulled them on, picked the frying pan up by its handle and carefully walked towards the back door, down the step and over the decking. She could feel the heat of the handle beneath her palms but luckily the padded oven gloves were nice and thick. She put the pan down on the gravel of the patio, where it settled on to the damp stones with one last dramatic sizzle.

Wendy watched the smoking pan and began to cry, huge hot tears of relief flooding down her face. 'Wendy?' She heard Ronan's voice behind her. 'I turned the smoke alarm off. Are you all right? I'm so sorry. I can't believe I was so stupid. I'd never do anything to intentionally hurt you or the kids, you know that.'

She ignored him.

'Wendy?' he said again. 'Talk to me.'

'Oh, Ronan!' she said, spinning around to face him. 'You could have killed us all. I know you didn't mean to, but that doesn't excuse your behaviour.'

'I'm sorry . . .' he began.

She strode past him, through the still-smoky kitchen, into the hall and back outside, wiping away the tears with the back of her hands.

'Is everything all right?' Nadia asked with concern. Wendy looked on the verge of tears.

'Yes, thank goodness. The frying pan was on fire. Everything's fine now. Nothing to worry about.' She put her arms around the boys, spooning one in on either side and sheltering them under her strong arms. 'How are my two big boys?' she asked in what she hoped was a calm manner.

'Mum, is the house going to burn down?' Steve asked, morbidly excited at the thought.

'No, love. It was a false alarm,' Wendy said.

'You have wet bits on your face,' Greg said, his face pale. The whole experience had obviously worried him. 'Are you crying?'

'No,' Wendy said, shaking her head. 'It's water

from, um, putting out the fire.' Luckily Greg seemed to accept this unquestioningly.

Steve rubbed his eyes and yawned. 'Can we go back to bed now?'

Wendy smiled at him. Nothing fazed him. She patted him gently on the head. 'Yes, love, of course you can.'

Greg looked up at her with a worried expression on his face. 'Is the house safe, Mum?'

'Yes. Your dad just had an accident with the frying pan.'

'An accident?'

'That's right.' Wendy didn't want to get into it. She was livid with Ronan, who was wisely keeping out of her way.

'Where's Dad?' Greg asked looking around. 'Dad!' he shouted.

'He's busy fixing the kitchen,' Wendy said. She had no idea what he was doing but the boys worshipped their dad and thought he could do no wrong. To her knowledge, they'd never seen him drunk and she didn't want their illusions shattered – not at this young age. He could be knocking back a swift whiskey right at this very minute, she thought, and then checked herself for being unkind. She knew that Ronan was distraught about what he'd done, but she wasn't going to let him off lightly. Chastising him in front of Nadia and the boys wasn't the answer, however. 'Now, go upstairs like good fellows and I'll be up to you in a few minutes. Nadia, can you see they get into bed? I need to clean the kitchen.'

'No problem,' Nadia said. She wondered where Ronan really was but didn't like to ask. Recently she had heard them arguing in bed late at night, usually after Ronan had been out, Wendy's raised voice cutting through the darkness. Nadia hated to hear them fighting but Nadia wasn't naive enough to think that all marriages were perfect.

Wendy saw the boys up the stairs and then went back into the kitchen. It smelt terrible and there were sooty black silhouettes on the wall behind the hob and the ceiling above it.

'My beautiful kitchen,' she murmured, staring at the smoke damage.

'Wendy?' Ronan lifted his head from the kitchen table where he'd been waiting for her. He didn't dare start to clean up without her – he might make things even worse. 'I'm so sorry. I'll clean up, you go up to bed.'

'Thanks for the offer,' she said, 'but I'll do it myself. You go on up. I'm come up when I'm finished. I'd prefer to do it on my own if you don't mind.'

'I'm so sorry, Wendy,' Ronan said again. 'You're right, I'm an idiot. I won't drink again, I promise. Ever.'

Wendy sighed. She knew it was an empty promise and she was too tired to have this conversation. She opened the cupboard under the kitchen sink and took out a tube of J-cloths and some cleaning materials. The kitchen walls would have to be repainted but some of the smoke stains might come off the units, she hoped. She'd do as much as she could now, and leave the back door and all the kitchen windows open while she was working – that way the smell might not be so bad in the morning. She eased a pair of tight-fitting yellow rubber gloves over her hands, squirted some cleaning fluid on to one of the cloths and set to work on the charred-black counter top beside the cooker.

'Can I help?' Ronan asked tentatively. 'Please?'

Wendy ignored him for a moment, then murmured, 'No, go up to bed.'

He pulled another J-cloth out of the tube. Wendy spun around, tears in her eyes. She was tired to the bone and she really didn't need this. 'Ronan, I need to be alone right now. Go on upstairs. Please, just go.'

'OK,' he said reluctantly. 'I'll see you in the morning. I'll ring a painter first thing. Is there anything else I can do?'

'No,' Wendy whispered. 'Nothing.'

'I'm so sorry . . .' he began.

'I know you are. That makes two of us. Goodnight, Ronan,' Wendy said quietly, turning her back on him again.

As she scrubbed at the wall behind the cooker with all her might, taking as much of the sooty shadows off as was humanly possible, she sobbed. It wasn't the first time Ronan had come home blind drunk, but he'd never endangered his family before. Usually he just fell asleep on the sofa with the television blaring, or came home with kebab stains all over the front of his shirt. Once he'd fallen asleep with a large glass of red wine balanced on his chest, which had subsequently fallen, staining all his clothes and the living-room sofa in the process. She'd had to get the sofa re-covered in the end. But this was different – and it had to stop.

The following morning, Wendy woke and turned to see if Ronan was awake, but he wasn't beside her. Then she remembered what had happened last night. She was sure she could still smell smoke, even in their bedroom with the door firmly closed. She had a raging headache and she felt as though she hadn't slept at all. She hadn't made it to bed until after five in the morning and her head had been so full of spinning thoughts that, exhausted though she was, she'd found it difficult to sleep.

She dragged herself out of bed. She could hear the boys and Nadia in the hall. Thank goodness for Nadia – what would she do without her? She suddenly realized how much she relied on the au pair and vowed to give her a pay rise and some extra time off.

Wendy grabbed her waffle-cotton dressing gown from the back of the door and put her weary arms through the generously large armholes. Was it her imagination or did it also smell of smoke? She sniffed it suspiciously. It wasn't the dressing gown. She ran her hands through her hair and held them up to her nose. It was her hair and skin – her whole body reeked of smoke. She opened the door and walked into the hall. She could hear voices coming from the kitchen. She padded down the stairs wearily.

'Morning. How's everyone after last night's little excitement?' she asked, slapping a big smile on her face for the sake of the boys. Ronan, Nadia, Greg and Steve all looked up from the kitchen table.

'Are you still mad with Daddy?' Steve asked astutely.

'Don't talk with your mouth full,' Wendy admonished. 'And no, I don't have time to be mad with Daddy. I have far too much to do today. And anyway it wasn't really his fault,' she added generously.

Ronan smiled at her gratefully. 'I phoned the painter. I told him it was an emergency and he's going to come over this evening.'

'This evening? Are you sure?' Wendy asked. Painters were notoriously difficult to pin down in Dublin.

'Yes,' Ronan assured her. What he didn't tell her was that he'd offered to pay the man a whopping 100 euros an hour for his trouble.

'Good. Well done.' Wendy was relieved. 'I have to have a shower now, I reek of smoke. Ronan, are you OK to take the boys to school?'

'Sure.'

Wendy nodded at him. 'Thanks. I have to drop my car in for a service. I'll be gone for at least an hour or so. And Mia and Gemma will be here at two.' She looked at her watch and sighed. No time for breakfast this morning, not if she wanted to shower, and she couldn't bear the lingering smell of smoke for one minute longer.

'Nadia, can you collect the boys later? I'll be putting Mia through her paces in the garage. And if you're in this morning, would you mind leaving the back door and the kitchen windows open? It's still very smoky in here.'

'No problem. And no worry, I make sure they do homework later,' Nadia said.

'And can we make chocolate buns this afternoon, Nadia?' Greg asked her, anticipation written all over his little face. 'Please? You promised.'

'Can we use kitchen, Wendy?' Nina asked.

'What time is the painter coming at?' Wendy asked Ronan.

'He said sixish.'

'As long as everything is tidied away by six that's fine. Thanks, Nadia.'

'No problem. I feed the boys early and we be go of kitchen by six.'

'Perfect.' Wendy smiled warmly at Nadia. Her English still wasn't quite there but she was getting better. 'Thanks, Nadia. I really appreciate it. Now, I have to have a shower and get going. I'm in a bit of a rush. See you all later.'

Ronan waited for his customary goodbye kiss but none was proffered. 'Bye, Wendy,' he said to her disappearing back. 'Hope the service goes well.' He was going to keep well out of her way until this evening, he decided. And in the meantime he'd do all those jobs around the house that he'd been promising to do – like putting up bookshelves in Greg and Steve's room and fixing the loo seat in the downstairs bathroom. Hopefully that would get him back in Wendy's good books. He'd forget about the song-writing session.

Shame, though, he nearly had his Eurovision song nailed. If only he could come up with some catchy lyrics.

Wendy drove to the garage in Deansgrange and parked in the designated area. One of the hazard lights on the dashboard had been flashing on and off intermittently for the last week and was worrying her, and one of the brake-light bulbs needed replacing. Unfortunately the service did take a large chunk out of her already jam-packed day. The answering machine at home was full of unanswered calls – several had come in this morning by fax – and her computer had seventy-seven unopened emails sitting on it. She also had to chase up several unpaid invoices, pay some bills in the Credit Union, do the Internet shopping which she hadn't got around to doing last night, ring the phone company about an annoying buzzing on the line, and pay her television licence in the post office – all in the space of one day. And that didn't include working with Mia in the afternoon and making alterations to Gemma's blue satin jumpsuit. Where was she going to find the time? Plus there was a fabulous Victorian house on show in Sandycove that she was dying to see. She could check it out online, she supposed, but it wasn't the same as seeing it in the flesh. But she really didn't have time today, that was for sure. Or on Saturday. She'd have to arrange a private viewing the following week. What an exciting life, Wendy sighed. Tonight would be another thrilling late night at the computer finalizing bookings, answering emails and sending out invoices, she supposed. She switched off the car engine and pulled the keys out of the ignition.

'Wendy Redden.' She handed the relevant documents to the man behind the desk in the garage office. 'My car's here for a service.'

He checked his desk diary and then looked up at her. 'You're bang on time,' he said. 'Can you go and wait by your car, please, and one of the mechanics will be out to you shortly? And if you can leave the service book on the front seat that would be great. Once he's taken the keys off you, you can wait over there if you like.' He gestured at a sofa.

'Thanks,' Wendy said. 'How long will it take, do you think?'

The man rubbed one of his eyes with an oil-stained knuckle. 'Hard to tell really. Depends what needs to be done. I'd say about an hour. Maybe an hour and a half tops.'

'Thanks, that's great.' Wendy was glad she'd brought some paperwork to do.

She went back outside and leaned against her Volkswagen Golf. It was a reliable little car and she'd never had any problems with it. It wasn't exactly the most luxurious thing on four wheels, but it did the job.

'Excuse me, Miss.' A young man dressed in oil-stained blue overalls walked towards her, wiping his hands on his thighs.

'Yes, sorry, can I help you?' Wendy asked him.

He smiled at her. 'Keys?'

'Yes, of course.' Wendy handed them over. 'One of

the hazard lights on the dashboard keeps coming on, and one of the brake-light bulbs has just gone. The one on the right.'

The mechanic nodded. 'No problem.'

The man in question was actually rather attractive in a rough-and-ready sort of way. He was tall and lean with strong-looking shoulders and a fine head of silky dark brown hair. And he filled his overalls rather well, Wendy thought.

Snap out of it! she admonished herself swiftly. You're a married woman and a mother of two. But I do miss the thrill of the chase, she thought wistfully as she watched the man drive her car into the test building. Ronan's a good husband but . . . A glimmer of the single, up-for-anything girl she used to be nudged its way into her mind and planted itself there. Wendy hadn't always been the sensible one in the family after all. She'd been wild in her own way, a fact she was strangely proud of now. Not that Gemma or Mia knew anything about her former life, of course. She'd always been careful to shield it from them.

Wendy sat down on one of the hard plastic seats in the waiting area and worked for a while before allowing her mind to wander. Damn the paperwork, she didn't have the energy to do any more. She was so tired; her lids felt heavy and her eyes gritty. She closed them slowly and sat back, resting her head against the wall behind her. She began to drift away, allowing her imagination to fly.

'Hello,' the mechanic said to her in her daydream. 'I need some help. Are you free?'

'Why, yes. How can I help you?'

He grinned at her. His overalls were gaping open. Her eyes rested on his firm, tanned chest, exposed to his waist. Not a hair in sight, Wendy noticed. Like a model from a glossy magazine. That's it, he's a model in his spare time. And he's in a band, she added. He's the lead singer. She'd always had a thing about singers.

'Follow me,' he said.

He led her by the hand towards a room at the back of the garage and closed the door behind them. Wendy looked around. There was nothing in it except a large desk and an office chair. He locked the door and gave her another wide grin.

'You're incredibly hot,' he said. 'Has anyone ever told you that?'

'Not for a long time,' Wendy said. 'So what's on your mind?'

'I think you know.' He moved towards her and stood in front of her.

Wendy could feel her breath quicken. The mechanic smelt of fresh sweat and his skin glistened in the light. His chocolate-brown eyes smouldered. She put out a hand and ran it down his taut chest. He grabbed her hand and pulled her towards him. She gasped. He began to kiss her passionately, his tongue probing her mouth forcefully. He moved her towards the desk and pushed her down on to its surface. She could feel the hardness of the wood against her back.

'Tell me you want me too,' he said in a low growl, pressing his body against hers.

'Wendy? Wendy Redden. Is that you?'

Wendy reluctantly snapped herself back to reality and opened her eyes. An attractive blond man was standing in front of her, smiling widely. He looked vaguely familiar but she couldn't quite place him.

'It's Des, you know, from Westport – Henry's friend? You look a little flushed – are you all right?'

'Um, yes, fine,' Wendy mumbled. She sat up and willed her cheeks to cool down. Of course, Des Sullivan. But he'd changed almost beyond recognition. He used to be the bad boy of the set they'd hung around with when the Reddens had lived in Westport, County Mayo, before Mia was born – all long, dirty-blond hair, black leather biker jacket, torn stone-washed jeans, crooked teeth and crooked smile. All the girls were mad about him, Wendy included, but he was always flitting from one girl to another. She noticed that he still had that tiny scar on his eyebrow – the one she knew for a fact that he'd got running through a glass door as a child, and not in a fight, as he'd always claimed to his peers.

'I'm not surprised you didn't recognize me,' he continued, sitting down beside her. 'It's been an age. I've been living in Sydney for years now. How've you been? Your family moved to Dublin or something, didn't they? It was all pretty sudden. Just after all that Henry business.' He gave a loud snort. 'That was the talk of the town, wasn't it? Probably still is.'

'Yes, yes,' Wendy said quickly. 'Dad got a job in Dublin. We moved when I was fourteen.' She really didn't want to talk about the past, especially her

Westport past. And *most* especially Henry Reilly.
Henry was her first real boyfriend; and it was all over
and done with, end of story. She'd loved him and
he'd broken her heart; he'd left her for the thirty-
seven-year-old mother of a friend of theirs, a woman
called Thelma Dickens. Henry and Thelma had run
away to Boston, never to be heard of again, leaving
two devastated families behind them. It was like
something from a bad American made-for-television
movie and no one could believe it. Henry was only
seventeen at the time and it had caused quite a stir in
Westport. Wendy had lost her head a little and she
certainly didn't want to be reminded of it now. It had
devastated her and she'd never really got over it, not
properly. Henry had no idea what an impact he'd
made on Wendy's life.

'You look great,' she said, meaning it. Des had filled
out a lot; his skin was tanned and his hair was
bleached blond from the Australian sun. Both his teeth
and his smile were still crooked, but this just added to
his appeal.

'Thanks. I'm enjoying being back in Ireland for a
bit.'

He didn't elaborate, so Wendy asked, 'And what
do you do in Sydney? Are you still working or have
you retired on your millions?'

He smiled. 'Not yet. I'm in computers.'

'Really?' Wendy asked out of politeness rather than
real interest. 'Programming?'

'Yep. Programming, servicing, troubleshooting, the
works. There's not much I don't know about computers

at this stage.' He stretched his long legs out in front of him and crossed his arms over his chest rather too smugly, Wendy thought. But he'd always been full of self-confidence, even as a teenager. 'There's good money in it, I've done OK for myself.'

'And what are you doing here?'

'Dropping my mum's car in to be fixed. It's making a strange noise apparently. I couldn't hear it myself, but you know what mothers are like. Always worrying.'

'No, I meant what are you doing in Ireland?'

'Oh, sorry. I'm over visiting Mum. She had a bit of an old heart attack recently so I thought I'd better see her before she, you know, pops her clogs.'

'I'm sorry to hear that,' Wendy said.

'Thanks. She's a tough old bird though, she's not going anywhere for a long time yet.'

'And where are you staying?'

'With Oonagh, my sister. Do you remember Oonagh? She's a couple of years younger than me.'

'Vaguely,' Wendy said.

'She lives in Bray, she married a Dublin guy a couple of years ago. Mum lives with her; she moved up after Dad died.'

'How long are you staying?'

Des shrugged. 'A couple of weeks. I'll see how it goes. I thought I'd check out the computer scene in Dublin while I'm here. Maybe see if there are any jobs going, you know? In case I decide to come and work here at some stage.'

'Are you thinking of moving back to Ireland for good?'

He shrugged again. 'Maybe. Might even settle down if I meet the right girl. Know any?' He looked at her intensely and raised his eyebrows.

Wendy blushed and looked away. Des hadn't changed. She held her right hand out in front of her. 'I'm married,' she said with a laugh, fingering her wedding band. 'With two children,' she added to cement it.

'Shame.' He smiled at her. They sat saying nothing for a few awkward moments. Eventually he broke the silence. 'How about a cup of coffee while we're waiting? Give us a chance to catch up. No strings. You can tell me all about your husband if you like.'

Wendy didn't quite know what to make of that last statement. 'I'm not sure,' she began. 'I'd better wait here. My car's nearly finished and . . .'

'Ah, come on. Live a little,' he cajoled. 'Just one cup of coffee. It won't do any harm. Unless you're in a rush?'

Wendy looked at his handsome face. She could do with a little distraction after the night she'd had.

He smiled at her, sensing her hesitation. 'And I won't mention Henry, OK? That's all in the past, isn't it? Man, did he make one bad decision. You're even better-looking now than you were then.'

'Thanks,' Wendy faltered, realizing that he was now officially flirting with her. 'But I don't think . . .'

Just then the mechanic walked into the office and

nodded at her. 'All finished,' he said, handing her the keys to her car.

'That was quick,' she said, remembering her day-dream and trying not to blush. 'What was wrong?'

'Nothing much. The brake fluid needed topping up,' he said, 'and I put a new brake-light bulb in for you. She's all set now. But you were right to bring her in. There's no point in messing around when it comes to brakes. Important things, brakes. Your brake-pads will need to be replaced soon enough. I'd give them another six months, then bring her in again.'

'Thanks.' Wendy smiled at his rather sweet use of the feminine adjective to describe her car. The mechanic handed her the keys and walked away.

She tore her eyes from his young buttocks and turned towards Des. 'I'm sorry, I really do have to go. I'm really busy today and . . .'

'No need to explain,' Des said. 'Give me your hand.'

'What?' she asked. And before she had time to protest he pulled a pen out of his pocket, held her left hand firmly and wrote a telephone number on her skin.

'Just in case you change your mind,' he said with a smile, letting her hand drop. 'About coffee.'

'Um, sure. Bye.' She avoided his gaze and practically ran out of the office. She put the key into the car door with shaking hands. Once she was sitting in the car she looked back at the doorway – she just couldn't help herself. Des was standing there, staring into her car. He lifted his hand and waved. Wendy felt flustered. She glanced in the rear-view mirror – she was very pink and her forehead was shiny. She waved back and turned the key in the ignition. The sooner she was out of there the better.

As she drove home, Wendy realized with a start that she'd run out of the garage without paying her bill. She'd ring them and apologize as soon as she got home. How embarrassing. But she had been rather distracted.

She wondered what would have happened if she'd gone for a coffee with Des. Maybe nothing. But maybe...? She felt a rush of adrenaline power through her veins, and then another warmer feeling suffused her body. With a shock she recognized it as desire. As she waited in a queue of traffic, she looked down at the number Des had etched on her hand in bold blue. After the number he'd written *Ring Me!*

Des Sullivan finds *me* attractive. Wendy smiled to herself, feeling deliciously empowered. Des Sullivan! As she sat at the traffic lights at Baker's Corner she ran her fingers over the blue number. She turned on the radio and tried to concentrate on what Ryan Tubridy, one of her favourite presenters, was saying. But it was no use, she was utterly distracted. At least it took her mind off more mundane things. And what if I did ring him? she asked herself. What would happen then?

6 'Knowing Me, Knowing You'

On Friday afternoon, Wendy stood on tiptoe in the back garden of Hollyhock House on Killiney Hill Road, trying to save her pink suede kitten-heeled sandals from sinking into the grass. She knew she shouldn't have worn them, they were going to get ruined, but they did go so well with her jeans and her pink silk kimono top and she loved them; they made her feel good and she could do with all the instant pick-me-ups she could find these days. She was staring up at the hillside in disbelief, Luke and Pat flanking her. A large white marquee was just about visible through the leafy trees.

'You're not serious?' Wendy was horrified. 'They said the marquee would be on the lawn at the top of the garden.' She pointed in front of her. 'That's not a garden, that's a bloody mountain.'

'Deadly serious,' Pat assured her. 'I'm really sorry, but it's all hands on deck, Wendy, or we'll never get the gear up there and ready in time. That marquee is on level ground, thank goodness, but there are some pretty steep steps to negotiate on the way up to it.'

'We need Ronan. Where's Ronan?' Wendy looked around a little frantically. She put her hands to her mouth and yelled, 'Ronan!'

'I don't think he'll be able to hear you,' Luke said, trying not to raise his voice. He understood Wendy's panic but she wasn't exactly helping the situation. 'He's in the marquee sorting out the power cables.'

'How big is the *garden* exactly?' she asked.

He shrugged. 'Four or five acres apparently. Mostly on a slope.'

Wendy raised her eyebrows. 'Tell me this is some sort of elaborate nightmare.' Luke and Pat watched as she visibly slumped in front of their eyes. Her usually rigid shoulders collapsed and she put her hand to her head. She looked crumpled, exhausted.

'Wendy?' Luke asked, concerned. He put his arm around her. He'd never seen her in this state before. It was rather unnerving.

'I'm sorry, Luke,' she said softly. 'I'm just having a bad day. I haven't had much sleep the last few nights. Ignore me. Sorry for being so short with both of you.'

'It's fine, Wendy, honestly. We'll manage. But we are going to need some assistance. Is there anyone you can think of who'd be free to help? Anyone at all?'

Wendy blew the air out of her mouth with a 'whoosh' and thought for a second. She shook her head. 'Not really. The local rugby team?'

'Do you know any rugby players?' Luke asked hopefully.

'No.' She sighed deeply and put her head on his shoulder. 'Oh, Luke, what are we going to do?'

He was a little disconcerted by her tone. Wendy was always so positive, so upbeat, and she always had an answer for everything. It wasn't like her to admit defeat.

'How about ... students?' he offered haltingly. 'They're on their holidays, aren't they?'

'Yes, I suppose so,' Wendy said, her head still resting on his shoulder.

'Where would we find them at this time of the day?' Pat asked, lighting a cigarette and pulling deeply on it.

Wendy lifted her head. 'I have no idea,' she said. 'Students,' she murmured. 'Students.' She thought about it for a few seconds and then her brain flicked into action. 'But I know someone who might. Give me one minute.' She punched a familiar number into her mobile.

'Where's Luke?' Ronan asked Pat. He was leaning against Pat's van – his heart was pounding in his chest and he felt as if he'd just run a marathon. Beads of sweat were popping out all over his forehead and he wiped them away with his forearm.

'No idea,' Pat said, looking around. 'No sign of Wendy either. When's Mia due?'

Ronan looked at his watch. 'Round about now,' he said. 'We're never going to be ready in time.'

The way things were looking, Ronan was right. The

guests would start to arrive in less than an hour, and the stage wasn't fully erected yet. The marquee company were working flat out to finish the job.

'Poor things.' Pat gestured towards several of the waiting staff, each carrying armfuls of large white dinner plates, winding their way up the hillside like black and white ants. 'There's a mini-kitchen at the back of the marquee, but the chef's doing his nut. Luckily all the courses are cold. There was supposed to be soup, but the catering company refused to let their staff carry the tureens up the hill – they say they're not insured to transport hot liquids like that.'

'Too right,' Ronan said. 'We'd better get back to work, I suppose. But I have no idea how I'm going to last the evening after all this exertion. I feel like my heart's going to jump out of my chest.'

'Know what you mean, mate,' Pat empathized. 'At least I don't have to sing. I don't envy you.' He ground his cigarette into the gravel with his boot, took a swig from his bottle of water, put the cap back on, wiggled the bottle into the pocket of his denim jacket and lit another cigarette. 'Lights next?' he suggested.

Ronan winced and nodded. At least they weren't as heavy as the amplifiers – *they* were going to be a killer.

Ronan and Pat heard engines powering up the gravel driveway and looked over. 'Someone's in a hurry,' Ronan murmured.

As soon as the two cars came into view Pat let out a hoot of laughter. 'It's Wendy,' he said, clappings his hand together in delight and relief. 'Followed by Luke. But what the hell?'

Ronan and Pat stared at the two cars in amazement. They were jammed with people – a large, unfamiliar-looking young man was sitting on another man's knee in the front of Wendy's car, and at least seven people were squashed into the back, including a beaming Nadia and a very excited-looking Greg and Steve. Luke's car was equally packed. As soon as the cars came to a halt, the doors sprang open and everyone poured out on to the gravel in a good-humoured wave of chatter and laughter.

Wendy walked towards Ronan, a smile plastered on her face. 'I've brought some reinforcements,' she said.

'No kidding!' Ronan grinned back. 'Where did you find them all?'

'In the Internet café in Dun Laoghaire. They're friends of Nadia's.'

Ronan leaned towards her. 'Are we paying them all?' he asked in a low voice.

'No,' Wendy said. 'But I will give them something for their trouble. Nadia talked them all into it. She's quite a popular girl with the local male population as you can see. At least two of them have introduced themselves as Nadia's boyfriend.'

Ronan laughed. 'Why am I not surprised?' He clapped his hands together again. 'Right, better put them all to work. We have a show to run.'

'Looks like Luke's beaten you to it,' Wendy pointed out. Luke had already started to direct everybody towards the side of the van. Pat was helping him.

'Daddy!' Steve and Greg came running towards

130

Ronan and wound themselves around his upper legs and waist. 'Isn't this fun?' Steve said, his eyes sparking with excitement. 'Nadia said we had to be good and help. What can we do, Daddy?'

'You can be my assistants, how about that?'

'OK.' Greg nodded.

'What's going on here?' Mia asked. She'd just walked the short distance from Killiney train station. 'Are the guests here already?' she asked, staring at Wendy's new army of helpers. Luke had lined them up and was passing out the AbbaFab equipment and giving them instructions. He'd already mentally hand-picked several tall, burly lads for the amplifiers. Pat was climbing up the hillside towards the marquee, his arms full of bags of electric leads, showing the Abba-Fab troops the way.

Wendy laughed. 'They're Nadia's friends. They're here to help us lug the equipment up the hill.' Wendy filled Mia in on what she'd missed.

'Sorry I wasn't here earlier to help,' Mia said.

'Not to worry, we weren't expecting you until now.'

'So when will the guests start arriving?' Mia asked.

'In less than twenty minutes. But there's a drinks reception on the lawn first, so they won't be in the marquee until later.'

'So the idea is to do a quick sound check and then we have a couple of hours off?'

'Correct,' Wendy said. 'I want to make sure you see the stage before we go on later. There'll be a big enough crowd and . . .'

131

'How big?' Mia cut in.

Wendy shrugged her shoulders. 'Couple of hundred.'

'How many?' Mia asked again. 'Exactly?'

'Nearly three hundred,' Wendy admitted. 'Much smaller than the Blackrock gig.'

'But that was only a few songs. This is a wedding. The newly-weds will be relying on us to make it the best night of their lives.' Mia bit her lip.

Wendy put her arm around Mia's shoulders and gave her a squeeze. 'You'll be fine,' she assured her. 'Stop fretting. Now for the mountain climbing.'

Wendy and Mia made their way across the garden and towards the path to the side of the hill. 'You're going up there in those?' Mia asked, pointing to Wendy's shoes.

'Mia, in my cruise-ship days I used to dance all night on the stage in six-inch heels.' Wendy smiled. 'If there's one thing I can do, it's heels.'

'I remember the photos,' Mia said. 'I used to borrow Mum's black feathery wedding hat and dress up in my swimming costume and dance around the house, pretending to be you.'

'Did you?' Wendy asked.

'Yes, for years.'

Wendy smiled. 'I didn't know. It's a pity we didn't have video cameras back in those days; I would have liked to have seen that.'

'You brought your gold costume home to show me one year, remember? You let me try it on. We have photos of that somewhere.'

'Of course. How could I forget? You nearly broke your ankle in my sandals.'

Mia giggled. 'I've never been good in heels. Unlike you.'

'Speaking of which, we'd better get going,' Wendy said. 'Follow me.'

Mia followed Wendy under the elaborate metal, flower- and silk ribbon- festooned decorative arch and up the steep natural stone steps that led towards the marquee. 'Mountain goats, eat your hearts out,' Mia murmured as they climbed up and up. They were followed by some of Nadia's friends and more catering staff, now lugging up the dessert plates and clinking boxes of cutlery.

After several minutes' steep climb, they finally reached the top. 'I can see why they put the marquee up here,' Mia said as she stood on the lawn, panting a little. 'Even if it is a bit of a trek.'

Wendy stood beside her. Stretched out in front of them was the shimmering blue expanse of Killiney Bay. It was a bright day and the sun was threatening to peep out from its scanty cloud cover at any moment.

'And I can see why they call this the Naples Bay of Ireland,' Wendy said. 'Look, there's Sorrento Terrace, the most expensive terrace in the country. I recognize it from the property pages. What beautiful houses.'

'Is that an outdoor swimming pool over there?' Mia asked, pointing into one particular back garden to their left.

Wendy squinted. 'I think so. Or else a rather large pond.'

'A swimming pool, imagine that.' Mia was impressed.

Wendy looked at her. 'Maybe you'll live in Killiney one day, Mia, you never know. And have a swimming pool in your back garden.'

'Maybe.' Mia smiled back. 'After I make my millions in AbbaFab, you mean?'

Wendy snorted. 'I wouldn't hold your breath.'

'Hey, girls!' Pat shouted over from the entrance to the marquee. 'They've finished the stage. Ready for your trial run? The amps are almost ready, Ronan's just wiring them up now.'

'Coming,' Wendy said. 'No rest for the wicked and all that.' She held her hand out to Mia. 'Come on, you. Enough sightseeing for one day.'

'Hi, Mia.' Luke strode towards them, his eyes fixed on Mia. He gave her a hug and a kiss on the cheek, then stepped back and smiled at Wendy.

'No kiss for me then, Luke?' she asked archly.

'Oh, sorry.' He leaned forward and kissed her too.

'Hey, hands off my wife,' Ronan shouted from the back of the tent. 'She's taken. Isn't that right, Wendy?'

'Do you want to do a quick run-through of some of the songs?' Wendy turned and asked Mia.

Mia looked at her sister. It wasn't like her blatantly to ignore Ronan like that. But she thought it best not to say anything. She was sure Wendy meant nothing by it. 'Yes, that would be great. And could we go over the dance routine for "Does Your Mother Know?"? I'm a bit confused about the turns.'

'No problem,' Wendy said. 'We'll do that first while

Ronan and Pat finish wiring up the amps.' She clicked towards the stage on the exposed wooden floorboards. They hadn't got around to laying the carpet yet. 'Ronan, we're just going to go through "Does Your Mother Know?" with Mia and Luke. Are the mics working yet?'

'No, it'll be another few minutes,' Ronan said. 'Do you need me?'

'No, you finish what you're doing.'

'OK. And we'll try and keep out of your way.'

'Great, thanks.'

'How are you today?' Luke asked Mia as they walked slowly towards the stage.

'Fine. Good, actually.'

'How was the head yesterday morning?'

'A bit muzzy but not too bad. Alva was in a bad way though. She was lying on the sofa moaning when I left. She rang in sick to work.'

Luke laughed. 'Poor Alva.'

'Come on, slow coaches,' Wendy said, staring down at Mia and Luke. 'Up on the stage with the two of you.'

'Yes, Boss,' Luke said with a grin. He climbed up and held out his hand for Mia. She took it gratefully. His grip was firm and she felt the power in his upper arms as he pulled her up.

'Thanks,' she murmured.

'Right, Mia,' Wendy said. 'As you know, Luke sings "Does Your Mother Know?", and Ronan backs him up. He usually sings to Gemma, but I think it's better if he sings to me today. It'll make things easier. So we'll swap the steps around a bit. You stand there . . .' But before she had a chance to finish, Ronan interrupted.

'It's probably best to leave the steps as they are,' he said. 'Save yourself the extra work. Mia will pick it up quickly enough. But, Mia, try not to laugh at Luke too much when he's singing to you, you'll put him off if you do.'

'Gemma always tries to make me laugh,' Luke explained to Mia. He shook his head, realizing what he'd just said. 'I shouldn't have told you that, should I?'

Mia smiled at him. 'Probably not. If it's a family tradition, who am I to . . .'

'That's all very well,' Wendy interrupted the banter. 'But I really do think that Luke should sing to me.'

'Why?' Ronan asked Wendy. She was in a very strange mood.

'I thought you were fixing the amps?' she said, glaring at him.

He shrugged. 'Sorry, I didn't mean to interfere. I was just trying to help. I'll get back to the amps.'

'I'm sorry, I didn't mean to snap at you, Ronan. I'm just trying to get things right. And to make things easy for Mia. But we'll do things as normal if that's what you'd prefer.'

'I don't mind, Wendy,' Ronan said, putting his hands up in front of him defensively, 'really I don't. You do what you think best, OK?'

Wendy nodded at him. 'OK. Thanks.' She turned back to Mia and Luke who were waiting for their

136

directions. 'Luke, you sing to Mia. I'll do backing with Ronan.'

'Sure,' Luke said. He took his place on the stage and showed Mia where to stand. 'Will I start singing, Wendy? Can Ronan accompany? It would make things easier.'

'Ronan, I know you're busy, but would you mind?' Wendy asked him.

'No problem.' Ronan jumped behind the keyboard and began to play the jaunty opening bars to the song.

Mia stifled a grin when Luke sang the first, rather cheesy line to her. *'You're so hot, teasing me, so you're blue but I can't take a chance on a chick like you, it's something I couldn't do.'*

Mia licked her lips suggestively.

'And I told you not to make me laugh,' Luke said, singing it to the music.

Mia giggled.

'And here's where you dance with your back to him,' Wendy said over the keyboard. 'When he says *"Girl, you're only a child"*. Turn your head, Mia, flick your hair and smile, good, good. You're supposed to be a young girl flirting with an older man.'

Mia did as requested.

Luke changed the first chorus from 'Does Your Mother Know?' to 'Does Your Sister Know?' and Mia couldn't contain herself. She stopped dead and gave a hoot of laughter. Then Luke started laughing and couldn't sing any longer. Ronan had to stop playing, he was laughing so hard.

'What was that all about?' Wendy asked with a frown.

'Sorry, Wendy,' Luke said. 'I couldn't resist it.'

'Well, it's not funny,' she replied, sniffing. 'And we don't have much time, so stop messing around. We need to get on with it.'

'Yes, Boss,' Mia said, then started laughing again.

'Mia!' Wendy said. 'You need to take this more seriously.'

'And you need to lighten up a little,' Mia said. As soon as the words had left her mouth she gasped at her own audacity. She had never spoken to Wendy like that before in front of anyone. Wendy gave a tiny squeak, then jumped off the stage and stormed out of the tent.

Mia looked at Ronan. 'Should I go after her?' she asked him.

'Best to leave her alone for a few minutes. She's pretty tired today. We had a bit of a problem with a frying pan on Wednesday evening and she was up most of the night cleaning the kitchen. She hasn't really caught up on her sleep.'

'A frying pan?' asked Mia.

'It went on fire,' Ronan said sheepishly. 'My fault. I put it on the hob and forgot about it. Wendy's not too pleased with me, as you can imagine. Listen, why don't we go through that song once more? Wendy's right, we don't have much time.'

Wendy listened as the strains of 'Does Your Mother Know?' rang out again. She was sitting outside on the

138

grass, staring down at Killiney Bay. She still couldn't believe that Mia had spoken to her like that, in front of Luke, Ronan and Pat. Her mobile phone was digging into her bottom and she shifted sideways and wiggled it out of her back pocket. She stared at it for a moment and then decided to ring Gemma.

'Hello?' Gemma answered. 'Wendy?'

'Hi.'

'Are you not working? What's that music in the background?'

'That would be the band practising without me,' Wendy said.

'Without *us*,' Gemma pointed out.

'Sorry, you're right. Without *us*.'

'And why are they doing that?'

Wendy explained what had just happened.

'Ah,' Gemma said. 'And I take it you're not well pleased with Mia for talking back to you.'

'It's not that!' Wendy protested.

'Really?'

'Well, OK, maybe it is a little. But I think Luke's having a really bad influence on her. She seems totally smitten, Gemma, it's really sad. She's being all silly and giggly. And he's not right for her.'

'I agree completely. But there's not much we can do about it, is there? Mia has to make her own decisions. I tried talking to her about Luke but she wasn't even listening.'

'When? You never told me.'

'On Wednesday evening, before you went on stage

in Blackrock. And I wanted to talk to you about it yesterday afternoon but I didn't get a chance. But you know, I don't tell you everything, Wendy.'

'Well, when it comes to Mia, you should. Maybe I should try talking to Luke myself.'

Gemma said nothing. She had no intention of telling Wendy *everything*, even when it came to Mia's life. Wendy sounded tired and Gemma didn't want to argue with her.

'Is everything else OK, Wendy?'

'Let me see, Ronan tried to burn the house down in the early hours of yesterday morning, as you know; I got little or no sleep last night, we've just finished hauling all our gear up a mountain, and Mia hates me. Apart from that, everything's just peachy. Listen, I have to go, Ronan's waving at me.'

'Wendy! You can't go now. You're obviously upset.'

'Everything's fine, I'm just a bit fed up. I'll ring you back later.'

'Promise?'

'Promise.'

'And take it easy, Wendy. I'm here if you need to talk. You know that.'

'Thanks.'

'There you are,' Ronan said as Wendy clicked off her phone. 'I was looking for you. Are you all right?'

'Yes. I am now. I just needed a little air.'

'Mia didn't mean to upset you.'

'I know she didn't. I'm tired, that's all. I shouldn't have taken it to heart.'

'Will you come back inside?'

'Sure.' Wendy pushed herself up with her hands and followed Ronan. 'I had to make a phone call,' she said to a rather startled Mia and Luke as she approached the stage. 'Now, where were we?'

An hour later, Wendy rang Gemma back. 'Gemma, it's Wendy again.'

'What took you so long? Now I want to hear all about the mountain climbing. You have no idea how bored I am, and I'm in desperate need of some real news. I'm sick to the teeth of reading about celebrities' vacuous lives and ridiculous problems. But that's all my magazines seem interested in writing about. And I've run out of books. It's driving me nuts.'

'Sorry to disappoint you, but the marquee is up a hill, that's all.'

'How disappointing.'

'But I did manage to corner Luke after our practice and have a word with him.'

'Really? Alone?'

'Yes. I asked him to check one of the hazard lights on my car. Complete fabrication, of course, there was nothing wrong with it. The others went to Dalkey in the van to find somewhere to eat.'

'And?'

'I don't think it went all that well to tell the truth,' Wendy admitted.

'Go on,' Gemma encouraged her.

'I asked him what his intentions were towards Mia.'

141

'You did not!' Gemma snorted with laughter.

'Why not?' Wendy asked defensively. 'What's wrong with that?'

'Intentions! That sounds like something a Victorian father would say, not a sister.'

'Yes, well.' Wendy sniffed. 'I was just letting him know I had my eye on him.'

'As if he hadn't noticed! Poor Luke, I'm starting to feel a little sorry for him. I was thinking about it after you rang earlier, Wendy.'

'And?'

'I think we have to let Mia make her own mistakes. She's twenty-four after all.'

'But she's a very young twenty-four,' Wendy said. 'You have to admit.'

'We're always saying that and you know, maybe that's our fault,' Gemma mused. 'And maybe it's time for us both to loosen the reins a little. Let Mia live her own life.'

'Ronan would agree with you. But I'm not so sure. She still needs us, Gemma.' Wendy's phone beeped. 'Hang on one second.' Wendy put Gemma on hold. Ronan had sent her a text message asking where she'd got to. 'Gemma, I have to go. Ronan's looking for me and I have to sort out the costumes and do Mia's make-up.'

'Bye then,' Gemma said. 'I'll talk to you tomorrow I suppose.'

'Are you OK? You sound a little down,' Wendy asked.

Gemma sighed dramatically. 'I'm just fed up with

being cooped up at home all the time. I hadn't realized how much of my time is taken up with work. I don't really have any other friends, Wendy. You lot are my friends, and my family for that matter.'

Wendy didn't know what to say. 'I'm sorry, Gemma, I have been trying to include you in everything. Training Mia in, for example. And you're welcome to come to as many weddings and gigs as you like, you know that.'

'Thanks. But it's not the same. I'll just be glad when my ankle's healed. But maybe you won't want me back now that you have Mia. She's much better than I am.'

'Gemma, you know Mia's only filling in for you. Yes, she's a great singer, I can't deny it, but she doesn't have your stage presence or your experience. So stop worrying.'

'Ah, pay no attention to me. I'm just feeling a little sorry for myself, I guess. And I know you have to go. I'll be fine.'

'Are you sure?'

'Yes, yes. Now go!'

A little later that afternoon, Mia and Wendy followed the housekeeper of Hollyhock House – a nice woman in her fifties called Mrs Tibbet – up the rather grand main stairs.

'Talk about a bathroom with a view,' Wendy said as soon as Mrs Tibbet had closed the door behind her, leaving them alone. Wendy looked around. She wondered if the housekeeper would give her a guided tour later. It was a stunning period house – many of the original features were still intact and she was dying to see the reception rooms.

'Look at that bath,' she said. 'Wouldn't you just love to soak in it?' The oversized oval marble bath had pride of place in the large room, positioned against the uncurtained sash window, commanding stunning views of the garden.

'It's gorgeous,' Mia agreed. She ran her finger over the curved rim of the bath, the white marble cool beneath her skin. 'It's a bit exposed though, isn't it? I'm not sure I'd want people spying on me in the nip.'

'Good point,' Wendy said. 'I'd put a crisp white canvas blind on the lower half of the window myself. And I'd paint the walls a soft cream instead of the blue. To match the bath.'

Mia murmured assent. She'd apologized to Wendy about her 'Lighten up' comment several times, but was still a little wary. Wendy had seemed fine in the restaurant, though, her usual chatty self. On the other hand, Luke had been rather quiet and withdrawn, which had unnerved Mia. She'd asked him several questions and he'd answered her rather shortly; he wasn't his usual charming and funny self at all. Maybe he was going off her. Maybe he had never really liked her in the first place. Or maybe Wendy had said something to him. Mia wouldn't put it past her. Luke and Wendy had arrived at lunch together in Wendy's car after all.

Mia watched as Wendy set her vanity case in front

of the large mirror, sat down on the upholstered bench and opened it with a click.

'*Heigh ho, heigh ho, it's off to work we go,*' Wendy sang under her breath. 'This evening's going to be fun,' she said as she dotted some cleanser on her cheeks, chin, forehead and neck.

'I hope so,' Mia said. There was a slight quiver in her voice which her sister recognized as nerves.

Wendy stroked cotton wool over her skin, removing her daytime make-up. 'I know so,' she said confidently. 'Sit down beside me. I'll budge over.'

'Wendy,' Mia began, 'did you say anything to Luke? In the car, I mean.'

'About what?' Wendy asked, staring into the mirror.

'About me.'

Wendy said nothing for a moment. Then she turned to face Mia. 'He's not right for you, Mia. He's too old.'

'Wendy, he's only four years older than me! You're five years older than Ronan.'

'Thanks for pointing that out,' Wendy said a little tetchily. She didn't like being reminded of the fact.

'And you have no right to tell me who I can or can't see. You're not my mother! So keep out of it, OK?'

Wendy was shocked. Mia rarely raised her voice to her.

'Sorry,' Mia murmured. 'But it's my life, Wendy.'

Wendy sighed. 'That's what Gemma said.'

'The two of you are always talking about me behind my back.'

'No we're not!'

'Yes you are. I'm not stupid. It's been going on for years. And I don't need you and Gemma trying to protect me all the time. Just stop it!'

'I know,' Wendy said. 'You're right. I shouldn't have said anything to Luke. I just wanted him to . . . oh, I don't know. Treat you with respect, I suppose.'

'I'm so embarrassed, Wendy. No wonder he was being so odd earlier. He probably thinks I'm not worth the hassle.'

'It won't happen again,' Wendy said. 'I promise.' She stroked Mia's hair. 'And he thinks the world of you. Nothing will change that. Nothing *has* changed that. He was probably just trying to play it cool in front of me.'

'Do you think so?'

'Yes.'

'And he really does like me?'

'What's not to like, Mia? You're wonderful.'

'Thanks.' Mia's heart lifted. Maybe Luke did like her after all. She smiled at Wendy. 'I'd better put some make-up on now.'

'So you forgive me for interfering?'

'Yes. But don't do it again.' Mia stuck her face inches away from Wendy's and glared at her, making them both laugh. 'Promise?' she said in her most threatening voice.

Wendy laughed. 'I promise. Here.' She handed Mia a thick white towelling band. 'Put this on to hold your hair back. Would you like me to apply your foundation?' Wendy rummaged in her vanity case and pulled out two tubes. 'Try mixing these two together, that should be a good colour for you.'

Mia rarely wore foundation and certainly not the heavier cream type. She took the tubes from Wendy and turned them over and over in her hands. 'Gemma did it for me the night before last. I guess I'd better learn how to do it myself. You guys won't always be around after all. Do you have a sponge?'

Wendy fished one out and handed it over. 'Good idea. It'll go on easier if you dampen the surface slightly.' She smiled gently at her sister. 'You've always had such beautiful skin, Mia. You're really lucky. Mine's like old leather at this stage. I used to sunbathe far too much on the cruise ship.'

'You were a sun goddess long before that,' Mia pointed out. She poured some of Wendy's moisturizer onto her fingertips and began to massage it gently into her skin. 'Like the time you were over from London on your holidays and you lay on tin foil in the back garden and got me to pour baby oil all over you? You got terrible sunburn and Mum had to bring you to the doctor, remember? She was so cross with you. "You're not a turkey, Wendy," she said. "There's no need to cook yourself." And we couldn't stop laughing at that and Gemma kept making gobble, gobble turkey noises. And then Mum got really cross with us for being silly.'

Wendy winced. 'Don't remind me. Some holiday! It hurt even to laugh. I had third-degree burns and I was in agony for weeks. I'll never forget spending most of the first few days lying in a cold bath; and even that felt scalding hot to me. My poor old skin. The things I put it through, all in the name of beauty. I shudder just thinking about it.'

Mia held the small wedge of sponge under the cold tap for a moment, then squeezed it out. 'Wendy?' she said as she put some foundation on to the back of her hand. It looked a little too dark for her complexion so she added a lighter dollop from the other tube and mixed them together. Wendy was right – it was almost the perfect shade. She really knew her make-up.

'Yes?' Wendy looked over at Mia. 'Do you need some help?'

'No. I was just wondering . . .' Mia tailed off.

'What?' Wendy prompted.

Mia was staring at the top of her own hand intently. 'Do you ever think about Mum?' she asked in a quiet voice, still staring at her hand.

'Of course,' Wendy said after a moment.

'You never talk about her,' Mia said.

'No. No, I don't.'

'Why?' Mia raised her head.

Wendy was leaning towards the mirror and carefully patting her crow's feet with a fingertip's worth of wrinkle cream. She held her hand in mid-air and looked at Mia. 'At first it hurt too much,' she said honestly. 'And then, I don't know. I didn't see much point in it, I suppose. She was gone and we had to get on with our lives.'

'But you never talk about her now,' Mia said softly.

148

'I'm sorry,' Wendy said. 'I don't know what to say, Mia. Would you like me to talk about her more?'

'It's not that,' Mia said. Then she sighed. 'Oh, I don't know what I mean. Ignore me.'

'No, it's obviously on your mind, Mia,' Wendy said, putting down the tiny pot of cream. 'And you're right, we should talk about Mum more. It's her anniversary soon, isn't it?'

'Yes,' Mia whispered. Miriam Redden had died in June, not that they ever mentioned the date, not really. Gemma and Wendy always made sure to ring Mia on the day, but Miriam was never mentioned. 'Seventeenth of June,' Mia added.

'Maybe we should do something this year,' Wendy suggested. 'Put flowers on her grave or something. What do you think?'

'Not flowers,' Mia said.

'Oh.' Wendy was stumped. 'Why not?'

'Mum didn't like cut flowers. She preferred plants.'

'You're right. I'd forgotten that. A plant then. A rose bush in a pot or something. What do you think?'

Mia nodded wordlessly. There was a lump in her throat and she didn't trust herself to speak.

There was a sudden rap on the door. 'How are you getting on, girls?' It was Ronan. 'Are you ready?'

'Not yet,' Wendy said. 'We're putting on our faces and we're not changed.'

'Right, I'll leave you to it. See you downstairs in what, ten minutes? The room at the back of the kitchen. Luke's with me.'

149

'Fifteen,' Wendy replied.

'Fifteen it is.'

Wendy and Mia listened as Ronan and Luke's muffled voices grew fainter and then disappeared.

'We'll do something this year,' Wendy promised. 'For Mum,' she added, just to be clear. She looked at Mia again. 'Are you OK?'

Mia nodded slightly. 'Yes, I'm fine. Sometimes I just miss Mum, you know. And I feel I can't really talk to you about it.'

'Well, you can,' Wendy said. She could feel tears prick the back of her eyes and she willed them not to spill. 'You can talk to me about anything. I know I'm not always the easiest person to talk to, but I do love you, Mia. And I'd do anything to make you happy. You know that, don't you?'

Mia wiped away a tear.

'Ah, Mia.' Wendy leaned over and put her arms around her. 'What is it?'

'I don't know,' Mia said, wiping back the tears. 'I really don't. Some days I just feel lonely. Is that stupid?'

'We all feel like that at times,' Wendy said soothingly, holding her close.

'But you have your own family. You have Ronan,' Mia said, sniffing slightly. 'And the boys. How could you possibly feel lonely?'

'Sometimes being lonely when you have people all around you is the most wretched feeling of all,' Wendy said. She shook herself inwardly. Mia didn't need to hear about her worries and insecurities. She needed a sensible, stable sister, not one riddled with self-doubt. 'But you're right, I have Ronan and my boys. And you and Gemma, of course. I'm very lucky, I know that.'

Mia had stopped crying now. 'I'm sorry, Wendy. I don't know where all that came from. I'm fine, really I am.'

'I know you are. But there's nothing wrong with having a bit of a cry now and again. It's good for you. Lowers the stress levels.'

'Really?'

'Absolutely.' Wendy ruffled Mia's hair affectionately. 'You'll be fine, Little Star.'

'Thanks, Wendy.'

'For what?'

'For always being there for me.'

Wendy suddenly felt a wave of guilt. She knew Mia wasn't being sarcastic – that wasn't Mia's style – but at that moment she realized that she was starting to become very self-absorbed. Mia deserved a lot more of her attention, and so did Greg and Steve. Mia was an adult, but she still needed mothering at times, whatever Gemma and Ronan said, Wendy knew that. But she wasn't feeling all that positive about her own life at the moment and she'd have to do something about that too. She needed to be strong and happy for Mia's sake, for the boys' sake. For Ronan's sake.

She wondered if she should talk to Mia, *really* talk to her? Tell her everything. But now wasn't the time. And who would benefit in the long run? Maybe it would only make things harder for everyone concerned. Gemma hadn't mentioned their Westport past in many,

many years and maybe it was best left alone. After all, every family had some sort of skeleton in the closet.

'I love you, Mia,' Wendy said eventually, her mind racing. 'Always remember that. I always have and I always will. Even if I don't always show it.'

'I know you do,' Mia murmured, touched but at the same time a little embarrassed by Wendy's declaration.

After sitting in silence for what seemed like forever, Mia pulled away from Wendy and picked up the make-up sponge again. 'Better get ready,' she said. There were so many things that she wanted to say, but she didn't know how to put them into words. Standing up to Wendy about Luke, and talking to her about Miriam had had a cathartic effect, however, and she now felt calmer and more content than she had in a long time. Maybe things would be different from now on, or maybe not, but at least she'd tried to voice her thoughts to Wendy. That was a start.

Wendy nodded wordlessly. She felt strange, as if all her nerve endings were raw and exposed. Emotionally open. Just like she'd felt after giving birth and the heady first few minutes with her brand-new babies. Everything seemed hyper-real, and she felt vulnerable and sensitive. At that moment she really wanted to talk to Gemma, but she knew it wasn't possible. They were due on stage in a short while and she had to collect herself before that. If she didn't, there was a distinct possibility that one of the more sentimental songs would send her over the edge.

Ronan gave a loud wolf whistle as soon as Mia and Wendy walked into the basement of Hollyhock House.

They were in the authentic 'Arrival' white jumpsuits, Wendy's with plunging neckline and gathered trouser legs, and Mia's complete with stainless-steel zips and dark pink edging on the collar and cuffs. 'Looking good, ladies!' he quipped as the girls stode towards them in their white platform boots.

'How are you feeling, Mia?' asked Luke.

'Terrified,' she admitted.

'Good!' Luke said.

Mia stared at him.

'Nothing like a bit of adrenaline to get the old blood pumping,' he continued. 'All the best performers are scared witless before they go on stage. It's a well-recorded fact. Even Agnetha herself suffered from stage nerves.'

'Really?' Mia asked, slightly mollified.

'Would I lie to you?' Luke winked at her and she smiled. She was more relieved to see that he seemed back to normal rather than to hear that the real Agnetha suffered from stage fright, but she kept this to herself. She looked over at Wendy and her sister smiled back at her.

'It's true,' Wendy confirmed.

'In that case,' Mia said, 'show me the stage.'

'That's better,' Luke said. 'Now, are we all set? The speeches are almost over and it's almost time for the bride and groom's first dance.'

'What are they dancing to?' Mia asked. 'I thought our first song was "Dancing Queen"? Strange choice for a waltz really.'

Ronan and Luke stared at Wendy. 'Did you not tell

her?' Ronan asked Wendy, trying to keep the shock out of his voice.

Wendy hit her forehead with the heel of her hand. 'Oops! I knew there was something. I'm so sorry, Mia.'

'What?' Mia asked.

'I never told you about the song, did I?'

'No. What song?' Mia asked. 'Would someone please explain what Wendy's talking about?'

'The bride and groom have requested a special song,' Ronan began, 'It's "their song" apparently.'

'Which means it's the bride's favourite song,' Luke quipped.

Mia's face drained. Please no, I really don't want to faint again, she said to herself as she willed her body to stay upright.

Luke, noticing her pallor and slight lurch, sprang into action and put his arm around her. 'Easy there, Mia. Why don't you sit down?' He steered her towards a chair by her shoulders. 'Wendy can sing the first song on her own. Really, there's no drama. It's only "Still the One", you know, the Shania Twain song?'

'I know that song,' Mia murmured.

'Sorry?' Wendy asked. 'What did you say?'

Mia raised her head and gave a half-smile. 'It's one of Alva's favourite songs, sad person that she is. She plays it all the time. I know it backwards.'

'Great,' Luke said. 'As long as you know it forwards, we're in business!'

'Excellent!' Wendy said with relief. 'Problem solved.'

'Now, ready for the ascent?' Ronan asked. 'Everyone got their ropes and crampons?'

They all laughed. 'We'll follow you,' Wendy said. 'And will you go behind Mia, Luke? I don't want her tumbling down the slopes in her boots.'

'My pleasure.' Luke grinned.

Wendy regretted her request as soon as she realized that Luke now had her blessing to check out Mia's bottom the whole way up the hill. But there's nothing I can do about it without drawing attention to myself, she thought crossly. And I did promise Mia I'd keep out of it after all. But I do wish her jumpsuit wasn't quite so tight around the bum.

Mia stepped on to the small stage that evening feeling a lot more confident than she had in Blackrock Park. She sang a little nervously during 'Still the One', not a song she'd ever attempted to sing before, regardless of Alva's drunken cajoling, but no one seemed to notice. And once the first strains of 'Dancing Queen' played, Mia was soon in her element. Gone was the slightly shy and nervous Mia, and in her place was the confident and self-possessed Agnetha. Wendy watched in wonder as Mia danced and strutted around the stage, throwing herself into the songs and imbuing them with such heartfelt emotion that Wendy realized that she herself had become quite blasé about the lyrics and decided there and then to put more effort into her own delivery. During

'Knowing Me, Knowing You', singing about 'walking through an empty house', 'memories, good days, bad days' and 'children', Wendy felt real tears in her eyes. And for the very first time in her long singing career she cried on stage.

AbbaFab left the stage to storming applause. They had sung two encores, finishing up with 'Take a Chance on Me' on Wendy's instruction, much to Mia's delight. During the song, Wendy changed the chorus lyrics to 'Take a Chance on *Mia*' as their mum had always done while singing along. And just like Miriam, Wendy had leaned in towards Mia and sung '*Mia*' in her little sister's ear every time the chorus said 'Me'. Mia had smiled to herself, delighted and touched that Wendy had remembered. She hadn't felt so close to her sister for a long, long time and if she closed her eyes, it almost felt like having her mum back.

'Girls, you were brilliant!' Luke said after they'd climbed back down the hill and were congregated around the van. A DJ had taken over for the rest of the evening, and was playing a selection of late-eighties hits at the request of the crowd. The band had caught their breath in the small catering marquee, unwinding for a few minutes before their descent, all on a high and eager to compare notes on their performance. 'And that was the best version of "Knowing Me,

Knowing You" I've heard in years. You'd almost believe that Wendy was really crying. What an actor!'

'Thanks,' Wendy said, trying to sound calm and level-headed. She was still a little shaken by her own uncharacteristically emotional reaction to the lyrics.

'Who's on for a pint?' Luke asked as he unzipped the top of his jumpsuit. 'Anyone interested in checking out a new club in town?'

Mia couldn't but notice his smooth, almost hairless chest and his taut stomach, both glistening with fresh, tangy sweat.

'Luke,' Wendy said, 'could you not wait till we're inside? There are ladies present.'

'Where?' he asked with a grin, looking around and feigning surprise. Wendy laughed and raised her eyebrows. 'Sorry, Wendy,' he said. 'But I'm boiling. It was sweltering in that tent. As I was saying, I'm off to the opening of a new club. A friend of mine, Bert, runs the place and I'm sure he wouldn't mind if I brought along a few friends if anyone fancies it.'

Wendy groaned. 'Wish I had your energy, Luke. I'm heading straight home to bed. The boys will be up at the crack of dawn tomorrow.'

'On a Saturday?' Luke asked.

'They don't have any problem getting out of bed at the weekend,' Wendy explained. 'School mornings are the problem.'

'I'm heading home with Wendy,' added Ronan, eager to stay in her good books. 'Early night for me too.'

'Where's the club?' Mia asked. She wasn't usually a big fan of nightclubs, but she was on a high, her head was buzzing and she didn't think she'd be able to sleep for hours and hours. Besides, she quite fancied the idea of spending some time with Luke away from Wendy and Gemma's overprotective eyes.

'In town,' Luke replied. 'Just off Grafton Street. It's called Atlas. Bert's promised me a booth in the VIP area if you're interested.'

'I might be,' she said.

Wendy looked at Mia. 'We're working tomorrow, you do know that, don't you?'

Mia nodded.

'That's not until the evening, Wendy,' Ronan said, eager for Mia to enjoy herself.

'I suppose you're right,' Wendy murmured. 'But don't get too tired, Mia.'

'Maybe I should just go home,' Mia began.

'You should definitely go to the club,' Ronan cut in, nudging Wendy in the side. 'Have a bit of fun.'

'Yes, of course you should,' Wendy added quickly. She knew she was being over-protective. 'I'd go myself if I wasn't so tired. You can tell me all about it tomorrow. And you should give Gemma a ring. If she's still up, I'm sure she'd be interested.'

'Good idea,' Luke said. He looked at Mia. 'Go on, it'll be a laugh.'

'Can I bring Alva?' she asked.

'Of course, bring whoever you like. The more the merrier.' Luke clapped his hands together. 'That's settled then. Let's go home, get changed and hit the

158

town, Mia. I'll pick you and Alva up in a taxi in an hour. And then we can go and collect Gemma if she wants to join us. How about that?'

She smiled at him. 'Sounds good.'

As Ronan and Wendy drove past the garage beside the Purty Kitchen pub in Dun Laoghaire, Ronan driving and Wendy staring out into the darkness, she was reminded of her car's service and of Des. She should have wiped his number from her hand and all memory of him from her mind, but she hadn't on either count. He had seemed very interested in her and it was flattering. No one had looked at her in that way for a long time, especially not Ronan. Maybe she'd give Des a ring. Just to meet for coffee, mind, nothing else. She could do with a little confidence boost, and what was wrong with a little male attention anyway? It wasn't as if it meant anything.

Who are you kidding, Wendy? she asked herself rationally as Ronan pulled into their driveway. Grow up. Coffee with Des isn't going to solve anything, in fact it's only likely to make things worse.

Later that night, lying in bed unable to sleep, Wendy turned towards Ronan. 'Ronan, are you happy?' She nudged him in the side. 'Are you awake?'

'Uh? Awake?' he grunted, still half asleep. 'I am now. What did you just ask me?'

'Are you happy?' she repeated.

Ronan opened his eyes. He could see the whites of Wendy's eyes staring at him in the murky darkness.

'Sure,' he said. 'Are you?'

Silence.

'Wendy?' He sighed. 'Is this about the other night? And the frying pan? You know I'm sorry. I was an idiot, a complete idiot . . .'

'No,' she said softly. 'It's not about that.' She'd just about forgiven him now that the kitchen had been freshly painted and was almost back to normal except for the annoying scorch mark on the ceramic hob, which was so far resisting all manner of cleaning products.

Ronan waited for her to elaborate, but she didn't. She put her head back on the pillow and closed her eyes tightly.

'Wendy?' he said softly several minutes later. But there was no answer. He gave up. He rolled over, closed his eyes and went back to sleep.

As soon as she heard him gently snoring, Wendy slowly swung her legs over the side of the bed and climbed out, taking care not to wake him. She pulled her dressing gown on and tied the belt firmly around her waist. She opened the bedroom door gingerly and crept into the hall, lingering for a moment outside Greg and Steve's door. 'Sleep well, my babies,' she murmured before making her way downstairs and into the kitchen.

She sat down on a kitchen chair and stared out of the window. There was an almost full moon outside, illuminating the deck and the neat patio garden. They had had grass several years ago, but Wendy had become sick of mowing it – Ronan's job of course, one

160

of many he never actually got around to doing. So she'd had the whole area paved and gravelled. The boys were always complaining about the lack of grass, but as far as she could make out, they only really missed digging it up to find worms to 'play' with. And as they'd quickly discovered, if they dug deep enough, there were still worms aplenty. Looking outside, Wendy suddenly longed for grass; she longed to stand in the garden in the dark and feel the cool, damp blades beneath her bare feet. She leaned forward and put her elbows on the table and her face in her hands. Large tears fell on to the wooden surface of the table. What was happening to her life and why did she feel so out of control these days? She stood up, wiped away the tears with the sleeve of her dressing gown, and walked over to the kitchen counter where she'd left her mobile phone on recharge. She flicked through the phone book and found the number she was looking for. It was late but she was sure he'd still be up.

'Hello?' Des answered. 'Hello?'

7 'The Name of the Game'

Sean's date, Sadie, was also crying on Friday night.

'Sean, that was such a lovely film. I can't believe Hannah died in the end, it was so sad, wasn't it?'

'Yes, very sad,' Sean said, trying to sound sympathetic. He'd felt more like laughing than crying at the end of the terrible Hollywood weepy, *Dying for Love*. The leads – well-respected actors, one of whom had even been nominated for an Oscar a few years back – should have known better. In Sean's humble opinion the film was brutal. But there had been no seats available for the one he had planned to take Sadie to, and *Dying for Love* had been the only other viable option. He wondered what Alva would have made of it. Alva had no time for sentimental films, which was strange, Sean always thought, as she had no problem with sentimental and far-fetched soap operas.

'So realistic too,' Sadie added.

Sean nearly choked on the dregs of his bottle of water. Realistic? Where else but on the silver screen would a stunning nurse in her late twenties fall for a rotund, balding man in his mid-sixties who was dying of cancer? And as for having the poor nurse die in a freak tree-felling accident in a redwood forest, what were the screenwriters thinking of? And was Sadie mad?

Sean grunted non-committally. 'Would you like a drink?' he asked before she had a chance to quiz him any further on the film. 'It was really warm in there, I'm parched.'

'Yes. But how about going into town? There's a new club opening this evening. I have an invitation to the launch. It's called Atlas, have you heard of it yet? It was all over the papers last weekend. It sounds cool. There's a huge globe beside the dance floor apparently and . . .'

Sean zoned out. Sadie loved the sound of her own voice, but luckily she didn't seem bothered that he was only half listening. A nightclub? He thought about it while Sadie prattled on. He wasn't normally a big nightclub fan. Alva tended to go clubbing with her friends from work, or Gemma (Mia wasn't a fan either), leaving him happily at home. But he should really start making an effort now that he was single again, he supposed. And tonight was as good a time to start as any. 'I'm not really dressed for it,' he said, gesturing at his plain white shirt and dark blue denims.

'You look great,' she said. She took in his wide shoulders, trim stomach and strong-looking legs admiringly. 'And you're with me anyway.' She clung to his arm possessively. He'd wondered earlier if she wasn't a little overdressed for the cinema. Her short, flirty red dress and matching red jacket and heels seemed a little over the top to him, but what did he know? He wasn't all that attuned to fashion, as Alva was always pointing out to him, like when he'd questioned her habit of wearing summer dresses over jeans. He wasn't sure if Sadie was what you'd call fashionable exactly: her hair was a rather unnatural ash white, as straight, shiny and still as a sheet of metal; her skin was a dark, nutty brown, as if she'd just spent a month in the Caribbean (which Sean knew for a fact she hadn't); and her thin, perfectly arched eyebrows gave her face a permanently startled look. Her cheeks were whippet-thin; her tiny, five-foot-nothing body doll-like, although she had remarkably muscular upper arms for a woman of her size. She was very attractive – there was no denying that – but there was something missing, Sean thought, although he couldn't quite put his finger on it.

Less than half an hour later, after striking it lucky with a taxi, they were in Atlas. Sadie oohed and aahed at the interior decor: the huge illuminated globe, the thick carpet underfoot, the generously oversized red and dark purple velvet sofas. She clung to his arm like a limpet, her head only just reaching his chest. 'Isn't this something?' she gushed.

'Would you like a drink?' he asked, gazing at the huge, brightly lit bar that ran the full length of the right-hand wall. He was gasping for a pint. And he hoped that with a drink to sip on, Sadie would stop talking so much.

'Yes, please. A white wine spritzer,' she said. 'I'll come with you.'

Sean wondered if Sadie would let go of his arm at any stage during the evening; she seemed inordinately fond of it. I'll have to fish my wallet out of my pocket to pay for the drinks, he thought, she'll have to let go of it then.

Alva and Mia stepped out of their taxi and started to walk up Grafton Street towards Atlas. It was a mild evening; just as well as they had both decided to wear dresses – Mia all romance heroine in floaty cream chiffon with a fitted denim jacket thrown over it to dress it down a little, and Alva resplendent in a plain but beautifully cut black number from an Italian designer (which had cost an arm and a leg but which she'd never actually worn) with a light, black ballet-style cardigan over her arms and tied just under her neat bust. Mia had sent Luke on in the taxi as Alva had only just jumped into the shower when he'd arrived and she didn't want to keep him waiting for ages. She'd also rung Gemma at home as her mobile wasn't switched on, but Gemma wasn't in the humour for a club, she told Mia, she was on her way to bed. Watching everyone dance would be most frustrating when she couldn't join in, she explained.

Mia and Alva linked arms as they tripped up the

cobble-locked pedestrian street in their heels, stopping every now and then to admire a particularly fine leather bag or pair of shoes in one of the brightly lit shop windows.

'Left!' Alva pulled on Mia's arm and steered her down a side street.

'Look at those lights!' Alva exclaimed as they approached the discreet doorway of the club. The sky above Atlas was a fiesta of multi-coloured strobes, criss-crossing each other with rainbow intensity. There was a clamour of smartly dressed people queuing against the redbrick wall of the street, chatting and laughing animatedly, all waiting patiently to be admitted. There were four bouncers outside the club, two stationed at the rather innocuous-looking plain black front door, and two roaming up and down the side street, talking to punters in the queue; recognizable only by their matching long-sleeved T-shirts, printed all over with a map of the world. Unlike stereotypical burly bouncers, the two men and two women were of normal stature, and each wore an earpiece and a wrap-around microphone.

One of the girls bounced up to Mia and Alva who were debating whether to join the queue or not. 'Hi, can I help you?' she asked politely.

'Please. We're friends of Luke Jackman's: he's on the guest list. Do we need to queue?' Alva asked the smiling woman.

'No, not at all. Follow me.' She led them towards the entrance. 'I met Luke earlier; he was in school with

Bert, he told me. These guests can go straight in,' she said to the woman to the left of the doorway.

'Thanks,' Alva said.

'Enjoy yourselves,' the woman said and bounced off again.

Once inside, Mia poked Alva in the ribs. 'Is it my imagination or was that the most polite bouncer you've ever met in your life?'

'No kidding.' Alva nodded. 'And look at this!'

The inside of the club was lit in soft, glowing shades of deep blue and purple. It was dark enough to be interesting, but not gloomy enough to be dingy. Swirling, exotic-sounding dance music drifted out of hidden speakers. The walls were decorated in swathes of red and dark pink heavy silks and there were fresh flowers on a dark wood console table to the left of a large stairwell.

'What's that smell?' Alva asked.

Mia sniffed the air. 'I don't know. Cinnamon? Vanilla maybe? Is this place for real?'

Alva shrugged. 'Seems a bit too good to be true. Has someone really opened a club with polite bouncers, tasteful decor and music that doesn't deafen you?'

'Maybe,' Alva murmured.

Two tall, identical-looking clean-cut men stood to the left of the stairway. 'Do you need to check coats?' one of them asked politely.

Alva and Mia shook their heads. 'No, we're fine, thanks,' Alva said.

'In that case, welcome to Atlas, ladies,' the other

167

man said, gesturing towards the staircase with a flourish of his left arm. 'Enjoy your evening.'

'Thanks,' Alva murmured. She looked at him and smiled. 'This is *Candid Camera*, right?'

'Sorry?' he asked.

'Nothing, don't mind her.' Mia put her hand in the small of Alva's back and guided her towards the top of the staircase. As they made their way down the stairs, they both noticed the thick carpet under their feet – manna to heel-wearers.

'Look!' Alva said pointing towards the middle of the room. In front of them was a huge floor-to-ceiling globe whose interior, softly glowing lights pulsated to the music.

'How cool is that?' Alva asked, very impressed. 'Hey, is that blonde girl Nicola from *Fair City*?' Alva knew all her soap stars intimately.

'Where?'

'On the dance floor. To the left.'

Mia stared over. 'It looks like her all right. But I've only seen *Fair City* a couple of times, so I'm not the best person to judge.' They walked past the globe and had another peek at the woman.

'No, that woman's hair isn't naturally blonde,' Alva said wickedly. 'Look at those roots. She's not as pretty either. And she's too short. Nicola's quite tall.'

'You're right. And look at that dress, it barely covers her.'

As they watched, the woman smiled at her dancing partner and swatted him playfully on the arm. The man looked very much like Sean. Alva focused her eyes on the man's face. It *was* Sean. What the hell was he doing here? And who was the Barbie doll dancing with him? Her stomach lurched towards the floor. She felt numb.

Alva stood rooted to the spot and dug Mia in the ribs. 'It's Sean,' she hissed.

'Where?' Mia looked around.

'On the dance floor. With the fake blonde.'

Mia looked closer. Alva was right. It *was* Sean.

'Over here!' They heard a shout behind them. Luke and another dark-haired man were waving at them from a small booth against the wall.

'Are you OK?' Mia asked Alva who was still staring at the dance floor. Barbie had now wrapped her arms around Sean's neck and his hands were cupped around her tiny waist. Alva felt as if someone had stuck a knife in her heart and was slowly turning it.

'Alva?'

'I'm fine. Let's just ignore them, shall we?'

'OK. But do you want me to say anything to Sean?'

'Like what?'

'I don't know. Ask him to leave maybe?'

'Don't be silly, it's fine. I'm over him, really. He can cavort with whoever or whatever he likes, I don't care.'

'If you're sure.'

'I am.' Alva nodded curtly. 'We'd better join the others.'

'Hi, girls.' Luke grinned as Mia and Alva approached. 'I was wondering when you'd turn up. Great place, isn't it? I saw you both checking out the dance floor.' He slid over on the dark red velvet sofa and patted the seat cushion beside her. 'Jump in.' Alva and Mia sidled in.

'Bert, this is Mia and Alva,' he said to the dark-haired man. 'And, girls, this is Bert. Bert owns Atlas.'

Bert winced. 'The bank does more like, but I'm delighted to meet you both. Ladies,' he said formally, standing up and brandishing his arm with a flourish, 'welcome to Atlas.'

'Or should I say, Mr Smooth?' Luke laughed.

'And what about you, Luke?' Alva said, looking Luke up and down. 'You're looking pretty smooth yourself.' She'd forgotten how attractive he was. Much better-looking than Sean. And he'd look incredibly good on my arm, Alva decided immediately. That would show Sean and Bimbo-features.

'Can I get you both a drink?' Luke offered.

'Please, drinks are on the house,' Bert said. 'Tell the barman you're with me, Luke, and he'll sort you out.'

'That's very kind of you,' said Mia. 'A white wine and . . .' she looked at Alva. 'What about you, Alva?'

'Do you think they have cocktails?' Alva asked Luke, her eyelids doing more batting than Babe Ruth in his glory days.

'Absolutely,' he said. 'What do you fancy?'

Alva raised her eyebrows slightly and smiled her most dazzling smile. 'A Sex on the Beach,' she purred. 'Or maybe an Orgasm. Or a Long, Slow Screw. What do you think?'

'I've never had any of them.' He laughed. 'So to speak.'

'You're making those up,' Mia said a little crossly.

170

'No, I'm not, honestly,' Alva insisted with a girlie laugh. She flicked her glossy dark brown hair back with a whip of her head.

'What about a Cosmopolitan, Alva?' Mia said quickly. 'I know you love them. Get her one of those, Luke.' She recognized that Alva was in full-on flirting mode and was keen to stop her in her tracks. I shouldn't have bothered inviting her in the first place, she thought. I want Luke all to myself tonight. Mia hadn't told Alva about her feelings for Luke. She'd agreed that he was attractive and good fun, but that was about as far as it had gone. Things had moved pretty quickly after all, she was only starting to get to know him. Nothing had happened yet, not really. But she realized now that she should have said something earlier. Alva *was* in a vulnerable state after all. Maybe she should say something now, she thought; that would probably be the best idea. Better nip things in the bud before Alva started getting any ideas. She'd talk to her as soon as she got a chance.

'Sounds perfect,' Alva said, looking at Mia. Was it her imagination or was Mia frowning at her?

'I'll give you a hand,' Mia said to Luke, jumping to her feet.

'Great,' said Luke, a little nervous at Alva's change of demeanour. She hadn't been so blatantly flirtatious the last time they'd met and he wondered if she wasn't a little drunk tonight.

Alva watched Mia and Luke walk towards the long chrome-topped bar at the far right of the large room. Then she whipped her eyes back to the dance floor, looking frantically around the club: she'd lost sight of Sean and the blonde who were no longer dancing. They've obviously gone somewhere private for some high-octane canoodling, Alva thought with a sick feeling in her stomach.

'Are you all right?' Bert asked her.

'Yes, sorry, I didn't mean to ignore you just now. I just spotted someone I know earlier and I was looking for him. So, how long have you been in the nightclub business?' she said, realizing that she'd been rude. Bert began to tell her about his previous business enterprises and Alva listened, trying to pay attention to what he was saying while her mind was elsewhere.

Mia and Luke reached the bar. Mia stood there and put her hands and her pulse points against the deliciously cool metal surface. 'It's hot in here,' she said to Luke.

He smiled at her. 'Sure is.'

'I'm not usually a nightclub fan, but this place is great. And Bert seems really nice.'

'Bert's great. We go back years. We were in school together and we meet up whenever we can. He has a young family so he's pretty busy most of the time.'

A new song came on, a remix of an early Madonna track, and Luke tapped a coin against the top of the bar in time to the music. 'I love this one,' he said. 'Want to dance?'

'What about the drinks?' Mia asked. They hadn't even ordered yet.

Just then Bert appeared beside them. 'I thought I'd give you a hand. Alva said she was fine on her own

172

for a few minutes. I need to have a quick word with one of the barmen anyway.'

'Great timing.' Luke slapped Bert on the back. 'Get the drinks in, will you? I haven't ordered yet. I'm taking Mia for a quick spin on the dance floor.'

Bert laughed. 'Go on.'

'Thanks,' Luke said. He took Mia by the hand and led her towards the centre of the room.

'I'm not a great dancer,' Mia said loudly over the music.

'That makes two of us.' Luke smiled at her.

He was lying of course, but Mia had just started to enjoy herself when Alva shimmied her way towards them. She sidled up to Luke, turning her back to him and looking over her shoulder while she moved to the music. She raised both hands to either side of her head, lifted her long, chestnut hair on top and let it drop back down in a swish, like a sleek living curtain.

Mia looked at Luke. He seemed transfixed by Alva, and Mia felt as though she'd been kicked in the solar plexus. She mumbled 'Excuse me,' to no one in particular, and practically ran into the Ladies. She locked herself into a cubicle and sat down on the closed toilet lid. She leaned forward and put her head in her hands. What had she been thinking of? Of course – Luke and Alva – what an obvious couple. Both stunningly attractive, with everything going for them. How could I have thought that Luke was interested in me, she wondered.

At the wedding gig earlier Mia could have sworn that Luke had been flirting with her, but it had obviously been no more than wishful thinking. He was just being nice and she had read too much into it. Maybe it was Alva he was really after. No wonder he'd practically insisted that she come out this evening.

Mia stayed in the cubicle until she felt a little better and then made her way back to the table where Bert was sitting, minding the drinks. She watched Alva flutter around Luke like an exotic butterfly and her heart sank even further in her chest. 'Can you tell the others that I'm going home?' she said, dragging her eyes off the happy couple. 'I'm exhausted. But best of luck with the club. I'm sure it will be a huge success.'

'Is everything all right?' Bert asked gently. Mia was staring at the dance floor and she seemed very out of sorts.

'Yes, fine, really,' she said. 'I was working this evening and I'm just a little tired. It was lovely to meet you.'

'And you. And please ask one of the bouncers at the door to order you a taxi. We have an account with a taxi company.'

'Oh, thanks. I'll do that.'

As Mia walked out she spied Sean just to the left of the staircase. Men! she thought as she made her way towards him. The woman clinging to his arm was tiny, and looked a little old to be dressed in such a provocative manner. The plunging lacing on the front of her red dress left little to the imagination, and, Mia thought in an uncharacteristically catty way, was certainly not a good choice for someone with such a droopy chest.

'Mia!' Sean said in surprise as she plonked herself in front of him.

'Sean,' Mia replied.

'Mia, this is Sadie,' Sean said, trying to sound less nervous than he felt. He hoped to goodness that Mia wouldn't say anything inappropriate. 'Mia's an old friend of mine.'

'Hello, Sadie. I'm also Alva's friend.' Mia looked at the woman, whose head was tilted up towards Sean, a simpering smile on her thin face. Mia took an instant dislike to her. 'And Alva's here,' she added, coming straight to the point.

'Alva?' Sean stared at Mia. 'Are you serious?'

'Alva?' Sadie asked, ignoring Mia and looking up at Sean. 'Alva, your ex?'

'Where?' Sean asked Mia, in turn ignoring Sadie.

'On the dance floor, with Luke.' Mia nodded over at the couple. Alva was doing her hair-lifting trick again and Sean winced visibly as he watched her sashay her hips suggestively to the music.

'Luke from AbbaFab?' Sean asked, unable to take his eyes off the couple. 'She didn't waste much time.'

'Would you like to dance, Sean?' Sadie asked, following his gaze on to the dance floor. She'd been single for far too long now and she wasn't going to let Sean go without a fight. Damn it, she could hair-flick for Ireland and she was far thinner than that girl.

Sean shook his head. He couldn't bear to watch

Alva enjoying herself with Luke any more. 'Let's just go home,' he said gruffly, turning his attention back to his date. 'OK with you?'

Sadie nodded. Going home with Sean was even better.

'Bye, Mia,' Sean said. He took one last look at the dance floor. Alva had stopped dancing and was staring over at them, as if sensing their collective gaze. Sean pulled Sadie even closer.

'Bye, Mia,' Sadie tittered. 'Nice to meet you.' Sean swung Sadie around and practically frogmarched her towards the bottom of the stairs.

'Good riddance,' Mia muttered as she watched Sean and Sadie leave.

Alva appeared beside her. 'So what did Sean have to say for himself?' she demanded.

'Not much,' Mia said. 'You've just driven him away. Enjoying yourself, Alva?'

'What's wrong?' Alva asked. Mia's eyes were sparking.

'What are you playing at?' Mia asked in disdain. 'I thought you wanted Sean back.'

'I do.'

'You're going a funny way about it.'

'He's the one who's with someone else!' Alva said.

'A very silly little someone who won't last the week. She's so not his type. And you've just blown it, Alva. And by the way, I'm going home. Alone. I'll see you later, or tomorrow, or whenever.'

'What do you mean, tomorrow or whenever?'

'I guess you'll be going home with Luke.'

176

'No, Mia. I won't be. In fact he's spent the whole time talking about . . .'

Mia cut in. 'Give my apologies to Luke for not saying goodbye, won't you? But he has been rather busy, hasn't he?' Mia ran up the stairs without looking back.

'. . . *you* if you must know,' Alva whispered the end of her sentence. Right now she felt very stupid and very lonely. What must Sean think of her? And Mia. And Luke. Her stomach lurched and she felt ashamed. She'd been so caught up in her own little world that she had failed to notice what was going on in Mia's life. Of course, she realized, Mia likes Luke, it's so obvious now. But it's too late to do anything about it. Why didn't I notice it earlier? I'm a terrible friend and Mia deserves better. I'm a horrible, horrible person.

At the top of the stairs Mia lingered for a moment. Was she overreacting? Luke and Alva had just been dancing after all. But she'd seen the way Alva was gazing at Luke, a look Mia had seen many times before, and she knew that if Alva had set her sights on him he didn't stand a chance . . . whatever Alva protested to the contrary. Besides, there was another gig tomorrow, well today actually, and she had no business being out at all really. She should never have agreed to it in the first place. Wendy had been right, as usual. Mia yawned. She suddenly felt dog-tired.

'Mia?' A bouncer appeared from nowhere.

She nodded.

'Bert asked me to order you a taxi. It will be here in about five minutes.'

'Thank you,' Mia said, almost tearful at Bert's kindness. If only other men were as thoughtful.

'I'm sorry,' Alva faltered as she sat back down in the booth with Luke. Bert was busy talking to a couple who had stopped to congratulate him on the club.

'Not to worry,' Luke replied. He lifted his drink and took a long gulp.

'I hope I haven't spoiled things,' Alva said. 'With Mia, I mean. She left in a bit of a state.'

'Why?' Luke asked.

Alva decided to come clean. 'Because I was flirting with you. And I shouldn't have been. But . . . I hadn't realized. About you and Mia, I mean. And Sean's here and I wanted to . . . it's stupid,' she finished lamely. 'I hope I haven't ruined things.'

Luke said nothing for a moment. 'Ruined things for you or for me?' he asked.

'Both,' she replied honestly.

'So do I.' He lifted his glass and drained the dregs of his drink. 'It's not always a good idea playing games with people's feelings like that, Alva,' he said after a moment. 'Especially not Mia's feelings. She's been a good friend to you.'

Alva felt about an inch tall. 'I know,' she said softly. 'I'm sorry. I had no idea that she, well, you know . . . that you guys . . .'

178

'How would you? And it's as much my fault as it is yours. I was just flattered that such a beautiful girl would want to dance with me. You're a great dancer and I got a little carried away, I guess. Talk to Mia. I'm sure she'll forgive you.'

'But what about you?' Alva asked. 'Will she forgive *you*?'

He sighed deeply. 'Who knows?'

'I'm so sorry.'

'I know you are. But, please, do me a favour?'

'Yes?'

'Is Sean still here?'

'No, he left just before Mia,' Alva said.

'Try talking to him about how you feel. Ring him tomorrow.'

'But he has another girlfriend now. She was with him this evening.'

'What's she like?'

Alva described Sadie in detail.

'That won't last the night,' Luke said. 'Trust me, I know her type. And from what you've told me about Sean she's not for him. Not after you.'

'Thanks,' Alva murmured. 'You know that's what Mia said.' She suddenly brightened. 'You know, you're right! You're absolutely right. I should talk to him.' She jumped to her feet. 'And there's no time like the present. Thanks, Luke.'

'I didn't mean . . .' Luke began, but it was too late. Alva was already striding away from him.

'Where's Alva off to?' Bert asked, looking over at Luke.

Luke shook his head. 'Don't ask. I think I've just made another big mistake.'

Alva could hardly contain herself in the taxi as it drew nearer and nearer Sean's house. Luke was right – Sean couldn't like that blonde woman, she wasn't right for him, that was obvious. He'd dropped her home of course, that was only polite, but now he'd be sitting up watching late-night television on his own, like he always did when he couldn't sleep. She would apologize for her appalling behaviour in Atlas, he'd admit that he'd been really jealous, and they'd hug, kiss and finally tear each other's clothes off. And then . . .

'Which way at the lights?' the taxi driver asked, interrupting her reverie.

'Right, please,' she replied. 'And then second left.'

He grunted.

Ten minutes later the cab pulled up outside Sean's cottage. Alva paid the driver, adding a generous tip – for good karma – and hopped out. The lights were on in Sean's front room: excellent, he was still up.

Alva stood on the doorstep, weak with anticipation. 'I'm sorry' was on the tip of her tongue. 'I'm sorry, Sean. Let's start again. I love you.'

Before knocking on the door, she had a quick peek in through the window; Sean never pulled the curtains properly.

*

'What's wrong, Sean?' Sadie asked in the taxi. He was staring fixedly out of the left passenger window, his right arm stiffly around Sadie's shoulders.

She put one of her hands in his and squeezed it tightly, her other hand snaking up his leg towards his crotch. 'Is there anything I can do to make you feel better?' she whispered in his ear, her breath hot and moist. She gave his ear lobe a playful nip and he winced.

'Sadie!' Sean nodded at the taxi driver.

She giggled. 'I'm sure he's seen it all before.'

An image flashed into Sean's mind, the image of Alva wrapping her lithe, toned legs around Luke's body. He couldn't shake it off. What had he done? Alva was so completely over him – that was obvious from her behaviour with Luke in the nightclub. But try as he might, he still couldn't get her out of his head. In fact, spending the evening with Sadie had convinced him even more that he belonged with Alva. But there was no point thinking about that now – it was too late. Alva was with Luke and he was with . . . He glanced sideways at Sadie. She wasn't the worst; she seemed to like him anyway. And he certainly didn't want to spend the evening alone, thinking about Alva and what he'd lost.

'Sorry,' he said, turning towards Sadie. 'I'm just a little tired, that's all. But let's wait until we get home. It will make it even better, I promise.' He threw her a smile.

Sadie's heart turned a somersault. Sean liked her.

Really liked her. She'd been worried that his ex-girlfriend had unsettled him, but that obviously wasn't the case. She stroked his leg and beamed up at him. 'I can't wait,' she purred.

As soon as Sean shut the cottage door behind them, Sadie was all over him like a giant cat, rubbing her body up and down his and licking his ear enthusiastically. 'Would you like a drink?' he asked her, trying to slow things down.

'No, but let's go into the kitchen,' she suggested. 'See what's in the fridge.'

'Um, OK,' he said with a gulp. He hoped this wasn't all going to turn a little *9½ Weeks*. He wasn't sure he wanted peanut butter and Nutella smeared all over his private bits, thank you very much. Let alone ice cream. In the early days, he and Alva had experimented with paint-on chocolate, but they'd both agreed that it tasted disgusting and that sharing a romantic dinner *before* sex was far more of an aphrodisiac than involving actual food in their lovemaking.

He led Sadie into the kitchen and she immediately opened the freezer section of the fridge and took out the ice-cube tray. 'Can I have a glass?' She smiled at him. 'Actually two.'

'What would you like to drink?' Sean asked.

'No drink,' she said. 'Just ice. And warm water.'

Sean handed her two tumblers and watched as she filled one with ice, each cube dropping into the glass with a hollow plunk. She filled the other with warm water. 'Follow me,' she said, walking back into the living room and putting the glasses down on the coffee table in front of the sofa. 'Sit down.' She put her hands on his chest and pushed him gently on to the soft seat. He leaned back and watched her, getting more and more nervous by the second.

'Sadie, what are you doing?' he asked as she knelt down in front of him and grinned, showing lots of her slightly off-white, rather large teeth. Sean was reminded suddenly of a rabbit. 'Sadie!' He almost jumped in fright as she leaned forward and began to open the buttons of his fly with her red-taloned fingers.

'Shush,' she said. 'You'll love this. I read about it in *Cosmopolitan*.' She reached back, took an ice cube in her mouth and began to suck on it.

'Sadie!' he said again. He tried to swat her hands away with his own, but Sadie was nothing if not determined. She took the ice out of her mouth, held the dripping cube between two fingers and sat up again. 'Will I turn off the light? Would that make you more comfortable?'

'No, it's just . . .'

'What?' She looked at him in amazement. 'It said all men love this. Just shut your eyes. I'll be gentle, I promise.'

'Sadie!' he protested for a third time as she popped the ice back in her mouth and delved both her hands rather roughly into his trousers. He'd had enough. What was wrong with him? Whatever the question, Sadie really wasn't the answer, and he'd just have to tell her to . . .

Suddenly there was a loud rap on the window.

Sean took both Sadie's hands firmly in his own and

pulled them away. 'There's someone outside.' He stood up, made his way over to the window and pulled back the curtains fully. He recoiled in horror as he recognized the face pressed against the other side of the glass.

'You prick!' he heard distinctly, even through his extra-thick double-glazing.

'Alva!' He ran to the door and wrenched it open. 'Alva!'

Alva looked over and stared at him, an expression of complete disgust on her face. She looked down at his crotch and then back up again. Without saying a word, she turned on her heel and powered off down the street, leaving Sean staring in her wake. He looked down. His fly was gaping open, his white boxer shorts framed by the dark denim. 'Oh, shit!' he muttered. What had he done?

'Sean,' Sadie called from inside.

Sean felt sick to the stomach. He was an idiot, a complete idiot. Alva would have no respect for him now and she'd be right. How could he have been so stupid? He had to do something. Something drastic. But what?

8 'Arrival'

'Mia, you have to start talking to me,' Alva pleaded the following Wednesday morning. 'We're living together, for heaven's sake, and I've apologized till I'm blue in the face. Please, this is getting ridiculous.'

Mia ignored her. She left the jumper she was carefully hand-washing dripping in the sink and walked out of the kitchen.

'Mia!' Alva followed her.

Mia walked into her room and closed the door in Alva's face.

'Mia, you're being really childish. Just talk to me. We need to sort this out. It's getting beyond a joke.'

Mia hadn't said a word to Alva for four days now and Alva was beginning to despair. They'd had their arguments over the years all right, but nothing like this. She waited outside the door for a few minutes but there was silence from inside the room.

'I'm going to work now,' Alva said finally. 'I'll see you later. I'll cook this evening, OK? Something nice.'

Still nothing.

Alva gave up. She grabbed her bag and jacket, and closed the front door behind her. 'Damn it,' she muttered, getting into the car and thumping the steering wheel with her fist. This can't go on, it's ridiculous. As she drove towards Dublin city, she decided to make one final effort to make Mia forgive her. And if that didn't work she'd move out.

Later that morning, Mia raised her head from her book. Someone was ringing her doorbell. It had better not be Alva again, she thought darkly. At first, she'd got quite a kick from sending her friend to Coventry, but now it was becoming rather tiresome. She wanted Alva to think about her behaviour in Atlas, but it had all got rather out of control and now Mia didn't know how to stop it. She couldn't start speaking to Alva again, just like that. Alva still hadn't apologized properly. Oh, she'd said sorry all right, but Mia didn't think she'd meant it, not really.

Mia got up and looked out of the window. Sean was standing on the doorstep, staring up at her.

'Can I come in?' he shouted through the open window.

'Depends,' she replied. 'Do you have any food?'

'Of course.' He grinned up at her. 'I'd hardly call in empty-handed this close to lunchtime, now would I?'

'I'll be down in a second.' Mia looked around the sitting room. Alva had made more of an effort than usual to keep it tidy, but there were still clothes draped over the back of the sofa and a pile of work-related folders spilling their contents all over the coffee table. But it wasn't too bad. And, in any case, Sean would hardly notice.

Mia left her flat, snibbing the door lock to make sure she could get back in, and went downstairs to the communal hallway. The owner still hadn't got around to installing buzzers for each flat, as he'd promised to do two years ago, but Mia didn't really mind running up and down the stairs to open the door for guests – it kept her fit. But she did feel sorry for old Mrs Carmody in the flat upstairs, who wasn't at her most mobile after two hip operations and had taken to lowering her keys through the window in a small basket whenever anyone came to call. Mia always smiled as she saw the basket swinging past her window on its way down to Mrs Carmody's guest.

Mia opened the heavy front door and stood back to let Sean in. 'To what do I owe this unexpected pleasure?'

'Can't an old friend call in without wanting anything?' he asked, feigning hurt.

'No.' Mia was no fool; she knew exactly what or who he wanted to talk about. 'Come on up.'

He followed her up the stairs and into her flat. 'I see Alva's still living here,' he commented, nodding at the sofa.

'Yes.' Mia said, leaving it at that.

He showed Mia a large brown paper bag. 'Salads and bread from the deli,' he said. 'Hungry?'

'Always. Want to eat now?'

He nodded. 'Why not?'

They climbed the few steps to the kitchen. Sean put the bag down on the table and began to fish out its contents. 'Potato salad,' he said, lifting out a large round plastic container. 'Apple and walnut; baby roast potatoes and rosemary; and that carrot one with the poppyseeds that get caught in your teeth.'

Mia laughed. 'Thanks, Sean, I know it's not exactly your favourite.'

'Bloody rabbit food,' he said. 'And pâté and bread.'

Mia handed him a breadboard and a knife. 'Will you do the honours?' she asked.

He nodded.

She put plates and cutlery on the table and filled two large tumblers with water from the fridge. 'Sorry, I don't have any juice to offer you.'

'Water is fine.'

'Thank you,' she said, sitting down at the table and looking at the spread. 'I was going to have a sandwich, but this is much better.'

'No problem.' He watched as she helped herself to some bread and smothered it with pâté. Then she heaped salads on her plate and began to tuck in.

'What?' she asked when she'd swallowed her first mouthful. Sean was staring at her blatantly.

'Aren't you going to ask me anything?' he asked.

'Like what?' She cocked her head and looked at him innocently.

'You know, about Saturday night. About Sadie.'

'It's none of my business, Sean,' she said evenly and took another large bite of bread.

'Mia,' he said, his voice a little mournful, 'I need your help. I've been really stupid.'

Still nothing from Mia.

'Mia, why are you being like this?'

'Like what?'

Sean waved his hands in the air rather aimlessly. 'Oh, I don't know. Uninterested, I suppose. As if you couldn't care less about me and Alva.'

Mia shrugged. 'Sean, I've had it up to here with "me and Alva". I thought you wanted to move on. What about Sadie?'

Sean winced. 'That was a mistake. I presume Alva told you what happened?'

'In the nightclub, you mean? I was *there*, Sean.'

'No, afterwards.'

'Afterwards?' Mia shook her head. 'No.' Alva had tried to tell her something about Sean and Sadie all right, but Mia seemed to remember that she'd walked out of the room in the middle of Alva's account, even though Alva had been visibly upset. Mia felt ashamed. It wasn't a nice thing to do to her friend.

'So you don't know?' asked Sean.

'No. Go on,' she said, curiosity getting the better of her. 'Tell me.'

Sean stared down at his hands which were pressed against the tops of his thighs. Then he looked up, a red slash of embarrassment spreading up his neck. 'Mia, it was terrible. I'm so ashamed. Alva called into the house and caught me . . .' He stopped suddenly.

'Yes?' Mia encouraged. He'd certainly caught her attention now.

189

'With Sadie.'

'Having sex?' Mia stared at him in astonishment.

'Not exactly, but close.' Sean explained how he'd answered the door in a rather compromising state.

'Poor Alva,' Mia murmured. 'No wonder she was so upset on Sunday.'

'She was upset?' Sean asked his voice an octave higher.

'Yes, of course she was. Don't sound so pleased about it. Hurting Alva is nothing to be proud of.'

'No, no, of course not.'

'Sean, what am I going to do with the pair of you?'

He shrugged. 'I have no idea. All I know is that I want Alva back. I do love her, Mia. Do you think there's any hope?'

Mia felt like laughing. They certainly deserved each other, that was for sure. 'What are you like?' she asked eventually.

'Would you talk to her for me, Mia? Please?' He put his hands together palm to palm in a prayer gesture.

'To tell the truth, I'm not exactly on speaking terms with her myself at the moment.'

Sean looked at Mia in amazement. 'She's still living here, isn't she?'

'Yes. But I haven't said a word to her since the early hours of Saturday morning. We had a bit of a fight.'

A smile played on Sean's lips.

'What?' Mia asked.

'You did that to me once.'

'Did what?'

'Stopped talking to me.'

'Did I?'

'Yes, in sixth year. When I made a joke in biology class about women being inferior to men, remember? You didn't say a word to me for two days.'

Mia blushed slightly. Now that he mentioned it, she did recall some incident in sixth year all right. 'What happened after two days?' she asked, her voice low.

'It was the weekend and I took you to the movies to say sorry. Something with Richard Gere in it, I think. Who, as you know, I can't stand. It was an act of great charity on my part.'

Mia nodded. 'Right. Well, this is different.'

'Is it?' Sean asked gently. 'I presume it has something to do with Luke from the band.'

Mia shot him a look. 'No, it doesn't!'

'I know Alva,' Sean continued, 'and she didn't mean to upset you, Mia. It had nothing to do with Luke and everything to do with me. I see that now, even if I didn't on Saturday night. She obviously didn't realize.'

'Realize what?'

'How you feel about Luke.'

'I have no interest in Luke!' Mia said strongly.

'Mia, don't be like that. It's me you're talking to.'

Mia sighed. It would be a relief to talk to someone about it. And she trusted Sean. And she was sick of being angry. 'Maybe I like him a bit,' she conceded.

191

'But, Sean, Alva was all over him. Hair flicks and all. I just couldn't take it. I thought he liked me.' She broke off, embarrassed at her outburst.

'He'd be mad not to,' Sean said gently. He put his hand on Mia's. 'Talk to Alva. I'm sure she feels awful, Mia. Let her apologize.'

Mia pushed the food around on her plate. 'It's not that simple,' she said.

'It is really,' Sean said. 'When she walks in the door, just say hello and take it from there.'

'I'll see.' Mia took a sip of her water and put it back on the table. 'So what about you?' she asked. 'Are *you* going to apologize to Alva?'

He sat back in his chair and gave a deep sigh. 'If she'll let me, yes.'

'And if she won't forgive you?'

'I have no idea. But I'll think of something. I haven't given up hope.'

'That's the spirit.'

Sean looked at his untouched plate. 'Haven't done very well on the eating front, have we?'

Mia shook her head. 'But I'm starting to feel hungry again now. Let's forget about Alva and Luke for a while and tuck in.'

Sean smiled at her. 'Good idea. And Mia?'

'Yes?'

'Thanks.'

'For what?'

'You know.' He nudged her shoulder affectionately with his. 'For listening. To Alva and me. I know it can't be easy sometimes and I think Alva . . .'

Mia interrupted him. 'Enough! Eat!' she commanded.

It was almost seven and Alva hadn't returned from work yet. Mia was sitting by the window waiting for her, attempting to finish reading another of her old favourites, *Rebecca*, by Daphne Du Maurier, but the type was swimming in front of her eyes and she couldn't concentrate on the plot. Sean was right – she'd have to start talking to Alva again and there was no time like the present. So she'd been waiting for her for the last hour. It wasn't like Alva to be home so late; Mia hoped nothing had happened to her.

'Ping!' Her thoughts were interrupted by a sharp rap on the window. 'Ping!' There it was again. Mia glanced towards the noise and recoiled in shock as a small stone hit the glass with another loud 'ping!'

'What the hell?' she muttered, rising from her chair and making her way towards the window. She jumped back in fright when she heard a loud bang outside.

'OK, what's going on?' She stared out, and suddenly her view was blocked by a barrage of colour as a cloud of red, pink, blue, green, yellow and purple balloons floated into her line of vision.

She opened the window and tried to push the balloons away so she could look down, but it was no use, there were too many of them. So she began to pull them into the flat through the window instead. Just as she'd succeeded in wrestling three of them in and had cut their rather tough ribbon-like strings with her teeth, allowing them to float up to the ceiling, she heard music from outside. It was one of her favourites, an old eighties song about lions sleeping in the jungle that Wendy used to sing to her when she was a child. Back from London for a two-day visit, Wendy had choreographed a dance for Mia and Alva, and Mia smiled as she remembered the happy summer day when she'd spent the whole afternoon with the two of them, learning the dance and the song. She pulled a few more balloons into the room and then looked down. Alva was staring up at her from the pavement.

'Hi, Mia.' She waved up, a hopeful look on her face.

Mia couldn't help but smile. 'Hi, Alva,' she shouted down. 'You're mad, do you know that? Come on up and help me with the bloody balloons.'

'Will do.'

The music, courtesy of Alva's car stereo, stopped, and seconds later Mia heard her friend bounding up the stairs. She practically ran into the living room where Mia was still struggling with the helium balloons. 'Do you like them?' she asked a little shyly, still wary of Mia.

Mia smiled. 'Yes. And they seem to like the high ceiling.' Sure enough, the balloons had all drifted to the ceiling, where they nestled around the central rose and plasterwork. 'Thanks. And where did you find that song? It's pretty old.'

'On a compilation album in HMV in town. I knew it would make you smile. You used to play it all the time when we were kids. Mia, I'm so sorry. Really I am. I behaved like an idiot and . . .'

194

'It's OK.' Mia let go of the balloons she'd been holding and they floated up to join the others. She gave Alva a quick hug and then drew back. 'I'm sorry too. Sean told me about that thing with him and Sadie. It must have been a shock for you to see him in that state, even if there wasn't really anything going on.'

Alva snorted. 'Nothing going on? Sean's trousers were practically around his ankles. I know what I saw, Mia.'

Mia thought for a moment. 'Things aren't always as black and white as they look,' she said eventually. 'Sean swears that nothing happened and I believe him. He sent Sadie home as soon as you left. He made a mistake, Alva. But we all make mistakes. Talk to him.'

Alva snorted again.

'What?' asked Mia innocently.

Talk to him? That was fine advice coming from Mia, Miss Grudge Holder herself! But Alva thought it better not to go into it. Mia had only just started speaking to her again after all. 'Nothing. But Sean and I are history, Mia. I have to accept that. It's just not meant to be.'

'Ah, Alva.'

Alva flopped down on to the sofa and brushed her hair away from her glowing face. 'I'll be fine, Mia. Really. I just need some time to adjust to being single again.'

'It's not so bad,' Mia said gently. 'Being single has its advantages, Alva. At least your heart never gets trampled on.'

Alva looked up. Mia had a strange expression on

her face. 'Luke's a good man,' Alva said gently. 'He also made a mistake. But don't punish him for it, Mia. He doesn't deserve it. It was as much my fault as his.'

Mia shrugged. 'It's irrelevant now. I'm not interested.' She stared up at the ceiling. 'Where did you get the balloons?'

'The Balloon Man shop in Dun Laoghaire, but stop changing the subject.' Alva took a deep breath. 'Mia, there are some good guys out there and although I don't know him all that well, I think Luke is one of them. If I can say that after what I've been through, then isn't there some hope?'

'Maybe,' Mia conceded.

'At least give him the benefit of the doubt.'

'Like you're giving Sean?' Mia asked archly.

'That's different!'

'Is it?'

'Totally. He betrayed me and our relationship.'

'But you're not together at the moment, Alva, and you certainly weren't on Friday night either. So how did he do that?'

'He just did.'

'Are you sure it's not a simple case of jealousy? Sean was with someone else and you're punishing him for it. Please, just swallow your pride and talk to him.'

'No!' Alva exclaimed. 'I can't.'

'Can't or won't? Just tell him how you feel.'

'I tried, Mia, remember?' Alva said with a wobble in her voice. 'You know I did. But *he* wouldn't talk to *me*. I think you're being a little harsh.'

'Sorry,' Mia murmured. 'You're right. But Sean called in earlier and I spent hours listening to him telling me how much he loves you and what a fool he was to let you go in the first place. I suppose it just annoys me.' She looked Alva in the eye. 'Alva, you love Sean and he loves you. Can't you get over all that's happened and give it one more try? None of this makes any sense.'

Alva shook her head. 'I can't, Mia. Maybe before Friday night . . .' she shrugged. 'Seeing him with Sadie like that, in our house, on our sofa; I feel sick just thinking about it. You say he still loves me, but how could he if he behaved like that?' Alva put her head in her hands. 'I know what you're going to say, that nothing actually happened. But don't you see? Men don't bring women home late at night for a little by-the-fire chat. Of course he was going to sleep with her. And maybe she turned out to be a little nuts and not his type. But don't you understand? She was in his house, our house. He *would* have slept with her if things had gone well. That's what matters. Not what he did or didn't actually do.'

'I hadn't really thought about it like that,' Mia admitted. 'And I suppose you're right. But can't you forgive him, Alva?'

'No, I don't think I can.'

Mia hugged her friend. 'Ah, Alva. What am I going to do with the pair of you?'

'Well, you can keep me busy for a start,' Alva said. 'Stop me thinking about it all too much. What are you doing this weekend? I still owe you lunch.'

'We're singing at a festival in Skibbereen. Want to come?'

'Where's that?'

'West Cork.'

Alva smiled. 'You know, that sounds ideal. I'm in Limerick on Friday and Saturday at a work thing. I could drive up and meet you there on Saturday afternoon if that suits.'

'Of course. That sounds great. I'm sure the others won't mind. And you can drive back with me on Sunday.'

'Perfect. And Mia?'

'Yes?'

'I am sorry.'

Mia smiled at Alva. 'You can stop apologizing. I believe you. Now, you promised to cook this evening, remember?'

'I did?'

'Yes, this morning.'

'Oh, right.' Alva thought for a moment. 'How about a curry?'

'Lovely. I didn't know you could cook Indian.'

'I can't. But I know a man who can.'

'Sean?' Mia asked hopefully.

Alva frowned. 'No! The chef in the Bombay Pantry. He does mean garlic naan bread too.'

Later that evening Mia was woken by the phone ringing. She lowered herself out of bed and staggered into the hall.

'Hello?' she said groggily.

'Hi, Mia.' It was Sean.

'It's almost one in the morning,' she said. 'Is anything wrong?'

'I'm so sorry, Mia. But I had to talk to you.'

'Go on.'

'It's about Alva.'

Mia sighed.

'Before you say anything, let me finish. I know you've had enough of the both of us, but I haven't given up. I've been thinking about it all evening. I need your help.'

'Yes?' Mia said, willing him to get on with it so that she could get back to sleep.

'Where will Alva be this weekend?' he asked.

'Actually, I think she'll be in Skibbereen with me. We're singing at a festival. Alva's coming down to join us on Saturday after working in Limerick,' Mia said in a low voice. She didn't want Alva to overhear the conversation. Luckily she was a heavy sleeper and was unlikely to hear them conspiring.

'Perfect,' Sean said. 'Skibbereen? That's about an hour's drive from Cork city, isn't it?'

'I think so.'

'Skibbereen,' he repeated. 'Great. You're an angel, Mia.'

'I don't know about that,' Mia murmured. 'Listen, I'm exhausted. Can I ring you tomorrow?'

'Of course, you go back to sleep. Talk to you tomorrow.'

Mia put the phone down, crawled back into bed

and switched off the light. And as soon as her head hit the pillow, she was asleep.

Sean, on the other hand, was having another bout of insomnia. But this time at least he had something positive to think about and a plan to concoct. Because he wasn't going to let Alva go without a fight.

9 *'Gimme! Gimme! Gimme!'*

'Come on, computer, please co-operate this time.' On Thursday morning Wendy pressed the power button on her laptop for the umpteenth time, scrunching her eyes tightly shut and willing it to behave. When she opened them again the screen in front of her was still full of illegible multicoloured lines.

She cursed under her breath and put her hands to her face. Not this morning, please not this morning. Unless she sent the invoices out immediately there would be a major cash-flow problem and no one in the band would get paid next month. Wendy knew for certain that their bank would be none too pleased if she and Ronan were late with yet another mortgage repayment. She'd already used all the excuses in the book on previous occasions, from having to organize several grannies' funeral arrangements (although it was hardly normal for anyone to have quite so many grannies), to sick pets and flooded bathrooms. I could always fall back on the cremated kitchen excuse, Wendy thought wryly. I haven't used that one before.

She took a deep breath and shut the computer down once more. She then opened and closed the lid of the laptop, trying to bring the screen back to life. This particular problem had happened once before, but had righted itself after a few minutes.

Wendy's work station was an old late-nineteenth-century clerk's desk, stained to look like mahogany, which she'd found in an auction house and bought for a song; much less than the cost of a brand-spanking-new but anonymous computer desk from one of the office supply furniture shops, with their unappealing wood-effect surfaces and wobbling legs. Ronan had sanded, stained and varnished it for her and it now sat proudly in the corner of the sitting room. It was, truth be told, a little large for the room, but it had real character and Wendy loved it. At the front was a panel of square cubbyholes and there were large, deep drawers on either side, ideal for holding some of her paperwork. She also kept a small utilitarian filing cabinet on castors beside the desk, which was wheeled under the stairs whenever they had company. And best of all, the desk had its original roll-top – restored to working order by Ronan – which when closed cutely hid away all Wendy's in- and out-trays and mountains of paperwork from Greg and Steve's prying eyes and sticky fingers.

Wendy's living room was her pride and joy. At present its walls were a tasteful shade of eau de nil, but she was about to change them again. She'd recently found the most delightful Designers' Guild curtain fabric, flamboyant pink, turquoise-blue and purple flowers on a plain white background – very retro, and jewel colours were the latest thing, after all. But she'd have to paint the walls to match. Plain white, she thought, white with a touch of blue maybe. Or that lovely Farrow and Ball colour she'd discovered in an interiors magazine only last week – pale powder white. It would cost an arm and a leg, but it would be perfect.

'Ronan!' Wendy yelled from her seated position. 'Ronan!'

She heard him run down the stairs. 'What's wrong?' he said as he walked into the sitting room.

'Were you asleep?' she asked suspiciously. I left you in bed over an hour ago, you lazy lump, she felt like saying, and you promised me you were about to get up. I've washed the kitchen floor, hung a full load of washing on the clothes-line, cleared the floor in the boys' room, extracted their dirty underpants and socks from under their beds; all this – and you've been bloody asleep.

Wendy gritted her teeth. She knew there was no point saying a word. Ronan would just apologize as he always did and nothing would change. And besides, she had more important things on her mind right at this moment, like her banjaxed laptop; a lecture on Ronan's domestic responsibilities could wait. It didn't usually bother her so much, but in the last few days her energy levels had hit an all-time low and domestic chores which she usually found easy had started to get on top of her.

'Were you using my computer last night?' she asked, trying not to sound accusatory.

'Yes. I was checking some sites for Steve on the Internet. He has to find out about the Egyptians for school. They're studying the Pyramids this week and next week they're doing . . .'

'Did you move the screen?' Wendy cut him off.

'The screen? I probably did. They both wanted to look at the site I found from the Ancient History Museum in Cairo and . . .'

'What did I tell you yesterday morning about the computer?'

Ronan gazed at her blankly. 'Sorry, Wendy, I don't remember.'

'I told you that there was a loose connection between the screen and the keyboard and . . .' She looked at him expectantly.

'And not to close the computer,' Ronan finished. He hit his forehead with the heel of his hand. 'Oh, Wendy, I'm sorry, I didn't think . . .'

Wendy sighed. 'Ronan, I have so much to do, I can't be without my computer today. I have to finish setting up the Skibbereen gig for one thing. It's next weekend and I still haven't given all our press details to the organizers.'

'Can't you ring them?'

'They need photos and biogs for the local papers and radio station. And it's all in here.' Wendy tapped the top of the laptop with her nails.

'Can't it be fixed?' Ronan asked. 'I'm sure there are

companies that do that kind of thing. I'll have a look in the Yellow Pages. Give me a few minutes to ring around, I'm sure I'll come up with something.'

'Thanks, that would be great. I'd really appreciate it. Sorry for snapping at you, I'm just under a lot of pressure. You know how it is.'

'Of course. And I'm sorry about the computer, really I am. It was stupid of me. While I'm in the kitchen, I'll make you some nice strong coffee. Would you like anything to eat? Have you had breakfast?'

'No, but I'm fine. I'll return a few phone calls on my mobile while I'm waiting.'

Ten minutes later, Ronan came back into the sitting room and handed Wendy a steaming mug of coffee and a round of hot buttered toast on a plate.

'Thanks,' she murmured, blowing on the surface of the hot liquid and taking a careful sip. 'Any luck?' She put the plate down on top of her groaning in-tray.

Ronan shook his head. 'Not yet. There's one company that can have a look at it all right, but they're really busy with their regular accounts at the moment. They can squeeze us in tomorrow afternoon.'

'Tomorrow!' Wendy spluttered. 'Are you serious?'

'I'm afraid so. But I'll keep trying other places.'

As soon as Ronan had left the room Wendy had an idea. She picked up her mobile phone, found Des's number and stared at it on the screen. Maybe it's fate, she considered. Wendy wasn't a great believer in fate, she tended to think that you made your own, largely by a mixture of hard work and being in the right place at the right time. But in this case she was prepared to suspend her disbelief, because it suited her to do so. Besides, she told herself, it's an emergency.

She made a deal with herself. If Ronan can't find anyone to fix the laptop, I *will* ring Des, she decided. And this time I'm not going to put down the phone as soon as I hear his voice. A shiver of excitement ran up and down her spine. It's business, she tried to convince herself. Strictly business.

'Ronan,' she called through the open door, sealing the deal, 'if you don't find anyone, there's someone I can ring. An old friend from my cruise-ship days. I bumped into him at the garage the other day.'

'Why don't you ring him now?' Ronan said, walking back into the room. 'I'm having no luck and I have to go out soon.'

'I will in a few minutes,' Wendy said. 'I just have to do a few other things first.' There was no way she was going to ring Des with Ronan standing beside her.

As soon as she was sure Ronan was otherwise occupied, Wendy picked up her mobile, her hands shaking. She pressed the call button before she had the chance to change her mind.

'Wendy Redden,' Des said, 'now there's a surprise. Did you ring me late on Friday night? Actually more like Saturday morning?' Wendy could picture the lopsided smile on Des's face.

'No, I did not!' she lied. Shit, shit, shit, she thought.

'OK,' he said, letting it slide. He knew she was lying. Out of curiosity, he'd rung the unfamiliar number back the following morning, and had got her voice on the message-minder. 'I was hoping you'd ring.'

'Des,' she said, grateful that he'd let it drop, 'I need a favour. My laptop's acting up. Do you think you could have a look at it?'

'Oh, sure, sure,' Des said lazily. 'I can have a look at it all right.'

'It's a bit of an emergency,' Wendy explained, ignoring his less than serious tone. 'There's a loose connection and the screen's gone all fuzzy. I can't read a word.'

'That's pretty common with laptops,' he said. 'What make is it?'

Wendy gave him all the details.

'Right,' he said. 'Here's the thing. It could be something simple, like you say, a loose connection. But it might need a new video card and that's a bit more complicated.'

Wendy groaned. A video card? That sounded serious.

'How urgent is urgent?' he asked.

'Very urgent. You have no idea.'

'I can come over and have a look at it this morning, if you like. There is one temporary option if you do need a new video card, so don't panic yet. I'll see what I can do.'

'I'd be so grateful, Des. Really.' She gave him the address and directions.

'You know I'll expect the favour returned, Wendy, don't you?' Des said, his voice treacle-thick.

'Um, this is just business, Des,' Wendy faltered. 'Ronan's here,' she blurted.

'Well, we'll have to save the pleasure for later then, won't we?' Des said smoothly.

'No, I don't think you understand . . .' Wendy began.

'Oh, believe me, I do,' Des murmured before cutting her off.

Wendy put her mobile down on her desk and put her hands to her face. She could feel her cheeks burning and willed them to cool down. What had she done? Emergency or no emergency.

'Did you ring your friend?' Ronan asked, coming into the room. 'Is he able to do it? Are you all right? You look a little flushed.'

'I'm fine, just hot.' Wendy stood up. 'Yes, he'll be here within the hour.'

'Thank goodness.' Ronan smiled at her. 'That was lucky, wasn't it? How do you know this guy exactly?'

'He worked for the cruise ship,' Wendy said vaguely. 'Administration.'

'I see.' Wendy had lots of different friends and acquaintances from her cruise-ship days and Ronan could never remember all their names. He'd stopped even trying long ago.

'Hopefully it'll be fixed by the time I get back. Do you want anything?' he asked kindly.

'Where are you going?' Wendy said in a slight panic.

'Town. With Pat, remember? I have a meeting with

Dino Fairfield, Mr Eurovision himself. It turns out he's Pat's brother-in-law. He's offered to listen to my song and give some helpful advice, I hope.' Ronan grinned. 'Exciting, isn't it?'

'You never said anything to me about it.' Ronan was forever having meetings with people in the music industry; Wendy found it hard to keep up. God bless his enthusiasm, she always said.

'I'm sure I did. I'll be back in a couple of hours. I'll be on the mobile if you need me.'

He kissed her on the cheek. 'Are you all right, Wendy? You look a little shell-shocked.'

'Um, I'm fine,' she managed.

What the hell was she going to do now?

'So where's hubby?' Des grinned at her as he strode into her hall a little later that morning. It seemed almost too small to hold his tall, self-assured frame.

'Upstairs,' she lied. 'Can I show you the computer?'

'Talk about getting down to business.' He cocked his head and looked at her. 'Like the boots.'

Wendy had changed out of her tracksuit and into a skirt and high-heeled boots as soon as Ronan had left. It would make her feel more confident, she told herself. She'd also slicked on some lip-gloss and run a brush through her hair. No point in looking less than professional, she reasoned.

'Nice perfume,' Des commented as he followed her into the sitting room.

'Thanks.'

Ronan had long stopped noticing her signature vanilla-based scent.

'This is the problem.' Wendy clicked on the computer and they both studied the distorted screen.

Des nodded. 'I'll get cracking.' He sat down on the chair in front of the desk and began to run his fingers along the join at the back of the screen.

'Would you like a coffee?' Wendy asked.

'Love one.' He gazed at her for a little longer than was strictly necessary.

'Back in a moment,' Wendy mumbled, and practically fell out of the door.

In the kitchen she stalled for time, taking a few deep, calming breaths before clicking the kettle back on to boil. Why is he having this effect on me? she asked herself. Get yourself together, woman. Get your computer fixed and stop this ridiculous behaviour before it gets you into serious trouble. Even if Des does find you attractive, you're hardly going to do anything about it now, are you? It wouldn't be right. What about Ronan?

As soon as the kettle had boiled, Wendy poured steaming water on to the coffee granules, put the two mugs, the sugar bowl and a small jug of milk on to a tray, and after taking another deep breath walked back into the sitting room.

'It's actually one of the fittings at the base of your screen,' Des said without looking up. 'It needs to be replaced, I'm afraid.'

'How long will that take?'

Des shrugged. 'An hour, tops. But I'll have to order the part for you and that could take a day or two, depending on availability.'

Wendy's face drained. She felt like crying. A few days – what the hell was she going to do now? She muttered an expletive under her breath.

'But while I'm waiting for the part I can hook up your hard drive to a different monitor. That way you can use your computer as normal.'

'Really?' Wendy was so relieved. She sat down on the sofa and put the tray on the floor in front of her. She began to laugh. 'Sorry, I just had to sit down there, it's been quite a morning.'

'You don't realize how much you depend on computers until something goes wrong, do you?' asked Des. He stood up. 'I have another monitor in the car. I'll get it. I was setting up some new computers in my brother-in-law's office this morning and I have two left over. I don't need to return them for a few days so I can borrow one of the monitors for your laptop.'

'Great. But do drink your coffee first,' Wendy said. 'A few more minutes won't make any difference at this stage and it'll get cold.' She was itching to get back to work but didn't want to appear rude.

Des sat down on the sofa beside her. 'Are you a bit of a workaholic by any chance, Wendy Redden?' he asked and then grinned.

She picked the tray up off the floor and nodded down at it, ignoring his question. 'Here's your coffee. Sorry it's only instant. I'm out of the real stuff.'

Des added a large splash of milk and wrapped both

his hands around the mug cosily. Wendy placed the tray on the floor again, then leaned down and picked up her own mug.

'So here we are,' Des said, staring straight ahead of him, a hint of amusement in his voice. 'Would your husband not like a cup of coffee?'

'No, he's fine. He's just had one,' Wendy said.

'I see.' Des took a sip.

Neither of them said anything for several minutes. Finally Wendy became uncomfortable with the silence.

'Thanks for coming over so quickly,' she said. 'I really appreciate it. Ronan spent hours this morning trying to find someone to help.'

'So I was the last resort,' Des said evenly.

'I didn't like to bother you on your holidays,' Wendy explained. 'And I didn't want you to get the wrong idea.'

Des raised his eyebrows. 'And what idea would that be exactly?'

Wendy stared at the floor. 'That it was anything other than strictly business.'

'Unfinished business,' Des murmured. He took another swig of his coffee and replaced the half-full mug on the tray.

Wendy held her breath. Unfinished business, what does he mean by that? What will I do if he tries to kiss me? I haven't kissed anyone but Ronan for so many years – will it feel any different?

Stop it, Wendy! she chastised herself. That's quite enough. He's not interested in kissing anyone, especially not you.

212

But he stood up. 'Thanks for the coffee. I'd better get back to work. I know you're anxious to be rid of me. I'll get the monitor from the car.'

Wendy watched him as he walked out of the room. She felt strangely disappointed.

Twenty minutes later, the computer was working again. 'Bless you,' Wendy said in delight as her familiar files popped up on to the new screen. It was slightly awkward as her keyboard now sat beside the new screen and not directly in front of it, forcing her to twist her neck and head slightly to read it, but it would be fine for a few days. It was working – that was the main thing.

'My pleasure.'

'And what do I owe you?'

'Wendy, you insult me. You don't owe me anything.'

'Please. You've saved my life. Let me do something.' The words were out before she had the chance to stop them.

'You can let me take you out to lunch,' Des suggested instantly, his eyes twinkling. 'How about that?'

'Um, I'm not sure ... I'll have to check when Ronan's free to babysit,' she said, fishing for an excuse.

'Why don't you go upstairs and ask him?' Des said smoothly. 'If he is upstairs.'

'Why don't I just get back to you?' Wendy said.

Des grinned at her. 'He's out, isn't he?'

'Um, yes,' Wendy admitted. 'But I didn't want . . .'

Des put his finger on her lips and pressed gently. 'Shush.' He took some of her long blonde hair in his

213

hand and brushed her face with it. 'Wendy, I won't do anything you don't want me to do.'

Wendy felt a frisson of excitement, mixed with a pit-of-the-stomach feeling of guilt. 'I don't want to do anything,' she gulped. 'Really.' She flicked her head to the side, pulling her hair out of his hand, leaving a few ripped-out strands lingering in his fingers. It hurt a little, but she didn't care.

'Feisty,' he said. 'I like that.' He put his hand behind her head; she could feel the power in his firm, strong fingers as he pulled her face towards his.

'Des!' she protested. 'Stop, please.'

'Just one kiss and then I'll leave,' he said. 'I promise. One kiss for old times' sake.'

Wendy faltered for a moment. What harm would it do, she asked herself, knowing full well that just one kiss never meant just one kiss. But she hadn't wanted anything so much for as long as she could remember. Her legs were practically buckling under her and the blood was pumping through her veins. She felt wanted, special, alive.

'Not now,' she murmured. 'Not here.'

'Just one kiss,' he whispered, leaning towards her.

She could feel his warm breath in her ear and it made her whole body tingle. He planted a tiny, fluttery, warm kiss on her neck, which melted on to her skin. He put his hands on her shoulders and gazed into her eyes. Wendy closed her eyes, willing him to kiss her properly, all her nerve endings tingling and her lips waiting to be kissed.

'Ring me,' he said in a silky-smooth voice.

She opened her eyes, mortified.

His eyes were caressing her face. 'I don't want to keep you from your work.'

'But . . .' Wendy began.

Des silenced her with a finger on the lips again.

'Later,' he said.

He turned away from her, opened the front door and left without turning round.

Wendy stood rooted to the spot, unable to move. Her blood was still pumping through her body, her lips still aching for his. She heard his car pull away. Finally she shut the door and rested her back against the wood. As if I could do any work now, she thought, her neck still poker-hot from his caress.

A few hours later, Ronan returned to find Wendy sitting at her desk, gazing into space. It wasn't like her; usually she was doing at least two things at once – talking on the telephone, the receiver lodged between her neck and her ear, leaving her hands free to type an email; or printing out some booking details while simultaneously filling in figures on her complicated expenses spread-sheets and talking to Sid in the tax office, the kindly official with whom she was on first-name terms due to her regular calls to his desk. As well as everything else, Wendy filed all the band members' tax returns.

'Is everything all right?' Ronan asked, a little concerned. 'Is the computer still broken?'

'No, Des fixed it, temporarily anyway.'

'Des?'

'My friend. You know, the computer guy.'

'You never told me his name.'

'Didn't I? It's Des. Des Sullivan.'

Wendy felt strange. She should feel guilty even saying Des's name out loud, especially in front of Ronan. But she didn't. She felt elated, reckless, dangerous and capable of anything.

'So you were able to work this morning after all?' Ronan encouraged.

Wendy really was in an odd mood. Usually you couldn't stop her talking about all the work she had to do. But now she'd gone all quiet and there was a wicked glint in her eye that he hadn't seen for a long time. When he'd first met her, the glint was often there, but the daily grind of work, running the house and looking after two lively boys had dulled her sparkle a little. Ronan felt very, very nervous. Something was up, he could sense it.

'Yes, yes,' she said distractedly.

She stood up and smiled at him a little too brightly. 'I have to go out for a while. I'm viewing a house.'

'Right now?' Ronan asked. 'Can't it wait? I thought you were snowed under with work.'.

'I am, but I need a break,' she said evenly. She looked at her watch. 'I won't be long; it's only in Sandycove, one of the big Victorian houses on the seafront. I'll be back within the hour. If the woman from the Skibbereen Festival rings, could you ask her if she received the attachments? I sent her two photographs – one black and white and one colour, a press release and some reviews.'

'Sure,' Ronan said. 'Anything else?'

'No, that's it. We have that corporate gig in Booterstown tonight, but they only want us to play for an hour. We're collecting Mia on the way.' She leaned over and gave him a peck on the cheek. 'See you later.'

'See you.'

As soon as Wendy had closed the front door behind her, Ronan looked out of the window. She crunched over the gravel in her boots, opened the car door and hitched up her snug-fitting leather skirt so she could get in without stretching it. He watched as she pulled the rear-view mirror down in order to check her make-up and only when satisfied turned the key in the ignition and reversed slowly out of the gateway, her brake lights still on. She'd left the handbrake on again.

Wendy wasn't wearing those boots or that skirt earlier, Ronan noticed with a start. He felt hollow inside. For a long time he'd suspected that he wasn't enough for Wendy, that sooner or later she'd realize how amazing she really was and would leave him for someone more exciting, someone who could give her the type of lifestyle she deserved. A life of luxury, allowing her to have everything her heart desired, from top-of-the-range leather bags to handpainted velvet cushions – all the things she lusted after in the glossy magazines she loved to read. And a house with many, many rooms that she could renovate and change to her heart's content. A house where velvet cushions wouldn't appear out of place.

If she was having an affair, how could he blame her? In fact, he'd suspected as much for a long time. Some of the house viewings had to be a ruse for clandestine meetings – surely no one could be that interested in other people's property, especially when they had no intention of buying?

This time he had to know for sure. He jumped to his feet. Within seconds he was also driving towards Sandycove.

Wendy's mobile beeped just as she pulled up outside Sandycove House, the imposing Victorian house on the seafront with its own designer-renovated, ultra-modern mews. She reached down and checked her screen. '*Thinkin of U,*' she read. '*I need U – ring me. D.*'

Wendy looked around her furtively. She was being paranoid; there was no one staring into the car. Why would there be? And it was only a text message after all. She stared at the screen. A shiver of delight ran up her spine. She'd heard about text flirting, but it was usually in the context of teenagers or famous football-ers. And it was pretty harmless, wasn't it? A bit of fun. She ran her fingers over the keys of her mobile. No, she decided. Not a good idea. She deleted the message quickly before she was tempted to reply and buried her mobile in the bottom of her bag.

'Wendy, is that you?'

Wendy was absorbed in the amazing white-walled, double-storey living room in the renovated mews at the back of the main house. Its wooden ceiling was punctuated with large skylights and light flooded the simple, minimalist interior. It was stunning.

She spun around on her heels. An elegantly dressed woman with long dark hair pulled back off her face in a sleek, glossy ponytail was smiling at her.

The woman cocked her head to one side. 'It's Nora, Nora Queen. Nora Valerio now, that's my married name.'

'Nora!'

Wendy was bowled over. Nora had changed beyond recognition. When working on the cruise ship she had had short, spiky, henna-red hair, a mahogany perma-tan, and a penchant for skimpy bikini-style tops and bum-hugging cut-off denim shorts – when she wasn't in showgirl mode, that was. Nora, Wendy remem-bered, had enjoyed a varied career as a pole dancer, post woman, and farm hand on her brother's farm in Donegal, ending up as one of the chorus girls in Wendy's show before disappearing off the face of the planet.

'Nora, you look great. Last time I saw you was on the *Emerald Star*. On the Mediterranean leg. You upped and left the ship without saying goodbye to anyone. Whatever happened? Where did you go? It was the talk of the ship at the time.'

Nora gave a deliciously deep and throaty laugh. 'A man, that's what happened. Isn't it always? Luca was one of the passengers, and you know what the powers that be were like about dating passengers. When we docked in Sorrento, he whisked me off the ship and we spent a wild week in the most adorable family-run hotel in Positano down the coast.'

Nora held out her left hand and an enormous diamond nearly blinded Wendy. 'He proposed at the end of the holiday and I said yes, of course. He was the best thing that had ever happened to me. Still is. We lived in Rome for a few years before moving back to Dublin last Christmas. We're married now, with our second on the way.' Nora patted her stomach and grinned.

'You wouldn't know it,' Wendy said. 'You always were annoyingly skinny. I bet you still eat like a horse too.'

'Sure do. Even more so now that I'm pregnant again. And what about you? Any family?'

'Two boys. Greg's six and Steve's five.'

'And you're in AbbaFab, aren't you? I see your photo in the papers from time to time. I'd love to hear you play, I adore Abba.'

'I'll send you tickets to one of our gigs,' Wendy promised. 'So what are you doing here? Are you moving house?'

Nora laughed again. 'Not at all. Luca works for my brother-in-law's estate agency. Lowan's?'

'Ah.' Wendy nodded. She recognized the estate agency's name instantly, it was one of the biggest and most successful in Dublin. She was au fait with them all.

'I fill in for him when he's stuck, showing the properties.' Nora lowered her voice a little. 'It's not really my cup of tea to tell the truth, but it gets me out of the house.'

Wendy sighed. 'You're so lucky. I love old houses like this, I could spend hours showing people around them. I'd love your job.'

'Really? Well, if you're ever interested, I'm sure Luca would take you on in a heartbeat. He swears by pretty women in their thirties. Too young and it's distracting for the punters, he always says. Bit of a dinosaur, my Luca is when it comes to being pc, but his heart's in the right place.'

'If I ever leave the band I'll seriously consider it,' Wendy said.

'Listen, we should meet up for coffee or lunch. I'd love to hear all about your family. You're married, I presume.'

'Oh, sorry, did I not say? Yes, to Ronan Borza, he's also in the band.'

'How funny, is he Italian too?'

'His father is, but Ronan's lived here all his life. I met him just after my mum died.'

'Oh, I'm sorry to hear that. You used to talk about her a lot on the ships; you two were pretty close. It must have been hard on you. And your sisters. You have two, don't you?'

'Yes, that's right. Well remembered. Gemma and Mia. It was hard on us all, but it's a long time ago now.'

'I suppose.'

A couple walked towards Nora, intent in their eyes. 'Here comes trouble,' she murmured to Wendy.

Wendy smiled. Nora always was a tonic. 'I'd love to meet up.' She handed Nora one of her cards. 'Give me a ring. We can do lunch.'

'I will.' Nora nodded, running her fingers over the tasteful white AbbaFab card with its gold lettering. 'Definitely. I look forward to it. I've never been a lady who lunches.'

'Me neither,' Wendy said. 'But for you, Nora, I'll make an exception.'

Wendy suddenly realized how little she saw of her old cruise-ship friends these days and made a mental note to look some of them up when she had the time. She sighed inwardly. If she ever did have the time.

As she walked back into the main house, she could hear the couple quizzing Nora on the unusual ceiling roses and original wall friezes. 'Italian or French?' they asked.

'Um, I'll have to check for you,' she heard Nora say.

Italian, Wendy thought to herself. She was tempted to tell the couple herself, but refrained. It wasn't her job after all.

As she wandered from room to room in the main house, admiring the generous proportions and the high ceilings, Wendy thought about what Nora had said. Would her husband really give her a job? Maybe she could squeeze it in during the day, after the paperwork and before singing. If she got up an hour earlier, it might just be possible. Wendy sighed. Who am I kidding? I already get up at six most mornings. I'm already wrecked enough without even more work.

As she walked into the bathroom, which needed a complete rehaul, often the case with older houses, she heard a muffled bleep. I wonder if it's Des again, she considered, the very thought making her smile. She whipped her mobile out of her bag and checked the screen. It was! As she read the message she blushed. It was pretty graphic this time, leaving her in no doubt of his feelings towards her. She was shocked but delighted. Imagine inspiring those kinds of emotions in anyone, she thought guiltily. This time she didn't delete the message. You never know, I might just need his number urgently, she reasoned. I'll keep it just in case.

Ronan sat outside Sandycove House in his car. He could see Wendy's car parked two spaces up. He felt terrible. How could he have doubted her? Of course she was viewing a house, she viewed houses most Thursday afternoons if she got the chance. Yes, normally in her tracksuit if that's what she happened to have on, but maybe today she just needed to change for some reason. He drove home feeling like a fool. What would Wendy have thought if she'd seen him? He was a paranoid idiot.

That evening Ronan drove Wendy and Mia to the corporate headquarters in Booterstown where they were playing. He'd been in a quiet, reflective mood all afternoon, but Wendy and Mia didn't seem to notice, they were too busy planning the weekend in Skibbereen. They were travelling down together on the train the following morning, while Ronan and Pat went on ahead in the van, and Wendy was giving Mia the final details.

'There's a press reception tomorrow evening,' she said, 'and we have to play one song. Then the official opening is on Saturday at twelve, followed by the gig itself on Saturday evening.'

'Has Wendy told you that she's cutting the ribbon, Mia? Along with the head of the Skibbereen Business Association,' Ronan said. 'Some fellow called Gubber O'Shea.'

'Really?' Mia asked. 'What fun! And what a name, is he really called Gubber?'

'Apparently.' Ronan gave a snort. 'He owns one of the local pubs.'

Wendy groaned. 'I'm sure he'll be ancient and he'll probably try to snog me. Might even slip me the tongue if I'm lucky,' she quipped.

'Wendy!' Mia was shocked. 'That's disgusting!'

'Sorry, little sis,' Wendy grinned. 'But it's true. I've met a lot of Gubber's type in my day and some of them are randy little buggers.'

'Wendy!' This time it was Ronan's turn to be shocked.

'Keep your pants on,' Wendy said. 'Gubber won't have his evil way with me, I can assure you.'

Ronan gripped the steering wheel tightly. He didn't

know how to deal with Wendy at the moment. She wasn't her usual self at all. She was extra feisty and some of her old energy seemed to have returned.

Unfortunately, Ronan thought he knew why she was behaving differently. He'd come across a graphic text message on her phone earlier and he was still reeling from the shock. He had no idea how the hell he was going to confront her, or deal with her explanation, for that matter. As far as he could see, he had nothing to win and an awful lot to lose by accusing Wendy of adultery without any solid evidence. But he knew in his heart that her mind was elsewhere, and this cut him to the quick.

At least he could keep an eye on her in Skibbereen, he supposed. There was something to be said for its distance from Dublin. And at some stage over the weekend, he decided, he would confront her about her affair. He couldn't go on like this. Thinking about Wendy with another man was torture. He'd just have to pick his moment.

10 'Eagle'

As soon as Alva arrived at the Ardilare County House in Limerick on Friday afternoon for the BodyFest event, she felt out of place. She was there to represent Bluewater, who were sponsoring the event, but she was beginning to regret offering to go. For starters, she seemed to be the youngest person in the main reception room by at least twenty years. She was surrounded by women in their fifties and sixties, and they all seemed to know one another. Then she noticed a few younger women as she looked around, and she began to feel a little less self-conscious.

She wasn't sure how much demand there would be for the streamlined Bluewater Cobra range though. As far as she could see, most of the women were wearing baggy grey or dark blue tracksuit bottoms, teamed with all manner of different tops – from skimpy vests that wouldn't look out of place on a Spanish beach to woolly jumpers and T-shirts emblazoned with all kinds of designs and pc logos such as 'Save the Whales' and

'Keep Dublin Bay Clean'. One small, red-haired woman was kitted out from top to toe in a rainbow-coloured tie-dyed creation and Alva had to make an extreme effort not to stare at her. Maybe the Cobra gear is just what they need after all, she smiled to herself. She spied a manned desk to the far left of the room and made her way through the chattering throng.

'Hi, I'm Alva Ryan,' she said to the white-haired woman behind the desk. 'From Bluewater.'

'Alva,' the woman said warmly. 'I'm Evie. We've been expecting you. It was so nice of your company to sponsor our event.' She gave Alva a generous grin.

Alva could feel her whole body relax. Maybe this wasn't going to be so bad after all.

'Carol, could you man the desk for a while?' Evie called over to another woman. 'I'm going to show Alva around. Alva's from Bluewater.'

Carol, also white-haired, and small and fit-looking, her toned body resplendent in dark blue leggings and a lighter blue vest top – all the more astonishing as Alva reckoned she must be at least sixty – came bustling over.

'Welcome.' Carol shook Alva's hand enthusiastically. 'We so appreciate Bluewater's sponsorship. With your support, we were able to fly in Alia Oberone from Amsterdam to give classes.'

Alva looked at her blankly.

'Alia's one of the most respected and influential yoga teachers in Europe,' Carol explained. 'You should go to her class this afternoon. It's ideal for beginners and you look pretty supple.'

'Supple? Really?'

Carol nodded. 'Certainly. You hold yourself well. Excellent posture.'

Alva was flattered. No one had ever commented on her posture before. 'I'll certainly check it out,' she promised.

'Follow me,' Evie said. 'I've set up some tables for you in the dining room. But feel free to move them elsewhere if it suits.

'Let's go and have a look,' Alva said, 'and then I can fetch the Cobra boxes from the car.'

'Cobra.' Evie smiled. 'Very good.'

'It's a yoga pose, isn't it?' Alva said, glad that she'd read the Cobra brochures carefully.

Evie smiled again. 'Are you a yoga virgin by any chance?'

Alva laughed. 'Is it that obvious?'

Evie nodded. 'But not to worry.' She touched Alva's arm gently. 'We'll have you sorted out by tomorrow.'

Alva wasn't all that sure that she wanted to be 'sorted out', whatever that meant. But she said nothing.

The space in the dining room was ideal and Evie helped Alva carry in the clothes from the car and set up the lightweight chrome travelling rail. They heaped the tops and jumpers in neat piles on the table and hung the trousers and longer tops on plastic hangers from the rail. Then Alva decorated the poster boards behind the tables with Cobra information and glossy photos of models wearing the clothes, and pinned up a price list.

Evie ran her fingers over a rich purple velour top with a generously-sized hood. 'This is rather lovely,' she said. 'Do you think it would suit me?'

Alva looked at Evie's conservative black sweatshirt and matching black leggings. 'Yes, definitely. Why don't you try it on?'

Evie pulled her sweatshirt over her head, dislodging her glasses, then eased on the Cobra top, pulling the hood over her short hair and zipping it right the way up.

'The colour's great on you,' Alva said.

Evie looked like a young girl, her big brown eyes peeping out from the depths of the hood.

'How much is it?' she asked.

'Nothing.' Alva smiled at her. 'It's a present.'

'No!' Evie cried. 'I can't accept it.' She scrambled to take it off, undoing the zip with a loud crack.

'Please,' Alva insisted, stopping her in her tracks. 'You'll be doing me a favour. Just tell everyone it's a Cobra top when they ask. Honestly, it's the best possible publicity for the range.'

'If you're sure,' Evie said hesitantly, fingering the velour.

'Positive.'

'In that case, thank you so much.'

'My pleasure.'

After a healthy but surprisingly tasty lunch of salads and quiche, Alva attended her first yoga class, with the aforementioned and rather strangely named Alia

Oberone. Alva wasn't usually one for exercise – even the word 'gym' practically made her break out in a rash – and she never walked anywhere if she could help it. After all, she reasoned to Mia and Sean whenever either of them scolded her for being so lazy, that's why cars were invented.

The class was being held in a large wooden-floored reception room, completely empty of furniture. Most of the women were clustered in groups against the walls, chatting quietly, but two were sitting on the floor with their legs stretched out in a wide 'V' in front of them, bending forward like ballet dancers limbering up. Alva gulped. She couldn't touch her toes on a bad day, let alone touch her head to her knees as they were currently doing.

'Don't mind them,' a tall, elegant woman with white hair piled on top of her head whispered to Alva, gesturing at the women. 'That's not what yoga's about.' The woman had a slight accent but Alva couldn't quite place it.

'Really?' she asked.

The woman nodded and continued, 'Yoga's not supposed to be a competitive sport. It's about finding your inner calm, finding your own sense of well-being. Some people would be better off joining a gym.'

'Is it good for dodgy backs?' Alva said, joking.

'It is actually.' The woman smiled gently. 'Very good. It's also good for restoring equilibrium in a busy life.' She looked Alva in the eye. 'Modern life can be very stressful, yoga is a great way to take some time out for ourselves.'

'That sounds excellent.' Alva smiled. 'I wasn't sure what yoga was going to be like, to tell you the truth. I've never done it before. I've always wanted to give it a go but ... you know what it's like. By the time I get home in the evening I'm usually wrecked. I tend to just slob out in front of the telly.'

'I know exactly what you mean. I'm prone to laziness myself.'

Alva was taken aback. The woman looked incredibly lithe and toned. Not slim exactly, but fit and healthy. Just how Alva would like to look in her sixties.

'I'm Alia by the way,' the woman said. 'And you are?'

'Alva,' she stammered.

This was the famous Dutch teacher – how embarrassing. Alva could feel her cheeks redden.

'Welcome to my class,' Alia said kindly, sensing her discomfort. 'I'm very honoured to be your first yoga teacher.'

Alva felt relief flood through her body. 'Um, thanks,' she mumbled.

Alia patted the small of Alva's back. 'Better get on with the class. See you later.'

She moved to the top of the room and stood there as still as a statue, with her hands in prayer position. Her head was bowed, the tips of her fingers resting gently on her mouth, her eyes fixed on the floor. Within seconds everyone stopped talking and gazed at her in expectation.

'Good afternoon,' she said in her calm yet strong voice. 'I'm Alia Oberone and I'm delighted to be here in Limerick for BodyFest. Let's get started, shall we? There are mats against the right-hand wall, so if you don't have your own, please take one. And then if everyone could find a space on the floor and lie down with their heads towards the centre of the room, we'll begin with some relaxation and breathing exercises before moving on to some asanas and breath-awareness exercises.'

Alva did as Alia asked and rolled out her pristine sky-blue Cobra yoga mat on the floor in a space between two other mats and their owners. Minutes later, she was following Alia's voice as it commanded her to focus her attention on different parts of her own body, from her toes to her fingertips. As she concentrated on the hypnotic voice and its instructions, she felt her body relax on to the floor. Her mind kept flitting away, but Alia's deep, soothing voice brought Alva's attention back to her body.

After the relaxation, Alia talked the class through a series of stretches and twists; her instructions were precise and easy to follow and Alva found that by concentrating on her breathing when her thoughts began to drift, her mind was almost totally focused on the moment, only lapsing now and again. Soon her niggles and worries were long forgotten as she focused on Alia's voice. As Carol had correctly surmised, Alva was more supple than she'd expected and was surprised to find her body responding well to the teacher's instructions.

'Now let's move on to the asanas, or body poses,' Alia said after giving them all a few moments to rest following the stretches. 'Remember not to push your body, let it tell you when to stop. And also remember your breathing. First, Tadasana, the Mountain. Stand in the centre of your mat, feet together, big toes and ankle bones gently touching. Arms hanging loosely but actively to the side. Gazing gently ahead. Concentrating on the breath.'

After a while, Alva was so caught up in the practice that she didn't notice the time pass. Resting after a fun pose called the Dog, which involved balancing her body on her hands and feet and moving her weight upwards and backwards, she glanced at her watch for the first time and was amazed to find that an hour had passed already.

After another hour, Alva began to wonder why she hadn't found the time to take a yoga class before. She'd toyed with the idea when yoga was the 'next big thing', somewhere after spinning and before Pilates, and was being offered in every gym and parish hall in Dublin, but had never quite got around to it. Now she felt more refreshed than she had felt for many years – tired yet energized. And calm; calmer than she'd felt for a long, long time.

During the final relaxation, Alia asked everyone to make a resolution, to repeat it three times and to do something about it in the weeks to come. Alva made two. One: to find a yoga class when she got back to Dublin and make it a regular part of her life; and two: to talk to Sean, to sort things out once and for all. Only then, she felt, would she be able to really move on with her life.

She opened her eyes and felt as if a huge weight had been lifted from her shoulders. She smiled to herself. She felt in control, ready to face anything.

As she rolled up her mat and popped it into its bag, Alia appeared beside her. 'Did you enjoy that?' she asked.

Alva beamed at her. 'Oh, yes. It was wonderful. Thank you so much. I'm going to find a class in Dublin when I get back.'

Alia thought for a second. 'Evie's class might suit you. She's based in Glasthule, is that near you?'

Alva smiled. 'What a coincidence. I'm in Sandy-cove, just down the road.'

Alia winked. 'No coincidence, fate,' she said, her eyes twinkling. She leaned in towards Alva. 'Let go of that stress,' she whispered. 'And face your fears. They might not be as scary as you think.' She squeezed Alva's arm. 'Will you be at my class tomorrow?'

'Try stopping me.'

'And one more thing.'

'Yes?'

'You'll have to give up the cigarettes.'

'How did you know?' Alva was flabbergasted. She hoped her breath didn't stink or something. Or maybe it was her fingers.

'It's affecting your breathing. I used to smoke too. But you *can* give up when you're ready to.'

'Um, thanks,' Alva murmured, not knowing quite what to say. 'I'll certainly give it some thought.'

Alia nodded at her and smiled. 'Good luck.'

Alva strode out of the class with her head held

234

high, her yoga mat in its bag slung across her shoulder. On her way out she heard the two young women from the class behind her who had been stretching before the class started.

'Did nothing for me,' one of them said in disgust. 'What about you?'

'Boring. And that bloody relaxation thing at the end, the resolve, what was that all about? I didn't get it. I think I'll stick to the gym from now on.'

Alva hugged her arms around her body and suppressed a smile. *I* got it, she felt like telling them.

That afternoon and evening Alva had great success with the Cobra range. As she had predicted, many people had admired Evie's new top and had also noticed Alva's smart yoga mat and matching bag.

'You're a godsend,' one woman told her after purchasing two pairs of cotton stretch trousers in a warm moss green and a matching hooded top. 'It's impossible to find nice yoga gear in Kildare where I live. I've been wearing these old leggings for years,' she said, pointing down at her legs. 'I'll be only too delighted to throw them out.'

As Alva was selling the range at a hefty discount – part of the sponsorship deal – everyone was delighted with the prices, and she felt reassured that she wasn't ripping anyone off, which enabled her to talk up her products with confidence.

The stand was thronged with women until seven, only letting up when food was served. Alva would have liked to attend another yoga class or one of the other sessions, much to her surprise, but unfortunately work came first.

She sat with Evie and Carol during dinner and they charmed her with tales of their children, husbands, dogs and friends. Both were yoga teachers with many years' experience between them, and Evie was also a baby-massage practitioner and sold special natural products for mothers-to-be and newborn babies' sensitive skin. They were quite a pair and Alva was entertained all evening.

Carol and Evie had jokingly fought over who would have Alva in their class, but Evie won out in the end, due to the close proximity of Alva's house and Evie's studio. It was only afterwards that Alva realized that, of course, she didn't actually live in Sandycove with Sean any more, but she was too embarrassed to point out her mistake. She'd find a nice flat in the general locality, she decided, Sean or no Sean. She loved Sandycove, it was home to her now, and Mia lived nearby, which was an added bonus. It was time to take charge of her life and to move forward.

Alva had planned to leave early on Saturday morning and meet Mia in Skibbereen for lunch. But first she wanted to attend one more of Alia's classes.

'Mia, there's been a slight change of plan,' Alva told her on the hotel phone on Saturday morning at half past eight.

'Jeeze,' Mia said sleepily from her hotel bed. 'What has you up? It's not even nine yet. It's not like you to be up so early on a Saturday.'

'I thought you weren't playing till tonight?'

'We're not, but I had a late one last night. I'll tell you about it over lunch.'

'Sounds interesting. But I won't be down until three or four. I want to take another yoga class this morning.'

'Yoga class? Are you serious? I thought you said yoga was for crusty vegetarians.'

Alva laughed. 'Did I? I was wrong. Listen, I have to run, the class starts soon and I have to take a shower. Talk to you later.'

'See you down here. We'll be in the Town Hall at a reception from three. After that we'll be back in the hotel, so try ringing my room. If I'm not there for some reason, try Wendy's mobile.'

'Mia, you really do need a mobile.'

'Yes, yes,' Mia murmured. 'See you later.'

'Great, see you in Skibbereen.'

Alva clicked off her mobile. Mia sounded in chipper form, if a little tired. Alva pulled her T-shirt over her head, shimmied her light cotton shorts down her legs and stepped into the shower. She closed her eyes and let the hot water caress her face. I'm going to be OK, she told herself. And for the first time in many days, she actually believed it.

11 'Another Town, Another Train'

'Mia!' Luke waved from the head of the queue in Dublin's busy Heuston railway station.

Mia made her way towards him, her large travel bag hitting her calves. It wasn't all that heavy really, just awkward, but she couldn't fit all her clothes into her small overnight case, so she was stuck with it. She swung the bag over her shoulder and continued.

'Where's Wendy?' she asked as she joined Luke in the queue, ignoring the irritated glances and tut-tuts of the passengers behind him. She knew she was queue-jumping, but she didn't want to miss the train to Cork. She'd cut it pretty fine, but luckily Luke had been a little more organized and was almost at the ticket desk.

'She's flying down later. Ronan rang me a few minutes ago. He's already on the road with Pat. Wendy has to do something this morning apparently. Some sort of last-minute thing.'

'What?' Mia asked in a slight panic. 'She didn't say

238

anything to me about flying down, and I was talking
to her earlier. What's happened?'

Luke shrugged. 'Sorry, I don't know any more than
I've just told you. Why don't you ring her?' He passed
her his phone. 'You really do need to get a mobile,
Mia.'

'I know, I know,' she said a little crossly. She keyed
in Wendy's mobile number and waited, but it went
straight to messages.

'Any luck?' Luke asked.

Mia shook her head. 'Her phone is switched off.'
She handed the mobile back to Luke.

'It's fine,' he said, putting his phone back into his
pocket and then nudging Mia gently with his shoulder.
'I don't bite.'

'It's not that . . .' she mumbled, her head lowered
slightly. She looked up and attempted a smile. 'I just
wish she'd told me, that's all.'

'Warned you, you mean?'

'No! Honestly, I don't have a problem with travelling down with you. Really I don't.'

'It might be nice to get to know each other a little
better,' Luke suggested.

'I suppose.' Mia was sceptical. Luke had shown his
true colours in Atlas and she wasn't sure how much
more she needed to know. 'Can you hang on here? I
want to get a paper in the shop.'

'Sure. Leave your bag, you'll be quicker that way.
I'll get you a ticket if the queue gets a move on. If I'm
not still here, I'll wait for you at the platform gate. It's
platform two.'

'Thanks.' Mia dumped her bag beside him and walked quickly towards the newsagent's. She browsed through the few shelves of bestsellers for a few minutes before selecting an entertaining-looking novel about an Irish female GP with a disastrous love life. She also grabbed a newspaper and two glossy magazines. If she was going to be stuck on the train with Luke for three hours, she'd need some ammunition.

There was no sign of him at the ticket office, and Mia found him waiting for her as promised, at the gate. He smiled as he saw her approaching and handed the tickets to the inspector, who glanced at them, looked at Luke a little suspiciously and then handed them back with a grunt.

Moments later they were sitting in the train. Mia spread her reading material out on the table in front of her. The mid-morning train was empty and they had the whole carriage to themselves.

'Help yourself,' Mia said, picking up the paper as soon as she was seated, bag safely stowed under the table, and gesturing at the magazines.

'Not quite my scene,' Luke said, perusing the covers of the first glossy. 'I don't have any man problems so to speak, and my breasts are quite big enough, thank you very much.' He read the cover of the second. 'But this sounds a little more interesting.' He read out loud: '"Learning to Live as One: letting go of your ex." Might be good advice for Alva, what do you think? We should save the magazine for her.'

Mia stared at him. Was he trying to be funny?

'Sorry,' he mumbled. 'Probably not appropriate.'

The driver made an announcement about the doors closing and seconds later the train began to move.

'You're stuck with me now,' Luke quipped. 'There's no escaping.'

'I can always get out at Thurles or somewhere.'

Luke shook his head. 'This one doesn't stop at all, it's the express.'

'I'll survive,' Mia said, sticking her head back in her paper.

Luke picked up a magazine and began to read. He was hoping that Mia would mellow in a little while. He'd been delighted when Ronan had told him about Wendy's change of plan this morning; he wanted to set the record straight with Mia, and saw the long train journey as the ideal opportunity. But it didn't look as if that was going to happen now. In a way he didn't blame her – he'd behaved badly and he had no one to blame but himself. He should never have danced with Alva like that; as soon as he'd realized she was flirting with him he should have made his excuses and left the dance floor. But to be honest, he'd been flattered by the attention. Alva was one of the best-looking woman in the place, bar Mia, and she'd had him in the spotlight of her wide and generous smile.

After a while, Luke tired of the magazine and put it back on the table. He stared out of the window. Nothing much to look at except green fields and more green fields.

He looked back at Mia. She was still buried in her

paper but at least he could see her face now as she'd lowered it a little. Her arms must have tired, he surmised.

'We could have flown down with Wendy, I suppose,' he opened. 'But it's probably quite expensive, especially at the last minute.'

Mia made an 'um' sound but said nothing.

'Skibbereen's going to be fun, isn't it?' he tried again. 'It's a lovely town. Have you ever been there?'

Mia lifted her eyes and glanced at him briefly this time. 'No.' She looked back at her paper.

'Anything interesting in the paper?'

'Luke! I'm trying to read.'

'And I'm trying to start a conversation.'

'I can see that. But it's early. I'm not in the mood.'

'It's not that early,' he pointed out. 'It's almost ten.'

'And I'm not a morning person,' Mia said. 'Why don't you go and see if the buffet car's open? I'd love a coffee. White, please, no sugar.'

'OK.' Luke climbed out of his seat. 'Don't miss me too much.'

'As if.'

Luke came back with two paper cups of coffee in his hands. He placed them on the table and sat down again.

'Thanks,' Mia said, prising the plastic lid off the top and taking a sip.

'What's it like?' Luke asked.

'Not as bad as I'd expected,' Mia admitted.

'Mia, will you please let me say something and then I promise I'll let you get back to your paper?'

Mia pre-empted him. 'It's fine,' she said a little wearily. 'I know what you're going to say. Don't worry about it. Alva was just trying to wind Sean up, I know that. I'm not in the least bit bothered, honestly.'

'It's not fine, Mia, is it? Or else you wouldn't be acting like this.'

'Like what?' Mia glared at him.

'You're clearly annoyed with me and I don't blame you. I felt awful after you left but I didn't know what to do.'

'I presume you just left with some blonde, like Sean,' Mia said archly. 'Isn't that what you all do?'

'No I did not!' Luke spluttered. 'I'm not like that, Mia.'

'Really?'

'Really.'

'As I said, don't worry about it. Now can I go back to my paper?'

'No, I haven't finished. I made a mistake, Mia. But we all make mistakes. I shouldn't have danced with Alva like that.' He ran his hands through his hair, making it stick up in funny little spikes. It quite suits him like that, Mia thought, then stopped herself. What did she care what his hair looked like?

'I've had a difficult two years,' he continued. 'And I'm just getting back on my feet again. I was a mess for a long time and that's why I haven't been in a serious relationship for a while. But I'm not afraid

243

to commit, Mia. That's not a problem for me. It's just . . .'

'Hold it right there,' Mia interrupted him. 'I really don't need to know any of this, Luke. Please. We're in the band together and that's it. Work friends. OK?'

'Is that really what you want?' Luke asked, his voice low. 'I thought there was something between us. I thought . . .'

'You thought wrong,' she cut him off again.

'What's up with you today? You're not yourself.'

'What do you mean?'

'You're usually so kind. The old Mia would have listened to me.'

'You don't really know me, Luke.'

'Maybe not. But I do know that you'd do anything for your sisters. You even replaced Gemma in the band when you didn't really want to. You've put up with Alva staying in your flat even though you haven't found it easy. And Ronan told me that Alva's joining us tomorrow night, so you must have forgiven her for hurting you.' He stopped for a moment and gave a small sigh. 'Mia, I'm so sorry if *I* hurt you. If I could turn back the clock you know I would. But please, just give me one more chance.'

Mia was shocked to find a lump forming in her throat. She was being terribly hard on Luke, but she didn't know how to forgive him. It was like Alva all over again. She shut people out to protect herself, she knew that. But only the people she was really close to, like her sisters, Sean or Alva, knew to keep knocking. Others just stayed permanently outside.

Luke sensed her confusion. 'Why don't we start again?' he suggested gently.

Mia looked at him. 'What do you mean?'

'Pretend we've just got on the train. Just me and you, no agenda, no past, no history. Just two strangers sharing a journey. Let's get to know each other properly. Don't shut me out, Mia. Please.'

Mia felt that lump again. Could he really know her so well after such a short space of time? They'd practically only just met after all. She nodded curtly. 'OK. Tell me something then. Something interesting about you that I don't know.'

Luke stared at the table top for a moment, then looked her straight in the eye. 'I was engaged,' he said evenly. 'Almost a year ago. We'd set a date for the wedding and everything.'

Mia was amazed. She didn't know quite what to say. 'Go on,' she prompted.

Luke sighed. 'She changed her mind, basically. Broke my heart. End of story.'

'What was her name?' Mia asked. 'If you don't mind telling me, that is.'

'No. Ciara. Ciara Halpin. She was a nurse in St John's Hospital, sorry, *is* a nurse in St John's. We met at a wedding, how ironic is that?'

'Lots of people do,' Mia said.

'Is that where Ronan and Wendy met?' he asked.

'No, they met in a pub. Well, to be precise, Ronan saw Wendy in a pub. He didn't actually meet her until later. He went out with Gemma first.'

'Are you serious?' Luke asked in amazement.

Mia nodded. 'It didn't last long. Then he went out with Wendy. They got married quite quickly, fairly soon after Mum died in fact. He'd been in love with her all along, apparently. He just didn't think she'd be interested in him.'

'And what about Gemma? How did she feel about the whole thing?'

'Fine, apparently. I was only young at the time so I don't really remember much about it to tell the truth. I think Gemma found him a little too sensible, too straight. But for goodness' sake don't tell him that.'

'Of course I won't.' Luke smiled.

'Gemma went out with one of Ronan's friends soon after the break-up,' Mia continued, 'so she can't have been all that bothered. I can't remember the exact details. But she's certainly OK about it now.'

'Ronan never said anything to me about going out with Gemma,' Luke mused.

'Why would he?' Mia said. 'It's ancient history.'

'I suppose. So what about you? Do you have a chequered romantic past like your sisters?'

'No.' Mia smiled gently. 'I've had a few boyfriends but nothing serious. Teachers in the music school mainly. And a French guy in college. Nothing like you. That must have hurt. Do you still keep in contact?'

'No. It's easier not to.'

'I understand.'

Luke gazed out of the window for a second. 'It's taken me a long time to get over Ciara.' He looked back at Mia. 'Life can be hard, can't it? But it's so minor compared with what happened to you. How did you cope, losing both your parents like that?'

Mia was taken aback. It wasn't something she was in the habit of discussing, even with her own sisters.

'Sorry,' Luke murmured. 'Maybe you'd prefer not to talk about it.'

Mia took a deep breath. Luke had told her about Ciara, which couldn't have been easy for him. She should at least make an effort. 'No, it's not that,' she said after a moment. 'I was very young when Dad died, so it didn't have a huge impact on me to tell the truth. But Mum, well, that was different. I was fifteen when she died and I adored her. She was everything to me.' Mia could feel tears prick the back of her eyes and she blinked them back.

'Stop if it's too much for you,' Luke said kindly.

'I'm all right,' Mia assured him.

He handed her a tissue and she dabbed her eyes gently. 'Wendy was twenty-nine at the time so she kind of took over. Mum had put her down as my guardian in her will, which came as a bit of a shock to us all, but Wendy took it in her stride. She's always been the practical one. I don't know what we would have done without her – she organized our lives like a military campaign and sorted everything out. I didn't have to worry about a thing.' Mia glanced out of the window for a moment and then looked back at Luke. 'She didn't really encourage me to talk about Mum much. "We need to get on with our lives, Mia," she'd say. She was right, I suppose. And it was her way of coping. We might have all gone to pieces otherwise. But I missed Mum so much and I couldn't really talk to anyone about it. We actually talked about it for the first time last weekend, me and Wendy. Isn't that funny? It's the anniversary of Mum's death soon and we're going to do something for it. Something special.'

Luke reached over and put his hand on Mia's. Tears were streaming down her face now. She felt stupid but she was powerless to stop them. She dried her cheeks with the sleeve of her shirt.

'What about Gemma?' he asked. 'How did she deal with it all?'

'Gemma was like me, in bits; she just didn't show it as much. Wendy was the strong one, the one who kept us all going. She still is.'

'It must have been hard on Wendy,' Luke said. 'All that responsibility suddenly.'

Mia nodded. 'No kidding. She was amazing. But, you know, I still miss Mum, even now.'

'Of course you do,' Luke soothed. He got up and moved so that he was sitting beside her. 'That's only natural.' He put his arm around her and she rested her head on his shoulder.

'Sorry,' she said, dabbing at her eyes again and giving a huge sniff.

'Don't be stupid. It's fine. It's good you can talk about it.'

They sat in silence for several minutes while Mia's tears subsided.

Finally Luke broke the silence. 'How are you feeling?' he asked kindly.

'Not too bad,' she said. In fact, she felt surprisingly good. She smiled at him, realizing that her eyes must be red and her face blotchy. 'I must look a sight.'

'Not at all.' He smiled back at her. 'You always look beautiful to me.'

Her heart skipped a beat and she could feel her cheeks begin to blush.

'Oh,' she murmured. She began to laugh. 'You really are a charmer, aren't you, Luke?'

'Don't make fun of me. I mean it, Mia. You're beautiful.' He kissed her tenderly on the forehead. 'Now, are you going back to your paper?'

She shook her head. 'I don't think so. Let's talk. It's far more interesting.'

'So I'm forgiven?'

Mia nodded.

Luke put his hand on hers and squeezed it. 'Good.'

Mia and Luke arrived in Cork city just after one and walked across the river towards the bus terminal. They were lucky; their timing was perfect and they only had to wait a few minutes for the direct bus to Skibbereen. By half past two the friendly bus driver had dropped them outside a hotel on the main street.

Mia looked around her as soon as the bus had pulled out. 'What a lovely town,' she remarked. 'It's pretty big, isn't it?'

'What were you expecting?' Luke asked, the hint of a smile on his lips.

Mia shrugged. 'A few shops, some pubs, a supermarket maybe – nothing like this.'

'Come on, you city slicker.' Luke took her bag off her and swung it over his shoulder with his own.

'Luke, I can . . .' she began to protest but he ignored her and strode up the street. She followed him.

'Almost there,' he said after they had walked a short distance, past O'Donovan's Bookshop and a large, bustling supermarket called Field's. Then he stood back against a shop window, put down the bags and pointed at a grey building. 'The Town Hall. That's where the reception is later.'

Mia stood for a moment, studying the Town Hall and the square in front of it, which was thronged with people. There were busy, cosmopolitan-looking shops along the interconnecting side streets – a deli called Kalbos, a peacock-blue-fronted shoe shop called Shoe Candy; and several upmarket clothes shops which Mia promised herself she'd have a browse in after the civic reception.

Luke watched her taking it all in and smiled. 'Dublin isn't the centre of the universe, you know. I grew up in a town just like this.'

'Really?' Mia was intrigued. 'Where?'

'A place called Oranmore, near Galway city.'

'But you don't have a Galway accent,' Mia pointed out.

'Ach, sometimes it creeps in,' Luke said, allowing

250

his voice to lilt. 'But I've been in Dublin so long now that it's been practically beaten out of me.'

The Town Hall clock chimed once and Mia and Luke gazed up at the clock tower. 'Bang on half two. We'd better get a move on,' Luke said. 'Wendy will be getting ants in her pants if we're not ready in good time.'

'You said it.' Mia laughed. 'You can tell me more about Oranmore later, OK?'

Luke picked up her hand and kissed it. 'I will, I promise.'

Mia frowned a little.

'Don't worry,' he said with a grin. 'I won't kiss you in front of your sister.'

'It's not that!' Mia protested.

'Yes it is. You should tell her about us.'

'Us?' Her heart soared. She hadn't been an *us* for so long and it felt strange. Strange but good.

'Yes, *us*,' he said, taking her slightly dreamy state for confusion. 'Me and you. You and me.'

'You know,' Mia said, thinking about Wendy, 'I think I will tell her. Today.'

'Good. Now, come on. The civic reception awaits and we still have to get ready. Our hotel is just down the road.'

'Would you let me carry my own bag?' Mia began, reaching down and picking it up, but he took it from her and swung it seemingly effortlessly over his shoulder where it nestled against his own.

I'd love to hold his free hand, she thought to herself

with a start. And he's such a gentleman, carrying my bag for me. She smiled.

'What are you smiling about?' Luke asked as he led the way down the road.

'Nothing.' Mia grinned back at him. She felt in remarkably good humour and was looking forward to later that evening when she'd find out even more about Luke Jackman.

'About time,' Wendy said as soon as they walked into her hotel room in the Skibbereen House Hotel. 'I was starting to worry.' She was in her costume, face bare and hair scraped back off her forehead with her customary white towelling head-band. With her hair like that and her skin *au naturel*, she looked years younger, Luke realized with a start, and far prettier. He'd never seen Wendy without her full complement of make-up.

'We had to get the train and the bus,' Mia said evenly, 'unlike some, who were travelling in the lap of luxury.'

'I'm sorry,' Wendy said. 'There was a problem at home this morning. Steve and Greg had a pillow fight; Steve hit Greg in the mouth and almost knocked out one of his teeth. I had to take him to the dentist. Couldn't be avoided, I'm afraid.'

'Is Greg all right?' Mia asked.

'Fine, thank goodness. He has strong teeth apparently. The dentist just pushed it back into place.' Wendy shivered. 'It gives me the creeps just thinking about it. Greg was really brave. But there'll be no more pillow fights in our house, that's for sure. How was your trip?'

Mia looked at Luke who winked at her surreptitiously, and then back at Wendy. 'Good, thanks. Where are Pat and Ronan?'

'Doing a sound check in the main hall. The reception starts at three so you two had better get changed quickly.'

Mia looked around the small double room. 'Where? Will I change in my own room? We haven't checked in yet so I don't have a key.'

'No,' Wendy said. 'I have everything laid out here and we're a bit short on time.'

'And Luke?' Mia didn't think she was quite ready to change in front of Luke, she'd be too embarrassed.

Wendy smiled at her. 'Luke has his own room, down the corridor. He can change there. Here's the key, Luke, and your costume.'

'Thanks.' Luke handed Mia her bag and then took the key and his costume from Wendy. 'See you in a minute,' he said, leaving the room.

'Oh, Mia,' Wendy said as soon as Luke had closed the door behind him. 'I shouldn't have dumped you with Luke like that without telling you. I meant to ring, but with Greg and everything . . .'

'It's OK,' Mia said. 'Honestly. Don't worry about it. We got on fine.' Mia opened her bag and fished out her boots and tights.

Wendy handed her her costume. 'Fine?' she asked, her eyebrows raised. 'Is that it? Fine? Is that all you're going to tell me?'

Mia hadn't said anything to Wendy or Gemma about the night at Atlas or the associated fracas, so she knew she was safe there. 'What do you mean?' she asked, feigning innocence.

Wendy leaned towards her and lowered her voice. 'He didn't try anything on, did he?'

'On the train?' Mia laughed. 'Wendy, are you serious? Of course he didn't. He was the perfect gentleman.' She whipped the plastic wrapping off her costume. 'Ah, karate suits again. Did you hear that crackle? I'm surprised we didn't see sparks flying with all that static electricity. I hope I don't get electrocuted on stage when I'm rubbing up against Luke.' She grinned at Wendy.

'Mia! Please tell me there's nothing going on between you and Luke.'

'You've got him all wrong, Wendy,' Mia said, slipping off her runners and pulling her jeans down her legs. She was very grateful that Luke wasn't present to witness her prickly stubble. At least it wouldn't show through the thick stage tights. She'd have to shave her legs later. 'Luke's a nice guy,' she added.

'Hum,' Wendy murmured. She had to restrain herself forcibly from commenting further, remembering what Gemma had said about letting Mia make her own mistakes. Her little chat with Luke obviously hadn't had the desired effect on him from all accounts, quite the opposite, in fact. So if something was going on, maybe it was all her own fault. Maybe by meddling she'd pushed them together.

Mia knew Wendy's mind was working overtime. 'You always analyse things too much, Wendy,' she said. 'Stop worrying about me. I'm fine.'

'But I do worry about you, I can't help it, it's my job,' Wendy said honestly.

'I know.' Mia gave Wendy a smile. 'I appreciate that. I won't do anything stupid, I promise. But I like Luke. And he likes me too. So can you just be happy for me? Please?'

'I'll try,' Wendy murmured. So there was something going on. At least she knew now.

'Thank you.' Mia sat down on a chair and began to ease the thick brown tights on to her left and then her right leg. She jumped up and pulled the top of the tights over her stomach. 'Very flattering,' she said with a grin. She put the tiny white skirt on and shimmied her hips. 'It's a bit short, isn't it? I wouldn't want to twirl too enthusiastically. Might give the photographers a bit more than they bargained for.'

'I don't think they'd mind too much,' Wendy said. 'The press like a bit of leg.'

Mia laughed. 'I hope I don't disappoint them.'

'Are you kidding? With your legs?'

Mia smiled. 'You're biased. You have to say nice things about my anatomy, you're my sister. We share the same genes.'

'Trust me,' Wendy said. 'There won't be any complaints.'

There was a discreet knock on the door. 'Ready?' Luke asked, his voice muffled by the wood.

'No!' Mia and Wendy chorused in unison.

'Hurry up then. Can I come in?'

'No!' Mia yelled.

'In a minute,' Wendy added.

255

Mia pulled off her long-sleeved T-shirt. Wendy handed her the white karate top and helped her put it on over her plain white bra, wrapping the thick blue belt tie firmly around Mia's waist and checking that she wasn't showing too much cleavage.

'Can I let him in now?' Wendy asked.

Mia nodded.

Luke walked in and smiled at Wendy and Mia, resplendent in his own matching white karate suit. 'What do you think, ladies?' he asked, putting his hands on his hips and spinning round. 'Will I do?'

'Just about,' Wendy said, surveying the back of the costume nervously. 'The seam across your shoulders is looking a little taut, Luke. I hadn't noticed until now. So be careful. No wild stage jumps for you, understand?'

'Wendy, we're AbbaFab, not Van Halen.' Luke laughed.

'Are you all ready?' Ronan said, coming into the room. 'Everything seems to be running on time and the press are dying to meet the girls.'

'Dying to get a look at Mia's legs, more like,' Wendy said.

'Probably true,' Ronan conceded.

'Stop that!' Mia said. 'You're making me nervous. And I'm not ready at all,' she squealed. 'I don't have my face on yet. Give me a few minutes.'

'Neither do I,' Wendy added.

'Hurry up, you lot,' Ronan said. 'Wendy, I thought you'd have them all organized by now.'

Wendy shrugged. 'Keep your shirt on, it'll be fine.

We'll be ready in a few minutes. Tell them Agnetha's putting her thigh-high boots on, that'll shut them up.'

Ronan looked at her. 'Fine,' he murmured. It wasn't like Wendy to be so *laissez-faire*. Especially regarding timekeeping. She was usually a stickler for punctuality.

The Town Hall reception went without a hitch and, as Wendy had predicted, the press were much taken with Mia's legs and other parts of her anatomy.

'Show us your famous bum, Agnetha,' one of the older men quipped after the band had finished their rendition of 'Dancing Queen' on the small stage at the top of the room.

Mia looked at Wendy, who smiled and shrugged. 'You really don't have to,' she whispered.

'It's fine,' Mia said. 'I'm not me, remember, I'm Agnetha. I'm sorry, you'll have to come to the show tomorrow night for that,' she said and smiled, fluttering her spider-like false eyelashes at the man.

'Oh, I'll be there all right, Agnetha,' the man said, 'in the front row. Try stopping me.'

That evening AbbaFab played a private gig for the Skibbereen Business Association, a short set lasting just over an hour. The band were all tired after the journey down and arranged to meet in the hotel bar for a nightcap, after removing their costumes and make-up, and having a rest. They'd been invited to join the Business Association for drinks following their set but had declined the offer, knowing it would lead to a long night of carousing and dangerously free drinks;

the locals were well known for their partying and their stamina.

The Skibbereen House Hotel was a comfortable four-star hotel only five minutes' walk from the centre of town, overlooking the River Illen. They didn't always stay in such nice hotels, but the owner was a member of the Business Association and the rooms had come as part of the package. Mia's room, a large and tasteful if rather blandly decorated double, had a view of the river, and her en suite held a deliciously large bath, which she'd filled with lashings of steaming water and some of the complimentary lavender bubble bath. She was taking a long soak in the fragrant suds, relaxing back against the cool ceramic end of the bath. She folded a hand towel and popped it under her head, its edge trailing in the water, something she never did at home, considering it an extravagant waste of a clean towel.

Mia loved hotel bathrooms with their abundance of clean, fluffy white towels to use and abuse as she liked; their wall-to-wall tiles which (as long as it was a decent hotel) didn't have grotty grey grouting and weren't hanging off the wall, unlike the ones at home; the tiny bottles of shampoo, bubble bath and paper-wrapped soaps; the dinky little shoe-shine and sewing kits; and most of all the fact that someone else had to clean up after her. Mia didn't feel too guilty about this. She'd worked for a summer as a chambermaid in a hotel in Dublin city so she'd certainly paid her dues. Even at her messiest, she'd never plummet to the lows that some people did when staying in hotel rooms, that was for sure.

As she shut her eyes and relaxed back in the bath, Mia thought about Luke. She was looking forward to talking to him again this evening. And maybe once the others all retired to bed ... Mia felt a warm glow in the pit of her stomach. She imagined Luke kissing her, his firm lips moving against hers, his strong hands caressing her shoulders. She imagined what it would be like to sleep with him. Mia hadn't had much experience with men in the past. She'd slept with one of her boyfriends, Yves, but she'd found it all rather disappointing to tell the truth. In her opinion, sex wasn't anything to write home about. After a few glasses of wine, Alva often told Mia what a great and considerate lover Sean was, although thankfully she never divulged too much information. But Mia had heard enough to understand that they had a healthy and active sex life, which they both enjoyed immensely.

She had hoped all along that she just hadn't met the right man yet. That sex would be wonderful with a special guy, one who loved her with all his heart and whom she loved back and trusted with all her being. Otherwise she wouldn't be able to relax and enjoy herself. Maybe Luke was the one?

Mia opened her eyes. Life isn't some sort of elaborate fairy tale, she chastised herself. And Luke isn't my knight in shining armour, coming to rescue me. *But*, a little voice in the back of her mind protested, *what if he is*? Maybe there is such a thing as Mr Right, Mia mused. Look at Wendy and Ronan. They've been together for years and they're still happy. Mia sat up. What time is it, she wondered. I'd better get out. Besides, I'm beginning to feel overheated.

She turned on the cold tap and splashed some water on her face, wincing as the cold droplets hit her warm skin. Then she climbed out of the bath and wrapped one of the huge bath sheets around her body. She pulled out the plug and listened as the water began to drain with a loud gurgle. She looked in the mirror; her face was red and flushed – not a good look – she'd been in the bath for far too long. After drying herself off and tying her damp hair back, she strode into the bedroom. She allowed the bath sheet to drop to the floor and dithered for a moment, completely naked. Simple white cotton underwear or the black lace? She decided on the cotton – the black lace would show through her dress – and put it on. Then she shimmied a pale blue summer dress over her head, slipped her feet into a pair of sandals and pulled a cardigan over her arms. It was a warm enough night, but not that warm. She dried her long hair off – which never took as long as people expected as it was so fine – slicked some lip-gloss on her lips and touched up her eyelashes with mascara. When she was satisfied with the result she took a calming breath and left the room.

'There you are,' Wendy said as Mia walked into the bar. She was sitting at a table with Ronan and Pat. 'We were wondering where you'd got to.'

'Where's Luke?' Mia asked before she could stop herself.

'At the bar,' Wendy said. 'Getting drinks.'

'I'll go and tell him what I want,' Mia said, eager for the excuse to talk to him alone.

'Hi, there,' she said, sidling up to Luke and giving him a tentative smile. She tried to banish her earlier, furtive bath thoughts of him from her mind, but all hope of this was dashed when he took her hand in his, raised it to his mouth and kissed it tenderly, his lips making her skin tingle.

'So you talked to Wendy?' he asked, surprised that she hadn't pulled her hand away.

'Yes.' Mia felt proud that she was able to answer him in the affirmative. She *had* talked to Wendy.

'Good,' he said simply. 'So what are you having?'

'Sparkling water, please.'

'Nothing stronger?'

Mia shook her head. 'It's been a long day. I feel ready for bed, to tell the truth.'

'So do I,' Luke murmured, gazing at her with unabashed longing in his eyes. Mia looked away. She could feel her cheeks burning.

'Sorry,' Luke said quietly. 'I didn't mean to embarrass you.'

'That's OK,' she replied, trying not to let her eyes meet his. 'It doesn't matter.'

'It matters to me,' he said. 'I want to do things right this time, Mia. After Ciara, I went through a bad patch, drinking too much, going out every night, having one-night stands, that sort of thing. I really wasn't myself for a long time. It helped to deaden the pain, I suppose. Sorry, I'd better order the drinks.' One of the barmen was standing patiently in front of Luke, waiting for him to order. After he'd done so, he turned back to Mia. 'I'm not explaining myself very well, am I? What I'm trying to say is I don't want to rush things with you. That's all.'

'You're not,' she said honestly. 'I'm not used to flirting and male attention in general, I suppose. I'm completely out of practice. I'm sorry, I'm sure you're used to far more sophisticated women than me. I must be a real let-down.' She gave a small laugh, regretting it instantly. What kind of idiot must he think I am? she wondered.

Luke smiled at her. Far from finding her awkward-ness and inexperience offputting, he found it rather endearing. 'Well, you'd better start getting used to *me*, Mia. I intend to be around for quite some time.'

Mia was taken aback. She smiled at him, relieved that he didn't appear to find her gauche. 'Oh really? And do I have any say in the matter? I might not want you around for very long.'

'No, you don't have any say whatsoever,' he replied firmly.

'I see,' she said with a laugh.

'Here are our drinks,' he said as the barman approached them.

'I'll carry some of them over for you,' Mia offered.

'Thanks. I'll join you in a minute. I'll just pay for them.'

'Thanks,' she said. 'I'll get the next round.'

'What were you and Luke talking about?' Ronan asked as Mia put a pint of Guinness on the table in front of him and a large gin and tonic in front of Wendy, making sure it was resting on a beer mat. Wendy was a stickler for things like that.

'Timing,' she said without thinking. 'In one of the songs,' she added.

'Which song?' Ronan asked. 'Maybe I can help?'

'No, it's fine,' Mia said. 'I think we've got it covered.'

'I think there's something going on between Mia and Luke,' Ronan whispered to Wendy as soon as Mia had deposited their drinks and walked back to the bar. 'Look at them flirting. And he just kissed her. Wendy! Are you watching?'

'Ronan, stop staring at them. And yes, Mia and Luke are together. She told me about it earlier.'

'You've changed your tune.' Ronan stared at her. 'I thought you were dead set against Luke going anywhere near Mia.'

'Things change,' Wendy said mildly.

'But . . .' he began.

'Ronan!' she said. 'Can't you just be happy for them?'

'Of course,' he murmured, picking up his own drink. 'I think Luke's a great guy and he'll be good for Mia. But *you* said . . .'

'Ronan, just drop it, will you? They're coming over.'

Ronan kept his mouth shut for the remainder of the night. He was upset that Wendy had snapped at him, but he'd talk to her about it later. And maybe confront her about his suspicions, if he could work up the courage.

An hour later Ronan couldn't stop yawning. 'I'm going to head up,' he said. 'I'm exhausted. Wendy, are you coming?'

'No,' Wendy said. 'You go on, I'll be up soon.'

Ronan thought for a moment. He didn't want to cause a scene. He leaned towards her and said in a low voice. 'It would be nice if you'd join me. Please, Wendy, we need to talk.'

'I have another drink on the way, Ronan, and I'm enjoying myself. It's usually the other way around, isn't it? Me going to bed early and you staying in the bar. But tonight it's different. For once in my life I don't have to get up early in the morning to deal with the boys and we have nothing on until lunchtime.'

'Fine,' Ronan said a little stiffly.

An hour later he was still lying in bed, wide awake, wondering what Wendy was doing. Was she still in the bar? Was she with someone else? He leaned over and switched on the bedside light. This was torture, he had to know. He got up and pulled on his jeans and shirt.

'Ronan!' Wendy said as he appeared beside her in the bar. 'What are you doing here? I thought you'd gone to bed.'

'I couldn't sleep,' he said. His eyes lingered on the empty glasses in front of Wendy, all smeared with her telltale dark red lipstick. 'How many have you had?'

'A few,' she said, and giggled.

'I have to check the equipment in the morning,' Pat

said quickly, standing up. He sensed trouble. 'So I'll be off. 'Night.'

''Night, Pat' Wendy waved her hand at him and gave him a bleary smile.

'I'm taking you up to bed,' Ronan said.

'Well, there's an offer,' Wendy quipped. She stood up, swayed a little and then sat down again. 'Oops,' she giggled.

'Come on,' he said. He put his arm around her and helped her up.

'Thanks, love,' she said, lurching into him.

'Where are Luke and Mia?' he asked, looking around.

'They've just gone up,' she said. 'Together,' she added. She looked at him. 'Bet you don't approve, do you? Sex before marriage is very, very naughty.' She giggled again. 'Not that I'd know anything about that, of course. Would I, Ronan?'

'Let's get you to bed,' he said, anxious to stop Wendy before she said anything else. So much for having any kind of meaningful conversation, he thought wryly as he helped her stagger out of the bar.

A few minutes earlier, Mia had rubbed her finger over the condensation on the side of her glass. It was warm in the bar and she was feeling a little flushed.

'Mia, don't take this the wrong way, but would you like to go up to your room?' Luke asked. 'You look a little hot. I could join you if you wouldn't mind and we could have a drink there.'

Mia considered this for a moment. She wasn't sure how she felt about having Luke in her room. The suggestion seemed to interest her and make her nervous in equal measures. Be brave, Mia, she told herself.

'OK,' she said with a gulp.

'It's not that late,' he said, sensing her unease. 'Maybe we could watch a film or something. What do you think?'

'I'd like that,' she said, relieved but also a little disappointed.

And, after saying their goodbyes to Wendy and Pat, that's exactly what they did. The hotel had a fine collection of films on its pay-per-view service, and as they flicked through the trailers, Mia wondered what Luke would say if she suggested a porn film. Not that she would of course. In fact, she had never even watched one, not a proper one anyway. In their teens, she and Alva had daringly taken out a few notorious films from the video shop (which didn't seem to mind what age its clients claimed to be), from *Betty Blue* to *9½ Weeks* (which neither of them had understood at the time), and watched them when Wendy and Gemma had been out singing, but that was about the extent of it. In fact, now that Mia thought about it, she really was quite innocent when it came to sexual matters. She wondered whether Luke would think her terribly childish and inexperienced. She hoped not. Anyway, she had no intention of suggesting a porn film, and wondered why she had even considered it.

Luke chose an American romantic comedy starring Julia Roberts and they settled down to watch it, taking some heinously overpriced chocolate from the fridge of the mini-bar. Luckily they'd had the foresight to bring some drinks up with them. Mia baulked at paying six euros for a bottle of water. She'd rather drink from the tap in the bathroom than pay that.

Luke arranged the pillows against the headboard of the bed. 'There you go,' he said. 'Ready for your own private viewing?'

Mia nodded. I know what I'd like to see, popped into her head before she could stop it. Mia, she chastised herself, stop that! She hopped on to the bed and leaned back against the soft pillows. He jumped up beside her and put his arm around her shoulders. 'Is that OK?' he murmured.

'Yes.' She snuggled in towards him and rested her head on his shoulder. 'Lovely.'

The film was entertaining enough and Mia tried to concentrate on the plot and characters, but her mind kept drifting back to Luke. Luke's arm, Luke's leg pressing warmly against hers. Luke's breathing, Luke's . . . damn it, she felt an overpowering urge to kiss him.

'Luke,' she whispered.

'Um?' he murmured, his eyes still fixed on the screen.

She put her hand out, raised her body a little and kissed him on the cheek. He smiled at her, gave her shoulder a little squeeze and then looked back at the screen again.

'Luke!' she hissed.

'You're missing a good bit,' he said, eyes still glued to the film, a smile playing on his lips.

'Luke!' she said crossly.

'I'm only joking.' He gave her his full attention. 'You're so cute when you're angry.'

'I'll give you cute,' she said, grabbing a pillow from behind her head. She swung her legs under her body and sat up on her hunkers.

'Are you threatening me, Mia Redden?' he asked. 'I'm a bit of a pillow-fight expert, I'll have you know.'

'Are you now?' she said, a glint in her eye. She swung the pillow and it smacked him in the jaw.

'Mia!' he exclaimed, rubbing his jaw and then picking up a pillow. 'You're asking for it. I warn you.'

'The Reddens are well known for their pillow-fighting expertise,' she said.

'I hear they knock each other's teeth out all right.' Luke laughed. 'I suppose a gum shield is out of the question?'

'Poor Greg,' Mia mused. 'But no face shots, how about that? Just in case it's a family jinx?'

'Deal.' Luke swung the pillow at Mia's waist with such force that it knocked her off her hunkers.

'You brat!' she shrieked. She jumped to her feet, sinking into the soft mattress, and gave him a blow to the chest. He retaliated with a bash to her upper legs. And so they continued for several minutes, laughing and shrieking until they were both quite breathless.

When she stopped to try to catch her breath, Luke rugby-tackled Mia around the waist and brought her down to lie flat on her back.

'Luke,' she panted, 'that's not in the rules.'

'Says who?' He smiled down at her. His face was

flushed and his breath was short and ragged. He kissed her firmly on the lips and then drew back. 'Is that in the rules?' he said.

'Yes,' she said. 'And so's this.' She put her arms around his neck and pulled him towards her. Their lips touched, gently at first, then with increasing force and passion. Mia's roaming thoughts were silenced, her mind totally and utterly concentrated on the moment. She'd never been kissed like this before – like it mattered, like there was nothing more important than getting every nip, every lick, every caress completely perfect. She used her fingers and hands to explore Luke's face, neck and shoulders, roaming over the rough and smooth landscape of his skin with her fingertips.

'Mia,' he murmured, coming up for air, 'you're amazing.' He gazed down at her and grinned. Then he began to plant tiny kisses on the nape of her neck, moving down towards her chest. His hands brushed back her cardigan and the top of her dress.

Mia stiffened. 'Stop!' she clamoured, her hands scrambling at her dress as she sat up.

'Sorry,' Luke said immediately. His eyes flickered nervously to hers. 'I didn't mean to . . .' He ran his hands through his hair and sighed. 'You're just so damn sexy, Mia. I couldn't help myself.'

'No, it's not your fault,' she said, 'it's mine. I'm not ready. I'm sorry.'

He sat staring at her. 'You're so lovely, Mia. I'd never do anything to hurt you, you know that. If you want to wait, that's fine by me.'

'Are you sure you don't mind?'

'Of course not.'

'Can we just kiss, Luke? Is that OK? Or is it terribly teenage?'

He grinned at her. 'No. I don't think so. It's sweet.'

'Sweet?' Mia frowned.

'That's the wrong word.' He thought for a moment. 'It's nice.'

Mia groaned. 'That's worse.'

'Sorry, I'm not expressing myself very well.' He took her hand in his and held it tight. 'Mia, whatever you want to do is fine by me. As I said before, I don't want to rush you. Kissing is absolutely great, brilliant. Really. It just feels a little odd to be talking about all this, to be honest.'

'Sorry, I think I get that from Wendy.' Mia yawned.

'That interesting, am I?' Luke smiled.

'Sorry.'

'No need to apologize, it has been a long day. Why don't I leave? Let you get some sleep.'

'No, no, it's fine.' Mia yawned again. 'Gosh, sorry. I've suddenly come over all tired.'

'You go to bed,' he said kindly. He leaned down and kissed her on the forehead. 'I'll see you in the morning.' He sat up and made to go, but Mia stopped him.

'I feel like I've wrecked everything,' she said, looking at him earnestly. 'I'm sorry for encouraging you and then asking you to stop like that. I wasn't trying to lead you on, I just . . .' She halted in mid-sentence and looked down at her hands. 'You must think I'm so stupid. I don't know why you're wasting your time with me, Luke. I'm an idiot.'

He put his hand under her chin and raised her face gently. 'Listen to me,' he began, 'I like you, a lot. And I don't think you're stupid, far from it. I think you're wonderful. You like to get to know someone before you sleep with him, that's nothing to be ashamed of. In fact, far from being childish, I think it's actually rather sensible. And it's really, really fine, honestly. This isn't just some fling for me, Mia. Do you understand that? And I hope it's not for you. It's not, is it?'

Mia shook her head. 'No. No, of course not,' she said, realizing as soon as the words had left her mouth just how much she meant it.

'Good.' He kissed her on the lips, firmly yet gently. 'Goodnight. Sleep well. I'll see you in the morning.'

She swung her legs off the bed.

'No, don't get up,' he said. 'I'll see myself out.'

As soon as the door closed, Mia suddenly felt very alone. Luke had said he didn't mind leaving, but she wondered if he really meant it. She gave a huge sigh. What was she like?

A moment later she heard a quiet knock on the door. What now? She went over to answer it, half expecting to see Wendy standing there, ready to question her as to why Luke had been in her room so late at night. But it was Luke.

'Oh!' She almost jumped backwards in surprise.

'I didn't get a proper goodnight kiss,' he said with a grin. 'And my bed's a bit uncomfortable to be honest. I was wondering if I could share yours? I'd like to wake up beside you, Mia. If that's OK with you. Nothing else.'

'Yes,' she whispered, standing back to let him in. A smile fluttered to her lips and she put her hand up to cover it. Her heart felt as light as a feather and she had to suppress the tiny bubbles of joy that threatened to gurgle out of her throat. 'I'd like that too.'

12 *Alva*

'I Do, I Do, I Do, I Do, I Do'

'Mia!' Alva called across the bar of the hotel late on Saturday afternoon. 'Over here!'

Mia waved and made her way towards Alva, impeded somewhat by several squat bar stools which had come adrift from the mothership of their tables.

'Hi, Alva.' Mia sat down beside her friend and gave her a warm hug and a kiss on the cheek.

'Sorry I'm late,' Alva said as she sat back against the upholstered seat. She studied Mia's face. 'What has you in such a good mood? You look positively radiant.'

Mia just smiled at her. 'Isn't it a lovely day? How was the drive from Limerick?' Without waiting for an answer, she whipped up the menu and began to read it. 'Gosh, I'm famished. Are you having something to eat? I had a huge cooked breakfast, so I didn't have any lunch. What about you? How about some lasagne and chips?'

'Mia, you're gabbling. What was the first question again?'

'Oh, sorry, was I? Sorry.' Mia shrugged and smiled again. 'I've no idea.'

In fact, she was finding it hard not to smile. Her mouth seemed to be hot-wired to her heart, which was zinging like it had never zinged before.

Alva looked at Mia carefully. Mia's cheeks were flushed and she seemed rather over-excited about something. 'You've had sex!' she said finally after noticing what looked suspiciously like stubble rash on the side of Mia's neck.

'No, I have not!' Mia said indignantly. 'I'm just in a good mood, that's all. It has nothing to do with ... you know.'

'Well, you've had something,' Alva said. She tried to catch Mia's eye, but she had buried her head in the menu.

'Mia! What is it?' Suddenly it dawned on Alva. 'Something's happened with Luke, hasn't it?'

'No!' Mia exclaimed a little too vehemently.

'That's it!' Alva cried. She knew when Mia was lying. She nudged her in the side. 'Go on, tell me what happened.'

Mia couldn't hold it in any longer. She had to tell someone or she'd burst. She'd been keeping it to herself all morning and the strain was getting to her. She'd almost rung Gemma several times before thinking better of it. Gemma would only tell Wendy after all, and then Wendy would want to talk about it. And she didn't want anything or anyone to bring her down to earth just yet, especially not Wendy. 'OK. I'll tell you. As long as you promise to keep it to yourself.'

'Cross my heart and hope to die,' Alva said. 'Go on!' She was dying to hear the news.

'I mean it, Alva. Don't breath a word of this to anyone, do you hear me? Especially not Wendy.'

'You can trust me, I won't,' Alva said.

Mia said nothing for a moment. She considered bringing up the Atlas night but thought better of it.

Alva caught Mia's eye. 'Are we OK?' she said. 'Mia?'

Mia nodded. 'We're fine.' There was no point in being petty. It had been a minor blip in their friendship and Mia was happy to put it firmly behind them.

'Really?'

'Yes. Now do you want to hear about Luke or not?'

'Are you mad? Of course I do.'

Mia took a deep breath and began at the beginning. She told Alva all about the eventful train journey and the late-night pillow fight. 'And that's about it,' Mia finished up. 'We kissed and then he stayed the night.'

'And?' Alva encouraged.

'Nothing happened, Alva. I know what's going through your dirty little mind, but we just kissed, that's all. It was lovely. I woke up and his arm was still wrapped around me.'

Alva knew from Mia's tone of voice that she was telling the truth. 'How sweet,' she murmured.

Mia laughed. 'That's what Luke said.'

Alva gave Mia a hug. 'Mia, I'm so pleased for you. I think it's brilliant.' She leaned towards her. 'Is he a good kisser?'

'Alva!'

Alva grinned at Mia. 'I bet he is.'

'I'm saying nothing. So tell me all about your yoga retreat. Was it awful?'

'No, it was great. I met some really nice women and I took a few yoga classes and really enjoyed them. I'm quite supple actually.'

Mia snorted. '*You!* Supple? Are you serious? Are you sure you have any muscles, Alva? You haven't exactly used them much.'

'I know, I know. But the teacher was fabulous and I really loved it. I'm going to sign up for classes back home too.'

'Wonders will never cease,' Mia said. 'My friend the yogi.'

'I wouldn't go that far.' Alva laughed. 'And I did a lot of thinking while I was there. Yoga really clears your mind, allows you to focus on the important things.'

'And?' Mia prompted.

'I'm going to talk to Sean. I want to sort everything out so we can both move on with our lives.'

'Good,' Mia said. 'It's the right thing to do, Alva.'

'I know it is. It just hurt so much – Sean dumping me like that – I didn't know how to deal with it. But from now on things are going to be different. I'm not going to take anyone or anything for granted ever again. I've lost one good man and I almost lost my best friend, both through my own stupidity. Neither of which are ever going to happen again, not if I can help it.'

Mia touched her shoulder against Alva's. 'You'll never lose me, I'm here for the long haul.'

'I don't deserve you,' Alva said.

'I know.'

'Hey!'

'Only joking,' Mia said with a grin.

'So what's happening this evening?' asked Alva, looking around. 'The town is really hopping. It took me ages to drive down the main street.'

'We're on stage from nine until eleven. There's some sort of Irish dancing competition before that, if you're interested.'

'I think I'll give that a miss, thanks very much. I'll just watch you sing, if that's OK. I'm really looking forward to seeing you on stage. I'm sure you're brilliant. I'm sorry I haven't made it to anything yet.'

'That's all right. You've been busy and it's not as if you can just arrive at someone's wedding or business do uninvited. You're here now.'

'You're brilliant, Mia. Do you know that? You have such a big heart. I'm lucky to have you as a friend.'

'Thanks,' Mia said. She was touched. 'Now, can we please eat?'

Alva watched AbbaFab belt out their first number, 'Waterloo'. Alva and Pat were sitting in the wings on

277

a flight box and Alva couldn't keep her eyes off Mia, who had been transformed by more than just make-up and a costume. She seemed a completely different person on stage: confident, fizzing with energy, dancing and singing her little heart out.

Alva felt a strange sort of lump form in her throat. Mia looked so happy and carefree. She realized with a jolt that Mia needed to be on stage, she'd always needed it, even as a child. It was part of who she was. It enabled her to be a different person for a while, to stretch her limits. And by suppressing her desire to perform since Miriam's death, Mia had been stifling part of her own personality, her safety valve. Being in AbbaFab is so good for her, Alva thought. And it's nice and safe because Wendy is there to back her up, and Ronan too. And now Luke. Long may it last.

As soon as the second song, 'Knowing Me, Knowing You', had finished, Pat stood up. 'Give me a yell if anything goes wrong,' he said to Alva, speaking loudly to be heard over the enthusiastic applause.

'Where will you be?' she asked.

'In the van.'

'Doing what exactly?' Alva asked, expecting him to be loping off to roll a joint, or to drink a beer at the very least. If she hadn't been glued to Mia's performance, she might have joined him.

'Ronan's writing a song for the Eurovision,' Pat explained. 'He has to submit it by Wednesday. He nearly has the lyrics nailed but they need a little more work. I promised I'd look over them, give him a few suggestions.'

'The Eurovision?' Alva asked in amazement. That wasn't very rock and roll. 'Really?'

Pat gave her a grin. 'There's decent money in it. Nothing to be sniffed at. And it's good exposure.'

'I suppose.' Alva wasn't convinced.

'He wants to write ballads, you see, for boy bands and the like.'

'Boy bands?' Alva couldn't contain her mirth.

'Alva, well may you laugh, but do you have any idea how much commercial songwriters earn?' He gave her some ballpark figures.

Alva's eyes opened wider and wider. 'Are you serious?'

'Not so funny now, is it? And once he has that market cracked it will leave us time to write some other stuff together. We have a few ideas for an Irish rock musical.'

Alva was impressed. 'That's great. But what about AbbaFab?'

Pat shrugged. 'It pays the bills. But it won't last forever.'

'I suppose not,' she murmured.

'See you later.' Pat walked away just as Ronan and Luke began to play the opening strains of 'Dancing Queen'. The end of AbbaFab – that didn't sound like good news for Mia. Then again, it was only supposed to be temporary while Gemma recuperated, Alva knew that. But whatever happens, Mia has to keep performing, Alva thought as she watched Mia interact with Wendy on the stage. I'll make sure of it, AbbaFab or no AbbaFab. She's a star.

'Pat! It's Sean, Alva's boy – um, ex. We met at one of Wendy and Ronan's parties.'

Pat stopped in his tracks and smiled in recognition. 'How are you? How are the house renovations coming along?'

They'd spent the evening discussing old houses as Pat had been thinking of buying a cottage in Wicklow which needed to be completely rebuilt. He'd changed his mind in the end, going for a town house near Bray instead, but Sean had been most kind and generous with his advice and had even offered to have a look at the house before Pat bought it.

'Good, thanks. Almost finished, I hope.'

'What brings you down here?' Pat asked. He looked Sean up and down. 'And what are you wearing under your jacket. Is that Luke's?'

Sean smiled. 'It is. And I'm here because of Alva. Is she here?'

Pat nodded. 'She's watching the show from the side of the stage.'

'I thought she might be.'

Sean told Pat his intentions. Pat smiled as Sean unfolded his plan and then began to laugh out loud. 'Are you sure?'

'Yes. Positive.'

Pat shrugged. 'In that case, follow me. If we get

280

separated in the crowd I'll meet you at the right-hand side of the stage. Alva's on the left.'

'Thanks, Pat.'

'I wouldn't thank me yet,' Pat said a little ominously.

Alva smiled as she caught the subtle change to the chorus from 'Take a Chance on Me' to 'Take a Chance on *Mia*'. Alva felt happy. It was good to see Wendy and Mia getting on so well. Alva knew that Mia worshipped Wendy, and nothing made Mia happier than pleasing her sister, who wasn't always the easiest of people to please. This evening was just getting better and better. In fact, Alva was getting quite emotional watching AbbaFab play and she wondered if it had something to do with Alia and her classes. Maybe my emotions have been all stirred up by the yoga, Alva thought. Whatever it is, I do feel rather strange.

She began to sway to the music and mouth some of the words. She'd forgotten how catchy Abba's songs were. I must buy one of those Abba compilation albums for the car, she thought. As the song finished she took a swig of water from the bottle at her feet. When she looked at the stage again she was surprised to see a man talking to Wendy and Mia. He was dressed in an Abba costume, one of the 'Arrival' jumpsuits, which was a bit too small for him. He looked familiar but she couldn't quite make him out under the stage lights.

'Ladies and gentlemen,' Wendy said as the applause

for 'Take a Chance on Me' petered out. 'This is Sean Malone and he has something to say. All yours, Sean.' Wendy handed him the microphone.

Alva nearly fell off the flight box. What the hell was Sean doing on the stage? Was this a joke? She stared at him in disbelief.

'I have a story to tell this evening,' Sean began. There were one or two groans from the audience. 'It won't take long. It's about a man who made a stupid mistake. That man is me.'

'Hey, we all make them, buddy,' Luke said into his microphone, and the crowd laughed.

'I had a girl, a wonderful, beautiful girl and I loved her with all my heart. And I'm here this evening, making an eejit of myself, to tell her that I'm sorry. That I love her.' He stopped for a moment. 'And to ask her to marry me.' He looked towards the wing where Alva was sitting and put his hand over his eyes in an attempt to catch her eye. 'Alva, what do you say?'

The crowd began to clap and cheer. 'Go on, ya good thing!' someone yelled.

Sean stared at Alva who was standing, rigid with disbelief. 'Alva?' he asked again.

She blinked, like a deer caught in the headlights. Had Sean really just proposed to her? On stage? In an Abba costume? What was he thinking of?

'Alva?'

Blood rushed to Alva's head. She felt sick and dizzy. Air! She needed air. She turned on her heels and ran out of the back entrance of the tent.

'Alva!' Sean said, dropping the microphone on the stage floor and following her. The crowd gasped and then a few people began to clap.

Mia's heart was torn. She wanted to follow Sean and find Alva, but she knew she couldn't. She also knew it was time for them to find their own way, together or separately.

'Are you OK?' Wendy whispered to her.

'I think so,' Mia said. 'And the show must go on, as they say. They'll be fine.'

Wendy nodded at her and then turned back towards the crowd. 'We thought you'd enjoy that little bit of drama,' she said into her microphone, rescuing the situation. 'It wasn't real, of course. And thank you to our wonderful actor.' The crowd clapped and cheered. 'Back to the music, folks,' she added. Luke began to sing 'Does Your Mother Know?' with as much energy and animation as he could muster.

After a few minutes of frantic searching, Sean found Alva at the end of the large field, leaning against a wall which separated the makeshift car park from a farmer's land. Her body was leaning forward, her hands supporting her weight, and she was staring at the river that flowed through the neighbouring field.

'That's the River Ilen,' Sean said softly as he approached her.

'Oh,' she said flatly. She continued to stare at the dark, slowly moving water.

Sean sat down on the wall and waited for a moment

283

before speaking. 'I'm sorry, Alva. It seemed like a good thing to do. I know how much you like grand gestures and all that.'

She snorted. 'Do I? I suppose you're right. But I don't necessarily like being on the receiving end of them, Sean.'

'Sorry,' he murmured again. He stared down at his hands. 'I've really messed up this time, haven't I?'

She turned her head and looked at him. He looked completely ridiculous in the Abba costume and she stifled a giggle. 'We're quite a pair, aren't we?'

'We are that,' he agreed.

She hopped on to the wall and they sat in silence for a few minutes. 'Do you really want to marry me?' she asked finally.

'Yes,' he said. 'Yes.'

'Why?' she asked.

'Because I can't live without you, Alva. Lord knows I've tried. You're under my skin. I love you – it's that simple. I can't help it.'

She nodded and stared at the river again. 'I know what you mean.'

'So what's your answer?'

'You're not serious?'

'Ah.' Sean shook his head and sighed.

'Ah, what?' she asked.

'I take it that's a no then.'

'Not necessarily.'

Sean looked at her. 'Is it a yes?'

She shook her head. 'It's a maybe. We have a lot of

things to talk about before we get to that stage, don't you think?'

'You're probably right. So what happens now?'

'I have to find somewhere to live for a start. Somewhere near you and Mia.'

'You're not moving back in then?'

'No. I think I need to live on my own for a while.' She smiled at him. 'Wash my own dishes, cook for myself.'

Sean was disappointed. 'Are you sure? I don't mind doing all that stuff, Alva, you know that.'

'I know, but it's not right, Sean. I think we both need to have our own space for a while. Let's get our relationship back on track first.'

'Our relationship? You mean you want me back?'

'Yes. I guess I do.'

Sean put his arm around her and drew her closer and gave a huge sigh.

'What was that sigh for?' she asked.

'Relief,' he admitted. 'I miss you so much, Alva. I wasn't sure if you'd have me back. Especially after that Sadie business.'

Alva thought for a moment. 'I wasn't sure if I could forgive you for that. But we all make mistakes. And don't let it happen again. Understand?'

Sean nodded. 'Alva, you're an amazing woman. I'm so lucky. God, how I missed you.'

She wrapped her arms around him. 'You're a good man, and I missed you too. You're part of me, Sean Malone. You're like my second liver.'

'You always were the romantic.' Sean laughed. 'Could you not have said second heart?'

'Livers are far more interesting organs.' Alva smiled at him. 'Sure, where would we be without our livers?'

'You're terrible,' Sean murmured. 'Now quiet, Alva. I want to kiss you.'

For once in her life, Alva did as she was told.

Later that evening in the hotel's nightclub Mia watched Alva and Sean dancing, their arms wrapped around each other, moving in rhythm to the music.

'They look so right together,' Mia said to Wendy. 'Don't you think?'

'Yes,' Wendy agreed. 'Do you think they'll ever get married, Mia?'

'I expect so. Not for a few years though. I think they have a lot more living to do first. Getting married so young isn't always a great idea after all.'

Wendy said nothing. Her eyes were fixed on Sean and Alva.

'Oh, sorry, Wendy,' Mia said as soon as she realized what she'd said. 'I didn't mean . . . you and Ronan are different.'

Again Wendy said nothing.

'Is Ronan all right?' Mia asked, gesturing towards him. He was sitting beside Wendy, his head resting against the back of the seat and his mouth open, snoring gently.

'He's fine,' Wendy replied tersely. 'He's just had too much red wine; it always sends him to sleep.'

'It's been a busy day,' Mia said, anxious to defend Ronan for some reason. 'And Ronan always works so hard.'

Still Wendy said nothing.

'Wendy, is something wrong?' Mia asked. Wendy certainly didn't seem herself.

Wendy sighed. 'No, everything's fine.' Her eyes were still fixed on Sean and Alva.

'You can talk to me, you know,' Mia said tentatively. 'I'm not a bad listener.'

Wendy looked at her sister and smiled. 'Thanks, but really, there's nothing wrong.'

'Excuse me, are you the girl from AbbaFab?' a tall, blond man stood in front of them and stared down at Wendy. 'I saw you earlier, I'm a big fan.'

Wendy looked up and smiled. He wasn't bad-looking really, if you overlooked the yellow teeth and the slight paunch. And he did seem to be rather taken with her if the eager expression on his face was anything to go by. 'Yes, that's right.'

'I'm Carl. Would you do me the honour . . . ?' he said rather formally, holding out his hand. 'I'd love to dance with you.'

'Why not?' Wendy said, standing up. 'Are you OK on your own here, Mia?'

'Um, sure. Luke will be back in a few minutes. He's at the bar.' Mia was completely taken aback. What was Wendy playing at? She made it a rule never to dance with fans. 'More trouble than it's worth,' she always said.

Mia watched as Carl began to swing Wendy around

the dance floor, oblivious to the fact that it wasn't exactly in keeping with the slow, melodic music. He was quite a good dancer for his size, Mia considered as she watched Wendy smile and laugh.

'Who's that with Wendy?' Ronan asked, rousing from his nap.

'An admirer,' Mia said honestly. 'He's called Carl.'

They both stared at Wendy and Carl.

'She seems to be enjoying herself,' Ronan said, a slight edge to his voice. He wasn't slurring his words, but he didn't seem altogether sober either.

'Ronan, is everything all right between you and Wendy? I don't mean to pry but . . .'

Ronan sighed. He'd love to talk to someone about his suspicions but Mia wasn't the right person. Gemma maybe. But certainly not Mia.

'Fine.' He patted Mia's hand. 'Everything's just fine.'

13 Wendy

'Head over Heels'

'Ronan, I'm off now.' Wendy popped her head around the kitchen door. 'I'll be back later. I'll grab a sandwich while I'm out.'

Ronan lifted his head from the paper. He was extremely tired this morning. The drive back from Skibbereen had taken even longer than it should have due to several sets of roadworks, with associated tailbacks, and Greg had been up several times during the night with nightmares about getting lost. He was a perceptive child and Ronan worried that he could sense the growing tension between his parents. 'Where are you going?' he asked Wendy, trying not to sound accusatory.

'Bank, post office, shopping centre to buy a new sports bra – my old ones are starting to look really grotty – chemist and supermarket. Nothing very exciting, I'm afraid.'

'What time will you be back?'

'Two or three. But you'll be out, won't you? You're going over to Pat's.'

'That's right,' Ronan nodded. 'You look nice, by the way.' He took in the navy dress which wrapped around her body and tied at the front, one of his favourites; the navy sandals with peep-toes; the freshly washed hair which hung loose around Wendy's face; the broad smile which lit up her expression.

'Thank you.'

Was it his imagination or did she seem a little uneasy? Nervous, even? 'See you later then,' he said.

'Bye,' she said breezily, before shooting out of the door.

Ronan stared at his paper but he couldn't concentrate, the words were swimming in front of his eyes. He shut his eyes tight and then opened them again. Maybe he was being paranoid. Just because Wendy was dressed up and obviously in a good mood didn't mean she was having an affair. Maybe the text had been a mistake, sent to Wendy in error or something.

'Stop it!' he muttered to himself. 'Try not to obsess.'

But it wasn't easy. It was all he could think about. He glanced at his watch. Pat would be expecting him. He folded up the paper and stood up. He wished he could get the picture of Wendy dancing with that blond man in Skibbereen out of his head, but he couldn't.

*

Wendy's heart was still thumping in her chest. She was sure that Ronan suspected something. It was the way he'd looked her up and down, she decided, his eyes lingering on her dress. Just as well he's not Superman, Wendy thought, a delicious shiver thrilling up her spine. Because if he did have X-ray eyes he'd see quite clearly that Wendy was wearing new and rather risqué underwear: a daringly low-cut black lacy basque with matching lacy almost-not-there knickers. Because she was not on her way to do mundane, boring shopping. Oh, no. She was on her way to a small, discreet hotel just outside Wicklow, where Des would be waiting for her.

They'd been texting each other all weekend and Wendy had finally relented and agreed to meet him, and not just for an innocent lunch either. She knew exactly what he wanted, because she wanted it too. Or at least she thought she did. She certainly wanted something, and maybe furtive sex with Des would stop the gnawing itch, the growing feeling that there was something wrong with her life and her marriage; that there was something missing. She was feeling rather out of control these days, as if her life was just ticking over and she was being pulled along in its wake, powerless to change anything.

Wendy had also been thinking about her teenage days in Westport ever since she'd bumped into Des in the garage, thoughts she'd tried to consign to the dumping ground of her memory a long time ago. What would Ronan do if he ever found out about Westport?

291

She shuddered just considering it. And as for Mia . . .
'Stop!' she told herself. 'I can't bear thinking about it.'
Maybe sex with Des was just what she needed. It
would certainly stop her mind churning over the past
and place it very firmly in the present.

As Wendy drove up the long gravel drive towards
the Glenford House, a small boutique hotel just outside
Wicklow town, she started to feel butterflies of anticipation in her stomach. She pulled up outside the large,
red-bricked house and the butterflies rose up to her
throat. She held back her excitement and tried not to
grin as she walked into the primrose-yellow hall, her
eyes resting on the glorious stained-glass arched window on the stair landing, the rich, jewel-coloured
damask drapes on the windows, the Victorian-looking
parlour palms in their huge tubs, and the rich, antique
mahogany furniture.

'Can I help you?' A woman appeared from
nowhere. A smartly dressed woman in a plain black
suit and crisply ironed white shirt. A respectable
woman.

'Yes, I'm looking for Des Sullivan. He's booked a
room.' Wendy willed her cheeks not to redden, but it
was no use. She felt as guilty as hell and wished now
that she'd worn different underwear. She knew this
nice woman could see right through her.

But the woman simply smiled.

'Ah, yes. Mrs Sullivan. It's your wedding anniversary, isn't it? How romantic. I do hope you have a
lovely afternoon. Mr Sullivan has arrived and is in

your room. I'll take you up now. He's already ordered champagne and lunch.'

'How lovely,' Wendy murmured.

Now she felt even worse. Wedding anniversary? Champagne? Her heart sank to the bottom of her shoes. What was she doing? As she followed the woman up the impressive staircase, she castigated herself. What kind of person are you, Wendy Redden? Lying to your husband, lying to this nice lady. Well, she hadn't lied exactly (she discounted lying by omission on this occasion because it suited her), but Des most certainly had.

'Here you are,' the woman said, leaving Wendy outside a door on the first floor. 'Happy anniversary.'

'Thanks.'

As soon as the woman walked away, Wendy opened the door. She was struck immediately by the strong, heady scent of hyacinths. Des looked up at her from the small sofa by the window. In front of him was a coffee table with a silver champagne bucket and an empty flute sitting on it. He was already sipping some of the pale, sparkling liquid.

'Hello,' he said in his silky-smooth voice. 'Isn't this place heavenly?'

Wendy nodded and closed the door behind her. 'Where did you find it?'

'On the Internet,' he said. 'It was recommended as one of the most romantic hotels in Ireland.'

'It's beautiful,' she said, still rooted to the spot.

'You look gorgeous.' He grinned wolfishly. 'Good

enough to eat. Would you like a glass of bubbly? It's rather good.'

Wendy nodded. 'Please.' If she was going to go through with this, she certainly needed some Dutch courage. 'And in case I forget to say it later, thanks for fixing my computer – you're a life-saver. Nadia told me you called by on Saturday. I really appreciate it. How much do I owe you for the work?' Wendy had been delighted to find her laptop working again on her return from Skibbereen.

'Nothing,' he said. 'On the house. A favour for a special friend.'

He lifted up the heavy dark green champagne bottle and poured expertly, tipping the glass sideways to prevent any frothing bubbles from cascading down the side.

'Come and sit down beside me,' he cajoled, patting the seat of the sofa.

Wendy placed her wrap on the back of the sofa and her bag on the seat and did as he requested, her heart quickening as she felt the warmth of his thigh pressing against hers through the thin material of her dress. He handed her the glass and clinked his own against it.

'To us,' he said.

'To us,' she murmured.

He took a long sip, then put his fingers into his glass, reached over and splattered some drops of champagne just under her neck.

Wendy jumped. The liquid was ice-cold.

'Des!' she exclaimed, her hand moving up to brush the champagne away.

'Leave it!' He moved towards her, cocked his head and began to lick up the drips. His tongue felt hot and rough on her skin and she winced. But she also felt remarkably aroused. She willed herself to fight it. Wedding anniversary, she reminded herself. What the hell was she doing here? Des wasn't . . .

Des silenced her racing thoughts with a long, sensuous kiss which tasted deliciously of champagne and something sweet. Wendy let herself be kissed, her body beginning to respond to his caresses, her mind befuddled with endorphins. Chocolate, she thought suddenly as Des's tongue caressed hers. That's what the taste was. Sweet, rich and dark.

As they came up for air, she noticed the chocolate-covered strawberries in a small silver dish on the table.

'Want one?' Des asked, following her gaze.

He took one in his fingers and played it over her skin, up and down her arms, lingering on her neck and finally popping it into her mouth while still holding its stalk. 'Suck the chocolate off,' he said.

She obeyed, the delicious taste filling her mouth.

'That's what I'm going to do to you,' he whispered.

Wendy could feel her whole body melt with desire. He stood up and put both arms around her waist, lifting her off the sofa.

'Des!' she said. 'What are you doing? I'm not sure I'm ready . . .'

'Shush,' he murmured.

He sat back down on the sofa and placed her on his knee, straddling him, their faces almost touching. He pulled her towards him and began to kiss her passionately, one of his hands pressing against the back of her head, making her feel trapped.

Wendy shook her head, forcing his hand away. 'Don't,' she said, her eyes flashing.

He nodded wordlessly and began to kiss her again. This time his hands roamed her neck and back, inching their way along the seam of her dress towards her breasts. She gasped as he cupped them firmly yet gently, playing with her nipples through the thin lace basque. Then he moved his hands down and began to snake them up her thighs.

Wendy tried not to squirm beneath his touch. She had terribly ticklish inner thighs. In fact, Ronan loved taking advantage of this fact and they often had tickling matches before or after sex. Ronan's side was his weak spot, just above his hipbone. Ronan. His smiling, kind face slipped into her head. Sex with Ronan was safe, comfortable and involved lots of laughter. Of course, it hadn't always been like that; in the early days it had been passionate and intense. But as the years had passed it had changed, they'd changed. Now they knew each other's bodies intimately and enjoyed pleasing each other. At least, they had done. Sex had been a little low on the agenda lately. She hadn't felt like it recently and Ronan hadn't forced the issue. In fact it was weeks since they'd last made love.

Wendy tried to concentrate on kissing Des. This was like the old days with Ronan. Her whole body was quivering under his touch, her nerve ends jangling with anticipation.

'Wendy?' Des said, drawing away. 'Will we move to the bed?'

Wendy gulped and nodded wordlessly.

He led her by the hand over to the huge four-poster bed and gently pushed her on to her back. He began to kiss her from the top of her head to her toes; quick, nibbling kisses that Wendy found a little irritating to tell the truth. She watched the top of his head as he took her big toe in his mouth. This did nothing for her and she stifled a laugh. She used to suck the boys' toes when they were babies – they loved that, she remembered. Her two little angels. They'd been darling babies, Steve especially with his unruly mop of white-blond hair.

Des started to tug a little roughly at the front of her dress. Wendy was afraid that he'd rip it. It was one of her favourites, which she'd picked up for next to nothing at an Irish designer's sample sale, and she was damned if she was going to let him damage it.

'I'll do it,' she murmured, untying it with shaking fingers.

As soon as she'd done so, Des pulled back the material and gasped. 'You're so beautiful,' he said, drinking in her pale, smooth skin, almost luminescent against the black lace, his hands roving up and down her flat stomach. He pulled her basque down, freeing her breasts.

Wendy suddenly felt self-conscious. She was practically naked and he was fully dressed. Plus it was broad daylight. However well preserved her body was, after having children it wouldn't stand up to much close scrutiny.

She pulled her dress around her. Des whisked it open again. 'I'm not finished,' he said in a husky voice.

Wendy began to unbutton his shirt. He helped her, his fingers faster than hers. She smoothed the shirt off his body and it fell to the ground. He had a firm, hairless and tanned chest and Wendy ran her hands over his toned shoulders. He leaned forward, opened her dress again and rubbed his chest gently over her nipples, sending waves of sensation crashing through her body. She scrambled at his jeans, opening his belt buckle and working at the fly buttons. He pulled them down his legs, kicking them off the end of the bed. He still had his socks on and Wendy noticed with a smile that they were Homer Simpson socks, similar to the ones Greg and Steve wore. She stifled a laugh.

'What?' Des asked, noticing her smile.

'Like the socks,' Wendy joked.

He leaned down and pulled them off. He didn't seem too impressed by her quip.

'At least you don't have matching boxers on,' she said.

Des glared at her. Then she realized that his shorts had a Man United logo on the waistband. She couldn't help but laugh. Des wasn't amused.

'What's so funny?' he demanded.

'My sons have almost the same shorts,' she explained. 'I'm sorry.' She tried to stop laughing but couldn't.

'Wendy!' he said in a whining voice.

She looked at him. His tanned cheeks were flushed, his hair was tousled and his teeth gleaming. Does he bleach them, she wondered. They look unnaturally white.

Wendy pulled her dress over her exposed chest again and sat up. 'I can't do this,' she said.

As soon as she said it she realized how ridiculous the whole situation was. She might have thought she could have an affair, but she was kidding herself. It just wasn't right. It just wasn't her. Not any more. Not ever.

'What?' Des demanded. 'I shelled out a small fortune for this room – champagne, lunch, the works. You're joking, right?'

She shook her head. 'No. I'm really sorry.'

Des looked completely defeated. 'But why?'

Wendy shrugged. 'I have no idea.'

'Is it me?' he asked a little petulantly.

'No. It's me.'

'And there's nothing I can do to change your mind?' He ran his finger along her leg. But instead of feeling turned on, she felt ticklish.

'No, I'm sorry.'

He said nothing for a long moment, then grabbed his jeans from the floor and stepped into them. 'I'm sorry too. But I don't fucking believe this, Wendy. You're a real prick tease, you know that? You always were.'

Wendy fastened her dress and stood up. 'That's unfair. I'm sorry I can't go through with this, but I did intend to, really I did. I just . . .'

'What? Changed your mind? Maybe you're just trying to get back at me for ignoring you in Westport, is that it? Some sort of retribution? Or are you trying to get back at Henry through me?' He laughed nastily. 'That's it, isn't it, Wendy?'

'No!' Wendy exclaimed. 'That's not true!'

'Are you sure?'

'Yes! I'd forgotten all about Henry until I met you in the garage.'

Des gave a hard laugh. 'I find that hard to believe. According to rumour he left you with a little reminder.'

Wendy's face paled. She was speechless with anger. 'Get out!' she screamed. 'Get out of my sight.'

'Touched a nerve, have I, Wendy?' he sneered as he grabbed his jacket. 'Don't worry, I'm leaving. My fiancée is flying in from Sydney tomorrow to meet Mum, so I won't be ringing you again. You're some piece of work, Wendy. I pity your husband. Does he even know about . . . ?'

Wendy gave a loud shriek and shoved him towards the door. 'Get out!'

'Take your hands off me,' he said. 'I'm going.' He slammed the door behind him.

Wendy crumpled to the ground and began to sob.

'Hello?'

'Yes.' Ronan answered the phone that evening.

'Can I speak to Wendy Redden, please?'

'She's in the bath. Can I take a message?'

'Please. She left her mobile phone in our hotel this afternoon. She asked us to ring her when we found it. Can you tell her it's in the safe and she can collect it whenever convenient. We found it down the side of the sofa.'

'Hotel?' Ronan said his mind racing. 'Sorry, what hotel?'

'Glenford House,' the woman said.

Ronan racked his brains. Glenford House, Glenford House? Wendy hadn't said anything about a meeting at Glenford House. Or had she? He couldn't remember. 'Ah, right. Of course.'

'Did you enjoy your wedding anniversary?' the woman asked.

'What?'

'Your wedding anniversary. The special champagne lunch. I know you had to leave early for a business meeting . . .' The woman tailed off, worried that she'd put her foot in it. Glenford House was often used as a discreet rendezvous for married lovers – lovers who often weren't actually married to each other. She'd seen it all in her time.

Ronan put her out of her misery. 'Thanks. Lunch was lovely.'

He put down the receiver and sank into the chair. What the hell was Wendy doing in a hotel all afternoon? And what was the woman talking about – a wedding anniversary? What wedding anniversary? The blond man from Skibbereen flashed into his mind. And then the penny dropped. Wendy *was* having an affair. He wasn't going mad after all. He felt sick to the stomach and angry blood raced through his veins.

He ran upstairs, taking the steps two at a time. The boys were in the living room watching television with Nadia. Of course, he thought, Wendy was in the bath washing away the evidence. She'd been avoiding him ever since she'd come in. He banged on the door of the bathroom.

'Wendy!' he shouted. 'Wendy, come out right now!'

'What's the matter?' she asked, hearing the edge to his voice. 'Are the boys all right?'

'Yes. I want to talk to you.'

'Can't it wait?'

'No. Glenford House rang. They found your mobile.'

Wendy gasped and put her hand to her mouth. She took a deep breath and tried to calm her heart which was threatening to beat out of her chest. How was she going to explain herself? She tried to think of a valid excuse but failed miserably. What the hell was she going to do? How could she have been so stupid? She should never have asked them to ring her at home, but she hadn't exactly been thinking straight at the time.

At least Des had had the decency to tell the woman at the desk that he'd had to leave urgently for a business meeting. But he hadn't settled the bill which had come as quite a shock to Wendy. Luckily she'd had her credit card on her or it would have been very embarrassing.

It was all such a mess. And for what? She began to

cry, hot, heavy tears running down her cheeks and dropping into the bath.

'Wendy, you'd better come out right now, I'm warning you!' He banged on the door again.

Think of something, she thought. Anything.

'Ronan,' she began. 'I can explain. I was at a meeting about a gig. They're thinking of holding weddings there and they need a band . . .'

'You're lying!' Ronan shouted. He banged on the door again. 'Why, Wendy? And who is it? That blond man from Skibbereen? Who?'

Wendy felt like laughing. Carl? As if she'd go near *him*.

'I know you're having an affair, Wendy. I have proof. I've seen the messages on your phone. There's no point denying it. And if you won't even talk to me about it, then our marriage is over. Do you hear me? Over!'

Wendy held her breath. Ronan didn't say anything else. She heard him march down the stairs. She jumped up and grabbed a large towel, sending a wave of soapy water sloshing over the edge of the full bath.

She unlocked the bathroom door and flung it open. Ronan was at the front door.

'Ronan. Where are you going?' she asked, panic-stricken.

He turned and looked at her, his face pale and his eyes glittering through the tears. 'I love you so much, Wendy. How could you . . .' He broke off and stared at her. 'But I can't take this.'

Wendy's heart lurched. Why had she hurt him so

badly? She had to tell him it had all been a horrible mistake, that nothing had happened. She began to run down the stairs, her hands clutching her towel around her body.

'Ronan!' she cried. 'Don't go. Ronan, I'm sorry. Please come back.'

Her foot tripped on something and she fell head first down the stairs. The last thing she remembered was Ronan's voice.

'Wendy!'

14 'One of Us'

Gemma and Ronan were sitting in the corridor of St John's Hospital.

'Wendy hates the lighting in here,' Ronan murmured, staring at his hands, clenched tightly together in his lap. 'She says it's too harsh. It shows up everyone's wrinkles.'

'She's right,' Gemma said gently, pleased that he was talking at last. He hadn't said a word for at least ten minutes and she was worried about him. 'It's not the most flattering, is it?'

Gemma had been sitting with Ronan for almost half an hour. He hadn't really told her what had happened, except that Wendy had fallen down the stairs and hit her head on the hard ceramic tiles of the hall floor. She had been knocked unconscious and still hadn't woken up. They'd arrived at St John's in an ambulance and Wendy had been whisked straight into the emergency rooms. The doctors were worried that she might have a haematoma or blood clot on the brain – Gemma had taken that much in when the doctor, a slightly crumpled-looking but nice man in his thirties called Dr Tobin, had spoken to her briefly about Wendy's injuries, but other than that they were all in the dark. Like Wendy. Ronan seemed to be in severe shock. He kept muttering to himself about being stupid and about a bag, but Gemma couldn't make out what he meant. When she asked him to explain, he just shook his head and put his face in his hands.

'Gemma! Where's Wendy? Is she all right? What happened?' Mia came flying down the corridor towards them, followed closely by Alva. Mia's eyes were wide and her face was pale, with two spots of high colour on her cheeks. Her hair was in a messy ponytail and she was wearing a denim jacket over an old tracksuit, which Gemma knew she wore in bed.

'That was quick,' Gemma said. 'You didn't get caught in traffic?'

'I drove in the bus lane,' Alva explained. 'It has its uses.'

'Wendy?' Mia asked, her eyes wild. 'Where is she?'

'The doctors are keeping her under close observation,' Gemma said more calmly than she felt. She didn't want to worry Mia unduly.

'Is she awake now? Can I see her?' Mia asked.

Gemma hesitated for a moment. 'Not yet, Mia. She's still unconscious.'

'Still unconscious? Does that mean she has brain damage, Gemma? Will she be all right? Tell me she'll be all right.' Mia began to cry, huge sobs racking her body. She brushed the tears away. 'Where's the doctor? I want to talk to the doctor.' She looked around. 'There's one over there.'

A young female doctor was talking to a nurse in the corridor.

Gemma put her hand on Mia's arm. 'That's not Wendy's doctor, Mia, so there wouldn't be any point in talking to her. Wendy's doctor is called Dr Tobin. He said he'd be back in a little while and I'm sure he'll have more news for us then.'

'I'll go and find him,' Mia said.

'It would be better if we all stayed here,' Gemma said firmly, thinking on her feet. 'Ronan needs us. Alva, would you get Mia a cup of coffee?'

'Of course,' Alva said, checking in her wallet for change.

'I don't want coffee,' Mia said in a tiny voice. 'I want to see Wendy.' She began to cry again.

'Why don't I go and find the doctor?' Alva said to Gemma. 'He might be able to put Mia's mind at ease.'

'Thanks,' Gemma replied. 'That would be great. Try asking in the nurses' office.' She pointed up the hallway. 'Up there and to the right.'

Watching Alva's back as she walked down the corridor, Gemma took Mia's hand in hers and squeezed it. 'Wendy will be fine, Mia. Try not to worry.'

Mia squeezed back but said nothing. Gemma offered up a silent prayer. She wasn't particularly religious, but she was prepared to try anything at this stage. Please God, make Wendy be OK. Mia couldn't cope if anything happened to her. Mia deserves a break, God. Please. She's a good kid. Tears came to her eyes and she blinked them away.

As Alva walked down the corridor, her runners squeaking on the hospital floor, Ronan looked up. The last time he'd been in this hospital was with Wendy when they were visiting Gemma after her ankle operation. Wendy's runners had made a similar noise on the floor, he remembered. He looked down again. Wendy. How would he survive without her? What if she never woke up? He began to rock backwards and forwards in his seat. He didn't care what she'd done, he still needed her. She was his life.

'Try not to worry, Ronan,' Gemma said, putting her arm around him.

He stopped rocking and looked at her. 'What if she dies?' he asked, his face racked with anguish. 'It's all my fault.'

'Hush, Ronan. She'll pull through. Wendy's a strong woman, you know that. And of course it wasn't your fault. She fell down the stairs. How could it have been your fault?'

'But it is,' he insisted. 'She fell because of me. She was running after me and she tripped over my bag, Gemma. I left it on the stairs. How could I have been so stupid? It's all my fault.'

'Why was she running after you, Ronan?' Gemma asked gently.

He put his head in his hands and stared down at the floor, rocking backwards and forwards again.

'She just was,' he said after a long pause. 'It's not important now.'

'What's Ronan talking about?' Mia whispered to Gemma. Her eyes were wide and Gemma knew that she was also in shock.

Gemma shrugged her shoulders. 'He's very upset, Mia. I'm not sure he knows what he's saying. Best just to leave him be, I think.'

Alva walked towards them with Dr Tobin in tow. Ronan looked up, his face hopeful. 'Is she awake?' he asked.

'No, Wendy's stable but she's still unconscious,' Dr Tobin said, coming straight to the point, for which Gemma was grateful. 'I know how concerned you must all be but I'm afraid I can't tell you much just yet. There is some swelling on the front right-hand side of the brain, at the point of impact. She probably has a skull fracture . . .' Mia gasped. 'But to be honest,' he continued, 'that's the least of her problems. The fracture isn't depressed, which is good, but we won't be able to tell the exact extent of it until we take an X-ray.'

'And what about the swelling?' Gemma asked. 'Is that dangerous?'

'I won't lie to you,' he said, his kind eyes locking with hers, 'it can be. But we're monitoring the intracranial pressure very carefully and she's on a ventilator to ensure a good oxygen supply to the brain.'

'Will she wake up soon?' Mia asked. 'Can I see her?'

'It's probably best to leave her alone for the moment,' he said gently. 'And hopefully she will wake up soon, though it's impossible to tell. But when she does wake up she may be quite confused and even have amnesia.'

'Amnesia?' Ronan asked. 'Will she know who we are?'

The doctor nodded. 'Yes, probably. Post-traumatic amnesia tends to affect the short-term memory. But sometimes patients can't remember the accident or what happened for days before it.'

Ronan thought about the implications of this, but said nothing. It was all too much to take in.

'Will she be OK?' Mia asked, tears streaming down her face.

Dr Tobin looked at Mia and then back at Gemma, recognizing her as the strong one. 'It's impossible to say, I'm afraid. But let's hope so.'

Mia could feel the blood rushing from her head and all around her everything began to move in slow motion. She staggered awkwardly and collapsed forward on to the chair beside Gemma. Dr Tobin and Alva lifted her properly on to the chair.

'Mia!' She heard Gemma's voice, foggy and distant. Gemma put her arms around her sister and held her close. Mia crumpled in a heap on to Gemma's shoulder. She could feel her sister's hands stroke her head and hear Gemma whisper, 'Wendy will be fine, Mia. She's as strong as an ox. You know that, Mia. She'll be fine, you'll see. She'll be fine,' over and over again like a mantra.

'I'll get some water,' Alva said, jumping to her feet.

Dr Tobin knelt down and put his hand on Mia's forehead, his palm cool and smooth against her flushed skin.

'You're very hot,' he said. 'How do you feel?'

'OK,' she murmured.

'Mia and Wendy are very close,' Gemma explained. 'Our mum died when we were young. Mia was only fifteen when it happened and Wendy pretty much brought Mia up.'

Dr Tobin nodded. 'You've had a terrible shock, Mia. Try to stay sitting.' And to Gemma. 'Has she ever fainted before?'

Gemma nodded. 'Quite a few times.'

'Recently?'

Gemma nodded again.

'Is she vegetarian?'

'No.'

'Still, she's quite pale. You might encourage her to get her iron levels checked. She might be a touch anaemic.'

'I will, thanks, Doctor.'

He stood up and gave Gemma a half-smile. 'You're welcome. I'll be back with any news.'

'Thanks,' she said again, continuing to stroke the top of Mia's head. She looked at Ronan who had just stood up. 'Where are you going, Ronan?'

'To stretch my legs. I need some air. I'll be back in a few minutes.'

'Do you have your mobile on you?'

He stared at her. 'Mobile?' he murmured, his eyes

glazing over a little. Wendy wouldn't be in this mess if it weren't for her damned mobile, he thought irrationally.

'Yes. Your mobile. Is it switched on?'

'Yes. Yes,' he answered a little vaguely.

'Good. We'll ring you if there's any news. Don't go too far.'

'I won't. Thanks.'

'Water,' Alva said, appearing in front of them. She opened a bottle of still water and handed it to Mia. 'Sorry it took me so long, the first machine I found wasn't working so I had to go upstairs. All very boring.' She looked at Mia who had already gulped down almost half the bottle and was taking a breather. 'You were thirsty. Are you feeling any better?'

'A little.'

'The doctor said she might be anaemic,' Gemma commented.

'Makes sense,' Alva said. 'Wendy was very anaemic after having the boys, remember?'

'Now that you say it,' Gemma said, 'maybe it runs in the family.'

'How long has Wendy been unconscious now?' Mia asked sitting up. She was starting to feel more alert.

Gemma studied her watch. 'Just over an hour.'

'Is that bad?' Mia asked. 'Is she in a coma, Gemma?'

'I don't know,' Gemma said. 'I only know what the doctor told us. I'm sorry.' She patted Mia's hand. 'I know this is hard for you.'

Just then Dr Tobin strode towards them. 'Good news,' he said. 'Wendy's just woken up.'

Gemma felt a flood of relief rush through her veins. Mia gave an audible cry of relief and sat up even straighter.

'But I must warn you,' Dr Tobin continued, 'she's a little confused. She keeps asking for Miriam. Who's Miriam?'

'Miriam was our mum,' Gemma explained. 'She's dead.'

'Oh, I'm sorry, you did say ... how stupid,' he faltered.

'Not to worry,' Gemma said kindly.

'Is Wendy's daughter here then?'

'Daughter?' Gemma's stomach lurched. No, not now, please not now, she begged silently.

'Yes,' he said. 'Wendy's asking for her daughter. Is she on her way?'

Mia stared at Gemma, whose eyes were fixed on the doctor's face. Gemma could feel her whole body trembling. She felt icy-cold. 'No,' she gasped. She tried to say more but the words stuck in her throat.

'Is she already here?' Dr Tobin asked, a little confused. He looked at Alva. 'Wendy keeps asking for her daughter, M ...'

'No!' Gemma cried out. But it was too late.

'Mia,' Dr Tobin finished.

Mia stared at Gemma. 'Gemma?' she demanded. 'What's he talking about? Gemma?'

Alva also stared at Gemma. Mia was Wendy's daughter? Was it true? She had heard of this happening in Irish families of course – it was common enough in the fifties and sixties. Everyone knew, or knew of,

313

a family where the grandmother had brought up an unmarried daughter's child as her own. But had it really happened in the Redden household?

'Gemma!' Mia said, her voice rising to a dangerous level. 'Is it true? Tell me! Gemma?'

Gemma said nothing. She opened her mouth to say something and then closed it again, still unable to force the words out.

Alva looked at Gemma's stricken face and knew the answer immediately.

'Gemma?' Mia continued, almost shouting now. 'It's true, isn't it? Why didn't you tell me before this? Years ago. Gemma?'

Gemma looked terrified. Mia was standing in front of her, the spots of colour on her cheeks standing out from her ashen face, her eyes black and flashing with emotion.

Alva knew she had to do something. She turned quickly towards Dr Tobin. 'Gemma will go and see Wendy now, Doctor. I'll take Mia outside for some air and we'll find Ronan.'

Dr Tobin had seen enough family dramas in his day to realize that he'd just stumbled into an emotional minefield. 'Of course,' he said. 'Gemma, this way please.'

Gemma put her hands in her crutches and rose to her feet. He put his arm around her shoulders and guided her slowly down the corridor, Mia staring in their wake.

'I won't forget this, Gemma!' she shouted at Gemma's back. 'I trusted you. You're supposed to be

my sister, for God's sake. Some sister you are.' Tears
were streaming down Mia's face and her body racked
with sobs. 'But you're not my sister, are you? Not my
sister at all.'

'It's OK now, Mia,' Alva said, trying to comfort her
but not knowing what to say. 'Let's go outside and
find Ronan.'

'But . . .' Mia looked like a crumpled doll.

'Come on,' Alva cajoled. 'Let's get some fresh air.'
She took Mia's arm gently and led her outside.

Gemma stood and waited at the nurses' desk as Dr
Tobin talked to the staff nurse. Wendy had been
moved into her own private room in the intensive care
unit, the nurse told him, and then asked him a question
regarding another patient's chart.

After a moment, Dr Tobin turned towards Gemma.
'Sorry about that. I'll take you in to see Wendy now.
Follow me.'

Gemma gasped when she stared through the small
window in the door of Wendy's intensive care room.
Wendy looked terrible. She had two drips attached to
her, one in either hand, and a small tube was feeding
what Gemma presumed was oxygen into her nostrils.
Her face was horribly bruised on the right-hand side
and the bridge of her nose resembled a war zone; both
her eyes were sunk into dark sockets and there was
dried blood in her hair.

'She was amazingly lucky,' Dr Tobin said. 'The X-
rays are back and she didn't break any bones.'

'What about her skull?' Gemma asked. 'I thought you said she had a suspected skull fracture.'

'No, she has a tiny hairline fracture, but nothing to worry about. She's one tough woman, your sister.'

'And the swelling?'

'She's awake and that's a very good sign. And the swelling seems to be reducing, which is excellent. But there's still a risk of bleeding and we'll have to keep her under close observation for the next few days. She's through the worst, though.'

'Is she very confused?'

'Yes. She keeps saying, "I was only fourteen". Does that mean anything, Gemma? Maybe you can shed some light on it. Did something traumatic happen then?'

'She had a baby daughter,' Gemma said in a monotone, staring at Wendy through the window. She looked back at Dr Tobin. 'Traumatic enough for you? The blonde girl outside, Mia, is her daughter.'

'Did she have the baby in Dublin?' he asked gently.

'No, in a small hospital near Westport where we used to live. We moved away immediately afterwards, to Dublin, and the baby was brought up as our sister,' Gemma said in a strangely even voice. It was the first time she'd ever told this particular piece of the Redden family history. But she'd rehearsed it so many times it was a relief finally to be able to say out loud the words that she'd had to keep repressed for so long.

'Mum thought it was for the best. I was only eight at the time, but I remember it vividly. Wendy didn't say a word for weeks afterwards. The birth went smoothly apparently, but it can't have been easy going through childbirth at that age. Or handing your baby over like that. Pretending nothing had happened.'

She put her hands on the door and leaned towards the glass. 'We've never really talked about it, to be honest. It was a taboo subject when Mia was around, obviously. I used to try and make Wendy talk to me about it in private, but she wasn't interested. She wanted to forget it had ever happened. Mia's her sister, not her daughter, as far as she's concerned. It's as simple as that. Her husband, Ronan, doesn't even know.'

Gemma gave a deep sigh and turned around to face Dr Tobin. 'I don't know how any of us are going to handle it.' She looked him in the eye. 'How is Mia going to handle it?'

'I don't know what to say,' Dr Tobin began. 'But Wendy is going to recover, isn't that the important thing?'

'Of course,' Gemma murmured. 'But at what cost?'

'It seems to me that Wendy has some explaining to do to her daughter,' Dr Tobin said, lifting his eyebrows. 'Don't you think? But not right now. She doesn't need any more excitement today, that's for sure.'

'I suppose you're right.'

'Let me know if there's anything I can do. But try not to say anything that might upset Wendy. She's still in a fairly fragile state. Her memory should start returning slowly, but it could be a very gradual process. Or it could happen in a matter of hours. It's hard to tell.'

'Thank you, Doctor, you've been very kind.'

'Let me know what happens, won't you? I'll check on Wendy later, but if you have any questions ask one of the nurses to come and find me. Otherwise, well, good luck with the family, um . . .'

'Secret?' Gemma suggested.

'Yes.' He smiled at her gently. 'Hope it all works out for you. Is this her husband?' Ronan was striding up the corridor.

'Mia said Wendy's awake, is she awake?' Ronan gabbled. 'Can I see her? Is she all right?'

Dr Tobin nodded. 'Yes, but she's a little confused. Maybe . . .' He looked at Gemma.

'I need to talk to her first,' Gemma interjected. 'She thinks Mum's still alive. I'm going to sit with her for a while, try to calm her down. It's better that way.'

Ronan looked at Dr Tobin.

'Maybe you'd like to sit in the relatives' room,' the doctor said. 'It's nice and quiet in there.'

Ronan nodded. 'And you'll come and get me as soon as Wendy's settled?' he said to Gemma.

'Of course,' Gemma promised. 'Where's Mia?'

'Still outside with Alva. She's crying. I couldn't make out what she was saying. Something about her mother. She wasn't making any sense, Gemma. Alva's having a cigarette and Mia's sharing it. I didn't know Mia smoked.'

Thank goodness for Alva, Gemma thought. 'She

doesn't,' she said. 'Must be the shock.' She looked at Wendy again through the window. She seemed to be stirring and her eyelids were flickering. 'I'd better go in now. I'll come and find you as soon as I've talked to Wendy.'

'Wendy?' Gemma leaned over the bed and studied her sister's eyes. They flickered again and then opened.

'Gemma? Is that you? Where's Ronan? Are the boys all right?'

Gemma felt a huge surge of relief. Wendy seemed to be back in the present. 'Outside in the relatives' room. And the boys are fine. They're at home with Nadia.'

'And Mia?'

'She's with Alva.' Gemma tried to keep her voice even but it was difficult. She wasn't sure if Wendy realized what she'd let slip to Dr Tobin.

'What is it?' Wendy asked. 'Have you been crying?'

'Just a little.'

'Tell me, what's wrong?'

Gemma looked at Wendy. 'Nothing. Really. Everything's fine.'

'Where's Mia?'

'Outside.'

'Ask her to come in. I want to see her.'

'The doctor said no more visitors for the moment. You're stuck with me, I'm afraid.' Gemma gave her a half-smile.

'What's happening? There's something going on.

Gemma?' Wendy tried to sit up but her head throbbed so badly that she was forced back against the pillows by the pain. She winced and put her right hand to her head, touching her bruise gingerly. 'My head,' she murmured.

'Wendy, take it easy. You've had a very bad fall.'

'Mia,' Wendy said again. 'I want to see Mia.'

'I'll go and get her as soon as the doctor . . .'

'I want to tell her the truth,' Wendy said, a sense of urgency in her voice. 'What if I'd died, Gemma? What if I hadn't woken up? What then? Would you have told her? Or would she have spent the rest of her days living a lie?'

'Wendy, I don't think . . .'

'She deserves to know the truth, Gemma. I should have told her a long time ago. Have I made a terrible mistake lying to her all these years?'

'I don't know,' Gemma said honestly. 'And there's no point worrying about it now. Maybe you should wait to talk to Mia until you feel a little better. Until you've had a chance to think things over. We've all had a terrible shock. Talk to Ronan first, see what he says. Maybe get some counselling.'

Gemma's mind was racing. She wanted to protect both Wendy and Mia, that was her job as their sister, wasn't it? Sister and aunt, she corrected herself. But things were spiralling beyond her control.

Wendy closed her eyes tight and then opened them again. 'Ronan,' she murmured. 'Oh, Gemma, I've done the most terrible thing. I have to tell you. I feel so guilty.'

She told her sister about what had happened just before the fall and what had or, to be accurate, what hadn't happened in the hotel earlier that day. Gemma listened in amazement. She knew Des Sullivan of old and wasn't all that surprised – he always was a bit of a chancer. But Wendy – the mind boggled. She couldn't think of anyone less likely to have an affair.

'Gemma, I've been such a fool,' Wendy moaned. 'I've ruined everything, haven't I?'

Gemma reached over and held Wendy's hand, careful to avoid the drip. She noticed a dark, angry-looking bruise on her wrist. 'You poor old thing,' she said. 'That looks nasty.'

'My body I can deal with,' Wendy said with a snort. 'But as for my head ... and I don't mean the concussion. What have I done to my marriage? To Ronan?'

'Ronan's in bits,' Gemma confided. 'He blames himself for your fall. He left his bag on the stairs apparently and you tripped over it. Explain what happened, Wendy. Talk to him. He'll forgive you, I know he will. He still loves you, that hasn't changed.'

'I'm so ashamed.' Wendy began to cry, but her eyes were so sore that it hurt to squeeze out every tear.

'Wendy, will I talk to him for you?' Gemma suggested.

'It's too much,' Wendy said.

'What's too much?'

'All of this. The affair, Mia. Because I'm going to tell her, as soon as I see her. It's only right. He won't forgive me, Gemma. It's too much.'

321

'Wendy, he nearly lost you. Don't you think that everything else will pale into insignificance?'

'I don't know.' Wendy was still crying. 'Oh, Gemma, I'm so tired.'

'I know you are. Try to get some sleep. Things will seem better in a little while. Try not to upset yourself.'

Gemma sat with Wendy, holding her hand firmly and dabbing away her sister's tears with a tissue. She didn't know what to do. Nothing she'd said to Wendy had seemed to help. This was something that Wendy would have to face on her own and Gemma didn't envy her.

Wendy drifted asleep and Gemma extracted her hand carefully. Wendy stirred a little and then settled back to sleep. For a moment Gemma wondered if she was supposed to be asleep. What if she never woke up? She felt anxious and pressed the call button. Within seconds a nurse arrived.

'Can I help?' she asked Gemma.

'She's asleep,' Gemma whispered, gesturing at Wendy. 'Is that all right?'

The nurse smiled at the worried-looking young woman in front of her. She checked the monitor beside Wendy's bed. 'Everything seems fine,' she said after a moment. 'I'll be back in a little while to check again. And Dr Tobin will be back in an hour or so. Try not to worry. Rest is the best thing for her at the moment.'

'Thank you. Can you tell me where the relatives' room is?'

The nurse gave her directions. Gemma looked at Wendy one last time and, satisfied that she was in good hands, went to talk to Ronan. She wasn't relishing it, but someone had to tell him about Mia, and it would be better for her to do it than Mia herself. Once she'd talked to Ronan, she'd tackle Mia. And if talking to Ronan was going to be difficult, talking to Mia was going to be even worse.

Gemma opened the door of the relatives' room.

'Ronan?' she said.

He lifted his head. Gemma sat down beside him.

Ronan looked at her expectantly. 'Wendy?' he asked.

'She's doing well,' she reassured him. 'She's asleep now and the nurse said that's everything's fine, that rest is the best thing for her at the moment. Her head hurts, but that's to be expected. Her memory seems fine.'

She paused, choosing her words carefully. 'Wendy's still a little confused but she remembers everything that happened last night. She's very upset, Ronan. She feels horribly guilty.' She looked at Ronan. He had a strange expression on his face. 'She told me about the hotel and about the other man,' she continued. 'But nothing happened. She couldn't go through with it. You know that, don't you?'

Ronan shook his head. 'No. I wouldn't listen to her.'

'She didn't know what she was doing, Ronan. Wendy knows she's made a huge mistake. She loves you.'

Ronan shook his head again.

'Please, just listen to me,' Gemma said.

'I suspected she was having an affair,' he said. 'But

I stupidly thought that if I didn't say anything, didn't confront her, it would all go away. I should have talked to her days ago. It's all too late now.'

'Ronan, it's not too late. Did you hear what I said? Wendy didn't have an affair. Yes, she thought about it, almost went through with it, but in the end she didn't. She knew it wasn't right, that it would ruin everything.'

Ronan looked at Gemma, his eyes glittering, 'Do you believe her, Gemma?'

'Yes. But the important thing is, do you?'

Ronan shook his head. 'I'm not sure what to think right now. I want to believe her, really I do, but . . .' He gave a deep sigh. 'Oh, I don't know. Things keep going through my head, you know?' He looked down at his hands for a moment and then raised his head again. 'But I don't know what I'd do without her.' He stopped for a moment. 'I need to see her, talk to her face to face.'

'She's sleeping now. Probably best to leave her. The nurse said she needs her sleep right now, remember?'

'As soon as she wakes up then,' Ronan said. 'I really want to believe her; I don't want to lose her, Gemma. But I just don't know if I can.'

'There's something else,' Gemma began. She hoped that once he talked to Wendy he'd see that she was telling the truth. She was about to drop another bombshell and she hoped he was strong enough to take it. But Gemma knew that if she didn't deal with it now, once Mia talked to Ronan things would be even more difficult. Better he should hear it now and have a chance to talk to Wendy first.

'I don't know how you're going to take this, Ronan, you've had such a difficult evening, but I have to tell you. It's about Mia. Wendy and Mia. And their, um, relationship.' Gemma paused for a moment, afraid to go on. How was she going to explain?

'Gemma, it's Mia you should be talking to, not me,' Ronan said, filling the silence. 'I already know that Wendy is Mia's real mum. I've known for years.'

'What? How?' Gemma was so shocked she could barely get the words out. Whatever reaction she'd expected, it wasn't this.

'Miriam told me a few days before she died. She was worried that something might happen to Wendy. She wanted Mia to know and she wasn't convinced that you'd tell her. She knew how much you love them both and how much you'd want to protect Mia. But it's part of who Mia is. Your mum knew that. In the end I think she felt that she'd made a mistake by bringing Mia up as her own, but it was too late to do anything about it. Miriam thought that all of you had enough on your plate, with her being so sick, without adding to it by telling Mia the truth. The last thing you all needed at that stage was extra emotional trauma. And I wanted Wendy to tell Mia herself. I believed that when the time was right she would. So I've kept it a secret all these years.'

'And what about Wendy? Have you ever talked to her about it?'

'No, Wendy has no idea that I know.' Ronan smiled at Gemma. 'I'm good at keeping secrets.'

'You're a dark horse, Ronan Borza, do you know that?' Gemma was still in shock.

He smiled again. 'And how are *you*, Gemma? This is a lot for you to take in, I know.'

'I'm all right. I'm worried about Mia though.'

'Go and find her.' Ronan stood up. 'I'll sit with Wendy if I'm allowed. We have a lot of talking to do. But now's not the time. I'll just tell her that everything's going to be all right and that I'll look after her. And I really do think it will be all right, Gemma.'

'I think so too,' Gemma said, trying to sound more optimistic than she felt.

Gemma walked out of the hospital and took a deep breath of the cool, fresh air. It was always so stuffy in hospitals, she thought as she looked around for Mia and Alva. She spotted them sitting on a bench to the right of the entrance. They were both staring straight ahead, puffing on cigarettes. Mia was blowing the smoke out almost as soon as she'd drawn it in, billows of it lingering in front of her mouth until she fanned them away with her hand. Gemma smiled to herself. Mia never could smoke properly. Alva, on the other hand, was drawing deeply and very little smoke was coming back up.

Gemma watched until Alva noticed her and waved her over. Mia glanced at Gemma and then looked away, refusing to meet her eyes. Gemma's heart sank.

'Hi, you two,' she said, standing in front of them. 'Enjoying your nicotine rush?'

Alva nodded. She dropped her spent cigarette to the ground and extinguished it under the sole of one of her runners. 'I must give up one of these days.'

Gemma said nothing. She'd heard that one before.

'I'll go,' Alva said getting up. 'I'll leave the pair of you alone. To talk.' She looked pointedly at Gemma.

'Don't go,' Mia said, looking up at Alva. 'I have nothing to say to *her*.'

Alva sighed. 'Mia, none of this is Gemma's fault,' she pointed out. 'Just listen to what she has to say.'

'Only if you stay.'

Alva nodded. 'OK then. But Gemma's . . .'

'Been lying to me for years,' Mia cut in, her voice full of anger. 'How do you think that makes me feel? I don't know what to think or who's telling me the truth.' She swung her eyes to Gemma's face and stared at her. Gemma could see the anguish behind Mia's glare and longed to be able to soothe her.

'I have nothing to say to you, Gemma,' Mia said. 'Just leave me alone. And Wendy too. I don't want anything more to do with either of you.'

'You don't mean that!' Gemma cried. 'We're sisters!'

'But Wendy's *not* my sister, is she? And neither are you! Why didn't you tell me, Gemma? Why did you never say anything? I've always trusted you to tell me the truth. My whole life is a lie. How could you let that happen?'

'It wasn't my place to tell you,' Gemma said, fighting

back the tears. 'It was Wendy's secret, not mine. It all happened such a long time ago. I was only eight when you were born, Mia, you have to remember that. I just went along with everything. I didn't have much choice. Mum thought it was for the best . . .' Gemma stopped when she saw the dark expression on Mia's face.

'I'll never forgive you,' Mia said in a chillingly calm voice. 'Never.' She stood up and with one last dagger look at Gemma, strode away.

'Mia!' Gemma said, walking after her. She put her hand on Mia's arm but Mia shook it off. 'Mia!'

'It's probably best to leave her be for a while,' Alva suggested. 'I'll take her home and stay with her.'

'Thanks,' Gemma said. She felt absolutely wretched. What am I going to tell Wendy? she thought. It's all my fault. I should have stopped Dr Tobin when I had the chance. I've ruined everything.

'It's been a very emotional day for everyone,' Alva said kindly. 'I'll take care of Mia. And I'll ring you later to let you know how she's doing.'

Gemma nodded. She was all out of words at this stage and she was desperately trying to fight back the tears. A few moments later she watched Alva drive out of the car park, a stony-faced Mia staring rigidly ahead of her in the passenger seat.

Only then did the tears begin to flood down Gemma's face.

15 'When All Is Said and Done'

Wendy was finally allowed home four days later, with explicit instructions from Dr Tobin to rest and to avoid anything stressful. He'd also forbidden her to even think about singing for at least three weeks, much to her horror. But even that failed to prevent her from attempting to do the paperwork. She'd asked Ronan to bring her laptop to their bedroom so she could work from bed, but he'd refused. She'd already insisted on ringing the insurance company herself to check her serious illness cover. Luckily, being her ever-efficient self, the premiums were up to date and she qualified for six weeks' benefit. After Ronan had consulted the other band members, including Pat, he'd withdrawn enough from the band's emergency coffers to cover everyone's expenses for a month. He'd then transferred this into each of their accounts. Wendy allowed herself a small rush of pride when she realized that the financial safety nets she had carefully put in place over the years were now being put to good use.

Nadia had taken the boys to school that morning and was proving invaluable to the family: as well as looking after the boys, she had taken over all the cooking, washing, ironing and housework. From this morning, when Wendy had arrived home from the hospital, Nadia had also checked on her every hour, replenishing her water jug and giving her snippets of news gleaned from the TV and the radio while Ronan worked downstairs.

'Wendy, the doctor said to rest,' Ronan protested when she asked for her laptop for the third time that day. 'And work is certainly not rest.'

'But I've so much to do!' Wendy protested. 'What about this weekend's gigs?'

Ronan stared at her incredulously. 'Wendy, please tell me you're joking. There's no way you can get up on a stage in two days' time, no way. I won't allow it. And you know what the doctor said.'

Wendy snorted. 'I meant to cancel them, Ronan,' she explained. 'I'm not that bad. My head still throbs a bit,' she touched the bridge of her nose gingerly, followed by the side of her head, 'and no amount of make-up, thick stage make-up included, is going to cover this lot.'

'I'm very relieved to hear you say it.' Ronan sat down on the edge of the bed. 'Please, you've been through a terrible time. I know you're not very good at doing nothing, but you have to, really. I've already cancelled some of the gigs and I can do the rest later. Now please just rest.'

'I'll try.' Wendy sighed. 'But my mind is working

overtime without work to distract me. And I keep thinking about what's happened. You know, I deserved to fall down those stairs. I'm a horrible person.'

'What! How can you say that?'

'Because it's true.' Wendy stopped for a moment and looked Ronan in the eye. 'I know you keep saying that we have all the time in the world to talk, but I'd like to start now if that's OK with you. We've been putting it off long enough. We need to clear the air. I can't just lie here thinking about it all, wondering about what's going to happen when we do talk.'

Ronan nodded. 'But are you sure you won't find it all too much? The doctor said . . .'

'I know, I know,' she interrupted, 'no work and no stress. But it's important, Ronan. I want us to get on with our lives, and until we face up to what happened I don't think we can. I certainly can't. Do you understand?'

He nodded again, silently.

Wendy waited for a moment before she spoke, collecting her thoughts. She stared straight ahead of her, her eyes resting on the soothing blue and green Monet water-lilies print on the wall opposite the bed. 'I haven't been happy for a long time, Ronan. And before you say anything, it has nothing to do with you, or us, honestly. It's all about me.' She gave a dry laugh. 'Goodness, I sound so selfish, don't I? And I was being selfish. Horribly, horribly selfish. I don't really know where to start to tell the truth.' She pulled her eyes off the painting and rested them on Ronan's

331

face. 'I've worked so hard over the last few years to make AbbaFab a success and I think I overlooked the fact that I had no life of my own outside the band. And I was just fed up with it all, I suppose. I wanted something for myself, something that had nothing to do with the band, or my life with you and the boys. And then I met Des O'Sullivan at the garage in Deansgrange when I was getting the car checked.'

Wendy glanced at Ronan. He was gazing at her intently. 'I know him from Westport, not from the cruise ships like I told you. He lives in Australia now but he was over visiting his mother. He invited me for coffee, but I said no. But he gave me his number and I kept it. He works in computers and I rang him when the laptop went mad.' She paused again, looking at Ronan. He deserved her complete honesty. 'But I was only looking for an excuse to get in touch with him. I would have rung him anyway.'

'Des is the guy who came to fix your laptop?' Ronan asked, needing to clarify things.

'Yes.'

'And?' he encouraged.

'After that Des started to text me. He made it obvious from the start that he fancied me, and he knew I was married, that didn't seem to bother him. He made me feel attractive, I suppose, wanted. I was flattered by his attention. At the start I never intended for anything to happen. It was a bit of fun, a distraction.' She stared down at her hands and fingered the white indent where her wedding ring usually rested. She missed her ring. The nurses must have taken it off

332

her hand in the hospital. 'And nothing did happen, not really. Not until the other day. At the hotel.' She looked up again. 'He kept pestering me for a date and eventually I . . .' She paused and then said in a rush, 'I met him in that hotel, Glenford House in Wicklow, the afternoon of my fall. The hotel that rang about my mobile. I'm not proud of it, Ronan, but I want you to know everything. It was so, so stupid. I don't know what I was thinking.'

Ronan's face drained. 'You were wearing your navy dress,' he managed eventually. 'The one I like.'

'Yes.' Wendy gulped and then continued, trying to get her confession over with as quickly as possible for both their sakes. 'But I couldn't go through with it. Once we were in the room we kissed, but it felt wrong, terribly wrong. I couldn't stop thinking about you. And I realized just how much I had to lose. Nothing else happened, absolutely nothing. I asked him to leave and he wasn't too happy with me. But he did and that was the end of it. I haven't heard from him since, thank goodness. He's probably back in Australia by now with his fiancée. I hope I never set eyes on him again.'

'And you left your mobile in the hotel room?'

'Yes. I was in such a panic to get out of there, I left it behind me on the sofa.'

'What if you hadn't forgotten it, Wendy? What then? Would you have told me eventually? Or would it have been yet another secret?'

'Secret?' she faltered. 'What do you mean?'

'Let's deal with this first,' Ronan said, leaving

Wendy hanging. 'If I hadn't found out, would you have told me?'

'I don't know,' she said honestly. 'But I do know this. It made me realize just how much I love you. And that I was the one with the problem, not you. You've always been a good husband, I know that now.'

'I've had my moments,' Ronan said. 'Like the fire . . .'

'No one's perfect,' Wendy interrupted. 'Forget about the fire. What I'm trying to say is that I'm sorry. For everything. And not just for the business with Des. For putting the band before my family, for snapping at you, for making you feel second best, for not being there for you . . .'

'Wendy!' Ronan said. 'You're the most wonderful woman I've ever met. You could run the country far better than any of our damned politicians; hell, you could be President if you set your mind to it. You're incredible. You never cease to amaze me.'

'But that's just it!' she said. 'I don't want to be President or run the country. I don't even want to run AbbaFab any more. I'm tired, Ronan. That's the truth. I'm tired to my bones. I want to stop being Superwoman and try just being myself for a change. And above all, I want to give our marriage another go. I know it will take time, but do you think you can forgive me?'

Ronan said nothing for a moment. Wendy felt as though her life was passing in front of her eyes and she held her breath.

Finally he said, 'I already have.'

She felt so ashamed. 'After everything I've done?' Tears ran down her cheeks.

He nodded. 'Yes. Losing you would be the end of me. Sitting in St John's, waiting for you to regain consciousness, was the worst hour of my life. I felt so out of control, so alone. You're everything to me, Wendy. You're all I've ever wanted. We make sense together.'

'I know,' Wendy whispered. She brushed back her tears. 'I'm so, so sorry. And I do love you.'

He shifted up the bed, put his arm around her shoulders and kissed the top of her head. 'I know you do.'

They sat in silence for a few minutes, Wendy crying gently and Ronan holding her. 'Hush now,' he soothed, stroking her head. 'It's all over. We'll put all this behind us and start again.'

'Thank you,' she murmured. 'And Ronan, do you know where my wedding ring is? I miss it.'

He pulled the ring out of the pocket of his jeans. 'I was hoping you'd want to wear it again.' He slipped it on to her ring finger, put his arms around her and gave her a gentle hug. Then he drew back and tenderly brushed her hair back off her face. 'Nadia will be back with the boys soon and they'll be dying to see you.'

'I'm just so tired,' Wendy sighed. 'I feel like I could sleep forever.'

'That's natural after a head injury.'

'I was tired long before that.'

'You work so hard, Wendy. I'm not surprised you're tired. You haven't had a holiday in almost two years and you take on so much. Singing, booking, everything really.'

'I've been thinking . . .' Wendy began. 'About the band.'

'Yes?'

'Would you manage without me for a while? I'd like to spend more time with Steve and Greg. I'd still do all the booking and everything, of course.'

Ronan looked at Wendy in surprise. 'I thought you loved performing.'

'I do. But I need a break. I could try finding someone else for you until Gemma's back on her feet. It won't be easy but at least the mad wedding rush is almost over. I'm sure I'd be able to find someone to fill in. Then when Gemma's on her feet again Mia could take over from me. Gemma and Mia would be brilliant together.'

'Is that really what you want?'

She nodded.

He patted her hand. 'You really have been doing a lot of thinking, haven't you?'

'Not much else to do confined in hospital and in this bloody bed.'

'True.'

'I met an old cruise-ship friend recently, a lovely girl called Nora, and she seemed to think that her husband might give me a job showing houses. He's an estate agent.'

Ronan grinned.

'What are you smiling at?' she asked.

'I was just thinking it would be the perfect job for

336

you. A licence to legitimately nose around other people's houses. It's a great idea.'

She thumped him on the arm. 'Ronan!'

'Good to see you're feeling a little better,' he quipped.

'There's something else,' Wendy said, a smile lingering on her lips. 'What about trying for another baby?'

'A baby?' Ronan was dumbstruck. Wendy had always said that her baby days were most definitely over. He'd always hankered after a larger family, but he'd learned to accept the fact that Wendy wasn't interested in going down that road again.

'Say something,' she said. 'What do you think?'

'You know I'd love another baby,' he said. 'But are you sure?'

Wendy nodded. 'Positive. I'm thirty-eight, Ronan. It's now or never. If I leave it any longer it could be too late.'

'Isn't there something you need to sort out first?' he asked. 'Your other baby,' he prompted gently. 'You have to talk to Mia.'

Wendy looked at him in astonishment. 'What?' she whispered. 'You know? I don't believe this. Did Gemma tell you? How long have you known?'

'I've known for years, Wendy. Gemma had nothing to do with it. Miriam told me before she died. I came to terms with it a long time ago. So you have nothing to worry about.'

Wendy was in shock. 'I can't believe it,' she whispered. 'You never said a word.'

'I promised Miriam I wouldn't. Not unless some-thing happened to you. And I always keep my promises.'

'I know you do. It's one of the reasons I love you so much. But I can't take this in. You knew? All this time?' She shook her head gently from side to side and winced at the throbbing in her temples.

Ronan began to stroke her head again. 'I'm glad it's all finally come out. Mia deserved to know the truth. It's part of who she is. And it's part of who you are too, Wendy.'

'*Deserved?* You mean she knows too?'

Ronan explained to Wendy about how Dr Tobin had inadvertently let the secret out in the hospital.

Wendy buried her head in her hands and began to moan. 'Oh no, not Mia. Little Mia. My Mia.' She raised her head. 'She must hate me, Ronan.'

'She doesn't hate you,' he said, 'she's just confused. She'll be OK. She needs to be left alone for a little while. You and Gemma have been living with this secret for years; to Mia, it's come as a huge shock.'

'Yes,' she murmured. 'Yes, of course.' Her voice changed. 'But has she rung yet? She must be so con-fused. I really need to talk to her, explain to her what happened when she was born, why I gave her away like that,' she said frantically.

'No,' Ronan said gently. 'She hasn't rung yet. You need to take it easy, Wendy. Try not to get upset. I'm sure she'll ring very soon. Just give her time. Gemma's been talking to her.'

Wendy didn't like the sound of that. 'What did Gemma say?'

'Just that Mia would come and see you when she was ready. That she needed some space to think things over.'

Wendy lay back against her pillows and rubbed her eyes gently. 'What a mess. And it's all my fault. When's Gemma coming over?'

'This evening, if you feel up to it.'

'I'll be fine. But Mia's . . .'

Just then they heard loud voices in the hall, an excited squeal and footsteps running up the stairs.

'Boys!' Nadia's voice rang out. 'Careful. We no need any more accidents in this house.'

'Too right,' Ronan murmured.

Greg and Steve burst into the room.

'Mummy!' Steve said throwing his arms around her. She winced as he kissed the tender part of her head. 'You still look like you've been in a fight.'

'Steve!' Ronan admonished. 'That's not very nice.'

Wendy laughed. 'It's fine.' She ruffled Steve's hair. 'It's good to see you both. It was far too quiet in the hospital without you.' She looked at Greg. He was staring at her.

'Does it hurt a lot, Mummy?' he asked solemnly. 'Your head looks sore.'

'It is a bit sore, pet. But it's getting better. Come over here and give me a hug.'

Steve moved over and allowed his brother to snuggle in beside Wendy.

'I'm glad you're back, Mummy,' Greg said looking up at her. 'I missed you.'

'And I missed you both too. Steve, could you ask Nadia to come up? I want to tell her something.'

A moment later, Nadia entered the room. She smiled at Wendy. 'The boys have been very good today,' she said. 'Very helpful.'

'I wanted to thank you, Nadia,' Wendy said. 'We wouldn't have got through the last few days without you. I do appreciate it. Really I do.'

'They are good boys,' Nadia said kindly. 'It was no trouble. And I decide to stay in Ireland for another six months. If you have me.'

'Of course we will!' Steve said quickly, throwing his arms around Nadia's neck.

'Steve!' Ronan frowned at him.

'Sorry,' Steve said. He stopped strangling Nadia. 'But can we keep her?'

'Of course.' Wendy smiled at Nadia. 'But I think the question should be, will she have us?'

Nadia laughed. 'You are not the baddest.'

'There's no such word!' Steve pointed out. 'No wonder you need to stay in Ireland. Your English is . . .'

'Steve!'

'I know, I know. Sorry, Nadia.'

'That's OK.' Nadia smiled at him. 'I used to it now. And it true. My English, how you say?'

'Sucks!' Steve added helpfully.

They all laughed.

'What are we going to do with you?' Ronan asked Steve, ruffling his hair.

Steve shrugged. 'I'll probably grow out of it.'

'We can always hope,' Wendy said and gave him a huge smile. 'But I kind of like you all just the way you are.'

16 'The Day Before You Came'

'Mia, can you hear me? Are you there?' Gemma
shouted up at the open window. She'd already tried
ringing the intercom, but there'd been no reply. Mia
hadn't answered her phone over the last few days and
Gemma was at her wits' end. Alva had assured her
that Mia was reasonably all right in the circumstances,
but she still didn't want anything to do with either
Gemma or Wendy at the moment.

Gemma felt as though her heart was breaking. It
was all her fault. Mia was right, she should have told
her the truth a long time ago. She felt wretched.
Wendy was home from hospital today and she was
going to visit her that evening. Gemma had no idea
what she was going to tell her. She'd have to lie, she
decided. Wendy was still in a fragile condition after
all. No stress, the doctor had said.

Gemma walked over to the front door and tried the
intercom one last time with no success. Then with a
heavy heart she walked slowly away on her crutches.

She was completely fed up with hobbling around, but she'd sent the taxi away in the vain hope that Mia would let her in. It had seemed to Gemma to be tempting fate by asking the taxi to wait. She made it up the hill and on to the main road, palms throbbing a little from the exertion and waited for the bus. It wasn't as if she had anything else to do that afternoon, after all. Life without AbbaFab was proving to be rather tedious and she had far too much time on her hands to think: about the past and about her future. She was dreadfully bored and itching to get back to work.

Walking slowly up her road after the short bus ride, Gemma was surprised to see Alva sitting in her car outside her door. Alva's head was lowered and she was engrossed in something. Gemma rapped on her side window. Alva looked up and smiled. She lowered her window.

'There you are,' she said. 'I wondered where you'd got to. I had to visit an account in Dun Laoghaire so I thought I'd call in here on my way back to the office. Lucky I had a paper to read.'

'You could have rung my mobile,' Gemma said.

'I did. You didn't answer.'

Gemma balanced on one crutch and pulled her mobile out of her pocket. 'I forgot to switch it on,' she said with a grimace. 'Sorry.'

'Not to worry. Can I come in for a coffee?'

'Of course.'

A few minutes later they were sitting at Gemma's kitchen table waiting for the kettle to boil.

'So how's Mia?' Gemma said.

'I was wondering how long it would take you to ask,' Alva said. 'Mia's OK.' She paused for a moment. 'Actually, to tell the truth, she's not great. But it's hard to get her to talk about it – you know what she's like sometimes. She just clams up.'

'Tell me about it,' Gemma said. 'I just don't know what to do. It's all my fault. I should have stopped Dr Tobin saying anything while I had the chance. I wasn't fast enough.'

'Ah, Gemma. Stop blaming yourself. If you ask me, Wendy should have told Mia years ago. It wouldn't have been such a shock to her then.'

'I know, you're right. I should have made Wendy see sense. Or told Mia myself.'

'Gemma! It wasn't up to *you* to do anything. It wasn't your secret to tell. You have to stop protecting your sisters. And this is all between Wendy and Mia now. I don't think you should get involved. I'm sorry to sound harsh, but Mia's a big girl. Let her fight her own battles for a change.'

'What are you talking about?' Gemma demanded. 'Of course I should get involved. And Mia needs my help. Wendy does too.'

'No, Gemma. They need your support, not your help. You can't fix this one, however much you try.'

Gemma seemed to slump visibly in front of Alva's eyes. 'But they're my family,' she murmured. 'What else am I supposed to do?'

'Get on with your own life,' Alva said gently. 'You must have dreams, ambitions. Don't you want to meet someone, have your own family?'

'Yes, at some stage I suppose.'

'Well, unless you stop living your life through Wendy and Mia you're not going to, ever. You'll be too busy trying to fix their lives instead of your own. When was the last time you had a boyfriend?'

Gemma opened her mouth to answer.

'A proper boyfriend, not just a fling?' Alva added.

'A few years ago,' Gemma admitted.

Alva raised her eyebrows. 'When we were kids you used to have to fight them off with a stick. Remember? What happened?'

'Things change,' Gemma pointed out. 'I haven't really had time . . .' she finished lamely.

'Don't let things change too much or you'll be left behind,' Alva warned. 'I've been doing a lot of thinking since Wendy's fall, Gemma, and I'm worried about you, all of you. I've known the three of you all my life and Mia's practically like a sister to me.'

'At least she has one real sister then,' Gemma said.

Alva smiled wryly. 'It's all a bit of a mess, isn't it?'

Gemma nodded. 'And I understand what you're saying, really I do. But I *have* to get involved, don't you see?'

'No, I don't.'

Gemma sighed. 'Then we'll have to agree to disagree, I'm afraid.'

'Just think about what I've said. Please?'

Gemma nodded. 'OK.'

Alva looked at her watch. 'Shoot. I have to go.'

'What about that coffee?'

'Another time. But thanks anyway. And Gemma?'

345

'Yes?'

'Mia's lucky to have you both. And I'm sorry if I was hard on you. But I'm only trying to help.'

'I know you are.'

'You stay there, I'll see myself out.'

As soon as Alva closed the front door behind her, Gemma felt her body slump. She put her arms on the table and rested her head on them. Her head was throbbing with thoughts. Maybe Alva had a point. Maybe it was time to let Wendy and Mia sort things out for themselves.

And then Gemma had an epiphany: maybe it is time for me to leave AbbaFab, she thought. Stand on my own two feet for a change. She smiled to herself. When I have two working feet, that is. A plan began to form in her head. It won't be easy, she thought, but sometimes taking a chance is worth the risk.

That evening, Gemma stood nervously outside Wendy and Ronan's house. She wasn't looking forward to this visit one little bit.

Ronan let her in.

'How's Wendy?' Gemma asked.

'Dying to get out of bed,' Ronan said. 'You know Wendy.'

'Only too well.' Gemma smiled. 'Is she upstairs?'

Ronan nodded. 'Do you need a hand getting up?'

'Are you offering to carry me?' she joked. 'I'm quite a weight.'

Ronan frowned. 'Um . . .'

346

'I'm only teasing.' She put his mind at rest. 'I'll manage.'

'That's a relief. No offence, but I'm not sure if my back could take it.'

Gemma slapped him on the arm. 'Don't be so cheeky.'

It took her a few minutes, but she got there eventually. Ronan followed behind her just in case. The stairs made him distinctly nervous these days.

'Gemma!' Wendy sat up in the bed and smiled widely at her sister. 'I'm so bored. Thanks for coming. How's the leg?'

'Fine. The plaster will be off soon, thank goodness. But not soon enough – I'm counting the weeks. Talk about being bored. I'm sick to death of hobbling around the place.'

'I can imagine. I've only been laid up a few days and I'm doing my nut.'

'But you're being a very good patient.' Ronan grinned down at her from the bedside.

Gemma sat down on the side of the bed and allowed her crutches to fall on to the carpet with a dull thud. 'That's better.' She rubbed the base of her palms together to ease them out.

'I'm sure you girls have lots to talk about,' Ronan said, turning to leave.

'Please stay,' Gemma said. 'I have something to tell you both.'

Ronan came back and leaned against the bedroom wall, his arms folded casually around his chest.

'Is it about Mia?' Wendy asked immediately.

'No,' Gemma said. 'It's about me.' She looked at Wendy and then at Ronan. 'I'm leaving AbbaFab.'

'What?' Wendy cried. 'But you can't!'

'Now you have Mia you don't need me,' Gemma pointed out. 'And I think it's time for me to move on and do my own thing.'

'But *I'm* leaving AbbaFab,' Wendy said before Ronan could stop her.

Gemma stared at Wendy in astonishment. 'Are you serious?'

Wendy nodded. Ronan started to laugh.

'What's so funny?' Wendy demanded.

'I'm not quite sure,' he admitted. 'Is this a good time to tell you both *my* news?'

'What news?' Wendy demanded.

'I've just got off the phone. My song has been accepted for the Eurovision song contest competition.'

'That's brilliant!' Wendy enthused. 'Congratulations, darling. You're so clever.'

Gemma looked at Wendy and then at Ronan. Darling? Wendy hadn't called Ronan darling for as long as she could remember.

'Good on you,' Gemma added. 'About time too. How long have you been entering the Eurovision competition now?'

'Hey, it's only been ten, no, eleven years.' Ronan snorted. 'No time at all. And I'm hoping to start writing full-time soon. Widen my song repertoire. Maybe write a rock musical with Pat.'

'But what about AbbaFab?' Gemma asked. 'I presume you're talking about leaving the band too. What about Mia and Luke?'

Wendy looked at Ronan and then back at Gemma. 'This is all news to me, Gemma. We haven't talked about any of this yet. But we can't *all* leave. It wouldn't be fair on Mia.'

'Mia's a big girl, Wendy,' said Gemma. 'She'll cope.'

'But . . .'

Gemma continued, 'Really, Wendy, she'll be fine. Changing the subject slightly, that's the other thing I wanted to talk to you both about. Mia. You and Mia to be precise,' she said to Wendy.

'Yes?' Wendy looked at Gemma expectantly.

Gemma took a deep breath. 'I'm sorry, Wendy, but she doesn't want to talk to either of us. Alva called in earlier and she says Mia's fine physically, but still very upset. I've rung her countless times and I've also tried calling in, but she wouldn't open the door. I'm at my wits' end, Wendy.'

Gemma heard a gasp. Wendy's face drained and she put both hands on the bed covers to steady herself. Gemma felt terrible. She knew she shouldn't have upset her sister. Her heart sank.

Wendy noticed the pained look on Gemma's face. 'I suspected as much,' she said. 'Thank you for being so honest. None of this is your fault. I'm to blame. Me and me alone. And I have to deal with the consequences.'

'Are you all right?' Ronan asked Wendy with concern.

'Not really,' Wendy admitted. 'But I needed to hear the truth. Mia's been kept in the dark for long enough. It's time for me to start facing up to my past, to shoulder my mistakes.' Her hands fluttered to her face and she pressed her fingertips to her eyes.

Gemma realized Wendy was crying. 'It'll be OK,' she soothed, shifting up the bed as best she could and putting her arms around her sister.

'I've been such a fool,' Wendy sobbed. 'I should have told her a long time ago. How could I have been so stupid? I thought it was for the best.'

'I know,' Gemma said gently, at a loss as to what to say. She looked over at Ronan but he shrugged slightly as if to say, I'm lost too.

'I'm going to call on Mia again this evening,' Gemma continued after a few minutes of holding Wendy and allowing her to cry. 'Hopefully she'll answer the door this time. Would you like me to talk to her for you?' she asked before she could stop herself. Alva had warned her not to get involved, but it was so difficult not to. Old habits die hard, Gemma thought wryly as soon as the question had popped out of her mouth.

Wendy shook her head. 'Thanks. But no. I need to talk to her myself.'

'I understand,' Gemma said softly and stroked her sister's head. 'I understand.'

'Hello?' Mia said tentatively into her intercom that afternoon, an hour after Gemma had called. She hoped it wasn't Gemma again. She had nothing to say to her.

'Hi, Mia. It's Luke. Are you busy? I'm going to take a walk down by the sea, shame to waste this sun. Want to join me?'

'Love to. I'll be down in a minute.'

Mia ran around the flat looking for her sunglasses. She knew she'd put them somewhere sensible, but she wasn't exactly sure where. 'Sunglasses, sunglasses,' she murmured, retracing her steps. She gave up after searching everywhere logical, grabbed her denim jacket from the coat hook in the hall and patted her jeans pocket for her keys. Satisfied she had them, she closed the door behind her and skipped down the stairs. She was determined to put the whole Wendy and Gemma thing behind her for the afternoon and have a nice time with Luke. But now she was starting to feel a little guilty for leaving Gemma standing on the doorstep like that. Still, Mia thought as she opened the main front door, she deserved it. They both did.

'Hi, Mia.' Luke bent down and kissed her on the cheek. 'You look lovely.'

Mia squinted up at him. 'Thanks. It's gorgeous out, isn't it? I walked to the shops earlier this morning and it was hot even then.' Then she remembered and patted the top of her head. She gave a small laugh when she realized that, yes, her sunglasses were perched there, held in place by her hair. She slotted them down over her eyes. That was better.

'What's so funny?' Luke asked.

'Nothing.' She smiled up at him and took his arm.

'You're in good form today,' he commented as they

351

walked down the road towards the sea front. 'All things considered.'

'Yes, I am.' Mia said, refusing to be drawn. Luke knew all about the Wendy revelation, Ronan had told him the details. Ronan needed to talk to someone outside the family, someone who would listen, Mia couldn't begrudge him that. But it was rather annoying that that someone also happened to be her boyfriend. Every time Luke tried to broach the subject with Mia, she'd closed up like a clam. Eventually he'd got the message.

'I presume you'd rather not talk about your sisters this afternoon?' he asked astutely as they walked down the road towards Monkstown seafront.

'Gemma and Wendy, you mean?' she asked, being pedantic.

He nodded.

'Correct,' she said shortly. And, changing the subject, 'I could kill an ice cream. Can we make a detour to the shop?'

'That's a great idea.'

Minutes later they were walking arm and arm along the hard, damp sand, licking their ice creams in companionable silence.

'What are you thinking about?' Mia asked eventually. 'You're very quiet.'

'Nothing really,' Luke said, not wanting to admit that he was pondering the Wendy–Mia situation. 'Ronan rang this morning.'

Mia remained silent.

'No, nothing like that,' Luke said quickly. 'There's

going to be a band meeting tomorrow. He has some-thing to tell everyone.'

'Really? What?'

'He wouldn't say. We'll have to go along and find out.'

'I'm not going!' Mia said immediately.

'Don't be silly, Mia. You have to go. You're part of AbbaFab now. You don't have to talk to Wendy if you don't want to. In fact, she may not even be there. She's supposed to be resting after all.'

Mia snorted. 'This *is* Wendy we're talking about?'

Luke nodded and smiled. 'She'll be there all right. But you have to go, Mia. It would be really bad form if you didn't. I know you're hurting at the moment . . .'

Mia spun on her heels and faced him. 'No you don't, Luke! You don't know how I'm feeling. No one knows.'

'Take it easy, Mia,' Luke said evenly. But Mia was having none of it.

'You really don't understand,' she continued, 'do you? My whole life has been one big lie. I'm not who I thought I was, I'm someone completely different. Wendy and Gemma have been lying to me for years and I trusted them. You have no idea how I feel.'

She pulled away from his arm, but he grabbed her hand and refused to let go.

'Luke! Let go of me.'

'That's where you're wrong, Mia,' he said. 'And no, I won't let go of you. Listen to me. I *do* know. I know exactly how you feel.'

Mia glared at him. 'How could you?'

'I'm adopted,' he said. 'My parents only told me when I was fifteen. I tried to find my birth mother but she emigrated to America just after I was born. I felt exactly like you do now. Hurt, let down, lied to, the whole works.'

Mia felt as if time had frozen. In one instant, everything had changed. Her mind was in a whirl. 'I'm sorry,' she said eventually, feeling ashamed. 'I had no idea. I don't know what to say.'

Luke shrugged. 'It's not something I'm all that comfortable talking about, to tell the truth, that's why I haven't told you before now. It took a long time for me to forgive my parents for lying to me all those years. They let me think I was their natural son.'

'Why?' Mia whispered. 'Why didn't they tell you?'

Luke stared out to sea. 'For the same reason Gemma and Wendy didn't tell you.' He looked back at Mia. 'They wanted to protect me,' he said. 'They loved me. And, as they admitted themselves, they made a mistake.' He looked at her again intently. 'And I had to forgive them for that. For not being perfect.'

'And did you?'

'Yes, eventually.' He paused for a moment. 'But my dad died before I had a chance to tell him.'

'Oh, Luke, I'm so sorry.' Mia felt terrible. Poor Luke, she thought, what must he think of me, whingeing on about Wendy and Gemma when he has family history of his own?

'That's why I'm telling you all this, Mia. I've never

forgiven myself, but it's something I have to live with. If I could change things, though, turn back the clock ... well, it's too late now.' He blew out his breath. 'Let's walk.'

Mia nodded, saying nothing. Luke was visibly shaken, and she tried to keep up as he powered along the sand. As she walked, she thought about Wendy. She felt a shiver run through her body. Luke was right: everyone had lied to her because they thought it was for the best – Miriam, Gemma *and* Wendy. None of them had meant to hurt her. Gemma had only been eight when she was born. Eight! Just a little older than Greg and Steve. It must have been very traumatic for her. And as for Wendy, Mia shuddered just thinking about it. Having a baby at any age was scary, but at fourteen ... Her eyes began to fill with tears and within seconds she was crying.

'Luke,' she whispered.

He stopped, and realized that she was crying, the tears sneaking down her cheeks under her sunglasses. He put his arms around her and held her tight.

'I'm sorry,' she said through her tears. 'I've been so stupid.'

'There's no need to apologize to me,' he said. 'But I think you should listen to what Wendy and Gemma have to say. Don't you?' Before it's too late, he wanted to add, but stopped himself. Mia knew what he was getting at.

Mia buried her head in his chest and continued to cry. Luke stroked the back of her head. 'Hush now,' he soothed.

After a while, Mia's tears stopped and she pulled away from him. 'Can we go home?' she whispered.

'Yes, of course.'

'And Luke?'

'Yes?'

'When we get there, would you mind staying with me for a little while?'

'I'd be happy to. I won't leave until you're feeling better.'

'Promise?'

'I promise.'

That evening, after a delicious meal cooked by Nadia and eaten on trays in Wendy's and Ronan's bedroom (a first – normally Wendy insisted that all food was eaten in the kitchen), Ronan offered Gemma a lift to Mia's house, which she gratefully accepted. He watched from the car as Gemma stood on the doorstep, waiting. Answer the door, Mia, he willed from his vantage point. Please, Mia. He wanted her to talk to Gemma, but he also wanted to get back to Wendy as soon as possible. She was still upset, although hiding it well, and he was worried about her.

Gemma tried the intercom for the second time.

'Hello?' Mia's voice asked tentatively.

'Mia? It's Gemma. Can I come in?'

Gemma heard a male voice say something to Mia in the background. It sounded suspiciously like Luke.

The door buzzed and Gemma pushed it open and

made her way slowly up the stairs. Mia's door was open and Gemma pushed it with one of her crutches.

'She's in the living room,' Luke said, opening the door properly for her and giving her a nod. 'Chin up,' he whispered, taking in her anxious expression.

Gemma gave him a small smile and a nod. Chin up. It was a curiously old-fashioned expression, but it fitted the occasion perfectly. She did just that, took a deep breath and crutched herself into the living room.

'Mia?'

Mia was standing at the window, staring out. She turned her head as soon as she heard Gemma's voice. Mia's eyes jumped around the room nervously before finally settling on Gemma's. She didn't say a word.

'Mia, I'm sorry,' Gemma said nervously, staying exactly where she was. 'You're right; I should have told you a long time ago.'

Mia scrunched her nose a little. 'Look, Gemma, I'm sorry too. I shouldn't have said those terrible things to you. None of this is your fault. Can you forgive me?'

'Forgive you? Of course.' Gemma was surprised. She wasn't expecting *this*. She moved closer to Mia, standing just beside her at the window. 'I know you probably have hundreds of questions. And I'll answer them all for you as best I can.'

Mia shrugged and gave a deep sigh. 'I know we have a lot of talking to do, Gemma. But right now, would you mind if we left it? I'm exhausted from it all, to tell the truth. And if I cry any more there won't be any water left in my body.'

'Fine by me,' Gemma said, relieved. 'There's plenty of time. I'm not going anywhere.' She stopped for a second. Alva's words rang through her mind. Stop trying to protect your sisters. Live your own life. 'And Mia, I'm not going to get involved in this any more – the whole situation between you and Wendy, I mean. You do what you think is right. I won't interfere. I promise.'

Mia was taken aback. She was waiting for the 'You must sort things out with Wendy' lecture. She wasn't expecting this. 'OK,' she managed.

'I'm going to go now,' Gemma said. She leaned over and gave Mia an awkward hug, her crutches getting somewhat in the way. 'I love you, Mia.'

'I love you too,' Mia said back, a lump forming in her throat.

'I'll see myself out now. You know where I am if you need me. Ring me when you're ready. Take care of yourself.'

'And you. And Gemma?'

'Yes?'

'I'll ring you tomorrow. Not to talk, mind, just to say hello.'

'That sounds good. Till tomorrow then.'

Gemma's eyes were full of tears as she walked carefully down Mia's stairs and towards Ronan's car. But this time they were tears of joy.

Luke proved as good as his word. He stayed with Mia until she fell asleep in his arms late that evening,

358

emotionally drained. After clearing the air with Gemma, Mia had agreed to talk to Wendy the following day after the band meeting.

Lying in Mia's bed, watching her breathing, Luke realized with a start that he never wanted to leave her, ever.

17 'Does Your Mother Know?'

The following morning Mia and Luke walked to Wendy and Ronan's house for the band meeting. Mia felt sick to her stomach with nerves, but she felt reassured by Luke's presence. They had talked late into the night; about his parents, what he knew about his birth mother, the long years of trying to find her, his fear of abandonment and his devastation when Ciara left him. And then Mia had shared her own feelings with him, something she'd never found easy to do. She felt so comfortable with him. 'I could get used to this,' she'd murmured as she dozed off to sleep in the safety of his arms.

'Hi, Luke, Mia. Thanks for coming.' Ronan opened the door wide and ushered them inside.

Everyone looked up as they entered the living room. Pat, Gemma and especially Wendy. Mia held Wendy's gaze for a second. She knew she should give her a smile, let her know that everything would be all right eventually, but she felt powerless to do so. Her lips were locked tightly together and she felt even more nauseous. Talking to Wendy was going to be one of the hardest things she'd ever had to do. But Mia knew she had to face her fear. Running away from it just wasn't an option. She could always shut Wendy out, she supposed, but then, thinking of Luke's situation, she chastised herself. I'm going to face this head on, she promised herself.

'I'm sure you're all wondering why I called this band meeting,' Ronan said, interrupting Mia's thoughts. 'Some of us have news that will affect the whole band,' he said, looking around the room. 'Where will we start?'

'With me,' Wendy said. She looked around the room, her eyes lingering on Mia's. 'I'm leaving the band.'

Mia gasped. 'What? But you can't!'

Wendy smiled at her gently. 'It's time for me to do other things, Mia. AbbaFab has been my life for many years now, but I need to start thinking of the future. I want to spend more time with Ronan and the boys.'

'But Wendy, you *are* AbbaFab,' Luke pointed out. 'What's going to happen to the band?' Wendy gave a brief nod to Gemma.

'I'm leaving too,' Gemma said, sounding a little nervous. 'I'm not quite sure what I'm going to do, to be honest. I've had an idea for a cabaret act and we'll see how that pans out. But I'm definitely leaving AbbaFab.'

'What about you, Ronan?' Luke asked. 'Don't tell me.'

Ronan nodded. 'Sorry, mate. I've decided to try and make a go of the song-writing lark. One of my songs has been accepted for the Song for Europe.'

'The contest that selects Ireland's Eurovision entry?' Mia asked.

'Yes,' Ronan said.

'That's great!' Mia said. 'Congratulations.'

'And I'm going to try my hand at writing a rock musical,' Pat added.

'That's all well and good,' Luke said in a slightly subdued tone. 'But what about AbbaFab? That just leaves me and Mia.'

'You're more than welcome to keep the band going,' Wendy suggested. 'You could find two extra singers and a new Pat.'

'I don't think so,' Luke said after a pause. 'Whatever about the singers, we'd never be able to replace Pat. And it just wouldn't be the same without all of you.'

'Thanks, mate.' Pat smiled at him and gave him a wink.

'What do you think, Mia?'

Mia shook her head. 'Luke's right. It's just wouldn't be the same.'

She felt deflated. Everyone seemed to have their lives mapped out for them, except for her and Luke. It just wasn't fair.

'But it's such a pity,' she murmured. 'I've only just started,' she began, not knowing quite what she wanted to say.

'What was that, Mia?' Ronan asked gently.

'I don't want to stop singing,' Mia said, surprising herself and everyone else by the strength of her conviction. 'I can't go back to teaching now. What am I going to do? I want to sing!'

Luke took her hand in his. 'We'll be fine,' he promised her. 'It's looks like AbbaFab has come to its natural end. Just like the real Abba. Isn't that right, Wendy?'

Wendy nodded.

'We'll find something else,' Luke continued. 'Whatever about me, Mia, you have a natural God-given talent.'

'He's right,' Wendy said firmly. 'You're brilliant.'

Gemma nodded. 'We all think so.'

'Really?' Mia asked. 'You're not just saying that?' She looked at Pat.

'You've got it, Mia,' he assured her. 'Star quality. You'll go all the way if you believe in yourself.'

'Thanks,' Mia whispered, staring down at her hands. She was touched. Pat didn't say much but when he did, he always told the truth.

'So is that it?' Luke asked. 'The end of AbbaFab?'

'I guess so,' Ronan said.

'It seems like such an anticlimax,' Gemma pointed out. 'The end of AbbaFab. Just like that.'

Wendy sighed. 'I know what you mean.'

'We should have a party,' Ronan said. 'And play one last time. When Wendy's better. And we can have two Agnethas.'

'Two?' Mia asked.

He grinned at her. 'Why not? And if Gemma's still

in plaster she can sing from a chair. We can do what we like. And our fans will love it.'

'Our fans?' Gemma asked.

'Don't sound so surprised,' Wendy said. 'We do have quite a number, you know. They're always emailing the AbbaFab website, asking when we're playing next. Speaking of which, why don't we play in the Singing Tree, where Ronan first discovered us?' She smiled over at Gemma. 'Where it all started?'

'Would we fit? It's quite a small pub,' Gemma pointed out.

'I'm sure they'd put a marquee in the beer garden if we asked them nicely,' Wendy suggested. 'My man has contacts.' She winked at Gemma and Gemma laughed. Ronan's cousin owned a marquee hire company.

'Great idea,' Ronan said. 'If everyone agrees, I can set it up.'

Pat nodded.

'Sounds good,' Luke said. 'Mia?'

Mia nodded too. She was trying to hold back the tears. She felt overwhelmed. It had been quite a week. First the Wendy revelation, now the break-up of Abba-Fab.

Ronan noticed her discomfort. He clapped his hands together. 'Who'd like a beer? I put the barbecue on just in case. Anyone up for a steak?'

Gemma laughed. 'Always thinking about your stomach.'

Ronan patted his stomach affectionately. 'But of course.'

Everyone stood up except Wendy, who remained on the sofa. 'Mia?' she said tentatively.

Luke squeezed Mia's hand. 'Stay and talk to her,' he said in a low voice.

Mia shook her head. She was almost shaking with nerves.

'Mia,' he said. 'It's time.'

'OK,' she murmured. She stayed on her feet as everyone left the room. Luke shut the door behind him and Mia suddenly felt claustrophobic.

'Mia?' Wendy said. 'Will you sit down?' She patted the seat of the sofa beside her.

Mia stared at Wendy for a moment. 'I'll stand.'

'Mia, please.' Wendy looked up at her and Mia noticed with a start that she was crying.

Mia shook her head.

'Mia.' Wendy looked her in the eye.

Mia held her gaze. And in that moment she realized that Wendy loved her. It was as simple as that.

'I'm so sorry,' Wendy began, tears rolling down her pale cheeks. Mia still said nothing. 'I never meant to hurt you. You have to believe me. I was so young when I had you, I didn't know what I was doing. If I could go back and change things I would. You have no idea how hard it was for me, living a lie for all those years.'

'*You* were living a lie!' Mia snorted.

'I know. And I'll never forgive myself for keeping it from you all that time. I made a mistake, Mia. A terrible mistake. I should have told you, but it never seemed to be the right time. I wish I could turn back the clock, but I can't.'

'Why did you give me to Mum?' Mia demanded. 'Did you not want me?'

'Of course I did. But I was fourteen, Mia. Fourteen! I had four more years of school ahead of me at the time.'

'But Mum could have minded me when you were at school. You didn't have to give me up completely.'

'It seemed the right thing to do,' Wendy said. 'For the family and for you. I wasn't thinking straight. I was in complete denial and I didn't tell anyone for ages. Gemma was only eight, remember. Mum guessed when I was just over seven months pregnant, and after that, she and Dad made all the decisions.'

'You could have been my proper mum,' Mia said. 'You could have looked after me.'

'It was what *I* wanted,' Wendy admitted. 'But Mum and Dad convinced me that it wasn't the right thing to do. They couldn't have any more children; having Gemma almost killed Mum, so I guess they saw it as God's will. They really did think it was for the best, Mia.'

'But you went along with it, Wendy. Even though you knew it was wrong.'

Wendy nodded. 'I thought keeping you was the selfish option. The other option was to give you up for adoption to another family. And that would have killed me. At least this way I got to see you every day. It was hard, but I saw you grow up. It made it a little more bearable for me.'

'But then you went away when I was three, to London.'

Wendy nodded. 'I found it harder and harder to cope with what I'd done as I got older. I realized that if I'd been a little bit more determined and a little older, sixteen or seventeen maybe, I could have kept you as my own. It became unbearable after a while and I had to get away. I couldn't live with the constant reminder of what I'd done. I went a little wild, to tell the truth, especially when I was working on the cruise ship. But I missed you so much. I thought about you all the time and I came back to see you whenever I could. And then when Mum died I got to look after you, like a real daughter. It was a strange twist of fate.'

Mia hesitated before she asked the next question. 'Who's my father, Gemma? I need to know.'

'A boy from Westport called Henry Reilly. He was a few years older than me. He's living in America now. He emigrated with a woman from the town.'

'What was he like?'

'Utterly gorgeous,' Wendy said honestly. 'He was tall and slim with white-blond hair, like yours, Mia. And the most beautiful skin. Even as a teenager, he didn't have one single spot. All the girls were mad about him. He loved music too, he was in a rock band called Tumbleweed and they used to play at parties. He had quite a voice. I always had a thing about musicians.'

'Does he know about me?'

'No, I never told him.'

Mia stared at Wendy incredulously.

367

'Don't look at me like that, Mia. He left Westport before I got the chance.' Wendy paused for a moment. 'But if you want to find him, I'll help you. His family in Westport might . . .'

Mia shook her head. 'Maybe sometime in the future. Right now, I think I have enough to be going on with, don't you?'

'Of course. Sorry.'

Mia leaned against the side of the sofa. She suddenly felt weary.

'Please sit down, Mia,' Wendy cajoled.

This time Mia acquiesced.

'So what now?' Wendy asked, wiping away her tears. She'd stopped crying but she still felt emotionally raw. This conversation wasn't exactly going as planned. She'd hoped that Mia would forgive her, they'd talk honestly, sort things out, and that would be that. But she recognized now that she was being naive.

Mia shrugged. 'I'm not sure. There are so many things I want to know, but right at this moment I can't think of any of them.'

'It's a lot to take in,' Wendy said gently. She looked at Mia. 'What about us?' she asked. 'You and me?'

'I don't know,' Mia said truthfully. 'I don't know what or how I feel, Wendy. I'm all over the place.'

Wendy took a deep breath. 'Mia, you're everything to me. You always have been. I love you more than anything in the world.' Wendy moved slowly towards Mia on the sofa. She put her arms around her, but Mia pushed her away.

'Not yet,' Mia said. 'I'm not ready, Wendy.'

Wendy felt as though she'd been stabbed in the heart. She moved away. 'We'll work this out, Mia,' She murmured. They sat side by side on the sofa in silence.

'It'll never be the same again,' Mia said. 'You and me. You know that, don't you?'

Wendy nodded wordlessly. Finally she said, 'But at least you know who you are now.'

'Yes. I always sensed something wasn't quite right, but I could never put my finger on it. As you say, as least I know who I am now.'

As they sat, Wendy felt the weight of her secret she'd been carrying on her shoulders for so many years lift, and suddenly she felt pounds lighter. She began to cry again. She smiled through her tears. 'At least one of us does.'

Epilogue
'Take a Chance on Me'

Fourteen Months Later

'Mia, I had to ring you. I have news.'

'Hi, Gemma. I can't stay on the mobile long, I'm on stage in a few minutes. I'm in the dressing room, sorry if it's a bit noisy.'

There was a busy hum of voices in the background.

'Not to worry, I'll be quick,' Gemma promised. 'Well, to start with, Ronan's song won the Song for Europe.'

Mia gasped. 'No, really? So his song will be in the Eurovision?'

'Yes!'

'That's brilliant! How exciting! I was so disappointed for him last year when he came second.'

'I know. And he has a really good chance of winning the whole thing. Johnny Logan has agreed to come out of Eurovision retirement to sing it.'

'What's it called?' Mia asked.

' "Sister, Miss Ya".' Gemma sang the jaunty chorus. ' "Sister, love ya; there's never been another quite like ya. Sister, miss ya; never, ever stop thinkin' of ya." '

'Catchy.' Mia giggled hysterically.

'Cheesy, isn't it? But it's so sweet it's bound to win. Wendy wrote the lyrics, can you believe it?'

'Um,' Mia murmured. It had been over a year since she and Luke had moved to London together to join the cast of the long-running Abba musical, *Mamma Mia*. Luke was still in the chorus, but Mia had progressed through the ranks quickly and was now understudy to one of the lead parts, the young daughter, Sophie Sheridan. She hadn't been home once in all that time to visit Wendy or Gemma. She'd given them a variety of excuses: 'The show's so busy, I can't possibly get the time off,' 'We have to paint the flat,' 'Luke's sick, I can't leave him,' 'I'm exhausted.' But the truth was, Mia just wasn't ready to face Wendy again. Not yet. She still had a lot of things to work through first. But Luke was helping, listening to her when she needed a friend, giving her advice when she asked for it.

Mia had also seen Alva recently when she and Sean had flown over to catch the show and for a 'non-honeymoon-honeymoon' as they'd jokingly called it. And they seemed more in love than ever, even if they were still arguing. But that just seemed to be their way.

'We're trying to find a way to live together without killing each other,' Alva had told Mia and Luke over dinner, while grinning at Sean. 'But it's hard. Sean's a very difficult housemate.'

'Pay no attention to Alva, she's a bit ratty as she's been off the cigarettes for a few weeks now,' Sean had retorted.

'And how's the cabaret show going?' Mia asked Gemma. Gemma now sang as Marlene Dietrich, Edith Piaf and other famous cabaret divas in clubs and at events.

'Great! I'm doing two nights a week now at the Olympia and lots of private gigs. I'm really enjoying it!'

'And your doctor friend?'

It turned out that Dr Tobin's mother was quite the cabaret fan. He'd been dragged along to a show at the Olympia Theatre, had recognized Gemma instantly and afterwards, somewhat smitten, had gone back-stage to find her.

'Excellent. Although he's always working. But I have even more exciting news,' Gemma continued.

'More exciting than the lovely Dr Tobin?' Mia laughed.

'Oh yes, far more exciting. Wendy had her baby. A girl.'

'A girl?' Mia faltered.

'Yes.'

'I have a sister?'

Gemma's heart stopped for a moment. 'Well, yes, Mia. You do. A little sister.'

'Does she have a name?'

'Sorry, of course. Stella. Stella Miriam.'

The line went silent for a moment as Mia took this in. 'Stella? Doesn't that mean star?'

'Yes,' Gemma said. 'It does. But Wendy said you'd always be her original Little Star, that would never change.'

Mia's heart thudded in her chest and tears flooded her eyes.

'Are you OK, Mia?' Gemma asked gently.

Mia wiped away the tears with her knuckles. 'Maybe I should come home,' she said, 'and meet little Stella. I'm due some time off.'

Now it was Gemma's turn to cry. 'That's a great idea,' she said joyfully. 'I'd love to see you and I'll tell Wendy. She'll be over the moon.'

Gemma heard a voice shouting in the background.

'Sorry, have to run,' Mia said, 'curtain call.'

'Break a leg,' Gemma said.

But Mia had already gone.